BELLANDI CRIME SYNDICATE

VOLUME ONE

ADELAIDE FORREST

ABOUT THE AUTHOR

Adelaide lives in her tiny house with her husband and two rambunctious kids.
When she's not chasing all three of them and her shepherd/husky mix around
the house, she spends all her free time writing and adding to the hoard of plots
stored on her bookshelf and hard-drive.
She always wanted to write, and did from the time she was ten and wrote her
first full-length fantasy novel. The subject matter has changed over the years,
but that passion for writing never went away. She has a degree in Psychology,
and prior to having her kids she worked as a therapist using horses in her treatment strategy and working with adults and kids with disabilities.
Adelaide started her journey as a published author in September 2019 with her
other pen name, Kenna Bardot, where she writes reverse harem. Having
achieved her passion of becoming an author, she's expanding with the launch of
Adelaide Forrest.

1
BELLANDI CRIME SYNDICATE
BLOODIED
HANDS
ADELAIDE FORREST

ABOUT BLOODIED HANDS

She was an innocent, caught in the wrong place at the wrong time.

Involved in a bank robbery that never should have happened in my city, Ivory found herself staring down the barrel of a gun. Only my protection prevented them from taking what has always been mine.

She should have stayed away. Instead, she charges back into my life like an Angel come to save me from my bleak existence. She has no place in my world where hardened criminals toy with the lives of the innocent. A better man would send her back to her quiet life.

Too bad I'm a Bellandi man through and through.

We always play to win, and what we win, we always keep.

Bloodied Hands is a full-length standalone novel with an HEA, but the series presents a better reading experience when following the suggested order.

This series contains dark elements, including over-the-top antiheroes who do as they please. Read at your own discretion.

SOUNDTRACK

"Dancing With Your Ghost" - No Resolve
"You Find Me" - The Sweeplings
"Stuff of Legends" - Daughtry
"Super Psycho Love" - Simon Curtis
"Even If It Hurts" - Sam Tinnesz
"Just Found Heaven" - Daughtry
"Sex & Stardust" - ZZ Ward
"Peace" - Alison Wonderland
"Notorious" - Adelitas Way
"As You Are" - Daughtry
"Secrets" - Written By Wolves
"Hurt" - Christian Reindl feat. Lloren
"I'm Dangerous" - The EverLove
"Guest Room" - Echos
"Ashes" - Braden Barrie

PROLOGUE
IVORY

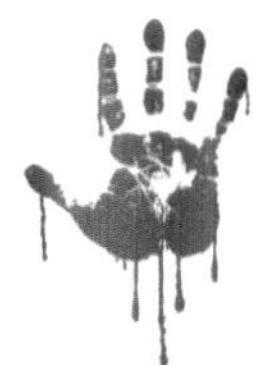

Twelve years ago.

I smiled up at Matteo, watching the way his eyes lit up with amusement as I giggled at him. He'd teased me, tormented me about the shyness I still felt when he touched me, although I'd given him my virginity a week prior. There was no way I could feel anything *but* shy, not with the way his stare had taken on a new brand of heat.

There hadn't been a repeat performance, even though I'd desperately wanted one. We didn't have a place to go, not without ruining my reputation, and Matteo maintained that I was too sweet for a backseat romp in his car.

I begged to differ, at least after what he'd shown me sex was like.

The humor in his eyes fled suddenly, disappearing to a cold mask I didn't enjoy seeing on his face when he stared over my shoulder. It wasn't unusual. That distant expression of his was what everyone else saw of Matteo Bellandi. When I turned his face back to mine and caught his eyes with my own, the smile slid from my face, slowly morphing to apprehension.

He stared down at me with the same cruel expression.

The one that he *never* used for me.

"We should talk, Ivory." Even his tone had gone cold. No life to it, his humor of only a moment ago a thing of the past.

I just didn't realize it would be the last time I felt like I mattered - like I was special.

Ivory.
Not his Angel.
But Ivory.

I flinched back, my hand leaving the smooth skin of his jaw as I stared up at him in confusion. I couldn't think of what I might have done to warrant such a change in behavior.

"What's wrong?" I whispered.

"Graduation is in a few days. It's time for us to go our separate ways." I would have sworn I knew Matteo - would have sworn I knew the boy I loved with every fiber of my being enough to recognize the tick in his jaw. The frustration eating at his face, even beneath the impenetrable coldness that he emanated.

I was wrong.

"Wh-what?" I stuttered, flinching when his arms released my waist and he stepped back to a more polite distance. I eyed the other students, hating that they were watching me have my heart ripped out. He blindsided me and judging by the whispers breaking out among the teens lingering on the front lawn of the school, I wasn't the only one.

"Come on, Ivory. You didn't really think I would go off to college in the fall with a High School girlfriend tying me down, did you?" He ran a hand through his hair, tossing a flirty smile over my shoulder at some unknown person behind me. He hadn't even finished dumping me, and he was already *flirting.*

"Why? Why did you-why did you fuck me if you were just going to dump me?" I hissed, steeling myself and trying to control the tears that threatened to make an appearance. No matter how shattered I felt, I couldn't let him see it.

"Have you looked in a mirror?" He smirked at me, as if taking my virginity and dumping me within a week was acceptable. "You're a hot piece of ass, baby. Getting in your pants was kind of the point of the entire year I spent getting you there. Now I've had it." He shrugged, and I winced.

I didn't know this boy.

I didn't know him at all.

"You don't mean that," I pleaded, my voice a hoarse whisper as I started to lose the battle with my own emotions. "You can't mean that," I repeated.

"Sweet, naïve Ivory. What world do you live in, so stuck up in that pretty little head of yours? The lion doesn't love the lamb, Ivory. Especially not just one of them when there's an entire field begging to be eaten." He shook his head at me, pressing a thumb to my quivering lips, the lips he claimed to love so much. "You weren't bad...for a virgin." A startled sob broke free. "See you around, Ivory. Hey, Shauna! Wait up!" he called, jogging around my frozen body.

Shauna.

The girl he'd been screwing before he started dating me. The one who had spent an entire year tormenting me that he'd finish with me soon enough, and he *always* went back to her.

I stood frozen, only snapping out of my trance when Sadie appeared at my side. "Hey, sweetie. Let's get you out of here, yeah?" she asked, and I think I nodded. Tears streamed down my face, but I couldn't understand why.

I wasn't sad.

I didn't feel *anything*.

Deep down, I knew that wasn't normal. I shouldn't be numb.

It was only high school, only my first love. There would be others, I tried to remind myself.

But even then, I knew no one would ever make me feel the way Matteo did.

I turned to leave, but Duke invaded my other side, ushering me off the lawn and *away* from the direction Matteo had gone. It didn't stop me from seeing him, his arm wrapped around Shauna with one hand tucked into the ass pocket of her jeans.

Still there was nothing but a vibration in my ears, as disbelief coursed through me.

I loved him.

And I'd been *nothing* all along. Nothing but another notch on his bedpost.

Sadie murmured to me, letting Duke tuck me into his side as they led me to his car in the parking lot. Sadie climbed into the back seat, leaving me to be the passenger. Duke drove with a hand resting on my knee, making circles with his thumb that should have been comforting.

It wasn't until we got to my house and they guided me to my bed that I broke down in sobs.

The bed he'd made love to me on.

Well, apparently the bed he'd fucked me on.

"Shh, it's okay sweetheart," Duke soothed, wrapping his arms around me and tucking me into his chest. "You're going to be just fine."

"I love him," I whined.

His body stilled, before he ran a hand through my hair. "I know, honey. I know you do. He's such an idiot." I vaguely knew of Sadie's sniffles behind me, where she ran a hand up and down my back supportively.

"I can never go back to school," I protested, realizing everyone had seen my very public humiliation.

"You will march your ass into that school tomorrow with your head held high and pretend you do not give the first fuck about him." I nodded in response, but we both knew it was bullshit. I wasn't Sadie. I wasn't strong enough to pretend something like that.

We lapsed into silence, my heart hardening with every tear that fell.

I would never be heartbroken again.

No man was worth *this.*

CHAPTER ONE

IVORY

With the tenderloin smeared in dijon mustard and wrapped in duxelle covered prosciutto cooling in the fridge, I set to laying out my puff pastry in preparation. I rolled it, needing that perfect quarter of an inch thickness so I wouldn't overcook my beef while I waited for the pastry to bake to golden perfection.

"You're insane, you know, that right?" Sadie asked.

"And why am I insane today, my darling?" I teased her, thanking the sweet baking gods that her sense of humor had never changed.

"Why are you making a Beef Wellington again? Your food isn't usually so pretentious, even with that fancy culinary degree of yours that didn't see much use." She raised her brows at me, as if daring me to contradict her.

I used my degree.

Just not in a restaurant or catering business.

"I'm doing a new series. Kind of a food bucket list, I guess. I'm torn between calling it *Food to Eat Before you Kick It or Famous Last Meals.* I had readers submit the best foods they've ever eaten and made my own recipes from what they submitted." I trimmed the edges of my pastry to what I knew I would need to wrap up my beef.

Contrary to what Duke might think, I cooked a recipe at least half a dozen times before it was ready for the blog. There was a reason that I was always happy to let him taste test, and by taste test I meant eat the entire thing once I had a feel for the flavor profile I'd created.

Eating the same thing over and over was exhausting.

No matter how amazing it tasted.

"Clever," Duke chuckled, always supportive of me and my passion. Though it wasn't surprising. Sadie was my kick ass and take names best friend who ran a boxing gym. Duke was a close second for the best friend status. The dreamer of our trio, he was a successful sculptor who had somehow defied the odds and made a real career for himself in an impossible industry.

In his head, if that was possible, well then so was my blog. And it had been, the whole thing grew faster than I could handle, and I found myself over-whelmed with trying to keep up with it. But whereas working in the restaurant and running a catering business had been purely exhausting, the blog was a good stress.

It distracted me from the fact that I wasn't getting any younger. Distracted me from the fact that I still hadn't fallen in love since my sophomore year of high school. I pulled the beef from the fridge, setting the plate down next to my puff pastry on my white marble counter. I'd bought the house just outside the city for a steal, knowing it was a dump. The affordable price left me with enough in my budget to fix it up slowly as I made money. Once I'd quit my job at the restaurant, money had been inconsistent and unreliable. Whether catering or with my blog, I could easily have a slow month anytime, so keeping my monthly expenses low was critical for me.

I paid cash for just about everything I did.

Slowly, my beloved house was coming together. I finished my kitchen and master bedroom, my sanctuaries in a house that was otherwise...shit.

It was otherwise shit.

But I loved my counters, and the natural lighting was perfection for photos for the blog. "It sounds interesting, I suppose," Sadie relented, and I smiled at her teasingly. It wasn't often that she relented her somewhat more assertive opinions. From Sadie, saying it was interesting meant the idea must have rocked.

I'd take it. Her lips pursed into a smile she tried to fight, giving away that she knew I saw right through her crap.

"When can I eat this thing?" Duke asked, eyes narrowed on where my hands oh so carefully lifted the beef and rested it in the center of my pastry. After a quick wash of my hands, I set to wrapping it up and sealing it tight. I brushed it, cutting the top to release air as it baked, and fought the urge to chuckle when Duke cleared his throat at me, still waiting for an answer.

Honestly, he should know better. I'd answer when I finished with my step.

"It has to bake for 40-45 minutes," I said after I'd placed the sheet in the oven and set the timer. He groaned, and I chuckled at him as I set to washing my fingerling purple potatoes in the sink opposite them. The task meant I couldn't see them, but after over a decade with them I knew exactly what they would do as soon as I turned around.

Make faces at me. Because we were mature like that.

I ignored it.

"Why purple potatoes?" Sadie asked when she finally realized she'd failed to get a reaction from me.

"They're a little denser and nuttier in flavor. Mostly, I just prefer them because they look so fucking pretty on the plate," I admitted. "For something as visual as the blog, and especially the more visual social media sites, that's super important."

"You keep cooking like this, and I'm liable to get fat." I snorted a laugh at her, pressing my face into the back of my forearm.

"Please," I laughed. For my 4'11" friend, who was so fit she could take out a full-grown boxer in minutes, getting fat was ridiculous. Stacked with lean muscles, even Duke was fit with forearms sculpted like a Greek God.

When I said he was a sculptor, I meant a mixed materials sculptor. He was just as likely to work with wood or metal as he was with clay. The man didn't discriminate, and some of those materials required some serious strength.

I'd tried to help him once.

Let's just say it hadn't gone well.

At all.

Now in his words I just sat there and looked pretty. I loved to watch him work but learned my lesson quickly and stayed out of his way.

As soon as I had the potatoes set to roast and popped them in my double oven, I moved on to setting up the place setting for the photos in my little breakfast nook. "Soooo...." I stilled. It was *never* a good sign when Sadie hesitated to speak her mind, and I knew exactly where she was going.

Where she was always going.

"There's this guy, he comes into the gym."

"Sadie," Duke warned on a growl. He was my fervent defender. I didn't need to date, not when it always ended in disaster.

"She can't stay a marriage pit forever!" Sadie hissed. "Eventually, she will have to open herself up to considering getting there with one of these guys, but the only way that will happen is if she *dates*, Duke."

"I hate it when you call me that." I winced, setting a plate down on the table a little too loudly.

"It's true, Ive." Her voice gentled as I made my way back to the space behind the island where my two friends sat, staring at me as if we were walking a very dangerous line. "Ben wanted to introduce you to his parents, and you bolted. Chris *proposed*, and you never saw him again. They were both amazing guys. You're a marriage pit. Too afraid to let anyone in."

"Stop it, Sadie," Duke said, eyeing the way my hands clutched the island like I could break it.

"It's been over ten years." Sadie's voice gentled with sadness, and I could feel what I hated to hear in her voice more than anything. The *pity.*

Because we both knew I was broken.

Broken in a way that I would eventually have to accept that love just would not happen for me.

Never again.

"Maybe it's time to look at what's right in front of you," she whispered cryptically, and I felt my brow tense in confusion.

"I don't see you with a ring on your finger," Duke snapped, and I raised my eyes to them.

"Stop it, both of you," I reprimanded them. "If I go out with this guy from the gym will you lay off?"

Sadie's eyes lit with hope, and she nodded. "You gonna give him an actual chance?" There was skepticism in her loud, honey-toned voice. I hated knowing that I'd put it there after twelve years of failed romances and first dates that went nowhere.

"Yes," I agreed. "I'm tired of being alone. It's time I tried to find a decent man, a good man. Someone who can give me a content life, if not an overwhelming romance." I gave a bitter smile, ignoring the pained look on Duke's face. He'd always encouraged me to practice self-healing, to put myself and my mental health before a relationship. I didn't want to disappoint him, but it was time to accept that some things just couldn't be fixed.

I was one of them.

"How's the gym?" I asked, washing some extra mushrooms. I needed the change of conversation desperately, and I knew Duke well enough to know he was too busy worrying about me to be the one to grant it.

Sadie allowed it, thankfully. She knew she'd pushed as far as was intelligent for one day. She twiddled with her loose, wavy dark brown hair as she turned warm honey brown eyes my way. "It's great. You know I love it there and business is booming."

"I'm sure prancing around in your tight little workout clothes has nothing to do with that," I chuckled. She returned the humor, shrugging like she didn't have a care in the world.

"Nobody said I wasn't smart. Mom and Dad miss you though. They said to tell you to stop by for dinner soon."

I smiled. "How about they come here?" I grimaced. Sadie's mom was great at a lot of things.

Cooking was not one of them.

Duke snorted out a laugh, the tension of my agreement to date fading into memory as Sadie and I burst into giggles. "Yeah, let's do that instead."

CHAPTER TWO

MATTEO

I zipped up my slacks, turning away from the pouty expression on the freckle free face of Jessica, staring up at me from where she'd knelt to suck me off.

Or was it Jennifer?

I shook my head, realizing just how little her name mattered when I'd never see her again.

I saw none of them again.

"Thanks, babe," I said, standing up and making my way to my office door. "Let a bouncer know if you need a ride. They'll call you a cab on me if your friend headed home without you." I shoved the door open, looking back at where she still knelt on the floor, wide eyes turned my way in disbelief.

"I just swallowed your load," she protested, and even I had to admit that there was something so unappealing in the tone of her voice. If she hadn't had those thick lips and the sleek chestnut hair to go along with them, I never would have looked past it long enough to get her mouth on me. "You didn't even get me off, and you're kicking me out?"

"Not at all," I drawled, stepping away from the door and going around the side of my desk to sit in my ergonomic office chair that was closer to a throne in resemblance. I spun around, facing the two-way mirror and looking down on the club floor below me. "You're more than welcome to go back to the party. It looks like a good night."

She stood, slowly jutting out her ass in her slinky, sequined mini that barely covered said ass. "Or I could stay. The fun doesn't have to be over. I have other things to offer." Her hands rested on the opposite edge of my desk, and I eyed them in distaste. The sight of her hands on my desk was enough to send me over the edge, completely distracting me from what should have been a delectable display of cleavage.

I inwardly cursed my cousin Lino. I rarely came to *Indulgence*, too caught up in running the other side of the business. He was one of very few people I could trust with my legitimate businesses, and despite his more carefree manner, he was dedicated to earning the biggest profit and running a tight ship. "Sorry, didn't think you were so dumb you couldn't tell I was done with you. I don't do seconds. I came, I'm done. That's all you'll get from me." I turned back to the paperwork resting on my desk, touching the touchpad on my laptop to bring up the digital file I needed to review.

She gasped, huffing her indignation at me when I didn't even bother to look away from my work. Her heels stomped against the hardwood floor as she stormed out of the office. "Shut the door!" I called after her, not even surprised in the slightest when she didn't listen.

"Women, am I right?" Lino said, leaning against the door frame and grinning at me.

"Oh, thank fuck, can I go home now?" I stood, grabbing my jacket off the back of the chair and shoving my arms in. "I can't handle the music here, not anymore."

"You're getting old, Matteo," Donatello announced, stepping into the room with Scar and my Uncle Gabriele following behind them with a smile.

"You're one to talk, old man." He grinned at me, remaining silent when it became obvious my Uncle had something to say.

"Got a new potential madam who wants to meet with you. High class, and I hear good things about her girls," he said.

"She here?" I asked, buttoning up my suit jacket.

"VIP section. Says she insists on meeting with you if you're planning to buy her out and add the girls to your roster." With a nod, we all left my office and Lino locked it behind him. Since we didn't talk business in public, unless we used it as an intimidation tactic, we walked in silence. I'd be damned if I lost money for someone running his mouth needlessly.

VIP was halfway up to my office, with the main floor visible for the VIPs to survey like they were in charge. They got to play at having power, while Lino and I ruled over it all with an iron thumb. The woman who sat in the VIP section stood immediately when we strolled down the steps. The middle-aged woman had wrapped her body up in a white pencil skirt and elegant black blouse. She'd styled her blond hair into a perfect updo, showing that she was the epitome of class, despite what was a rather questionable profession.

Criminal, if we were being honest.

She was in good company.

Two younger, equally high-class women flanked her, and I knew from a glance at them they were two samples of the product she offered in her stable.

The brunette looked vaguely familiar, and I knew it was possible I'd had her before. But my tendency toward brunettes with big lips meant they blended together.

Except for the only one that mattered.

The other, a stunning African American woman, smiled at me demurely.

Like there was any fooling the man who was looking to buy the rights to her pussy. None of us were innocent, and a coy smile couldn't have fooled the devil in that scenario.

"They're pretty," I said, gesturing for the women to take their seats. The brunette stayed standing, but the other two sat gracefully. I took my seat across from them, not even glancing away when my Uncle and Lino sat on either side of me. "How do I know they're any good?"

"Would you like to sample the merchandise?" the madam asked, giving me a humorous smile. "If these two aren't to your liking, I can assure you I have a wide variety. We could arrange an appointment." I considered it momentarily but decided that professionals weren't likely to have what I was looking for.

No one did.

I turned a glance Lino's way, silently asking if he wanted to give either of them a go. He shook his head, surprising me. Lino was normally much less particular about his bed partners than I was, so a freebie with a professional was right up his alley. I knew whatever had happened with Samara that he'd needed me to cover for him, it must have been big. He'd been in love with her for as long as I could remember. His best friend. The daughter of his father's house-keeper. I knew better than to mention her with Uncle Gabriele around. The women we protected were not on the tolerated list of discussion topics, not when Gabriele would threaten them if we so much as hinted at exploring something real with them. The brunette climbed into my lap, perching on my knee as if she belonged there.

I fought the urge to bristle. I didn't enjoy being touched, outside of what was necessary to get off. Cuddling was not my style, and for that reason I never had sex with a woman in a bed of any kind. The last bed I'd had sex in had been in High School, and if I had anything to do with it that would be the last time.

The only time I'd ever made love.

"You don't have to pay me," the brunette whispered. "Like last time. You were so good; I'll give it to you for free again." I turned a cold glare her way, not reacting when she flinched back and nearly fell off my lap.

"I don't do seconds," I hissed, and she nodded meekly, returning to take the seat next to her employer. "I'll send a few of my guys over to your stables tomor-row. They'll pay; I don't like men who expect freebies from the girls they run. If they're impressed, then we can meet again to discuss the possibility of expanding my existing operations."

"Yes, Mr. Bellandi. Thank you for your time." The woman was smart, I gave her that. She stood, extending a hand for me to shake and then the three of them were off.

I stood, nodding to Lino with a look that communicated that we *would* have a conversation about Samara the next day. "I've arranged a date for you with Luca Morelli's daughter, Elena. You're taking her to dinner tomorrow," my Uncle ordered.

"No, I'm not." There was no inflection in my voice, nothing to betray my annoyance at his constant interference with my love life.

"She's a good match, beautiful, and she knows exactly what we expect of her because her father's in the life. It's time you choose an appropriate match to continue your family line. You need a successor," he argued, blocking my path when I moved to leave.

"No, I don't. Lino can take over if something happens to me. We've had this discussion before, and I will not marry someone I don't care for just to appease your insecurities about the future of this family. I couldn't have the one I wanted, so now I just won't have anyone at all." With my monotone rant over, I shoved past my Uncle and made my way down the steps to the main club floor. After navigating gyrating bodies, only of the ones too wasted to realize they were standing in the path of a predator, I made my way out the side door and was grateful to find Donatello already waiting. How the man was always exactly where I needed him, I'd never know, but I wouldn't take it for granted either. We slid into my Aston Martin, and I drove through the streets of Chicago on the way back to my manor outside the city.

CHAPTER THREE

IVORY

My lungs heaved as I pushed, telling myself just a bit farther. I'd taken my regular route, pushing my speed faster than my usual jog. Something in me had woken up that morning needing to run, needing that feeling of exhaustion that could only come from a too-strenuous workout. I could have hit the gym instead; I was positive Sadie would love the opportunity to beat my ass into fighting shape.

Normally I might have taken her up on it, but the bucket list series for my food blog, *A Dash of Sass*, had propelled the blog from paying the bills to insanity what seemed like overnight. I didn't have time for a run, but damn if I'd give it up. I needed the blankness that came with a hard run, nothing but the ache in my legs and not enough air in my lungs.

I passed the park on my left, hooking a right onto 111th Street and passing Sadie's gym. Finally giving in, I slowed to a stop, catching my breath with my hands on my knees to rest. After a brief pause, I picked up a walk, pulling my phone out and turning off the music in favor of pressing it to my ear and dialing my mom when I saw she'd called me.

"Hello," her familiar, airy voice answered.

"Hey, it's me," I wheezed.

There was a brief pause, "are you running again?"

"Oh, for the love of God, mom. We've been through this," I argued with a chuckle as I passed another jogger I recognized from my daily runs. He smiled at me, and I returned it. I didn't know the guy's name, but I could tell you at exactly what time in the morning he hit the corner of 111th & South Trumbull.

He was cute, all lean and tall with a mop of blond hair on his head and a kind smile.

I'd long since stopped caring how much of a fright I must look when he saw me every day, already two miles into my run by the time we crossed paths. "I just don't think it's safe for a young woman to be out running alone like that. Dad and I can get you a treadmill if it's about the money. We have some saved up."

"Ugh, no," I groaned. "It's not the money. I hate running in one place. It takes the fun out of it."

"Fine. Just be careful, please," she pleaded, and I resisted my chuckle in the face of her genuine concern. As an only child, my parents worried far too much about my safety.

They also worried far too much about my lack of a husband and family.

Saying they wanted to be grandparents would be an understatement.

"You're coming to dinner tonight, right?" she asked, and I shook my head at her with a huff of laughter. It was Sunday. They usually came over to my place mid-week, but Sundays had always—and would forever—be my mother's territory. She wouldn't even give it up to her "fancy chef daughter."

"Yep, I'll see you tonight, okay? I'm about to go into the bank."

"Okay, sweetheart. Love you."

"Love you too, bye." I hung up, feeling appreciation for my meddling mother and father. Even when they were sticking their noses into my love life—which they no longer did too often after setting me up on too many failed dates with their friends' sons—they meant well. They meant the best.

They'd just been head over heels in love for too long to consider the possibility of love not being meant for me. I didn't have a soulmate.

That didn't mean I had to be alone.

I walked into the bank with my phone in my hand, emitting a long, low groan when I only made it a few feet inside.

People crowded the interior, to the point I could barely see the front of the line from my place at the back.

Didn't anybody work normal business hours anymore? I'd thought having an unusual profession would work to my advantage, but so many people mid-morning was just one more sign of the way the workforce in Chicago was changing. I took my place in line behind a middle-aged woman, who gave me a sympathetic smile, undoubtedly having had the same reaction when she walked in only a few moments prior.

I pulled out my phone and stared down the screen as I scanned through all my unaddressed social media notifications. I couldn't keep up with it all anymore. The blog had officially gotten away from me with its success, and while the money was fantastic, I needed to consider hiring a social media manager to take that element off my hands.

I didn't bother looking back when the door opened behind me. With the crowd already in there, it stood to reason that the door was revolving.

"Nobody move!" a male voice yelled from the doorway. A woman screamed, and I turned back to find three men standing just inside the door, black ski masks covering their heads and AK-47's in hand. My phone dropped to the floor in shock as one man used a gun to hit the security guard in the face where he stood frozen. I jolted in place from the sound of my phone hitting the floor, bending down to snatch it up. Even in that moment, I appreciated my expensive, protective case. Usually it was water damage or food that the case saved my phone from, but I supposed bank floors worked too.

Two of the men moved to the tellers with bags, while the other stood guarding the door. "Everybody in the corner!" he yelled, and the crowd scurried over quickly.

I couldn't say what possessed me to do it, but as everyone else attempted to hide behind each other and be as small as possible, I threw my shoulders back and stood tall. An elderly woman shuffled her way over, fidgeting with her walker in her hurry to comply with the orders of the bank robber watching us pointedly. I took her arm, giving it a reassuring pat as we left the walker in favor of getting her into the corner.

"Thank you, dear," she said with a shaky sigh, patting my arm when I'd maneuvered her into the corner. I nodded, shoving my phone into my jacket pocket finally and making my way over to grab her walker. After just a few seconds of standing without it, it was clear that the woman needed it for stability.

"Get back in the fucking corner," the man at the door warned, deep brown eyes peeking out from the holes in his ski mask as he glared at me.

"She needs the walker. That's all," I placated, holding my hands out in front of me to show I wasn't a threat. Though admittedly, if a guy with a really big gun was concerned about me then we had definitely entered backward land.

"She'll live." He pointed his gun at me, and I flinched and ignored the whimper a woman behind me released at the prospect of the gun being turned on the hostages.

"Fine. Be a douchebag. I mean, you are robbing a bank obviously, but it takes a special brand of asshole to leave an elderly woman without her walker," I mumbled, unsure what exactly had come over me. The others behind me were afraid, and so was I. But I was also just *pissed*. There was no way I would die without ever being loved, especially not shot full of holes in a fucking bank robbery.

Though, if I didn't shut my mouth that might happen regardless of how I felt about it.

Instead of firing the gun, I watched as the man's chest shook with laughter. He lowered the gun and tipped his head at me. "By all means, go ahead. I wouldn't want to add asshole to my rap sheet, sweet thing," he drawled, and I bristled.

I had a feeling I'd fucked up.

Regardless, my feet carried me the extra distance until I wrapped my hands around the walker. A hand landed on the other side when I moved to lift it, and with a nervous swallow I turned my face up to glare at the robber staring down at me with amusement dancing in his eyes.

When our eyes connected, his eyes narrowed, and the amusement fled. It was rather comical to watch whatever was passing through his mind as the thoughts were so very visible on his face even when I could hardly see it. "Ivory?" he asked. I froze at the sound of my name on his lips.

"Do-do I know you?" I stuttered in shock.

"No. No, of course not," he said, stepping back a few steps and backing his way toward the door. "Time to go! Now!" he yelled to his friends.

Why I couldn't just let him leave, I'll never know, but my curiosity had me pressing forward, somehow convinced he wouldn't hurt me after whatever he'd realized. "How do you know my name?" He backed away so quickly that he nearly tripped over his own feet, his eyes wide with fear.

"Tell him we didn't know. Never would have done this if we'd known you were here. Never. Make sure he knows we didn't touch you, yeah?" His buddies' eyes widened as they looked at me, seemingly as lost as I was. They fled out the door regardless, hopping into a van waiting at the curb.

"But I don't understand. Tell who?"

"Bellandi. Tell Bellandi it's all good." He hustled out the door without another glance back leaving me with only one question.

Matteo.

How the hell did a bank robber know my high school boyfriend?

CHAPTER FOUR

The next few hours passed by in a blur of police interviews and news cameras shoved into my face as I tried to escape the insanity of the scene that followed the robbery. To say the police wanted to know my connection to Matteo Bellandi had been putting it lightly, and they were disbelieving and disappointed to find that I hadn't had one in *twelve fucking years.* My heart stuttered in my chest. I'd never thought to see Matteo again, and honestly after what he'd done to me, that was for the best. I couldn't say how I'd react.

Would I still love him? Would he still take my breath away? Would I hate him? What if I didn't care about him either way? Then what excuse did I have to hide behind when I just couldn't fall in love with someone?

I realized with a start that I was nervous. And it seemed far worse than the typical nerves that went along with seeing an ex and wanting to prove you were better off without them. It was more than wanting to avoid shrinking back into that weak, pathetic, *broken* girl he'd made me into.

Even after twelve years, I was still in love with the ghost of a man who had never existed. I was still in love with the lie Matteo had shown me, and what happened after I saw the real Matteo would always haunt me.

Always.

I pulled my gently used Toyota Yaris up to the house in Barrington Hills where I knew Matteo's family lived back in high school, feeling beyond awkward. I'd never been to the estate when we dated, Matteo preferred to keep me separate from his family life that he'd explained as "complicated." He'd been to my house. He'd spent time with my parents, but he'd never allowed me the same courtesy.

That should have been my first sign that something was wrong with our relationship.

Even never having been there, it was common knowledge where Matteo lived. His family's wealth was legendary, so much so that some people speculated that their business practices were shady, but most attributed that to jealousy. There was no family as synonymous with success as the Bellandi's.

I'd known going to the estate was my best bet as soon as I realized my curiosity couldn't let me forget the incident in the bank without finding out why there was *any* connection between Matteo and I. I wanted him out of my life, scrubbed completely from any trace of him. Call it a near death experience, but I was determined to move on once and for all.

And to do that, I needed answers.

Massive wrought-iron gates sat blocking the driveway, making me release a sigh of frustration. I *so* did not belong on that estate.

A security guard at the gate stopped me, and I rolled down my window with a smile. "Can I help you, ma'am?" he asked, giving me a once over that stated he found me unimpressive.

Ouch.

I wasn't wearing Versace or anything, but I had dressed and done my makeup to prepare for facing the man who broke my heart all those years ago. Like any sane woman would do. "I'm looking for Matteo Bellandi," I smiled.

"Baby, whoever you are he doesn't do seconds."

"I—what?" I asked, throwing the car into park once I realized that getting inside would not be as simple as I'd hoped.

"You know. He never does the same woman twice. No matter how good she sucks cock, so stop thinking you're different." He shook his head, looking at me like he couldn't believe I had the audacity to turn up on Matteo's doorstep.

"I'm not—"

"Turn the car around and be on your way."

"You don't understand—"

"Really? Because you look exactly like all the other bitches he brings around."

Okay, double ouch.

That one got a physical wince. From what I'd seen in school, he appreciated variety. So I didn't exactly know what *that* was about, but I wasn't touching it.

Nope. No way.

"Look Mister, I'm not looking for another round. I just need to speak to him. Urgently. Just," I sighed, pinching the bridge of my nose as he turned to walk away. "Tell him Ivory Torres is trying to get in touch with him," I called, shaking my head and wondering if answers were worth this shit.

"What the fuck did you just say?" he whispered, snapping to a stop and turning back to me.

"That I don't want another round?" I asked, flinching when his steps prowled toward me. His hand touched the roof of my car, his upper body leaning down to put his face level with the window as his wide brown eyes met mine.

"Your name. What did you say your name was?" His voice raised a bit, not to the point of yelling, but enough that I knew he meant serious business.

"Ivory Torres?" My voice was barely a whisper, and I felt a piece of me shrivel when, yet another strange man recognized my name in connection with Matteo.

What the fuck had I gotten myself into coming here?

"The Ivory?"

"Umm, well I suppose so. It's not exactly a common name, is it?" I grimaced with an uncomfortable chuckle.

He turned his back on me without another word, going to the guard booth and picking up his cell. I ran a hand through my hair aggressively, feigning casualness as I did my best to eavesdrop.

Because you're damn right I fucking eavesdropped. I was surprised I didn't stick my head out the damn window.

"Yeah, boss. Ivory Torres is here for you." A pause of silence while the man on the other end of the phone spoke. "You got it." He ended the call with a touch of his finger to the screen and hit the button to open the gates. They creaked open slowly, acting every bit as heavy as they looked. I ran my hand through my hair again, biting the corner of the inside of my lip and losing some of the nerve that fueled me to drive there. "Go on through, drive right up in front of the house at the circle and someone will show you where to go."

"I—okay." My hands went to the steering wheel as my eyes fixated on that gate. Even when it opened fully, I didn't shift my car to drive.

"I'm sorry, Miss Torres. Meant no disrespect to you. You won't get any going forward." I turned wide eyes his way finally.

Because there was zero chance, I'd be seeing him *again*.

Fuck that.

"I—okay," I repeated, putting my car in drive and going through the gate in a daze.

I was in trouble.

I was in so much trouble. My Uncle would kill me, if he ever found out I was here. My father would kill me too. What the fuck had I been thinking driving up to the house of someone who had criminal connections like I was invincible?

Fuck.

I thought about turning around and escaping the way I'd come, but the gate closed behind me and running away now that Matteo knew I was there felt humiliating. I drove my car up the rest of the driveway, feeling my eyes bug out when the house itself came into sight. It was massive, in a way that was unnecessary—ridiculous even. An intriguing mixture of white stone and grey brick, I felt minuscule in my tiny car. Pulling up in front of the house where the guard at the gate had directed me, I found an older gentleman standing on the stone steps with a bright smile on his face. I shifted into park slowly, taking a deep breath and releasing it on a sigh as I turned off the ignition. Grabbing my purse out of the passenger seat, I opened my door and unfolded myself as gracefully as I could manage. The last thing I needed to do was flash someone my goodies at Matteo's house. I was getting the distinct feeling that was *not* the kind of man I was looking to attract.

"Miss Torres, I presume?" a man greeted as I shut the door and stared in shock at the house. "My name is Donatello. I manage Mr. Bellandi's home. If you'll follow me, he's asked that I see you to his office."

I nodded wordlessly, letting him lead me in the huge dark wood doors and into the sprawling mansion. I'd obviously known he was wealthy, but I'd never imagined this. I knew I was stalling. But I couldn't stop my eyes from darting around the foyer in awe. I'd never seen wealth like this before, let alone stepped inside a home of that caliber. The floors were tiled in Mediterranean tile; the walls painted off white with huge archways connecting the rooms in the place of doors.

"Best not to keep him waiting," he said with a polite smile.

I nodded, picking up my pace as I followed him. A curving staircase led upstairs, but we bypassed that in favor of stepping around it to a narrower archway that led into a hall. "Matteo still lives here?" I asked. I couldn't see that. We were a decade out of high school. The man nodded. "I never got the impression he got along with his father," I added, deciding there was no harm in exposing how little I truly knew about the man of the house.

"His father passed some time ago. The estate is much more practical for security reasons than the Penthouse in the city where he lived prior, and so he moved back here after his death." He didn't seem hesitant to reveal Matteo's personal information to me, and I had to wonder if that was common. Surely, a man of Matteo's stature would be interested in confidentiality.

I agreed, thinking back to the gate and the walls surrounding the property. I had a feeling it was nearly as secure as the White House. We stopped in front of two impressive, heavy wood doors. With a smile back at me, he tapped his fingers against it twice. I drew in a shuddering breath, hating the audible way it displayed my fear of what might wait for me behind those doors. Once again, I questioned if I was making a mistake. Perhaps I was better off not knowing, not seeing, not feeling again.

Because the truth was, I had felt little of anything since he'd broken me.

"Enter," a deep, masculine voice returned, following Donatello's knock. My heart stalled, having thought never to hear that voice again. It had changed, deepened, become more commanding as if there was almost no trace of the boy, I'd loved remaining. And yet somehow, my soul recognized it on some deep level that nearly brought tears to my eyes.

After all the time that had passed, just the sound of his voice through a closed door was enough to bring me to my knees.

Donatello opened both doors with a flourish, waving me forward with his hand and a bow of his head. I took a deep, steadying breath before I managed to will my feet to move into the room.

My eyes darted around the opulent space, reflecting on the way the decor in that house made me feel cheap in my forest green button up and short white petal skirt with silver rivulets all over it. I felt out of place and realized I'd never belonged in Matteo's world.

No wonder he dumped my ass.

At least my heels made me feel classy, looking stunning and strappy all wrapped around my ankles in forest green suede against the dark hardwood floor. "Ivory." There was a smile in his voice, and I turned to the left where the room curved to find him staring at me from behind his desk, pen still in hand. Though his head tilted down to look at the paper he'd been writing on, his eyes fixated on me with startling intensity.

The breath whooshed out of me, confronted with that impossibly handsome face. In high school, he'd been all about clean edges, the blond-haired All-American boy next door with the stunning blue eyes and boy muscles packed onto his frame however he could. A decade later his hair was darker, browner than blond, and it only made those piercing azure eyes of his seem brighter. His once clean-cut face was covered in some cross between stubble and a very short, well-groomed beard. He'd bulked up, his lean frame a thing of the past with no issues packing on muscle now that he'd aged, that much was visible even covered by the designer suit he wore. He was everything he'd been in high school, intimidating and unattainable, but now he was just *more*. The pen fell to the paper in front of him with a clatter that drew me from my stare, and I shook myself a bit. "Ivory," he whispered again, standing with a smile and walking around the desk to approach me. His lips found my cheek in greeting, and I winced when the contact sent a shiver through me. "You're as beautiful as I always knew you would be."

I flushed, staring up into his intense gaze. He stood too close, far too close, and I shifted back a step pointedly. "Thank you," I murmured awkwardly. Years ago, there'd been obvious affection in the way he looked at me, humor always in his eyes when they landed on me. That was absent, *gone*, only an almost dark, unsettling intensity remaining. "You look good too," I returned. The smirk he gave me communicated that he was arrogant enough to know just how much of an understatement that was.

Lie of the century.

His smirk melted into a grin. "What are you doing here?" His words were harsh, but his tone was gentle, almost mystified, and laced with his own disbelief.

I understood it very well. Standing in front of him after all those years of pain was a surreal experience, I had no desire to repeat. I wanted to get it over with and be on my way.

"I was at the Byline Bank in McKinley Park this morning when three armed men wearing ski masks came in to rob it," I said in answer, deciding to just be blunt with the situation. I was growing increasingly suspicious of whatever might have brought criminals to identify me in connection with Matteo.

He stilled, his body freezing in a way that felt unnatural. He didn't so much as twitch aside from the movement necessary to form his next words. "Did they touch you?" His voice was carefully controlled.

"No. As soon as one of them got a good look at me, he begged me to tell you they didn't know I was there. That they couldn't have known I'd be there, and to tell you they didn't touch me."

"Ivory—" His face gentled, movement returning to his body suddenly. He leaned further into my space, and I backed up another step. I would not allow him to cross that line, not after everything he'd done. All I could do was get my answers, say my peace, and move on with my life finally.

"Why would bank robbers know my name? And why would they panic because of you?" My arms crossed over my chest, and my teeth sank into that spot at the corner of my mouth that had practically become a chew toy under all the stress of the day.

"You're under my protection. You have been since high school." His voice hardened slightly as his gaze traveled down to my crossed arms. He didn't appear to appreciate the posture, or the attitude behind it, but kept his mouth shut about it.

"Right," I grumbled. "Well, let me make something very, very clear then. I do not want your protection." The remaining gentle look disappeared in favor of hard, cruelly handsome lines. "Remove it, and I will go on living my life like you do not exist just as I have done for twelve fucking years."

"Be very careful," he grumbled under his breath. His nostrils flared at me, what had once been a relaxed posture tensing as he stood taller.

"I want nothing to do with you or whatever the hell it is you're involved in where criminals are afraid of you. You let me live my life without interference, and if I get gunned down in the street then so fucking be it," I hissed, glaring up at him. The muscle in his jaw ticked, his glare turning positively glacial. "It will be better than being a part of whatever this is," I mumbled, turning on my heel to leave.

The doors I'd entered the room through had closed, courtesy of Donatello no doubt. I'd been too wrapped up in the enigma of a man behind me to notice.

It wouldn't happen again. I swore it on my soul, I would never see Matteo again.

He wasn't worth it.

I barely had my hand wrapped around the handle before Matteo's palms pressed against the wood beside my head, and he leaned into me—caging me in.

Fuck.

I'd forgotten what it was like to have a man make me feel short. At 5'7" I wasn't the tallest woman, but I was no slouch. It took a large man to make me feel tiny. Matteo's 6'5" was effective.

"You've been very foolish coming here," he murmured, near my ear. His breath tickled the flesh, sending a shiver racing through me. "I let you go twelve years ago, and it was the most difficult thing I've ever done. Did you really think I would do it twice?" I ignored my confusion at his words. Like he'd walked away for any reason other than wanting to fuck around.

"There's a difference," I gasped as his mouth trailed over the side of my neck in the whisper of a caress. Barely there, so subtle that with anyone else I might have wondered if it was a figment of my imagination. But I knew Matteo's lips, knew his mouth, knew his scent.

"What's that?" The humor in his voice even sounded arrogant. He knew how affected I was by his touch, and I stilled my body and willed it to shut the hell up.

"I wanted you then," I hissed. "I don't anymore."

"Ah, my Angel, you expect me to believe you have not missed my touch? That you are not already wet for me?"

Why did that voice of his have to be so deep, so *fucking sexy?* I wanted to turn around and rip out his vocal cords, just so I couldn't torment myself with the prospect of him using it to seduce other women who looked like me.

"Fuck you, Matteo." I grumbled, yanking my head away from his wandering lips.

"You should be careful, Angel. I'm a dangerous man now. I do not tolerate disrespect." He stepped away from me, as if the sound of that nickname in his voice wasn't enough to bring the threat of tears to my eyes. As if the teasing torment of his breath on my neck had been nothing but a game. "I have business to tend to tonight," he said as he straightened his suit like he was a gentleman and not a deviant who'd just violated my space. "I'll pick you up at seven tomorrow for dinner."

"That will never happen." I laughed, turning to look at him over my shoulder only briefly. He had to be kidding me.

"*Cara mia,* you will be ready and waiting, or I will feast on you instead."

I gasped. "Go to hell, Matteo."

"I've lived in Hell for twelve years, Angel mine. It is time for me to feel the sun again." With that, he moved to sit in the chair behind his desk.

"What does that even mean?" I asked, and he tilted his head to look at me thoughtfully. "You don't even know where I live," I pointed out, turning the sterling silver knob on the door and pulling it open.

"Ivory," his voice called out, and I paused in my steps to go over the threshold. "I mean it, Angel. You will be ready for dinner at seven."

"Or what?" I whispered, raising my chin and turning to face him. "I won't have sex with you. I won't ever make that mistake again."

"We will see about that," he smirked, picking up his pen once more. "You're too naïve to know when you're playing a very dangerous game. I am not a man you say no to."

Donatello appeared in the doorway, eyeing the tension between us. "Miss Torres, may I be of some assistance?" he offered, seeming to want to dissipate the anger pulsing through the room. My heart thudded in my chest. I couldn't say what it was about Matteo's threat, but I knew he meant to make good on it. However, that would happen.

"No, thank you," I snarled, feeling badly for the older man as I turned and stormed toward the door. "I'll show myself out."

"Ivory!" Matteo called behind me, but I kept walking. I didn't stop, even when I heard Donatello's steps following me.

"Miss Torres," he pleaded, but I ignored him as I fumbled through my purse to dig out my keys. I had a moment of panic where I thought the gate wouldn't open when I got to it, but as soon as I put my car in drive it started to open. Whether it was Donatello or Matteo who ordered the guard to let me out, I didn't care at that moment.

I was too concerned with the fact that if he'd wanted to keep me there, *he could have.*

There was one thing I was sure of; Matteo was even more dangerous to me than he'd been twelve years ago.

And there was no way in Hell I would ever see him again.

Over my dead body.

CHAPTER FIVE

MATTEO

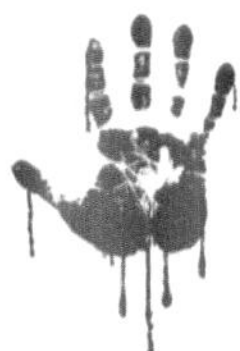

I turned my glare Donatello's way. A lesser man would have cowered under the weight of it, although it wasn't actually aimed at him. Not intentionally.

That right was reserved for the angel who'd just fled like I wouldn't follow her into the pearly gates themselves to drag her back with me. "Send Scar to follow her home and get me everything she's been up to for the last twelve years." My older friend nodded, turning and striding out the doors with his cell to his ear - already calling Scar no doubt. "Don? I want him on her 24/7 but tell him to be discreet for now."

He didn't speak, just nodded his understanding as he made his way out the front door. Scar was already waiting at the curb, one of the BMW's being pulled up by another one of my guys.

Satisfied that he would catch up with her, I turned back to stride through the halls of my too-empty house, all while the knowledge that it wouldn't be so empty for too much longer settled in me. I'd have Ivory there regularly soon.

There was no other option. She'd settle into her new reality, eventually.

She didn't have a choice, since I wouldn't let her go again.

Seeing her again had been like a punch to the gut. She'd been beautiful, even in my decade old memories, but somehow, she was even more stunning standing in front of me, all grown up with no remaining trace of the youth she'd been at sixteen. All that sleek chestnut hair that I knew shone auburn when the light hit the strands just right hung down to her narrow little waist in layers, bisecting her where her lithe body tapered out to the hips that seemed to defy the odds. The Portuguese side of her heritage somehow packed all the right curves onto her slight frame, like her body just couldn't decide if it wanted to be slim or curvy. Her mother's French influence had given her the beautiful ivory skin that was her namesake, that generous dusting of freckles across her nose and cheekbones only drawing attention to her sea-green eyes.

Any of the little details that comprised Ivory would have been enough to make her memorable, but it was the thick, lush lips that had haunted my life for over ten years. Whether she wore them relaxed or pillowed, spread into a blinding smile, or wrapped around my cock while she drove me wild with her innocence, I could never get the image of them out of my head.

By the time Donatello returned to my office, I'd sat down in my chair and started tapping my pen against the desk idly in my impatience. It wasn't characteristic of me; distractions weren't something I allowed in my life.

It was too dangerous when one wrong move was the difference between life and death, not just for me but for the people who counted on me.

Donatello took a seat on the other side of the desk, quirking an eyebrow up at me. He'd never actually met Ivory, couldn't have had the opportunity when I'd refused to bring her around my family for her own safety.

But he knew of her—had seen her. Even then, he'd been one of the two confidants who knew just how obsessed I'd been with my angel.

"How long will you be entertaining Miss Torres this time around?" His amusement faded for something close to disappointment. He knew as well as I had that I'd broken her when I ended things the way I did. Back then, I had to rely on he and Lino to make sure she was coping.

Healing.

Moving on.

All the things I'd never been able to do.

I knew that he'd be disappointed in me if I forced her to experience that all over again just for a few quick fucks. I stared back at him in response, and that disappointment faded and replaced with a pleased grin. "Right."

"I'll be needing an appointment on Jeweler's Row. I want something custom and quick." I picked up my pen, finishing the paperwork on my desk with a quick flourish of my signature before handing it off to Donatello to send out with a messenger.

"I'll make the arrangements." His eyes crinkled in the corners with his bright smile, and I shook my head even as my own lips tipped up slightly.

"Nothing but the best," I reiterated, and he nodded in a wordless representation that it didn't need to be said. He stood to leave me to my work, undoubtedly having plenty of his own to do now that he needed to run twelve years' worth of data on Ivory and find me the best jeweler in Chicago who could work on my tight schedule.

"I'm proud of you, son," he said, his voice cracking with the emotional weight of the bond that held tight between us. My father hadn't been a loving man, had tolerated *no one* loving me. That hadn't been enough to stop Donatello from showing me rare moments of affection when I earned them.

Lino saved me from having to respond when he shoved the door open and burst into the room. He was literally the only person who got away with it, but even being who he was my hand twitched toward the pistol in the top drawer of my desk. "Heard you saw Ivory?" he asked, plopping his ass down into the seat that Donatello vacated.

I pinched the bridge of my nose between two fingers and released a sigh. "For fuck's sake, she just left fifteen minutes ago."

"What can I say? Your guard has a big mouth. He was all excited that he'd finally laid eyes on *the* Ivory Torres. Nervous wreck about it too, worried she's going to demand his head or some shit." He leaned forward in his chair, stripping off his own suit jacket and making himself comfortable.

Shit. He was in for the long haul.

"Why would he be worried about that? Did he touch her?" Even I wasn't immune to the menace in my voice, something I rarely noticed. It happened too frequently to give a shit, but when Ivory was threatened, well, *that* was a different story.

"Nah, just told her she looked like every other bimbo you bang. Before he realized who she was, anyway."

My fists clenched beneath the desk, and I swallowed loudly. "He said what?"

"Shit, man. I thought you'd closed that door a long time ago," Lino whispered, seeming to finally alert himself to the dark energy pulsing around me.

"She came back to me. That's my sign she's mine, so I'm taking her." I shrugged, turning my attention to where Donatello watched our exchange with a mixture of horror and amusement. "Who's at the gate today?"

"Christian," he answered hesitantly.

"Right, tell Ryker to make it very clear to Christian exactly what happens when someone runs his mouth to my woman. I want him alive, but I want him to know what the consequences are for calling her a whore."

"Woah, I think you're overreacting—" Lino objected, and I turned my glare his way. "How could he have known, Matteo? You spent twelve years looking for her twin to warm your bed."

"Does it look like I give a fuck?" I hissed, turning back to the spreadsheet waiting for me on my computer. I needed to run through the numbers from the last shipment, and I needed Lino to update me on the latest numbers from the businesses, and I needed it done before I went to inspect the cleanliness of the new brothel my men had sampled.

I might run escort, but I only ran the best of the best. Women who made six figures a year and would be free to retire young and live a good life if they were smart.

For the first time since I'd taken over, a voice questioned me.

Because Ivory wouldn't like it. When she found out that was.
But she'd deal with it.
She didn't have a choice.

CHAPTER SIX

IVORY

The deep breath I took before I opened the front door wasn't nearly enough to prepare me for the shit storm I was about to walk into. I knew that.

But there was nothing else to be done for it.

My father flung the door open with a sudden jerk, grasping me around the back of the neck and pulling me into his arms with a shudder. "Christ. Jesus fucking Christ almighty," he mumbled into the top of my head.

"Daddy, I'm fine," I protested in a mumble against his chest. The press of his shirt against my face muffled my voice, nearly suffocating me. "Well, at least death by hugging is better than being shot," I joked, and I heard my mother's gasp from somewhere further in the house.

How she'd heard me, I'd never know. The woman had eyes and ears everywhere.

"Ivory Leonora!" she cried, and even without being able to see her I knew she pressed her hand to her chest in outrage. She was nothing if not dramatic.

"It's true," I announced, giving my father a shove until his arms fell away. Even at 59, the man was fitter than most 40-year-old men because of his own inability to sit still. The number of times I'd heard him say, "idle time is wasted time," during my youth would make most of his Air Force buddies cringe.

My mother's arms closed around me as soon as I could breathe in peace, and I sighed. I couldn't blame them for their concern. Seeing your daughter on the news as police ushered her out of a bank following an armed robbery wasn't something most parents had to experience.

I'd called them back before going to Matteo's house, making sure they knew I was okay once I'd realized I'd been on the news. Still, the whole thing seemed to be far more traumatic for them than it was for me, and I'd been the one staring down the barrel of a gun.

"My baby," she cried, tears soaking my shoulder where she'd rested her face. I was taller than my mom, even when I didn't wear heels. Having gone straight to their house for dinner after seeing Matteo, I hadn't changed out of my impress-the-ex outfit.

Though I regretted dressing to impress.

Like a lot.

I shrugged off the anxiety plaguing me. I'd figure out how to deal with Matteo's threat in the morning, because there was no way to ponder it with my father staring at me.

Where my mom saw everything that happened, my father saw every thought inside my head.

Safe to say, I hadn't gotten away with anything as a teenager. Well, except for the one time I'd had Matteo in my bed in high school. After that experience, I'd gone the straight and narrow for a few years until I graduated. After that, well, that had been a different story.

My father cleared his throat. "All right Alice, you've coddled her enough. Let the girl in the house."

"Me? You suffocated her!" Mom protested, though her arms relented and released me finally. With a groan, I walked off into the house, leaving them in their own entryway to bicker as usual. They had a special love, the love people dreamed of finding. That didn't mean that they weren't as sarcastic with each other as possible before they got all kissy and gross.

I did *not* need to be around for that part.

Mom's fried chicken sat on the granite counter, waiting for her to move it to the huge oak table in the dining room. I grabbed it and moved it over, with the sounds of their arguments fading into the background when the humorous jabs at one another started to ease into affection. By the time they made their way into the kitchen, I was pulling the collard greens out of the pot and putting them in one of mom's serving bowls. "Oh honey, you didn't need to do that. I would have used the white bowl," she said, coming up and taking the macaroni and cheese out of the oven.

"Of course," I snorted. "If I'd used the white bowl, you'd have wanted the orange one. Anything to be the opposite of what I pick, contrary woman."

She huffed at me and started to object. "I am not—"

"Woman, you're the most contrary person on the planet," Dad announced, pulling out his seat at the head of the table. "Who the hell cares what bowl the food's in? You going to start taking pictures of it too?"

"Honestly, Martim. These things matter." I took my seat to Daddy's right, serving myself and listening to him gossip about which flight attendant was hooking up with his co-pilot. Apparently, it was quite the scandal—what with the woman being 26 and the pilot in his 50s. Normally, I put on a good show of listening to him sound like a teenage girl, but that day—given everything that had happened—my head just wasn't interested in his idle gossip. I poked at my food, barely eating and contemplating what I would do about Matteo the next day despite my resolution to forget him for the time being.

"Okay, what gives?" Daddy asked.

"What do you mean?" I mumbled, snapping out of my trance and forcing a bite of fried chicken into my mouth.

"You seemed fine about the robbery, my little warrior," he teased, reaching over and pinching my cheeks. I stuck my tongue out at him. "So why are you so in your head now?"

I sighed, dropping the chicken to my plate and biting the corner of my mouth while I contemplated what story I could tell my parents about Matteo. There was no way I'd ever admit I'd gone there, especially because a criminal had known him. "I talked to Matteo," I said vaguely.

My mother stilled, and I glanced at my father to watch his brow furrow. I was under no illusion that he didn't know what Matteo I meant, so I knew his next question was his attempt to give me time to rethink the course of our conversation. "Matteo who?"

"You know, Matteo Bellandi. From high school." I shrugged, as if discussing the boy who'd made me cry myself to sleep for weeks could ever be a casual occurrence.

"And where did you see him?" Mom asked, she forked some greens into her mouth, chewing as if she found them distasteful, but there was no doubting the fact that it was Matteo she found disgusting.

"I didn't," I lied. "See him, I mean. He saw me on the news and reached out to see if I was all right or if there was anything he could do. That's all." My eyes glanced at mom's curtains on the big picture window behind her, seeing that the rods needed dusting. "If you need me to come over and help with the housework, I can do that. I know you have trouble reaching some high places." I changed the subject deftly, knowing mom would bristle at the insinuation that she couldn't clean her damn house herself.

She started to do just that, but Dad's deadly serious voice interrupted her. "I do not think so, young lady. You are not changing the conversation like it doesn't matter that piece of shit somehow got your phone number. You're getting a new one. End of story." He stabbed a piece of macaroni and cheese, shoving it into his mouth angrily.

"What good would that do? With the assets the Bellandi's have access to, he could just find that number if he wanted it," I pointed out. Whether Matteo had my number yet was irrelevant. I'd known for twelve years that he could find me if he'd wanted.

He just hadn't wanted to.

"Ivory—"

"Besides, do you realize what a hassle it would be to change my number? I run my business through it." I shrugged, ignoring his pointed glare.

I sent mom a pleading look, that she took with a sigh and directed my father's attention elsewhere with the promise of further gossip about work. I tuned in better, feeling his eyes on me too attentively for my taste several times throughout dinner.

But we survived without mentioning Matteo again, and when I went home after dinner that night, I was even more determined to make sure I never had to tell them anything about him again.

It was better that way for everyone.

Especially me.

✳✳✳

My white dress with big tropical coral flowers floated around me with the breeze, and I thanked the heavy cardigan I wore for keeping it down. As a rule, floaty skirts were dangerous in the windy city, but that never stopped me.

Sadie said I had an aversion to pants. I couldn't argue against it. I wore them only when it was necessary to fight off the cold, which was why I wore a dress despite the chill to the Spring air.

I hurried into the restaurant, not even surprised when I found Duke and his family already sitting and waiting for me. I'd changed my clothes last minute after spilling my pet leopard gecko Smaug's water bowl all over myself like a complete idiot, and me running late following some random catastrophe wasn't as rare as it should have been.

Duke turned to face the door, his down-turned blue eyes meeting mine as he shook his head and a smile played at his mouth. I shrugged with a grin of my own, hurrying over and taking the empty seat next to him. Leaning in, I placed a kiss on his cheek and smiled at his mom and brother.

His mother returned the smile, her eyes warming as she looked at the two of us. She'd made no secret of hoping the two of us would end up together one day, and I knew she analyzed every move we made around one another to notice any subtle difference. If we'd ever crossed that line, she'd know before we told her. That much was obvious, since the woman missed nothing where her sons were concerned.

"Hey, Gendry," I murmured.

"What? No kiss for me?" Duke's older brother chuckled, and I narrowed my eyes at him in a glare.

"Why don't you kiss my a—"

"Okay! So good to see you, Ivory, my dear. Should we remember we are in a restaurant and have a nice brunch, without the lot of you bickering like you're still children?" Amelia cut me off. When she turned her face back to the menu in her hands, I stuck my tongue out at Gendry. "I saw that," she drawled, her lips quirking up even though her eyes never left her menu.

Creepy.

"How do you do that?" Duke mused, opening the menu that sat on the table in front of me. I ignored the hint, not even glancing at the menu. Asshole just had to make fun of me every Monday when we met for brunch.

"It's a mom thing. You'll understand one day, Ivory," she said pointedly, and I snorted water back into my glass. Because I was a lady like that.

"I think I'm missing a certain requirement for having children," I chuckled. The waiter saved from whatever response she might have when he came over.

"Can I get you something to drink, miss?" he asked, and I gave him a smile that was probably a little too happy. I needed a drink for the way the conversation was about to turn. As much as I loved Amelia, I just couldn't sometimes.

"A mimosa, please." Duke chuckled, his face hitting my shoulder. I knew I was practically begging the waiter to bring me my drink tout suite, and there was no way anyone missed the tone.

"Are we ready to order brunch?" the waiter asked, totally barely cracking even a bit of humor.

Oh, he was good.

"Nope, just the mimosa for now!" I announced, flicking Duke in the forehead until he reared back with a flinch.

"That hurt!" he protested, rubbing at the spot with a crease in his brow.

"I'll have the nutella french toast with a side of bacon," Gendry said, handing his menu to the waiter. I turned my glower his way. "She'll have the crab benedict, hollandaise on the side." Not only had he thrown me under the bus by ordering *his* food, but the bastard had ordered mine.

It wasn't even like I could protest that he'd ordered wrong, because he hadn't. It was the same thing I got every week. I handed my menu to the waiter, shrinking back in my chair to pout while Amelia and Duke ordered their food. "I'll be right out with that mimosa, ma'am," the waiter announced before he turned to flee the table.

"How did I go from a miss to a ma'am? Did I age ten years in the last five minutes?" I teased, desperate to deflect Amelia away from the pointed way she looked at me.

"You two aren't getting any younger. When are you going to give me grand-babies?" I sighed, leaning forward to bang my head on the table. The woman had a very, very thick skull for this determination that Duke and I were meant to be an item.

"Shouldn't you be pressuring Gendry?" Duke asked. "He's older."

"And he also has never brought a girl home. I can't exactly pressure him when he's determined to remain eternally single, can I?" Amelia steeped her hands, and as soon as the waiter dropped my mimosa in front of me, I took a long swig.

"I've never brought a woman home either, mom," Duke laughed. Amelia raised a brow, turning her attention my way. "Ivory doesn't count. You know we aren't dating."

And we never would. I'd been friends with Duke since second grade. There was no way we would ever go there. "I don't understand you two," Amelia shook her head, sipping at her water in a polite way that made my gulp of mimosa seem vulgar. "I wonder who the kids will look like."

Oh, for fuck's sake.

It would be one of those days.

"I have a date," I interrupted. "Tonight." It didn't matter that I had no intentions of going on said date, but it was enough to deflate Amelia to sighing.

Duke stilled beside me. "Sadie set that up fast."

"Not him. Different date," I answered vaguely.

"Where did you meet this one?" Amelia asked with pursed lips. A look passed between her and Duke, and I ignored it. Neither one of them were fond of my failure of a dating life, for very different reasons. Duke worried I'd get involved with the wrong man and get hurt. Amelia hated everyone who wasn't her son.

"I've known him for a long time," I evaded. They both let the subject drop, and Gendry was nice enough to steer the conversation toward work and the tension melted away.

As much as I hated Amelia's insistence to make something out of nothing, Duke's family was as close to me as my own.

They were my family too, and when his hand rested on my thigh and he took my hand in his, I knew they always would be.

No matter what a colossal fuck up he might think I was when he found out about Matteo.

CHAPTER SEVEN

I flipped back and forth through the pages. The folder Donatello had handed me felt obscenely light, and I knew there was no way in Hell he'd included everything there was to know about Ivory for twelve fucking years. I'd wanted to give the man the benefit of the doubt, since he so rarely did anything less than a thorough job. A quick scan confirmed there was something missing. A mishap with the printer no doubt.

I shoved the papers back in the file folder, standing from my desk chair and going in search of the man. There was a matter of hours before I would pick Ivory up for our date, and I needed all the information I could get.

God knew I would need it.

The sound of Donatello's voice reached me, his voice a loud hum as he puttered around in the kitchen with fixing lunch for my guys on duty. I tossed the folder on the island counter, not angrily, but impatient as I ever was. "Where's the rest?" I asked, slipping my hands into my pockets. He turned from the stove, quirking his lips at me and shaking his head like he couldn't quite believe it himself.

"That's all of it."

"It can't be. She's an adrenaline junkie, and you expect me to believe that she's spent the last twelve years cooking and moving from one failed career to another until she finally settled on a blog? Ivory's way too social to be content with a career like that. She'd never survive not being surrounded by people nonstop, not unless something happened." I shook my head, picking a kalamata olive out of one of Donatello's little bowls that he kept pre-measured ingredients in. The man was meticulous.

"I looked at everything," he admitted, rolling out the dough for what appeared to be his Mediterranean flatbread. "There was nothing there, Matteo. From what I can see, that adrenaline junkie you remember disappeared without a trace at eighteen."

"What happened at eighteen?" I reached for another olive, shaking out my hand when Donatello smacked me away with the rolling pin. I narrowed my eyes on him, and he grinned back at me. The old man knew he was one of three people who could get away with something like that and live to tell the tale.

"No idea." He shrugged, setting down the rolling pin in favor of combining his toppings in a small bowl. "Before that, as you saw in the folder there were some parties. She snuck into a club at least once and got caught. Went out joyriding with a college guy who had a motorcycle when she was a junior, normal teenage stuff." My fists clenched at the reminder she'd been with other men. Even if there was no evidence to suggest she'd been sexually involved with the biker, I knew from looking through her file there'd been others.

I had no right to be pissed. No right to be jealous since I'd been the one to walk away from her.

That didn't make me feel any less murderous.

"She wouldn't have just stopped."

Donatello twisted his lips up into a grimace. "Did you consider the fact that maybe she was only an adrenaline junkie because of you? You encouraged that part of her, without that influence she might have settled into an easy life. It would explain why she went through so many career changes before she found a successful one."

"And not being social now?" I pinged my eyebrows up, watching him coat the dough in olive oil with a silicone brush like it was an art canvas.

"Well, for what it's worth, that seems like it may have changed immediately after you left her. She remained close to Ms. Hicks and Mr. Bradley, but her friendships with others dwindled by the time the next school year started. Given what my granddaughter says about school, I suspect that once you dumped her, she lost her popularity and the bulk of her friends. She was never the it-girl by her own merit, but because of your interest in her. Once you moved on—"

"So did the rest of the school. Fuck," I groaned. I always seemed to underestimate just how cruel women were to one another.

"I imagine being betrayed by you, and subsequently by most of the people she considered her friends, would be enough to make her hesitant to put herself out there again. Perhaps less trusting of strangers." Donatello sprinkled the topping mixture and feta cheese on the flatbread before shoving it in the oven.

I sighed, knowing his theory probably had merit. Ivory had never taken rejection well, and she'd always been too trusting. While part of me wanted to be pleased that she'd learned that valuable lesson, I hated that they had ostracized her because of me. I'd never wanted to hurt her, let alone cause other people to hurt her too. "You realize it's ridiculous that you cook a fucking flatbread for my security, right?"

He froze. "Do they not like my flatbread?"

I shook my head with a smile. "They like it, Don, but they're killing machines. You'll give them a complex with that shit."

He sighed in disappointment. "I dislike it when you curse."

"Of all my sins, cursing is the big concern?" I chuckled.

He rolled his eyes, shooing me out of his kitchen. I didn't have the heart to point out that once I'd moved Ivory in with me, it would become her territory. "It is the most unnecessary."

"Did you get me a jeweler yet?" I teased, even as I backed out of his space. I'd let him enjoy it while it lasted.

"She'll be here noon tomorrow."

I grinned at him, and I knew it was the one I wore when I'd conquered something impossible. "Perfect."

CHAPTER EIGHT

IVORY

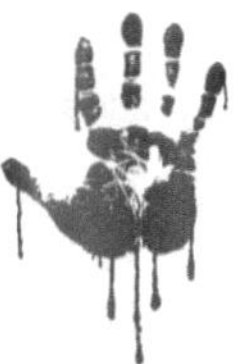

It was normal for Duke to walk me home after brunch. The restaurant wasn't far; it was midday, and I walked just about everywhere if I could. That didn't stop him from thinking I needed an escort. Since his house wasn't far from mine, he'd taken to hitching a ride to the restaurant with his brother so he could escort me home.

He'd tried walking me there in the beginning, but you know, he got sick of asking if I was ready yet. I got sick of him asking if I was ready yet. It was better for both of us he wasn't there to nag me in the morning.

I hated waking up.

The silence between us wasn't typical, and I knew he could tell that I wasn't telling him everything that needed to be said about my date. Duke knew me as well as anyone. So, on the way home, I called Sadie. I needed her advice on what to do about Matteo, so she might as well save me the trouble of explaining twice. She'd been putting in a ton of extra hours at the gym since her dad had handed over the reins but was fine to skip out. It wasn't like she did training or worked the front unless someone was out, so she had more freedom to set her own hours.

Her empty car was in my driveway by the time we made it there. Not surprising since she and Duke were both prone to using their keys nearly as often as I used mine. Flashing a quick, awkward smile for Duke, I led the way up the steps to my little cottage of a house. The door opened, since Sadie never locked the damn door.

Sadie had her ass planted on one of my bar stools at the island, as she flipped through the notes, I made for the next few recipes I'd be sharing on the blog. "I want to eat this one," she said, stabbing a finger into the page for my swiss chocolate mousse cake. It wasn't uncommon that she and Duke would call dibs on specific recipes, as if there wasn't always plenty of food for both, anyway.

"It will go straight to your ass," Duke smirked, ducking when Sadie hurled the binder at him.

"Hey!" I protested, scurrying to pick it up and shoving loose pages back in - praying to all that was holy that they weren't mixed up. I did not have time for that shit.

"You! What was so important, Miss Cryptic Phone Call?" She spun on the stool, jabbing that finger in my direction.

I chewed on the corner of my mouth, casting a glance at Duke out of the side of my vision. His jaw tensed, that strong, angular bone structure of his high-lighted in the light flooding in my windows. "Why don't we sit?" I sighed, making my way over to the couch. Sadie hopped off the stool, plopping into her favorite armchair dramatically.

"Will there be yelling?" she asked, eyeing Duke where he stood too still. I knew he'd be pacing back and forth any second.

I nodded. "Safe bet."

"Oh, for fuck's sake, Ivory. What did you do?" I paused before answering, considering my words carefully. Perhaps there was a way to get through the coming storm *without* mentioning Matteo's name. Duke dropped his head to his chest, mumbling under his breath. "Why? Just why?" I knew he wasn't talking to me; his mumbles were always directed to himself.

I ignored them.

"I uh, just need advice. Best way to get out of a date."

"Just text him and say you changed your mind," Sadie answered, scowling at me like I'd lost my marbles. I'd canceled plenty of dates in the past.

"Well, I don't have his number, actually," I pointed out, wiggling my toes in my heels. The polish on one of my toes was chipped, and I immediately scowled at it.

"Please tell me you're kidding me," Duke hissed, and the telltale sound of his shoes thudding over my hardwood floors announced the pacing had begun. "Why exactly are you going on a date with a guy if you don't even have his number?"

"Well, I mean—" I paused with a sigh. There wasn't much to be done for avoiding his frustration. "I didn't *exactly* agree to go on the date at all." I drew out the first words of the statement, rushing the rest out in a mumble in a pathetic hope it could somehow be misinterpreted.

No such luck.

He froze, and Sadie turned wide eyes his way. As irritating as his pacing might have been, we both knew it was terrible when he was still. "Excuse me?" That voice was a deadly whisper, and while my friend was volatile and emotional, quiet was something he rarely ever achieved. When he was silent, it was just bad.

"Honey—" Sadie tried to soothe him, sensing the shit show hovering just under the surface.

"Why is there a date in the first place if you didn't agree to it, Ivory?" he asked.

"He told me we were going out. Said he'd pick me up at seven," I whispered.

His eyes closed, and his voice remained a whisper for the next words. "You told him where you live?"

"No! Don't be ridiculous," I protested.

"Then what is the problem?" Sadie asked. "He can't exactly pick you up if he doesn't know where you live." Her voice melted into a laugh, but Duke's face didn't change. He knew I wasn't quite so dramatic that I would risk his anger for no reason.

I winced, twisting my lips into what I knew was a very unattractive grimace. "I'm not so sure that's true in this case."

"What does that mean?" Duke's voice dropped further, and he crossed his arms over his chest as he strode over to stand in front of me.

I tilted my face up to look at him fully, giving him my best innocent expression to placate him. "I—well, he's probably capable of finding out where I live pretty easily," I admitted.

"Who?" Duke's voice trembled, and I knew he had a very good idea.

"Duke—" I started.

"Who is the fucking date with, Ivory?" he warned.

"Matteo," I whispered against my better judgment. Duke's body went taut, and he stared down at me in disbelief before storming through my living room and out my back door to the yard.

Okay, that seemed dramatic.

"Honey, where did you see Matteo?" Sadie's voice asked softly, and I didn't miss the way she stared after Duke. Like his pissy fit was more important than getting me out of the stupid date I didn't want.

"The robbers at the bank, they recognized me somehow. Begged me to tell Matteo that they didn't hurt me. I wanted answers so I—"

She cut me off with a gasp. "Oh no, please tell me you didn't!" she shrieked, drawing Duke back into the house. His shirt sleeves were rolled up, his normally neat blond hair all messy.

"Didn't what?" he asked, slowly. "What did you do, Ive?"

I steeled my shoulders. I didn't care if it had been stupid in hindsight, I wouldn't be treated as if I was a child incapable of making responsible decisions because I'd made *one* mistake. "I went to talk to him. I wanted to know why they would recognize me."

"Jesus Christ," Duke hissed. "What were you fucking thinking?!"

"I thought that I had a right to know!" I yelled back.

"You also had a right to just be grateful that they didn't shoot you in the face and leave it at that. If someone is connected to criminals, you do *not* go to their house and make demands!"

I stood, storming my way into the kitchen and grabbing a cutting board out of it.

I needed to cut something.

I figured a vegetable was probably better than Duke's pretty face.

"Well, I did. It's done," I sighed, pulling a cucumber from my fridge and tossing a container of Duke's favorite homemade hummus onto the island.

"Okay, okay," Sadie stood, giving Duke a wary glance as she stepped up and leaned onto the counter. "Don't get dressed. Put on some sweatpants, throw your hair into a knot on your head, and look a mess. Matteo Bellandi does not take a woman on a date when she looks more prepared for a movie night at home."

"Okay, okay that works. I can do that," I sighed in relief. I grabbed the peeler from the island drawer, making quick work of the cucumber. I knew she was right. Matteo probably took his dates to high-class restaurants and made them think they had a future before dumping them on their ass when he was done with them.

"Pack a bag," Duke interrupted, taking a furious bite out of a cucumber as soon as I sliced it. "You're staying with me for a few days."

"I can't do that. I have to work. I have photos to take tomorrow. Your kitchen isn't my favorite for that," I argued, shaking my head and discounting it immediately. There was no way I would be forced out of my home.

"Then I'll bring you back and hang out with you while you work tomorrow." Once he'd made quick work of the cucumber, he put the cover back on the container of the hummus and shoved it in the fridge. I widened my eyes at the counter, before turning them his way when he snatched the knife out of my hand and brought it and the cutting board to the sink to wash.

Since when did he wash my dishes?

I shook my head, turning and leaning back on the island. "You only have one bed."

"We'll make it work," he shrugged, acting far too casual considering his outburst before.

I did not like the sound of *that*.

He shoved the cutting board and knife in the strainer, turning to Sadie. "You want to pack for her?" Sadie stifled a laugh, because even she knew this was uncharacteristic behavior for Duke. He wasn't pushy. He wasn't an asshole.

His hand hit the railing of the stairs, and his foot was on the first step when I called out to him. "I'm not going, Duke."

His eyes hardened as he turned his glare to me. "You are."

"No. I'm not letting him chase me out of my house just because he said he'd pick me up for a date." I omitted the other stuff he'd said about making a dinner out of me if I wasn't ready. That definitely wouldn't help the scenario at the moment. "Look, if he shows up. If anything escalates, you're close. I know to call you. Odds are, he won't even turn up. I can't imagine I'm worth the effort of tracking down my address. It's not like he's lacking for company." I knew I was placating Duke, but I hated the protectiveness he constantly showed over me with men. Like he was determined that *every* man who was interested in me was a douchebag, just because Matteo had been. He sighed, dropping his head to stare at the stairs.

"Fine," he grunted. He turned, striding out the front door without another word.

"Well, that could have gone better," Sadie said.

I nodded.

"Yep."

***

How was it I didn't own a single pair of bummy sweatpants?

Sadie would stage an intervention if she found out.

The only yoga pants I owned were leggings and hugged my legs and butt way too much for me to face Matteo in. In all fairness though, I hated pants. When I was at home, I lived in skirts, dresses, or pajama shorts. I eventually tracked down a pair of pajama pants my mom had given me in one of her tirades about being dressed appropriately for a home invasion. Because wearing pants instead of booty shorts would protect me if someone decided he wanted to rape me. That said, I did like the fabric, big watercolor flowers on a black background with a wide, grey waistband and they were loose and comfy.

For pants.

I'd shoved an old, loose grey tee over my head, kind of hating the way it hung off one shoulder. But it was the baggiest shirt I owned, so it would do. My trusty slippers were stuck on my feet, and I was far too unsettled to relax. Smaug had taken up residence on my shoulder, just hanging out and enjoying the ride while I paced in a mimic of Duke's earlier movements.

My phone chimed with a text, and I unlocked the screen to see a message from Duke asking if Matteo had shown. A glance at the clock confirmed it wasn't even seven yet. Typing out a quick response, I did my best to keep my snark out of it.

"I know, I know," I said to Smaug as I walked to the kitchen and grabbed a bottled water out of the fridge. I chugged the contents, feeling thirsty.

Who was I kidding? My mouth was the Sahara.

"I'm being ridiculous. There's no way he'll show." I shoved my hair into a bun on top of my head just to be safe, careful not to dislodge Smaug. He glared at me although I'd taken care. "Don't look at me like that, Mister," I scolded him.

I jumped at the sound of the doorbell, glancing at the clock on my stove with wide eyes. Smaug's little claws dug into my skin through the t-shirt, and he looked at me—an echoing panic in his adorable little face.

Seven on the dot.

"Coincidence, right?" I asked, swallowing and making my way to the door. A glance through the peephole confirmed it was, in fact, Matteo Bellandi standing on my step and looking as breathtaking in a black suit as he had the day before. If I hadn't known better, I'd have sworn Smaug shrugged his shoulders at me. I backed away from the door, wondering if there was any way to hide the fact that I was home.

I could just *not* answer the door, right?

"Open the door, Angel," his hard voice demanded, an unmistakable edge to his tone.

"I don't think I will," I shouted through the door, clapping a hand over my mouth as soon as the words left me.

So much for that.

"Ivory, we can do this the easy way or the hard way. It's your choice." Something thudded against the door, and I peeked out to see him leaning against the frame on one hand, his face just above the peephole.

"What's the hard way?" I whispered, and I fully thought he wouldn't answer.

"I pick the lock," he didn't hesitate to say, and I blanched.

"You wouldn't dare! That's breaking and entering!" I backed away from the door, realizing it might not matter that much to him if bank robbers feared him.

Fuck. I totally should have gone to Duke's.

I hated being wrong.

I really, really hated it.

"I'll call the police!" I shouted, nabbing my phone off the island of the kitchen and hurrying back to the door. The sound of metal scraping on metal sounded through the door, and I flung it open on a gasp. Two odd little metal sticks stuck out of the deadbolt, and I barely had time to turn amazed eyes Matteo's way before he backed me into the house. Slamming the door shut behind him, he advanced until my ass hit the console table next to the foot of the stairs where I kept my keys and such. He ripped the phone out of my hand, glancing at the screen where Duke's text was open and tossed it onto the table behind me. I swallowed when he put his hands on the wall next to my head, caging me in.

"If you think the cops are dumb enough to get between me and my woman, think again. There isn't anybody in this world who will save you from me." I stared up at him, wincing as Smaug's claws continued to dig into me.

Safe to say, he wasn't a fan.

Matteo let his arms drop from the wall, his eyes giving me a once over, and he pinched the bridge of his nose between his fingers and sighed as his eyes caught on Smaug. "Ivory, the fuck is that?" The exasperation in his voice was a little too like Duke's every time I brought Smaug to his house.

"He's a gecko, and his name is Smaug," I objected, reaching up with one hand and holding it out for the lizard. He gladly abandoned his favorite perch, wiggling his way into my hand. I ran my thumb over the back of his head to soothe him, before turning and walking away from Matteo in favor of setting Smaug in his tank where he'd be safe from whatever storm was brewing. As soon as I had the lid on, Matteo spoke.

"Good. Now go get dressed. Our reservation is for eight."

I turned to him, my reflection shining off the stainless steel of my fridge in the kitchen. "Are you insane?"

He shrugged, seeming to genuinely consider the answer. "It's possible."

"Get out," I scoffed, shaking my head and moving around him to get to the front door. I swung it open quickly, gesturing him out the door. When he just raised a brow at me and didn't move, I sighed to keep myself from stomping my foot.

"I made reservations at *Vecchio*," he said pointedly. I knew in that moment he'd done his research on me. The only time a man would rub reservations at the hottest new restaurant in town in a woman's face was if he knew she was a food-addict.

I eyed him suspiciously. "They're booked six months out," I argued, crossing my arms over my chest. "Did you blow off some other girl to harass me into going with you?"

He chuckled. "No, sweetheart. It is safe to say that I do not take women to dinner."

"Oh well, keep with that tradition then, yeah?"

"I know you want to go. I can see the gears turning in that pretty head of yours." His voice lightened to genuine amusement as he watched me struggle to ignore that temptation. *Everyone* talked about that place, but it was impossible to get in.

"Unless you're willing to let me take someone else there and use your reservation? I'll pass," I hissed, and the amusement fled those harsh features.

"You go to dinner with another man, and we will have a very, *very* serious problem, *Cara mia*." I flinched back at the menace in his tone and felt my brow furrow as I stared at him. There really was no trace of the boy I'd loved in the man in front of me.

And something about that drained all the fight right out of me. I fought back tears, unwilling to let him see just how much he still affected me. "Please, just leave," I begged.

He was indifferent to my deflation, or he just didn't care. He stepped forward, crowding into my space and shoved the door closed again. "Go get dressed," he whispered, and I thought I might have caught a moment of regret in his blue eyes as he looked down at me more gently.

I shook my head, chewing on my lip and suddenly finding my floor fascinating.

I needed to mop.

"I don't want to scare you," he whispered, his fingers catching under my chin and lifting until I met his intent gaze. "But you will go to dinner with me. Now, you can either change, or you can go in pajamas. Your choice."

I glared at him, jerking my face out of his grip. "Go to Hell."

He sighed, biting out a "fine." The next thing I knew his hands were on my waist, and he lifted me off my feet. My stomach hit his shoulder, and I breathed out a sudden oof.

"What are you doing?" I hissed, squirming on my perch as he turned for the door. "Matteo, I'm not even wearing shoes!" He shrugged, jostling me as he pried the door open. I couldn't believe he'd hauled me over his shoulder like I was nothing, the fucking Neanderthal. "Okay!" I relented. "Put me down, and I'll change!" He closed the door, and I could feel the smug grin on his face even before I saw it.

"Ten minutes." I widened my eyes at him, turning and fleeing up the stairs to my room to hunt down something that would be appropriate for Vecchio without looking like I'd put in effort. I didn't even have time for effort.

Because I had ten fucking minutes.

***

It ended up being a good thing I didn't have time. Matteo couldn't wonder if I'd gotten ready for him or if I'd tried to look my best.

He already knew I hadn't.

I'd grabbed the first little black dress I found in my closet, and it was really a gamble which one I'd throw over my head.

I might have had a slight addiction to them.

I'd only had time to swipe on quick eyeliner and mascara, thanking the eye makeup gods that for once they both cooperated. A red lip tint followed, and I tore my hair from its bun to fall loose around my shoulders. A change of under-wear and bra, and I shoved the dress on over my head and slipped my feet into my favorite strappy yellow heels for a pop of color. I couldn't ever go all black with my clothes.

I didn't stop to think about my dress until I started walking down the stairs, using the railing to secure myself when my legs felt like they'd collapse beneath me. But the moment Matteo looked up from the phone where he'd been typing vigorously, I could feel the way his eyes trailed up every inch of my bare legs.

I glanced down at my chest, feeling my breathing constrict when I realized I wore *that* dress. The one every woman had in her closet - the one that existed purely for the purpose of seducing a man. A sweetheart neckline, with every-thing above it disguised with a delicate and feminine lace. The dress was sleeve-less with an asymmetrical hem lined in a wide band of lace. One side? Appropriate length, but the ruched and shorter side was the shortest thing I owned. The lace on that side was wider, offering some level of modesty that wouldn't have been there otherwise, but the color of my skin was unmistakable as it peeked through. It wasn't scandalous, and was entirely appropriate for Vecchio, but I shouldn't have worn it for Matteo.

I never would have chosen it if I'd had time to think. I swallowed as his blue eyes met mine, seeming impossibly dark suddenly, like two sapphires glittering at me dangerously. "You're breathtaking," he murmured, holding out a hand for me as I approached the last step. I took it with an exhale, trying to forget the way my skin had heated when he stared at it. Like a man dying of thirst, who'd seen water for the first time in days. Like he couldn't believe I was real, nothing but a mirage.

I shrugged it off, knowing it meant nothing.

Nothing ever meant anything to Matteo Bellandi.

"Should we go?" I asked, and Matteo nodded. I hurried over to my coat closet, nabbing my black bolero jacket and shrugging it on. I glanced at my purse, knowing it was too big to bring to dinner with me. I tore a clutch off the top shelf of my closet and tossed in my phone and debit card quickly. When I went to the door, Matteo snatched the keys out of my hand and guided me out the front door as he turned off all my indoor lights. I hit the switch for the outside light, watching in fascination as he locked my door for me and checked the door twice to be sure it was shut tight.

"You need a security system," he nodded gruffly, pocketing my house keys. He took my hand, tugging me toward the dark grey car in my driveway. I didn't stop walking but gasped at the sight of it. Because even though I knew nothing about cars, I knew it was sexy as hell.

"What is that?" I whispered, and he glanced back at me with an arrogant smirk. He knew damn well how sexy that car was.

"It's an Aston Martin," he said, and I rolled my eyes.

Of course, it was.

I did not understand what that meant, aside from it being another indicator of how far apart we were in terms of the worlds we lived in. "Do you want to drive?" he asked, and I gave him a wide-eyed look.

"No, thank you," I whispered. He opened the passenger door, helping me navigate my way inside gracefully.

The door shut with a thud, and I buckled myself in. Everything I remem-bered about Matteo showed the ride itself might be a terrifying experience. The driver's side door opened, and he dropped into the seat with a smooth glide that looked entirely at home in the luxury car. He grinned at me when he closed the door. "I have to say I'm surprised. I'd have thought you'd have jumped at the chance to take her for a spin."

I nearly flinched, assaulted with memories of driving his Mustang in high school and pushing every limit he set for me. Instead, I steeled my features into a cool mask and shrugged. "You know nothing about me anymore."

He winced visibly, shifting the car into reverse and backing out of my tiny little driveway. It was comically short compared to the curving road you took to get to his estate. When he put the car in drive, I let the purr of the engine relax me into a semi-comfortable state. I could do this. I could get through dinner and then send Matteo on his way after making it clear I wasn't interested in being one of his good-time girls.

No problem.

Staring out the window, I didn't see when he reached for me. But I felt it when his hand skimmed my thigh, grabbing my hand in his and holding it while he drove. His skin rested on my bare flesh, and I felt goosebumps rise from the contact. I tried to free my hand from his grip, but he held steady, not even releasing me when he shifted gears— instead taking my hand captive with his to do it. "Let go," I ordered.

"Nope, I don't think I will," he said, keeping his eyes on the road and not even bothering to glance my way.

"This isn't a date," I hissed.

"Of course, it is," he laughed. "I'm taking you to the nicest restaurant in the city. You look beautiful. I've been inside you. It's a date, Ivory."

"Twelve years ago doesn't count, Matteo. Plenty of men have been inside me now," I lied. Obviously there had been more than just him, but my numbers were still embarrassingly low for my age. At least when I wanted to toss them in his smug face.

"*Never* talk to me about the other men you've been with," he ordered in his deadly voice. "I will not be held responsible for what I'll do to them if I'm forced to think about it."

"You really are insane. Did you think I'd become a born-again virgin after you dumped me?" I chuckled, shaking my head. His grip on my hand tightened, not crushing but *vibrating* with fury. Somehow, he kept himself from hurting me.

"Angel—"

"Not an angel, Matteo. Not anymore. You ruined me, remember?" I hissed, shifting my legs away from our hands when he tried to rest them there again.

"I didn't ruin you," he growled. "I made you mine. In a way that no one else will ever be able to do." He dropped my hand, having no place to rest them comfortably. I tucked it under my thighs, not willing to risk him grabbing it again.

"And then promptly threw me away. Congratulations," I laughed. "You must really value your belongings." He was silent for a moment, and I could feel the tension radiating off him. When he pulled into the parking lot of the restaurant and drove straight up to the valet, I was shocked when he hopped out of the car so quickly.

"Do not open that door," he ordered the valet who'd moved to assist me out with a pointed finger in warning. The glare he gave the valet was enough to make the poor boy look like he might pee himself. Tossing his keys at the other one, he slammed the door and strode around the car on quick, efficient steps and pulled open my door himself. I took the hand he offered, pivoting my legs out until I could let him lift me up and out of the car. My hands smoothed my dress down just to be safe as I turned a polite smile to the boys watching us from the hood of the car. Their gazes were too intense, too shocked.

"You've been here before." I winced at the accusation in my voice. I didn't own Matteo. I had no right to be jealous, even as the thought of him bringing another woman to the nicest restaurant in town to wine and dine her slid through my veins like something insidious. He put a hand at the small of my back and guided me up the front steps. Even though the restaurant was technically outside the city, the crowd still lingered out the door. The natural stone building was stunning, like something out of a movie as he led me in the front door. That traitorous hand of his never left my back, somehow feeling far too intimate despite the dress that separated us.

"Mr. Bellandi," the hostess said with a blinding smile. "It's so good to see you again." She ignored me completely in favor of turning hazel eyes up at him with a flutter of her lashes. "Will you be needing a seat at the bar tonight?" I didn't bother to control my eye roll. Women could be such bitches. "Or I could probably squeeze you into Kendra's section, if you'd prefer—"

"I have a reservation for two," Matteo cut her off, glancing down at the podium meaningfully.

"Oh. How nice of you to take your—" she paused dramatically "—sister to dinner?" I snorted. Full on fucking snorted in the entryway of the nicest restaurant I'd ever been in.

You couldn't take me anywhere, I swear.

The hostess finally hardened her gaze into a glare she narrowed on me. Matteo's voice dropped low as he whispered to her. "My woman. Now, apologize." I swallowed uncomfortably, glancing at the pissed off man next to me.

"I—I'm very sorry, miss," the hostess stuttered, turning frightened eyes my way to avoid Matteo's wrath.

I shrugged, suddenly feeling sympathetic enough to let her off the hook. "It's fine, really. I'll be done with him tonight, so feel free to make plans with him after he takes me home." I smiled at her, and she blanched back at me. Matteo's growl was unmistakable, as was the way the hostess flinched back.

"Alex, take their coats," the hostess called, and a boy came from the coatroom. Matteo's stiff fingers helped me out of mine, and he handed them to the boy with venom written all over his features.

"Do not even attempt to make plans with me later," Matteo said before the hostess could get a word in edge wise. "Ivory here doesn't seem to realize the seriousness of our relationship just yet, but I assure you, I'll be remedying that."

The hostess nodded, grabbing two menus and strutting off toward what I could only assume would be our table. Matteo's hand pressed into my back a little more forcefully, like the frayed edges of his control were slipping in the face of my sass.

Still, he pulled out my chair like a gentleman, and I was about to slide into it with a polite thank you when a man's voice caught both of our attentions. Matteo went ramrod still, the only motion he made was to grasp me around the waist as he pulled me into his side forcefully.

"Matteo!" The man made his way towards us, only sparing a glance for me before he turned his dancing brown eyes back to Matteo. I'd been dismissed after only a glance, but for once I couldn't say I minded. Even in that moment where our eyes had connected, something about the way the dark brown of them glinted gave me the creeps. The way Matteo kept me plastered to his side only confirmed that he was *not* someone I wanted fixating on me.

"Adrian." Matteo's voice was flat, no emotion to him when he answered. They shook hands, postures tense.

"I'm glad I ran into you. I wondered if we could discuss—"

"Not tonight," Matteo said sharply, his arm tightening around me until I had no choice but to turn my body in to face his. Feeling awkward, I raised a hand to rest on his chest. The motion had the unintended benefit of soothing something raw inside Matteo, and even though his body only relaxed a fraction, I felt it in every inch of my body that was plastered to his.

"Understood." Adrian turned dark, dancing eyes to me. Suddenly, he seemed to find me *very* interesting, and his eyes passed over me from head to toe. "And who might this be?"

"Ivory," I answered, forcing my lips to curl into a tentative but polite smile.

Adrian held out a hand, and I placed mine in it when I realized I had no reason not to, nothing that could be perceived as anything other than an insult, anyway. Raising it to his lips, he pressed a kiss to the back of it. "You are a rare beauty, Ivory." Matteo growled, whether at the words or the sight of Adrian's lips on my skin I would never know, and Adrian turned wide eyes up to him with a smirk.

"Oh, I see. It's like that, is it?" Matteo didn't answer, but Adrian dropped my hand, regardless in the face of Matteo's eerie silence. Adrian's smile was no less intimidating as he looked down at me again. "It was lovely to meet you. I'll let you two enjoy your evening." He turned, striding back to what I had to presume was his own table. I sat finally, letting Matteo push my chair in for me.

"What was that?" I whispered as he took his own seat across from me.

"Adrian is a business rival," he answered shortly, opening his own menu. I didn't continue my questioning immediately, as the waiter came and took our drink order. Matteo ordered a bottle of wine, that I had to assume was insanely expensive. I ignored it, letting him act in his high-handed way.

It was one dinner; I reminded myself.

Eat some delicious food and then get out.

"Do you know what you would like?" Matteo asked after the waiter left.

I widened my eyes at him dramatically. "Are we really not going to talk about whatever that was?"

Matteo sighed, setting his menu on the table and turning his attention to me finally. "It was business, and you *Cara mia*, are not part of my business. I would like it to stay that way."

"Because I'm so naïve I couldn't possibly understand your business?" I hissed.

"No, because it is much safer for you if you're not involved. I may be many things, but I will always do whatever it takes to keep you safe."

The waiter came back, saving me from having to respond to the ridiculous lie of that statement. The polite smile he turned down at me was polite, all clean-cut charm. "What can I get for you, Miss?"

"The spring risotto," I said with a smile.

"An excellent choice." The man gave me a bright smile, before turning to Matteo. "And for you, Sir?"

"The bistecca fiorentina." Matteo's voice was short and curt, and I looked up to see him glaring daggers at the waiter. "She's not on the menu, so don't look at her like she's a piece of meat."

I gasped. "Matteo!"

"I apologize," the waiter whispered backing away from our table. "I didn't intend—"

"Go," Matteo snapped.

"What is wrong with you?" I hissed at him as soon as the waiter left. I could feel eyes on me from all around the dining room, and my cheeks heated with the realization that his moment failed to go unnoticed. Matteo nodded to someone over my shoulder, and I turned to find another Italian man nodding back at him. "Who is *that?*"

"My security," Matteo grunted.

"That poor waiter didn't deserve—"

Matteo held out a hand, silencing me with his domineering bullshit. "He wanted to fuck you."

"Maybe I should let him," I taunted, standing from the table.

"Sit down," he ordered, but I ignored the command I heard in that too-sexy-for-his-own-good voice.

"I'm going to the powder room." I shook my head as I walked and followed the sign to the back hall of the restaurant. Miraculously, there was no one in the bathroom, and I vented to myself as I went about my business. "Fucking ridiculous man. Like I needed a man to chase off someone because he *looked* at me. What kind of caveman bullshit is that?" I came out of the stall, surprised to find a woman standing at the sink when she hadn't been before. She smiled at me, kindly not commenting on my tirade that she must have overheard. I'd just finished washing my hands and accepted the hand towel from the attendant, when the door opened, and Adrian appeared in the mirror behind me.

"Get out," he said to her. She slid her eyes to me, before seeming to decide better and fleeing the bathroom.

I swallowed, turning around to face the man who'd strolled right into the ladies' room like he belonged there. "Any chance you haven't realized this is the women's bathroom?" I whispered, and he threw his head back and laughed. It was a shame there was something so *off* about him, because if it hadn't been for that, he'd have been attractive. Not Matteo-level sexy, but handsome in his own right. Deep golden skin and dark hair, he was the epitome of tall, dark, and handsome. Even as he stepped closer to me, getting right in my business until I leaned back on the counter with both hands. He drew up one hand, letting his fingers trail over my cheekbone gently, and he watched the contact intently. "So exquisite. I can see what drew him to you."

I swallowed again, jerking my head away from his hand as much as I dared. "Matteo won't be pleased to know you touched me," I whispered. A few hours ago, I'd have said it was an exaggeration, but after seeing the way he reacted to men even looking at me, I couldn't be so sure.

"I imagine not, no," Adrian grinned. "That's part of the fun, you see? Though I imagine we'll have plenty of fun in our own right. I had to be sure you knew that I am interested and willing to risk the wrath of Bellandi should it mean you are the reward."

"That's flattering," I huffed. "But I'm afraid I'm not interested."

"Ah, sweetheart. It's adorable that you think—"

He broke off when the door flung open, Matteo's enraged energy filling the bathroom as he rushed in. The man he'd referred to as his security followed behind him, looking exasperated but pissed off too. "Take your hands off my woman," Matteo snarled. "Or I'll remove them for you."

Adrian stepped back, raising his hands as if he was innocent. "We were only talking, Bellandi," Adrian placated with a shit-eating grin.

"She does not exist for you. Get that through your fucking skull." Adrian smirked back at him, and Matteo's face turned positively feral. "This is not something you want to test me on, Ricci." Adrian didn't utter another word as he strode to the door, but he paused long enough to wink at me just before he left. Matteo cursed, balling his hands into fists. "Scar's on her. Round the clock," he ordered the security man. He nodded, turning and striding out of the bathroom, seeming content to go about his duty as Matteo ordered. "Are you okay?" Matteo turned to me, his hands cupping my cheeks. Momentarily distracted by how good they felt—especially compared to the icky way my skin crawled when Adrian touched me—it took me too many precious seconds to draw away. I needed him to not touch me. Needed to never remember what it felt like when his hands were on me.

"I'm fine," I nodded, taking a deep breath to compose myself. It hadn't been bad. He'd barely touched me. It was nothing like the last time.

I'd be fine.

Matteo studied me, sighing at whatever he saw on my face. Taking my hand, he guided me back to the table. We settled in, and our food followed within minutes. I did my best to steady my shaking hands, drawing a fortifying breath into my lungs. The glass of wine on the table proved too tempting to ignore, and it took everything in me to not spill it all over my dress. "Did he touch you, Angel?" Matteo's low rumble should have been frightening, but for whatever reason in that moment he wasn't the monster who haunted my nightmares. He showed me a glimpse of the boy I loved, the fake boy who had never existed, letting the terrifying enigma of a man drift away.

"Nothing too serious." I gave him my best effort at a reassuring smile. He hadn't touched me in any way that should have been traumatizing but given my history—given the way I reacted to the touch of men I didn't know—it was too much.

Being with Matteo already had my body strung tight, lingering on the edge of some cliff that I just knew I could never let myself fall over. To do so would be to fall to my heartbreak again. "You're shaken."

"It's not every day that pushy ass men seem to fixate on me." I twisted my lips into a saccharine smile, almost hoping that he would take the bait and stop with the sympathetic, almost caring act.

We both knew it was a lie when all was said and done.

"You can tell me, you know. Whatever it is that—"

"Can we not? Please? Whatever it is, is none of your business." He stared at me like he might argue, before finally tilting his head down in a nod.

"Very well, *Cara mia*. Tell me about your blog."

I sighed, not even pretending to hide my distaste that he would have done such thorough research on me. "What's there to say? It's a blog. I post recipes and photos of my food; people try them and love them. I make money through advertising mostly, but also some affiliate programs and stuff like that. You know, I use so and so brand of spatula and get a kickback from it."

"Seems like a smart way to make more money. Is a food blog common?"

I tilted my head in thought. "They aren't uncommon, by any means. You can find them all over the internet, but not everyone makes a full-time income from them. It all depends on how determined you are and if having it be your job is something, you're even interested in to be honest." The waiter brought out caprese salad, not even once glancing in my direction.

I felt a growl threaten in my own chest, because it wasn't enough that Matteo acted like a wild animal, but apparently, I needed to as well. I picked up my fork and ignored Matteo's self-satisfied grin that he turned on the waiter. There was something so feral in it, I couldn't blame the poor guy when he scurried off in a hurry.

"Are you always so territorial over all your dates?" I asked, stabbing a piece of tomato and shoving it into my mouth without preamble. The light drizzle of balsamic over it burst on my tongue pleasantly.

"I don't date," he answered with an eyebrow raised. "I don't even bring women out in public, so it would be hard to be territorial. Aside from you, I can't think of a single woman that I would object to seeing her take another man to bed as soon as I finished with her." My mouth was only inches from my wine glass, but thankfully I hadn't taken that sip just yet.

I had a feeling I'd have spit it all over the table.

And my food. That would have been unforgivable.

"Well that's, um, interesting," I faltered. How did one respond to that kind of confession?

He chuckled at my discomfort, taking a sip of his own wine. Watching his throat work while he swallowed the liquid shouldn't have been an aphrodisiac. It appeared, that literally everything about Matteo screamed sex. It was most unfortunate. "I don't have any use for women in my life. I don't particularly enjoy conversing with them, and I most definitely don't enjoy the way they view me as a meal ticket."

"You just enjoy fucking them and then tossing them aside? I guess some things never change." I hissed the words, watching as Matteo's jaw clenched in fury.

"What I did to you is nothing like what I did to all the women who have filled the void in your absence. I know it will be difficult for you to believe, but I did what I had to do at the time. One day, perhaps you'll understand. But do not compare yourself to others. You're nothing like them."

I swallowed, running my tongue over my teeth after I set my fork down, having finished my caprese salad. "And how am I any different? Just because I was a virgin?"

"You're different because you mean something to me, because you meant everything to me." The waiter collected our plates, and I fixed my gaze on the glass of wine in front of me.

"If that were true—"

Matteo cut me off, grasping my hand in his. "Not tonight, Angel. Soon, but not tonight."

I nodded, drawing my hand back to my side of the table. Matteo allowed it, seeming no more interested in having a physical altercation than I was. It was unfortunate enough that the tenseness to our conversation wasn't missed by the people dining closest to us. "Donatello told me your father passed," I said to break the silence that started to spread. "I'm sorry."

"Don't be," he chuckled. "The world is better for my father being gone."

I swallowed, because that didn't bear good things for the kind of man Matteo had become, given that I knew even as a child he was groomed to take over his father's businesses. The Bellandi Corporation had been passed down through generations from what anyone could tell. "I'm kind of surprised you never ended up married to Shauna." I laughed, and a twisted sort of humor filled Matteo's face.

"What in the fuck would make you think I'd marry Shauna? She wasn't particularly the most pleasant to spend time with." He was right, even people who Shauna didn't torment knew she was catty and cruel—just as likely to stab you in the back as she was to smile to your face.

"She used to tell everyone you were engaged. That your families had arranged for the two of you to be married like we live in the dark ages. Uniting two proper Italian families," I cringed with a scoff.

Matteo swallowed, "Ah. Well that was true enough before you, but I refused and given Shauna's propensity for sleeping around it wasn't difficult to navigate my way out of it. Old Italian families like mine, things like that matter. There are unfortunately certain expectations for our women, and if those aren't met than negotiations become difficult." I stared at him, not completely comprehending. "Last I spoke to her father; she'd moved to New York to try and start fresh. I've no idea how that worked for her."

The waiter delivered our dinners, and I dug into my risotto with a slow, savoring bite. The creamy flavor practically melted on my tongue; the hint of cheese delectable. My eyes drifted closed on a moan. When they opened, it was to Matteo's darkened blue gaze on my face. I cleared my throat awkwardly, taking a sip of my wine to dispel some of the tension I felt. "The whole Italian thing is that important to your family? It just seems so...dated? People inter-marry all the time."

"Not in families like mine. My father was unorthodox, taking my mother for a wife. I guess they felt like they needed to make up for that by ensuring I settled down with a good Italian woman." I cut through my stalk of asparagus, popping the bite into my mouth. It hurt to have it confirmed that he would always be destined for an Italian woman, because no matter what happened or didn't happen between us, Italian I was not.

"Your mother wasn't Italian?" I asked to dispel the awkwardness of what his confession did to me. I knew we wouldn't ever really be together, obviously I knew better than to have expectations or even hopes where Matteo was concerned, but to hear it so blatantly spelled out struck something in me down. I shoved it away. I could feel the hurt later, but in front of Matteo, I was determined to make him believe me unaffected.

I didn't want him.

Couldn't want him.

He shook his head, slicing a bite off his steak. He held out his fork, offering me a bite of the meat in the same way he always had back then. Ever the foodie, I always needed to try everything at the table. At least if I'd never had it. I shook my head, the smile on my face horrified. He leaned across the small, intimate table for two, and the forkful hovered just in front of my mouth. Knowing it would be a bigger scene than I felt like causing to continue to deny him, I had no choice but to open my mouth and accept the beef in. Matteo slid the fork inside, eyes fixated on the motion as my lips sealed around it and plucked it off the fork. I hummed my approval as the intense flavor coated my tongue, and I chewed.

After a moment's delay, he sat back in his chair and resumed eating. "My mother is Norwegian," he admitted. "She and my father had a fling when she was in the city for college. Brief, sex motivated. She got pregnant with me, so they had no choice but to get married really. Given my family's conservative values, there was no way to avoid it even with her heritage." That explained how Matteo had lighter hair than Lino, and I imagined the rest of his Italian family. "They hated each other. Spent most of my childhood fighting, until my mother decided she just didn't care. As soon as my father died, my mother left town and never looked back."

"She left you?" I whispered.

"We were never close, and she felt trapped in her marriage with my father. So once she was free, there was nothing keeping her here."

"Except for her son," I hissed as I finished my last bite of risotto.

"Not all women are meant to be mothers, my Angel. Neither of my parents were suited to the role. Thankfully, their hatred of one another kept them from repeating the mistake. Would you like dessert?"

I forced a smile for his sake, trying to rein in my hatred for him in the wake of his confessions. No wonder love was so foreign to Matteo. He'd never been loved in his life, never even seen it. I felt sorry for him, because I knew that no matter how much it had hurt, the love I'd experienced had been a bright light in my life. "No. As much as it pains me to admit, I couldn't eat another bite."

He laughed, requesting the check from the waiter and turning the conversation to inquiries about Sadie and Duke even though I knew he didn't care what they were up to. He'd hardly tolerated either of them in high school when they were a necessary evil to being with me. Sadie was too nosy, too in my face and bubbly and demanding for Matteo's tastes, and Duke was a man. Even then, Matteo had always been possessive to the point of excess.

While we waited for the check, the stares he gave me were disquieting in intensity, as if something was coming and he was trying to get a read on my reaction.

I just hoped the thing that was coming was him dropping me off at home and never looking back.

It didn't seem likely.

***

We'd ridden back to my house in silence. Matteo's body vibrated with tension, whatever affected him so much at the end of our dinner still visibly pulsing through him. He didn't try to hold my hand in the car, but that could have also been because I sat on it. When he pulled into the driveway, I held out a hand for my keys. "Thank you for dinner," I said politely. "It was nice to catch up."

It was as clear a dismissal as I could manage without being outright suicidal with the man who looked ready to snap at any moment. He glanced at my hand with disgust in his eyes, shoving his car door open and stepping out.

As soon as he slammed it shut, I winced.

"Poop," I whispered to myself, watching as he prowled around the car. I hadn't paid enough attention to realize he'd shut the ignition off, but I figured that probably didn't bode well for me. Likely meant he didn't mean to just see me to my door. "Double poop scoops."

My door opened quickly, and I unbuckled myself and let him guide me out like the gentleman he liked to pretend to be. His hand took up residence at my back, guiding me up the steps to my house as the car door closed with a thud behind me.

My breathing was erratic, and I fought to control the rising panic.

He couldn't seriously think I would sleep with him.

Could he?

He dug my keys out of his pocket, and I let out a sigh of relief when his eyes met mine. They were more relaxed than I'd seen him all night, more at ease with whatever was going on in his head. I reached out to take them from him with a smile, my breath freezing in my lungs when he turned away and used them to unlock my door himself. When he pushed the door open lightly, he gestured me inside. Pausing in the threshold, I turned to say goodnight in one last bid to keep him outside my house. Outside my sanctuary where he didn't belong.

His eyes were soft when my gaze met his, soft and dark and full of the promise of all the things I believed the last time I'd let him have all of me.

"Goodnight, Matteo," I whispered, putting a hand on the door and standing my ground.

"Aren't you going to let me in, *Cara mia?*" he asked, and his voice vibrated with something dark. Something dangerous. Something I didn't understand in the slightest but knew well enough to fear.

"No," I whispered, stepping back and slamming the door in his face. I gasped when his foot blocked it from closing and backed up as he prowled inside. He didn't turn to face it as he closed it gently behind him, stepping closer to me slowly. "Don't you dare touch me," I hissed, taking another step back. That *fucking* console table jabbed into my ass, and I stumbled, glancing to the side and looking for a different escape route.

"Are you afraid of me, my Angel?" he asked as his body pressed tightly into mine. I whimpered, even through his suit I could feel every ridge of muscle packed onto his frame. He was a stranger to me; his body was nothing like the one I'd known once upon a time. "Because you should be."

"What do you want?" I whispered, hating how weak my voice sounded as I spoke.

"I'll never hurt you. Surely you know that." His voice cracked and his hand slid underneath the curtain of my hair to cup my face in his hand as he ran his thumb over my cheekbone. It was the same one Adrian had stroked, and I could practically feel him erasing the other man's touch with his own as possession glittered in his eyes. "I should walk away. Leave you to your life."

I swallowed, not having the guts to agree with him. As prepared for it as I was, as much as I knew it was the smartest outcome for me, the thought of watching him walk away from me like I didn't matter for a second time was devastating. His forehead hit mine, blue eyes staring into my soul from so close that I felt like he saw every crack—every hole I'd worked so hard to cover up over the years. No matter what a train wreck I knew whatever this thing with Matteo would be, I still couldn't look away. "I won't. This time around, I can keep you safe. I have to believe that," he whispered, but I got the distinct impression he was trying to convince himself of it more than me. "I'm not letting you go, Ivory. Do you understand what I'm saying?"

"No," I whispered honestly. Because I had a feeling that I really, truly, had absolutely no concept of whatever was happening. No control over it, not an ounce of real understanding.

"You will soon enough," he murmured, tilting his face until his lips pressed against mine softly and silenced my protest. Nothing but a light, teasing touch of his lips to mine, his gaze captivated mine even as heat flared through me from the smallest touch. He pulled away with a groan, his eyes closing and disconnecting me from that blue-eyed stare that threatened to steal away my sanity. His other hand came up to bury in my hair, tilting my face the way he wanted me. When I gasped, the pressure of his hand at my scalp and the sensation of him controlling me so thoroughly too much for me to handle, his lips crashed against mine.

There was no gentleness in that kiss, no trace of the man who'd softly memorized the feel of my lips on his from a moment ago.

All that remained was a dominating force. His hand where he cupped my cheek forced my mouth to open for him, and his tongue darted inside to tease mine. I whimpered, hoping the sound would alert him to the fact that he was taking too much, pushing too hard too soon.

Scaring me.

I was totally and completely trapped, surrounded by him. That was not something that I could handle. Not with him. Not with anyone.

My whimper seemed to fuel him on, his hand leaving my face to drift down my body in a slow, smooth caress that lit my nerve endings on fire. I'd thought they'd died a long time ago, but they flared to life with the subtlest touch from Matteo, even while I fought to maintain my sanity.

It was Matteo.

Not a stranger.

While I convinced myself of the fact that I was safe enough and would walk away from whatever happened, Matteo groaned into my mouth. I realized at some point I'd started kissing him back. He pulled back enough to nibble at my bottom lip, and I moaned although I'd hated myself as soon as the sound left me. His hand slid around from my waist to my back, tugging me tighter to his body and then he slid it down and over my ass. My hips wiggled against him shamefully, and he squeezed the mound. Then he hoisted me up with one arm under my butt, setting me on the console table that I wasn't sure could support my weight.

His lips fused to mine again, expert strokes of his tongue against mine as he shoved my thighs apart and inserted his hips between them. With all of him pressed against me, it was impossible to miss the bulge in his pants as he ground it against me. His hands ran over the bare skin of my thighs as he shoved the dress up my legs and hooked his fingers into the waistband of my thong. When he moved to tug it down, I jerked back from him. My head smacked against the wall, but I didn't care as concern crossed his features. I shoved him away with two hands at his chest.

"Get off me," I protested, and his hands left my legs. His expression was torn as he stared at me, and I could see him trying to work out the kinks of how to get what he wanted. "You need to leave. Now." He stepped back just enough that I could hop off the table and shove my dress back down my thighs. "This isn't happening."

He sighed, running a hand through his hair before he nodded. "You're right. It's too soon." I knew my face must have morphed into one of shock. "I lost control. I miss you, Angel," he pressed one last soft kiss to the corner of my mouth, before turning and striding for the door. "I'll see you in the morning."

He opened the door, closing it behind him and was gone. I hurried over to lock it, breathing a sigh of relief when there was something separating us. My back hit the door when I spun around and panted in a miniature panic attack.

Because what in the fuck was wrong with me?

CHAPTER NINE

IVORY

I woke up slowly, feeling so warm. Usually, I woke up cold. For years, I'd tossed and turned so much during the night that I would either wake up being suffocated by my blanket or freezing and the blanket on the floor. There was a definite weight pressing into me, but it was a comfortable one rather than the strangulation of being tangled in a comforter.

A sigh of contentment reached my ears, and I was still half-asleep enough that I had to consider if I'd been the one to make it. Snapping my eyes open suddenly, I panicked and tried to squirm out from whatever, *whoever,* laid on top of me.

In my bed.

When I'd most *definitely* gone to bed alone, after getting reacquainted with a certain battery-operated friend in my nightstand drawer.

"Angel, Angel," Matteo soothed me, holding me underneath him tighter as I struggled. I calmed minutely, freezing in place when I realized that my ass was rubbing against his groin, *his very hard* groin, in my inability to get out from under him. "Shh," he purred, taking my chin in his hand and turning my head back at an uncomfortable angle so he could see me. His lips came down on mine, soft and soothing even as my panic renewed.

"What are you doing in my bed?" I hissed, jerking away from his hold, and finally squirming out from under him. Judging from the position, he'd been lying on his stomach and covering my left side with his body, his leg cocked over both of mine.

"I don't like to wake up without you." He shrugged, watching me as I tugged the comforter up to cover my breasts. I wasn't naked, thankfully, but the tank and shorts I slept in with nothing underneath left absolutely nothing to the imagination.

"So you broke into my house and crawled into bed with me while I was sleeping?!"

He smirked at me, the fucking bastard. "Well, I couldn't very well climb in while you were awake, now could I?"

"You—I," I stumbled, lost for words. There was no remorse on his face, absolutely nothing to show he felt guilty for invading my privacy and doing god only knows what to my body while I slept. "You had no right."

"I have every right," he said, shocking me so much that my mouth snapped closed. "You're mine. You should get used to spending the nights together, Angel." My eyes drifted down to his chest, realizing he was shirtless for the first time once my panic had abated a bit. As much as he'd terrified me, as much as I wanted to hurt him for violating my bed, I didn't fear Matteo. I couldn't muster up any fear that he might hurt me physically, no matter how stupid that might have been. He'd always made me feel safe, like being within his arms was the *only* place in the world where nothing could hurt me.

My eyes didn't know where to settle as they darted around. His shoulders were broad, sculpted with biceps that must have been as thick as my thigh. His pecs were perfectly formed, and even sitting the muscles of an impossibly defined eight pack stood out and tempted me to lick every ridge. The tattoo on his chest caught my eye, a quote I recognized from Aristotle referencing the night following the light of day. When my eyes darted back up to his face, I knew he hadn't missed my reaction to seeing him. He stood from the bed, revealing thick thighs corded in muscle. Only a pair of black boxer briefs covered him, and they barely contained the *fucking anaconda* of an erection I remembered all too well. I swallowed with nerves as he leaned over me in the bed.

His face gentled, and he cupped my jaw and stared down at me in that intense way of his. "This is happening, Angel." His lips touched mine briefly, and then he turned and swaggered his way into my en suite bathroom.

I sat there, disoriented and freaking out for a minute. When the shower started up, I was up and fleeing my bedroom in case he decided he wanted company. I didn't dare change my clothes for fear of the creep appearing the moment I was naked, so I snagged my huge, baggy sweater that I curled up in when I read. Shoving my arms in, I fled down the stairs, only coming to a halt when I found two men sitting and drinking coffee at the island. I stumbled back a step, preparing to flee out the front door when they spun and saw me standing there.

"Miss Torres," one said, setting his mug down. "Is everything all right?" I stared at him, slight relief crashing through me when I realized he was the man Matteo had said was his security the night before. He stood, approaching me like I was a wounded animal. "Has something happened to Mr. Bellandi?" he asked, and I shook my head frantically.

"In the shower," I mumbled, not acknowledging his other question. What kind of question was that, anyway? How could things be all right with three men I didn't know in my home? I glanced down at my mostly bare legs, feeling suddenly exposed, but neither man's gaze ever drifted away from my face. "What are you doing in my house?"

The man tilted his head, a small smile crossing over his features as he shook his head. "I go where Matteo goes, ma'am. We weren't introduced last night. I'm Simon, Matteo's head of security."

"Okay, so you're his security. Ignoring the fact that you both *broke into my house,*" I paused to roll my eyes, ignoring the chuckle from both men. "Then who is he?" I gestured to the other man who sat at the island, dutifully drinking his coffee.

"That's Paolo. We call him Scar," Simon said with a polite smile. "He goes where you go." I blinked, stepping back from both men in favor of getting to my front door.

I was in way over my head.

I snatched my keys off the console, striding for the front door with another shake of my head. "Miss Torres?" Simon called, and something in his voice made me turn back to glance at him the moment my hand hit the doorknob. "It won't do you any good."

"What?" I whispered.

"Running. It won't matter. He'll never stop. Do yourself a favor, and just settle into your new life instead of fighting it, yeah?" My blood chilled at his words, and panic flooded my veins.

"Ah, you're scaring my Angel I see," Matteo said from the top of the stairs. His legs made quick work of hurrying down them to meet me at the foot of the stairs. Touching his lips to my cheek briefly, he kissed me goodbye like a husband leaving for work. As if our relationship was normal, and he hadn't broken into my home while I slept. I turned to face him, and I knew he could see the apprehension in my face. "Don't worry, Simon and I are leaving. I have business to see to." I breathed out a sigh of relief. "Try not to give Scar too much shit, okay?"

"You can't be serious!" I protested. "I'm not letting you put some babysitter on me."

"Bodyguard," Matteo corrected in a deep voice that left no room for argument. "Scar, why don't you take up position outside for the time being? I don't think Ivory is ready to have a house guest just now."

"Yes, boss," Scar grunted, chugging the rest of his coffee and sliding past me to get to the front door quickly.

"Is he just going to stand out there all day?"

"He'll do perimeter checks periodically. Aside from that he has the SUV." I hesitated, feeling horrible that the man would have to just sit out there, but steeled myself against the feeling. I wouldn't let an intruder remain in my home just because it was less comfortable outside.

"See you later, Angel," Matteo said, pressing a quick kiss to my unmoving lips and then he and Simon were gone without another word. Matteo's Aston Martin and what I presumed was Simon's SUV backed out of the driveway, and Scar's voice reached me from the remaining SUV when he rolled the window down.

"Go back inside, Miss Torres," he said, his voice void of any form of inflection. I nodded, stepping back into my house. I went for my phone.

I needed Sadie.

***

Sadie sat at my island again, her customary place. Having had the two unfamiliar asses perched in the seats that my two best friends had claimed so long ago sent another pang of discomfort through me. She was far too quiet, though it was probably to be expected. She hadn't gotten the full story yet, only as far as the fact that I had in fact gone on the date.

She didn't know that I'd woken up to Matteo mostly naked in my bed.

Or that he'd invited two strangers into my home, because he had no boundaries when it came to me or my privacy.

I nabbed the onion from my drawer, setting it down on the cutting board a little too forcefully. "What are you making now?" Sadie asked, and I didn't miss the suspicion in her voice.

"Spring risotto," I said. "The recipe was fantastic, and I want to see if I can replicate it while it's still fresh, you know?"

My front door opened, and Duke's face filled my vision when he crowded into my space quickly. He took my face in his hands, his eyes boring into mine, and then they darted to glance all over my face as if he'd be able to see trauma. "I told you. I'm fine," I hissed.

"You also told me you wouldn't go on the date," he accused, and I winced.

"I didn't have much choice." My voice was a weak whisper. I so didn't want Duke to be present for the conversation I needed to have with Sadie. He would lose his mind.

"What does that mean? And what's with the beefcake screening your visitors? Christ, Ivory," he turned, plopping into his customary bar stool.

"He's her security, apparently," Sadie said, sipping her green smoothie through her straw.

"What the fuck? Why do you need security?"

"That's a really good question," Sadie concurred, and I knew I would not get out of admitting the entire story. Not now that I'd started.

"Can we just talk about this later?" I asked Sadie pointedly as I finished chopping my onion.

"Nope, not happening, Ive." Duke crossed his arms over his chest. I fished my pan out, slipping butter in and hanging my head once the heat was on.

"There was a slight incident at the restaurant," I admitted. "One of Matteo's business rivals became interested in me, cornered me in the bathroom. Matteo seems to think he's dangerous, so for the time being I'm stuck with Scar."

"Shit," Sadie muttered, and I watched as Duke's eyes flared. He stood from the stool, striding around the island to turn off the heat on my stove.

"Pack your shit, Ive."

"Duke-" I protested. We'd been here before.

"No, I let you try it your way. Do you see how well that worked out?" He pointed outside, where I could practically feel Scar watching our interactions through the mirror.

"I can't."

"Do not tell me you're getting sucked into his web again!" Sadie jumped up, hands on her hips. "Do you remember what happened last time? You were so happy with him, and fell so hard, and he *crushed* you!"

"I'm not!" I ran my hands over my face. "I just, I don't think it will matter if I'm here or at your house. You don't know the full story yet." I knew my grimace was visible and watched as Duke's face morphed in anger.

"What, Ivory?" Sadie's voice gentled, seeming to realize I was balancing delicately on the edge of sanity.

"He was here this morning when I woke up," I whispered.

"The goon? I figured he turned up at some point, since he's outside now," Duke said, and I turned wide eyes his way.

"No. Not Scar, I mean him too." I sighed, even I knew I was doing a shit job of explaining a shitty situation. "Matteo."

"What did he want? Introduce Scar?" Sadie asked, and I knew she was as confused as Duke looked.

"Matteo was in bed with me when I woke up," I spat out.

"You slept with him?" Sadie hissed, looking at me like I'd lost my mind.

"No! I went to bed alone," I explained. "He—I think he picked the locks. Crawled into bed with me while I was sleeping. Scar and Matteo's security guy were down here when I tried to leave. They told me it would be pointless to run. That he would never stop," I gasped, feeling the weight of their stares on me.

"Holy shit," Sadie whispered and her brow furrowed.

"Duke?" I asked, watching as his face hardened to a point I'd never seen before.

"He was in your bed with you? After he broke in?" I nodded, feeling tears pool in my eyes when he turned and strode out of my house without another word.

"Duke!" I yelled, chasing after him.

Sadie grabbed my arm, stopping me from following him out the door. "Let him go. He needs to cool off, think things through. You know how protective he is of you."

I nodded, feeling like I'd fucked up again.

I shouldn't have told them.

"What are you going to do?" she asked.

"I don't know, Sadie. This time I really don't know."

CHAPTER TEN

MATTEO

I couldn't wait to get back to Ivory, but the life I lived stopped for no one. Taking a day off to spend with my angel just wasn't possible, especially not with Adrian sniffing around her like a rabid dog. Donatello poked his head in my office while Lino and I were going over some upgrades to one of the apartment buildings I owned within the city. "Paolo called. Mr. Bradley has left Miss Torres' home. In a fit, evidently."

I smirked. "I can't imagine he's pleased to know I'm back in her life."

Lino outright laughed. "Safe bet there. Wonder if he ever tapped that," he mused, and I leveled him with a glare. A lesser man would have cowered, but my beloved cousin only laughed in the face of what was a very real danger to his life. "When do I get to see her again? Is she still as hot as she was in high school?"

Donatello stepped between us, likely saving Lino from very serious pain. "She will be my wife. You will not speak of her in that way again."

Lino's eyes widened, and he barked out a laugh. "Holy shit. Didn't realize you were *quite* that serious about it, man. I just enjoy pushing your buttons."

"I think I'd like to break your pretty fucking face," I growled.

"I would advise saving that anger for people who want to harm Ivory," Donatello inserted, distracting me from turning Lino's face into a bag of meat. "With Ricci's interest, a message needs to be sent about what happens to people who cross the line with her. It's your best chance of keeping her safe if you truly intend to install her at your side permanently."

I picked up the paperweight from my desk, the one fairly personal touch I allowed in a room that saw crime daily. The sea green globe reminded me of Ivory's eyes and had become a fixture in my life soon after I'd walked away from her. "Well, Ryker got a lock on the guys who robbed the bank. He's waiting for you if you'd like to convey a message," Lino said with a smug look. The bastard had been sitting on that information, withholding it from me the entire time he sat in my office, and we discussed apartment building renovations like I gave a shit about the specifics.

"Call him. Now. Tell him to grab them and meet me at the warehouse," I ordered, already striding out of the office. I grabbed my phone out of my pocket, dialing Ivory's number. I'd programmed mine into her phone when I'd snuck into her bedroom the night before, so her voice was predictably guarded when she answered.

"Of course, you went through my phone. Leaving no stone unturned when it comes to invading my privacy, huh?" I smiled, loving even that bit of fight and sass she had that hadn't been there before. I'd loved her innocent, but the slightly harder woman she'd become would be better prepared to live a life at my side.

"I'm taking you out tonight. I'll be at your place at six." She started to protest, but it fell on deaf ears when I hung up the phone with a grin.

My little angel was about to be mine again, in every sense of the word.

And she had no idea.

***

It was a struggle to wipe the smile off my face when I made it to the warehouse. The warehouse was located inside my territory, a necessary evil when you wanted to be sure no innocent bystanders heard victims scream. Riverdale was one of the worst areas of Chicago, and it was a very rare occasion that someone was foolhardy enough to play the good Samaritan in that area. Regardless, the abandoned building wasn't welcoming in the slightest, but the locked room that had once served as a freezer was fantastic for ensuring nobody ever stumbled across someone I needed to keep around for a while.

I should have been surprised to see Ryker's van parked in the back.

I wasn't.

As soon as the man found them, I had little doubt he'd set things in motion to get them here. He was efficient, his obsessive tendencies required nothing less. But there was nothing he hated more than an innocent woman getting wrapped up in a dangerous situation that she had nothing to do with. Even if I hadn't demanded blood because they'd put a gun in my woman's face, Ryker would have.

He had strange values, considering he was my most violent enforcer and nothing fazed the man. I'd seen him do some fucked up shit and never blink. But he didn't do women or kids.

Said that was the one thing his woman could never forgive. Not that he had a woman, or at least, not one who was aware he'd claimed her, since she was already married to another man.

I shook my head, because obsessive didn't cover it.

The man was a stalker.

I knocked on the steel, exterior door, and Ryker opened it up quickly. "Took you long enough," he grunted, turning and striding away. I turned the deadbolt, locking out any trespassers.

"I was on my way when Lino called," I snorted, and he leveled me with a dark grin.

"I may have already had them in my van." He shrugged his nonchalance, but it was fake. His steel-blue eyes glittered with excitement.

There was a reason the man was my best enforcer. Violence simmered in his blood, an unending rage that never seemed to quiet. I'd never asked where it came from. Even I didn't dare. Ryker was not the man you asked questions about himself. He was loyal, friendly with me and my other guys, but his life started when he joined up. He didn't have a past, was a ghost before he came to me.

That was something I understood.

So we didn't push. People who did ended up dead.

"How many?" I asked. I hadn't been able to ask Ivory exactly how many men had thought to rob the bank. I'd been flooded with too many emotions after over a decade of feeling nothing—suddenly overwhelmed by rage and fear and relief and real lust.

"Four. From what I can tell, three were inside and one was the getaway driver. He never even laid eyes on your girl. Should we let him live?"

I hummed. "We'll see how I feel in the moment." Ryker smirked, and I knew he was relishing the fact that for once, I would enjoy the violence I took part in. Too often I was just a cold spectator, rarely getting involved myself unless I needed to send a very serious message.

Not this time. Not when it came to my Angel.

When he opened the door to the freezer, I let my face slide into that cold mask that the rest of the world knew. "Mr. Bellandi!" One man started in as soon as I filled the room with my presence. Ryker stepped off to the side, leaning against his table where he kept his tools. His ass hit it, and he grabbed one of his picks that he normally used to insert under fingernails. The crazy fuck set to cleaning out under his own nails with it, and if I'd been in any situation where I could have, I'd have laughed my ass off at the horrified look one of the more bloodied men shot his way. "We didn't touch her. I swear!" the man blubbered on.

"Yeah? Tell me how it went down," I challenged, crossing my arms over my chest and staring down the four men strapped down to wooden chairs that Ryker would throw in the incinerator after he finished up. I listened to the most bloodied man rattle on through his story, admitting that he'd pointed his gun at Ivory, but realized who she was as soon as he got close enough. Every muscle I had tensed, picturing what her terror must have looked like as she stared down the barrel of a gun for wanting to help an old lady. I could imagine the slime ball in front of me probably had filthy thoughts while he stared at her. Knowing the way Ivory seemed to draw people into her orbit, had there been need of a hostage, they'd have taken her.

My Angel.

Visions of her broken and bleeding body flashed in front of my eyes, and I reached behind my back to grab the handgun I'd tucked in there before leaving the estate. As soon as I held it in front of me, flicking off the safety, the man began to tremble. "Please, please no." I stepped forward, pressing the gun against his forehead. The stench of urine struck me, his pants wet as terror undoubtedly took over.

"You scared my woman. Can you imagine how she must have felt now?" My voice sounded colder than normal, even for me.

"Yes! Yes, she must have been terrified," he blubbered.

"And yet, she didn't piss herself. One Hell of a woman, if you ask me," Ryker chimed in from the sidelines, watching with interest.

I smirked at him, silently confirming everything he suspected of Ivory. He'd meet her for himself soon enough, and it filled me with pride to know that my friends, my men, would lay down their lives to keep her safe. I'd come a long way from the scrawny little boy who'd had to leave her for her own good.

I'd burn the world down if it meant she was safe.

I pulled the gun away from his face, watching as it morphed with relief. I fired a shot into his thigh, relishing in the way he screamed out his pain. Blood welled from the wound, turning his jeans an even darker hue. "You shot him!" One other protested. "You fucking shot him." I nodded to Ryker, who set down his tool and joined me as I shoved the gun back into my pants after hitching the safety on. Stripping off my suit jacket, I tossed it over the back of one of the spare chairs we kept in the corner. I undid my cufflinks, rolling up my shirt sleeves. Couldn't get them bloody before my date.

My fist connected with the nose of the man who seemed to think a gunshot wound to the thigh was the end of the world. The sound of a nose crunching beside me meant Ryker had taken to giving the men a stern reminder of exactly who I was.

Who Ivory was by association.

"I'm feeling generous," I announced. "You get to live." I struck again, hitting the soft flesh of the man's belly. He groaned his pain, and I glanced out the side of my eye to see the man I'd shot panting so hard he steadily approached unconsciousness. "The only reason you're not dead is because you brought her back to me. I'm feeling thankful for that."

"Yes, Sir," the smartest one grunted, taking Ryker's next punch like a pro. We set to giving them a reminder they would never forget.

No one touched Ivory. No one looked at her wrong.

Or they'd end up dead.

Or beaten to shit at the very least.

CHAPTER ELEVEN

IVORY

My phone rang on the counter, and I jumped so hard I nearly sliced my finger off while chopping chives. That stupid man had me afraid of my shadow.

I wiped my hands off quickly, swiping the screen to connect the call even though I was really, really tempted to ignore it. "Hello?"

"Hey, Angel," Matteo's gruff voice said over the line. "I'm on my way to you."

I sighed, rubbing my temple in frustration. "I'm working. I can't go out tonight."

"I have a feeling you'll be trying that excuse often. What are you making?" I shoved down the twinge of excitement at the prospect of Matteo eating my food. I loved feeding people, to where I preferred cooking for dates and boyfriends rather than having sex with them. At least I knew I was good at cooking.

"Prime rib," I said hesitantly, glancing at the oven and roast that would be ready to pull out within a few minutes.

"What a coincidence," he said, and I could hear the smirk in his voice. "I love prime rib, and I can't imagine you'll eat it all yourself."

"I was planning on bringing some to Duke. His muse has been insane lately, and he forgets to eat if I don't feed him," I responded, wincing when Matteo's snort sounded over the phone.

"I'll just bet he does," he said mysteriously. "I'll be there in fifteen."

"Matteo!" I called out, hissing out an annoyed breath when he hung up on me again. I glanced over at my camera sitting on the dining room table, asking myself why I'd bothered with putting off cooking until so late that my pictures would suck.

Oh, right. I'd wanted the excuse to not go out with Matteo.

The timer went off, and I grabbed my oven mitts to pull the prime rib out of the oven. The wire rack over the pan served as an effective cooling rack, and I transferred it to set over a cutting board so I could use the drippings to make my au jus.

With that finished, I snapped my photos of all the completed components before I sliced into the prime rib and prepped up three plates. One I popped into the fridge for Duke, knowing I'd shoot him a text that it was waiting for him if he got hungry. I'd just finished wrapping up Duke's plate when my front door opened, and I spun around quickly.

"I locked that for a reason," I pointed out, staring at Matteo's stunning face as he stripped off his suit jacket while he prowled toward me. He tossed his jacket, so it landed on one of the stools at the island, stepping into my space until his torso pressed into my chest. I gritted my teeth, staring at the spot where his white dress shirt was open at the top. Even all wrapped up in a fine suit and with the potential to be a gentleman, Matteo somehow managed a small rebellion from the norm that hinted at just how ungentlemanly he could be. The lightest dusting of hair peeked out from the bottom of the opening in his shirt, yet another reminder that the boy was gone. Replaced by a beast of a man who was nothing but bad for me. His hand reached out, running a thumb over my bottom lip as he tilted my face up to his. Soft, coaxing lips touched mine, and I had to fixate on remaining still. I wouldn't make the same mistake I'd made the night before, wouldn't kiss the devil in front of me.

He pulled back, an evil knowing in his eyes as he stared down at me. He knew exactly what game I was playing, that my lack of reception to his kiss had nothing to do with being unaffected and everything to do with trying to prevent myself from falling under his spell. "I told you, you need an alarm system." He took my hand, guiding me over to the breakfast nook where I'd set the plates and put out a bottle of Cabernet Sauvignon. I knew it wouldn't be up to Matteo's standards, but I wouldn't have bothered if I'd been able to stomach not having wine with prime rib. I didn't want him to read into it, but Cabernet was just perfect. He put me in a seat, somehow knowing it was the seat I always sat in, with my back to the windows so I could see my kitchen—my inspiration. He took his own seat, pouring the wine into our glasses without commenting on the wine itself.

"Would an alarm system keep you out?" I asked after the silence grew too large for my tastes.

"What do you think?" He grinned, a flash of teeth that spoke to just how animalistic the man was.

I sighed, rolling my eyes to the ceiling. "Then what exactly is the point in having one? If it doesn't keep intruders out of my home?"

"I'm not an intruder, Angel. Soon enough, you'll welcome me into your home and bed. We both know these little games will be futile." He picked up his fork and knife, slicing through the prime rib that melted like butter in his hands.

I couldn't blame it.

Popping the meat into his mouth, he paused, chewing thoughtfully before emitting a deep moan of satisfaction that made me press my thighs together. "That's fucking incredible."

I shrugged, picking up my glass and sipping at my wine. "It's just prime rib."

And it was. Just great prime rib.

"You're gifted. Truly." Matteo's voice was astonished, as if he was seeing something about me for the first time. It suddenly felt too intimate, which was ridiculous. My cooking was far from a secret. Thousands of people read my blog every day, but something about Matteo had always seen beneath the surface to every facet of my being.

"Why are you doing this? Forcing your way into my life? Surely, there must be other women who could satisfy whatever need it is you think I'll meet—"

His fork dropped to the plate, and he stared at me until I fell silent under the force of that glare. "I am doing this," he paused, heaving a deep sigh. "Because you are mine. It's as simple as that."

"I haven't been yours for a long time, Teo," I protested, wincing at the way the name I'd once called him felt as it left my lips.

"You've always been mine, *Cara mia.* Even when we couldn't be together." He said it like it was so obvious. But the reality was he had spent over a decade fucking other women and leaving me to be with other men. That was not the man I wanted to belong to.

"I'm not interested in whatever weird kind of relationship you think it is we have. An open relationship? Something where you come back whenever you feel like it? Neither of those scenarios appeal to me, Matteo. I'm sure there are plenty of women content with what you're offering, and there's nothing wrong with that if it works for you. But I'm not that girl." I gave him a sad smile, setting down my silverware. I was finished—eating, playing his games, all of it. "I believe you know where the door is." He took another bite of his prime rib, defying me and my wishes to the last. When he'd finished his plate, he stood, watching me as I finished cleaning up my kitchen. It was an obsessive thing, always needing to clean the space down after every use. He glanced at my sage off-shoulder maxi dress, and his eyes tracked down to take in the nude heeled boots on my feet.

"You're comfortable in those?" he asked, and I furrowed my brow in confusion.

"Yes, though I'll take them off as soon as you leave." He knelt at my feet in front of me, shoving my dress up enough to inspect the shoes. I nearly lost my balance when he took one foot in his hands, twisting it gently to inspect the heel.

"They'll do. Let's go." Scooping up his jacket, he shrugged it back onto his shoulders but left the front unbuttoned. Like a crazy, elegant rebel.

"I'm not going anywhere," I protested. He seemed to consider his options and then nodded as if he was conceding defeat. With a heaving sigh of relief, I flinched when he stood directly in front of me and his hands grasped my hips in his hands. After he truly settled there, he lifted and heaved me up onto his shoulder. I grunted, smacking his back in struggles that went ignored as he turned and walked toward my entryway. He turned off the lights as he went, grabbing my keys off my console table and making for the door. "Matteo!" I shrieked. "Put me down!" Stepping out on to the front porch, he didn't seem to care that we must have been attracting attention from my neighbors—that they would likely call the police to report an abduction. "I need my phone at least. My purse." He swatted me on the ass with a resounding thump. It wasn't painful in the slightest, not through the combined fabric of my underwear and my dress, but the principle of it was shocking, regardless.

"Don't need them," he grunted, sealing my door shut with my own keys. When he turned and strode for the Aston Martin, I increased my struggles.

"Stop! Let me go! The neighbors will call the police, you know."

Matteo chuckled, turning me around so suddenly I felt dizzy. "You calling the cops?" he asked, and I had to wonder which neighbor he was harassing.

"No, Sir. Wouldn't dream of it, Mr. Bellandi. I didn't see nothing," my friendly, older neighbor Mike said, and his front door closed with a thud.

Traitor.

I imagined him retreating inside it, leaving me to the mercy of a man that he feared himself.

"Matteo, please," I begged as he pried open the passenger door.

"Get in the fucking car, Ivory," he ordered, setting me to my feet next to it. I nodded my submission, sensing something different playing beneath the surface of Matteo's sanity in that moment. Something had put him over the edge, and I suspected that it was me.

The only real question was what would he do about it?

I sat and pivoted my legs into the car, flinching when the door slammed closed. I had the brains to realize opening that door would likely be a very poor decision, so I sat with my hands in my lap. Matteo was in the driver's seat only a moment later, reaching across the center compartment to lean into my space and buckle me in himself. With a purr the engine started, and he pulled out of my driveway too fast for my liking. I gripped the seat next to my legs, trying to control my panic. "Matteo—"

"If you *ever* let another man *touch* you, I'll kill him," he snarled, his voice so menacing I froze in horror. That voice left little doubt to the fact that he meant every word, summoned straight from the pits of Hell. "We are not in an open relationship. No one touches you. No one touches me. It is you and I from here on out. Am I understood?"

I nodded, staring at my legs as he spoke.

"The words, Ivory. I need the words."

"Yes, Matteo. I understand," I whispered, fighting the urge to cry. I wouldn't let him know how much he'd frightened me. I may not have been the strongest of women, may not have been perfect, but I would be damned if I showed him my weakness. I'd survived him once, and I would do it again, but the second time around I would prove I could do it without letting my heart get involved in whatever twisted games he wanted to play.

He fell silent, driving us through the city, as I tried to reinforce my resolve.

Because I couldn't let him break me.

Not a second time.

❋❋❋

I don't know where I expected a man like Matteo to take me on a date. Somewhere exclusive. Somewhere classy.

I never would have guessed he'd bring me to Millennium Park. We pulled up onto the side of the road, and Matteo was out quickly and approaching the three men standing on the curb and waiting for us. I recognized Simon and Scar immediately, but the other man beside them was a stranger to me. Matteo tossed the stranger his keys, and I couldn't hear the words that the two of them exchanged from my place inside the vehicle. Matteo strode over to my door, tugging it open with a smooth elegance that spoke to his proper upbringing. He gave me his hand and pulled me free from the car with less patience.

I officially ranked lower than the car in that moment. He guided me down the sidewalk and into the park with his hand at the small of my back. The Aston started up behind us, the strange man whisking it away to park it somewhere safely no doubt. As we made our way in silence, Matteo's expression was steely every time I glanced at him out of the corner of my eye. Shivering in the cold, I tried to discreetly cross my arms over my chest and rub some warmth into my mostly bare arms.

"Here, Miss Torres," Scar said from behind us. He shrugged out of his suit jacket, holding it out for me. My lips tipped in a sheepish smile, turning and reaching out a hand to take it.

"No," Matteo said from my side, shaking his head at Scar, who nodded and slid his arms back into the sleeves. Matteo stripped out of his own, draping it over my shoulders until I was suddenly cocooned in his scent—enveloped in the warmth from his body. I shuddered as his hands rubbed up and down my arms now covered in his jacket, releasing a sigh when his lips hit the top of my head. I could only hope that the cruel, dangerous Matteo had vacated his body in favor of the version of him I could handle.

Somewhat.

We resumed walking, picking up a brisk pace after Matteo glanced at his watch. A huge crowd had already formed, but Matteo and his guys made quick work of maneuvering us through it to get to the center near the back where the more relaxed listeners sat in lawn chairs compared to the ones who waited next to the stage. I was grateful for the width of the heel on my boots, and I realized with a start that was what Matteo had inspected back at my house. He'd been checking my ability to walk on grass. It was an oddly considerate, intimate, thing for him to have considered, particularly coming from the man who claimed he didn't even take women to dinner.

He guided me to a huge blanket on the ground, where another man in a suit stood guard. Matteo sat on the blanket, looking altogether unreal. Wearing an expensive Italian suit, handsome beyond belief, he emitted raw power even sitting on a blanket in the park. I sat down next to him, curling my legs to the side. Matteo's security moved behind us, remaining standing, and I tried to ignore them. They gave us enough distance that I knew they wouldn't be eavesdropping or anything of the sort, but it still somehow felt intrusive. Like their presence was just different from the hundreds of people around us.

I was distracted from the awkwardness when a song I recognized well started from the stage. The artist's voice rang loud and clear, and the listeners silenced immediately as my favorite indie musician played one of his first hits. I swallowed back my growing apprehension that Matteo seemed to know so much about me, because there was absolutely no chance that it was a coincidence. We sat in silence, listening to the artist sing about a woman who needed someone to lean on, about a woman who had gone through life alone for too long. I could feel Matteo's eyes on the side of my face, but I refused to look at him. He sighed, repositioning my body until I fell onto my back. My head landed on his thigh, and his fingers took to stroking my hair. Tilting my head away from him, I looked toward the stage. We were far away enough that I couldn't see much beyond the more avid fans who stood close to the stage, but it was better than acknowledging Matteo. His attentiveness in combination with the lyrics of the artist's songs was too much, it made the situation feel like a critical moment in my life.

A crossroad.

My heart pumped in my chest, despite what should have been nothing but calming. "You can trust me," he whispered. I huffed a laugh, resuming my determination to ignore him after the minor slip up. "I know things didn't end well before. There are things you don't know. Things you *can't* know just yet. I did what I had to do for your sake, Ivory, but leaving you was the hardest thing I've ever done. It broke something inside me, and if you haven't figured it out yet, that boy you loved no longer exists."

"I'll bet. You sure looked broken when you went off to fuck Shauna," I hissed.

He winced, looking ashamed for the first time I think I'd ever seen. Even in high school, Matteo had been unapologetic for his behavior, taking what he wanted when he wanted it. The boy who never heard the word no, the boy who had the world waiting in the palm of his hand if he so much as said the words. "I needed you to hate me," he whispered brokenly, and my head turned to face him and meet his eyes.

"You succeeded," I whispered back. "I've never hated anyone as much as I hate you."

His hand cupped my cheek as he stared down at me, a thumb trailing over the freckles on my cheek he'd once found so fascinating. "I'll fix it. I promise."

"No one can fix this, Teo," I murmured, hating how pathetic my voice sounded.

How broken.

"Just watch me," he challenged. I shook my head, returning to silence to listen to the music for the rest of the concert. I let it seep into my bones, remind me of what it felt like to be alone. I'd lived alone for so long, the prospect of not having to be for once appealed in a way I never expected.

I was so lonely that even a man I hated seemed like a decent option to cuddle me while I slept. To hold me still while I battled in my dreams. I determined that as soon as Matteo left me, and I knew he would eventually, I would stop looking for perfect.

Perfect didn't exist.

All that mattered was that I found someone who loved me.

Someone who held me.

Someone who knew me, because he asked me questions.

Safe. Content. That was what I needed.

Not a stalker who broke into my home and knew things about me that he shouldn't have known.

✱✱✱

My eyes were droopy, taking me back to the days of my childhood where I could not be a passenger in a car at night and stay awake. It just didn't happen. "Where are we going?" I asked, staring out the window as Matteo turned in the opposite direction of my house.

"Home," he answered evasively, his hand clenching the steering wheel tighter as he shifted gears and merged into traffic on I-90.

"My house is in the opposite direction, Matteo. Take me home," I protested, glancing over at the side of his face where his features glittered like the hardest granite. My eyes snapped wide open as unease became very real.

"My bed is bigger."

"I didn't invite you to join me in mine," I hissed, shaking my head in disbelief. I wanted to call for help, wanted to call Duke or Sadie to come pick me up.

But I didn't have my phone.

"I don't even have my purse, or my phone Matteo. I need those things. Please take me home," I begged. He grunted, pressing a button on the steering wheel.

"Boss?" Simon's voice came over the speaker.

"After we're safely in the estate, I need you or Scar to go to Ivory's. Get her phone off the kitchen counter and her purse. Bring them to the house." He glanced over at me, his eyes glittering in the light coming off the dashboard given how dark it was outside. "And a change of clothes for her to wear home tomorrow."

"Anything else?"

"That's all." The line disconnected, and I stared at him in disbelief.

"You can't just tell me I'm staying the night! I have the right to say no." My face twisted when he turned hardened eyes to me.

"We're done with these games. It's time for you to accept that I am not going anywhere, Angel." His voice softened, as if realizing just how much he was asking of me. "I want to move forward with the rest of our lives."

"And you just don't give a shit about what I want? That's promising for our future," I spat, and watched as his jaw clenched. I shut up, feeling like I'd done nothing but test Matteo's limits all night. He was angry with me, frustrated, and I truly didn't know the man well enough to know if that was just bad or if it was terrible for me.

The boy I'd loved never would have hurt me, but he was gone. A lie that had never really existed, one that Matteo admitted was gone forever.

I didn't speak until we pulled up to the gates of the Estate, the guard nodding to Matteo wordlessly before he opened it. Matteo drove in, and when I turned back to see the gates closing a feeling of hopelessness settled inside me. There'd be no escaping his fortress unless he wanted me to. We both knew that. "Matteo," I whispered.

"Quiet, Angel," his voice was low, a barely there whisper that increased my anxiety. Men like Matteo didn't need to yell to be terrifying. They could convey their dissatisfaction without a word, by just existing. He pulled the car to a stop quickly, hopping out and pulling me from my seat.

Donatello stepped out the front door. "Mr. Bellandi. Ms.Torres. Welcome home."

I resisted the urge to point out that it wasn't my home. That it never would be, and Matteo spared me from having to respond when he answered. "We're not to be disturbed. When Simon or Scar return with her things, put them in my office please."

"Certainly," Donatello nodded, watching with wide eyes as Matteo took my hand and pulled me into the house. We traipsed over the tile floors, and he pulled me up the winding stairs. I had to fight not to trip, my dress too long and my boots not prepared for the speed with which Matteo took the stairs. He didn't let me take in the landing at the top of the stairs, just turned down one of two hallways and led me all the way to the end.

The master bedroom was a very different style than the rest of the house. Modern, clean lines done in a combination of dark grey and tan, I had to wonder what prompted the difference between that room and the rest of the house.

"I never bothered remodeling the rest of the house," he answered my silent question. "But this room I did as soon as I moved back in after my father died."

"It's lovely." I shifted awkwardly, doing my best not to glance at the massive platform bed on the back wall.

"Get ready for bed." He jerked his head to a door to the bathroom behind me. I took it as my reprieve, retreating into the space and locking the door behind me. It was a continuation from the bedroom, white and grey marble with tan elements through the space. A huge deep soak tub, and a massive shower made for orgies dominated the space, but a massive two sink vanity caught my eye. I stepped in front of the mirror, trying not to think about how many women Matteo had caught in his web in that bathroom. I washed the makeup off my face, attempting to calm my raging heart and convince my eyeballs to remain in my skull, given they looked wide enough they might bolt at any moment.

I could do it. I had slept in a bed with Matteo the night before, unknowingly, but I'd survived. The next morning he'd take me home, and I'd get the fuck out of dodge. It was only one night. I stripped off my socks and shoes, stacking them in the corner.

A brand-new toothbrush in its packaging sat on the counter, and I used it all while wanting to keep my bad breath to spite him. When I went back to the bedroom, after hyperventilating for a few moments, Matteo stood next to the bed. His back was to me, and he stared out the window sipping a scotch. His suit was draped over one of the armchairs in the room, all his beautiful olive skin on display and only his ass covered by his skintight boxer briefs.

He turned, setting his tumbler on a coaster on the little table in the seating area. I took a step back as he prowled toward me, flinching when he only reached out a hand to clasp a strand of my hair. "You expect me to believe you sleep in your dress?"

"I don't have any clothes." I swallowed.

"That's because you won't be needing them until morning," he murmured, pressing his lips to mine briefly. "Take off your dress."

"No. I don't want this, Teo. I don't want you—"

"Ah, *Cara mia*, you always were a terrible liar," he chuckled.

"I'm not lying! This isn't—" I broke off, gasping when he leaned forward and pressed his lips behind my ear. His breath tortured my skin, making me shudder. "You're bad for me."

"Yes," he agreed. "But you're mine, regardless." His hands grasped the fabric of my dress, bunching it until it was a mound around my hips.

"Teo, stop," I whispered but the vehemence, the fear had gone. Nothing remained but anticipation. Because no one had ever made me feel the way Matteo had the night, he took my virginity.

No one had ever worshiped me the way he had.

"Tell me you aren't wet for me," he whispered, teasing my neck with the slightest scrape of his teeth against my weak spot. Even after all these years, he remembered exactly where to touch, where to kiss, where to bite to drive me wild. Even though I'd only had him inside me once, that didn't mean we hadn't done everything else over that year we spent together. "Come on, Angel. Lie to me again."

I didn't speak, didn't think I could put the words together to tell him I wasn't. And he was right, it would have been a lie, anyway. When his fingers brushed against me, I was ashamed of how shockingly wet the gusset of my panties was as it pressed into my skin. Matteo groaned, the sound vibrating against my neck until he pulled back to press his forehead to mine as those skilled fingers toyed with me through the thin barrier of my underwear. "It means nothing," I whispered, closing my eyes to shut out the intimacy of his stare.

"You want me to believe that any of the other assholes you've let touch you ever got you this wet when they've barely touched you? Your body knows me, just like mine knows you," he whispered, removing his hand in favor of pressing his torso to mine so I could feel the steel length of his erection.

"It means nothing," I repeated on a sigh.

"It means everything, Angel," he said, voice soft, nearly reverent as he tugged the dress up and over my head. I wanted to fight him, wanted to keep my arms firmly pressed to my side, but nothing worked. My body had always been putty in his hands.

Nothing had changed.

Big calloused hands stroked down my sides, a tremble in them as they graced over my hips and grabbed my ass. He lifted me, staring up at me with eyes full of emotion I suspected reflected in mine.

My eyes burned with the threat of tears. Because even with all we'd changed —even after he'd hurt me—after twelve years of just existing, Matteo was the only thing that could make me feel.

I loved him. Exactly as he was, no matter what he might have done or become. Matteo would always be the one who owned my heart, and that was exactly why I needed to stop. I needed to get his hands off of me. But somehow, as he carried me to his massive bed, my legs wound around his waist with a mind of their own. As conflicted as my mind might have been, my body had no such qualms as it quivered at the slightest stroke of his thumb against me.

He dropped me to the bed, and I bounced on my back only once before Matteo was sliding between my spread legs and leaning over me. His lips found mine, coaxing me to open for him when he traced my lips with his tongue.

He swallowed my whimper when I opened for him, pressing into me and tangling his tongue with mine. I'd expected him to be savage when he got his way, to take what he wanted, but he was the same as he'd been in high school when he finally got me in bed. He went slowly, taking his time, building my need through nothing but the feel of his skin against mine. I ran my hands over his chest, feeling the tightly corded muscles jump beneath my hands. When I curled my hands around his neck, twirling my fingers into the spot where his hair met the nape of his neck and pulled him closer, only then did he deepen the kiss beyond his initial exploration. Our mouths fused together, and I arched my back when his hand slid up my spine to find the clasp of my bra. He pulled away from me just enough to rip it off me, before he was back where he belonged, nibbling at my bottom lip. He smiled at me, cupping one breast in his hand until I arched further, pressing my flesh into his hand in a silent plea. He kissed the front of my throat, slowly kissing his way down until he hit my collarbone. Pulling back, he stared down at me for only a moment, and I watched those stunning blue eyes darken as he reached out his other hand to toy with my other breast. He pinched the nipples, worshiping the flesh while he stared at it like he couldn't believe he had his hands on me.

"Teo," I whispered, and I knew my voice conveyed every bit of my need when he growled at me. His hips slid further down the bed, and I immediately missed the press of him against me. Until he lowered his mouth to one of my breasts, sucking the peak inside and ravishing it with his tongue while he enveloped it in warmth. When he pulled away, the cool air of the room was a sharp contrast, making me writhe when he repeated the action to the other. "Please," I begged, and I immediately had a moment of hatred for myself.

He sensed it, erasing the logic when his lips kissed down over my stomach. His tongue found that spot, right in the hollow of my hip where I instantly squirmed beneath him. He sucked the flesh into his mouth, nipping and torturing it until I knew he'd leave a mark. Fingers grasped my underwear, and he knelt up and pressed my legs up so he could strip them off my legs. As soon as he released my legs, his mouth was between them. "Oh my God," I whispered, my legs thudding to the bed around him, and I stared down at his head as he worked me over.

Matteo didn't lick a woman's pussy because he felt obligated, or at the very least not mine. I might have argued he enjoyed it more than I did if he wasn't so damn good at it.

That talented tongue explored every part of me, thrusting in and out until I whimpered. When he turned his attention to my clit, it was so he could slide a finger inside me. I clenched around him on a cry, feeling the way he moaned in response vibrate through me. He withdrew that finger, only to add a second and curl them to stroke that spot inside me that made me quiver.

"Teo," I whimpered, and the sound of his name seemed to push him over the edge. He wrapped his lips around the bundle of nerves at the apex of my thigh, sucking gently. My legs tightened around his head; my hand buried in his hair to hold him exactly where I wanted him as I shattered in a blinding orgasm that stole my ability to function.

I laid there, panting and trying to regain my ability to move. When I opened my eyes, it was to Matteo shoving his own underwear down his legs and kicking them off. He pulled his fingers free of me and spread my legs wide from where they'd wrapped around his head. Sliding up my body, his hips lined up with mine so he could grind his length against my wet core. His lips found mine in a bruising, claiming kiss that seemed even more primal because he tasted like me. He reached down, sliding himself through my wet and notching his head at my entrance. Pulling away from my lips, he groaned, "Tell me you're mine."

Still recovering from my orgasm, I nodded in a daze.

"Words, Angel. Give me the words."

"Yours," I murmured, cupping his cheek with a delirious smile and tugging him down to kiss him again. He slid inside me slowly, filling me until there wasn't a single inch that couldn't feel him.

"Fuck," he groaned against my mouth. He reached down, wrapping my legs around his hips. Our foreheads pressed together; our mouths not quite touching as he started to move inside me. Even without his lips on mine, I could taste him, taste *me* in his breath on my face. One of his hands grabbed mine, our fingers intertwining while he wrapped his other under my shoulder to hold me where he wanted me. He slid in and out in slow, hard thrusts.

Matteo didn't fuck me; he'd never fucked me.

He made love to me, eyes on mine the entire time. There was no doubt who was inside me. No doubt about who owned me in that moment.

Matteo was all around me, an extension of myself.

The other half of me.

Tears stung my eyes again, and I buried my head in his shoulder to try to hide them.

He cupped my cheek, pulling me so he could see me. His face twisted in pain. "I'm here now," he murmured in what seemed to be a reassuring voice.

But it was just another reminder.

He was here now, but there would come another day when he wasn't. Another day when he broke me and tossed me aside.

I smiled at him and nodded, determined to guard my heart from everything my body seemed incapable of denying.

I loved Matteo, exactly as he was.

But he'd never be mine.

Seeming to sense my growing distance, Matteo reached between us, pressing fingers to my clit to bring me back to the place where I focused on the sensations between us. I moaned, not even trying to resist what he offered me. Tossing my head back, I came on another cry, clenching around him like my life depended on keeping him inside me.

Above me, Matteo groaned, sinking teeth into my shoulder as he flooded me with heat. We lay there for a few moments, neither one of us moving to disconnect. Because who knew what would happen when we did, and reality came crashing down.

Eventually, he had no choice but to pull free of me, and the spill of fluid that followed made me glance down my body in horror. "You didn't wear a condom," I whispered. I couldn't believe I'd been so stupid. I'd just trusted that a man like Matteo would be smart enough to wrap it up.

"No," he said simply, not looking concerned in the slightest as he stood and strode for the bathroom. I laid there, feeling beyond lost until he returned.

Using a wet rag, he cleaned between my legs—his eyes fixated on the action. "What is wrong with you?" I whispered. "Why wouldn't you put on a condom?"

He looked at me, momentarily surprised, as if *I* was an idiot for expecting he'd wear one. "Nothing between us. Ever," he grunted, tossing the rag to the side of the room. "I'm clean. I know you are." I clenched my eyes shut, hoping he wasn't lying. Being on the pill, I shouldn't have had anything to worry about if he was honestly clean. "Really, Ivory. You're the only one I've ever had without a condom. You're safe. I would never risk you like that." I nodded blankly and stood. "Where are you going?"

"Bathroom," I said, and only partially because I needed a moment to myself. As oddly sweet as it was for him to clean me, I couldn't not use the bathroom after sex.

It was a convenient excuse to go hate myself in private.

CHAPTER TWELVE

MATTEO

It took Ivory too long to turn her brain off and settle into sleep. I could tell because she was still. I'd only spent one night with the woman, but there was no doubt in my mind that the way she thrashed in her sleep was a common occurrence. Even in sleep, she'd seemed relieved when my body pressed hers into the bed, holding her still. That beautiful face of hers calmed from the stressed, tense state it had been in when I'd entered her room.

Given how peacefully she slept with my weight on her, I was hesitant to leave her, but I needed to get her phone in case there'd been an emergency while we'd had our date, and the sun was already rising over the horizon. I hadn't bothered with the curtains, usually I was up before the sun. I removed myself from Ivory's body, silently hoping that her peaceful sleep would continue even without me. One day, I would understand the cause, but I knew better than to push too hard, too fast.

My Angel was stubborn.

And for whatever goddamn reason, I found that sexy as Hell.

I tugged the curtains closed quietly, slipping into my boxer briefs and stepping out of my bedroom. Making my way downstairs, I headed for my office. I'd put her phone on the nightstand before I slipped into the shower. I knew having it would comfort her, delude her into thinking it offered her any protection from me.

The truth was, I could do whatever I wanted to Ivory, and there wasn't a person on this Earth who would *dare* to stop me. Her endless bag of shit sat on my desk, and a quick glance confirmed that her phone wasn't sitting next to it conveniently. I had no choice but to dig into the monstrosity. It was a first for me, but I'd heard horror stories of what men found in their women's purses.

As soon as I opened it, I realized it wasn't on top of the pile of shit.

That would be too easy.

Rummaging through, my hand grasped a medicine packet. My heart leapt into my throat. Her file had shown no illnesses, so I tugged it out with growing horror. I should have been relieved to see the birth control. From any other woman, I'd demand it. But knowing that Ivory was protected from pregnancy didn't fill me with any relief.

A pregnancy was one more way to ensure that she was mine, completely.

In a way that no one would ever have with her.

I lifted my phone, snapping a picture of the front and the back of the packet before replacing it in her purse. It didn't matter that it burned me to do it. When I found her phone, I turned and went back to my sleeping woman, suddenly determined to experience my first morning sex ever.

CHAPTER THIRTEEN

IVORY

I'd been in a daze all morning. After Matteo had woken me up with his mouth between my legs, he fucked me until all I'd wanted to do was curl back up in his bed and sleep for the rest of the day. With a sexy as hell chuckle, he reminded me that I probably had work to do. Though he made it clear he didn't object to me staying in his bed all day.

I wanted to slap myself. I'd let him touch me, let him have me again, let him finish inside me without a condom. I didn't understand what it was about Matteo that turned me into an incoherent mess who couldn't string together two letters to say 'no.'

I was so distracted that I'd had to turn the stove off and walk away, because I would get nothing pretty enough to photograph unless I found an outlet first. I'd taken to cuddling with Smaug, running my finger over his scales and watching with amusement as he closed his eyes in contentment. He really was the weirdest, most affectionate lizard I'd ever seen. While I'd never really thought of myself as a reptile person, I melted the second I saw him at the pet store and brought him home.

Even if he ate mealworms and crickets.

Blech.

The knock on the door seemed like a welcome reprieve, even as I wondered who would drop by. Duke was pissed that I'd gone out with Matteo again and not answered my phone for nearly twelve hours, and I couldn't keep bothering Sadie with my emergencies while she was working at the gym. So, I hadn't told her about my sleepover yet.

The courier standing on my front porch wasn't someone I'd ever received deliveries from before, and I squinted my eyes at him in the bright sun. "Can I help you?"

"Miss Torres?" he asked, and I nodded. "Sign here."

I took the clipboard, scrawling my signature quickly and then accepted the small box. Carrying it over to my trusty island, I shrugged at Smaug's look of curiosity as he peered down at the box. With a sigh, I peeled back the gold wrapping paper.

A note rested on top, and I picked it up, reading the handwritten words with growing horror.

It reminded me of you.

Exquisite.

Adrian

His phone number completed the note that I set to the side like it was diseased.

It probably was.

My trembling fingers lifted the white gold necklace out of the gift box. I may not have known much about jewelry, but I knew the stones in that necklace were diamonds. *Fifteen* of them in a Y shape that would dangle between my breasts.

I swallowed nervously, dropping the necklace back into the box and then wincing. That thing probably cost more than my car. The note followed, before I folded the box back up as best as I could.

Even if I'd been interested, I had no use for jewelry like that. But I *wasn't* even remotely interested in a man that would corner me in a bathroom and terrify me.

Picking up the box, I strutted my way outside to where Scar sat on guard duty in his car. He rolled down the window, looking on edge when he took in my bare feet. "You should go inside, Ms. Torres. It's cold."

I dropped the box in his lap. "I don't want this. Might as well make yourself useful if you must stalk me."

I turned and went back for my door. "Shit," he hissed, and I glanced back to see him already calling someone on his phone.

It didn't take a genius to guess who it might be.

CHAPTER FOURTEEN

MATTEO

I felt like my bones would burst free from the confines of my skin. Rattled in a way I'd never been, *pissed* in a way I couldn't recall ever experiencing. He'd touched my woman, and when I'd warned him, I meant business where she was concerned, he'd sent my woman a fucking gift.

As soon as I parked the Aston in Ivory's driveway, I shoved my door open. It felt like I should have run to where Scar stood guard on her porch, but my steps were careful, controlled. If I didn't contain the monster who was out for blood, I'd frighten Ivory beyond what a gift from Adrian must have already done. As soon as I was on the porch, Scar pulled the small jewelry box from his suit pocket, his jaw clenched tight and his nostrils flaring.

On anyone else, the display of anger over Ivory might have made me feel territorial, but I knew Scar. I knew him well enough to know that the man was trustworthy, and his interest in Ivory was purely related to his dedication to me and my family. He'd been nothing but a street rat when we'd taken him in, a little pickpocket who'd been abused in every way a man could imagine—just another victim of the failed system that let kids like him fall through the cracks every day. I took them in, gave them a purpose.

Even if it was one that the U.S. Government didn't agree with.

While I wouldn't say my crimes were without victims, I did my best to keep the innocent out of it.

The note crumpled in my hand as I read it and stared down at the necklace in the box. I hadn't even given my woman jewelry yet, and this fucker thought he could buy her affection with a predictable gift. I dropped the crumpled note back in the box, turning to Scar where he stared down at me. I nodded, and he pocketed it. "Keep it. Consider it your bonus for making sure he doesn't get near her."

"Yes, Boss," Scar smirked, and I knew the man was thinking how much it would piss Adrian off to line my man's pockets.

"She's permanent. Got any objections to being her detail long-term?" I asked, and his eyebrows raised.

"Permanent like—"

"Like a ring is being custom made at this very moment, and she'll have my kid as soon as I can swing it."

He chuckled, a rare sound for the more stoic man. "She know that?"

"Not yet," I shrugged, because Ivory's opinion on the matter was inconsequential. "Let's go."

I opened the door, not even surprised when I found it unlocked. I didn't suppose Ivory thought there was much point when I'd just break in as soon as I got there and she had her own personal security, but I added it to the list of conversations we needed to have.

"Is it safe to assume that you'll deal with him for me?" she asked, slamming around in her kitchen. There wasn't a food item in sight, so she wasn't cooking. I realized quickly that she was scrubbing the cabinets, as though she didn't already keep them immaculate for her blog. I, perhaps wisely, refrained from commenting. Next to me, Scar's lips quirked at the sight of the leopard gecko clinging to her shirt. She'd probably forgotten the poor thing was there, jostling him around in her cleaning frenzy. I sighed, stepping up to her and holding out a hand. It surprised me when the thing was more than happy to abandon Ivory in favor of the safety my hand offered. She stopped cleaning finally, glancing down at her lizard and pouting at him. "I'm so sorry, Smaugy," she cooed, taking it from my hand and bringing him to his tank while she whispered to him. "I forgot you were there, baby." She set him in the tank, and I fought the urge to laugh as the lizard glared at her.

Who could have known a lizard would have so much personality?

"I'll take care of it," I answered finally, like she'd been asking. We both knew I'd handle it. "From now on, you don't answer your own door," I said, and she leveled me with a glare. "Scar will be in the house with you, except for when he feels it necessary to check outside the house. You stay with him at all times. You do not drive yourself anywhere. You do not walk anywhere alone. He is always on you, understood?"

"That cannot be necessary—" she started to argue, breaking off when she saw the serious expression on my face. "I think you're being a little extreme over a bit of jealousy, Teo," she whispered.

My heart broke, hating that I would need to crush a bit of that remaining innocence in her. "He's not a good man, Angel. I've seen what's left of women after he's finished with them, and he's looking to pawn them off on the next asshole who wants to use them. He is *not* a man you want anywhere near you, and now he's fixated. I will make sure he gets over you real quick, but in the meantime, I need you to do your part and stay with Scar."

"He sells them?" She whispered, her voice cracking. "Like prostitutes?"

"Sex trafficking." She swallowed, nodding slowly as she closed her eyes in pain. I knew what question would be next; it was the only logical path her mind could take while she was still so in the dark about who I was and what I did. "You said he was a rival. Do you sell people too?"

"No," I said firmly, and even though it was true, the bitter stain of a lie twisted my insides. I ran women, but they were all paid for their services and chose to be there. It was a very different crime than what Adrian did.

I just couldn't be certain Ivory would see it that way when the time came.

"Okay," she nodded, relief making her chest swell with the inhale of breath she took.

"One day, you'll understand everything I do, Angel," I sighed, drawing her into my arms. "Just not today." She nodded, not even bothering to argue, and I knew that the reality of the threat Adrian posed to her was settling in. "You'll stay with Scar?"

"Yes." She nodded enthusiastically, and I felt my face harden at the bit of fear I'd put in my woman because of this piece of shit's determination to fuck with me. When I drew away, Ivory's eyes glanced down at my arms, where I knew my shirt sleeves were rolled up, ready to bloody Adrian for what he'd done. I had abandoned my suit jacket in my haste to get to Ivory, left behind in my office. I was only grateful I'd had the foresight to leave my gun in the car.

She didn't need to see that yet.

"Is that—" she started, and I knew she'd ask about the tattoo on my left forearm.

"I'll see you later. Stay with Scar," I ordered, nodding at the other man as I fled the house.

It was not the right moment to explain the tattoo I'd gotten the same day I broke her heart.

✳✳✳

Adrian's home was a stone monstrosity right in the middle of the city. A complete and total attention-grabbing statement, like the man thought owning a home in it meant he owned the city.

He didn't, because it was mine.

I strolled up to the door, gun tucked in hand and not caring who saw me. This city was mine, and there wasn't a person in it who was stupid enough to fuck with me when I meant business.

Not a person except for Adrian Ricci. The stupid fuck.

Even his security didn't dare shoot me, not without direct word from their boss. Even in the unlikely event they killed me, my men would revolt, and the city would descend into complete and utter chaos. No one wanted that.

The door opened before I could knock, and I shoved it wide and shouldered the butler out of my way. "Where is he?"

"Mr. Bellandi, perhaps—"

I pointed my gun at his forehead, staring down at him with glacial eyes that showed just how little I would care if I shot him dead. "Where the fuck is Adrian?"

"Office at the end of the hall," the man whimpered. "Could you perhaps holster your weapon? There's no reason this needs to be a violent affair."

"I disagree." I stormed through the wood-paneled halls, a deception on Adrian's part to try to convince his business associates of the illusion that he came from old money.

Like them. *Like me.*

But Adrian Ricci was nothing but a motivated thug who thought because he made money on the backs of others suffering, that somehow entitled him to the luxuries that the old bloods enjoyed.

But we all knew the truth.

He was nothing. He lived as nothing, and one day, he would die as nothing.

I shoved his office door open, wondering how pretty his classical cream painted walls would look covered in his blood. "Matteo," he said, standing with a smile, even while I leveled my gun at him. "Come now, whatever it is you think I've done—"

"Stay the fuck away from my woman. I thought I made myself very clear that she does not exist for you."

"Ah, I see Ivory told you about my little gift then. How very disappointing," he sighed. "Really though, Matteo. Can you blame me? All is fair in love and war, and the woman is positively enchanting. Such fire!" he exclaimed. "I wonder what she'll be like when she's broken. How pretty those eyes will look when they're vacant. Like a beautiful, little doll."

I crossed the distance between us in favor of shoving Adrian up against the wall with my arm to his throat. "You will *never* touch her."

He grinned up at me, a direct challenge in his gaze. Drawing back my hand that held my gun, I used it to break his nose. "Fuck," he groaned, smiling again through blood-soaked teeth.

"Mr. Ricci?" one guard who'd undoubtedly followed me in asked from the door.

"It's all right, Jesse," Adrian assured him. "Matteo and I are just having a difference of opinion. Women. That trap between their legs makes all of us go a little crazy, isn't that right?" With a snarl, I repeated the strike, leaving no part of Adrian's face unbloodied. When my gun pressed against the underside of his chin, I knew that killing him would be the best thing for Ivory. I may not walk away, but she'd be safe regardless, and the calm in his eyes even as they swelled up told me he wouldn't be leaving her alone without my forcing it. Lowering the gun, I fired it into his right hand, the same one that had touched Ivory without her permission.

"Touch her again, and I'll shoot your dick off next time. You won't have much need of my woman without it."

He roared out a laugh, swaying when I released my hold on his throat and sucking in a full, unhindered breath. "I always knew I liked you, Bellandi!" he called as I turned and strode out of his office and home without another word.

I dialed Scar as soon as I was in my car. "She doesn't leave your sight if she's out of that house. Understood?"

"Yes, Boss. I guess it didn't go well."

That was an understatement.

CHAPTER FIFTEEN

IVORY

After Matteo left, I tried to ignore Scar's presence in favor of cooking. When he realized he was making me uncomfortable, an audience I hadn't asked for, he'd excused himself to go give himself a tour of the house, muttering something about needing to be prepared and know where everything was located.

Because that wasn't ominous.

I set to rolling out the dough, letting myself smash it a little thinner than I normally might have for sticky buns. I needed the outlet, and I'd just use this batch to test out the flavor for this replication. I rolled them mindlessly, shoving them in the oven.

I *never* left my kitchen a mess. It was one of the few things that had stuck with me from culinary school and my subsequent days working in a restaurant. I rebelled nearly every other way, because if I wasn't an *actual* chef than who gave a poop? But with cleaning my kitchen, I was a neurotic.

So, when I went to flop into a chair at my breakfast nook, I knew I was shaken even before my trembling hands touched my face. I lost track of how long I sat there, lost track of everything around me. It wasn't until the doorbell rang that I jolted out of my stupor, glancing at it nervously. When I was about to stand, Scar appeared from the hallway and shook his head at me. I remembered that I wasn't allowed to answer my door and flopped back into my seat in a sort of empty frustration. I picked a point on my wall, staring at it in fascination when I found the slightest of cracks in the paint. "It's Mr. Bradley. Would you like me to open the door?" Scar asked lightly. I nodded at him, hearing Duke's voice the moment it opened.

"What the Hell are you still doing here?" he asked.

Scar grunted; the sound oddly devoid of inflection. While he might have looked like a hard man, he'd been nothing other than polite and even warm to me. He seemed oddly capable of anticipating and dealing with my moods, like I was more than a nuisance his boss ordered him to watch over until he finished playing with me.

"Christ, Ivory," Duke said, striding past me and pulling my oven open. He cursed, hunting for a potholder and dropping the sticky buns on the stove top with another curse. "What were those supposed to be?"

"Sticky buns," I whispered.

"Well, they're burnt buns now." I must have forgotten to set the timer. He came to stand in front of me, after the beep of my oven turning off filled the too quiet space. "You all right?" he asked, kneeling so that his face filled my vision. I nodded, smiling at him slightly. Duke's hands rested on my bare thighs just above my knees, feeling too warm against my cool skin. "You're freezing," he whispered.

"Ms. Torres, I'm afraid I have to suggest that Mr. Bellandi won't appreciate Mr. Bradley's hands on you," Scar input, raising a brow at me. I glanced down at Duke's hands, confusion settling over me.

"He's my friend," I said, and Scar sighed and nodded. His expression communicated that he still didn't believe it would be something that Matteo would tolerate, but in that moment I couldn't have cared. Duke didn't appear to either, instead taking to rubbing his rough, artist's hands over my cold skin to warm me up. "I'm fine," I reassured him.

"This really has you freaked out," he whispered. "Why don't you come stay with me?"

Scar's face pinched into annoyance, but I took care of it when I answered Duke. "I think I'm safer here. This isn't the guy you can protect me from."

"What the Hell has he got you wrapped up in?" Duke hissed, and my eyes darted over his shoulder to find Matteo standing in the doorway. I hadn't heard the door open, and Matteo held a key in his hand. A key to my house, I presumed, though how he'd gotten it was beyond me.

"Take your hands off her," Matteo ordered, and Duke stood up quickly, turning to face Matteo for the first time since high school, I realized. Duke's attractive features that lent toward the boy next door all grown up were no match for the savage beauty that was Matteo Bellandi. He still didn't have a suit jacket, his sleeves rolled up to his elbows hastily, and a few splatters of red dotted the chest of his white shirt. He looked like a criminal which I was suspecting he was more and more with every day that passed. Ice-blue eyes glittered as he glared at Duke, sizing him up and finding him lacking.

"You don't get to come in here after twelve fucking years and put her in danger. She deserves better than you'll ever be able to give her, Bellandi," Duke hissed, all the vehemence he'd built up in the years of watching me fade into half a life wrapped up in that tone.

Matteo smirked at him, the blue eyes I loved to watch warm for me glittering hard and cruel gems. "You still haven't made a move, huh?" he asked Duke, who froze solid in front of me. I turned my head to look at Duke, wincing when his shoulders sagged. The reality of what I hadn't seen struck me when he turned a sad glance my way.

"You broke her. I keep waiting for her to be ready for a relationship, but it never fucking happens, because of what you did to her," he spat at Matteo, confirming the truth that shook me to my core. "I love her enough to wait. Even for twelve years."

"Duke?" I whispered, staring up at him. He turned to me, looking down at me with a grimace.

"This isn't how I wanted you to find out."

I backed away a step, just knowing I needed space. "Why didn't you tell me?"

"Would it have mattered?" he hissed. "You've always been so wrapped up in him, that you never even saw me."

I winced again, hating that he was angry at me when he hadn't bothered to be honest. "Don't," Matteo growled. "You do not get to upset her because you were too much of a coward to make a move."

"Matteo!" I gasped, hating that he would be so cruel in a moment that was probably critical to my ability to maintain a friendship with Duke.

"Fuck you," Duke hissed, striding for the door. He paused, looking back at me with nothing but sadness. "Call me if you decide you want to be more than just a fleeting fancy for Matteo Bellandi."

I dropped into my seat as he left, wondering how the fuck my boring life had gotten so messy.

CHAPTER SIXTEEN

IVORY

Scar glared at me as we got ready for our morning run. The last week had passed with the same routine, a run in the morning, I went about my day, and then Matteo would show up in time for dinner. We'd either eat at my house and he'd spend the night, or he'd take me out and we'd end up at his. It was almost comfortable, predictable. I couldn't imagine Matteo's life followed that routine too often, but he gave me the distinct impression that he was doing everything he could to lull me into a sense of normalcy after I'd lost Duke.

It wasn't like he was dead or anything, and he'd answer my texts—mostly one-word answers—but the ease of our friendship disappeared. He hadn't dropped by since Matteo outed him, and I couldn't blame him. Not while knowing that at the very least Scar would be at my house with me. He'd been humiliated, his feelings for me revealed by the worst person in his mind. I knew that.

It didn't stop his absence from hurting me. Even Sadie had been mostly absent, likely spending a good deal of time with Duke and encouraging him to channel his emotions into his art rather than a less productive rage.

So in the face of all that, Matteo seemed determined to show me what a relationship with him could look like. I'd stopped fighting his presence, because until they resolved the Adrian issue, he was a necessity. I'd even stopped fighting his power over my body, because I might as well get some great orgasms out of the situation before he packed up and left my life without a trace. Again.

But I did everything possible to remind myself that it was temporary. That Matteo *would* leave me, and I'd be left to pick up the pieces. My resolve only strengthened with time, the more Matteo chipped away at my armor with his strong presence and made me want things that would never happen. I resolved to find some kind of solution to making him move on sooner than later when it would hurt more but had no idea what that would be.

"You need to vary your routine," Scar pointed out as I opened my front door. He turned with a copy of my house key in hand, locking up behind me.

I'd long since gotten used to everyone having a key to my house. If they'd wanted to hurt me, they would have already. "I like my routine."

"It makes you easier to track, easier to follow. Your predictability makes you an easy target for people who might want to harm you," he grunted, picking up a jog beside me. The massive, hulking man hated running with me, but he did it anyway. He even managed to not slow me down too horribly, given the length of his legs and the way one of his strides equaled two of mine.

"You want me to run at a different time of day?" I asked, slowly building my pace. "It wakes me up to start my day. That's the point."

My breathing was steady, my body going to that place of focus that running always brought me to. "At the very least you should change your route. Makes it less predictable."

I considered it. "I don't want to get lost," I admitted. Even though I'd lived in the area for a few years, I didn't venture off the main roads. There was still a distinct possibility that I'd wander somewhere I shouldn't be.

"You'll have me," he grunted, his own breathing far less steady than mine.

"I won't always have you," I huffed a laugh. "You can't spend the rest of your life looking after me. Matteo will need you to do something else, eventually."

"He won't leave you unprotected." We turned the corner, heading up the road that would take us by the park. I could feel his eyes on me, even as I pointedly kept mine fixated on the park next to me. "What exactly do you think this is?"

"What?"

"Your relationship with Matteo. You still think he will walk away?" Under any normal circumstances, I would have been grateful for the interruption that saved me from answering.

Those were not normal circumstances.

My body jolted as I crashed into a man who jogged out of the park entrance. He emitted an "oof," catching me with stabilizing hands on my hips when I nearly fell on my face. "Easy." My body stilled, horror crashing over me when I recognized the voice that spoke from above me. Tilting my head back, I came face to face with what I *thought* might be Adrian Ricci. In all honesty, it was difficult to tell.

His face was beaten, bruised with a gash through his cheekbone, a split lip, and a bandage over his nose where it had been broken. Two purple bruises surrounded his cruel looking brown eyes. "I—Adrian?" I asked, stepping back far enough that I forced him to release his hold on my hips. One of his hands was wrapped in a bandage as it left my body hesitantly.

He winced dramatically. "I realize I'm a sight at the moment, but I assure you I'm all right."

"What happened to you?" I asked against my better judgment. I didn't need to know the details of what happened to Adrian, not given his business.

If what Matteo said was true, he deserved everything he got.

"Matteo didn't mention he came to my home and beat me bloody for sending you a little gift? Went into a jealous rage, in fact. Most men wouldn't dare, but Bellandi is untouchable." He shrugged, as if to brush off the revelation.

Matteo had beaten the shit out of him.

I remembered the blood on his shirt that day when he'd come back and destroyed Duke. I'd been so distracted I'd forgotten all about it. "That's enough," Scar hissed, tugging me behind him and blocking me from Adrian finally. I wondered what had made him wait so long, deciding that Adrian didn't pose much of a threat to me with him right there and on a crowded street in the middle of the morning.

Still, his words about changing my route seemed even more necessary, given what couldn't have been an accidental meeting. Adrian had followed me, stalked me, and learned my routine. Exactly for this purpose.

It sent a chill down my spine.

"We were just talking," Adrian held up two hands, feigning innocence even as he winked a bloodshot eye at me.

"Think very carefully if this is a war you want to begin. There are plenty of things that Matteo lets you get away with when he can't be bothered to care. This will not be one of them." Scar nudged me, pushing me to turn back the way I'd come. I started walking in that direction, going slowly so I wasn't far from Scar's protection.

"To the victor go the spoils of war," Adrian said, a smile in his voice. I turned back to look at Scar, finding Adrian's eyes on me. "I look forward to seeing you again, little doll." Scar caught up with me, pressing a hand to my back and urging me to leave Adrian behind us. When I finally turned away from him, it was with mounting terror over what was coming.

He wasn't giving up.

✳✳✳

Days passed, with my life a static, suspiciously routine pattern of events. But the constants in my life remained absent, until the day Sadie sat on my stool, finally back in the spot she'd been neglecting in favor of talking Duke down from the ledge. I felt Duke's absence fiercely, the text that I was making his favorite brownies going unanswered entirely, where he normally would have raced to my house.

"Did you know?" I asked her, pouring the batter into the brownie pan from my stand mixer.

She raised a brow at me, acting like it was ridiculous to think she wouldn't. "*Everyone* knew, honey."

"Everyone but me," I sighed, putting the pan in the oven and closing it. I stepped around the island, plopping onto a stool instead of immediately washing the bowl. Sadie looked at me with wide eyes, and I knew it didn't get past her as seriousness settled over her features.

"He never made a secret of it. You just didn't want to see it," she whispered, reaching over to pat my hand. "Now that you know, what do you plan to do with that information?"

I felt my jaw slacken, shocked she'd even suggest what I thought she was suggesting. "What do you mean?"

"Well, you could give him a shot," she suggested. "He loves you, Ive. Always has. He may not make you feel like Matteo always has, but he won't hurt you. You could do a lot worse."

I nodded, because she was right. "I know, but it's just—it's *Duke*. He's my best friend. It would be like dating you."

"I mean, I'm sure Duke and I have very different equipment. Can't say I've ever gone there, but—" she giggled, and I laughed with her. "He's not unattractive."

"I know, but we grew up together. How can I cross that line?"

"Kiss him. That's the best way to see if there's chemistry, find out if you can see him in another way," she suggested. My eyes bugged out of my head, envisioning the image of Duke touching me that way.

It didn't fit, no matter how much I might wish it did. I didn't want to hurt Duke, and I *had* promised I would find a man who could love me and give me a content life.

It just wouldn't be him.

"I can't do that to him. Subject him to a life with someone he knows will never—" I broke off on a whisper. "I need an easy, simple date. Something with no expectations, just to show myself that someone else can make me feel like Matteo does. Set me up," I begged. "That guy from the gym you were planning on before this whole Matteo mess started."

"No way in Hell! You do not need to involve another man in your mess right now," she laughed, standing from the stool and grabbing water from the fridge.

"It's exactly what I need! A distraction from unrequited love and dangerous sex machines. Pleaseeee," I whined.

She sighed, staring at me in disapproval. "All these years of having to force you on dates, and you choose now."

"Don't pretend you didn't keep Duke's feelings from me. You both kept something from me I should have known. You owe me." I wasn't beyond playing on her sympathy, because if I knew Sadie, I knew that the guilt of keeping that from me for so long had been weighing on her. It was probably part of what possessed her to stay away for so long following the revelation.

"Ughhh," she groaned. "Fine, but this makes us even. If Matteo kills him, I'll take it out on you," she said menacingly, the warning clear in every feature of her exotic face.

"Deal," I said. I couldn't contain my excitement even in the face of Sadie's threat, which I didn't take lightly. She'd beaten me up with fitness before, she knew how much I hated it. She'd get me in the ring again and kick my ass.

But the freedom of knowing I was my own woman, and I could do what I wanted, was worth it.

I hoped.

CHAPTER SEVENTEEN

IVORY

It wasn't often that I got to see my uncle.

So, when he came to visit, I held that time as sacred. As his favorite, okay only, niece, it was my responsibility to him.

And so, it was tradition that riding in the car with him on the way to the restaurant, I claimed the front seat. I didn't even care that it stuck my parents in the back; they were used to it. Uncle Adam *always* drove, a consequence of whatever Rambo stuff he got up to when he took off to places unknown to do things most of the government didn't even have the clearance for.

My Uncle was a badass.

"Where were you this time?" He'd been a Marine, some special task force or something. I'd been only a teenager when he'd retired and opened up his own private security firm.

"Florida," he said, casting an amused look my way.

I chuckled. "Well, that's horribly ordinary."

"Oh, it was torture. Having plumbing, modern amenities, and a roof over my head to protect me from the elements. I tell you; I'll never take a job like *that* again." He shook his head, pursing his lips.

Sticking my tongue out at him, I muttered a quick, "Smart ass."

"Ivory! Don't call your uncle names. That's my job," Mom inserted from the back. Adam pulled up to the valet, and we all hopped out of the car. Mom and dad had never used a valet, like me, but Adam did things in style, and we'd learned long ago to just roll with it. Because when he was around, he paid.

That simple.

When the valet took his Mercedes away, we stepped up and into Angel's, the little Italian place Mom and Adam loved so much. It wasn't within Mom's price range normally, so she only got to have it when Adam came to visit.

We always came when he was in town. The name had been a bittersweet reminder in the first few years after it opened, but I'd eventually moved on over the term. The restaurant boasted some of the most authentic Italian food in the city, and that was saying something for Chicago.

Stepping in the front doors always felt like being transported to Naples, not that I'd ever been, but I could *imagine.*

What was different about that night from all the other nights, was the man who came striding in when my mom gave our name to the hostess.

"Angel," Matteo whispered, bending down and pressing a quick kiss to my lips as his hand cupped my elbow. I floundered, staring up at him in shock.

Because, please sweet lord tell me he hadn't just kissed me in front of my family.

Please.

A quick glance at my father's reddened face confirmed that he, in fact, had.

Well then.

Poop scoops.

"Uh, what are you doing here?" I asked, stepping back from him and hoping he'd release his grip on my elbow.

No such luck.

"I saw the reservation and thought I should reintroduce myself. It's been a long time since I saw your parents," he said with a polite, gentlemanly smile on his face.

"How did you know we had a reservation here?" I whispered. His stalking really knew no boundaries.

"It's one of my restaurants." He shrugged, because owning a restaurant was just a throwaway business detail in the great lineup of things the Bellandi family owned.

"Of course, it is," my dad snorted, echoing my sentiments.

"I don't believe we've met," Adam stepped up, holding out a hand for Matteo to shake. His face was hard, set in stone. Even though Uncle Adam had never met Matteo, I knew that he knew exactly who he was. My uncle made me his business, and there was no way he wouldn't have kept tabs on the guy who fucked me over.

"Matteo Bellandi. You must be Ivory's Uncle Adam." Matteo took his hand, and it was subtle, but there was obviously a struggle for dominance working between the two men as they stared each other down.

"I didn't realize you two were an item now," Adam said with a grimace.

"We're not—" I started, cutting off when Matteo's hand tightened on my elbow.

"It's fairly new," Matteo smiled. "But I recognize the real deal when I have it."

"You didn't the first time," my father muttered, his jaw clenched tight. My mom's eyes were wide, staring at where Adam faced down with Matteo. She seemed to know there was something different from my uncle's usual protectiveness where I was concerned, something just *off* about the way Adam glared at Matteo but also looked at him like he might be a formidable opponent.

No one stood up to Adam.

Ever.

So that Matteo could and still smile while he did it, well, that was insanity to my mother. I could see the gears turning in her head, wondering about all the rumors that surrounded the Bellandi family. "Honey, you didn't tell me you were seeing someone," she said finally, a tight smile curving at her lips.

"It's new, like Matteo said. Didn't think it was smart to get you all excited," I lied, because the reality was, I never intended to tell my parents I was seeing Matteo. My father snorted at my choice of words, knowing damn well excited was a euphemism for pissed off.

Was that what they called it when someone inserted himself in your life and you couldn't escape?

Dating my stalker.

My parents would have been so proud if they'd known.

"Your table is ready, Mr. Bellandi," the hostess inserted, politeness stamped on every one of her features. I wondered if Matteo had slept with her too, but there was no trace of familiarity or jealousy on her face when her eyes met mine. If he had, he'd made sure she knew the score ahead of time and could be professional in the face of his girlfriend's family.

Regardless of how I felt about the temporary nature of Matteo in my life, I appreciated the discretion for my family's sake. They wouldn't take well to having my boyfriend's conquests rubbed in their faces.

Especially not with my history with Matteo.

"Lead the way, Ms. Favre," Matteo gestured, and it was a horrifying realization that he hadn't just stopped by but had every intention of staying for dinner.

"Matteo," I whispered, catching his attention as he guided me in to follow the hostess. "This is not an appropriate time. You can't just insert yourself to dinner with my family, especially not on the rare occasion I get to see my uncle."

"Ah, so you were intending to invite me to meet him another day during his visit?" he asked, guiding me to one end of the table. He sat me in the seat to the right of the head, smoothly lowering himself into the chair at one end. That in and of itself made a statement.

"Well, not exactly," I sighed.

"I thought as much. As you don't seem to want to make the introductions, I took the liberty myself." I could feel my uncle's eyes on me as he took his seat at the opposite end of the table. Normally he didn't care about posturing, and he would have taken the seat next to me.

I knew besides challenging Matteo; he took that seat precisely for the purpose of keeping tabs on me through the meal. Next to me, he might not see everything, but on the other end of the table, he saw Matteo and I perfectly.

I resisted the urge to bash my head on the table, staring at my empty wine glass in frustration.

I needed alcohol.

Lots and lots of alcohol.

My mom and dad sat next to Adam, leaving the seat between my mom and Matteo unoccupied. He didn't seem bothered when he took my hand in his, holding it openly on top of the table for my family to see.

A waiter came, delivering wine into all our glasses without being ordered, and I narrowed my eyes on Matteo's high-handed bullshit. Then I took a few very unladylike swallows of the delicious bordeaux. Matteo's jaw clenched as he watched me drown my inhibitions in my glass.

"So, Matteo, how's business?" My uncle asked, his voice sounding cordial. I knew better. Knew that beneath that fake veneer was a man who would kill Matteo if he thought I was in danger.

And he'd never go to prison for it.

I realized that was why I couldn't let on to my family that I was anything other than a thrilled participant in the ruse of a relationship Matteo crafted. As much as my feelings conflicted over Matteo, I just couldn't live with him being dead either.

That was why I'd never even considered calling Adam in the first place, but his sudden, unplanned visit did suddenly seem all too convenient.

"Business is booming. I own several properties, restaurants, nightclubs. I do very well. Your niece will never want for anything." Matteo smiled, the edges fraying as he addressed my uncle. Knowing Matteo, he knew exactly who Adam was—knew what he'd done. He knew that Adam likely had a thorough understanding of whatever illegal dealings Matteo had, and I knew the two men were on opposite sides of the law. In Matteo's defense though, Adam had never truly operated within the realms of the law either.

How you went about saving lives was insignificant, as long as you did. That was his philosophy, and it always had been.

"What made you come visit?" I asked, turning a beaming smile Adam's way. "It's not like you to just drop in without planning." His lips crooked in a bemused smile, and he shook his head at me in the same way he did every time he told me I was too smart for my own good—too good at reading people to waste away in my own kitchen. He wanted me working for him, always had. Getting a feel on his potential clients. For the first time, I considered it.

I had a feeling I'd want to leave Chicago whenever Matteo decided he was done with me.

Too many memories.

"I had a case end sooner than planned. Figured I'd come surprise you all."

"Coincidentally, as soon as you could get away after I was involved in a robbery?" I smirked, and he grinned at me.

"Complete coincidence," he lied. "I would like to know what they have done about it. Have the police found them?"

My father snorted.

Ah that was where I got my refined behaviors from.

"I suspect you know more about that than us," Mom laughed.

"Wasn't asking you," my uncle said, turning raised brows to Matteo. I turned to face him too, watching as he lowered his Bordeaux to the table after a generous sip.

"It's been handled." He shrugged, and my father stilled at the table, taking it as further confirmation that Matteo was dangerous.

Mom looked to Adam like she expected him to protest, require information about how it had been handled. But Adam merely looked thoughtful for a moment, before turning his attention to the menu in front of him.

"Good," he murmured. "Good to see someone around here is at least capable of getting shit done." Mom's horrified eyes looked from me to Adam, finally stopping when my dad cleared his throat.

"I think I'll have the lasagna," he muttered, and the conversation ended there.

I turned to Matteo, panic coursing through me.

What the fuck did he mean it had been taken care of?

He shook his head, signaling me to hold my tongue for the moment.

For once, I listened.

I listened, and I guzzled more wine.

I didn't need alcohol. I needed to be shit-faced to deal with that hell of a dinner.

CHAPTER EIGHTEEN

SADIE

My fingers hovered over the keypad on my phone.

Could I really do this to her?

The answer was easier than it should have been.

I could, and I would.

Ivory was far too stuck in her own little world to realize that she had two men on her hook. She couldn't just bury her head in the sand and pretend they didn't exist while she added another man to the mix.

Hopefully, this would be exactly what she needed to pull her head out of her ass.

I dialed the first number, tossing back a shot when it rang.

"Yeah?" Duke's voice grunted on the other end of the line.

"Ivory's going on a date," I blurted, determined to keep my voice strong. I knew Ivory would be pissed if she ever found out, but I would always do what it took to protect her.

Even from herself.

"I told you, I don't want to hear about that shit," he snapped and slammed something around. Undoubtedly some metal scraps in his shop as he worked off his rage.

"It's not with Matteo. It's someone else. You should go, stop her from doing something stupid. She doesn't see you that way; it just doesn't come naturally after being your friend for years, so you need to *make* her see you that way if you want it to go anywhere."

"Is this one of those grand gesture things women are always talking about?"

he returned, a smile in his voice. The metal stopped clanging, and I knew he was considering it.

"Grand gestures, come to Jesus moment. Just get your ass to *Indulgence.*" I hung up, giving him a ten-minute head start before I dialed the number Scar had been all too willing to give me.

"Bellandi," the voice on the other end said.

"Matteo?" I asked.

"Who is this?" His voice went taut, and I took it he didn't get very many phone calls from women. That pleased me.

"Sadie. I thought you'd want to know that I helped Ivory sneak out tonight. Scar's sitting downstairs, completely oblivious that she stepped out and took a cab."

"What?" he whispered, and that voice was menacing.

"I'm in her room pretending to be her to buy her time, but you should probably just head over to *Indulgence.*"

"What the fuck is she doing in my club?" His voice went deep, menacing, and I worried about the guy that was on the date with Ivory. I convinced myself it would be fine. I'd warned him not to get touchy.

"She's on a date," I laughed, hanging up the phone. It rang when he called back, and I ignored it in favor of taking another sip of Ivory's wine. When Scar's phone rang downstairs, and I heard the front door slam, I considered how easy it would be to divert their attention and sneak her out again if the need arose.

I filed that bit of information away in case we needed it.

CHAPTER NINETEEN

MATTEO

I didn't know what the fuck Ivory was thinking.

Had I not clarified that I'd kill any man who touched her?

And yet, I sat in my Aston, cursing traffic as I tried to get to her from the meeting that had occupied me later than I liked. I scoffed, the thought of Ivory challenging me by going on a date with another man insane to think. Nobody else would have dared, but if she'd made one thing clear with this little stunt?

It was that I'd been too gentle. Given her too much time to adjust to the reality of my return into her life.

That would change.

Effective immediately.

By that time tomorrow there would be no doubt in her mind that I meant every word when I told her she was mine. Every word when I explained I would never let her go.

Pulling up in front of the club finally, I tossed my valet my keys as I climbed out and strode off without another word. The Aston was inconsequential in comparison to Ivory with another man.

"Mr. Bellandi?" the boy asked, hushing immediately when I didn't spare him a glance. My bouncers threw open the doors, and I prowled into my club, ignoring employees vying for my attention.

I didn't give the first shit about any of them. My eyes scanned the dance floor, looking for my deviant little angel. People crowded into the floor, admittedly a security nightmare for Ivory, even if she hadn't been with another man to begin with. The pulse of bodies was too much, would make it impossible for Scar to protect her unless he was practically on top of her. I caught sight of the huge man, standing guard against the wall. Following his eyes toward the center of the floor, my heart stopped when the crowd parted to reveal my angel.

I froze momentarily as she threw her head back and laughed at something the man across from her said. He miraculously danced with her without touching, something I found odd given Ivory's metallic emerald green dress looked painted on. It left her legs bare, the length of them standing out in the stilettos she wore. Delicate straps led to a scoop neck that showed a hint of the beauty I knew was hidden just underneath.

I growled, flinching when Scar touched my shoulder reassuringly.

"He hasn't touched her once," he admitted and the sincerity in his voice took me off guard. Something in me loosed, knowing I wouldn't need to murder a man in front of Ivory.

Even I knew that might be just slightly too much at that point in our relationship.

But that wouldn't save my Angel from the wrath she incurred.

Especially not when Duke appeared in her space.

CHAPTER TWENTY

IVORY

It had been far too long since I'd been dancing.

I'd loved it, once upon a time.

And then I'd become a statistic. One of the millions of women who found themselves out of their depth in a dangerous situation with men who didn't give a shit about the word no.

I hadn't gone dancing since.

Hadn't been able to trust men or trust my recklessness.

That all changed the day Matteo came barging back into my life, even though I'd been the one to barge into his home. He was the most reckless thing I could ever do, not the alcohol pouring through my system or the way the music energized me as I moved to the sound of it. My date, Patrick, was nice. He kept his hands to himself, which, for a date in a nightclub, I had to say was surprising, but very much appreciated.

"You're the life of this club with those moves," he yelled, letting me hear him over the din of the music despite his respectable distance.

I threw my head back and laughed, because we both knew it wasn't a compliment. I wasn't a horrible dancer, but I was too enthusiastic in my excitement to give in to the sensations pounding through my body. The adrenaline of feeling like I was part of something, part of a crowd, for even just a little while.

A figure emerged from the way the crowd formed, slipping through any gaps he could find. My eyes landed on Duke, watching as he panted with exertion. Whatever he'd been doing, he'd rushed it. His jeans were stained, his tee-shirt beaten and one I recognized from his collection that he wore only in his studio.

Duke wasn't the nightclub type to begin with, but there was no way he'd show up in studio clothes if he decided to go out for a night on the town.

"Duke?" I asked, and he sucked back a deep fortifying breath. "What are you doing here?"

He didn't answer, suddenly crashing into my space. His hand caught me around the nape, sliding underneath the curtain of my hair. I knew he'd find it slick with sweat, but he didn't seem to care. I stared up at him with wide eyes, and I knew what was coming.

I wished I could stop it, but something in the look in his eyes prevented me.

He needed it. He needed to know.

The least I could do was give him that.

Because the truth was, I already knew I'd never love him the way he loved me.

It wasn't possible when someone else already owned me.

Heart and soul.

One more deep breath, his cornflower eyes staring into mine intently. They drifted closed, his lips touching mine tentatively at first. I didn't move, didn't dare do anything. I had to let him see, had to show him. He'd spent too long waiting, too long *wondering* what might be.

It was time for Duke to move on with his life.

When I didn't shove him away, his confidence grew, and his lips pressed into mine more firmly. The tip of his tongue traced my lips, and I opened for him just enough for him to kiss me. The art, the passion, with which he worked translated into his kiss. A skilled seduction where he used his mouth as the only conduit.

But there was nothing, no spark.

Because only Matteo could make me feel.

When he pulled back, his eyes opened slowly, a mix of awe and apprehension flitting through them. "You didn't feel it?" he asked. I shook my head, looking down as tears filled my eyes. "I'm sorry, Duke. You know that I'd change it if I could."

"It's because of him? You're choosing a criminal over me?" His voice sounded harsh, and I knew that the rough wrath of Duke's temper hovered just under the surface, waiting to unleash when he was alone and could show the real hurt.

"No. I know Matteo and I will never last," I explained. "I'm choosing you over me." His brow furrowed, and I stepped closer to his embrace, wrapping my arms around him supportively. "You deserve more that I'll ever be able to give you. I love you too much to trap you in a relationship with me, when I know I'll never be able to love you the way you love me. I don't want that for you."

His arms tightened around me. "What about what I want?"

"You'll find someone better for you." He stiffened, pulling away. His eyes darted over my shoulder, and he nodded silently with a huff of laughter before turning on his heel and disappearing into the crowd.

My spine tingled, something like apprehension sliding up it suddenly and pooling in my chest. The press of a body against my back came out of nowhere, making me stumble forward. A massive hand wrapped around my throat, trapping me, and panic flooded through me. My hands stretched up to claw at that hand, as Patrick stepped forward.

"Hey man, let her go!" he protested.

"It's quite fortunate that I think having his heart crushed is punishment enough. Otherwise, Duke would be a dead man. Get rid of the extra, naughty angel," Matteo's voice growled in my ear. I sighed in relief, my panic abating with the feeling of safety that came from Matteo. As pissed as he might be, and I imagined he really, really was, he wouldn't hurt me.

Not really.

"Let go of me, Teo," I whispered, giving Patrick a reassuring smile where he eyed us in a mix of fury and concern. "It's okay. I know him," I yelled.

"I suggest that you get the fuck out of my club while you still have all your limbs," Matteo grunted at him. His voice might have remained quiet, had we not been in a club. But with the music thudding overhead, he had no choice but to shout the command. Heads turned our way, watching the exchange. Patrick's eyes widened, but he nodded before abandoning me to Matteo.

I sighed, frustration mounting. I hated feeling owned, like property that belonged to Matteo and couldn't think or act for myself. "Did you forget about something?" he asked.

"Hmm, nope," I whispered, trying to ignore the way Matteo skimmed his free hand over my hip.

"You are spoken for, my love. Very much in a committed relationship. It is very fortunate for your date that he didn't touch you. Otherwise, it would have been the last thing he did."

I froze, feeling Matteo's grip on my throat tighten in warning. "Things are about to change. It's time for you to accept what is happening with us."

"There is no us! There will never be an us!" I yelled back at him, not even caring about the people watching.

"Ah, but you're wrong, *Cara mia.* There very much is an us. There has always been an us, and there always will be an us. You will never let another man touch you," he barked the order, releasing my throat in favor of taking my hand and yanking me toward the exit.

"Wait, I don't want to go anywhere with you!" I snarled, attempting to pry his fingers off my hand as I stumbled after him.

"That's most unfortunate for you. No one here will stop us."

"Matteo!" I shrieked, glaring at Scar where he took up his place behind us. The night air was cold as it hit my skin, the wind ripping through the street. The valet raced to get the car as Matteo draped his suit jacket over my shoulders. "*My* jacket is inside. At least let me get it before you cart me off like an animal."

Matteo nodded to Scar, who turned and stalked back into the club. When the Aston pulled up in front of the club, Matteo didn't wait for him. Instead, he shoved me into my seat and slammed the door closed before taking his own seat and stealing me away into the night.

***

Matteo drove too fast.

He always drove too fucking fast, but nothing could compare to when he was full blown, *pissed off.*

"I cannot believe you were so stupid to go out without Scar. Do you care nothing for your safety?" he growled, turning blocks to head for the highway.

"I was fine!" I protested, shaking my head at his ridiculous behavior. I wasn't a reckless child, if I wanted to go to a club for once, then that was what I would do.

"And what would you have done if Adrian showed up?" Matteo asked, and I pursed my lips. I'd been confident no one could follow me since Scar hadn't even noticed me sneaking out, but there had been risk involved on that front.

It was just worth it, to have a single night of freedom from the confines of my life with Matteo.

"I can't have someone following me all the time, Teo," I whispered. "I need space, room to just be and the ability to do what I want."

"Yeah? Well, you can kiss that goodbye," he laughed, a dark, hollow sound that grated on my nerves.

"What does that mean?" He was silent for a moment, and I began to wonder if he would bother answering me or if I'd just wake up to some surprise restriction without asking my consent. He shoved the sleeves of his shirt up one by one, frustration written in every feature of his face. His bone structure was unique, sculpted, and radiated strength with his chiseled square jaw, and that *always* made him look intimidating to some extent, but the way he pursed his lips in that moment only aggravated it.

"Things are changing. You'll see what I mean once I make the arrangements." I considered asking but decided against it. If Matteo didn't want to tell me something, give me preparation, then he wouldn't. I could beat my head against a wall, or just accept that we would argue whenever he made those arrangements.

My eyes went to the tattoo on his forearm opposite me, watching the way the muscles corded as he gripped the wheel. "Why do you have that tattoo?" I asked.

His eyes darted down to it, and he veered off the road to pull into an empty parking lot of one of the many businesses lining the streets as we made our way out of The Loop.

"What are you—?" I stopped when he threw the car into park. He stripped off his seat belt, his body turning to face me ominously.

He took my hand in his, touching my fingers to the tattooed flesh of his forearm. I traced the lion's face with my fingers, circling the clock face that hid the face of a lamb in its intricate details. "I got it the day I broke up with you," he admitted, shocking me. "As a reminder."

"A reminder of what?" I whispered. I suddenly knew that I didn't want to have this conversation. My apprehension over it had made me procrastinate in asking, because why would I want to know why Matteo had immortalized the worst moment of my life on his skin.

"That the lion should never get involved with the lamb, because it's only a matter of time before the lamb is hurt." I huffed a laugh, pulling my fingers away suddenly. If I'd expected a sweet answer, something to hint that everything had been a lie, that had been anything but. "Not because I broke your heart, Angel. My life is complicated. It's dangerous, and it always has been. Walking away was the best way to protect you from the consequences of it. Every time I thought about going to you, about taking you back, that tattoo reminded me why I had to stay away."

Tears pooled in my eyes, and I shook my head. I wouldn't let him in again, and I worked to rebuild those walls between us, the shaky ones that seemed to fail every day. "Don't."

"It was always you, Ivory. Always," he whispered, pressing his forehead to mine. "You're the only thing that could hurt me. The only thing they could use to break me. That is why you need to do what I tell you. You must stay with Scar. It's the only way I can keep you safe."

I nodded, numbness flooding my system as I fortified my walls. Matteo sighed, aggravated. He'd always known when I worked to build up my walls, always sensed them the second they went up.

It was what made him so effective at tearing them down.

"Fuck it," he grunted, shoving open his car door. My eyes opened, staring around us. The lot was dark, not a car or a person in sight. I flinched when my door opened, and Matteo unbuckled me hastily.

"What are you doing?" I asked as he pushed me to lie over the center console. Maneuvering my legs, he twisted me about until I knelt on the seat. "Teo?"

"Hush, Ivory," he whispered, sliding my dress up my thighs and over my hips to reveal my black thong. "Fucking Christ, you're beautiful." His hand came down on the cheek of my ass in a loud smack that made me cry out, and I felt the searing pain immediately. He repeated it to the other side, and I whimpered. "You do not let another man touch you. Never again, Ivory. I gave Duke a pass because he won't be a problem again, and because I know you would hate me. I will not be that generous going forward." His hands stroked over my hot, burning skin, and I resisted the urge to squirm when that heat shot straight to my core and transformed into a deep, dark arousal that should have humiliated me.

Instead, I thrust my ass back at Matteo, letting him know just how I felt about his spanking. "Shut up and fuck me."

He chuckled, "my little angel likes being spanked? I'm not surprised. You'll take everything I give you, Cara mia."

I nodded, whimpering when his hand gripped the waistband of my thong and pulled it down my legs as far as he could until it got caught at my knees. He left it there, two fingers thrusting inside me and finding me already wet and waiting. The sound of his zipper broke the silence behind me, and only a few seconds passed before his fingers withdrew and the smooth, velvety head of his cock replaced them. A hand wrapped in my hair, making me arch my back to take him deep as he surged inside in a single, hard thrust that I felt bottom out against the end of me.

"Teo," I gasped, the fingers of his other hand bruising my hip with the force of his hold on me.

"You'll take it," he ordered, using his grip on my hair and my hip to tug me back until I fell out of the car. With his cock still planted firmly against me, he positioned me so that my hands supported me on the seat. My heeled feet hit the ground, feeling all too shaky to support myself, but Matteo didn't give me any reprieve. He pulled out and snapped his hips back in quickly, releasing his hold on my hair finally in favor of keeping my ass tipped up the way he wanted it. The skin of my ass tingled, something more than the recovering sting from his strike against me. A glance over my shoulder confirmed his eyes were fixated on where we connected, watching himself sink in and out of me in a fast rhythm. I knew I must have looked obscene, standing and bent at the waist to the point I nearly folded in half, and it wasn't easy to hold still and let Matteo take what he needed. His palm slapped down on my ass again, and I screamed, tossing my head back. "This pussy is mine."

"Yes, Teo," I whimpered, and in that moment, it couldn't have been a lie. I clenched around him, my body loving the domination in his voice and the way he gripped me.

She was a traitor when it came to Matteo.

Just like my heart.

"Your mouth is mine. You will never let another man put his lips on you again. Understood?" he barked an order, shifting his hips so he dragged over that spot inside me with every thrust.

"Yes, Teo," I repeated on a whimper. My body tightened, my orgasm crashing over me. He never stopped, never even paused, just forced his way through my orgasm with punishing thrust after thrust.

"This ass is mine," he whispered, and one of his hands abandoned my hip in favor of pressing his thumb to the part of me that no one had ever touched. I whimpered, wiggling against his grip on me. "I'll claim it soon, Angel. All of you belongs to me. I was the first man to take your mouth, the first man to take that sweet little pussy, and I'll be the first man to claim your ass too."

He slowed his pace, and I glanced back to watch him stare at the dirty way he touched me, *claimed* me while he fucked me with his monster of a dick.

"Shit," I moaned, not wanting to reveal that the strange, foreign pressure against me felt *good*. It was dark, forbidden, something I'd never thought to like.

But I did.

"Do you want to know a little secret?"

"Hmm?" I hummed, exhaustion claiming my calves from the angle and the heels.

"I'll be the last man to take all those things too," he groaned, finding his own climax within me. His hand hit the roof of the car, supporting his weight as he lost his control for that one moment where Matteo ever let go. The one rare moment of vulnerability he only showed when he came. I couldn't see his face, but I felt it all the same.

When he finished, he helped me slide my thong back into place and straighten my dress. Then we went home.

CHAPTER TWENTY-ONE

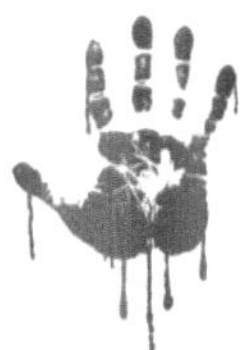

When I'd gotten in the car with Scar, I'd *thought* we were just going home after letting Sadie work me over at the gym for two hours. She was itching to kick my ass after the scene with Duke, and I couldn't particularly blame her.

I wanted to kick my ass too.

What was wrong with me I couldn't feel chemistry with my admittedly handsome best friend who I knew would do whatever he could to keep me from being hurt?

Ugh.

So, when Scar turned the wrong way and merged onto the highway, I cursed and turned to look at him. He'd tried to convince me to sit in the backseat of the SUV more times than I can count, but I never wanted to feel like I was being chauffeured around. It made me feel like a rich man's mistress, which wasn't far from the truth, but I detested it all the same.

"Where are we going?" I asked him, groaning and flipping my head back into the seat. He didn't answer, just sat there all stony and silent with his eyes on the road. "Did it maybe occur to either of you I don't feel like going to Matteo's? He rarely summons me this early, anyway. What's going on?"

"I think it's best I leave it for him to explain," Scar grunted and the muscles of my body tightened.

"Oh God, is it bad? Did something happen?" More silence. "Whatever," I sighed, trying to calm myself. "He's probably just done with me. Ready to end this bullshit."

Scar snorted out a laugh, and I realized I'd rarely heard the man laugh. Even though I was comfortable with his presence, and I knew he found me amusing, I'd never once made the man laugh.

That was unacceptable.

"I'll miss you; you know. You're always welcome to come over if you need food. I'm good at feeding people, if you couldn't tell. You eat a lot. Who feeds you when you aren't stuck with me?"

He shook his head like I was ridiculous.

Now *that* he did all the time.

"I'll have plenty of your cooking, Ms. Torres."

Well, *that* sounded ominous.

I crossed my arms over my chest, watching as the city streets turned to the slightly less urban streets that led to Matteo's estate.

I was a sweaty mess, going to Matteo's where I didn't even have clothes to change into.

The drive passed in stony silence, Scar knowing damn well that I wanted to ask questions, and me knowing he wouldn't answer them. He was a loyal bastard; I'd give him that.

Besides, I had a feeling asking questions about Matteo was a slippery road. I'd taken to the strategy that burying my head in the sand and waiting until he was done with me was the best way to walk away without being completely shattered when it was over. Whatever he did for a living, I didn't want to know.

Nope.

Ostrich I was.

Scar rolled down the window as he pulled up to the gates of the estate, and the guard stepped up to the window. He stood outside, unusual as they normally stayed in their little house until we pulled up.

"Busy day," he muttered to Scar, glancing at me across the car. "Good afternoon, Miss Torres," he smiled politely. It was the same guard who had been working when I'd first naively come traipsing into Matteo's domain. I had since learned his name, after he'd returned from vacation, anyway.

"Hi, Christian," I said with a hesitant smile. He'd been nothing but polite since the first time, abnormally so, but I hadn't been able to shake the reminder I looked like all the other girls Matteo banged.

Euw.

He cleared his throat, turning an oddly amused look Scar's way, and the sullener man only glared back. "Go on in," Christian said, stepping back from the car and hitting the button to let us into the estate. As we drove up the long, winding drive, it became obvious what Christian had meant by a busy day.

Someone was moving.

My heart thudded in my chest, unable to believe that Matteo wouldn't have mentioned he was moving, unless he planned on dumping me or he was in trouble and had to get out of dodge.

But why would he have me brought to the house?

A moving van passed us on the drive, another sitting in front of the house as two men hopped out of the front. We pulled up behind them, and they opened the rear doors to reveal a van packed with boxes.

"Uhh kay. Did Matteo get married or something?" I asked Scar, who smirked at me from the side. He was out of the car the next moment, and I followed him, albeit hesitantly. I did *not* belong at Matteo's house under the best circumstances, but my dirty running shoes were particularly unsightly against the opulent tile of the foyer. My high-waisted running shorts and sports bra weren't much better. Boxes covered the foyer, and two staff I recognized in passing collected things from the foyer and brought them up the stairs or to the living area and kitchen as we made our way to the hall to go to Matteo's office.

Scar knocked on the door, turning to murmur to me. "I really don't feel like chasing you. Keep that in mind, yeah?" he grinned, shoving the door open at Matteo's command. I froze at the threshold, staring up at Scar.

"Why—why would I—" I broke off when Scar shoved me into the room, and I barely caught myself before I stumbled. The door closed behind me, and I eyed Matteo as he stood from behind his desk. "What's going on?" I asked him, crossing my arms over my chest and preparing to harden myself. Matteo wouldn't know that he hurt me.

Not the second time around.

"Come sit with me," he gestured to the couch against the wall and facing his desk. I eyed it warily, knowing it hadn't been there before. It was white, modern but a light contrast to all the masculine grays and browns of his office. A little coffee table and ottoman hybrid sat in front of the couch, looking like a perfectly cozy space to curl up and work if I ever saw one. I went as he took my hand and guided me to the couch, plopping down next to him. I didn't even care that I might dirty up the fabric, since I'd likely never see it again.

"The issue with Adrian is proving to be more difficult to solve than I originally foresaw. Given your stunt last night," he broke off, eyeing me in frustration, "I no longer believe it's safe for you to remain in your home for the time being."

"I knew—," I paused, feeling everything in my body tighten as his words sunk in. "What?"

"Adrian remains as fixated as ever, and you're determined to put yourself in dangerous situations by sneaking out past your security. I need you to remain where I can keep a closer eye on you." I tugged my hand free from his grasp.

"What the fuck does that mean?" I whispered.

"Angel," he whispered, and I stood from the couch. Darting to the door, I raced for the foyer and threw open one of the boxes. The staff stared at me, and I vaguely knew of them snickering when my jaw dropped, and horror settled over me.

My stand mixer sat there, gleaming like sea glass in the light streaming down through the massive skylight.

Backing away a step, I stared at it, blinking while I wrapped my head around what was happening. With a shake of my head, I made for the front door.

This was *insane.*

He was insane.

Scar stepped in front of the door, crossing his arms over his chest and looking formidable as he blocked my path. "Move," I ordered, walking into him and trying to shove him aside.

"Can't do that, Ms. Torres," he grunted. "Told you, I don't much feel like chasing you."

"Angel," Matteo said somewhere behind me, and the sound of his footsteps against the tile made my body jerk with every step closer he came.

"You can't do this," I whispered, feeling like I might break.

"I'll do what I have to do to keep you safe," he murmured back, a hand reaching out and brushing my hair away from my shoulder.

I whirled on him, shoving at his chest to the sound of gasps around me. "You do not get to move me out of my home! What is wrong with you?!"

"You should have thought of that before you went out alone last night."

I shoved him again, hating the fact that his body barely budged. "I'm going home. I expect my things will be returned today."

"You really think Scar is all that stands between you and freedom? You have no car. The only exit from the property is guarded, and there is a guard on each door of the house itself. You no longer go *anywhere* without my permission, *Cara mia.*" His voice dropped low, dancing over my skin like a caress.

"You can't do this!" I yelled, tears welling in my eyes. I'd expected Matteo to break my heart, but I never would have thought he'd do it like this.

Never like this.

"Ah, my love, I believe it is already done." Matteo turned and strode for his office, leaving me floundering in the middle of the foyer with an audience.

"Ms. Torres?" Donatello asked, stepping up to me and putting a hand on my shoulder. "Do you have any specific requests for where you want things in the kitchen? I'll see to that personally. Normally the kitchen is my domain, but I very much look forward to having company."

I shook my head, feeling the first tear fall as he patted me on the head and stepped away. I turned, eyes connecting with Scar's where he stood at the door.

"You knew," I whispered, betrayal making my heart clench. I meant it when I said I'd miss the sullen man who had come to mean something to me.

And he'd brought me to a prison.

His face contorted briefly, as though the sight of my tears bothered him.

But it didn't.

None of them gave the first shit about me.

"He'll keep you safe," he whispered, and each word was like a blow to my gut.

"Ivory," a vaguely familiar voice whispered next to me, and I turned my head to look up into Lino's familiar brown eyes.

"Lino?" I asked stupidly, wincing when he wrapped an arm around my shoulders.

"Come on, sweetheart. Let's sit you down."

He guided me to the living room, settling me on the couch next to him. Donatello delivered a glass of wine a moment later, giving me a sad smile and eying me warily.

"How are you?" I asked Lino after chugging the contents of my glass. Donatello took it, refilling it in front of me and handing it back.

"Better than you at the moment, I expect." The sheepish smile he turned my way was a welcome sight, and I even returned it.

"Samara?"

He winced. "Going through a rough divorce."

I nodded. It had been years since I'd seen her, but the man she'd gotten herself hitched to had never been a good man. "I'm surprised it took so long."

"You know her, she's stubborn." I nodded. "Like you," he added.

I glared at him. "I just want to go home."

"You *are* home," he said, tucking me into his chest when fresh tears welled in my eyes.

✱✱✱

Lino had long since gone back to Matteo's office, doing whatever it was the two of them called work where Matteo's employees were completely content to watch me cry over being trapped in his house. Staff moved around me, unpacking my things without regard for what I might want. They didn't even ask me where I wanted everything to go—the only person who had bothered with that being Donatello.

I suspected they knew I'd say to keep everything in boxes.

Locking myself in the bathroom, I thought over my options.

I only had two.

Let it happen.

Or call Adam.

The phone in my hand rang when I pressed his name on the screen, and I had to wonder if I knew what I was doing.

I just wanted to go home, but alerting Adam might be like declaring war. He was unpredictable and there was absolutely no way to know how he might react to me being a prisoner in Matteo's home.

"Hey pretty girl," he answered, affection always in his tone. When I was silent, I could feel the way he radiated tension through the phone. "Ivory?"

"I need your help," I whispered, sobbing over the line.

CHAPTER TWENTY-TWO

MATTEO

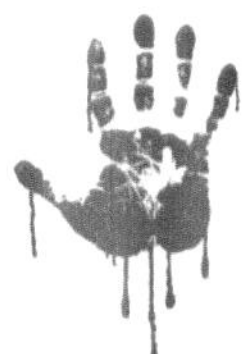

Ivory knew the moment her uncle arrived, if the wide eyes she threw my way when I stormed out of my office were any sign.

"You think you're clever, don't you?"

She didn't respond, staring at me silently as she stood from the couch and making her way to the door. I blocked her, stepping into her path and catching her up in my arms. "He will *not* take you from me. Do you understand?"

"You already lost me, so what does it matter," she hissed, the wildcat in my stubborn little angel rising to the surface after her temporary shock.

I looked forward to her wrath when I took her to bed later.

But in that moment, I needed to remind her who called the shots. I stepped back from her, going for the door. Her sneakers squeaked against the floor behind me, a reminder she hadn't changed after her arrival although all her clothes were being unpacked systematically. "She doesn't step foot outside," I ordered Scar, passing through the space he allowed before he closed it to block Ivory in.

"Yes, boss," he grunted, absorbing Ivory's slap to his chest.

"Let me out! Matteo!" she yelled, and I closed the door behind me to drown out the sound.

I didn't need her uncle thinking she was being tortured.

"Bellandi," Adam greeted, crossing his arms over his chest and attempting to stare me down. He knew I wasn't so easily intimidated, but he still had to try. "I'm taking Ivory with me."

I knew there was a gun in his holster, the man went nowhere unarmed. But I didn't even consider needing to proceed with caution. He was too smart to pull a gun on me in my turf.

If he did, he'd be dead. Shot down by any of the guards undoubtedly on edge after I gave the order to let him in the gate.

"Ivory is with me now."

"I know your reputation. I know what you do. Ivory isn't the woman you involve in that kind of shit, Bellandi. You know that and I do."

"She's mine. Always has been," I grunted.

He sighed, nodding. "I know, but you threw her away. Now she wants to leave, and you have to let her."

I pulled the tiny box from my pocket, fingering the velvet and holding it up so he could make no mistake about what it contained. He eyed it warily, a deep sigh rattling in his chest. He hung his head, knowing what it meant for a man like me.

Men like us didn't let go of what was ours.

Not when it came to wives.

"Fuck," he whispered, and the way he warred with himself almost made me feel bad for the poor guy.

"If you hurt her or let anything happen to her, I'll make her disappear, and even you will never find her. Got me?" Adam asked, glaring at me.

I nodded. I could live with those terms; after all, it was much easier than I'd anticipated it would be to convince him.

"She loves you," he sighed. "Always has. She's scared, but I have to believe she'll find a way around that."

"I'll make sure she does," I said, reassuring him. I'd always envied the relationship Ivory had with her family. The way they loved each other and wanted what was best was admirable.

"Can I see her?" he asked. I nodded, stepping back to the door and watching as Scar opened it.

Ivory raced out, flinging herself into her uncle's arms. "Thank you!" she said, breaking my heart when she took solace in him. Solace from me.

"You call me if he hurts you, yeah?" Adam grunted; voice thick with emotion. Ivory backed up, staring up at him in confusion.

"Wh—what?" she stuttered.

"This is the safest place for you, honey. Adrian Ricci is no joke. You do what Matteo tells you," Adam grunted, wincing when she tugged fully from his grasp. "Love you," he murmured, turning and going for the driver's side of his car.

"Adam!" she yelled as he climbed in. "Adam!" she screamed when he started the car and inched down the driveway.

I stepped up behind her, wrapping arms around her waist and containing her when she lunged for the car with horror in her eyes.

My angel broke, crying while I held her in my arms and wished there'd been another way. That she'd let me ease her into it.

But it didn't matter.

We'd always end up with her living with me.

I couldn't regret it being sooner than I planned.

CHAPTER TWENTY-THREE

Waking up trapped underneath Matteo's weight had become far too comfortable. Normally he woke up before me and stayed with me until I woke up. It was an unspoken thing between us, that he insisted on doing it so I could get my first quality rest in years. I didn't want to talk about it—didn't want to acknowledge the fact that Matteo was far too astute not to suspect there was a reason for my restless sleep.

Not when the reason felt so insignificant. Some women survived much worse. Some women dealt with the true trauma that came from horrific circumstances.

They were stronger than I was. Stronger than I would ever be.

So, when I woke up the next morning to the familiar press of his chest against my back and his leg draped over mine, I revolted against the feeling of comfort. Even with how angry I'd been yesterday, how broken I'd felt knowing he would completely disregard my wishes, I hadn't been strong enough to resist when he rolled me underneath him and made love to me.

At least that's what I would have called it, if Matteo was capable of love.

He wasn't. The day before had made that clearer than ever.

"It's time we talk about this," he grunted, pulling off me and rolling me to my back. My sleep camisole revealed more than it hid, and I brought my arms up to cover my silk covered breasts.

"Talk about what? That you've completely ignored what I want?"

"Ivory," he warned, and I blinked up at him with the most innocent expression I could muster.

"We're not doing this," I mumbled, rolling my eyes and moving to escape the bed.

Grabbing me around the waist, he shoved me down onto my back again, inserting himself between my legs and pinning my arms to the bed by my head when I struggled. "Whatever the fuck happened to you fucked you up. You thrash around in your sleep. You fucking beg for it to stop."

"Don't—" I warned, turning my head from side to side.

"I want to help you, and I can't do that if you don't tell me who to kill," he growled.

"Matteo—"

"Who, Ivory?"

"I don't know! Okay. I don't know who he is." My voice trailed off, unable to meet Matteo's gaze.

"Tell me what happened. Every time he bothers you at night, you bring another man into our bed." I turned furious eyes to him, finding him looking at me apologetically. "I didn't mean that the way it sounded. Our bed is ours. Just you and me, Ivory. Let me help you erase whoever he is."

"It's your bed, not ours," I snarled instead, determined to hold on to my anger over being moved in without permission.

"Are your clothes in the closet? Your toothbrush at the sink?" His face turned to stone as he spoke.

"Teo," I whispered.

"Am I inside you every night and wake up with you in my arms?"

"Teo, that's not—"

"Answer me, Angel."

I grimaced. "Yes."

"Then this is *our* bed. That will not change."

I sighed, finally relenting. I so did not want to have a discussion with Matteo about his lack of boundaries and his ability to lie. We both knew it was only a matter of time before he kicked me out of his home when he got bored. Maybe the reality of cracking me wide open would prove I wasn't worth all the intrigue he seemed to think I was. "You know that moment when you first fall asleep? Where you're still aware, but everything is fuzzy and warm. Little bits of reality filter through the fog, but most everything is lost."

He tensed above me, staring at the side of my face since I refused to look at him. "Yes," he whispered.

"That's the best way I can describe what being drugged felt like. It reminds me of how that felt and what happened, so when I hit that part of sleep, it makes me panic, but I'm just so used to it that I guess I don't wake up anymore," I admitted.

His forehead touched my temple, and from the corner of my eye I saw his eyes slide closed. "Drugged?" His voice was a hoarse whisper along my skin. I nodded. He couldn't possibly mean to make me discuss the gritty details. "What happened?"

The breath that rattled out of my chest was rough, filled with disbelief and fear. "I went to a club alone. Sadie hadn't turned twenty-one yet, and Duke just hated the whole club scene. One minute I was fine, drinking and dancing, enjoying myself. The next thing I knew I was stumbling and fuzzy. Someone caught me, said he'd find me a place to rest it off. I was too out of it to protest. I just didn't understand what was happening."

"Jesus. *Fuck*," Matteo groaned, his face contorting in pain.

"He didn't rape me. He didn't have a chance. He propped me up against one of the walls in a darker corner of the club and supported my weight. I was in and out of consciousness, but I know he moved my underwear aside. *Touched me*. Someone caught on to what he was doing and chased him off, she said he had his pants undone when he ran off, and I just fell to the floor. She and one of her friends who was a bartender set me up in a back room and saw me through it. I didn't want to involve the cops, not when I'd been so stupid, and they respected that."

"He touched you," Matteo growled. "Drugged you and planned to rape you."

"It wasn't that bad. It's silly. I just, that feeling of losing control over my body was the worst thing. I couldn't even fight him. People surrounded me, and I still had no way of making anyone know that I was in trouble. Falling asleep reminds me of that, and I know that's a ridiculous association. But it's never gone away," I explained with a shrug.

"What did he look like? What club?"

"It doesn't matter, Teo. It was a long time ago, and I remember nothing about him. Everything was blurry. I barely even remember what Verona or Evie looked like if I'm honest." That was one reason it would have been so stupid to involve the police. There was nothing to go on. Even Evie hadn't gotten a very good look at the guy, and it wasn't like a rape kit would have been productive. Just traumatizing.

I hadn't dated for over a year after that. Hadn't gone to my gynecologist. I'd only touched myself when necessary for hygiene.

"No one will ever touch you again," Matteo promised. I smiled at him sadly even though I believed him.

Matteo would let no one else touch me as long as I was his.

We'd been here before.

And one day soon, I'd have to relearn how to live life without him.

✳✳✳

Several times over the two days since Matteo had moved me in, he'd suggested I do my blog posts and such from the couch of his office. Apparently it was the purpose for it, but he also clarified that there may be meetings where I needed to vacate when he and Don or Lino or when one of the countless other guys who worked for him needed to have private conversations about the business.

I wasn't the type to be forced to move once I'd settled in for the more tedious back end stuff of my business. I hated doing it to begin with, so I wasn't about to move once I motivated myself to do it. Because of that, I'd neglected to join Matteo in his office while I worked, preferring to sit in the kitchen with Don for company. I was coming to associate Matteo's office with bad news anyway, between the day I stupidly strolled in there like I had any control and the day he told me he was moving me in.

I was happy to avoid the misfortune that happened in there, thanks.

So, when Lino finally emerged from the office after a long two-hour meeting, I barely looked up at him when he strolled into the kitchen. "He wants you," he said, and I assumed he was talking to Don. Matteo didn't summon me to his office regularly, as opposed to the other man who appeared to handle many matters for Matteo. "Ivory, sweetheart. Talking to you." There was a smile in Lino's voice, and my eyes darted up to meet his in shock. I closed my laptop slowly, smiling at Don.

"Will this bother you if I leave it for now?" I asked.

He glanced at it and shook his head. "No worries, Ms. Torres." I brushed my hands over the fabric of my easy sage dress as I stood and made my way down the hallway.

Foreboding crept down my spine as I walked down the hall, and I took deep breaths and tried to convince myself it was only because of what happened the last time Matteo called me to his office. I wasn't a child. Wasn't about to be reprimanded by the principal. This was a man I slept with every night. Yes, he was a man who admittedly did things I didn't approve of without concern for my thoughts, but he wouldn't hurt me.

Not so soon after the stab of betrayal of moving me out of my own home and trapping me in his estate.

Knocking on the door, I waited for the familiar voice to summon me in before opening it. Matteo wasn't alone, a middle-aged man stood next to the desk. I walked in, smiling for him when he nodded.

"Ivory," Matteo said, standing and wrapping an arm around my waist. He pressed a chaste kiss to my cheek, turning his attention to the strange man. "This is my personal physician, Dr. Marchesi."

"Are you sick?" I asked him, and he chuckled at me. His eyes didn't meet mine, and that foreboding feeling slithered through me again. "What's going on?" My eyes turned to the corner when the doctors' eyes darted there. A massage table sat in the corner, and my brow furrowed. I didn't understand why a physician would give me a massage.

"He's here for you," Matteo said.

"But I'm not sick," I whispered.

"He's going to help me keep you safe. Just in case." Matteo's voice dropped to a whisper, and my eyes darted to the medical bag sitting on the coffee table where Matteo intended me to work.

"I don't understand."

The doctor pulled something from his bag. He held it between two gloved fingers, so small I could barely see it from across the room. "It's a microchip. Just a little tenderness for a day or so following insertion, much like a flu shot, then you won't feel a thing."

Horror dawned on me, and I backed up a step only to have Matteo tighten his arm around my waist and plaster me to his side. "No. No fucking way."

"Angel," Matteo whispered, and I turned wide eyes to him.

"You can't be serious! I'm not letting you put that thing in me!" Struggling against his grip, I shoved at him to let me go.

"You need to be still. We don't want to hurt you more than necessary," Matteo warned. My eyes returned to the doctor, watching as he loaded the chip into a syringe with a fat needle.

"No! Teo, please!" I begged, backing away. I couldn't explain the dramatic reaction, but in the face of being microchipped like a dog after being taken from my home, it was too much.

I felt trapped.

Trapped in a way I'd never been before, like I might never know freedom again.

"Lino!" Matteo yelled, and my panic increased. Matteo's grip tightened on me, and I thrashed in his arms as he hauled my back against his chest. Lino, Don, and Scar rushed into the room and made their way toward us.

"No!" Matteo maneuvered us to the massage table, letting Scar help guide him until my stomach pressed to the table gently.

Even manhandling me, they were gentle about it.

I screamed again, wincing when Lino pressed a hand to the back of my head and stroked it affectionately. "It will be alright," he murmured, pressing my face forward into the face cradle. His other hand pressed to my left shoulder, holding it down firmly. Matteo's hand took up residence on my right shoulder, and the other two men grabbed my legs and held me perfectly still. I felt my chest shaking with the force of my crying and wished I could stop, but I was so angry that there was no stopping the tears.

Another hand pressed against my back, and the sound of scissors snapping together reached my ears before my dress suddenly loosened around me slightly. "I recommend here," the doctor said, pressing a finger into the fleshy part to the right of my spine. "It makes it impossible for her to remove herself."

I mumbled against the pillow. What the hell did this guy think I was? A superspy?

I was n*ever* cutting anything out of my skin.

Good God.

"That works," Matteo grunted as I wiggled in their hold. "Get it done." The needle pressed to my skin, and I whimpered.

"Shhh, sweetheart," Lino comforted me, and I didn't miss the fact that it wasn't Matteo. He knew there was no forgiving this.

Especially not after our conversation the day before.

With a slow glide, the needle pressed in, dropped the microchip under my skin, and pulled back. A hand pressed something to the entry point, no doubt to stop the bleeding until the doctor taped a bandage to it. When the sound of latex gloves being removed from his hands caught my attention, the pressure at my legs and shoulders finally relented.

I didn't move.

"Get out," Matteo barked, and I heard footsteps as they all hurried to do just that. When the door closed, Matteo finally turned all that intensity on me again. "Angel," he whispered. His hands wrapped around me, pulling and rearranging me until I sat on the table. I still didn't look at him, seething behind my tears. He reached out a hand to cup my cheek, wincing when I flinched back from him.

"Don't touch me," I hissed.

"Ivory—"

"I'll never forgive you," I whispered, finally looking at him. I had to wonder why it had been necessary—why he'd needed to break whatever good we'd had in our fucked-up history.

"You don't have a choice," he murmured back, icy eyes staring into mine.

"That seems to be a common theme with you," I huffed a laugh. Guilt flashed across his features momentarily, before he wiped all expressions from his face. "You were right. I never should have come here. I was happier without you."

I stood, forcing my way around him. He didn't move, didn't follow.

But his roar of rage echoed behind me as I escaped. Glass shattered, and it sounded like something flipped. I emerged into the kitchen, snatching up my laptop and ignoring Donatello's apologies. I couldn't even meet his eyes as I fled the room.

I hurried to one of the guest rooms upstairs, locking myself in and collapsing onto the bed.

I couldn't even go home.

CHAPTER TWENTY-FOUR

Our interactions with each other had been fleeting for two days. I worked in the kitchen. He worked in his office. We ate dinner in silence. He went back to working while Donatello and I cleaned up.

Then I ran to the spare bedroom and locked myself in. Somehow, I woke up in his arms in his bed the following morning both days. How he maneuvered me there without waking me, I'll probably never know. As soon as I woke up, he wordlessly stood from the bed and got ready before burying himself in his office again.

I stood in the kitchen, staring at the ingredients set out in front of me and preparing myself for the experiment I was about to undertake when Matteo's yell echoed through the house.

"I don't fucking care what you do with it! Just get it out of here!"

I hesitated. His office was officially on my no-no list of places to go, but there was *something* so *broken* in his voice as he shouted, that my feet moved on their own accord. I rounded the corner, passing people who stared at me in horror.

My eyes landed on the doll as soon as I walked in the room.

The size of a child's doll, she almost looked like she could actually be a child's plaything.

If you only looked at her face.

And ignored the lace teddy that adorned her body.

My eyes darted to the scrap of red lace sitting next to her, an identical, life size match of what she wore.

"Ivory," Matteo whispered. "Go back to the kitchen, Angel."

I only spared him a moment's glance before it drew my eyes back down to the doll. Her sea-green eyes were vacant and empty, surrounded by ivory skin and perfectly layered chestnut hair. Freckles dotted her cheeks and nose, and it didn't take a genius to figure out exactly who she was supposed to look like.

Me.

"What is that?"

"Go, Ivory."

"Where did you get that?" I snapped, ignoring the sympathetic way he stared at me. I knew Matteo well enough to know when he was protecting me, and that expression on his face was answer enough about where the doll came from.

"Everyone get the fuck out," he grunted, and the office cleared instantly. The door closed behind them, and Matteo strode to me and caught me up in his grasp. "He won't touch you," he murmured, as if it would distract me from the missing doll. One of his security people had snatched it up as he fled the room, no doubt the one who messed up and brought it into the house.

"Teo," I whispered, feeling raw in the face of the way that doll made me skin crawl.

Hefting me up into his arms, I barely protested as Matteo carried me over to the couch and sat with me in his lap. I buried my face in his neck, breathing in the familiar scent there and letting it comfort me.

The thing about Matteo for me?

I couldn't be near him and not want him.

Ever.

It was why I kept my distance from him. I knew I had zero self-control where he was concerned and being pressed up against him—feeling him harden beneath me as I straddled his hips—only proved that the feeling was mutual.

Nothing should have been sexy in that moment. Not after being given a creepy doll and lingerie from a man I'd given no indication of interest.

But Matteo was a different story.

He always had been. I pulled out of his neck, crashing my lips to his in a torrent of need. His hands worked my dress up my hips as my hands went to the zipper of his trousers.

I wanted him.

I needed him.

And in that moment, I would not question it.

I needed the reminder I was alive.

Not just a thing to be used and discarded, but a real, live person with feelings and thoughts. I needed to exist, and Matteo was the greatest adrenaline rush I'd ever had.

I freed him from his pants stroking him as he shoved my panties to the side. Rising, I notched him at my entrance and slammed down onto him so hard he groaned. "Easy, Angel."

He knew as well as I did that taking him, even with foreplay, wasn't an easy feat. Taking him with no preparation after zero sex for two days was just plain foolish.

But I needed that pain, the feeling of being ripped open from the inside.

I needed my body to match what he did to my heart. To my soul.

I needed him to understand what he did to me, and I wasn't foolish enough to think I'd ever hurt Matteo the way he hurt me. He'd have to have a heart for that to be possible.

His hands at my hips tried to steady me, but I swatted him away and rocked my hips back and forth quickly. I knew my pace was frenzied. I knew I was acting like a crazy person as I used him, but I couldn't be bothered to care.

Eventually, he settled, seeming to sense that I needed *exactly* what I was taking. He put his hands back on my hips and slid them up and under the fabric of my dress, not stopping or encouraging me so much as just wanting the contact with my skin.

I chased my orgasm, loving the way my clit rubbed against his pubic bone in that position, and feeling like maybe, just maybe, for one moment I was in charge of something. My hands on his chest steadied myself as I exploded into an orgasm, trembling around him and feeling him find his own release inside me.

I didn't let the intimacy of our simultaneous orgasms touch me. Not the way it normally did.

As soon as I caught my breath, I stood and smoothed my dress back down. "Ivory," he whispered, reaching for me. Something in my expression seemed to make his own darken.

I knew what he saw as he looked at me. Something I expected I hadn't been able to achieve since the moment he came back into my life.

But in that moment?

I was safe within my walls.

Not even Matteo Bellandi could touch me.

I turned and strode out of the room, going to the guest room and taking a shower to scrub myself clean. Matteo didn't bother to follow me.

✳✳✳

For a couple of days, the distance between Matteo and I remained firmly planted like a void. I ended every day with him inside me despite it, with him trying to force me from my shell with the intimacy of sex and the sensations only he could wring from my body.

But that's the thing about sex. It could only be intimate if I allowed him to touch more than my body, and after the way he'd betrayed me that wasn't happening.

For the first time in my life, it felt like my heart was safe from Matteo.

I *hated* it.

It should have been a comfort, should have reassured me I'd walk away unscathed when he decided he was finished me. Instead, it just left me feeling cold.

Alone.

Again.

So, when Matteo had suggested I could go to *Indulgence* with Sadie while he handled some business with Lino, I jumped at the chance. I was desperate to get out of that house, desperate to have some semblance of freedom. Going dancing with my friend was a welcome change.

I didn't always expect Matteo to have me surrounded by security.

I never expected to be trapped in the VIP area where he could watch me from his tower of an office.

I decided right then and there as I watched that I really, *really* hated any offices where Matteo was concerned. Watching brunette after brunette strut her way up those steps and act like she had a right to Matteo, listening to them tell Simon that he'd want to see them.

That they're special.

Newsflash.

They weren't. Not even one of them.

After the first few, Simon took to pointing me out and informing the girls that Matteo was spoken for with a live-in girlfriend, and just like that, women glared at me from every corner of the VIP. When I glanced down at the regular part of the club, for ordinary nobodies like me, I wished I could go be anonymous with them. Until I saw women pointing up at me with harsh expressions and speaking in one another's ears.

"Why am I here?" I asked Sadie, flopping onto an empty seat.

"Beats me. This sucks," she groaned. They allowed Sadie to go down to the dance floor. Just not me.

"What the fuck is the point of a club if I can't dance?" I snarled, catching Simon's attention.

He shrugged at me with a smile. "Boss' orders, Ms. Torres."

I groaned, flopping back against the cushions dramatically. A new girl wandered into the VIP, easily admitted access for whatever reason.

If I had to guess?

It was because she was *gorgeous.*

Inhumanly gorgeous.

I wanted to hate her but staring at her clear blue eyes and chestnut locks only gave me a different idea. I waved her over, patting the seat next to me. She took it with wide eyes, seeming entirely grateful to be saved the awkwardness of being on her own.

"Thank you!" she gushed, perching next to me.

"Have you ever met Matteo Bellandi?" I whispered, and Sadie eyed me curiously. Simon's eyes rested on mine in fixation too, but I didn't care.

"No. I've heard he's beautiful," she whispered, as if Matteo's looks were a secret.

As if.

It seemed the entire brunette female population of Chicago was very well acquainted with Matteo's appearance.

And his dick.

I fought back the surge of possessive jealousy. He wasn't mine, and never would be.

"So, this might sound weird, so bear with me," I laughed. "But do you want to fuck him?"

"Oh, for fuck's sake," Sadie groaned, smacking my shoulder. I winced, turning a glare her way.

"I—what?" the girl asked.

"I live with Matteo, girlfriend by force, I guess. Anywayyyy," I noted her shocked expression and realized I needed to save this conversation from crazy town. Stat. "He's a cheater. Already cheated once, but says he's changed. Blah blah you know the spiel."

"And you want to prove he'll cheat again?" she asked.

I nodded, opening up just enough to admit that Matteo had gotten to me before everything went to shit. "I want it done, before it hurts more, you know?"

"Oh honey, I mean. If he's as good looking as I've heard, then it's not exactly a hardship, is it? Are you sure you can handle knowing—?"

I nodded, though I knew there was a grimace on my face. "I want to know if he gives you *any* sign of interest. If he takes your number, gives you his. Whatever. I need to know."

She nodded, and I forced Simon to let her up the stairs. He played along, smirking the entire time like he was in on some huge joke.

Sadie took my hand, pulling me from my seat. "Let's go."

"Go where?"

"Dancing." She shoved past two bouncers who just trailed after us in dismay. "They won't touch you. Matteo would cut off their hands if they did. So we will not sit here so you can wait and watch him be seduced."

I swallowed, nodding. As soon as we hit the dance floor, I made it my resolution to *not* look at Matteo's tower. I didn't want to know. Didn't have any interest in finding out how Matteo liked to fuck the girls he took in his office. He'd admitted he didn't have sex in beds except with me, but the office saw some action.

I hated it by extension.

I threw myself into the action of dancing, trying actively to lose track of time. Song passed after song, and when there was no sign of the gorgeous girl returning to the VIP room from Matteo's tower, I felt something inside me shrivel and die.

There would be no doubt in my mind about what happened in that office, not with the time she'd spent there.

When my eyes slid away from the tower slowly, I met Simon's eyes briefly. Even his gaze was knowing, all traces of amusement gone from his features as he stared down at me. I didn't expect the anger making his face tense; the disappointment making his shoulders drop.

Hands touched my waist from behind, and barely a second passed before Scar stepped into my space and physically separated the guy from me.

I forced my best, most convincing, *bullshit* smile to my face as I turned to look at whoever had been brave enough to touch me with bouncers and bodyguards all around me. He was cute, if not oblivious to the *off-limits* aura my guys gave anyone who got too close. "It's okay," I said to Scar, stepping into the stranger's orbit. I took his hands and placed them back on my hips as I resumed the rhythm of the music.

"Ivory—" Scar started, and I smiled at him. He didn't seem to know what to do with that smile, faltering in whatever he'd been about to say. My eyes darted back up to the Tower, and Scar winced when my eyes found his again.

"It was only a matter of time, Scar," I whispered, and his face twisted with confusion.

Like Matteo had really convinced his guys I mattered—that I was important. He probably had to, if he expected them to risk their lives to protect me.

But the secret was out. I was just another in a long line of forgettable women who would mean nothing to Matteo. His jaw tensed, but he nodded, stepping back and letting me turn my attention to my stranger.

I smiled again, shoving down that broken part of me. I didn't get to be upset.

This was my doing.

The stranger smiled at me, and once we had room to move, he picked up the sway of his body and moved in tune with mine. Sadie found her own dance partner, moving close to me in the crush of bodies so we all enjoyed the music as a group.

A prickle of unease tingled down my back, but I was determined to ignore it. Until people dancing around us froze, and Sadie's hand grasped my arm. Turning to look at her, I saw her face etched with horror. "Ivory," she whispered, grabbing the stranger's hands and shoving them off my body. My eyes met Scar's next, and he smirked at me and crossed his arms over his chest.

My body pivoted slowly, eyes tracking through the crowd where they stared at me.

Matteo stood on the stairs that connected the VIP area to the main dance floor. His hand gripped the railing tightly, so much that it looked painful.

His face was etched in rage.

Those beautiful features looked monstrous in the flashing lights of the club as his darkened gaze found mine. Lino followed behind him, dragging the girl I'd sent down with a tight grip on her arm. Her eyes found mine, wide and full of fear. Her lips mouthed the words, "I'm sorry."

"He didn't take the bait," Sadie whispered in horror. "So, what was he doing up there?"

I glanced over at her, wondering the same thing. When Matteo took the first slow step toward us, it was not the body language of a man who'd fucked up and fallen for a woman's tricks and gotten laid.

It was the movement of a man who'd been wronged.

A man hell-bent on destruction.

I turned, shoving at the stranger. "Go," Sadie whispered, and the poor fool just stared at her. "If you value your life, you'll leave this club right now and never come back." That caught his attention, and he backed away slowly before picking up his pace and fleeing for the door.

I felt Matteo's presence. Felt every step he took until he stood directly behind me. He didn't touch me, didn't speak. But I knew he was there, heard the ragged intake of each breath.

"Matteo," I whispered, glancing to the side to look at Lino and the woman I'd selfishly sent into a situation I'd never had a hope of controlling.

"Do you think this is a game?" he whispered with a dead voice that probably concealed his rage from anyone who didn't know him. I watched with wide eyes when my stranger was stopped at the doors, bouncers ushering him toward a hall at the back of the bar.

"You're taking this too far, Bellandi," Sadie hissed. "This is too much."

"Do you know who I am, Sadie?" Matteo asked her slowly, and I watched as my friend gulped and nodded. "And you knew this when you called to inform me that Ivory had a date, no doubt?"

Pure, unfiltered betrayal rushed through me, and I turned to stare at her. Not only had she kept secrets from me, but she'd been the one to tell Matteo I'd gone on a date?

"Ivory," she whispered, stepping into my space. Matteo blocked her with an arm at her chest, forcing her to keep her distance.

"Ivory does not exist for you. Not until she understands the severity of what is happening here."

"You can't do that!" Sadie shouted.

"How could you?" I whispered to her, and I thought for sure the sound would be lost to the music. By some miracle, the music was nothing but a dull pound in the background, lost to the potent silence and the crush of people staring at us.

"I can, and I will."

"He doesn't have to. I don't even want to look at you," I hissed, flinching when Sadie winced. She nodded as if she'd expected that and turned and walked away. The bouncers didn't stop her and shove her into some back room to wait for their boss' wrath.

Matteo finally touched me, his fingers brushing the hair off the back of my neck delicately. "The next time you send me a woman," he paused, and my breath hissed between my teeth in anticipation of the crash. The admission that he would touch her, the pain that would break me all over again. "I'll make her and whoever the fuck you think to let touch what's mine, watch me fuck you," he hissed, wrapping his tight grip around my arm and pulling me into his body. I staggered, lost for words, because that had *not* been what I expected him to say. When he turned and pulled me toward the staircase, I fought against his hold.

"Teo," I whispered.

"Shut the fuck up, Ivory," he snarled. He kept pulling me until I stumbled in my heels on the third step. Then he looked at me, grasping me around the waist and tossing me over his shoulder. I shrieked, my hands going for my ass to make sure I wasn't hanging out of my dress. He smacked the back of my thigh, and I whimpered in shock. "I wouldn't expose you. That pussy is mine."

I gasped, smacking at his back in outrage. We passed Simon who chortled despite Matteo's glare.

Up and up we went until we stood outside the door to his tower of an office. "I don't want to go in there," I whispered, and he paused.

"Why?"

"I'm not naïve. I know you've had women in there before. They were all looking for seconds, and it was obvious you'd invited them up."

"I wasn't a saint, Ivory."

"I don't want to be another one of them, Teo." My voice broke, and I buried it in my hands.

"You could never be one of them." He stepped into the office against my wishes, kicking the door closed behind him and locking it. He didn't hesitate to bring me straight to the wall of glass overlooking the club, a King in his kingdom. He set me down, turning me to face the glass. Security convinced everyone to return to the fun, and the music cranked up loud again, but I didn't miss the way everyone's eyes seemed to fixate on the glass even as they drank and danced.

His hands grasped the bottom of my dress, tugging until he revealed my thong. Shrieking, I shoved his hands away. "What are you doing?"

His hand came down on my bare ass in a hard slap, and I screamed. "Matteo!"

"He had his hands on you." His voice went deathly quiet, and it took everything inside me not to tremble. Those strong, somehow callused hands stroked over the sensitive skin where he'd struck me, and heat bloomed in my core in response.

I hated how much I liked it—hated that I had to resist the urge to arch my back and press my ass into his touch. "I thought you fucked that woman. I didn't think you'd care."

Wrapping his hand around my throat, he slowly guided me back until I had no choice but to support my weight on the glass with my hands and the back of my head touched his shoulder. His free hand fidgeted with my thong, shoving it down my thighs one side at a time and inching it down like he couldn't bear to release his hold on my throat. "Teo," I rasped.

"Shut up, Ivory. Just shut the fuck up and listen for once." I stilled, snapping my mouth closed. The sound of him unzipping his pants behind me made me whimper, anticipation of what was coming like a pulse in my veins.

I thought I'd had everything Matteo had to give. I thought I made him lose control sometimes.

I'd been wrong.

He shoved inside me in one hard thrust, not giving my body time to adjust to the feeling of fullness that came with him being inside me. "This is where I belong," he groaned, keeping me still and keeping himself planted deep.

So deep.

It felt like I could feel him in my soul. Etched there permanently in some strange tether that tied us together through the years.

Over lifetimes.

Like nothing could ever keep us apart.

"I will *never* touch another woman again, Angel." His words were soft, menacing beneath the surface. The real Matteo that few ever got to see playing at the surface instead of hidden down deep. "I'm yours, Ivory." Tears stung my eyes when his lips touched my cheek, the soft pressure too much to handle at that moment. "And you're mine."

I nearly sobbed.

Because I wanted that.

I wanted to be his, and for him to be mine.

But to love Matteo was to be broken. I knew that better than anyone.

And I couldn't do it again.

"I'm not a good man." He pulled his hips back, thrusting in so hard he rammed against the end of me. A mix of pleasure and pain shot through me, and I gasped in his hold.

"Teo."

"I don't care if you want to leave me. I won't let you," he growled in my ear as he fucked me in slow and deep, hard strokes. "Do you know why, Angel?"

I shook my head, too incoherent to form words as he worked me over. His free hand wrapped around my front, pressing between my thighs to feel the place where we connected. He cupped me, touching himself as he slid in and out of me and made me mindless. The palm of his hand pressed against my clit and threatened me with an orgasm that hovered just out of reach.

"Because I love you. I have loved you since the moment I laid eyes on you." He shoved deep, pausing there and letting me think for just a moment. "Nothing will ever take you from me."

"Stop," I pleaded on a whisper, and from the way he slid out of my pussy and then glided back in, he knew I didn't mean to stop fucking me.

"I'll never stop," he whispered, that hand abandoning my throat finally in favor of cupping my cheek and turning my head so he could look at me. "Tell me you understand."

"Please, stop," I begged, clenching my eyes shut, so I didn't have to look into the piercing blue of his eyes. Even his eyes told lies.

Even his eyes deceived.

"Look at me," he commanded, and my eyes snapped open of their own accord. "You will be my wife." My body acted on its own, fighting in his grasp until his length slid free and I stumbled forward into the glass. "You will be the mother of my children." He stalked toward me, gathering me up in his arms even as I slapped at him like a cornered animal. He spun until my ass hit his desk, and he shoved everything onto the floor as he pushed me onto my back. Forcing my legs wide, he plunged inside me again and my back arched in pleasure despite the panic flooding through me. When I moved to rise, his hand went back to my throat, pinning me to the desk with pressure that threatened instead of hurt.

This was not the Matteo I could fight. It wasn't the Matteo I could plead with.

This was the criminal who took what he wanted without remorse. His face came into my space, staring at me and our breaths mingled. He shoved one knee high, keeping it positioned with his hand on the back of my thigh.

And then he fucked me.

Brutally.

Until I sobbed beneath him, and I would have sworn I would feel him imprinted inside me for the rest of my life. "Teo, please," I whimpered.

His lips crashed to mine, ending my halfhearted protest. Even as I feared the man staring back at me as he ravaged me, an orgasm built between my thighs. I tried to reach for it, wanted it to wash away the taste of pain Matteo gave as he slid in and out of my tender pussy.

He pulled his mouth away, glaring down at me. He pressed his thumb to my clit, but didn't move it, just tormented me with the promise of what could be. "Tell me," he growled.

"Tell you what?" I whimpered. "Teo, please."

"Tell me you're mine."

"I'm yours!" I shrieked, willing to admit just about anything in that moment.

"Tell me you love me." I froze, staring up at him in horror. "Tell me, *Cara mia*."

His face softened, something in the beast receding as he stared in the face of my panic. "Tell me," he pressed.

"I love you," I cried, tears falling from my eyes to tickle my ears. "I never stopped," I admitted and hated myself for it. His thumb made a single circle around my clit, and I erupted beneath him to the sound of his arrogance.

"I know," he murmured, and after a few more slow, languid thrusts he flooded me with his heat.

Even after we both caught our breath, Matteo made no move to separate from me, pressing his chest against mine and cradling me.

It was like he knew my foundation had been rocked.

That he'd changed my world with three little words.

I just hoped they weren't lies.

CHAPTER TWENTY-FIVE

IVORY

The smells from the kitchen made even my nose tingle with excitement.

The Ragu Napoletano was something I'd made occasionally, but never for a true Italian like Matteo.

Arms wrapped around my waist, Matteo's face nuzzling into the crook of my neck. "That smells delicious," he murmured, nipping at my skin softly. "But not as good as you."

I swatted him away playfully. "Get out!" I giggled when the scruff on his face tickled my jaw. "I mean it! You'll make me overcook the Strozzapretti."

"So make more." He shrugged, his shoulders jostling me as if he truly didn't care.

"Are you insane? No. Be gone, you slut."

"Your slut," he smirked, and one of his hands took mine in his. He turned me to face him, staring down at me intently in a way that scared me.

"Is everything okay?" I asked, biting my lip. His free hand left my waist, darting into his pocket. The thumb of the hand that held mine captive stroked over my left ring finger as he stared at it in fixation.

The smile he gave me when our eyes met again was breathtaking. A full, disarming smile that stole the air from my lungs. He held my eyes with his, and the cool touch of metal against the skin of my finger made my body freeze.

"What—what is that?" I asked, eyes darting down to the huge teardrop shaped diamond settled around my finger in two intricate, diamond studded bands of rose gold.

"Pick a date. I want to know by tomorrow."

"I—what?" I asked, feeling like my jaw was on the floor.

"A date, Angel," he chuckled. "I'd prefer a summer wedding, so we need to make arrangements quickly."

"A year is plenty of time—" I started to explain, because I had no need for a big wedding.

Wedding.

"You misunderstand me, *Cara mia.* I'm not waiting until next year to make you my wife."

"But it's already the end of May!"

"As I said, pick a date." He gave me that beautiful smile again, and I almost wanted to smack him for the way he enjoyed my floundering.

"You can't just put a ring on my finger, you know? You didn't even ask me if I would marry you!" I argued, shrinking back into the counter as much as I could.

"Asking would imply you have a choice." He smirked, giving me a glimpse of that dark possessiveness that always seemed to linger beneath the surface.

"Matteo," I warned. "I think we should slow down."

"I'll not waste another moment of my life without you as my wife, Ivory. Pick a fucking date," he growled, and I winced. With a sigh, I nodded. I was learning. Maybe I wasn't the fastest learner, but I knew well enough to know when to push and when not to. This was clearly one of those moments I shouldn't touch.

He smiled again, pleased with my concession. "Thank you. Don't overcook the Strozzapreti," he said, turning and striding back to his office like he hadn't turned my world on its head again.

Like marrying me had always been a foregone conclusion, and I suppose for Matteo it had. After all, he didn't care if I said no.

We were getting married.

His wife.

Ivory Bellandi.

Fuck.

CHAPTER TWENTY-SIX

IVORY

"Where are we going?" I grinned at Matteo as he swerved the Aston through the highway traffic just outside the city. We'd spent a few days in bliss, ignoring the world and getting lost in each other whenever we could manage. Matteo still worked, I had a feeling that would never change, but I'd finally set foot in his office long enough to work from the couch.

Offices no longer seemed terrifying.

Was he perfect?

Absolutely not.

He was dominating, controlling. He manipulated me to get his way and forced my hand when I didn't do something he wanted, but I realized that everything he'd done was to protect me.

Could I really be angry that he loved me enough to keep me safe?

He was all I'd never dared to dream for.

I didn't want to waste any more time.

He eyes met mine across the center console, his hand tightening around mine briefly. He glanced at an exit sign before moving into the right lane to take it. "Don't freak out."

I froze solid. "Why would I freak out? What did you do?" I'd only just come to terms with the last time; I did not need a new thing to be pissed about.

"We're going to my uncle's house for dinner," he admitted, and everything inside me tightened. I'd never met his uncle before, but I'd caught snippets of information from conversations Matteo and Lino had. I knew enough to know he wasn't a kind man.

"Say what now?" I asked, turning to him and feeling my eyes harden when he glanced at me in amusement.

"You had to meet him sometime, Angel," he laughed.

I glared at the corner of his eye, that spot where just the faintest trace of crow's feet were forming on his face. Even the tiny trace of aging only emphasized his dangerous features. "You're right. I probably did," I agreed, and the relief in his face was comical. He seriously thought he was off the hook. "But not today! Not without knowing what's coming. You blindsided me, you asshole!"

He barked out a sharp laugh, reveling in my growing comfort with him. In Matteo's words, it often grew boring having people just do what he said all the time.

I was anything but boring.

"Can you blame me?" he asked.

"Why was this necessary? Now I'm panicking!" I groaned, tearing my hand out of his grip.

"Which is exactly why I didn't tell you until we were almost there. I didn't want you fretting all day when you could be happy with me."

"That's almost sweet," I admitted. "But mostly selfish I think."

"It was completely selfish," he consented with a rogue grin. I smacked his arm, trying not to think about the time before we'd left the house where he'd ambushed me in the shower.

Where I'd gone to wash the sex off me.

That had been an exercise in futility.

"What if he hates me?" I whispered, and Matteo winced.

"He won't be your biggest fan," he returned, and I groaned.

"Why?"

"You aren't Italian. He wants me to marry a friend's daughter, and he thinks —" Teo paused, thinking over his words, and I knew the next statement would be about whatever his secret business enterprises entailed. "He thinks love is a weakness. That I should marry someone I'm prepared to lose one day."

I widened my eyes at him as he turned down a long driveway. "What's the point?"

"To have children." He shrugged. "That's the entire point of marriage to my uncle, after Lino's mom died, anyway."

"What happened to her?" Lino never talked about her. I hadn't known for sure she'd died but had guessed as much.

"There was an accident. Men targeting my uncle ran them off the road. He lived, she didn't."

"God, Teo," I whispered, horror rolling through me. "What are you involved in?"

He didn't answer, pulling up to the security gate in front of an estate slightly smaller than Matteo's. The driveway wasn't as long, not as winding, and the house itself was boxier than the sprawling structure that Matteo lived in.

But whatever the family business was, Matteo's uncle benefited from it greatly.

"Go on through, Mr. Bellandi," the guard said when Matteo rolled down the window, and the Aston rolled through the gate as it opened.

"Breathe," he chuckled. "My uncle not liking you has *nothing* to do with you. Being sweet won't change his opinion. Looking your best won't change his mind. And I don't give the first fuck what he thinks of you, because I choose you. That's all that matters." We pulled up in front of the house, and something unwound inside me. There was a lot less pressure when I knew his dislike of me was already a foregone conclusion. "I won't let him disrespect you."

"Okay," I whispered. Matteo turned to me, inspecting me. Satisfied with whatever he saw, he climbed out of the car. Regardless of what Matteo said, I was grateful I lived in dresses. My sky-blue wrap dress was timeless and classy, and probably the one thing I might have contemplated wearing to meet Matteo's uncle, anyway.

With both his parents gone, the disapproving Uncle was the closest thing to parents he had left. Lino liked me, I thought. So, there was just the Uncle left to sway. Maybe he'd come around eventually, right?

I couldn't imagine spending my life with a man, to have half his family hate me for the entirety of our time together. "About me being your wife," I started as soon as he opened the car door for me. He pulled me out, tucking the hair behind my ear on one side.

"Mhm," he murmured, shutting the car door with a soft thud.

"I don't want to be a problem for your family. You don't have to feel obligated to make me promises, Teo. Not every relationship is built to last, maybe—"

"Don't," he hissed, the hand that closed the door staying planted firmly so he trapped me against the car. "Nobody obligates me to do anything. Ever."

"But maybe this is better off as a short-term relationship. We don't have to muddy it up with things like divorce and kids—"

"There will never be a divorce," he grunted, grasping my hand in his and tugging me away from the car. "I will only marry once, Ivory."

"So, let it be with someone—"

"Enough." His voice was a whisper, but the warning was clear. I didn't even know why I bothered to argue with the man sometimes. So stuck in his own way that he'd never consider when someone else offered him a viable option.

"Okay," I whispered back, knowing fully well I'd resume the conversation another time.

I plastered an easy smile on my face, determined to make the best impression despite whatever Matteo's uncle might think of me. Matteo knocked on the door, as cool as ever, and I snuggled into his side. The last thing I wanted when his uncle formed his opinion of me firsthand was for Matteo to be distant because I'd pissed him off. A bit of his coolness melted as he grasped me around the waist and smiled down at me momentarily, but I knew the rest of his attitude wouldn't change. He was in work mode, the same calculated way he behaved the moment he set foot in his office or when talking with one of his guys who he didn't trust as much.

At first, the persona had terrified me, especially combined with my residual hatred of his office itself. But after being around him in that mode more often, I was insanely attracted to it. The dark waves of dominance that poured off him appealed to something in me, the part of me who had floundered on her own and worked to find herself loved the comfort in which Matteo just was who he was.

When a middle-aged Italian woman answered the door, she nodded to Matteo respectfully before turning surprised eyes to me. "Mr. Bellandi. We weren't aware you were bringing a guest." Panic crossed over her features, and Matteo continued as if he wasn't bothered by it. Stepping into the house like he belonged, he dragged me with him. The woman's eyes darted toward the living room, and voices sounded from the space. Matteo's eyes narrowed at the sound of a woman's tinkle of laughter.

"What did he do?" Matteo growled, clasping me tighter around the waist.

"He invited Mr. Morelli and his daughter," she whispered, eyes clenched. Her tension racketed up my own until I gasped when Matteo used the hand at my waist to guide me into the living room without preamble. Lino stood off to the side, totally and completely devoid of all the playfulness I was so used to seeing in him. His serious mask had been in place before we'd even entered the room, but it faded momentarily when he approached us.

"Ivory, sweetheart, you look beautiful as always," he said, pressing a kiss to my cheek affectionately. He and Matteo exchanged a look, and it was clear who Lino would side with when the battle lines were drawn. Judging from the disbelieving glare the three other occupants of the room leveled me with, I had to guess that moment was approaching.

Quickly.

"Matteo." His uncle grimaced. "What's this?"

"I could ask you the same thing, Gabriele. I'm fairly certain I made it very clear the last time we saw one another that I was not interested in your arrangement regarding Elena." I felt the wince that went through my body as my eyes met hers, knowing that the beauty on the couch with the big brown eyes was my competition as far as she was concerned.

She smiled, completely unconcerned with Matteo's dismissal. Whatever arrangement Matteo's Uncle Gabriele had in mind; love wasn't a part of it. She stood from her perch on the blue velvet sofa, crossing the distance between us to press her lips to Matteo's cheek in greeting. I fought to maintain my composure, knowing I needed to appear unconcerned with the beauty before me. If Matteo wanted her, he would have her, no doubt.

I didn't want to think about the fact that he could have already.

"It's always lovely to see you, Matteo," she practically purred. "Who is your friend?"

I bristled at the blatant dismissal, feeling murderous as she reached out a hand to touch his forearm in familiarity. I didn't understand how I'd gone from trying to shove a woman at him to feeling possessive, but I suspected it had something to do with the heavy, weighted ring sitting on my finger.

"Elena," Matteo said coolly. "This is my fiancé, Ivory."

Her eyes widened, and she turned her back to us momentarily to shoot a meaningful glare to Gabriele. "You assured me I would be his wife."

"You will be," the Uncle reassured her, ignoring the glare Matteo shot him. "She is merely a passing fancy. You know how men are."

"The ring on her finger tells a different story," she spat, eyes darting to my left hand where Matteo used it to drag me into his side. "Such a pity. Come daddy, I believe we've been misled enough for one day." The other man followed his daughter out the door.

"Lino, take Ivory into the dining room," Matteo said, and my eyes turned to him. I wanted to argue that my place was beside him, but the menace on his face communicated that this was exactly one of those moments where I just needed to get the Hell out of his way.

"Of course," Lino agreed, holding out an arm for me to take. I stepped away from Matteo, letting him guide me to the door at the back of the room.

"Not one more step, son," Gabriele snarled with a vicious bite that made me want to shrink into Lino for protection. "If she's so worthy of being your wife, then she will need to get familiar with situations like this. Will she not?" he turned to Matteo.

"Don't you dare," Matteo returned, and his hand went behind his back.

Both men moved so suddenly that I couldn't possibly follow the movement. All I knew was one moment they glared at each other, the next they each had a gun in hand and pointed at the other. I gasped, and Lino cursed under his breath.

"She is a weakness. I should have gotten rid of her the first time she distracted you from what's important." He shifted his gun to the right, taking his aim off Matteo and leveling it on me where Lino guided me to the door.

I winced, feeling Lino shove me behind him so I wasn't staring down the barrel of the gun. "Killing her now would be a mercy compared to what they'll do to her to hurt you."

"She's not mama, father," Lino begged. "Matteo won't let anything happen to her."

"Put down your fucking gun before I kill you," Matteo threatened, and the quiet rage in his voice sent fear through me.

What the fuck had I gotten myself mixed up in?

Gabriele huffed. "You'd shoot your own uncle? For pussy?"

"I'd shoot you for calling her that. I'd make you suffer if you hurt her," Matteo growled. Gabriele lowered his gun, tossing it onto the coffee table and raising a hand as if he was no longer a threat.

I exhaled a sigh of relief, releasing the desperate grasp I had on the back of Lino's suit. I didn't even remember grabbing him, remembered nothing aside from the terror that I'd lose Matteo.

I couldn't lose him.

"She had better be fertile," his Uncle grimaced, staring down Matteo's fury. I had to admit, it took a brave man to push his luck in the face of all that was Matteo.

Matteo's features twisted, and the sound of the gun going off was deafening in the living room. My hands flew to my ears, covering them instinctively. "Fuck," Lino grunted, staring at where his father clutched his arm in agony.

"You fucking shot me."

"You ever threaten my woman again, and it will be far worse than a flesh wound. Come Ivory," Matteo demanded, and I rushed into his side. Even though I was terrified of the glimpse I'd gotten into that beast that lurked under the surface, I knew Matteo wouldn't hurt me.

I felt that in my soul.

It didn't stop me from trembling as I burrowed into him though. He guided me out of the house, and I resisted the urge to ask questions. I got into the car, Matteo in the driver's seat, and didn't even argue when he pulled me over the center console and crushed me to his chest. "Teo, what—?"

"When we get home. I'll explain everything when we get home." He set me back to my seat, and I buckled up.

"Why not now?" I asked when he put the car in gear and started down the driveway. The gate opened at the end, and we escaped Gabriele's manor in one piece.

Or two.

"I can't have you trying to run. I need you locked down first," he admitted, and my heart clenched.

"It's bad, isn't it?"

"Do you love me?" he asked.

"You know I do."

"Then that's all that matters."

I hung my head, tears threatening to fall. Matteo had shot someone.

His own uncle.

And he didn't seem the least bit remorseful. "That's not the first time you've shot someone, is it?"

"When we get home."

I released a quiet sob, turning my attention to stare out the window.

I was so fucking screwed.

❋❋❋

The door to Matteo's office closed behind him with a quiet click. He turned to face me, a thousand emotions flitting across his normally impassive face. "You need to understand that what I'm about to tell you will change nothing."

"Teo, you're scaring me," I whispered, stepping back as far as the space would allow when he prowled toward me. He caged me between him and the desk, touching my cheek so gently I might have thought I imagined it had my eyes been closed.

"Anyone but you would be right to be afraid. Anyone but you would have to be stupid not to be, but I'll never hurt you, Angel," he whispered. "I wish I could be a better man for you, but I'm not, and I can't be."

"Why can't we just leave? Go somewhere and be someone else?"

"This is all I know. They raised me to run the family businesses, and I can't abandon that legacy. I'd always be a threat to whoever tried to take over, and we'd never be safe. Not really."

"I don't understand." I shook my head, staring up at him with glassy eyes.

He sighed, touching his forehead to mine. It felt final. It felt like he knew, no matter what he demanded, that whatever came next would cost him.

That it would cost him *me*.

"My family has run this city since my grandfather was in charge. Nothing happens here without our say so."

"You make it sound like you're some kind of mob boss." I shook my head with a dark chuckle, my smile fading when his eyes caught mine. He didn't laugh. Didn't flinch. "No. That's ridiculous."

"We call it more of a syndicate, but the premise is the same," he said, voice low.

Quiet, as if waiting for me to scream.

"But mobsters deal drugs and sell weapons!" I whisper hissed. "They sell women, and you told me you didn't do that."

"I told you I didn't take part in sex trafficking. The women who work for me are willing and very well compensated—" The sound of my hand striking him across the face echoed through the otherwise silent office. I stared at him in horror, waiting for the beast to strike. But to my amazement, he only nodded. "I deserved that."

"You think?" My eyes went to the ring on my finger, staring at it as tears slid down my cheeks.

"Don't even think about it," he snarled at me, pulling my attention away from the ring that suddenly felt like a shackle to a life I didn't want.

"I don't want to be a mob wife."

"Too fucking bad. I told you, this changes *nothing*," he stressed, pressing into me tighter. "I do what I can to keep innocent people from getting caught up in this world, Ivory. I'm not a good man, but I'm not the worst there is. Me in charge is what's best for the city."

"You shot your own uncle!" I protested.

"He disrespected you!"

"Was it the first time you've shot someone then?" I asked with a grimace, because he and I both knew that I didn't want to know the answer to that question. I needed to bury my head in the sand and pretend the day never happened.

"No," he admitted.

"Have you killed before?" I whispered, and his face shuttered as he stared at me.

"Don't ask me questions you don't want the answer to, Angel."

"Oh God," I cried, flinching away from him. But I had nowhere to go. Nowhere to run. "You're a murderer," I whispered.

"In my life, it is kill or be killed. I have done what I need to do to survive."

"This is why you left me, isn't it? You need a good little Italian wife to make your mob happy. Fuck, I'm so stupid," I winced.

"No. My uncle believes that women are a weakness. People only use the ones we love against us, and to protect Lino and I he forced us to stay away from the women we love. He threatened you, and I had no choice but to walk away to keep him from hurting you, Angel. Believe me. Nothing else could have ever made me leave you."

"You expect me to believe you *broke me* to protect me? I wasn't worth walking away from this shit?! You chose this over me, Matteo. You do not get to sugar coat that. The wealth, the power, God. Is that all that matters to you?"

His hands grasped me around my waist, twisting me around until he bent me over his desk.

I gasped, swatting at his hands behind me as he hefted my dress up over my ass. The hand at the back of my neck kept me pinned in place, unable to even begin to fight him. "Stop it!" I shrieked, flinching when he tore my thong down my legs.

"And what about you, Angel? What happened to my adrenaline junkie who couldn't get enough of the rush of doing something wrong? Who loved to drive my fast cars without a license and dared any cop to fuck with her?" His fingers pressed between my thighs, finding me already growing wet in response to his skilled manipulations of my body.

"I was a stupid child!" I yelled. "I did stupid shit, and it got me in a stupid situation."

"No, the only thing you did that was stupid," he said, releasing himself from his pants and pressing inside me slowly until he filled me to the brim. "Was doing something like that without me to protect you." He groaned, and I heard him fumble around in a drawer of his desk.

"What are you doing?" I whispered; my head turned the wrong way.

"Before you go accusing me of shit I didn't do, I've never fucked anyone but you in this house. This is for all those nights when I'd sit here, working late, and imagining your pretty fucking lips wrapped around my dick." I had no clue what he was talking about, but it came a little clearer the moment a bottle uncapped, and cold liquid trickled down between my cheeks.

"Matteo!" I gasped, squirming away when he pressed his thumb against that forbidden place.

"I'm going to show you just how good it can feel to be bad, *Cara mia.*"

"Teo!" I screamed, wincing when that thumb popped inside the outer ring of muscle and pressed inside me. His cock worked my pussy, sliding in and out of me in slow, intoxicating strokes that teased my g-spot without ever sending me over the edge.

"You are mine. This pussy is mine." His thumb left my ass, leaving me with a bizarre empty feeling until he replaced it with a long finger and pressed in mercilessly.

"It hurts," I whispered.

"This ass is mine," he continued as if he hadn't heard me. "You say it hurts, and yet your pussy is strangling my cock and so fucking wet I can hear it." He added another finger, making me burn from the inside out. That same dark pleasure I got when Matteo did things, I shouldn't like set me on fire, coiling in my core and waiting to explode.

"Let me come," I begged, not even recognizing the deep rasp of my own voice.

"You come when you take my cock in your ass." He gave another teasing roll of his hips, tormenting me in all the best ways. "You ready for that?"

"Just do it already," I hissed, feeling strangely brave in the face of what I was so sure would tear me in two. That dark side of me craved the things Matteo did, the way he took control of my body and demanded what he wanted without preamble.

He groaned, pulling his fingers free. He abandoned my pussy in favor of rubbing lube all over himself if the squeezing sound of the bottle behind me was any sign. With both his hands used, he finally had no choice but to let go of my neck. I turned my head to look back at him, watching him. For the first time when I looked at him, I knew exactly who he was. Exactly what he did.

It changed nothing. Didn't change the fact that I loved him with every fiber of my being.

I hated myself for it, knowing I could love a monster capable of such unforgivable sins.

When the head of him pressed against my ass, I tried to relax. While I may not have had anal before, I knew enough to know tensing up was not in my best interest. He stilled me with a hand at my hip, guiding himself inside slowly and making me whimper beneath him. The stretch was uncomfortable, outright painful even, but the way pleasure built with every minuscule thrust into me was undeniable. Wrapping a hand around me, Matteo worked his fingers at my clit in slow, tantalizing circles, adding more pleasure to the mix to overwhelm the pain. He paused, pressing his forehead to my back momentarily when his balls touched my pussy. "You like this," he groaned, and the slickness coating his fingers was undeniable. He pulled back, pressing back in slowly.

"Fuck!" I moaned, wiggling my hips to get more friction from his fingers.

"Not yet," he ordered, stilling me with a slap to my left butt cheek.

"You said I could come when your dick was in my ass. Did you not get the memo that it's in there? Because I sure as fuck did," I argued. He chuckled, humor in every little inflection of that deep voice.

"Oh, I sure as fuck got that memo, Angel." He pulled back, picking up his pace when I didn't protest. His strokes were still soft, downright delicate compared to the way he normally took my pussy, and I could feel his eyes watching the spot where he entered me so gently. "You look so fucking beautiful taking my cock in your ass."

"Fuck you, Teo," I groaned, and his fingers left my clit in favor of pressing two inside my pussy. "Oh God," I cried, thrusting back against him. "Please."

That thumb of his pressed to my clit, and I detonated around him on a cry. Heat scorched my insides when he followed me over the edge, and we stayed in place long enough to catch our breaths.

Matteo pulled free and brought me to shower without another word.

I felt like I'd changed. Like the Ivory I'd been before was gone, replaced by a woman who would let a murderer fuck her ass and love it.

It left me feeling numb.

Because I didn't recognize myself when I looked in the mirror. Matteo was content to hold me close, smothering me so he knew that I hadn't left. He didn't say it, but I could see the panic in rare moments. I knew he didn't want to lose me anymore than I wanted to lose him, so one of us would have to concede.

I knew it would be me.

It always was.

CHAPTER TWENTY-SEVEN

MATTEO

Ryker stood just inside the door, welcoming me inside with a nod. "Is he alive?" I asked.

Another nod in response, but the tension pouring off him was tangible. It impressed me the man was still alive.

The dealer who had shot his woman's husband had been a very idiotic man.

There was no doubt in my mind that he wouldn't walk away with his life. Even if I'd been so inclined, which I wasn't, there would be no way to talk Ryker down from the cliff. Not after I'd seen the pictures of Calla sobbing with her two children clinging to her.

"What are you going to do about the woman?" I asked as we walked toward the freezer. Her husband hadn't been a good man, the crooked cop that he was, but she hadn't had the slightest clue about that. So wrapped up in the picture perfect life they lived, she never saw the darkness that lurked beneath the surface in the man she'd married and shared a bed with. She didn't know him. Not in the slightest. The reality made me grateful that the truth was out with Ivory. No matter how much the truth of who I was had hurt her, the pain was done. She could heal, and there would be no more secrets between us.

Not that she'd ever find out about, anyway.

"She needs time," he answered gruffly, one of the rare twinges of emotion crossing over his face. Only that woman and those kids could bring out anything that even remotely resembled humanity in the enigma that was Ryker. "They aren't ready."

"No, they're not," I agreed. "It would take a cruel man to uproot them right now."

He nodded. "She hasn't worked in years. Never needed to. I'll send money. Take care of them until they're ready to understand."

He opened the freezer door, schooling his harsh features back into the mask of indifference that he was so gifted at. I wondered if it was conflicting for him. He didn't want Calla and the kids to suffer but having Chad out of the way undoubtedly freed up the place he wanted to fill more than anything.

I stepped in behind him, glaring at the beaten pulp that remained of the overzealous street dealer who worked for me. His eyes were nearly swollen shut, but even with all that, he still recognized me the moment I walked in. "Mr. Bellandi," he sobbed.

"Who gave you permission to kill the cop?" I asked.

"No—nobody, sir. He saw me dealing, was gonna arrest me. I didn't have no choice!" the guy sniveled, greasy hair hanging down to his shoulders in a matted mess of blood and his own filth.

"Tell me, what do you think is more valuable to me? A low-time street dealer who buys more of his own product than he sells or a cop on my payroll who makes evidence disappear? Hmm?"

He winced, fat tears rolling down his blood-stained cheeks. "I didn't know!"

"Even if he wasn't on my payroll, do you think it's more of a hassle for me to get you out of prison for dealing? Or for killing a cop?"

"I'm sorry. I didn't think—"

"Clearly," I spat. "His wife and kids are important to my friend Ryker. I'll let him decide what to do with you. But allow me to make one thing clear. You'll never see the light of day again, so you can save your apologies. I'm not in the habit of employing idiots." I turned, striding for the freezer door. Ryker nodded at me, a little satisfied smirk playing at his lips.

However, he ended the dealer's life, one thing was for sure.

It wouldn't be pleasant.

The dealer's screams started before the freezer door closed behind me and cut the sound off completely.

As soon as I was out of the warehouse, I climbed into the Aston and went home.

It would be the first time I did something unsavory after Ivory learned the truth. She'd given me a look when I left the house at ten at night that communicated exactly what she suspected.

I guess the good thing was that I didn't need to fear she'd think I was having an affair.

Bright side.

I drove in silence, hoping she'd be sleeping by the time I got home. If she asked, I'd tell her the truth. But I still wanted to keep her as sheltered from that side of my life as possible.

She was everything good, soft, and sweet. I loved that about her and intended to do anything I could to protect it.

Even if it meant keeping her in the dark.

When I finally pulled up in front, the house was quiet, nobody but my security moving around the property. I nodded at one of the door guards, moving into the house wordlessly. The sight of Ivory curled up in the center of my bed, tangled in the blankets, made my heart heavy.

I couldn't stand it when she tried to sleep without me, the way her brain felt the danger that came with not being wrapped up in me.

I stripped out of my clothes, showering as efficiently as I could. Even though I had done nothing, hadn't even put hands on the man, I couldn't sully Ivory with the filth of my decisions. I wore my bloodied hands like armor but would never allow them to stain her.

When I was finally clean, I climbed into bed with her, my boxer briefs on just for safety. I didn't tolerate Ivory sleeping naked if I could avoid it and didn't do it myself either. With my lifestyle, the risk of there being an emergency in the middle of the night was too great. I pulled her into me, rolling her under my body like every other night. Her brow immediately settled, relaxing into a content expression even in her sleep.

I knew exactly how Ryker felt about Calla.

Because Ivory was the only thing that made me feel human.

I breathed her in, savoring the humanity that only she could give me.

And fell asleep faster than I ever had after leaving the warehouse where all my greatest sins happened.

CHAPTER TWENTY-EIGHT

MATTEO

"Matteo. Mr. Atticus Revere is here to see you. Shall I instruct Pete to open the gate?" Donatello rarely interrupted when I was working, particularly after Ivory started spending her computer time in my office with me.

He never knew when we might be preoccupied.

I wasn't even sorry.

"Yes." I nodded, concern pooling in my stomach. There weren't many men who had my respect enough to worry me when they dropped by unannounced.

"Atticus Revere?" Ivory asked, her lips pursing as she thought her way through the name. "Why do I know that name?"

"He's a pro-football player. Quarterback for Minnesota." I stood, helping Ivory gather up her notebooks. "You can meet him, if you like, but we'll need a few moments. I'm sorry, Angel. I wasn't aware he'd be dropping by."

She shrugged. "I should start making lunch, anyway. How do you know a Pro-football player?"

"My father put him through school. Even when he was in high school, he was an incredible athlete, apparently. But his grades weren't good enough to land a scholarship. My father always loved football. Wanted to see the kid do well, give him the chance he wouldn't have if he hung around Chicago." My father had been a cold man, uncaring most of the time. But God help the man who tried to come between him and his football.

I set Ivory's things on the coffee table when Rev swaggered into the office with an easy smile. I returned it, moving forward to shake his hand. "Good to see you, Bellandi."

"You too. This is my fiancé, Ivory," I introduced, holding out an arm and inviting my angel into my side. She accepted, gladly pressing herself into me.

"Fiancé?" Rev raised an eyebrow in surprise with a huff of laughter. "I didn't think it'd been that long since we spoke."

"It hasn't," I agreed. "I suspect you'll understand one day."

"It's nice to meet a friend of Teo's," Ivory murmured, pressing a kiss to my cheek and gathering her things. "But I suspect you came to talk business. I'll get out of your hair. Would you like to stay for lunch?" she asked, bringing a smile to my face.

"You're an idiot if you say no," I informed Rev, and he chuckled in that easy, laid back manner he learned from his Southern daddy.

"She a good cook?" he drawled, and Ivory smiled at me smugly.

"A chef actually. The best, but I might be biased."

"Then shit yeah, I'll stay. Won't pass up a good, home cooked meal."

"Great," Ivory agreed with that smile that made my breath catch. She retreated from the office, closing the door behind her and letting us get down to business.

"So, what brings you by?" I asked, sitting down behind my desk and leaving Rev to get comfortable in a chair in front of it. He steepled his hands over his knees, leaning forward to look at me intently.

"I'm retiring."

"Okay," I nodded. Thirty-five wasn't an unheard-of age to retire from pro-sports, and I wasn't an unreasonable man. While Rev's contract with my father had ensured a small cut of Rev's pay came to me, I by no means required it.

I had plenty of money of my own.

"That's it?" he asked, and I chuckled.

"You've more than paid off your school loans at this point. Out of curiosity, what prompted the retirement? I thought you'd play until you dropped dead."

He sat back in his seat, a smile of disbelief flitting across his face. "My kid's in high school, man. My ex just moved to this new town in Colorado, and I ain't gonna miss another minute of his life, you know? Time to settle down."

"Admirable," I agreed. "I wish you the best of luck, Rev. You deserve it. Let's go see what my woman is cooking up."

I wasn't a good man. Was far too hard most of the time. But for a man who did everything he could to hold up his word? A man who worked his ass off and just wanted to spend time with his son?

I could pretend for an hour or two.

CHAPTER TWENTY-NINE

IVORY

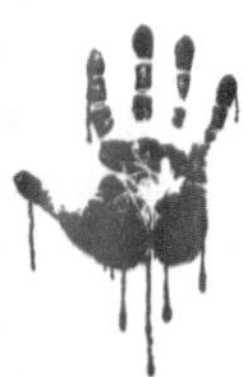

I was going crazy.

Literally.

I could feel my sanity slowly slipping away the longer I spent in that house. The more days I spent cooped up like a prisoner.

I hated feeling like the world wasn't a safe place and wondering if I'd ever look at it the same. How could I? When I was set to marry a mob boss of Chicago.

Fuck, that still sounded insane.

I shook my head, snapping out of my trance when my engagement ring clinked against the mixing bowl I pulled from the cupboard. I slipped it off my finger, setting it on the bottom shelf of the cabinet for safekeeping while I cooked.

Wearing jewelry was one of those things that I couldn't overlook, even if I rebelled against my culinary training in a lot of ways. Because it was unsanitary and made me feel gross.

Matteo had a sick sixth sense about when I took that ring off.

If I didn't think it would make me paranoid, I'd suspect him of putting a sensor in it.

But that was crazy, right?

Sure enough, he stepped into the kitchen and snatched my ring out of the cupboard in favor of shoving it back onto my finger. He stared down at me, eyes full of rage that we were about to have that damn conversation again.

Yeah, well, I was sick of it too asshole.

I tore it off my finger, shoving it back into the cupboard. "It bumps into everything," I protested. "Not to mention it's gross. Do you know what germs get on rings like that? Nope. Not happening."

Matteo's eyes narrowed on me, studying my face. "You're pissed off today. Are you feeling okay?"

I squinted back, daring him to comment. I'd been hit with sudden spells of nausea the last couple days, at the most random moments. Nothing severe, and the moments passed almost as quickly as they appeared, but I could see the control freak in Matteo rebelling against the notion that something could be wrong with me.

"I told you, I'm fine. I just need fresh air. I need to run, but you won't let me leave the fucking property!"

"Christ, Ivory. The property is huge, you act like you can't run out there."

"It's not the same," I whined. "Please, Teo."

"Not yet," he sighed. "I haven't heard shit about Adrian in over a week. I don't trust it."

"Fine," I groaned, turning back to the counter to mix. If I couldn't exercise, maybe dark chocolate brownies could fix it.

"If you're looking for a workout, I can help with that," he chuckled, stepping into my back and running his lips behind my ear.

"Oh how convenient," I laughed. "I don't think sex is safe anymore. I mean, I could get hurt, you know?" I mocked him, testing his limits. He and I both knew that sex with him wasn't such a workout for me. He put me where he wanted me and took it.

"You can run the show," he whispered, and I froze, turning to face him.

I narrowed my eyes in suspicion. "For how long?" He twisted his lips in thought, and I fought the rising chuckle. "Don't hurt yourself."

"Ten minutes," he offered.

I chuckled, "thirty."

"Fuck woman, what the Hell are you going to do to me that will take thirty minutes?"

"Should we find out?" I whispered, giggling when he turned for the stairs to our bedroom.

✳✳✳

Matteo lasted thirty minutes *on the dot* before he hauled me up from between his legs, rolled me underneath him and slid inside me. He fucked me until I came on a scream, only then finally letting himself find his own release.

"I wasn't done," I protested with a pout.

"Woman, thirty minutes was up. You were done."

"What were you, counting the minutes?" I giggled, but the serious look he leveled me with made me roar with outright laughter.

"How the fuck else do you think I managed not to come down your throat?" I bit my lip. I never liked blowjobs, never enjoyed swallowing, but something about Matteo was intoxicating, and I wanted him everywhere I could get him.

His gaze darkened, and he cursed. He rolled off me, muttering about how I would drain him dry as he went to the bathroom. I got dressed, deciding that while my jaw had been the only thing to really get a workout, I would make those brownies, anyway. By the time I made my way back to the kitchen, a tiny, delicate trinket dish sat on the counter. I bit my lip, resisting the urge to smile. Gilded in gold around the edges, it was hand painted in a marbled pattern of icy blue and sea green.

Slipping my ring off, I dropped it in the bowl before washing my hands and starting to work on my brownies. When Matteo emerged from his office a few minutes later, he whispered in my ear briefly. "Back on your finger as soon as you finish, yeah?"

I nodded with a smile.

It wasn't about the dish.

It was about him listening to me, respecting my wishes on something, even if it might seem small.

First, he let me be in charge for sex, at least for a little while, then the dish.

Matteo was learning to compromise, and I knew our relationship would be all the better for it.

***

The funny thing about boundaries is that they constantly fluctuate.

I should have known Matteo would let me leave the house if it suited his needs.

Evidently, informing my parents of our pending nuptials qualified as important enough to venture off the estate. With two bodyguards anyway.

I'd wanted Matteo to stay home. Knowing my parents' hatred for him, it seemed like the most natural solution to delivering what they would never consider to be good news.

So when I knocked on the front door, it was the only sign that my parents might get that something was off. Usually if they were expecting me, they'd leave me to let myself in. And I would.

I'd wanted to take off the engagement ring, give us some time to settle them into Matteo's unexpected presence before they were blindsided with the sight of the massive rock on my finger. Matteo had put his foot down, claiming that the woman who would soon be his wife wouldn't be hiding her engagement ring *ever.*

"Ivory, honey, what are you doing knocking—" My mother broke off, staring wide eyed at Matteo. "Mr. Bellandi."

"Matteo, please." He smiled, and I watched my mom melt in the face of it. When we'd been in high school, my mother had adored Matteo and loved the way he doted on me.

She'd been nearly as crushed as I was when he broke my heart. My father had always disliked him, as most fathers hate their daughters first real boyfriend, and the way things ended set the tone for every other relationship in the future. No one would ever be good enough for me in my father's eyes. Men only used and abused and hurt.

It was why I'd never bothered bringing anyone else home to my parents.

"Of course," my mother smiled. "Would you like to come in?"

"Please." There was no hesitation in his voice, only the slightest edge of victory. He knew as well as I did that, he'd be able to win mom over again. She was the easy one.

"Martim?" Mom hollered, stepping back to let us move into the small home they'd lived in all my life.

"What, woman?" Dad yelled back, and mom rolled her eyes at me.

"Ivory brought a friend!" We moved into the kitchen, following mom to where she was finishing up with dinner. "Can you test the pasta for me, sweetheart?"

I stepped away from Matteo, moving to the stove and scooping out a piece of spaghetti to taste. I felt mom's eyes on my finger nearly immediately and tried to ignore them. She reached over, snatching my hand in hers. "Ivory," she gasped. "You're getting married?" I nodded shyly, preparing for the tirade. Instead, she wrapped her arms around me and clung to me tightly. "Oh, my baby. I'm so happy for you!"

I gave Matteo wide eyes over her shoulder, wondering what the Hell kind of twilight zone I'd landed in. "You are?"

"Oh, sweetie, I know he hurt you. But no one else ever made you happy the way he did, and that's all I want for you. Besides, I'm ready for some grandbabies." She turned her excitement to Matteo. "You will give me grandbabies, right?"

He grinned happily. "As soon as I can manage it, Mrs. Torres."

I choked on my spit, hacking up my lungs like the lady I was. "We haven't talked about kids yet, mom."

"Well, that's all right. You have time before the wedding to work those things out." She waved us off and the other reality sat heavy on my chest.

"Actually, Mrs. Torres, we're getting married July 6th."

"But that's like a month away," she whispered, and my father chose that moment to step into the room. He narrowed his eyes on the ring on the hand my mom still clutched in hers, his face turning red.

"No offense, ma'am, but I've spent too much of my life without Ivory as my wife. I plan to remedy it as soon as possible."

"Like Hell you will," my father growled.

"Martim!" Mom hissed.

"You broke my daughter. I won't let you do it again."

"With all respect, that's not your decision to make," Matteo said calmly, matter-of-factly. He knew as well as I did that my father's approval was not something he would have for years.

"Daddy," I whispered. "I'm not broken. I never was. Broken-hearted, yes, but I wasn't broken."

He hung his head. "I watched you. For years I watched you keep every man at a distance, because of how he hurt you."

I stepped away from my mother, touching my father's shoulder affectionately. "I didn't do that because I was broken," I admitted, saying the words I had never even dared to speak to myself. But they were the truth, regardless. "I knew, even back then, that what I had with Matteo was special. I knew that I'd never find it again, because I was only capable of falling in love like that once. Not looking was just easier than being disappointed constantly."

"He hurt you," Daddy whispered.

I nodded, feeling tears sting my eyes. "He did," I agreed. "But we were just kids, Daddy. If I can forgive him, why shouldn't you give him a chance to show you why I did?"

My father nodded slowly, turning to Matteo and holding out a hand for him to shake with a sigh. "You hurt her again, and I'll have Adam make sure they never find your body."

Matteo nodded solemnly. "I'll die before I let anything hurt her ever again."

They released hands, helping mom carry things to the table while I checked the pasta.

And we settled into our slightly awkward, first-of-many family dinners.

❋❋❋

There were two more people who needed to know about the wedding, and one of them needed to be the one to approach me.

No matter how things may have turned out, what Sadie had done in calling Matteo to inform him of my date had been a betrayal.

It was one I knew I would forgive her for, but not before she apologized for it at least. My two best friends not knowing that I was getting married, when I'd always seen them every day, was proving to be too much for me. I was an emotional mess, the isolation mixed with the frantic questions from the wedding planner at odd times throughout the day, were going to my head. I needed a brief reminder of someone who had always been a constant in my life.

So naturally, I took to harassing Duke like a maniac. I called him five times a day, even knowing I looked like a crazy person. He'd ignored my calls and texts for long enough, and it was time for both of us to grow up and face the conversation like adults so we could work on mending our friendship.

He'd finally caved, relenting to my emotional plea over the phone for him to come to the estate. I'd completely expected him to refuse to meet me here, but given the security threat from Adrian, Duke seemed more concerned with my safety than with his pride. I figured that had to be a good sign, coming from my hotheaded friend.

Still, when Donatello escorted Duke into the kitchen where I stood wringing my hands in nervousness, the cool expression on his face made me flinch. His normally perfectly styled dirty blond hair was a mess, his smooth face covered in stubble. He shrugged, glancing down at the work clothes he didn't normally wear out of his studio. "I've been working," he explained. "Turns out getting your heart stomped on is good for the muse."

I winced, stepping around the island to stand directly in front of him. "I'm sorry," I said, throat tightening with the threat of tears. "I don't want to hurt you."

He stared down at me, cornflower blue eyes tormented. "Then don't. We can leave town until things die down. Go somewhere Adrian can't touch you." He reached out a hand covered in cuts and scars, calloused and rough, to touch my cheek. I leaned into it briefly, drawing in a deep breath to try to gather my strength to deal with the outcome of my admission.

"We're getting married," I said, steeling my spine.

I watched as his brow furrowed, realizing that given his offer to run away with me, those words had been insensitively vague, but I didn't know what else to say as he stared at me. I stretched up my left hand, taking his hand in mine and squeezing it supportively. I knew the moment he felt the band around my finger, watched as the confusion melted off his face. His eyes landed on the ring, his lip trembling briefly as shock widened his eyes. "You're *marrying him?*"

"In July."

"Ivory." He croaked, leaning down to press his forehead to mine. "How am I supposed to deal with this? I can't watch you marry him, sweetheart. You're making a mistake."

"Then it was my mistake to make," I whispered back, hating the way his eyes hardened at my words. He pulled his hand back, taking his face from mine and stepping away.

"You don't know what he's capable of. He's—"

"I know everything," I said shortly. I might not have been privy to all the details, but I knew *more* than I ever wanted to know about Matteo's businesses.

"You what? Do you hear yourself? The Ivory I know would never be okay sharing her body with a criminal! He hurts people for a living," Duke rasped, staring at me in a way I'd never felt from him.

Judged.

Less.

Somehow, he'd built up this fantasy in his head where I was perfect.

I wasn't. I was a mess, a shell of a woman too afraid to love, because no one would ever live up to the real deal.

No one would ever be Matteo Bellandi.

"You're one of my best friends, Duke. I don't want to lose you, but I won't let you treat me like there's something wrong with me. I love him. I have always loved him, and you know that. What he does for a living"—I paused, shrugging and flopping my ass onto one stool at the island.—"It's not ideal, but I'm not doing it. My part as his wife is just to love him, and I'd be lying to myself if I said that having his love wasn't enough for me."

"Christ, Ivory. I've *never* been your friend. I've always been waiting for you to come to your senses and *see* me."

I closed my eyes, drawing in a ragged breath. "One day, you will meet someone who makes you feel the way I feel with Matteo, and suddenly you'll understand. Finding *that* is what you should have been doing all these years, not waiting on someone who'd already found her person."

"I'm so sorry I wasted my time then. Hopefully this other woman is too smart to fall for some guy's bullshit. Are you so naïve to think he loves you? Christ."

"I do," Matteo's voice announced from the hall that led to his office. I looked to him, watching as Duke spun quickly to face the man he'd always treated like an enemy. In high school, I hadn't really understood.

But hindsight was everything. Duke had been jealous, chasing a relationship he'd never have for over a decade.

"If you did, you'd let her go. She's better off without you," Duke accused.

"Hmm," Matteo mused. "And why do you think I spent so many years without her in my life?" Duke's head jolted, like me, he never could have guessed that Matteo might have been anything other than a cheating dog back then. "As much as you might hate me, I understand it. Losing Ivory is like losing the sun. You had a decade to claim her, Duke. A decade with me out of the picture where you could have made Ivory yours. You could have been married, started a family in that time. But you never told her how you feel, and that's because you *knew* she didn't feel the same."

Duke winced but surprised me by nodding solemnly.

"I want you in our lives. I want you to be Uncle Duke to my kids. Please," I begged. "Don't make me choose."

Duke turned, crushing me into his chest and hugging me tightly. Lips touched the hair on my head as I broke down in tears. "I won't make you choose, sweetheart," he whispered. Matteo let him hold me as I cried, but I felt his eyes on us every moment.

Thinking. Calculating.

Protecting me always.

CHAPTER THIRTY

IVORY

"I'm all for you working here whenever you want, you know that," Matteo grunted, and I smirked into my laptop, not even bothering to glance up at him. "But for the love of God, could you let me work, woman?"

I broke into giggles, crossing my ankles over the arm of the couch where I'd draped them to give Matteo a perfect view as my sundress rode up my thighs. "I don't know what you're talking about. I'm minding my own business, working myself."

He gave me that panty-melting grin that literally no woman in the world would be immune to. "Is that so?"

"Mhmm," I hummed in response, crossing and recrossing my legs so that my thighs rubbed together in a desperate bid for friction. I didn't know what the Hell was wrong with me, but I'd wanted sex constantly in the few days since we'd told my parents about our engagement. I almost felt bad for Matteo.

"I can't have sex with you again, Angel. You've drained me dry." I pouted at him, finally turning to face him and the unbelievable happiness written plainly on his face.

I smiled back at him. "I can't help that I want you so much. Maybe you should stop working out. Eat more of my brownies," I teased.

"Oh, so you'll stop jumping my bones every ten minutes if I lose my abs. Is that what you're saying?" I chuckled, setting my laptop on the coffee table and prancing over to plop my butt on his desk in front of him.

"Like you wouldn't be upset if I changed my body," I accused.

"Angel, I love you. Your body is a bonus, yes, but I'll love you however you come."

I tried not to melt, because an admission like that for a man like Matteo, who could have anyone, meant so much to me. "Hmm, it's a good thing, really. Marriage is forever."

"It is," Matteo agreed, capturing my lips with a sweet kiss.

The door opened behind us and Donatello cleared his throat. "I'm sorry to interrupt."

"What do you need, Don?" Matteo asked, leveling the man with a stern look. I knew Donatello had never had to knock before I'd come to the estate, and everyone was having some adjustments to the changes in rules regarding privacy. I forgave him for the awkward moments when he forgot, but Matteo was a little less lenient.

"Ms. Hicks is here for Ms. Torres. Should I have the guards let her in?"

I glanced to Matteo, daring him to say no. I knew at the club in his anger he'd told Sadie she wouldn't see me. I'd honestly mostly forgotten about it in all the drama that ensued after that, given her betrayal and the fact that we weren't speaking, anyway. Him refusing to allow me to see Sadie would violate my trust, another heavy-handed attempt to control me, and with the way he looked at me, he knew that. He knew if we would have a real chance at this marriage, then I needed to make my own decisions so long as they didn't endanger me. "Do you want to see her?" Matteo asked me on a whisper.

I nodded to both men, giving Matteo a relieved smile that he'd made the right choice. "I'll let the guards know," Donatello said, bowing out of the room to give us a moment of privacy.

"You and me, Angel. I know Sadie comes along with you, just don't let her talk you out of this." It almost sounded like an insecurity, a question of whether my friend could convince me that the relationship we were building was unstable. There was a time when a stranger could have convinced me it wouldn't last, but that time had gone.

Somewhere along the line, I'd started to believe that Matteo loved me as much as I loved him—needed me to feel whole. Maybe it was in the way he clung to me at night and slept later than he should so he knew I could rest peacefully. Maybe it was the way he had called my Uncle to let him know he'd made things official and invite him to the wedding. Maybe it was the way he'd agreed to bury the hatchet with Duke so he could be a part of our lives, despite Matteo's possessiveness.

Whatever it was, I knew without a doubt that it was *real.*

"Just yell if you need anything," he murmured, leaning into my space again to give me an affectionate kiss.

"Always." I stood from the desk, smoothing his papers for him and retreating from the office. By the time I made it to the kitchen, Sadie sat in one stool waiting and Donatello was nowhere to be seen. She'd taken Smaug from the tank Don had set up for him against the wall where the kitchen connected with the dining room, snuggling him in the way she didn't like me to see. Nobody could resist the tricky little bastard. Even Matteo was growing fond of him, and Don was a goner.

"So, this is the great Bellandi Estate," she sighed, eyes darting around the room as she took in the pristine, gourmet kitchen.

"Did you come to sightsee?" I said, every bit of the bitterness I still felt over her betrayal coming through those words. It was enough to make her wince.

"You know I didn't," she sighed, finally turning to look at me. When our eyes connected, relief seemed to flood through her. "I was half worried I'd come, and you'd be miserable. Heaven knows that he's intense and controlling enough to smother you."

I crossed my arms over my chest to stare her down. "And yet, you called him when I went on a date. Did you call Duke too?"

"Yes," she admitted. "You did that thing where you just bury your head in the sand and keep digging your hole! You needed someone to force you to deal with the problems instead of just pretending they didn't exist."

I sat down on the stool next to her with a sigh. "I needed to do that," I agreed. "But that wasn't your decision to make. I should have been able to come to that on my own."

"I'm sorry," she whispered. "I wanted to tell you a hundred times, but you're never home anymore—"

"Matteo moved me in here the day after the club," I sighed. I didn't want to remember those days and the tumultuous storm of emotions. Having my will stripped away, locked up in a glorified prison, was not a feeling I wanted to relive.

"God, I'm sorry, Ive. I'm sorry it hurt you, but you look good. You look happy. So I don't regret it. The way he looks at you...." she trailed off with a secret little smile. "I hope one day I find someone who looks at me like that."

"Intense? Like he wants to eat you alive? Is that what you mean?" I giggled, and the tension broke as she burst into laughter along with me.

"I guess so, yeah. Things are good?"

I grinned. "Yeah, you could say that. He's...intense. I don't think I've ever met someone as strong-willed as Matteo, like everyone in his vicinity just has to do everything he says. I know he has power, and that's part of it, but there's also just that something about him, you know?"

She laughed. "Yeah, he's dangerous. Not just because of the title, but he just gives it off."

I fiddled with the ring on my finger, turning to face her finally with tears in my eyes. "It's a good thing you finally came to your senses and came to apologize. You were running out of time to pick out a Maid of Honor dress."

"I was, what? What?!" she shrieked, snatching my hand to stare at the ring. "You're getting married?"

"July 6th," I grinned.

"Holy shit!" I could hear Matteo's chuckle drift in from the office.

"Eavesdropping creep!" I hollered at him, and the chuckle transformed into a roar of laughter. "Come on, let's go for a walk outside where the stalker can't listen in."

I took her out the front door, going around the rose garden on the side of the house. I'd never spent much time in it, mostly just run past it in the mornings. I knew I'd need to remedy that, because it was gorgeous. "So, tell me about the sex. I need to live vicariously through you. I'm in a dry spell."

I rolled my eyes, Sadie had always been a little more open to casual sex than I had, but the recent dry spell had lasted six months. Her opportunity for sex hadn't changed. What had changed was her willingness and desire for something more, but she wasn't ready to hear that. "It's pretty much constant. I mean, I always knew we were attracted to each other, obviously. But lately I swear all he has to do is look at me, and I'm dragging him off to bed."

Sadie laughed her ass off. Her voice was teasing when she spoke. "You're sure you aren't pregnant, right?"

I smiled back at her, even though I knew my body froze solid. "Of course not. You know I'm on the pill."

Except I'd been due for my period the day Matteo proposed. I'd spotted a teeny bit a few days after, so hadn't thought anything of it. I'd gotten so wrapped up in the wedding and being happy that I never realized it didn't come.

"You okay?" Sadie asked. I wanted to hide it, wanted to pretend that my world wasn't crashing down around me, but I couldn't. I had to know, and since I couldn't leave the house, she was my only chance.

"No. I don't think so," I whispered.

"Woah, what happened?" Sadie was suddenly in my face, but I forced a smile in case one of Matteo's men were watching us. I didn't doubt it in the slightest.

"I missed my period. I didn't—I didn't even realize."

Sadie stilled next to me, her face breaking out in a grin. "Holy shit!" she whispered. "You're pregnant! I'm going to be an Auntie."

"Would you be quiet? We don't know for sure—"

"Honey, when has your period ever so much as been late?" Her voice turned more somber when she realized I wasn't as excited as her.

"Can you go to the pharmacy? Get me a test? I don't want Matteo to know until I *know*."

"I'll be right back, okay?" I nodded, and she walked calmly to her car. I knew Sadie enough to know by the tensing of her shoulders she wanted to run. She wanted to fucking sprint, but she wouldn't risk outing the secret before I was ready.

Matteo telling my mother he wanted kids soon was a very different thing than me getting pregnant before we were even married. He would kill me. I couldn't imagine there hadn't been situations in the past where women tried to trap him with a baby. Even in high school, people joked about it.

As soon as she left, I made an excuse to Matteo that she just had to run a quick errand and would be right back. I faked a smile the entire time, leaving him to his work meeting with Lino and Donatello in favor of baking my stresses away.

✳✳✳

Sadie came back, disguising her purchase with a bag full of all my favorite chocolates. "I thought you might need them while we wait," she blurted, and I gave her a grin before breaking out into laughter when her eyes landed on the double chocolate chip cookies waiting on the tray to go into the oven. She brought her purse into the bathroom with her to wash her hands, conveniently slipping back into the kitchen without it.

God, I loved this girl.

"I'm just going to use the bathroom," I said after I put the cookies in the oven. "Make yourself at home."

"Always do," she grinned, catching my hand briefly as I made my way to the door. "No matter what happens, we'll figure it out, okay?" I nodded at her, tears pooling in my eyes.

I already knew what the test would say. All the symptoms, the missed period, every thing was a glaring point of evidence against me.

I couldn't believe I'd missed it.

So when I closed myself in the bathroom, I tore open the test without hesitation. I'd chugged two bottles of water in the brief fifteen minutes it had taken Sadie to run to the pharmacy.

Because I was desperate to know the truth.

Whoever decided that it was a great idea to pee on a stick was an asshole.

Sadie had even been generous enough to buy me an ergonomic one.

Because I was obviously at risk of developing carpal tunnel in the five to ten seconds I had to pee on the damn thing.

I rolled my eyes as I capped it and set it on the counter, proceeding to wash my hands too thoroughly. I counted in my head, an endless cycle of seconds that never seemed to end.

It didn't seem possible that two minutes could be so long.

It brought me back to all those speeches in high school, the torment of required time frames when all you wanted to do was race through the words as quickly as possible and get it over with.

When I finally counted to 120, I did it again. Just to be safe, I mean, who knew how fast I'd counted? Right?

With a few deep breaths, I looked in the mirror, fixating on how pale my face looked compared to the deep wood tones and amber tiles. I hated this bathroom, and if Matteo and I made it work, I decided I'd immediately change it. I spent more time in that bathroom, positioned between the kitchen and Matteo's office, throughout the day than I did in the gorgeous master bathroom upstairs.

Finally deciding I couldn't distract myself anymore, I glanced down at the test on the counter.

Digital, it left absolutely nothing up to interpretation.

Not with the way the word glared up at me in stark, bold letters.

Pregnant.

Even having known what the test would say, I swallowed my sob. I'd never felt so conflicted, never wanted something so badly despite knowing it had the potential to ruin my relationship with Matteo. He was all I'd wanted for so long; it was completely disarming to realize that for the very first time, there was something I wanted more.

This baby. Even knowing it was nothing more than a tiny collection of cells in my womb, even knowing there was likely nothing resembling a baby to it yet, I wanted that baby more than anything.

I loved it in a way I'd never known could be possible.

I made sure the test was clean, carrying it out to Sadie.

"Oh my God," she whispered, her eyes filling with tears of joy. I nodded back at her, feeling beyond happy. "He's an idiot if he isn't over the moon, but I don't think you'll have that problem," she whispered, taking the purse I carried out to her.

"I hope you're right."

"You going to tell him now?" I nodded. "Okay, call me if you need me." She crushed me to her in a tight hug that I felt in my soul. No matter what happened, I'd always have Sadie.

And I hoped Duke.

I'd be okay.

I just hoped I'd still have Matteo.

✳✳✳

As soon as she left, I took a few deep breaths and started my way down the hallway, pregnancy test still in hand. It was fairly unusual for Matteo to work with the door open, let alone have meetings, but the light streaming through the crack in the door was there, regardless. I realized with a start that I'd been the last one to leave the office, and it must have been me who left it open. I hoped they hadn't heard any snippets of my conversation with Sadie, but my hopes dashed when I heard Matteo's annoyed tone as he snapped at Lino.

"I don't understand what's taking so long!"

"These things take time, Matteo," Donatello soothed him, that fatherly tone to his voice. "We've talked about this. It will happen. You're both young and in your prime. Without the pills, you just have to be patient." I froze in my steps, the first inkling of something being horribly wrong making me listen to know for sure.

"How long has it been since you swapped out her pills for placebos?" Lino whispered to him. "It can take months. Some people are just less fertile than others."

I gasped, covering my mouth quickly as my body started to shake.

It couldn't possibly be what it sounded like.

There was no way Matteo could do something like that to me.

And yet, it made too much sense. I wasn't naïve. I knew that the pill wasn't foolproof, but I'd never so much as had a pregnancy scare before. To get pregnant within weeks of Matteo returning to my life?

"Six weeks," Matteo grunted in response to Lino's question, and it felt like something within me shriveled and died. Any chance we'd had at having an open and honest marriage, any chance I'd felt I might have had where he respected the boundaries of a normal relationship.

Just gone.

Having heard enough, I shoved open the door and stepped into the office. Three sets of shocked eyes turned my way, Matteo's icy blue ones closing briefly as he clenched his jaw. "Please tell me it's not true," I whispered, watching as his eyes drifted down to the pregnancy test still clutched in my hand.

"Get out," Matteo muttered, and neither Lino nor Donatello put up a fight, taking the opportunity to happily flee what was no doubt about to devolve into something ugly. "Angel," he murmured softly, stepping around his desk and looking like he might touch me. He reached out a hand, slipping the test from me so he could read the damned word that changed our lives.

That he'd changed without my consent.

"Did you change out my birth control pills?" I whispered, and his eyes darted up to look at me finally, so much joy swimming in them as he clutched the test tightly. "Please, Teo. Tell me you didn't do this." My voice broke, devolving into a sob.

He reached for me, cupping my cheek in his strong hand. "I can't," he whispered solemnly despite the happy little smile that continued to tip his lips up. His eyes went to my stomach, and his hand followed. He stroked it over my dress, acting like he could already feel the life growing inside me.

The life he'd put there, without a single thought for what I might want. "How could you do this?"

I stepped back, and he snapped a tight jaw and weary eyes back up to me. "I did what I had to do. I told you, I'm not wasting any more time. We both want a family together."

"We never talked about it!" I hissed. "I never gave you any sign that I'm ready to be a mother! What if I didn't even want the baby?"

"I know you, Ivory. I knew as soon as you were pregnant, there would be nothing anyone could do to keep you from giving that child everything. Please, just try to understand—"

"When did you do it?" I asked, shaking my head and closing my eyes. I couldn't listen to him rant about how he'd known I would want this. I tried to think of what our relationship was like six weeks ago, but all I could think was that it was different. I fought the relationship at every turn.

"The morning after you first spent the night here, I saw your pills when I went to get your phone. That was when I put it in motion, and I replaced them within a few days."

"That was the first time we had sex," I snorted in disbelief. "You fucked me once and thought it entitles you to knocking me up? What is wrong with you?"

I ran my hands over my face, trying not to see the way his face tightened, that familiar possession running over his features as he stared down at me. He stepped into my space, and I winced at the feeling of his chest touching mine. "You have always been mine," he growled. "I wanted you bound to me in every way. I have done nothing but *be* clear that I would not lose you this time. I wanted you to be the mother of my children. I knew that in high school! Now, I'm a thirty-year-old man. I made it fucking happen, because I'll be damned if I waited for you to come to your senses. If I'd left you to come to terms with our relationship on your own and hadn't pushed you every step of the way, we'd have been forty before we got married."

I winced, stepping back out of his space and shaking my head. "You're wrong. If I trusted my instincts, we wouldn't have gotten here at all. And all you've done with this is prove those instincts right! I can't trust you, and I won't marry a man I can't trust, Teo," I whispered, moving to slide the ring off my finger.

"Don't you fucking dare," he hissed, making me stop. I turned on a huff, striding through the house to pack a bag. "Ivory!" he yelled, behind me. I passed Scar in the hallway, and he gave me wide eyes at whatever pissed off expression he saw on my face.

"We're leaving in ten minutes," I told him.

"Uh, is that cleared with the boss?"

"Fuck your boss," I spat. "So help me, Paolo, if you don't take me I will make your life a living Hell." I raced up the steps to the master, ignoring the sound of Matteo thundering after me.

"What the Hell are you doing?" he asked, hauling ass into the bedroom behind me as I hauled out my suitcase.

"I'm leaving. I can't do this with you." I tried to focus on the angry. Tried not to break down into tears as his betrayal felt like it stabbed right over the same scar tissue from the last time he'd ruined everything we had.

Sniffling against the tears making my throat ache, I ignored him in favor of shoving random clothes into my suitcase. "You can't leave," he whispered, the first sign of real regret coloring his tone.

"I can't even look at you right now. What you did, I—I don't know if I can ever get over that."

"You don't want the baby?" he whispered.

I spun around, staring him down fiercely. "Of course, I want the baby! I don't want you!"

He flinched, as if those words hurt him as much as I'd intended. But they couldn't because he didn't care what I wanted. "You don't mean that," he murmured, stepping into my space slowly, hesitantly.

"You hurt me," I whispered. "You promised you wouldn't hurt me again."

His face crumpled. "I'm sorry, Angel. I'm so sorry I hurt you. I just needed you to be mine completely. I couldn't bear the thought of losing you. Don't go. Just stay, and we can figure it out."

"You have to let me go home. I just want to go home for a while and think things through."

He sighed, nodding reluctantly and pressing his forehead against mine. "Take Scar with you."

"Okay," I whispered, turning and zipping my suitcase hastily.

"Ivory?" he asked when I reached the bedroom door. "I love you, Angel. I love the baby. More than anything else in this world. Take some time, think things through. But you'll come home. I won't accept anything else."

I swallowed, darting out of the room and down the stairs. Somehow, Scar knew I was cleared to leave, and he hustled me to the car where he let me break in silence.

CHAPTER THIRTY-ONE

IVORY

The sound of my doorbell was jarring against the classical music playing in the background.

I hated it, but Sadie had read it was good for the baby.

I fought down the vomit that threatened at the smell of bacon as I made Scar breakfast. I didn't want him to know that cooking has become a chore. That I couldn't even enjoy that anymore, because the smell of food made my stomach roll. I couldn't have him reporting how ill I'd gotten to Matteo.

Despite hiding it, I knew the moment the doorbell rang, knew my time was ending.

The problem was, I was no closer to deciding what to do with myself. No closer to deciding if I'd ever be able to forgive Matteo for what he'd done. My hand rubbed my stomach out of habit, as if the baby could give me all the answers.

It surprised me he'd given me a few days. I didn't know if that was a sign that he was having second thoughts, or if I should look at it as a gift he gave me out of true remorse.

Scar nodded at me when he looked through the hole in the door, confirming what I already knew. I nodded back, even though I knew it was pointless. Scar would always do what Matteo told him to, no matter how I might care for the broody man. He'd quickly joined the ranks of people I love, and it hurt to know that when it was all said and done, I'd always be second to Matteo.

It shouldn't have hurt. He'd been Matteo's first.

But everything hurt.

He opened the door, leveling the man behind it with a glare I didn't expect and standing directly in the way so he couldn't enter. "Are you here to fuck it up again?" I startled, removing the bacon to a paper towel lined plate and turning off the stove in disbelief. I'd never heard Scar talk to Matteo with anything but respect.

"If you're stupid enough to stand between me and my woman, then maybe I need to think about cutting you loose. I don't employ stupid people," Matteo warned, and then his footsteps came into the house and the sound of the door closing followed. I didn't turn around, didn't want to look at him.

I wasn't ready. Not for this.

I still didn't know what I was doing.

"How are you feeling?" he asked, and I heard him tap his fingers on the island behind me.

He was too close, only a couple steps away, and even just the vague sense of him being there was enough to weaken my resolve.

I missed him.

So fucking much I wanted to strangle myself. There had to be something wrong with me. "She throws up about a hundred times a day," Scar answered helpfully, and I winced.

I guessed I wasn't as stealthy as I thought I was.

"Shut up and eat your breakfast," I teased, putting a plate in front of his usual seat at the island. He took it, digging into his eggs with vigor.

"Is that true?" Matteo asked, and I finally had no choice but to face him. The dark circles under his eyes came as a surprise, I'd never seen Matteo look anything other than perfect. It shouldn't have surprised me though, they were flawless copies of mine. The return to not sleeping well had not been kind to me.

"They should rename morning sickness something like all day misery," I answered with a little smile. It never stopped, even as early in the pregnancy as I was. I really hoped that wasn't an indicator of a rough pregnancy.

"Have you been to the doctor? Did they say there was anything they can do?" he asked, and his eyes darted down to my stomach where the island hid it.

"My appointment isn't until next week, but it's normal, Teo," I whispered. "Some women don't have morning sickness at all, and others just get hit hard."

"Come home, Angel." He rounded the island until nothing separate us but a few inches of space. "Let me take care of you. Let Don do the cooking. It can't be helping."

I eyed Scar warily, noticing the tension in his body. I knew it would be easier for him if I returned to the estate, knew he wouldn't be so stressed about making sure I was safe.

I wanted to go home, but how could I just forgive something that was so unforgivable?

The way he'd broken my trust, it wasn't something I would have tolerated from anyone else. I didn't have the answer to the question that I had to ask myself. Did I love him enough to forgive it?

The thought of a life without him was terrifying, going back to being that void of all the feelings only he gave me. "I am home," I said instead, and watched from the corner of my eye as Scar's entire body locked solid.

"Your home is with me," Matteo scolded, stepping into my space until he wrapped his arms around me.

"I'm not ready for that. I'm not ready to forgive you."

"So come home and let me prove to you I'll take care of both of you! Christ, Ivory. I just want to give you the world." He whispered the words, and Scar took that as his sign to abandon his plate in favor of doing a perimeter check.

"I don't want you to take care of me! I never wanted that."

"Then what do you want, Angel? Tell me, and I'll give it to you. I swear!" I almost melted at the desperation in his voice, almost caved into the way he curled into me like the possibility of losing me brought him to his knees.

"I've never chosen you," I whispered, finally feeling like I had the words to explain the conundrum that tore me in two. "Every decision, every step to be together or not be together, you've made it. You decided we were going on a date in high school, and that was that. Then you dumped me, and I had no say in that either. When you claimed me again, you didn't care that I told you I hated you. You didn't give a shit that I was terrified of you and wanted to run for the hills. You pushed and pushed and moved me into your house against my will. And I forgave it," I whispered. "I tolerated it. But now, you took away my right to choose this baby. I'll never have that moment where the man I love tells me he wants to have a baby. I'll never get to make love to you and hope that *that* was the moment we made a child together. So now what do I have? I'm just a woman living a life that she didn't *choose*, Matteo! I want to choose you. That's what I want."

He pressed his forehead to mine gently, his face scrunching up in pain. "So I can't pick you up and drag you home?" I chuckled at his attempt at what I assumed was a joke, but I never could tell with Matteo.

"No," I sighed back, letting him press his lips to mine softly. I resisted the urge to lean into him. It conflicted me enough for both of us, the last thing he needed was me showing him just how desperate I was for him.

He nodded, letting his hands touch my belly. "I'll be back to check on you in a couple of days. Call me if you need me for anything." Then with a deep sigh, he turned and strode out of my house. Scar replaced him within minutes.

He went back to eating his eggs even though they were cold. "You okay?" he asked.

"You want fresh eggs?" I asked him, ignoring the million-dollar question that I felt a little closer to answering.

"Nah. These are fine." I shook my head and turned to scrub my pans.

***

That cleaning continued. I'd made the switch to all-natural cleaners we picked up at the store when we'd fled Matteo's house. Just enough supplies for us to survive.

And for me to clean relentlessly, if we were being honest. I didn't have enough cookware to go crazy, had no baking dishes to speak of. If I'd thought Matteo wouldn't have had a coronary at the prospect of me bringing more belongings to the home, he didn't want me in, I might have asked for some. But that was not a battle I thought worth fighting.

My thoughts plagued me as I scrubbed, wondering if I would *ever* really have a choice where Matteo was concerned. Obviously, the choice with the baby was gone. It was coming whether I was ready for it or not.

But if I decided that I didn't want to marry Matteo? Didn't want to raise our child together?

I knew he'd take away my choice again. He made it very clear that he would do whatever it took to have me as *his* in every sense of the word.

Did it really count as having a choice, if I'd lose the opportunity to choose if I made the wrong decision?

I didn't think so, and that thought plagued me.

Could I raise a child with a mobster? Could I bring up a child in a world as dangerous as the one Matteo inhabited, where I couldn't leave the estate without a bodyguard for safety?

It seemed impossible. It wasn't the life I wanted for my baby, and as much as I might love Matteo, my child's life had to be the most important consideration.

But the only way for the baby to be safe from Matteo's enemies would be to leave Chicago, sever all ties with Matteo permanently. No one could ever know he had a child.

And that made my heart hurt.

Car doors slamming outside made Scar's head snap to attention, and he instantly went alert. "Call Matteo," he ordered as more cars slammed. I grabbed my cell, dialing Matteo quickly as Scar pulled his gun from his holster. My fingers shook, but I dialed him as quickly as possible. "Get down, Ivory." Scar whispered, going to the window to peek outside.

"Angel?" Matteo said over the line.

"Matteo, there are people here—" I started, but Scar snatched the phone.

"Adrian and about a dozen men are outside. Ivory is going out the back," he snapped, handing the phone back to me. "Go, Ivory. Keep your head down but fucking run." Matteo's voice shouted in the phone, but I stared up at Scar in horror.

"I won't leave you!" I protested.

"Yes, you will," he announced, touching a hand to my stomach delicately. "Go,

Ivory," he whispered, shoving me toward the back hall that led to the back of my house. I scurried, keeping my head down so no one would see me through the windows. The phone in my hand echoed with the furious sound of Matteo's voice calling for me, and I brought it up to my ear.

"Teo," I whispered as the first tear fell in my terror.

"Fuck, *Cara mia.* We're on our way. Just get out of there."

"I love you. I'm sorry. I'm so sorry," I whispered as I hit the back door.

"Don't you dare. I love you, Angel. I'm coming for you, and I'm never letting you out of my sight again, you understand me?" The door crashed open, the sound of it carrying through the house. I was out the back door when the sound of yelling carried through it, followed by gunshots. "Fuck! Ivory!" Matteo shouted, but I didn't answer.

With tears streaming down my face, I got to my feet and ran through the yard. "I've got her!" a male voice shouted, and I sobbed.

Weight hit my side, and I went flying and landed sprawled out on my back with my hands curled around my stomach protectively. "Matteo!" I cried, reaching for the phone I dropped.

A male hand reached down, plucking it off the ground and I followed it up to stare into Adrian's crazed, dark eyes. "Goodbye, Matteo." He grinned, dropping the phone to the ground and stomping on it until it crunched, and the call disconnected. I gaped up at him in horror. "Hello, beautiful. Fancy seeing you here." I started to stand, getting to my knees warily and eyeing him.

"Adrian, what are you doing?" I asked, and then he was wrapping a hand around my upper arm and dragging me through the yard. "Help!" I screamed. "Somebody!"

He made no move to stop me. Didn't seem to care that someone would have heard the commotion. He hurried me through the house, because there was one person, I knew he wouldn't want to face.

Matteo.

God, what if I never saw him again?

Bodies scattered my living room, and the sight of Scar lying motionless among them was enough to make me collapse despite his grip on me. I barely touched my fingers to his face, shaking at the sight of all the blood covering his chest. "Scar?" I asked, hoping like Hell he'd wake up and just look at me. "No. No, please," I begged, fighting off Adrian's arms as they wrapped around my waist. "No! Let go of me!" I shouted, twisting to claw at his face. When a nail broke the skin of his cheek, those eyes darkened, and I froze in horror. I didn't even see the fist he aimed for my temple.

All I knew was the sudden explosion of pain.

And then black.

CHAPTER THIRTY-TWO

MATTEO

My blood roared in my ears, drowning out the sounds of Lino shouting at me from the driver's seat as he navigated through traffic. My men's SUV's surrounded us, racing for the only thing that mattered in my life.

My angel and my unborn child.

In the hands of that mother-fucking sadistic piece of shit.

I should have never allowed her to leave the estate. I should have never *touched* her.

"Matteo!" Lino shouted, finally drawing my attention away from the dead silence coming through my phone. "Talk to me, man. What's going on?"

"He has her," I answered, feeling a deadly, killing calm settle over me. I knew it wouldn't last, knew that as soon as I saw for myself that Ivory was gone from her house the rage would return.

But until that moment I embraced the monster. Let it take over me as I coordinated with my men.

The second we pulled up in front of Ivory's house, the house I'd left only an hour before, I was out of the car before it even stopped. "Matteo!" Lino shouted, throwing the car into park and following me. I didn't know what he was so worried about, it was obvious that Adrian and his men were gone. Not a single vehicle remained, just random bodies left to rot on Ivory's floor as I threw myself in the open front door.

In the middle of the chaos, Scar laid there—entirely too still. Lino went to him, checking for vitals, but a few of the men went to check the rest of the house. "Ivory!" I yelled, racing for the backyard, unsure if it should relieve me that I didn't find Ivory laying there.

She was alive but being with Adrian was far from a blessing. As soon as he put his hands on her, she'd wish she was dead.

He would hurt her. He would *break* her.

I couldn't let it happen.

Lino stepped out into the yard, looking around in dismay. "We'll find her," he said.

"She has a tracker," I reminded him, never more grateful that I'd disrespected Ivory's wishes than in that moment. "Get the guys ready."

"Scar's alive," he said, making my head jolt in shock. "Riddled with bullets, but somehow the stubborn fuck is still alive. Bruno and Marino took him to Doc."

"Good," I nodded, pulling out my phone and opening the app that would show me Ivory's location. They were still moving, but it would take me time to assemble enough of a team to stage an invasion wherever they landed. "I want every man we have."

"You've got it. I'll call Don, get him on it too." I gave a last nod, calling the one other man I wanted at my side. The one man I could trust to make sure Adrian suffered a very slow, painful death while I tended to my angel.

As much as I wanted to deliver his punishment personally, I knew Ryker would be a far worse punishment than I could ever dream to be.

And that would have to be enough.

"Yeah?" he asked when he answered the phone. Simon stood at the front door and nodded to me as I made my way back to the car, hopping in the driver's seat to be ready to go with me wherever I went.

"Adrian Ricci took Ivory. I need you to give him the worst death imaginable," I hissed into the phone as I made my way back inside her mostly empty house.

"When and where?"

"Get your ass to her house," I said, rattling off her address. "We're mobilizing now." I kicked one of his men's bodies for good measure, wanting to make even their corpses suffer for the part they played in taking Ivory from me. The number of them was a sign of just how hard Scar had fought to protect her, taking out half a dozen men on his own before they took him down.

"On my way."

CHAPTER THIRTY-THREE

IVORY

I woke up.

Slowly.

Disoriented.

The pillow beneath my face wasn't mine. It didn't smell like Matteo, and the fabric of the pillowcase was far too luxurious to be the cheap set I'd picked up at the store with Scar. My face throbbed as I moved, and my head swam the moment I peeled myself off the pillow.

Deep wood-paneled walls stared back at me from the edges of the room, a navy comforter draped over me. I touched the side of my head, wincing at the pain radiating from there and the dried blood that seemed so coarse against my fingers.

I ignored my swimming head, shoving the comforter off me and got to my feet slowly. I swallowed my nausea as my stomach rolled once I was standing, determined not to vomit until I figured out where I was.

The first door I came to was a bathroom, and I stared into the mirror at the huge, mottled bruise at my temple that covered my brow bone and the top of my cheekbone. The blood seemed to be from a minor cut, and I ignored it in favor of finding my way out of the bedroom.

Seeing the bruise, I knew without a doubt Adrian must have knocked me out. Everything came back to me in a rush of panic.

Scar was dead.

I swallowed back my tears, knowing I needed to find a way out of that sadistic fuck's home. That was what Scar would want. I could mourn him once I was safe, could tell him how sorry I was that my stupid decisions had gotten him killed.

I liked to think he would forgive me.

But I didn't think I'd ever forgive myself.

The door opened quietly, and I slipped out into the hall. For once, I was pleased my feet were bare. It let me slip through the house silently. The hall was an endless parade of closed doors, and I found my way to the staircase easily. I sprinted down it, the front door in sight.

I did not understand what might wait for me outside. I couldn't imagine Adrian would lock me somewhere and leave me unguarded.

All I knew was that I had to try.

My hand was only an inch from the front door when Adrian's voice made my skin crawl. "Going somewhere, my love?" he asked, and I froze in place. I spun to face him, noting that he looked more manic, more crazed than normal. His normally slicked black hair was a mess, sticking up at all angles like he couldn't keep from taking his frustrations out on it. "Ah, sweetheart. Your beautiful face," he whispered, stepping toward me with an expression of concern. Like he hadn't been the one to hurt me. "I wish I hadn't needed to hurt you. I never want to hurt you, Ivory."

"Matteo told me you like to hurt women." I stepped away, retreating until my back hit the door, and I was trapped.

Reaching out a hand to run his fingers over the bruise, his brow furrowed when I whimpered at the pain it sent shooting through my skull. "Whores. I like to hurt whores. You are not a whore, my little doll. You are pure. Innocent in a world of filth."

"I'm not innocent," I argued, shrinking further into the door. "I'm not some virgin—"

"You are loyal. Loving. Warm. All the things that made Bellandi choose you as his wife, yes?"

"Matteo chose to marry me because he loves me," I argued, probably stupidly. I shouldn't argue against the points the man gave for not wanting to hurt me, but I also figured he wouldn't risk Matteo's wrath over someone he thought of as a common whore. My eyes darted around the entryway of the house, taking in the oversized windows that reflected the woods surrounding the house.

Nothing but woods.

Where the fuck was I?

"And there is a reason he fell in love with you, out of all the women who throw themselves at his feet. Something about you, little doll, that just draws men like us in like moths to a flame." Those dark eyes of his glittered as he stared at me in fixation, an intensity that might have rivaled Matteo's, if not for the unhinged quality that Adrian had.

Where Matteo's fixation always felt like coming home, even in his darkest moments, Adrian's was nothing but haunting. "Matteo will come for me," I whispered.

"He'll have to find you first." He grinned, looking confident in his intention to hide me away. I felt my lips twitch but disguised it with a grimace. I owed Matteo an apology for fighting him so intently on the tracker he'd put beneath my skin.

I felt nothing but gratitude for it in that moment.

"And what is it that you plan to do with me?" I let my lip tremble, because I knew it didn't take long to break someone. And having Adrian's hands on me might be my breaking point.

"I want what he has. I want his businesses, his control of the streets, you as my wife, and to see you swell with our child." He stepped back from me, moving to the couch visible from the door, completely unconcerned that I might try to run out the door. He raised a brow, as if daring me to try it.

I knew I wouldn't get far. Not with how arrogant he was, and I knew in that moment that my best odds laid in waiting for Matteo to come.

And I knew he would.

He would always come for me, that I knew.

"I can't give you Matteo's businesses."

"I think you underestimate what he would do to see you returned to him safely. Once he has signed everything over to me, I'll kill him." He shrugged, as if Matteo's death didn't truly matter.

My lungs seized in my chest. "You can't," I begged finally stepping away from the door and approaching him somewhat. I kept my distance, stayed away from the couch and stood on shaky legs. "I won't survive if you kill him."

"You'll do whatever I tell you to do," he barked as he lit up a cigar and poured himself a scotch. "Because if you do, I'll let you keep your baby." I flinched, staring at him with horror-filled eyes. My hands wrapped around my waist on instinct, protecting the baby from the monster who would threaten something that hadn't even *lived*.

"H—how?" I stuttered. It didn't seem possible. I'd told only Sadie, Duke, and Scar about the baby.

"I bugged your friend Sadie's home." He grinned, pride in every feature of his exotically handsome face. If he hadn't been so deranged, he might have been attractive, but as it was, he just couldn't ever be anything but terrifying. "Imagine my surprise when she went on and on about being a godmother to her best friend's baby."

"You can't—" I started.

"I've no desire to hurt your baby, my doll. It is my insurance to be sure you do as you're told. If you behave, you can keep it, and I'll even claim it as my own. If you don't, well, I could sell it for quite a hefty sum. So many sick people in this world that would love a baby."

I blanched, and I knew my face must have paled when I dropped into the armchair with a gasp. "Please," I whispered.

"As I said, I have no desire to do that. Hopefully, the child will be a girl, and no one need know she's not mine since she won't cause problems with the succession." He stood, smoothing his suit as if he were some classy, elegant businessman and not a monster who trafficked women and children. *People.*

He sold people, and for the first time in my life, a lust for blood pumped in my veins. I wanted him to suffer, wanted to watch him bleed out for the children he hurt. For the threat to *my baby.* I knew Matteo would have plans to handle it and probably be able to ensure he suffered more efficiently.

But it didn't stop me from wanting to be the one to do it when he approached me with an arrogant swagger to his hips. He'd thought he'd trapped me. Cornered me in a way that I could never escape.

He didn't know I was a survivor, and he didn't know I'd promised myself a long time ago that I would *never* be somebody's victim again.

His hand tilted my head up to look me in the eye, his thumb stroking over my injured cheek gently. "Come to bed, my doll," he drawled in a voice that was nothing but a mockery of men who knew how to seduce a woman to their beds.

I stood, trying to rein in my venomous glare when he smirked at me triumphantly. My vision lined with red, the call for his blood something fierce within me.

Call it a mother's need to protect her child. Call it a self-defense mechanism. Whatever came over me in that moment destroyed any perceptions I had of myself as a peaceful person. I never wanted to hurt anyone. Never wanted to resort to violence.

Where had that gotten me?

I opened my mouth to speak, releasing a gasp when gunshots made the windows vibrate. He narrowed his eyes on me, looking at me like I'd betrayed him and given away our location. When the gunfire sounded closer to the front door, he moved. I bolted, going for the stairs and a place to hide safely.

The hand he dug into my hair prevented me from getting far, and I screamed as he used it to force me back to him. An arm wrapped around my throat, until finally he pulled a knife from his pocket and held it to my throat, making me still immediately.

Deep breaths. I centered myself, those breaths becoming everything I would need to keep a clear head in the next moments. Sadie was at the forefront of my mind, and I swore I would never stop going to the gym with her and even stop complaining about it if I walked away alive.

The door burst open, and Adrian spun with me still in his hold, and my head cocked back as far as I could to avoid the piercing of the tip of the blade against my skin. Adrian raised a pistol, aiming it at the door as Matteo stepped inside. His eyes narrowed on the knife against my throat. "Adrian, put down the gun," I said on a wheeze. "You know he'll never let you walk away after this."

Matteo leveled his own gun on Adrian, but I knew from the look in his eye that he would never fire. He'd never risk me like that. "I don't need to walk away to break him," Adrian whispered, and I moved.

I kept my hands close to my body, raising them slowly until I was a breath away from touching his arm. I grabbed his forearm just as he tensed to slit my throat, pulling down and to the left while I cocked my right shoulder. My head slipped under his armpit, and I used his own twisted arm to stab him in the side three times.

Still he fought, and I knew from Sadie's lessons that the adrenaline pumping through him meant he hadn't even *felt* the wounds yet. I focused on that wrist, twisting until he released the knife and turned to thrust it up under his chin.

The gun dropped from his hand instantly, and the gurgling sound he made would haunt me for the rest of my life. But it didn't stop me from speaking to him, the last sound he ever heard my voice. "You shouldn't have threatened my baby." I yanked the knife free, watching as he flopped face first to the floor and the puddle of blood surrounding him grew. His lifeless eyes stared up at me, like a little broken doll. Horror spread through my veins, unable to believe what I'd done.

Unable to believe that I didn't feel one bit of remorse for killing a man.

"Ivory," Matteo whispered, and I looked up at him. Blood coated my hands and my dress. "You're bleeding." I nodded, glancing down to my left hand where the knife had cut into my palm in the struggle. "Let's get you cleaned up and have that stitched, okay Angel?"

"Take me home," I whispered, feeling everything return as the haze of adrenaline faded. The pain, the horror over what I'd done.

"After we go to Doc," Matteo answered, wrapping an arm around me and guiding me from the house.

I didn't know when I started trembling. All I knew was that it didn't stop for a long, long time.

CHAPTER THIRTY-FOUR

IVORY

The trembling continued, accompanied by silent tears streaking down my cheeks. "Angel," Matteo murmured, wrapping me up in his arms in the back of the car while Simon raced along the streets. Matteo had torn his jacket and held it to the wound in my hand, while I shook in his arms. "You should have just gotten away. If you hadn't been in the shot, I could have killed him."

"Fuck you," I whispered through chattering teeth. "He took me from my home. He threatened to sell our baby. I'm going to be a mother, and I will do whatever it takes to protect this baby," I whispered, glaring at him.

His mouth molded into a smirk at my ire. "You were a badass, Angel."

I groaned. "Don't give me your shit right now. I just stabbed a man."

"Rather fantastically," he laughed. "Never would have thought you had that in you, my angel."

I glared at him mockingly. "Maybe I'll stab you next."

"What? Why?" he chuckled, and Simon made a noise while he tried to suppress his own laugh.

"Because you're pissing me off. Being all snuggly when I'm covered in blood. Fucking psychopath, that's what you are! I bet you're all turned on too, like a creep."

I could only describe the face he made as one of absolute glee as his body shook with his roar of laughter. "You wouldn't be entirely wrong."

"Gross!"

"Ivory?" he asked, and I turned to find him staring down at me. My breath caught from the emotion in those blue eyes as he pressed his forehead to mine. "I fucking love you. Whether you're my angel or a knife-wielding badass."

I rolled my eyes, "I love you too, Teo." His lips claimed mine in a slow caress that couldn't be described as anything other than making love to me with his mouth. I sighed into the contact, realizing just how much I'd missed it during our separation. As soon as the car stopped at the estate, Matteo tugged me out and into the house.

"How is he?" he barked at the two men gathered in the foyer.

"Stable," one said, nodding his head to the living room. I turned, my eyes landing on Scar's prone body laid out on the massage table where the doctor had put in my tracker.

"He's alive?" I whispered, and Matteo nodded, glancing at me uneasily.

"I didn't want to get your hopes up until I knew for sure." I slid out of Matteo's hold, moving to his body and staring down at his bare torso as I counted the bullet holes in his body.

Six.

He'd taken six bullets to protect me.

It was a miracle none of them aimed for his head. "When will he wake up?" I asked, turning wide eyes to the doctor who stood over him and looked exhausted.

"When he's ready," he breathed. His eyes examined me from head to toe. "Any of that blood yours?"

"Yes," I whispered.

"Go shower. Be quick about it. I'll look you over as soon as you're out." Matteo took my uninjured hand and started to guide me away, but I gave him pleading eyes.

"I don't want to leave him."

"We'll hurry back, Angel." Pressing a kiss to Scar's forehead briefly, I let Matteo take me upstairs to shower.

✳✳✳

My eyes never left Scar's chest, watching the rhythmic rise and fall as the doctor stitched up my hand. "It will scar," he warned, and I shrugged. It wasn't the first time I'd cut my hand with a knife, and it wouldn't be the last. If I walked away from being taken by a crazed human trafficker who wanted me to be his wife with nothing but a scar, then I'd consider myself lucky. "Let me have a look at that head."

"It's nothing," I sighed.

"Doesn't look like nothing." I relented, turning in my seat so the doctor could poke and prod the wound. "Any loss of consciousness?"

"Yes. I don't know how long I was out, but I woke up in Adrian's bed." The room filled with Matteo's fury almost instantly, even from where he stood coordinating with his men regarding the cleanup at my house and Adrian's.

"Do we need to do an exam?" the doctor asked carefully.

"No." I shook my head. "He didn't touch me like that."

"You're certain? Maybe when you were unconscious?" I stilled, not having thought of the possibility.

"I don't—wouldn't I feel it? If he raped me?"

The doctor nodded. "Most likely, but there are no guarantees with these things. I'd like to do an exam—"

Matteo's bellow echoed through the room, and then he was punching numbers into his phone. "Ask the fucker if anybody touched Ivory while she was unconscious." He put the phone on speaker, and another man's screams of agony filled the room.

"Who is that?" I asked.

Matteo replied briskly. "Adrian's second in command. We took him alive."

Another man's cold, deadly quiet voice came over the phone as the screams died down. "Did anybody touch her? Was she raped or touched in any way when she was unconscious?" he asked, presumably to the man he tortured. I paled, and the doctor patted the back of my head to get my attention. Shining a light in my eyes, he sought to distract me while he checked for a concussion.

"No! We dropped her in the bedroom and left her to sleep it off! I swear! Normally, I'd have thought for sure Adrian would rape her, but he was different about this chick. Obsessed, man."

"You believe him?" Matteo asked the phone.

"Yeah, I do. He's singing like a canary, and so far everything checks out." I sighed in relief, and the doctor sat down next to me, patting my hand.

"You've got a nasty concussion, not surprising. I want you to take it easy for a few days, no cooking, nothing that strains your concentration like reading or long hours of television. Tylenol for the pain."

"Okay," I whispered.

As soon as he stepped away to deal with some other minor injuries, I turned back to Scar. Gripping his hand in mine, I finally allowed myself to break.

Everything hit me. My resounding relief over not being raped. My hope that Scar would wake up soon. The terror I'd felt when I first heard those gunshots. "Why isn't he in the hospital? Shouldn't he have a breathing tube or something?" I whispered when Matteo wrapped his arms around me. Tears fell steadily as I sobbed, leaning over Scar.

"Draws too much attention. Besides, it's not the first time he's been shot, Angel. He'll pull through just fine. Doc didn't even have to put him under."

He quieted, continuing to hold me through my breakdown.

Just held me.

Like he didn't have a million other things he needed to be doing, his hands slid under my shirt and caressed my stomach with nothing but relief in his touch.

We sat there for hours, despite Matteo trying to draw me away to bed. "I can't leave him. Not again," I said every time.

After the room emptied, everyone else finding their way to their beds, that was the moment when Scar's groan echoed in the silence. "Scar?" I whispered, hoping to God he'd open his eyes.

"Hey, man," Matteo smiled into my neck.

"Ivory," Scar groaned, jolting where he laid like he might sit up.

I touched his shoulder, applying just enough pressure to keep him lying down. "I'm here," I whispered. "I'm fine. Thanks to you." The sniffle I made sounded particularly pathetic in the quiet room.

"I'm going to go grab some guys to help him into a guest room, Angel," Matteo murmured, ducking out and leaving me to stare at Scar.

"Don't cry," Scar mumbled. "Hate it when you cry."

"I thought you were dead. Adrian dragged me through the house, and you were just there. And there was so much blood."

"He got to you?" Scar's voice went taut.

"I'm fine, Matteo came quickly because of the tracker." I nodded, watching as his eyes went to the bruise on my face.

"Not quick enough. He make him suffer?"

"Ivory killed him," Matteo said, pride infused into his voice. "Bloodthirsty thing." I chuckled, completely appreciating the fact that Matteo seemed determined to turn my killer status into a joke. It somehow made it feel less real. Less like I'd stabbed a man four times like a vicious monster. "Come on. Let's get you to bed so the guys can help Scar to his bed. He needs to sleep."

I nodded, pressing a kiss to Scar's cheek as Matteo guided me away. "You're lucky I trust him. Otherwise I'd kill him for the way you're fawning over him," Matteo grunted, and I laughed all the way to bed where Matteo rolled me underneath him and held me for the whole two seconds it took for me to pass the fuck out.

EPILOGUE
IVORY

Not being able to drink at your own wedding was shit.

Like seriously.

I guess I should have just been glad that I wasn't sporting a huge baby bump, still in my first trimester. Matteo had been kind about it, agreeing not to drink with me.

Damn right I'd taken his offer. If momma couldn't get drunk then neither could he.

I smiled at the thought, staring up at my husband as he twirled me around on the rented stage on the estate property, the rose garden to our backs.

There had never been a discussion about where we would get married, we never even talked about whether the wedding was still on after everything that happened with Adrian Ricci.

I never once considered leaving Matteo. After all, I was a killer now too, regardless of the circumstances. I could have let Matteo kill him for me, I'd known that even at the moment. But something dark within me knew that I needed to do it myself.

Matteo had never once looked at me as anything but his equal since that day, and even though I often suffered from horrifying nightmares, I wouldn't have changed a thing.

Lino twirled Samara around the dance floor beside us, laughing despite the shadows under Samara's blue-grey eyes. I knew that her ex-husband was giving her trouble with the divorce, but Lino refused to talk about it much.

To be honest, I got the impression Samara didn't tell him much. He'd never done well with hearing the specifics of her relationships. I suspected he kept her as solely a friend for similar reasons to why Matteo had pushed me away.

That would change once the divorce was final. With every day that passed, something more and more possessive thrummed beneath Lino's skin. Like a beast hovering below the surface, just waiting for the right time to strike and claim Samara once and for all.

I couldn't wait. They'd always been perfect for each other, for as long as I'd known them both.

"How long do you think it will take Samara to realize what's going on?" I asked Matteo, making him vibrate with laughter.

"I think," he whispered, "that if she dances with one more man who isn't him tonight, he just might make sure she knows who owns her before the night is over."

Sadie caught my eye and grinned, tormenting Duke by making him dance with her. "I agree," she chuckled with emphasis. "If you don't want them to dirty up all your surfaces, you might need to get your shank hand ready."

"Sadie!" I hissed, throwing my head back on a laugh. Dad's eyes found mine, shining as he watched me. I looked away as my own tears threatened. He'd already turned me into a blubbering mess during our father daughter dance. There was no way I could let him do it again. Even Uncle Adam had given Matteo a pat on the back, the two of them reaching an easy friendship despite the differences in the way they approached the law. With me knowing the truth, Adam was the first to relent that I was a big girl, and only I could decide about what crossed boundaries for me. Sadie twirled Duke away, drawing eyes from our other guests. I didn't have the heart to tease Duke that he should be leading.

It would take a very strong man to lead Sadie anywhere.

I loved the girl to death, but she was terrifying.

And stubborn.

And both things had saved my life, all the relentless lessons she'd given me for self-defense, drilling me with the most dramatic and outlandish scenarios she could come up with. Without her, I could easily have died.

Without her, I wouldn't have a husband and a baby on the way.

We owed her everything.

"Has it been everything you wanted?" Matteo whispered, smiling down at me. The stars twinkled in the night sky, the lights hanging from the house and worked into the rose garden echoing the romantic feel.

"All that matters is you're my husband. But yes. You've given me everything I could ever dream of having."

"Well then, my wife," Matteo growled. "I think it's time that we went to bed." He swept me up into his arms as I giggled, hiding my face as our guests stared at us.

"Oh God," I cried, kicking my legs. He didn't care. Matteo's feet carried us to the house and inside, ignoring the hooting and cheering behind us.

"Go get him, girl!" Samara shouted, shrieking when Lino moved to grab her.

The house was empty, except for a few guests waiting in line to use the bathroom. "There's no one to save you now," he teased, taking the steps slowly.

"Who said I wanted saving?" I whispered, pressing my face into his neck and breathing him in.

If there was any one thing that comforted me above all else, it was the way Matteo smelled.

Like him. Like his soap.

Like me.

I'd never considered myself possessive aside from Matteo, but if he ever smelled like another woman or touched another woman, I just might need my shank hand.

He set me down in our bedroom, turning me to face away from him. Matteo's hands drew down the zipper at the back of my dress, oh so slowly.

Teasing me.

My own fingers released the clip that kept my hair pulled to one side, reveling in the way Matteo's lips skimmed the back of my neck. The A-line dress pooled at my feet in a puddle of white. I turned, facing Matteo so he could get the full experience of my lingerie. He'd been nothing but gentle since my concussion, making love to me every chance he got but never giving me the rougher parts of him I loved.

I wanted to test his control, feel it snap. The strapless corset hugged my growing breasts perfectly, and I backed onto the bed with a little smirk on my face. Rubbing my thighs together, I watched Matteo loosen his tie and strip off the jacket of his tux. His smirk matched mine. I should know, since I'd learned it from him.

Watching him strip off his tux was a thing of beauty, revealing sculpted inch after sculpted inch until he wore nothing, and I had to fight the urge to pounce on him.

My pregnancy was a gift and a curse to Matteo, giving me a sex drive impossible to keep up with.

He gave it a good run for his money, but I worried that I'd distract him from his work. He climbed into the bed with me, sliding into the cradle of my thighs and taking my mouth in a passionate kiss. Those kisses melted any resolve I could have ever put up, any wall I could have ever built between us.

Those kisses were love.

Pure, untainted love.

No secrets, nothing standing in our way.

"I don't deserve you," he murmured, trailing lips down over my collarbone. "But I will spend the rest of my life proving that you're mine, anyway."

A smile graced my face, watching as his fingers worked the little closures at the front of my corset. "You don't have to prove anything, Teo," I whispered. "Because I choose you. Always." His eyes flashed to mine, relief and longing mixed in those pools of blue. I hadn't realized how much he needed those words. How much I'd hurt him by saying I needed to choose him, as if it wasn't a foregone conclusion.

To Matteo, it had been a condemnation, a denial of the love that vibrated between us like an electric current.

But I'd have loved him for the rest of my life, even if I couldn't be with him. *Always.*

He was inside me, part of me in every moment.

And I knew that nothing would keep him from me. Not even a rival gang member. He tore the corset away, yanking the panties away until they tore beneath the force of his desperation as that control snapped.

I reached a hand between us, guiding him inside me so we moved in tandem. He surged inside, filling me to the brim and filling my ears with the sound of his pleasured groan. I wrapped my arms around his shoulders and drew him down to kiss me, lifting my hips to accept his thrusts. "I love you," I whispered against his lips, staring into his eyes like I might connect with the deepest parts of his soul.

"I love you too, Angel." One of his hands came up, cupping my nape as we shared the air between us, and his other palmed my ass in his hand. His chest touched mine, brushing against my breasts and stimulating the oversensitive flesh.

There was nothing but us, nothing but his skin on mine and the place where we connected. His lips touched mine, tongues tangling in an intimate embrace that sent me spiraling over the edge until I dragged Matteo with me. Heat filled me as he came, and it was in the moments after sex that I whispered the name of our child.

"Luna if it's a girl."

"Luca for a boy," he murmured, pressing his forehead to mine as we laughed.

"How did I get so lucky?" I teased him, thinking he'd scoff at me like he always did.

"Love finds a way," he whispered back, shocking me with the easy smile that took over his face.

That it did.

✳✳✳

Thank you for reading Bloodied Hands! I hope you enjoyed Matteo and Ivory's story. Please consider taking the time to drop me a review. Hearing from my readers means the world to me.

. . .

FOR MORE OF Matteo and Ivory, download the exclusive extended epilogue for a glimpse into their life 1.5 years later. Get it here.

CONTINUE READING FOR LINO & Samara's story in Forgivable Sins.

2
BELLANDI CRIME SYNDICATE
FORGIVABLE SINS
ADELAIDE FORREST

ABOUT FORGIVABLE SINS

Samara

I burn for him, but Lino will never be mine. Faced with the reality that I could never have the man I loved, I made the wrong choice and settled for the worst kind of man. When his gambling problem puts me at risk, Lino steps in to protect me.

There's just one problem.

Lino has a darkness inside him. One that could unravel everything he's built and drag him down to the pits of Hell. I won't risk him in that way, especially not when everything I thought I knew about us changes.

Lino

I've loved Samara since I was a boy, since the very moment when I first heard her sing. But my father's cruelty knows no bounds, and I made the biggest sacrifice of my life to protect my Little Dove.

Everything changes when her ex-husband shatters the safety I worked so desperately to build for her. Suddenly the safest place for her is right in my arms where she always belonged.

And I won't stop until she's my wife.

SOUNDTRACK

"Damage" - Outr3ach
"You're No Good" - Hidden Citizens
"What It Takes" - Adelitas Way
"Feel Something" - Adam Lambert
"Ego" - Smash Into Pieces
"Too Late" - Folded Dragons
"Drown" - Martin Garrix
"Conquer" - MAGNUS
"Worst of You" - Maisie Peters
"Power Over Me" - Dermot Kennedy
"Beyond Today" - James Gillespie
"BOOM" - X Ambassadors
"Grace" - Lewis Capaldi
"Coldest Water" - Walking on Cars
"Stay" - The Score
"Dreamin" - The Score
"ICFTI" James Gillespie
"Champion" - Elina
"Power" - Isak Danielson
"Make Believe" - The Faim
"Hold Me Up" - Sam Tinnesz
"Leading the Pack" - Sam Tinnesz
"Fighter" - Jung Youth, Sam Tinnesz
"Be Legendary" - Pop Evil

"Silence" - No Name Faces
"Warriors" - League of Legends
"Conversations in the Dark" - John Legend
"Protector" - City Wolf
"Everything or Nothing" - Willyecho
"The Fear" - The Score

PROLOGUE
LINO

Nineteen years ago

Samara sat at my mother's piano, pressing the keys quickly and lightly as she sang a soft melody. I recognized it as one of the popular pop songs the girls at school listened to, but the sweetness of her voice made it seem like the song belonged to her and no one else.

Gentle. Clear. Haunting.

Even then, I felt everything inside me tighten as something snapped taut and vibrated through me.

I stared at her as she faltered when she caught me watching her from my place next to her on the bench at the piano that nobody ever used.

Not since my mother's accident years ago.

The shy smile on her face made me beam at her, but instead of teasing her like I might have ten minutes ago, I reached forward and tucked her frizzy copper hair behind her ear so she couldn't hide the blue-grey eyes she covered with thick-rimmed black glasses.

"Your voice is pretty," I whispered, trying to straighten my shoulders to look taller. I wasn't short for my age, but my cousin Matteo was taller than me already and girls flocked to him. He said chicks liked tall boys. Even eleven-year-old chicks, apparently.

"Thank you," she replied, her cheeks turning pink with the blush that so often covered her face. She smoothed her hands over her green skirt, moving to stand and put some distance between us, but I stopped that by grabbing her right hand in mine and running my thumb over the odd heart shaped birthmark on her palm.

"One day when we're married, you'll sing to me every day," I said, watching as the smile faded from her face and her pursed mouth parted in shock.

"When we're married?" she whispered, the blush fading in favor of her golden skin paling.

I nodded. "I'm going to marry you."

She huffed in laughter, but I knew Samara well enough to know I'd made her uncomfortable with my declaration. She was my best friend and had been for years already.

I also knew she had years to face the inevitable reality that I meant every word.

My father cleared his throat, and I turned to see him standing in the doorway with his arms crossed over his chest. I deflated immediately but smiled to reassure Samara. I knew she worried about our friendship, knew she worried that my father's disapproval of her being a part of my life would have consequences for me.

But there was nothing I wouldn't do to have Samara in my life.

Even face my father's wrath.

"It's okay," I whispered. "I'm sure your mom will be done soon. I'll see you at school tomorrow." She nodded, casting a wide-eyed glance to my father before she darted off to the attic where she, her mother, and her brother, Yavin, lived. She had to pass my father to fit through the narrow doorway, and for a moment panic coursed through me that he might touch her.

Hurt her to punish me.

But she escaped unscathed. I knew I wouldn't be so lucky.

"I thought I told you to stop hanging out with the cleaner's kids," he snapped, and I knew Samara wasn't far enough to have avoided hearing him. It was intentional. Everything with my father was a deliberate action, all part of the greater games he played to gain control over everyone in his life.

I'd have to talk Samara down from the edge again, because every time he pulled this stunt she didn't want to come between a father and his son. I didn't have the heart to tell her that my father's fists were already between us and there was no room for anyone else in that gap. Not when she still mourned the loss of the father she couldn't even remember, and not when she was the one who fussed over my cuts and bruises.

"And I told you, Yavin and Samara are my friends." I stood from the bench, closing the keylid gently and reverently. All my strongest memories of my mother were at that piano, and I knew one day, I'd have the same kinds of memories with Samara.

"You told her you would marry her. Let me be very, very clear, Angelino. That will never happen. Not so long as I'm alive. No son of mine will marry a Jewish brat." I kept quiet, because I knew there was no point in arguing with him. But one day, I'd do whatever it took to find a life that was happy. A life where my father didn't dictate my actions.

I wasn't surprised when his long legs carried him across the room to close the distance between us. The slap of his hand against my left cheek was no shock either, and I barely flinched. He'd done much worse. "Am I understood, boy?"

I grimaced, sucking my teeth as I murmured, "Yes, father."

It hadn't been the first time I lied, and it would be far from the last.

CHAPTER ONE

SAMARA

I ran.

I ran harder than I ever had before. My bare feet left a trail of blood with each step on the stairs.

Slipping on the hardwood, I skidded into the door with a painful thump that made my already tender stomach concave from the force of the doorknob. Blood coated my fingers, and I whimpered when I couldn't get a grip on the lock. It wouldn't turn. Wouldn't open.

A groan and thud sounded at the top of the stairs where I'd left the bedroom door wide open in my effort to make a hasty escape. "Samara! You stupid cunt!" he roared at the top of his lungs, and I whimpered again, finally dragging my nightgown up to wrap it around the knob and pull it open. Fresh, cold air blew the door open further, blasting me in the face. On one side of my head, the hair billowed in the wind. On the other, it stayed plastered to my scalp in a bloody mess.

His blood.

Out the door. My feet thudded against the pavement, sprinting for the neighbor's house. Pavement turned to grass. The stab of each blade in the cuts on my feet echoed with the frigid night air stabbing at my lungs as I gasped for breath. I fell on the front step, finally screaming for Linda to open her door. Everything hurt. My soul hurt, my heart hurt, my body hurt.

He was coming.

Drunk. Desperate.

"Linda!" I screamed, standing to bang on the door more frantically.

She gasped when she tore it open, and I fell inside into a puddle of nothing but blood and bruised flesh.

"Samara!" he yelled again, but the door closed and locked, cutting off the rage in his voice.

Safe. Safe behind closed doors.

For now.

My eyes snapped open, and I shot to a sitting position in bed. My empty bed, with my new mattress.

It didn't matter. Every time I opened my eyes, I still saw the broken mirror on the floor, the blood on the base of the lamp that I'd used to bash him over the head with. Too fevered, my body felt slick with sweat as I shoved the blankets off. I curled my legs in, crossing them and trailing a finger over the scars on my feet. Thick, hideous white lines that covered the soles from my toes to my heels.

It took hours for Linda to pull out all the pieces of glass.

It had taken almost as long to wash the blood off me, out of my hair, out from under my nails.

I still didn't feel clean. Still woke up every day with the feeling of blood coating my skin and the stain of his touch on me.

I stood to shower, making my way into the bathroom. I avoided looking in the mirror as I went. I didn't want to see my pale face staring back at me or see the vacant look in my terrified eyes. That look would stay until I washed the nightmare from my skin.

Washed his touch down the drain until I was clean again.

Another day, another nightmare of my doing. My phone chimed with a text message from the bedroom, and I felt my lips curve into a hesitant smile. I didn't need to check it to see who it was from or what it would say.

My daily good morning message from Lino was one thing that drove Connor mad during our too-long marriage. Most days, I'd said good morning to my best friend before my ex-husband even when he was in bed next to me. Now it drew me out of the memories, and it pleased me to know that even though Connor was part of my past, Lino remained.

I got in the shower, taking a deep breath and forcing myself to belt out an upbeat song while I washed away the sweat. There was no one to hear me, no one to tell me to just stop because he couldn't stand the sound of my voice. Just me and my demons, taking back our power.

It would be a good day, despite the rocky start.

I just knew it.

***

MY KNEE-HIGH BOOTS clicked on the granite tile floors of Lamb & Rowe. Such a stark contrast to the way my bare feet slid across my hardwood floor in my dream.

My memory.

People nodded as I passed, the file folder in my hand filled to the brim with charts and my monthly summaries for my boss. Summaries on all the people who stared at me, nodding in respect tinted with apprehension.

I fought down the urge to smirk when I stepped into the elevator that would take me to the top floor, remembering what the bankers thought when Jasper Rowe first hired me. It hadn't mattered that I had a ring on my finger, because news spread through Chicago like wildfire, and I had foolishly married a partner in my last firm.

But it didn't matter. My work ethic spoke for itself, and while Jasper and I were friendly, there was absolutely nothing romantic between us. I was his rock, professionally.

Stepping out of the elevator into Jasper and I's sanctuary, I dropped my phone on my desk quickly and made my way to his private office. I knocked on his door, letting myself in with no concern or hesitation even before he could respond. "Don't forget you have your lunch with Carson Davis in an hour."

"Good morning to you too, Samara." There was an unmistakable smile to his voice, and I looked to him with a raised brow. His blond hair was perfectly styled as usual, and his honeyed skin glowed like he was well-rested. So, I couldn't decide what had made him come to work so late. The man worked constantly.

"It's noon."

"It's 11:56 actually," he returned, and I dropped the folder on his desk and crossed my arms over my chest. The position made me feel a little more capable of breathing in the black turtleneck I'd put on that morning to accompany my grey wool skirt. He grinned at me, and the lightest grey eyes I'd ever seen twinkled with mischief as he leaned back in his chair and didn't even bother to open the file. "Your assessment?"

"Mark Dobson's accounts aren't doing as well as they easily should be with the amount of hours he logged last month. It might have something to do with the rumors he's sleeping with Jim Clarke's wife during that time."

Jasper's stare blanked as he looked back at me, but I recognized the sudden rigidity to his frame. "That's a very serious accusation based on rumors." Even though his words might have seemed cautionary, the man knew me well enough to know I was far from interested in office gossip.

I nodded to the folder, and he sighed and slid it open. The photos I'd printed from the high-tech security tapes spoke for themselves. "Fuck," he groaned, scrubbing a hand over his face. "That is way more of Dobson's ass than I ever needed to see. If this gets out...."

"I've approved a $3,000 bonus for Mack in the security office for a signed NDA that he's not to speak of what we found on those tapes or you will own him for the rest of his life. We went through all the extra hours Mark logged, and I took care of the film from inside and around his office during those times. The photos are the only evidence. File them away for insurance, and then my suggestion would be to remind Dobson that if he breathes a word of his involvement with Mrs. Clarke, it will mean he makes the affair public record. He will blacklist himself from the other firms in the city following his termination here if this gets out."

He sighed but nodded. "I'll need to talk to Kelly first, but she always agrees with you. Pitbulls, both of you."

"I'll call her assistant and get you a meeting on the books for whenever we can fit it in today, and I'll schedule Dobson's termination for first thing tomorrow morning. You also had a cancellation with Christopher French, and Dobson is free until 10 a.m."

He took a sip of his coffee, placing it back in the exact spot on his desk where he kept it. Everything had its place in Jasper's life. Then he turned to lock the photos in the safe tucked behind the portrait on the back wall of the office. "Is there anyone who can pick up the slack until we can hire a replacement?"

I nodded, continuing when he didn't see me. "I'll divide the main accounts between Johnson and Romero, two each, and distribute the less demanding accounts between Skorzeny and Evans."

"Perfect. What would I do without you?"

"Crash and burn, most definitely. It's incredible you made it this far in your life without me, honestly. I'm off to lunch. Do you think you can hold down the fort until I get back?" He turned around with a laugh, mimicking the smirk on my face with his own.

"I'm sure I'll manage somehow, Miss Mahoney."

"Peachy." I turned on my heel, striding to my desk to grab my purse and head down to meet Lino for our biweekly lunch. I'd just locked my file drawer with all my confidential information when the elevator doors opened. Even if I hadn't known that Jasper had no appointments until later in the day, I'd have known who strutted out those doors anywhere.

I didn't even have to look at him to feel the air change with his presence and hear the confidence in the gait of his step. His dress shoes tapped against the floor as he made his way to me. Glancing over, my eyes traced those shoes up and over his body encased in grey and up to the devastatingly angular face that made women chase after him everywhere we went. His full lips tilted into a stunning smile when our eyes met, the deep brown of his almond eyes shining as his strong brow softened.

The bastard had worn my favorite grey three-piece suit, fitted to perfection over his lean but muscular form. Since I'd started the process for my divorce all those months ago, it felt like Lino and I were playing with fire, like something shifted in our friendship.

But we both knew it couldn't. I wouldn't let it happen.

I was done with men. Done with the hurt they caused. Not to mention my brother would revolt if he knew I got involved with Lino. He and Yavin partied together, worked together. Lino might have been my best friend, but Yavin filled a role that I never could. There was no chance that my protective best friend would take me into the underbelly of the world where they lived, and that meant I stayed on the sidelines. Never really a part of his world, and never really out of it either. "Will you ever listen when I tell you to wait in the lobby?" I asked, smiling at him with a shake of my head as he leaned in to kiss my cheek.

Normal. Expected.

So why did it feel like his lips lingered, like he breathed me into his very soul?

And why did my heart flutter like when we were children?

"When will you learn that I do what I want, Little Dove?" He brushed my copper hair over my shoulder, reaching down to take my right hand in his. His thumb stroked the birthmark on my palm, something he'd done since we'd been children. It seemed mostly involuntary at this stage in our lives, something he did completely out of habit. I rolled my eyes at him but let him keep it in his as he led me to the elevators. Not for the first time, I wondered how things would have turned out if Lino had kept the promise he made all those years ago. The one that made me write Mrs. Samara Bellandi in my journal for years after.

But when high school came, he dated.

He dated everyone but me. I couldn't blame him, not with the way girls threw themselves at both Matteo and Lino. I wondered if maybe he was waiting for me to turn sixteen, but sixteen came and went. Then high school came and went.

Then college.

Eventually, I'd just accepted that Angelino Bellandi would never marry me, and I'd given myself to the first man to treat me like I mattered.

The elevator doors closed us in, and the air suddenly felt stifling. I still felt that pull, that irrational draw to Lino. While I'd convinced my heart that being his friend, having him so thoroughly immersed in my life was enough, my body was another story. His thumb still traced my palm, still stroked my skin so delicately, like he thought I might break from the slightest pressure.

He'd never know that I'd survived much worse pain. He could never know. I wouldn't be responsible for what happened to him if he did something there was no turning back from. I knew without a doubt, if he found out about the times Connor had hurt me, I'd lose Lino forever. Lose him to the darkness that lurked just beneath the surface.

I wouldn't be the cause of that, not when it had been my stupidity and stubbornness that led me to that place.

"Where did you go just now?" Lino asked, jolting me out of my thoughts. I turned my head up to look at him, feeling his gaze examining every piece of my face. As if he could see my injuries. See the internal scars I wore that I never allowed him to see. He frowned at me, and I knew his head ran through all the possibilities of what he might need to do to protect me from whatever made me lost in thought.

"Nowhere of significance," I shrugged. "Work this morning was complicated. I had to investigate a rumor, dispose of the evidence to prevent damage to the company's reputation. I'm just distracted is all."

His brow tensed, tarnishing that sexy businessman persona just enough for the devil to show in his face. "You could come work for me."

"I like my job. I rock at my job. I love my job."

"But it's stressful. I could give you a more low-key position." The elevator doors opened on the bottom floor, and we hurried through the lobby to make it to where I knew Lino's driver and his bodyguard would wait on the curb. I nodded to both men, getting friendly smiles in return.

"Miss Mahoney," Georgio, the bodyguard, murmured respectfully and climbed into the front seat after giving a silent nod to Lino. I rolled my eyes at the ridiculous display as Lino pulled the door wide for me to climb in, the unspoken agreement that I couldn't open my own damn door and Lino's insistence on being the one to do it. I settled into the back seat and buckled in, turning my attention to Lino as soon as the doors closed behind him.

"I need to stand on my own two feet, Lino, and you have to let me," I whispered.

A contented sigh escaped when he reached down and grabbed my legs to pivot me in my seat. He slid the zipper down on my boot, stripping it off to press his thumbs into the arch. We would quickly come to the season where it needed to stop, where I wore pumps to work and wouldn't have socks to protect the secret of my scarred feet.

Since Lino had spent years massaging my feet, my shoulders, taking care of me in every sense of the word, he would know without a doubt that the scars hadn't always been there. "You would be. It's not like you're not a hard-worker."

"No, Lino," I said firmly, tugging my feet back and sliding the one back into my boot. He stared at my legs, his hands hanging in mid-air like he couldn't quite believe I'd stopped him mid-massage. Truthfully, neither could I.

"Okay, what's going on with you?" he demanded, and I knew if there hadn't been seatbelts involved, he'd have been in my face. "You're distancing yourself from me. I want to know why."

"Don't be ridiculous. I am not distancing myself from you. You're my best friend." I wished I could tell him the truth, wished that I could explain the guilt I felt for keeping secrets from him. The playful moments between us faded more and more every day, and I missed the bond I had with my best friend like a lost limb.

We rode the rest of the drive-in silence with Lino's frustrated energy vibrating next to me. Even the two men in the front seat looked uncomfortable as they glanced back at us warily. Finally pulling up to Angel's felt like a relief, where I normally treasured any time, I could spend with him.

I got out of the car quickly, ignoring the way Lino looked ready to kill me. I knew damn well he liked to open my door for me, but I'd meant what I said about needing to stand on my own two feet. The divorce, the complete and total failure of my marriage, made me feel like a failure, and I needed to prove to myself that I wasn't the problem. That I wasn't too codependent on my best friend. That I wasn't to blame for the way Connor's anger had simmered and erupted in our final months together.

Lino growled as he stepped up beside me, pressing a hand to my lower back to guide me inside. The hostess knew him well since he took me to Angel's at least once a month. I tried not to think about the other women he'd probably taken there too, tried to tell myself it didn't matter.

Placing my napkin in my lap, I tried not to flinch when he barked at me. "Is it the divorce?"

"Why would you think that?"

"Would you stop answering all my questions with a question and give me a goddamn answer, Samara? Is he still giving you trouble?" The waiter who filled our water glasses seemed to be comfortable with our conflict, turning a blind eye to it until Lino glared at him and he got the message to disappear.

"He doesn't want the divorce. I knew this would be a struggle. He has all the resources, and I'm just me," I sighed. I knew what would come next.

"I'll handle it. This has been going on for far too long, and it's time to just be done with it. You need to be free of him finally and start looking toward your future."

"No. I don't want you to get involved," I argued.

"Little Dove—"

"Do not Little Dove me."

His features softened, which was always the unintended consequence when I stood up to him. "You never told me what made you file for the divorce."

I pursed my lips, nibbling on one corner and deciding on what I might tell him to justify the seemingly abrupt decision. "He started gambling, was gone most nights. I just don't want to live my life like that, wondering where he is. If the money is really going to gambling or if it's going to hookers or blow. And then wondering if it even matters. That's not the life for me."

"Christ, Samara. You should have told me." His face twisted into a pained expression, and I reached out a hand to grasp his in mine. I gave him a small smile to reassure him. "You should have told Yavin." The mention of my brother was sobering, because I knew exactly what it would cost the two most important men in my life if they knew the truth.

The real truth.

And it terrified me.

"What could you have done? My marriage failed. Even if I sent you to stalk him and find out what he was up to, the moment I needed to send you to spy on him would have been the end. I won't be with someone I can't trust, financially, emotionally, and sexually." His hand spasmed, and I fought back my laugh. "Now can we please for the love of God just enjoy our lunch? Please?"

"Anything for you, Little Dove," he whispered, and my heart clenched in my chest at the words I wished were true. I fought back the resentment I felt.

He'd do anything for me.

Except give me him.

CHAPTER TWO

LINO

My employees skirted away from me as I made my way across the empty club floor. Normally, I might have cared to present a better, friendlier, persona.

But in that moment, I did not give the first fuck.

"What's wrong, Lino?" one of the new bartenders asked, stepping up next to me and hurrying to keep my pace in her sky-high heels. She was still training, and I cast a glance over her shoulder briefly to find the manager who should have occupied her time.

My feet froze in place as I spun to glare down at her. "What did I tell you about calling me that? I'm your boss. You are to address me as Mr. Bellandi."

She looked up at me through her eyelashes, not seeming to realize she hadn't earned the right to the familiarity she seemed to think we had. I wasn't dumb enough to think she hadn't heard the rumors I was in the habit of screwing my employees. It didn't change the fact that the rumors were bullshit, especially since I'd spent the last ten months not screwing *anybody.* "You seem tense. I could help you with that." The sultry smile on her barely legal face did nothing but annoy me.

"Proposition me again, and you're fired. I am not just a walking dick for you to use to get off. Get yourself a vibrator and call it a day." I stormed off to the sound of her gasp behind me, not paying any attention to the huff of laughter that echoed from the sidelines where my more intelligent employees deftly avoided my simmering rage.

No one else dared to stand in my way as I climbed the steps up to the offices. As soon as my feet hit the second floor, my eyes darted over to meet Enzo's hazel ones. The powerhouse of a man leaned against the door of his office with his arms crossed over his chest, grinning at me like some kind of evil shithead who enjoyed my suffering far too much for comfort.

"How's Samara?" he asked, eyes twinkling with mischief that only brightened in the face of my glare.

"Shut the fuck up."

"That good, huh? She divorced yet? I think your dick might fall off from lack of use if she doesn't hurry it along." My feet stayed planted to the floor just in front of the top step.

"Can we maybe not talk about my dick?"

"Aw, she's giving you delicate sensibilities. That's cute."

"Enzo," I warned.

"Seriously, though. How's she doing?"

"Your interest in my woman does not give me the warm fuzzies." I took a few steps down the hall, making for my office. He followed even as I sighed in annoyance. The man was relentless.

"You're a menace. You need to get laid for all our sakes." I shrugged, because even I couldn't argue with that. Only Samara could reduce me to a celibate puppy, but she was worth every bit of the wait. I wouldn't touch her until she was free and clear of that piece of shit ex of hers.

Speaking of. "Get me a meeting with Campbell."

"The investigator? Why?"

"She's hiding something. I want to know what." I didn't wait for a response, storming the rest of the way down the hall and closing myself in my office with a slam of the door that let everyone know I was *not* to be disturbed. I barely resisted the urge to shove all the stuff off my desk in my fit of rage.

Samara had been keeping secrets from me for months, maybe even longer. As long as I'd known her, she'd been an open book with me. For her to be cryptic for months and then reveal some bullshit story about his gambling being the cause for a sudden divorce meant something serious had happened.

And if I found out he'd laid a hand on her, there'd be nothing left for Ryker to chop up and burn by the time I was done with him.

The knock on the door came only a minute later. "Campbell will be here tomorrow at 2," Enzo said, not daring to open the door. I didn't bother to answer.

Not while I still vibrated with the fury that Samara would keep something important from me. As soon as she was mine, fully and completely, we'd be having a *very* serious conversation.

And it couldn't come soon enough.

CHAPTER THREE

It felt like everyone's eyes fell on me as we waited in the elevator. That was always the consequence of Lino coming around.

He intimidated everyone around him in ways that most men could never dream of doing. Even though he was lighter, less severe than his cousin Matteo, he just commanded the surrounding air.

Us mere mortals never stood a chance of not being drawn into that orbit. The intoxicating combination of danger and sex-appeal was irresistible to anyone who laid eyes on him, but when you combined those things with the unique affection he showed me? I'd never stood a chance. I'd fallen in love with him when I was too young to even understand what romantic love was, and while I'd long since let go of those feelings and accepted that we would be nothing more than friends, it didn't stop the people at work from looking at me as though I was on the verge of metamorphosis.

"Good afternoon, Miss Mahoney," one investor murmured with a bowed head as the elevator let him off on the floor below Jasper's office.

"Good afternoon," I mumbled in return, suddenly eager to make it to the relative peace and privacy that my desk offered. Having everyone stare at me because of something work-related was one thing, but I'd never been comfortable with the attention my friendship with Lino brought.

Users.

Abusers.

Jealous women.

Nothing good could come from any of them, and I demanded my own respect. Not the respect I gained because of my association with someone else.

I let out a sigh of relief when the empty elevator deposited me on the top floor, but it was short-lived. "Samara?" Jasper called from his office where he'd propped the door open. I moved in to stand in his open door, my eyes darting out the window at his back to the sprawling view of Chicago. Lamb & Rowe occupied the top floor of the building, one of the taller ones in the city. Jasper turned, following my gaze to stare at the building a few blocks away. The refurbished warehouse that held *Indulgence,* where Lino ran the Bellandi business from behind his desk in the upper office, was striking in the urban backdrop otherwise filled with steel and glass. Even lower than the skyscraper Jasper occupied, it was just as impressive.

With a sigh, he turned back around to face me. "I don't want to tell you how to live your life."

"Then don't," I snapped, crossing my arms over my chest defensively.

Pinching the bridge of his nose, he groaned. "Angelino Bellandi is not the man you need, Samara. Don't tell me you're getting involved with him."

"We're just friends."

"I don't like it. After Connor, the last thing you need is someone with a reputation like that—"

"Lino would burn this city to the ground before he let anything hurt me, Jasper." The words tumbled from me in a rush, true even if I had no desire to voice them.

"Then why is Connor still alive and giving you trouble? Why isn't he dead and buried where he belongs?" The vehemence in Jasper's voice still caught me off-guard every time, but there was no doubt about the cause.

After the assault, I'd mostly hidden out at my house until my feet could heal and the other injuries could disappear. Given I'd never missed two days of work in a row since I'd started at Lamb & Rowe, Jasper hadn't bought the excuse that I was sick and checked on me. He'd promised to hunt Connor down himself, and the only way I'd been able to dissuade him was by promising that Lino and Yavin had that covered.

I couldn't look at him, not as realization dawned on his features. The way my black boots contrasted the marble floors suddenly seemed fascinating. "You lied to me," he hissed in disbelief. When my eyes finally met his, it was to find his hands clutching the arms of his desk chair so tightly it might snap. "He has no fucking idea, does he? No clue what that piece of shit did to you?"

I shook my head silently, watching as his jaw clenched.

"Your brother? Does Yavin know?"

"No," I whispered.

"Did you think keeping the truth from them would stop them from raining Hell down on this city when they find out? No matter what you tell me, that man—" He spun in his chair, thrusting an arm out to point at *Indulgence* through the window—"is obsessed with you. You are fucking blind if you don't see that."

"Don't be ridiculous," I scoffed.

"You're only prolonging the inevitable. When he finds out, and Samara, he *will* find out, you had better hope that he loves you enough to shield you from the flames," Jasper huffed. "I can't even understand what you were thinking. Lying to me about that, and then not telling them. You're smarter than that."

"I thought that I wouldn't let any of you pay the consequences for my decisions. I married him. I stayed with him after the first time he hit me, and then the second and the third. I forgave him. Nobody else did that, so when it escalated, I had no one to blame but myself!"

Jasper paled, standing from his chair abruptly. "Don't you dare. You are not responsible for what he did."

"You're right. I'm not, but I am responsible for the fact that I was there. I ignored the warning signs, and I paid the consequences for that. Now, it's done. Now, I can move on, and I want to do that with my best friend, brother, and boss walking free and not visiting them behind bars!"

"Samara," he whispered, his brow furrowing as if my words hurt him physically.

"I already ruined *my* life. I won't ruin theirs too." Turning on my heel, I strode out of the office and closed the door behind me.

My desk chair was a welcome respite, and I tucked myself into it and woke up my computer. After a few deep breaths, I felt stable enough to get through the rest of my day.

And I did just that.

CHAPTER FOUR

LINO

Campbell had the sense to look nervous as he stepped into my office at Indulgence. No matter how much I wanted to give him his latest job and send him off to do it, we both knew I couldn't ignore the way he'd failed with Ivory. The man wasn't dumb, and he had long since heard the news that Matteo had claimed her in every way a man could claim a woman.

I knew that Matteo had relayed him a message too.

"Sit down," I said, gesturing to the seat on the other side of my desk. I barely glanced up from the contract sitting on my desk, letting him wait for a few moments. "Matteo isn't pleased."

"I couldn't have known about the robbery before him. She went straight to his place after it happened," he protested.

I raised an eyebrow at him, finally glancing up into his ruddy face. "Ivory Torres was assaulted in a club nearly a decade ago. Why wasn't Matteo made aware of this?"

He blanched. "I—I didn't know. She never filed a report."

"You were supposed to keep tabs on her," I pointed out.

He laughed. "Keeping tabs and stalking are two very different things. Bellandi only wanted to know if she was in danger, otherwise she was persona non grata, and he didn't want to hear about it. I didn't follow her every step of her life, and if something happened, then there would be no way of me knowing. She never saw a shrink. Never went to the police. There was nothing to find, Lino."

I nodded, because I'd expected an answer like that. As much as Matteo loved Ivory, in their years apart even the mention of her name was enough to send the man spiraling into a violent rage. He wouldn't have wanted to know about her daily life, about the men she may have dated. It would have driven him crazy. "I need you to look into someone for me."

"What's the name?" he asked, pulling a small notepad out of his back pocket. Old-fashioned as always, but he was damn good at his job.

"Connor Walsh."

"Why does that sound familiar?" he asked as he jotted the name down. His pen looked ancient, and the way it scratched at the paper made my skin crawl.

"You ran him a few years back. I need an update now that they're getting divorced."

"Ah, the one who married your pretty friend. Samara Walsh?"

"Mahoney. She never took his name."

Campbell chuckled. "Well, from the impression I got that must have pissed him right off."

"I'm sure a lot of things about Samara pissed him off," I agreed. "She's not exactly the type who belongs with a domineering bastard like that, but she's a grown ass woman and has to make her own decisions. Or so she likes to remind me, anyway."

Another chuckle, and I'd known Campbell long enough to know he commiserated with me. His own wife was like an older, more stubborn version of Samara. There should be a special club for men like us, who had women who drove us crazy, and we loved every second. Because even while we loved it, I knew my Little Dove made me want to tear my hair out.

Frequently.

But I very much looked forward to the day when she could tear it out for me.

While she was underneath me. Right where she belonged.

Damn the consequences.

"Alright, I'll run a background check," Campbell said.

"No. I want surveillance. I want to know where he goes, what he does. If he so much as looks at Samara wrong, I want to know about it. He's fighting the divorce, and she's keeping secrets from me. I want to know exactly what they are."

"You want me to look into her too?" Campbell asked, and even though I thought about it, I decided against it.

"Let's start with him. If she finds out I had her followed, she'll lose her shit. If nothing comes up with him, then we'll reconsider."

"Good plan. I'll start today." He stood from the chair, making for the door without so much as a glance my way to say goodbye.

"Campbell? You find something, I want to know as soon as you find it. Got it?"

"You got it Mr. Bellandi."

I nodded, dismissing him out the door of the club.

***

The Bellandi Estate was far too much house. How Ivory had adjusted to living in it so smoothly given her circumstances was beyond me. She waddled around in the kitchen, ignoring the way Donatello fussed over her and begged her to go sit down. But the woman was already past her due date and pissed about it.

"Angel, would you sit before you give Don a heart attack, please?" Matteo chuckled from his seat on the island stool next to me. I nearly laughed out loud, considering how much he'd hovered when she'd first started showing what seemed like a lifetime ago.

"You heard the doctor. Movement is good for me, walking helps bring on labor sometimes," Ivory protested, walking to the other side of the kitchen to grab the sugar she needed for whatever chocolate deliciousness she was mixing.

"I don't think pacing around in the kitchen is what he had in mind. A walk around the property in the fresh air would be more accurate."

"Have you been outside today, you hermit?" After the stand mixer stirred for her, she poured the batter into the pan and let Don bend to put it in the oven, thankfully.

I wasn't sure she could bend that far anymore.

Matteo grinned at her back as she strutted over to Smaug's tank, lifting him out gently and cooing at him affectionately. The lizard was more spoiled than most children. "I haven't, no. Why would I when I have everything I could ever want in my kitchen?"

"Daww," I teased. "I'm so glad I'm everything you could ever want, Teo."

"Don't call me that," Matteo warned, waving a finger at me. My eyes tipped over to Ivory where she continued to pace about the kitchen and only spared her husband a single, bored glance.

The joys of pregnancy.

"It's freezing outside, so the kitchen it is. Little Luna needs to come. I am not having a C-Section, do you hear me Matteo Bellandi?" Her face hardened into a glare that would terrify most men. Matteo was braver than me, or just plain stupid. Personally, I thought the latter.

"Whatever you say, *cara mia*," he murmured in that gentle voice I'd thought I would never hear from my hardened cousin. Satisfied with his agreement, Ivory nodded and kept walking. Smaug snuggled on the shelf her protruding belly presented, clinging to her sweater lightly. He hung out there more than on her shoulder since her belly had gotten big enough, staring up at his owner in awe like he knew exactly what kicked at him periodically from inside her stomach.

Some people had guard dogs. Luna had a guard gecko.

Totally normal.

Matteo turned a bright grin my way, and I knew what that meant. "How's Samara?"

"She's fine," I said shortly. I grimaced at him, silently trying to warn him it was not a subject we needed to broach.

"Just fine? Not jumping your bones yet?" he asked, drawing a little giggle from his wife. How Samara could be so oblivious to what was happening between us when everyone around us saw it so clearly, I would never know. Sometimes it felt like she'd built walls so tall that she couldn't see over them.

"I'm waiting until the divorce is final. I won't make her mine when she still has a husband." I shrugged like the timing was inconsequential, even if it killed me more and more every day that I held true to the promise I'd made myself. I'd wanted to claim her as soon as Matteo claimed Ivory for himself, knowing my cousin would have my back and help me protect Samara the way he protected Ivory.

Instead, I'd done the right thing. It was vastly overrated, but after wasting this much time, I couldn't bring myself to break my vow. "The divorce still isn't finalized?" Ivory asked, and I hated the way her voice morphed with concern. She'd only met Connor a few times in passing before they separated, since she and Samara had barely spoken before she reunited with Matteo, but even she hadn't formed a positive opinion of the man.

"She said he's fighting it, and since he has all his resources at his disposal, he's holding up the process." I shrugged, because that was as much as I knew, even though it frustrated me to no end. There had been a time when Samara told me everything, and even the things she didn't say outright, she said in every other way. But the past couple years she'd been distant, like some secret plagued her, and she couldn't open up to me the way she once had.

I hated it.

I'd been patient, but that time had come to an end.

"And why haven't you backed her up?" Matteo looked at me like I'd grown a second head.

"I've been respecting her boundaries. She asked me not to get involved, and I wanted to give her that, stupidly." I huffed a laugh. I didn't say it, but I remembered how close Matteo had come to losing Ivory because of his willingness to cross boundaries that shouldn't have been crossed.

"I hate to say it," Ivory whispered, clenching her eyes closed like it pained her to admit. "But it's been over nine months. I think it's time that you interfere. Just don't tell her I said that. Girl code," she said with a humorless chuckle.

Donatello left the room, and I knew it was because he had no interest in talking about Samara. He loved her like a daughter, had watched her grow up in the same way he'd been there for Matteo and I. The prospect of interfering in her life without her consent wasn't something he would take lightly. Even if he would ultimately side with Matteo and I when it came to her safety.

"I'm already working on it," I admitted. The way Ivory's face filled with relief made something in my chest tighten. I'd waited too long to interfere. If Ivory thought so, then I really had given Samara too much time to figure it out on her own.

"Good. Connor really gives me a bad feeling, Lino. I'll feel much better when all the ties are severed."

"You and me both, sweetheart," I agreed.

Maybe I'd finally start sleeping again once I knew Samara was mine. I had a feeling I'd have a much greater incentive to stay in bed when I couldn't sleep at the very least. Having her waiting there for me would mean I never wanted to leave.

CHAPTER FIVE

SAMARA

Making my way into the Bird Lounge on Tuesdays was something that never seemed to get any easier. The memory of the days when I'd gotten up on the stage and sang was nothing but a distant memory that ate at me every day. It was one that I wanted to change, something I wanted to take back after the years of Connor convincing me I couldn't sing. The guitar in the case at my side felt weighted, and I pointedly had to ignore the glances of the few people who still recognized me for the regular I'd once been.

Singing had never been a career path for me, even when I'd let Lino convince me I had a voice worth listening to, but that didn't mean that my soul didn't miss the way it felt to sing on stage. Even if Lino had never come to the *Bird Lounge* with me, I saw him everywhere. Felt his presence in the very venue, given that I'd chosen it for the name.

His Little Dove singing at the *Bird Lounge.*

I'd always thought to bring him there one day, to show him what I could do when someone believed in me.

When he believed in me.

But those days were gone, Lino's position in my life solidified with all the years wasted between us and all the bittersweet memories I had of him as my best friend.

So watching someone perform on the stage, the stage I knew I wouldn't perform on that night the moment I walked into the door, I settled into my chair as an observer. Her voice was deep, raspy. Seductive rather than the clear twang of my own. Everything I wished I had for myself. I sipped at the beer I'd grabbed from the bar, smoothing a hand down my fitted skirt. The sleek fabric was a contrast to the cashmere sweater that hung off my shoulders loosely, and the fabric inched up my thighs when I crossed my legs.

A glance over to the bar confirmed the man who had been watching since I entered still sat there with his eyes on me. I ignored it in favor of feeling the music pulse through my veins. I felt the moment he stood, far too aware of all the men in the room. I wished I could go back to the days when I didn't feel like a victim swimming in shark-infested waters. I wished that I could erase the scars the assault left me with.

"You getting up there tonight, sweet thing?" he asked, helping himself to the other chair at my high-top table. I smiled politely, inching as far to the opposite side as my chair would allow.

"Not tonight."

"You brought a guitar. Just like every Tuesday." His green eyes angled down to look at the case propped against my chair.

I fought down the discomfort of him having seen me before. Lots of people went to the *Bird Lounge* for open mic night. It didn't mean he was a stalker or meant to harm me. "Not feeling it tonight," I whispered, feeling my pulse quicken when he leaned closer into my space.

"My friend over there says he heard you sing once. Said your voice is as pretty as you are. I told him that wasn't possible. How about you prove me wrong?" he pushed, his hand coming so close to mine that it almost touched my beer bottle.

"I'm not interested in proving anything to anyone," I hissed. "I sing when I want to. Not on command."

"Aw, don't be like that, baby," he murmured, reaching toward me until his finger skimmed against my forearm. I flinched back, standing from my stool quickly and gathering up my guitar. "Hey, where are you going?" He was to his feet before I could make my retreat, blocking my path to the door. I knew it was ridiculous. He couldn't hurt me in a room full of witnesses, but the inability to escape, being trapped, was too familiar to the way Connor had cornered me all those months ago.

"Let me leave." My voice shook with the words, and I knew a crowd was forming, to my horror.

His hand touched my arm again, successfully gripping lightly. There was a genuine apology on his face, seeming to realize he'd frightened me somehow. "I didn't mean to scare you."

"Let go of me, please."

"Sweetheart," he whispered, his brow furrowing in confusion.

"I believe she said to let her go. Given she's Bellandi property, you might want to listen," a male voice interjected, and I turned to find Rex staring him down from the bar. "You alright, Samara?"

The offending man dropped my arm quickly at the mention of the Bellandi's, and I turned to give Rex a grateful smile. "I'm good, honey," I whispered, ignoring the pointed look he gave me as he studied the way I rubbed at my arm as if I could wash the other man's touch off me. "I best be getting home. I'll see you."

And like the coward I was, I adjusted my grip on my guitar and bolted out the door. "Mike will walk you to your car!" Rex called, and I didn't bother to argue. Mike took up his place at my side as we made our way outside, a silent sentry that I appreciated in the face of the realistically minor altercation inside.

"You okay?" he asked when we reached my car.

"Yeah, just jumpy. One of those days, you know? Got a bad feeling," I lied, giving him a self-deprecating shake of my head. He slipped his card into my hand.

"You call me if you need anything, Samara. My sister," he paused, seeming to consider if he should voice whatever thoughts coursed through his head. "She was jumpy like that after a bad breakup. He out of the picture?" he asked.

"I'm working on it," I admitted, not even bothering to deny the silent accusation behind the weight of his comparison to his sister.

"You call me if he gives you a hard time again. A man like that deserves to know what it is to be a punching bag for someone bigger than him." I huffed a laugh, because bigger was an understatement. Mike was a massive mountain of a man who made even Matteo seem small, when you considered pure size, anyway.

"Yeah, Mike. I'll call you," I agreed, hefting the car door open.

"Liar," he accused. "You'll take a beating before you call me. Ain't no shame in asking for help when you need it."

I turned wide eyes his way, having never heard the normally calm, mellow man sound even remotely annoyed. The snap to his voice seemed uncharacteristic of him, totally at odds with the man I'd known casually for over five years. "You don't know a damn thing about my situation. He's out of the house, doesn't touch me. I got myself into this without help, and I'll do this without help too."

"Bellandi claims you as family. Why isn't it already taken care of?"

"Because I'm not actually family. I take care of my own problems, and I don't need a man to fix my problems for me." I dropped into the seat, looking back up at Mike through the open door. "I'd appreciate your discretion. This is something I just need to take care of on my own. Can you respect that?"

"Of course. Not gonna take your choice away from you."

"Thank you, Mike," I whispered in relief.

"Don't thank me," he grunted, tapping on the roof of the car before backing away. "Just use my number."

CHAPTER SIX

LINO

I sat behind my desk, staring at the screen as if it would manifest a report from Campbell. It hadn't even been ten hours since I'd set him on Connor Walsh, so expecting him to have found something groundbreaking in that time was ridiculous and impatient. Even for me.

It was late, another late night at *Indulgence*, although it was a Tuesday and not as busy as Thursday through Saturday. The window at my back showed the club floor, the door to my office closed to keep the music out.

I didn't want to deal with anyone's shit.

I didn't want to be there at all, but I'd been putting in extra hours so I could step back and let the managers step up more and hire a new one to oversee. With Matteo's permission, we'd decided that *Indulgence* was ready for me to be less involved with the day-to-day operations and add it into my more passive business interests where I acted as the distant owner, even though Matteo was technically the owner of all the Bellandi properties.

My conversation with Samara's next-door neighbor earlier in the day had *not* gone well. I'd thought it would be easy enough to visit the woman and pry gently into the last few days of Samara's marriage. If there was nothing to hide, it should have been that simple. So the fact it had been anything but left me feeling restless and aggravated. She'd given me nothing.

Not a fucking thing.

Closed up like she guarded the most precious treasures along with Samara's secrets, and under different circumstances I would have appreciated the loyalty she showed my woman. Just not when that loyalty stood in my way.

The knock at the door sounded, and I turned away from the spreadsheet I was neglecting on my computer with my inability to focus. "Open." Enzo stepped in, closing it behind him. "What did you find?" I asked without preamble.

He sighed, dropping into the chair so suddenly I thought it might break under his weight. "Nothing. The woman doesn't have any skeletons in her closet that would make her dislike the Bellandi name."

"Then why the Hell wouldn't she talk to me?" I grunted, dropping my head forward to rub at my eyes.

"Did it occur to you that maybe you intimidated her? Walking up to her house in your suit and tie and looking like you own Chicago, throwing around the Bellandi name the way you did? From what I've seen, she's sharp as a tack." Enzo argued, amusement sparking in his face as he stared at my annoyance. Even with him though, hidden beneath the veneer of entertainment, I could see the gears turning.

He knew Samara vaguely. Knew of her more. Knew enough to know that if she was keeping secrets from me and Yavin, it had to be bad. "The woman didn't even blink when I told her I was a friend of Samara's. She knew damn well who I was before I introduced myself and was ready to slam the door in my face the second she laid eyes on me. What the fuck kind of trouble has Samara gotten herself into that she wouldn't come to me for help?"

The look of apprehension that crossed his face was completely terrifying. "Maybe she's not in trouble at all," he said hesitantly. "Have you considered that, you know, maybe she's dating someone and just isn't ready to have you and Yavin breathing down his neck?" I felt the snarl that graced my face, even before Enzo's uncomfortable chuckle filled the room.

I looked away from him, casting my gaze down to the crowd of people dancing. If I wanted, I could have gone down to the floor and had my pick of women to bring up and have my way with. But I didn't want that, because for the first time in my life, having Samara was a distinct possibility. If I'd been celibate for months on end and found out she'd been dating, I'd lock her up and throw away the key.

There was *nothing* that I would let stand in my way of claiming my woman finally.

No one.

Not even Samara herself.

"She's not dating," I said definitively. The alternative was just not worth considering. Because I wouldn't be responsible for what I would do if I had to go back to the knowledge that someone else had put his hands on my woman, and worse, that I'd allowed it in my desire to have her divorced before I made her mine.

Like a fucking idiot.

I decided at that moment that regardless of Samara's wishes, I *would* step into her divorce proceedings. A little poke to the right judge, and I'd owe a small favor. It would be entirely worth it to have Samara in my bed where she belonged. Where she'd always belonged.

"I just want you to be prepared for all the possibilities here. You're all ready to go charging in like a white knight and rescue her, but there could be another explanation," Enzo said carefully. He stood from the chair, rounding it and making his way to the door. The man was intuitive enough to know that his final blow would set me over the edge, that I wouldn't want to even look at him until the morning at the very least. "She could just not feel the same way."

"I'm no white knight," I huffed a laugh, even as rage built inside me. The woman had me turned inside out, and I hadn't even kissed her yet. Had never had the pleasure of feeling her lips on mine, and yet she'd had me wrapped around her finger since I'd been ten years old.

"I know that, but does she?" Enzo asked, and then he opened the door and disappeared through it, leaving me to my thoughts.

He left me with the agonizing thoughts about what expectations Samara might have about a relationship with me. She wasn't like Ivory, thankfully. I'd made no secret what the Bellandi family did, but she also knew that I ran the legitimate businesses and that her brother worked that side with me.

She probably did not understand that I wouldn't just ask her on a date, had no clue I planned to insert myself in every facet of her life as soon as she was divorced. Likely the night the divorce was final. I was the one who first greeted her every morning, even though it meant setting my alarm for hours earlier than I needed to wake up. I was the one who snuggled with her on the couch when she had cramps and the one who rubbed her feet when she killed them wearing heels to work.

I was the one who took care of her, who sheltered her and encouraged her hopes and dreams.

Me. Not Connor.

Because she always had been, and she always would be *mine.*

No matter what a piece of paper said.

CHAPTER SEVEN

SAMARA

Lino's oversized band tee hung nearly to my knees, the name of his favorite band stretched over my chest loosely. Having showered off the slimy feeling that the man from the Bird Lounge had left me with from only the simplest of nearly harmless touches, I couldn't wait to crawl into bed and sleep what remained of the night away.

But as I left my bathroom, toweling my hair dry as I walked, I thought I glimpsed light from the open doorway. Snatching my glasses off the nightstand quickly, I shoved them onto my face to confirm that I wasn't on edge and para-noid. I grabbed my phone in one hand, the bat I tucked under my bed in the other and crept into the hallway slowly.

As quietly as I could.

My bare feet padded across the floor, thoroughly dried and giving me the traction I needed to get through the hall without a sound. The light came from my office, the office I hadn't set foot inside all day, and as I peered around the doorway to peek inside, I knew why.

Connor knelt beside my desk, ticking away at the digital safe as he tried to guess the code. I hefted the bat up higher, drawing in a deep, shuddering breath. "What the fuck is it you think you're doing?" I asked, stepping into the doorway. I held the bat in my hands tightly, channeling all the fear I felt into that grip. I wouldn't let him come into *my* home and scare me, wouldn't show him that what he'd done still woke me up at night.

Barely sparing me a glance, he punched the safe in frustration before turning his full attention to me. "Rowe always gives you a huge bonus for the holiday. I need the money."

"And you thought I'd keep thousands of dollars in cash sitting in a safe in my home? He's not a criminal, Connor. He pays me by direct deposit like any normal employer." I rolled my eyes, unable to believe that I hadn't been able to see his descent into desperation for exactly what it was during our marriage. He'd been smart, attractive, charming. What remained of him was nothing like the man I'd married, nothing but a shadow of the addiction that plagued him.

"No, that's just the guy you spread your legs for like the good little whore you always were." He stood, unfolding his suit clad body to leer down at me.

I bit my tongue, because arguing that I wasn't Lino's whore and never would be was pointless. He hadn't gotten it through his head in our nearly five years of marriage, and he wouldn't learn now that we separated. "Just get the fuck out," I hissed. "Or I'll call the cops and tell them exactly why we're getting a divorce."

"The cops ain't gonna come and kick me out of my house, Samara," he laughed. "My money pays for it."

"We both know your money hasn't paid for jack shit in years," I argued, stepping aside from the office door in a clear invitation for him to leave. "Besides, we had a deal. You stay the fuck away from me, and I don't press rape charges and stain your precious family name with something 'unsavory' like that." He stepped around the desk, and I held in the tremble that threatened to take over my body. I wouldn't let him see what being near him did to me, wouldn't let him know that having him in my home with no one else to interfere was enough to make my pulse race. I just wanted him out of my space.

"I *need* that money, Mara," he whispered, something in his voice cracking. I ignored the moment of pity I felt, knowing that it was just another ploy to play on my compassion, on the fact that I had at one point loved him.

"Save your self-pity for someone who gives a shit. That isn't me anymore," I whispered, gesturing him out the door with a nod of my head. He nodded, twisting his lips in a way that communicated that I wouldn't like his next words.

I should have expected it. Should have seen the madness playing just beneath the surface of his calm.

But I didn't, and I barely had time to hit him in the torso with the bat when he reached out for me. "Fucking bitch!" he grunted, grabbing the bat in his hand and yanking it out of my grip to toss it to the side. "You will get me that money. You owe me for all the years I tolerated you fucking around on me."

"You're delusional," I yelled, taking a step back and tugging at where he held my forearm in a bruising grip. "Let go of me!" The panic in my voice might have horrified me under different circumstances, might have made me think twice. I didn't want him to hear it, but I knew I wouldn't survive another rape.

The first one had nearly broken me.

With a twist of his body, he flung me to the floor of the office, so I landed on my stomach and scrambled to get to my feet. The way he chuckled behind me made a rock settle in my stomach. "Where's your precious Lino now?" he hissed, and I flipped over to my back and scooted back away from him in the face of that sound.

When he straddled my hips, I felt a single moment of relief that he wasn't forcing my legs apart. That his fingers weren't prying my legs open to take what I wouldn't give. That relief fled with a sharp gasp when both his hands wrapped around the front of my throat and pressed down, squeezing until my vision went hazy, and I couldn't get a single breath. I kicked my legs, bucked my hips. But there was no reprieve.

No air.

He'd kill me. I knew it wouldn't be long before everything went black.

"You're going to be a good girl and get me everything you have in your account, aren't you, baby?" I tried to nod, tried to speak past the rock in my throat that let nothing pass. His hands tightened further, punctuating the affectionate term I'd hated every time he used it with a squeeze that made my head spin and darkness creep in at the edges of my vision. "I'll be back for it tomorrow and if you don't have it, I'll find another way to make that money off you. You understand?" I tried again, heaving in a deep, shuddering breath that made my body heave with coughs when he released me. "Good girl," he sighed, standing to his feet and straightening his suit like he hadn't nearly killed me.

I didn't watch him leave, but somehow heard the path of his footsteps as he made his way down the stairs, even as my ears rang and the feeling returned to my body like being stabbed with a thousand needles repeatedly. I didn't move, couldn't find the strength to make my arms work for what seemed like an eternity.

When I finally turned my head, I found my phone resting where I'd dropped it by the door and maneuvered myself to my hands and knees to crawl to it.

Linda was number four on my speed dial, and she was the only person I could call with this. The only one who wouldn't set off a manhunt of epic proportions.

"Samara?" she asked, her voice thick with sleep. I knew it had to be late; it had been late to begin with when I'd gotten home from the lounge.

"Need h-help," I breathed. My voice was barely a whisper, hoarse and foreign sounding. Like it didn't belong to me.

She came anyway.

CHAPTER EIGHT

SAMARA

Linda had me curled up in my bed, thrusting pain medicine at me along with a bottle of water. I wanted to resist, wanted to tell her I didn't think I had it in me to swallow the pills, but the thunderous look on her face had me accepting them, anyway.

"He could have killed you. This has gone too far, Samara." Where she might have been gentle with me, after months of watching me battle with him in divorce litigation, this was the final straw for my hardened neighbor.

I nodded. "I'll figure something out in the morning. I promise." Her eyes narrowed to the thinnest slits when faced with the haggard sound of my voice. She shook her head at me, the lines on her aged face looking more weathered than usual in her concern.

"You're not alone. We'll figure it out together," she sighed finally as I forced the pills down. She thrust the bag of frozen peas into my hands, and I fought to contain my wince when I pressed it to the delicate flesh of my throat. She glared at it like my throat was at fault for Connor's assault.

"Is it that bad?" I asked.

She nodded and her silver hair shook around her chin as she didn't even bother to sugarcoat it. "It's already bruised. You won't be going to work for some time, I suspect. Unless Jasper Rowe wouldn't think it odd if you suddenly wore a turtleneck every day." I shook my head, because even if I could hide the physical signs of the injury, there would be no disguising the pathetic rasp to my voice.

I laid back, resting my head on my pillow and only letting the ice *barely* touch my neck. Laying on my back with the pressure of the ice on my neck sent a pulse of terror through me, and I shot to sitting upright again. "You should rest, honey."

"I won't be able to sleep," I admitted, and she sighed before curling up in my bed with me. She turned the television on and pulled up my streaming service to settle in with her favorite reality dating show. I huffed a laugh, wincing in pain. "You could have asked what I wanted to watch."

"Hush. I'm your guest," she said as she made herself comfortable. "It's only good manners to let me watch what I want since I wouldn't even be awake if you weren't so stubborn." Eventually losing myself in the show, I set the peas on my nightstand and settled in on my side.

As I was drifting off to sleep, I vaguely heard Linda talking to someone and must have smiled in my sleep.

She was always talking to her shows.

CHAPTER NINE

LINO

I hated hiring people, hated reviewing resumes. I looked forward to the day that my manager handled such matters for me, and I never had to concern myself with the matters of employment. The shadow that appeared in my office wasn't mysterious, but I worked hard to ignore the way Enzo lurked in the doorway, no doubt on his way out for the night. Given the ridiculously late hour, most of my employees had already gone home for the night. "You need to go home," he ordered, snapping my gaze away from the computer where my eyes nearly glossed over from staring too intently. I shook my head, rubbing the heel of my palms into my eyes to clear my vision.

"Just a bit longer," I argued, wanting to wrap up my glance over of the resumes that had come in the last few days. Knowing it would bring me one step closer to a more normal, regular work schedule, I felt eager to persevere and get it done. I needed to be ready to give Samara the relationship she needed, the kind she would want and be proud of. A man who was there in the evenings to dote on her, to spend time with her, but still provided for her and made her life easier.

I'd spent too many years of my life living for the Bellandi name—living for the business and the success that we strove for constantly. It was the only thing that mattered when family was business and I had no hope of ever being with the woman I'd loved for as long as I could remember. But with a real chance at happiness finally on the horizon, the hope that pulsed through me was foreign. Unknown.

And it was everything. She was everything. My past, my present, my future.

"You can't keep pushing so hard for something that may or may not happen, man," Enzo sighed, scrubbing a hand over his own face.

"It not happening isn't a possibility for me. I proceed like I will soon have a wife in my home because no other outcome is acceptable," I warned. "You should refrain from discouraging me for a few days. I'm not feeling generous where you're concerned after earlier."

Enzo laughed, and I hoped I would soon get to watch him fall to a woman who was everything he never dared to dream for. I would very much look forward to the day when a woman knocked him on his ass and he never fought back. "Okay, okay." He held up two hands to placate me. "You'll get married and have six kids. You've got it."

I went to tell him he would one day be struck by a woman who just felt like the other half of his soul, but never got the words out. The sound of my cell ringing made both of us turn concerned glances at it as it vibrated along the cherry surface. The time on my computer read 3:39 a.m. I knew we both wondered who would call me at that time at night, and my first instinct was Ivory was in labor. But the name on the screen made my pulse race for an entirely different reason.

I snatched it off the desk, taking the call without hesitation. "Little Dove?"

"I—is this Angelino Bellandi?" I barely recognized the exhausted voice of Samara's neighbor as she whispered, something akin to deep-rooted, genuine fear hovering in her words.

"It is. Is Samara okay?" I asked, and I was already on my feet. My suit jacket already snatched off the back of my chair and shrugged onto my arms.

"She will be, but no. She's not. She'll be furious with me when she finds out I called you, but—"

"You did the right thing. What happened?" I asked, cutting off the older woman. I had no patience to listen to her rambles, not when my thoughts were a mess of horror. Fear. True fear was something I couldn't remember feeling, probably not since my mother had died. Or perhaps it had been the day I turned sixteen and my father told me that if I ever touched Samara, he would slit her throat while I watched. But in that moment, there was nothing but pure, blinding fear.

"Connor broke into the house. He, shit," she hissed and paused. "He strangled her, Mr. Bellandi. This has gone on for too long, and I can't just sit by and watch her suffer in silence."

My body stilled, halfway to the door of my office. The tremble started in my hand; the phone vibrating against my head as I struggled to contain the sudden rage that made my vision turn black. "What the fuck did you just say?" I whispered, and every muscle in Enzo's body locked solid at the sound of the menace in my voice.

I sounded like a savage.

I sounded like Matteo.

"It's bad, Mr. Bellandi. She's finally asleep in bed, but she can't stay here. That much is clear," Linda whispered, and I could almost picture her staring down at my little dove where she slept. She was another person who Samara sucked into her orbit and refused to release—another one drawn to the genuine sweetness that she presented.

"She doesn't know you called me," I said in realization as my feet finally carried me to the door as my body became unlocked. Enzo slid out of the way, closing the door to my office behind me and locking it before he hurried to catch up as I thundered my way down the stairs. Under any normal circumstances, the stairs wouldn't have been enough to even remotely wind me. But with my anger a tangible venom in my veins, my heart felt like it might implode inside my chest.

"No." She said the word carefully, as if she knew she'd stepped on a landmine and did not understand how to defuse the bomb without losing a limb herself.

"She was fucking strangled, and she didn't call me?" I accused, my jaw clenching as I thought about what else she might have kept from me. "Why the Hell isn't she in the hospital?"

There was a pause on the other side of the line that confirmed the woman knew more than she was willing to tell me. "She refused to go to the hospital. She always does, but I suspect you and Samara will need to have a very in-depth conversation about her marriage to Connor before you can understand what I mean, Mr. Bellandi. Should I presume you're on your way?"

"Yes. You can presume that," I bit out, hanging up the call as Enzo slid into the driver's side of my car. He didn't need directions, didn't need to be told that I was in no state to drive. He just slid into the position where I needed him, no matter that it was outside his job description and nearly four o'clock in the morning. As soon as I was in the passenger seat, he peeled out onto the road and made his way to Samara's home.

What had been her home for years, anyway. I already knew she wouldn't be living there ever again. She'd be fucking lucky if I ever let her out of my sight again, given exactly what she'd been hiding from me.

She'd officially used up my patience with her lies and secrets.

And I wouldn't tolerate another second of it.

✳✳✳

The BMW pulled into the driveway smoothly, no matter how quickly Enzo took the turn. I hadn't even shut the door behind me before the front door opened, and Linda stood in the doorway staring me down. With a resigned sigh, she stepped back as I thundered my way up the front steps of Samara's tiny house she'd loved so much when Connor bought it for her. "Where is she?" I hissed.

"She's sleeping. She should remain that way for the time being." The woman's voice was light, gentle as I made my way to the stairs at the back of the house. "You need to prepare yourself for what you'll see, Mr. Bellandi," she added, closing the door softly as Enzo finally made his way inside. "There are bruises. I thought it might be prudent to warn you before you saw them for yourself." The banister creaked as my hand clenched, the sound of the wood straining under the pressure of my fury a warning that I needed to control myself. The last thing I needed was to scare my Little Dove, especially when she was already vulnerable.

Hurt.

Schooling my features, I nodded to her and released the banister. "Find out everything she knows," I ordered Enzo, and then continued my way up the stairs. The bedroom door at the top was cracked open, the soft glow from the television illuminating the space just enough. I'd not been in her bedroom since she'd moved in with Connor before they married, but the nostalgia of it hit me with a sudden fierceness. I'd spent many nights curled up in bed with her when we were younger, escaping the fear of my father's fists by hiding away in her bed. It had been that way even when I'd been too young to understand what it meant. That she was my home.

On any other occasion, walking into the room she'd once shared with a man who wasn't me would have been enough to drive me mad with jealousy. But the sight of Samara's tiny form curled up in the center of the bed, her knees held tightly to her chest as if she couldn't bear to be alone even in her sleep, was enough to bring me to my knees for another reason altogether. I perched on the edge of the bed, reaching a hand over to tuck her copper hair behind her ear so I could see her face more clearly. Even in her sleep, she looked disturbed.

Trapped.

In a way I recognized, because I'd seen it on my face too many times as a child when I looked in the mirror. There was nothing I wouldn't do to erase that look from her face permanently, but as my eyes drifted down to the purple marks on her delicate golden skin, I knew that I would burn the city to the ground if that was what it took to find Connor.

I curled myself around her, tucking her back into my front to comfort her. When she jerked in my hold, a panicked gasp rattled in her throat. "Shh, Little Dove. It's just me."

She whimpered, and the sound of pain that escaped her in a long, low groan was enough to make a growl rumble in my chest. It took everything I had to keep my body from vibrating with the fury that took over every muscle, tightening everything in me until I could release my tension on Connor when I tore him limb from limb. "What are you doing here?" she rasped, attempting to pull away, but the motion lacked energy and enthusiasm in the way I'd have thought Samara capable of. I wanted to think maybe she enjoyed being in my arms as much as I enjoyed having her there, but I suspected it was just another sign of the pain that wreaked havoc on her body.

I drew my phone out of my pocket, texting Enzo to have Linda come and pack Samara a bag when he finished discovering what she knew. "I think the better question would be, how long do I plan to play with Connor before I slit his throat?" She winced, and I suspected my words may have gone too far. Still, she didn't escape my hold, and barely spared a glance for Linda when she stepped into the bedroom quietly.

"You called him," she whispered, burrowing the side of her head farther into the pillow. Linda didn't bother to respond, and there was no shame in her face as she set to packing Samara's things. It was good to know that one of them had the sense to involve me, even if it had come too late. But Samara's reaction concerned me.

Desolate.

Resigned.

As if there was nothing worse than me knowing the truth, nothing worse than whatever justice I might mete out. Samara had never made me feel like less, even though she knew what the Bellandi family did. The possibility that she might hate me for killing someone who hurt her was too crushing to consider. Linda zipped the suitcase up, depositing it at the foot of the bed and staring down at Samara, who refused to look at her. "One of these days, you'll understand. You'll have a girl you love like one of your own, and if someone ever dares to hurt her, you will do whatever it takes to protect her."

Samara nodded, but even that motion didn't have her usual zest. I suspected there was more to it than her sore throat but didn't press. We didn't move until Enzo came up to collect the suitcase, and then I climbed out of the bed. I drew Samara into my arms, lifting her and carrying her out of her room.

My Samara would have protested. Would have claimed she could walk, that she wasn't an invalid. This Samara allowed it without a word, snuggling her face into my shoulder and sighing contentedly.

A broken dove.

She didn't so much as flinch when I crawled into the back seat with her, and Enzo pulled out in favor of making our way to my house.

CHAPTER TEN

SAMARA

I stared at the floor of the BMW. Lino's hand rested on my bare thigh in a hold I knew he meant to be soothing. Just above my knee, it was nothing inappropriate. Nothing that should have made my body come alive, especially not given the fact that I'd nearly been strangled to death less than two hours before.

But it did. Somehow, instead of feeling calming, his touch felt like a claim. Like a brand.

Distantly, I knew the air was cold, could hear the heat pumping in the front to warm it up. Lino stripped off his suit jacket and wrapped it around my shoulders, but it didn't matter. I couldn't feel the cold, anyway.

What I felt were his eyes on me, felt the awkward stretch when he looked to Enzo for advice. I knew Lino so well it wasn't funny, knew every mannerism and quirk. I knew his expression that signaled that exact moment when my fun-loving friend faded away to be replaced by the ruthless businessman who got his way no matter the cost.

I also knew the way his body sat too still in the middle seat next to me was merely the calm before the storm. I could feel it simmering beneath the surface and waiting to erupt. I knew it was only for my sake that he postponed the explosion. The thing I'd never wanted to happen had come to pass. Even if he didn't know the whole truth yet, he no doubt would soon enough.

Connor was a dead man.

And I would be responsible for the stain that left on my best friend's soul. The knowledge was a punch to the gut, knowing that I'd be the downfall of the person I loved most in the world.

My heart thumped in my chest, a staccato rhythm as the same word pounded in my head on repeat.

Fuck. Fuck. Fuck.

He wasn't meant to know, wasn't meant to ever see me so weak. My body felt like it was frozen solid as my brain raced with all the things I could say to save us from the situation we shouldn't have been in. But there was nothing left, no lies to tell. Only the truth remained.

"Samara," he murmured, attempting to catch my eye by ducking his face into my vision. I ignored him, finding that spot on the carpet much easier to focus on, much easier to sink into the numbness that made everything just a little less painful. "Little Dove, look at me," he ordered gently. Taking my chin in his hand, he ignored the flinch that startled me. Hands too close to my throat, too close to wrapping around and squeezing. "I'd never hurt you. You know that." He twisted my head until he could look down into my face, but still I couldn't bring myself to meet his eyes. Those warm brown eyes were too knowing, too familiar. Every time he looked at me, it felt like he saw inside my soul. I didn't want him to see just how broken I'd become. Not when I knew he'd be looking for it. "Jesus, fuck," he groaned, pressing his face into my neck. His body trembled, vibrating with fury suddenly as if he could see it even without my eyes on his.

I let him hold me, let him maneuver us out of the car so that my bare feet never touched the cold floor of his garage. The smell of him filling my nostrils felt like a familiar comfort, all spiced vanilla and clean man. I wanted to sink into the way it felt to be cradled so delicately in his arms. To feel like I mattered to someone in a way that was irreversible.

Inevitable.

After spending so many years under the thumb of someone who sought only to control me, to use me and manipulate me, the thought of having the power that came with love and affection over Angelino Bellandi was enough to push back a little of the numbness. A little of the haze.

When my eyes opened, it was to find him looking down at me. His breath shuddered when my eyes met his finally, my arms tightening around his neck in response. "There you are, *vita mia*," he murmured.

"What does that mean?" I whispered, the hoarseness of my voice making his nostrils flare briefly. He reached the top of the stairs, turning into one bedroom and setting me on the bed gently. Sitting on the edge, he looked over at me where I curled in on myself.

"My life." My heart clenched, and a whimper stuck in my sore throat. I wanted that. More than anything, I wanted to be everything to him in the way that he had *always* been everything to me. "You'll be safe here. Enzo will stay until I call in one of the other guys to watch over you. He'll be right downstairs if you need anything."

My eyes widened, darting up to his to find him standing from the bed. "Where are you going?"

"I have to find him," he grunted. "He doesn't get to just walk away after what he did to you." I grabbed his hand, pulling until he sat back on the bed with me.

"Please don't leave me," I begged. I didn't know why it felt so important that he stayed with me, but with him finally knowing the truth about my marriage, I needed him. Needed to know that he wasn't walking away, needed to know he wasn't as disgusted with me as I was for everything I'd tolerated. It wasn't rational, even in that moment I knew it.

But as the panic seized my lungs, I climbed into his lap and straddled his hips with my legs so I could wrap myself around him like a monkey. "Samara." His voice went ragged, as if I tormented him by making him stay with me.

"Please, Lino," I whispered with a broken sob. "Please don't go. I need you."

"Okay," he sighed, tipping his head forward to press his lips against the top of my head in a gentle kiss. The closest to the real thing I'd ever get from him, I knew. If it was all I could have, it would be enough. It would have to be.

He stood, keeping me in his arms in a show of surprising strength. I'd known he was strong, of course. The way his suits fitted over his arms and chest left no doubt to that. But there was something about a man who could stand without help, bearing my weight on top of his, that seemed so unreal. So far-fetched.

So Lino.

"Let's get you washed up, and we'll get some sleep. You will never go to sleep with his touch lingering on your skin again." I nodded my assent into his neck, feeling his hands tighten around my thighs briefly. He strolled us into the connected bathroom, setting me on the bathroom vanity and detangling himself from my limbs. Shyly, crossing my legs together, I tried not to think about the fact that I'd been wrapped around him.

That Lino's hips had been between my legs.

"Can you stand to shower?" he asked, eyeing the bathtub and separate shower in consideration.

"Yes. I want to wash him down the drain, not sit in water stained by him." He nodded, reaching in to turn on the massive granite shower, before coming back to me and lifting me down off the counter and sliding me down his body until my feet touched the warm tile floor.

He swallowed, something flashing over his expression briefly before he pulled back and started unbuttoning his crisp white dress shirt. "What are you doing?" I squeaked.

"Helping you shower."

"You—what?" I watched him strip the shirt off his shoulders, and my eyes caught on the tattoo on his chest, an eye staring back at me. It was realistic, blurring out in a puff of fog and abstract tribal details with the only pop of color the iris itself in a pale grey tinted with light blue. My hand reached out to touch it, fingers brushing over the eyelashes that fanned out from the eye. Lino gasped softly, so subtly I nearly missed it. "What is this?"

"My everything. Everything I spent years protecting. Everything I want for myself." I furrowed my brow in confusion and looked up at him, finding him grinning down at me in amusement. "You'll understand one day soon, Little Dove. For now, let's get you clean."

"I can do it," I protested weakly, flinching when his fingers tickled the flesh of my thigh as he reached for the hem of the shirt I wore. I saw the moment he seemed to recognize the band logo staring back at him, and a rare moment of smug satisfaction crossed over his handsome, angular face.

"You sleep in my shirt often, *vita mia?*" I resisted the urge to cross my arms over my chest, too off-kilter with his proximity and those traitorous fingers dancing against my skin. The smile he gave me both infuriated me and made my pulse race. Such was the devastating beauty of Lino's perfect teeth and full lips tipping up to reveal that one dimple to the right of his mouth. "Did you sleep in this when you were with him?"

My face went hot, suddenly feeling like wearing a friend's shirt to bed had been inappropriate. It wasn't like I'd imagined Lino when I was with Connor; it wasn't like I'd used the man I'd once called my husband to fill the void. But regardless of the fact that our relationship had never been romantic, if I'd been forced to choose between Connor and Lino, even in the happiest moments of my marriage, there was no doubt who I'd choose. Lino was just a part of me.

The other half of me. Even as friends.

"You wore my shirt." He drew said shirt up, but it got caught on my arms when I shoved it down.

"I can shower alone," I hissed, fighting him when he tugged again.

"Little Dove, you can barely stand on your own. There's no way I'm leaving you to shower alone." Using his free hand, he lifted my arms up so he could maneuver it over my head. I couldn't breathe. Couldn't find the path to functioning, not with my naked torso open to his eyes and so close to touching his bare chest. "Relax. You can trust me."

I nodded, sucking in a deep breath. Exhaustion was real, something that came closer and closer to overtaking me with every second I spent objecting. I knew if we didn't get the shower over with soon, I'd be dead on my feet. My chest heaved with the breath, my nipples scraping against his skin gently and sending a tingle straight to my core. His eyes never left my face, never ventured lower to the sight of a naked woman practically in his arms.

It was all the confirmation I needed that Lino would never be more than a friend, would never see me as anything other than a best friend and the baby sister of his other friend. He backed away half a step, his fingers unfastening his pants, so they dropped to his feet, and he went through the awkward motions of stripping them off and freeing his feet from his socks and shoes. I didn't glance down, didn't dare look to see if he wore underwear or what he might look like if he didn't. My emotions spun, exhaustion bringing them all to the forefront.

The man I'd always wanted didn't even see me. So, I determined that I'd school myself against his charm and not see him either. A nurse. He became a nurse about to give me a professional sponge bath.

In the shower.

Naked.

With a quick swallow, I slid my fingers inside the waistband of my bikini underwear and let them fall to my feet. I looked away from Lino, taking my first step on my own since before the assault.

When my legs wavered, he was there, catching me against him. Those strong hands grasped around the backs of my thighs, lifting my feet off the ground just enough that he could shuffle us into the massive shower and under the rain shower head in the center. As soon as my coppery hair was drenched, clinging to my shoulders like a wet rat, he turned me to face away from him.

I was grateful for the reprieve. Avoiding eye contact was nearly impossible when he was so close. Touching me. A bottle cap popped open, and his fingers soon slid through my hair and slowly massaged my scalp so thoroughly that I think I moaned and let my eyes drift closed. "It smells like you," I whispered.

"My shampoo typically would." The humor returned to his voice, but it felt strained. Like being so close to me naked was painful. I could only imagine it felt similar to seeing your sister naked, given the way he hadn't reacted to me. I'd thought something had been shifting in our relationship, thought it wasn't just me who felt the sudden urgency and desire since I'd announced my divorce.

But it appeared I was wrong again when it came to Lino. I doubted it would be the last time.

"Is this your room?"

He stilled, as if realizing suddenly that something was weighty. Something in this moment meant something to him, but I had no idea what it might be. Just that I knew him well enough to hear the gears turning.

"Yes, Little Dove. This is my bathroom. That was my bed."

"Why wouldn't you bring me to a guest room?"

"Tomorrow. We'll talk about those kinds of things in the morning. After you've told me the truth, I'll give you *my* truth." I swallowed as he rinsed my hair, knowing that the time had come to be honest. But in the morning. For the night, I just wanted to forget. To pretend that, just maybe, there was a version of life where Lino could be mine. Where someone could cherish me the way he did.

Where I mattered.

So, when he worked conditioner through my hair, I settled into the feeling of his hands brushing against my back, of his fabric covered groin brushing against my ass. The hot water felt like heaven against my skin, but nothing compared to the way Lino ran a soapy loofah over every inch of my body. He didn't hesitate, didn't hover in any key place and was downright methodical about the way he cleaned me, but nothing could take away the fact that he was caring for me. That he loved me enough in his way to suffer through something like this with me.

For me.

By the time he inched my legs apart to run the loofah over the most intimate parts of me, I was so relaxed I was half asleep and my body jolted with a moan. He stilled, waiting, and I felt his breath at my ear.

Like my hips had a mind of their own, they tilted back and pressed my ass into his thighs. "Samara," he groaned on an agonized gasp. His hand returned to washing me quickly and drew away to rinse the soap off me. Suddenly fighting back tears, I caved to the tiredness seeping into my bones and let it wash away the pain.

The rejection.

The water turned off, and he stepped out to grab the towel and dry me off. I let him guide me into the bedroom in a daze, barely cooperating when he slipped one of his shirts on over my head. A minute later he tucked me into bed, and only a few moments passed before he crawled in behind me and wrapped me up in his arms.

It was the fastest I'd fallen asleep since the night Connor had assaulted me.

And for the moment, sleep was all that mattered.

CHAPTER ELEVEN

SAMARA

Sunshine peeked through the windows where the curtains didn't close. I groaned, feeling the vibrations of it in my throat like an open wound. The moment my eyes opened, I remembered where I was. Remembered the night before.

Drawing myself up to sit, I took in the space that was Lino's bedroom. Having never been in it before, never having a cause for it since he'd bought the house after we were too adult to cuddle in our sleep without consequences, I didn't know what to expect.

It was obvious he hadn't designed it alone. The walls were painted a dark blue-grey, masculine and dominant. Though there was little clutter, an intricate shelving unit seemed to be crafted into the wall to my right. Nightstands sat to either side of the bed, and a sitting area with leather arm chairs was set up over by the biggest window. I could picture him sitting there and looking out as he drank his morning coffee, and the thought brought a smile to my face.

But Lino was nowhere to be found. He'd promised not to leave me, hadn't he? The actual conversation from the night before seemed fuzzy, and I thought back to the painkillers Linda had given me. Coupled with the soreness in my body, it was a wonder I remembered anything.

And I remembered certain sensations in vivid color.

Grabbing my glasses off the nightstand where Lino must have put them after I'd fallen asleep, I stood and made my way to the bathroom slowly and went about my business. Swiping toothpaste onto my finger, I at least got rid of some of the grimy feeling I'd woken up with. I was making my way back to the bed, trying to think of an alternative to walking downstairs in a t-shirt with no underwear on, when the door swung open and Lino walked in. Dressed casually in his favorite sweatpants and shirtless, I fought the urge to drool over the grooved abs I hadn't wanted to notice the night prior. "What are you doing out of bed?" he asked, his brow furrowing in that frustrated way of his. Clutched in his hand at his side, the purple case of my phone was vibrant in contrast to his grey sweats.

"Is that my phone?" My brow furrowed as I looked up at him in confusion.

He shrugged, slipping it into the pocket of his pants unapologetically. "What are you doing out of bed?" he repeated.

"I need clothes. Did you put my suitcase in a guest room?" I asked, and he shook his head at me like I was ridiculous. "I don't have underwear on, Lino."

"Oh, believe me. I'm aware. Get in bed and I'll grab you something. Underwear and leggings?"

"You are not about to go rummaging through my clothes," I argued, taking a step toward him.

"Watch me," he hissed, some of the anger I knew must have been lurking under the surface during our moments of peace last night coming out to play. "Get in bed or so help me I will put you there myself."

With his harsh words, something that Lino rarely showed me, I climbed into the bed carefully and shot him a glare. "Happy?"

He huffed a humorous laugh and turned to a door that opened into his closet. He was back quickly with a pair of underwear and leggings, helping me glide them up my legs to my mortification. "Lino, you don't need to—"

"Hush, Samara. I'm taking care of you. Deal with it."

"I'm injured, not dead. I can put my own fucking underwear on, thank you," I hissed, slapping his hands away when he grasped me around the ass and pulled me to stand so he could pull them up the rest of the way.

Kneeling at my feet, he looked up at me. Beneath the anger simmering on his face, I could see the anguish. "Did you look at them?"

I shook my head, not needing to ask to know that he meant the bruises. I could feel them pulsing just under my skin with an ache that couldn't be ignored, but I would never admit that to Lino. Not when he seemed so intent on spoon feeding me for the next three years. Before I knew it, he lifted me off the floor and into his arms. Wrapping my legs around his waist for stability, I clung to him. With everything less hazy than before, being carried felt more intense. Strange and erotic all at once, but the thunderous look on his face quelled any rising desire in me. When he went in the open bathroom door and stopped in front of the mirror, I unwound my legs from him, and he dropped me slowly until my feet touched the floor.

"Look at them." He grunted the words, voice deepening in the way I knew there'd be no arguing with. I turned away from him to face the mirror, letting my eyes settle on the deep purple marks covering my throat. When I met his eyes in the mirror, they were wild with fury. "That is more than a simple injury. He almost killed you," he growled.

"I'm right here, Lino," I whispered, my heart clenching as his eyes closed and he nodded, pressing his lips to my hair as if he needed the contact to know that I was real. When I turned to face him, he lifted me into his arms again and I didn't bother to protest.

"Has he hurt you before?" he asked as soon as he settled me onto the bed and sat next to me. I didn't want to look at him, wanting to keep taking the coward's way out, but I also knew that I owed him an explanation.

"Not like this," I whispered, and I knew it was the wrong thing to say when his face twisted in fury again. "It was always little things. Grabbing me, slapping me once or twice. Nothing big enough to make me think he was capable of this." Even as I said the words, they felt like a lie, but I wasn't ready to get into the night that I'd told Connor I wanted a divorce.

"Why didn't you tell me?" he asked, and his voice made me inch closer to him on the bed so I could cup his cheek in my hand. Even as tears pooled in my eyes, I plowed forward.

"I never wanted you to know. You're the only person who looks at me and sees someone who's strong. Who stands up for myself. I didn't want to lose that," I whispered, my throat tightening with my attempt to fight back my tears.

"Surviving this only makes you stronger," he argued.

I nodded, because I'd long since realized it was true. Surviving after Connor's assault had required a strength I didn't know I possessed, especially since I was determined to do it without telling my family or Lino what had happened. "I couldn't stand the thought you would look at me differently. The thought that you might pity me for what happened when it was my own decisions that put me there in the first place, that was something I couldn't bear. So, I kept it from you. I kept it from everyone."

"You are not responsible for what he did," Lino hissed, tugging back from my hold on his face with a sudden ferocity.

"I didn't say that. But I chose him. I *married* him, Lino. I let him tear me down for years and strip away everything that mattered to me except for you. He destroyed the way I saw myself, and I let him. If I couldn't even defend myself or stand up for myself, then I had no business asking you to risk everything to defend my honor that I didn't deserve to hold on to."

Lino's deep eyes darkened, and he finally shook his head before sliding closer to me. "You're wrong. You're mine to protect, and you need to trust me to do that. Promise me you won't ever keep secrets from me again," he ordered. "I mean it, Samara. No more."

"And what about you? You said that you'd give me *your* truth after I came clean. Does that mean you're keeping secrets too? And I'm just supposed to accept those?" I snapped, crossing my arms over my chest with a huff.

"I'll tell you my secret when you're feeling better. It's not a secret, so much as something you just refuse to admit to yourself, but that's alright. Things are about to become very, *very clear* between us. Do you know what I'm talking about?" My eyes widened, and I bit my bottom lip to fight the tremble.

"No," I whispered truthfully. Before he'd helped me shower like nothing more than a nursemaid, I might have thought the darkened gaze as he stared at me nestled in his bed could be lust. But following those actions, there was no way that could be possible.

"You will," he said simply, grabbing the television remote off the nightstand and pressing a button. A flat screen dropped from the ceiling, and he put on a popular fantasy show for me to immerse myself in. "I'm going to go grab you something to eat, and some drinks to stash in the mini-fridge for a few days. Some of my guys are downstairs, working out a plan for canvasing to find Connor. They won't bother you up here, and I don't want you going down there."

"Ashamed of me?" I whispered, hating the way my voice betrayed how frayed the edges of my emotions were.

"Never, but you need to rest. I want your ass in my bed for at least two days. You need something and I'm not here, then you text me and I'll get it for you." He snagged the blanket, pressing a hand on my shoulder until I laid back in the bed and he helped prop pillows up behind me. Tucking me in sweetly, I sighed in contentment as the warmth of his forest green bedspread coated me. "Watch some tv. I'll be back in a few minutes." He dropped my phone on the nightstand.

"I really think we should talk about why you had my phone." The words themselves sounded sleepy, but I tried to shove back the wave of exhaustion that came with being so cozy.

He didn't answer. Instead, he kissed the corner of my mouth, leaving me dumbfounded, and then I watched him strut for the door. The shoulders were my favorite body part on a man, and Lino's strong, broad shoulders did not disappoint. It was the sight of his ass in those sweats that made me want to take a bite out of it though.

"Stop staring at my ass!" he called as he rounded the doorway.

"Stop shaking it then, pussy tease!" I called back with a laugh.

✳✳✳

Why did men always insist on interrupting reading a book *just* when it got interesting? I'd learned two things over the last two days I'd spent in Lino's bed. First, he had a sixth sense for when I was about to read a sex scene and would put a stop to it.

Lino left the bed in favor of running into the adjacent bedroom. I turned my eyes away from the kindle in my hands to watch him go, but he was quick to return. He took the kindle out of my hands to set it on the nightstand.

"Lay down," he ordered, and I fought the urge to roll my eyes. I did what I was told anyway, because the second thing I'd learned was that Lino needed to tend to me. I didn't have the heart to tell him I thought it was probably more for his benefit than mine. With my head tipped back on the pillow, I exposed my throat to him. Trusting, never even considering the vulnerable position it put me in. There was no one that I trusted more than Lino.

So when his cream covered hands touched the cords of my throat gently, I didn't so much as flinch. I watched him, absorbing the way those deep eyes of his fixated on the bruises as if his touch alone could erase the stain Connor had left on my skin. When his hands reached around the column of my throat, he leaned forward to press his forehead to mine and our gazes finally collided. "I'm okay," I whispered, my voice hoarse with emotion even though I wanted to moan in pleasure as he worked the cream into the back of my neck. I was less sensitive there, more a muscle ache than strangulation pain, and the way his calloused fingers worked the flesh delicately was like pure heaven.

He held my eyes as he whispered, "I almost lost you."

"You could never lose me," I said back stupidly, giving away far more than I normally allowed about my own emotions for him. Safe distance, *friendly* distance had always been key to ignoring the way everything reached a crescendo when he touched me. With him in my face and his hands on me, there was no distance.

I would easily lose myself in him if I didn't get control over it.

And that would only lead to heartbreak.

He closed his eyes, taking the intensity of his gaze away enough that I felt like I could breathe. "Turn over," he whispered, pulling back to his knees. I wanted to argue, wanted to preserve my sanity by fighting back and putting some distance between us, but the promise of whatever else Lino might have in store for me was just too much to resist. I turned onto my stomach, listening to another bottle popping open behind me. One of his hands slid inside my t-shirt, gliding over the flesh at the small of my back and inching it up to where my bra might have been if I'd worn one. When the other hand touched me, I gasped from the cool oil that coated those hands.

I was no stranger to massages from Lino, but they usually came through the barrier of clothing. To have his hands on my skin, rubbing up and down the sides of my spine gently and kneading the tight muscles, sent an all new intensity of sensation crashing through me.

Skin on skin, everything seemed *more*.

My body came alive, as if his hands were enough to make me hear his focused breathing. To feel the heat of his body as he straddled my thighs. To feel the press of his groin against my legging covered ass. I wanted it to be real, wanted it to be more.

But even if Lino had wanted that, I couldn't.

I was done with men. Done with the pain they caused and the lies they told. No matter how much I loved Lino, he was a man at the core, and he'd hurt me with his lies once before.

After all, I wasn't Mrs. Angelino Bellandi like he'd promised.

We spent a few long moments with him fixating on the tense muscles beside my spine, and I wanted to mourn the loss of his body when he swung his leg over and climbed off me. Even if my more logical self knew, it was better to be done with it. That space between our bodies was good. Was normal.

We needed to get back to normal.

I rolled to my back before moving to sitting and pulling my knees into my chest. "You don't have to stay here with me, you know," I whispered when he returned from washing his hands in the bathroom. There was another tube of ointment in his hands, and he sat next to my feet.

"I enjoy taking care of you," he murmured. When he grabbed one ankle, I flinched. I should have known he missed nothing when it came to me, and armed with the knowledge he had, he would have turned to analyzing every mark on my body. He pulled a little harder, waiting until I relented to give him my foot. The tube in his hand turned out to be scar cream, and he rubbed it on the soles of my feet. Holding me steady while I squirmed, he seemed immune to my ticklishness. "What were you planning to tell me happened here?"

"I hadn't worked that out yet," I admitted as he massaged it into the raised, fleshy scars.

"And what *actually* happened?"

"It doesn't matter. It's over now, so there's no point in us rehashing all the details—"

His head snapped up, his jaw clenched and nostrils flaring like a cornered animal. "It's worse than strangling you?"

I dismissed him with a chuckle that sounded as fake as it felt. "I don't know what gave you that impression." He switched to the other foot, but his eyes never left my face.

"Why else would you not tell me? After strangling you, I would think anything else would be inconsequential to admit. What the fuck happened?" His thumbs pressed into the arch of my foot more harshly, his annoyance pushing him to that ledge I knew he walked daily in his business life where he became a ruthless king.

"Lino—"

"I will find out, Samara. So help me God, I will fucking find out. And if it doesn't come from your mouth, I'll lose my damn mind. I rarely get angry with you. Do not test me." I knew he meant every word, knew that now that he knew there was something to find he would be relentless until he learned the truth. It didn't matter that I'd never gone to the hospital, that there was no official record. Linda knew, and Jasper suspected.

"I stepped on glass."

His glare was nothing short of pure fire, but the words stuck in my throat. "Samara," he warned.

"The night I told him I wanted a divorce. He wasn't pleased. I didn't realize he was drunk, or I would have waited. He was always quicker to outbursts when he'd been drinking, but he hid it so well. I never even suspected until he got close enough for me to smell it on him." Finished with my feet, Lino's hand ran up the back of my calf, the barest of pressures that I could barely feel through my leggings. I knew the restraint it took for him to touch me so gently, knew that he overcompensated and tended toward overly soft touches to avoid hurting me. "I fought him off. Tried to get away, and we broke the floor-length mirror that we kept in the corner of the bedroom. When I got away, I stepped on the glass in my hurry to run out. I ran all the way to Linda's, so the glass was deep by the time we dug it out."

"Hence the scars," he sighed.

"Hence the scars," I returned, thinking for just a moment that he might let it be.

"You said you were sick. Said that it was the stomach flu, which is the only time you won't let me near you. I knew you were lying, but I thought you just needed time after coming to terms with the divorce. I gave it to you like an idiot." The breath hissed out of him, like he couldn't believe he'd given me space I *had* needed.

"I did need space. Giving it to me was the right thing to do," I murmured in my best attempt to soothe him. "No matter what caused me to need that space, nothing changes the fact that I needed it."

"He hurt you? Aside from the glass, you said there was a fight?" I winced, closing my eyes to avoid looking at him. "It's my job to take care of you. I need to know, *vita mia.*"

"He said I was his. That I would only ever be his, and he wanted to prove that. So he grabbed me, pushed me down and—" I paused with a grimace. No matter what I did, how my face contorted, the words just wouldn't come. I'd never said it out loud, never admitted it. Linda had known from my injuries, known from the way I'd winced when I lowered my body into the bathtub that Connor had taken something I hadn't freely given.

Lino went solid, his hand freezing on my calf and fingers digging into my leggings like he just couldn't restrain himself any longer. "Say it," he whispered, staring at my face. "I need to hear you say it, Little Dove." His voice was broken, even with the rage contorting his features.

I closed my eyes, shutting out the vision of his anger. It was the only chance I had of ever admitting what haunted me in my sleep. Or what *had* haunted me. I hadn't had a nightmare since I started sleeping in Lino's arms. He always had been my safe place.

My home.

"He raped me," I admitted, fighting back the burn of tears behind my eyelids. I had to hope the explanation was enough, because I wouldn't be able to suffer through all the painful details. Not with him.

Lino's fingers spasmed on my leg before his touch disappeared altogether. My eyes flew open as the bed shifted with the loss of his weight, and I watched as he slammed the bedroom door behind him. "Lino!" I cried, wanting to chase after him. But I knew that even in his happier moments the past few days, getting out of the bed on my own was the fastest way to piss him off so I straightened to kneel, staring at the door like it would burst open any moment and I listened.

The distinct sound of thumps sounded from a few rooms down, and his anguished roar echoed through the walls. I lifted my hands to my face, pressing them against my lips to steady the tremble as my tears finally broke free and streaked down my cheeks in a flurry of desperate emotion. I wanted to fix it and needed to fix the pain I'd caused.

But I couldn't. I knew better than anyone that there was no *fixing this.*

The door opened slowly as he stepped back into the room, his face blank as he sat on the edge of the bed with a sudden drop of his weight. I stared at him, unable to go to him and make it better and just trapped by my own self-hatred. My eyes landed on the bloodied knuckles of both of his hands, the skin torn to a mess and his hands trembling despite his empty expression. "Lino," I sobbed, reaching out a hand to hover over his in horror.

"Come here," he whispered, his voice matching the emptiness of his face. I nodded, crawling forward on my knees until they touched his thigh. His face turned to mine suddenly, and the expression in his eyes nearly sent me flinching back. They were full of anguish, full of *rage* so intense that my heart stuttered in my chest.

Then he touched me, grasping me around the waist and with a hand behind my neck. He lifted me up and into his lap so that I straddled his legs, and his arm crushed me against his chest. His face went to my neck, tucked into the curtain of my hair as he breathed me in, and I cried into his shoulder.

He stayed like that for what felt like an eternity, just holding me while my brain raced with trying to figure out what was happening. "He was already dead for what he did to you, but now he'll suffer before I finally grant him the mercy of death." His breath tickled my neck, feeling menacing in the face of his declaration.

"No," I hissed. "I don't want that—"

He pulled his face from my neck, staring down at me in disbelief. "After everything he did, you're still protecting him?" Lino's rage boiled over the top, written in every feature of his harsh expression.

I reached out hesitantly, grabbing him around the nape of his neck. "I'm protecting *you*," I said in a ragged whisper. "He isn't worth the risk, the stain on your soul or the possibility that you could be caught. I won't lose you because of him."

He looked at me like I was insane. "You think it will leave a mark on me? Hurting him?"

"Of course, it will. Murder is murder, Lino. No matter what he's done—"

He let out a breath that was ragged. "Making him hurt the way he hurt you will be the greatest honor of my life." He pulled back suddenly, lifting me off his lap so he could stand and left me sitting in the center of the bed, wondering what the Hell had just happened. When he came back, his knuckles were washed clean of blood, though the ragged strips of flesh still looked raw and painful. When he reached out to pluck me off the bed, I didn't argue. I just wrapped my body around him again and let him carry me out of the bedroom and take me downstairs.

"What are we doing?"

"I'm making you dinner." He plopped me into one of the stools at his massive island, and I watched as he pulled frozen puff pastry from his freezer. I smiled at him knowingly, because puff pastry meant one thing.

He was cooking me bourekas.

My head spun with the sudden change of atmosphere when he grinned at me. He only made me bourekas when he wanted something.

I just didn't know what it was.

CHAPTER TWELVE

LINO

The last thing I wanted to do on the heels of Samara's confession was leave her side. There was no doubt in my mind that she was opening herself up to the future we had, even if she wasn't ready for the words themselves. Her body spoke for itself, and the way she instinctively wrapped herself around me and sought me out in her sleep told me everything I needed to know.

Samara and I were on the same page.

She was mine. Mine to protect and mine to love. Mine to worship and adore. Mine to touch and kiss and fuck.

Just like I was hers. Hers to look to for shelter and affection. Hers to wrap around her delicate little finger.

But the knowledge of what Connor had done to her was just too much for me to handle. She needed to be free of him, and I had the ability to make that happen. I just had to leave her side to do it.

"I need to ask you something," I murmured, setting my fork down. Samara sliced at the last grilled tomato of her breakfast, narrowing her eyes at me as if she'd had enough of my questions.

"What's that?" she asked.

"What did he want when he attacked you the other night?"

The tension left her body in a sudden burst of relief when she decided that line of conversation was safe. Well, relatively safe compared to the other topics we'd covered since the attack. "Money," she admitted.

"What happened to his trust fund?" I gathered up my plate and made my way to the sink to rinse and drop it in the dishwasher.

Samara scrunched her nose up when I turned to look at her while I waited for the answer. The motion lifted her glasses up just slightly, and I wanted to take them off and kiss the lines they hid on her nose. "He burned through that about a year ago."

"The gambling." I nodded, knowing it made sense. Even if his trust fund had been massive when I'd looked into him when Samara started seeing him. "Was the money to gamble more? Something else?"

"I don't know," Samara whispered, chewing the last bite of her toast thoughtfully. "I didn't care enough to ask."

"Okay, I'll touch base with my guy and see if he has anything for me. Then I need to go out for a bit today. Enzo's going to come monitor things here while I'm gone." She stood, bringing her plate to me with her expression, silently daring me to say something about it.

"That isn't necessary. I'll be fine on my own," she argued. "I don't need a babysitter."

"He's not a babysitter. Enzo will be here for your protection today, and I'll talk to Matteo about having a man on you at all hours. Let him pick someone he trusts." I took the plate from her hands when she bent down to put it in the dishwasher. Doing it for her and kicking it shut, I raised a brow at her before I swept her up off her feet and brought her to sit in the living room. I'd have much preferred her to stay in bed, but I couldn't have Enzo looking at her in a bed.

Nope. Just no.

"I can walk," she pouted as her grey legging covered ass hit the cushion of my leather sofa.

"And I can carry you."

"Is Enzo going to carry me around too?" I gritted my teeth, knowing from the innocent expression on her face she had no clue just how much she risked by prodding at my jealousy that way. I'd done what I could to hide it from her since high school, anyway. Once I'd forced myself to stop chasing her dates off, I had no choice but to accept that she *would* date. That she would take men to her bed, eventually. Men that weren't me.

"No. He's not. The only way you leave this couch is to go to the bathroom, and it isn't far. Aside from that, Enzo brings you whatever you need." I stood, staring down at her and daring her to fight me on it.

A mischievous smile spread across her face, making my breath stall in my lungs. She was so fucking beautiful it hurt sometimes but knowing that we walked along the precipice of her finally becoming mine helped to ease that pain. As soon as she was ready, I'd have all that beauty staring up at me while I made her mine in the way she'd always been meant to be. She grabbed her favorite pillow, the one I kept specifically for her even though it stood out like a sore thumb in my living room. With my clean, almost industrial lines and tan and black furniture, Samara's deep purple throw pillow and matching fuzzy blanket were probably the only personal touches in the house.

Before I'd become a celibate man waiting for Samara's divorce, more than one woman had looked at them with accusing eyes. I'd never explained, not when I didn't owe any of them the truth, that they belonged to my married best friend. They all knew that the only space they could fill in my life was purely sexual, and they were okay with that. I'd been nothing but honest about being unavailable, and many women were willing to use me to meet their own needs.

Quid pro quo.

Laying out on her side like the unintentional siren she was, she stretched and nuzzled her face into the pillow. The most beautiful part of Samara was that she had absolutely no idea the effect she had on men. Part of that was my fault for chasing boys off so much in her formative years. "What if I need something from my suitcase? Should I send him up to the bedroom?"

"Yes," I grunted, but I knew she was going somewhere with it.

She bit her lip, confirming it with that subtle mix of shy and playful that was so endearing. The playful side of Samara rarely came out with anyone else, always so concerned with what someone might think of her to drop her guard. But not with me, with me she always spoke her mind, always felt comfortable to just be who she was. I loved knowing that I gave her that, that in the face of all the goodness she brought to my otherwise dark, work-centered life I could give something back to her.

"So he should just go rummage through the suitcase with my underwear in it if I need a sweater?"

I think I growled, ripping the sweatshirt off my head and tossing it at her. She giggled, looking shocked as she stared up at me. "What if I need socks?" she pressed. With a hiss of frustration, I turned to leave the living room. "I suppose I should probably put on a bra?" she called, making me turn back to look at her. Her arms crossed over her chest, trying to hide the breasts that were fairly large for her 5'4" frame. Samara was all tits and ass, a body made for men to drool over. I'd known of course that she hadn't been wearing a bra. I could feel it when she curled into my side in her sleep or when she'd been snuggled in my lap or laid out underneath me. I just hadn't let myself think about the fact that I could have my hands on the breasts I'd spent my teenage years dreaming about with just a tug of her t-shirt. Having seen them in the shower, perky with dusky nipples that made my balls ache, didn't help anything in the slightest.

I turned back, racing up the steps to bring her a bra and socks. I rummaged through her suitcase, wondering if Linda had specifically chosen the laciest underwear she could find or if Samara just didn't own a lot of variety. I both hoped and dreaded that it might be the latter. I'd spend all my time inside her.

The woman would be the death of me. There was no doubt about that.

***

Talking with Campbell had only made my already bad mood that much worse. His initial probe into Connor's finances had revealed that things were likely far worse than even Samara knew. They'd kept separate bank accounts at his insistence when they were married, and it appeared that was probably the only thing keeping Samara from outright bankruptcy. Not only that, but the fucker was in deep with Tiernan Murphy. A ruthless loan shark who operated in the void Matteo left, he gave money to people with families and kids who depended on them and didn't give the first shit about the fact that it frequently blew back on innocent people. Since Campbell hadn't been able to find a single trace of Connor anywhere, I knew I'd have to call Ryker in to help.

I'd already planned on going to see Judge Ed Ryan, but the new information about Connor's debt made that trip even more urgent. It wasn't beyond Tiernan to expect a wife to settle her husband's debt on her back, and if the fucker took a step into Samara's space, I knew I'd start an all-out turf war.

Judge Ryan was as tough as they came and typically favored the Bellandi's. As much as he hated all the crime in the city and the rising gun-violence, he was also practical enough to see that while Matteo operated outside the lines of the law; he kept the city from delving into absolute chaos. Men like Tiernan Murphy wanted that chaos, and Matteo was the only thing standing in his way. Not to mention, Judge Ryan had a daughter a few years younger than Samara and I. I knew he would do anything to protect his precious girl, and if I could play to that sensibility and paint a vivid picture of what Samara had suffered at the hands of her ex, I stood a decent chance of getting her divorce granted that day.

A quick call confirmed he was home, and it gave me the perfect opportunity I needed for my request. His home was opulent, the elite of Chicago's one percent. The Ryan family came from a long line of benefactors to the city. Ryan's lack of a son to pass it all down to had once been the gossip of Chicago, but he'd slowly navigated himself away from the family business in banking and served as a judge, raising his daughter to give back to the city and put the city first in her life.

The tenacious young woman ran a charity for the city's children, orphaned by gun violence. She had a soft spot for her kids, and the city worshiped her for all that she did to help them. With her long raven hair and bright green eyes, she was the pretty poster child every nonprofit could only dream of.

The problem had quickly become that some stains on the city were determined to use her to control her father. He wouldn't tolerate it. Hired security to protect her and consulted with Enzo regularly to keep the security systems and training for her personnel up to date. She was the revolution, and not everyone wanted that to come.

One of the guards I knew by name let me in through the front gate, and another I didn't recognize opened the front door once I pulled the BMW up to the end of the drive. "Mr. Bellandi, he's expecting you," he called. I hurried to make my way inside the mansion as the guard closed my door. It would not be in my best interest to waste Judge Ryan's time. There was nothing he hated more than waste.

That went for time as much as food.

Just not when it came to his family legacy and opulent home. We all had our quirks, I supposed.

Striding through the entryway, I made my way down the hall to the left until I stood in the open door of his office. His daughter Irina stood in front of the desk, pointing something out to him briefly. Seeming to hear my approach, she turned to face me with a bright smile. "Mr. Bellandi. How nice to see you."

"It's good to see you too, Irina," I said, genuine in my joy at seeing her. I'd given to her charity frequently, had gotten to know the woman in passing, just well enough to know that she was one of the good ones.

"How's Samara?" she asked, having seen right through my bullshit the first time she laid eyes on Samara and I together at one of her charity functions where I often brought her as my date.

"She's why I'm here actually," I said, glancing toward her father where he sat behind his desk and eyeing our interaction. "Her ex has been jerking her around with the divorce. I need it taken care of today."

"Well, hello to you too, Angelino," Judge Ryan said with a grin, gesturing to the seat opposite him.

"I'll leave you to it," Irina ducked out of the room, knowing full well that she had no place in her father's business when it came to his position as a judge.

"Hello, Judge," I sighed, dropping into the seat when he eyed it again.

"Surely you know that interfering in divorce proceedings is a little outside my specialty." He eyed me warily.

I glanced around the office, appreciating the finer points of his masculine space that tended toward very traditional lines. It may not have been to my personal taste, but that didn't mean it wasn't something I could appreciate, regardless. "I wouldn't ask if it wasn't important."

"And this has nothing to do with your feelings for the girl?" His look of disbelief said he knew that to be bullshit.

I sighed. "Of course it does, but it's complicated."

"Enlighten me, or I'm afraid I can't wade in without understanding what I'm getting into. You're a businessman. You know my reputation is on the line for every one of these favors we negotiate. I need to know that it won't blow back on me."

I spit it out, not having any choice but to just admit the truth in the face of his threat not to help me. I didn't know any other judges well enough to go to them with a request like this. "He was abusive. Raped her when she asked for the divorce. Three nights ago, he broke into the house and strangled her. Turns out, he burned through his trust fund and needs money to pay off Tiernan Murphy. I need her divorced from Walsh before Murphy comes looking for retribution. It's the best way to keep her safe."

He sat back in his chair, blinking at me. "He hurt her?"

I nodded back, eyeing my hands that clenched into fists. "She can't go to work because she's bruised so badly. Her feet are scarred from stepping on glass when she tried to get away from him after the rape."

He sighed, rubbing his hands over his aging face. "Granting the divorce will only do so much good in the eyes of Tiernan Murphy. Without something to protect her, he'll still try to use her as leverage. Murphy doesn't pass up a woman like Miss Mahoney when he gets her under his thumb."

"I know. She won't be Samara Mahoney for long. I'll do whatever it takes to protect her. You know that."

"You'll marry her to protect her?"

"I'll marry her, because I love her. But yes, I'll marry her *now* to protect her," I agreed. "Once she's Samara Bellandi, not even Tiernan Murphy would dare to touch her."

"Have you informed her of your pending nuptials?" he asked, but he was already reaching for the phone at his side to make the appropriate phone calls.

"Not yet." I shrugged, even though anxiety swirled in my gut. I meant it when I said that I would do anything to protect her, even manipulating her into marrying me through threats.

I just really hoped it didn't come to that for the sake of our marriage.

"I wish you the best of luck with *that*, my friend," the judge chuckled, dialing his phone. I tuned him out when he started talking to someone on the other line, finding out who was responsible for Samara's case and negotiating his way through it with as little information as possible. I appreciated his discretion, because I knew Samara would kill me if the abuse became common knowledge thanks to my interference.

I didn't want her on my bad side, even if the thought of going toe to toe with her was a welcome one.

Especially once she was my wife.

By the time he ended his phone call, there was a Divorce Decree waiting for me to pick up at the Court. Samara was free, and I was free to make her mine.

Fucking finally.

CHAPTER THIRTEEN

SAMARA

Hanging out with Enzo hadn't proven to be too horrible. In fact, he reminded me of Lino. At least, when Lino wasn't bogged down in stress because of my life and the decisions I'd made. He was humorous, thoroughly entertaining, even though he looked like a beast.

I'd met him occasionally, but never seen him in anything other than a suit. So when he'd turned up in jeans and a simple black V-neck with motorcycle boots on his feet, I'd had to do a double take. The word Ride stretched up the underside of his right bicep, Die up the left. I had to imagine there was a creative way of squeezing the Or in under his clothes, and I nearly felt curious enough to ask. The only thing that stopped me was Lino's strange behavior before he'd left the house.

I didn't pretend that I ever knew what went on inside my best friend's head. He was a mystery, but for him to seem so *jealous* was unheard of.

So Enzo and I spent a few hours watching segments of action movies from Lino's collection, debating how difficult stunts might have been. I seemed to be firmly in the camp of "that shit isn't possible." Enzo was in the camp of, "looks like fun."

Insane. He was insane, but I suspected he did it to entertain me. To distract me from everything going on. I knew, in some vague sense, that he'd been the driver who drove from my house to Lino's the other night. I also knew he was kind enough not to comment on the bruises or the night in question. He didn't act like a babysitter, just went about waiting on me hand and foot in a way that made me feel less like a burden.

So when Lino came home, I was half asleep on the couch, with Enzo sitting in the recliner I knew Lino often favored. The relaxed cadence of Lino's voice was full of relief, and just enough to draw me back from the edge of sleepy land. "Hey, *vita mia*," he murmured, bending down to stroke his fingers through my hair.

"Hey," I murmured back sleepily.

"How'd it go?" Enzo asked. I turned my gaze his way to find him standing and stretching out his behemoth body.

"It's done," Lino said cryptically.

"What's done?" I asked. I didn't know what possessed me, because I knew better than to ask questions about Lino's business. Nothing good could come of it.

"Your marriage." He grinned at me, handing me a piece of paper that I sat up to accept. The bold words stared back at me, making me gasp in shock.

Divorce Decree.

I was divorced. Finally, totally and completely free of Connor after nearly a year of fighting, all because I couldn't bring myself to admit what he'd done to me. "I'm divorced?" I asked, turning my wide eyes up to him.

"Yes, you're finally divorced." His eyes turned to liquid fire as he stared down at me. I couldn't even guess at what passed through his head, and the moment ended as quickly as it started when Enzo cleared his throat.

"Right then, I should be off." He approached us, leaning down to touch my shoulder. I couldn't help my reaction, still half stuck in the disorientation that came with waking up and having my world rocked by my own divorce.

I flinched back so sharply I jostled the sofa. Shame instantly took over. Because I hated reacting that way to a man who had been nothing but kind to me. My breath came in a wheeze, and I opened my mouth to apologize.

"It's alright, darlin'. Don't you worry about it. Healing takes time. I'll see you when you finally show your face at the office." He turned a knowing grin Lino's way before striding out of the living room. I wanted to call after him and tell him I knew he wouldn't hurt me, but my voice seemed stuck in my throat.

"It really is okay, Samara," Lino soothed me, holding out his arms. I nodded, taking the invitation to stand and wrap my arms around his neck. He lifted until I was high enough on his body to switch his hold down to the bottom of my thighs, and the feeling of his fingers so close to the most intimate parts of me should have felt more intrusive. Should have felt scary given the way I'd reacted to Enzo's hands on my freaking shoulder. But instead, all I felt was comfort. Every inch of me that touched Lino never felt anything but safe, and I hoped that would never change.

"How did you get the divorce pushed through?"

"I have friends in high places. Called in a favor with Judge Ed Ryan," he answered, my body barely moving as he strode up the stairs. He kept me so still, so stable in his arms that there was no room for fear. I trusted him not to drop me, trusted that he would do everything in his power to catch me anytime I fell.

I took comfort in the fact that he was my rock, my constant in life that I could always depend on. Even if our relationship was never meant to be more that friendship, there was something truly beautiful in the way we loved each other so fiercely without the complication of sex. He felt like my partner far more than Connor ever had, and I supposed I should have listened to that voice instead of saying I do to a man I had no business marrying.

I'd aimed too high, disappointed him when I couldn't be the perfect society wife he needed. Drove him to drinking and gambling out his regrets for the choice he made in marrying me. But I'd learned my lesson, learned that some-times a person was truly better off alone.

So I didn't have a man waiting in my bed every night. That was what vibra-tors were for, and if I wanted to find someone to have sex with, that possibility was always there. I got the companionship I needed from Lino.

Everything else was optional.

"There's more good news today too," he whispered as he carried me.

"Hmm?" I asked, sleepiness already setting in after the momentary jolt to my senses.

"Ivory had the baby a couple hours ago. She and Luna are doing just fine." He nuzzled his nose against mine with a genuine, joyful grin on his face. I'd missed seeing it and hated myself for the fact that my situation had taken it from him—even temporarily.

"That's good. Has Matteo given them a few moments of peace before he starts peeing on them both?"

His quiet chuckle lit up his eyes, and I realized that watching the transforma-tion from so close was even more spectacular than all the times I'd seen it with more distance between us. "I think the hospital staff would discourage it. They're probably safe until they go home."

I gave him a mock gasp, all too aware of the way his eyes fixated on my mouth. "How dare the hospital staff discourage caveman traits? That's discrimi-nation, that is."

When he walked into the bedroom, he dropped me on the bed gently. His eyes were still warm on mine as he murmured, "Get some sleep, Little Dove. You're going to need it soon." He turned to go shower off his day in the bath-room. I curled up, resting my face on the pillow he used every night so that his scent surrounded me. Not even his ominous warning was enough to push away the comfort that enveloped me and drew me in.

I was asleep before he got out of the shower.

Divorced. Single.

Free.

CHAPTER FOURTEEN

LINO

Matteo's home never seemed forbidden. Not like it had when my uncle had been in charge and ran the house like a prison. Despite the security that Matteo stepped up after Ivory came back into his life, the guards were friendly and valued the trust given to them. Matteo rewarded loyalty and good employees, and they often enjoyed rather cushy jobs for being mobsters.

Guarding a mansion behind a twelve-foot fence and gate was about as safe as it got when it came to safety. Even if they had to brave the cold winters of Chicago to check the property or do their rotations outside. So, it was no wonder that as soon as I walked in the door, Scar grinned at me.

The house was jovial on the most casual days.

The day after Luna was born was a special circumstance.

I didn't want to intrude on their family time, or distract from Ivory's recovery, but Matteo had called me over to meet my baby cousin.

There was no saying no to an invitation like that.

I'd wanted to bring Samara with me, but I thought seeing the bruises on her throat might cause Ivory distress. Matteo had said the birth went as smoothly as anyone could have ever expected, his Angel handling childbirth as well as she handled shanking villains who threatened unborn babies.

Scar wasn't what I would have called a softy, though Ivory brought that out in him. But watching the man walk around cooing to the newborn cradled in his arms was downright comical.

I reached out for the beautiful girl, glaring at the kitchen when Don's voice called out. "Wash your hands, you filthy animal! You will infect her with some disease, and I'll kill you myself!"

Scar chuckled quietly, his chest vibrating with his attempt to hold in the sound so he wouldn't wake Luna. I grunted, making my way to the kitchen and stripping off my suit jacket to roll up my sleeves.

I made a point of showing Don how I washed every crevice of my hands. "Fucking Ryker went right for her. That man has more blood under his fingernails than a mortician, but he thinks he can just grab the moon girl? Not on my watch." He waved the knife in my face as he chopped up cucumbers for Ivory. It appeared that her craving didn't just go away when she gave birth.

I supposed it was preferable to the pickle craving. Don had made more late-night pickle runs than I could count.

That and banana yogurt with dark chocolate chips in it. The woman was a nut.

I highly suspected Matteo would never touch a banana anything again.

As soon as my hands were washed to Don's preference, Scar finally handed over the baby. "Well, hello there little Princess," I cooed at her, tucking her head into my arm and bouncing the way I'd seen Scar doing. She didn't stir, just let me take hold of her while she slept.

"Where's Ivory?" I whispered as I stared down at the bundle in my arms. Faint chestnut hair like her mother, with long and dark lashes even though her head was mostly bald. Those little lips came straight from her mother, pursed into a perfect angelic pout as she slept. But the nose was all Matteo, and I knew from his rambling last night that she had his blue eyes. The perfect combination of the two of them, all wrapped up in a lilac baby blanket and sleeping soundly. Hopefully, she would keep the blue eyes. She felt tiny in my arms, and I instantly wanted a dozen of them for myself.

"Sleeping. Little Luna kept her up most of the night. It was a rough first night home," Don answered, but there was nothing but affection in his voice as he stared at the baby in my arms. No frustration that his own sleep had probably been interrupted since he lived on the property as well.

"What are they doing home from the hospital? Shouldn't they be under observation or something?" I asked, because even I knew it was uncommon to come home the next day.

It was Scar who answered, and I really should have seen the answer coming. After Ivory's run-in with Adrian Ricci that had resulted in Scar getting shot, Matteo took no chances where her safety was concerned. "You know Matteo. Security risks. He has a doctor coming to check on them both twice a day to be safe, but everything looks good so they're safer here."

"Makes sense," I nodded, staring down at the other woman he would no doubt take no risks with. The poor thing would probably be under lock and key for most of her life, if not all.

I didn't blame Matteo one bit.

Ivory came down the steps slowly, and I watched as Donatello hurried over to her side. "You know you shouldn't do the stairs alone. We could have brought her up to you."

She chuckled, waving the older man off in favor of stepping up to me and holding out her arms with her brow raised. I found I didn't want to relent, the little one felt far too good in my arms. Like a baby belonged there.

I'd have to remedy that as soon as I could get Samara on board, and as soon as I dealt with my father.

With a sigh, I handed Luna over to her mother. The baby opened her eyes the moment she sensed Ivory, looking up at her with an obvious love that only a mother could receive from a newborn. "Matteo and Ryker are waiting in the office," Scar said finally, hovering over Ivory. She smiled up at her bodyguard, reaching up to pat his cheek when he cooed at Luna.

The obvious friendship, the strength of the bond they'd formed was one I could only hope Samara would form once I assigned her a full-time guard. I just hoped it didn't take anyone getting shot to form it.

With a wave and a kiss on Ivory's cheek, I made my way down the hall to Matteo's office with Don at my heels. Scar stayed behind, never far from Ivory's side even in the privacy of their home unless Matteo was nearby. Somehow Ivory was entirely comfortable with his presence, like he was just an extension of her. Even when they didn't interact, they were at peace in one another's presence, and I had to hope that she would somehow be able to convince Scar that he deserved the kind of love she'd found with Matteo.

The kind of love I had with Samara.

The kind of love that never went away, that waited until it was safe. The kind of love that existed because of sacrifice.

Real.

When we entered the office, Matteo stood with a broad smile. The proud father, silently asking if I'd seen his precious girl. The best thing he'd ever made. "She's perfect," I said, stepping up and giving him a brief hug and pat on the back. "Completely perfect."

"She needs cousins," Matteo joked, but his words echoed the thoughts I'd had in the kitchen.

"I'm working on it. As soon as Samara's ready, she'll have one." Matteo grinned, and I felt my lips tip up into an answering smile. After so many years of wanting Samara and knowing she was beyond my reach, that it wouldn't be safe to make her mine with my father's threats hanging over my head, it seemed completely unreal to know that she was finally so close to being mine.

Ryker cleared his throat. "I'm happy for you. You know that," the man said gruffly, scratching the back of his head as if he wasn't prepared for the celebrations. Still stuck waiting for Calla to grieve her loss, I knew the two of us getting our women had to be bittersweet. He'd given Calla a year, and he still had over four months left on that sentence to wait before he claimed her. "But I want to get down to what we're doing with Walsh." His eyes glittered, and all I felt in the face of his vengeance for Samara was grateful.

I knew Ryker, even if he was unofficially family. He was family. He wanted to make Walsh suffer nearly as badly as I did.

"He's mine," I snarled, the beast rising to the surface in the face of someone else taking that vengeance from me. I'd allowed Connor to marry Samara against my better judgement. Given him the most precious gift in this world, and he'd hurt her. He'd hurt her worse than I could have ever imagined him capable of.

"I can help," Ryker argued, crossing his arms over his chest. He was shorter than me, only slightly, but his body mass made my leaner definition seem pathetic. He and Enzo should have sparred more often, because the result was always terrifying.

"You can," I agreed. "I want you to find him for me. Samara needs me right now, and I don't like being away from her. God knows you're a stalker, so you should have no problem tracking him down. Campbell lost all trace of him; he has been asking around but isn't getting anywhere. I hope you have better luck."

I dropped down in my favorite seat in the office as Ryker stalked to the door. "I'll find him," he grunted. "Can't promise he won't be bloody when you get there, but I'll find the fuck."

"That's fine, just make sure he's still breathing. I think I'll have to get creative with my punishments for him," I sighed.

"We know anyone who's gay?" Ryker asked Matteo, and Matteo grinned at him cruelly.

"I have someone in mind."

"Then I say we give him a taste of his own medicine," Ryker said.

"I don't give a shit how you do it, but when you find him you make sure he fucking suffers for what he did to my girl," Don ordered, and the more harsh tone of his voice would have been unexpected under any other circumstances. But not when talking about the man who'd hurt Samara. The man on his own was peaceful, not a violent bone in his body, despite his attachment to us, but for Samara he'd have dismembered Connor himself.

I chuckled, because this office was the only place I could give in to such thoughts and not be judged for them. Worse yet, could *act* on them without consequences from any of the other guys. "How's Calla?" I asked.

The smile slipped off Ryker's face. "She's getting there," he said, and he slipped out the door.

"I can't decide if I feel bad for Calla and the kids, or if I'm happy she has someone to love her like that," I admitted.

Donatello laughed. "Have you ever met her?"

"No," I admitted. "You?"

"Yeah. Once, bumped into her ex at the store with her one time. Ryker's got his hands full with that one."

"Hellcat," Matteo grinned, confirming Don's words.

I only hoped she didn't wear off on Samara when the time came for them to meet.

CHAPTER FIFTEEN

SAMARA

Lino tossed the shrimp into the pan with the buttery scampi sauce. Just the smell of it made my mouth water, even if the chef hadn't been the sexiest man I'd ever seen. He had a shirt on, something that seemed a little like a travesty, but the sight of his grey sweats hanging off his ass and the snug black t-shirt fitted to his shoulders was almost as good.

Almost.

The black apron he donned was always the icing on the cake though, but I didn't dare comment. I'd learned a long time ago not to question the apron, something I didn't think he felt comfortable enough to wear in front of anyone else. Though, I'd never heard of him cooking dinner for anyone before. I'd heard tales of him cooking with Ivory, but given that happened at the Bellandi estate, I doubted he risked the hit to his reputation by wearing an apron.

I loved it.

As soon as he'd cooked the shrimp to perfection, he tossed the linguine into the pan and finished cooking it in the buttery sauce that I just hoped I didn't dribble all over my super fancy pajamas. I was pure class like that.

If I'd owned a shirt with a clever saying about life needing to have order in the chaos, I'd have a stain on it. That was just me.

"How are you feeling?" he asked, turning around finally and twirling some linguine and shrimp onto my plate. I didn't waste any time picking up my fork and shoving some into my mouth even though it scalded my tongue. The moan that slipped free would have been indecent if I'd been naked.

Hell even dressed it bordered on indecent. Lino raised a brow at me, as if to point out the obvious. "That's hot," he added, crossing his arms over his chest and rinsing the pan out. Then he took his seat at the island next to me, bumping my knee with his pointedly.

"I feel good. I think I could go back to work, maybe tomorrow?" I suggested.

Lino laughed, tentatively twirling his linguine like a gentleman. And here I was eating like the troll from under the bridge. "That's funny."

"Why is that funny?" I turned to him, wanting to stare him down when he pissed me off.

"I can see you're feeling better," he chuckled, pointing a fork at my face. "The attitude has returned, but your neck is still bruised. How do you plan on explaining that?"

"I'll wear a turtleneck," I said with a shrug.

"No. You will return to work when the bruises are gone and not a day before."

My fork dropped to my plate with a clatter, my glare turning glacial. "And since when are you the boss of me?"

He dropped his own fork, turning a matching glare my way. "Since I got a call in the middle of the night that someone strangled you! That's when. You're playing under my rules now, *vita mia*. You lost your right to make decisions concerning your safety when you failed to call me the moment he hurt you, the *first time*."

I winced, whispering his name.

"No. I don't want to hear it, Samara. Do you have any idea what it feels like to know that you kept that from me? I thought we were honest with each other, but I find out you've been lying to me for years. Not telling me that your *husband* was hurting you?" He scoffed. "I'm trying to be understanding, but I can only take so much. For now, the only way I'll be able to function is if I know you're safe because I control your safety. I suggest you accept that."

I blanched, staring at him in horror. Lino had never pushed beyond my boundaries, he might push me right up to the line, but the moment I pushed back he would find a compromise. For him to push past that line meant I'd really, truly fucked up, and that the consequences hadn't just been mine to bear in the end.

My secrets had hurt him. I couldn't fix that, but I could give a little to help him cope in the aftermath.

"Okay," I whispered. He gazed at me with wide eyes for a moment before turning back to his food. I followed suit, and we fell into a slightly uncomfortable silence until we finished.

Given his mood, I didn't want to push too hard. Even before his outburst Lino had been weird. Ever since he got back from Matteo's house the day before, something in him seemed even more intense. Like he wouldn't let me out of his sight, in spite of the fact that my body was healing. In fact, sometimes I got the impression his sense of urgency stemmed from the healing.

Like a clock was ticking down to something, and I had absolutely no clue what.

Or maybe I just didn't want to know, didn't want to think about the fact that he looked at me like I might slip through his fingers.

How could I, when I'd been wrapped around his finger since childhood?

I wanted to understand. Wanted him to look at me the way I'd always dreamed he might, but it was far better for my health that he didn't. I wasn't ready to be just another one of his mistakes. Above all else, I'd never survive Lino looking at me like I was just another woman. He might not have been mine, but I meant something to him in a way that no other woman did.

As his best friend, I was a permanent fixture in his life, not just yesterday's one-night stand.

After dinner, Lino let me walk to the living room on my own—watching every step like I might step on a landmine. If I hadn't been so stressed about the change in him, I might have found it comical. But just when I reached the couch, when I was ready to plop onto my spot and snuggle up with him, Lino stopped me with a gentle but insistent hand at my waist. I turned to find him staring down at me, something meaningful in his gaze.

Finally giving me something, he let out a massive sigh. "What's wrong?" I asked.

His hand reached up, tucking my hair behind my ear. "Do you have any idea how long I've waited for this moment? And now I can't find the fucking words, no matter how many times I practiced this."

My lip trembled so hard that I bit it. "I don't understand."

"You're divorced, finally," he said.

"So you said."

"You need more time to heal, but you're well on your way," he added.

"You are kind of freaking me out," I laughed.

"You aren't helping." He grinned at me, shaking his head. "I'll be patient. I can let you come around to the idea over time, so long as we're on the same page about where we're headed."

"What the fuck are you talking about?" I giggled, tipping my face down to bury it in his chest as my body shook with uncomfortable laughter.

That hand of his snagged my chin, lifting until my eyes found his again. With another breath, he whispered, "Fuck it."

And then his head descended, his lips brushing against mine in a whisper of a kiss. Barely a touch, barely *anything*. And yet my body hummed to life, my lungs filling with air for what felt like the first time ever.

Like Lino alone could breathe life into me. I pulled back with a gasp, biting my bottom lip as it tingled. His eyes smoldered as he stared down at me, the arm wrapped around my waist refusing to release me. "Little Dove," he whispered.

"Stop. We can't do this," I hissed back, shoving against his chest in a moment of panic. He couldn't cross that line, couldn't lump me in with the others who didn't have him.

I had to have him in the only capacity I could keep him, because the thought of going through my life without him at all was too painful to consider.

"We can, and we are," he announced, curling his hand around to the back of my head. Grabbing a fistful of my hair in his fist, he tipped my head back and claimed my mouth again. The second kiss was harder, more forceful. As his torso pressed into mine, the masculine, clean scent of him filled my lungs. He tilted my head, putting me exactly where he wanted me as more pressure applied to my lips, near the point of bruising.

Gone was my best friend who thought I was amusing. He'd been replaced by a conqueror. He didn't relent, didn't stop. Not until long after I submitted and opened my mouth to his.

The first stroke of his tongue against my lip made my knees tremble, and when he plundered on to drink from me like a starving man, I felt like I might collapse.

No matter my feelings, this was Lino. My friend for as long as I could remember. My rock.

My head swam with the implications of what that kiss would mean until he erased all thought but the way he felt against me as he lifted me off the ground and carted me to the couch. That hand never left my hair, never relented, but I didn't even mind the bite of tenderness that came from my abused neck.

I couldn't mind *anything* when Lino's lips were on mine.

When he sat down, my legs straddling his hips, I finally tore my mouth from his. I whimpered, touching my forehead to his as I stared down at him in confusion. "Why?" I asked. This was a bad idea. It could only end in disaster, and even though I tried to remind myself of all the consequences this would have, nothing could permeate the haze he'd created in me.

His answer was nothing but a breath that I felt against my over-sensitized lips. "Because you're mine."

I shoved him away again, shaking my head to clear the fog. "This isn't happening. I can't be yours."

"You'll always be mine, Little Dove," he murmured, and then he set out to show me, tugging me down to his lips more gently, but taking, nonetheless. I didn't fight the third kiss, just gave him everything he wanted. He smiled against my lips in approval, sliding his tongue against mine in a slow glide that turned me into a puddle in his lap. When he'd finally had his fill, he tucked his face into my neck and let my thoughts dance around inside my head.

He didn't bother to try to talk me through what was happening, but I could feel his smug satisfaction with every trace of his fingers up and down my spine. He soothed me without words but didn't seem interested in offering verbal comfort.

He'd said his piece, and for a man like Lino it was as simple as his declaration implied.

I was his.

∗∗∗

I felt like I walked, okay sat, around, electrocuted like a live-wire after Lino's life-altering declaration the day before. Every part of my body tingled with the need that I felt building inside me, that it had been far too long since I'd gotten any kind of real sex just wasn't helping.

Before Connor's assault, it had been nearly a year since we'd had sex.

I would go crazy with Lino's little touches seeming far more meaningful after the kiss the night before, that precipice of insanity loomed closer than ever. I didn't know what to expect, hadn't known if he'd try to get lucky. But he'd simply gone about his night as if nothing had changed once we'd untangled from each other, getting ready for bed and tugging me against his front to spoon while we slept. Admittedly, the time had probably passed where I needed to sleep in his bed. Not that I ever had, but I hadn't been willing to broach the subject with him before.

I slept better with him than I ever had without.

Now, the thought of going to a guest room seemed like a dangerous topic. So I decided I'd stick my head in the sand and see how it played out. If I got my sleep on, got some cuddles, that didn't mean it *had* to mean I accepted more. Right?

So when the front door vibrated with the force of someone banging on it when we watched a movie on the couch the next evening, I jolted from my spot on the sofa. The electricity that Lino had sparked in my blood made everything seem more intense, more real, and my reactions felt too extreme given the circumstances. Lino sighed, standing and seeming to steel himself for a fight. "Lino! Open the fucking door!"

I turned horrified eyes to Lino. "Is that my *brother?!*"

"Yes," he said, striding for the door. I rushed to my feet, chasing after him even though I knew it would not make him happy.

"What is he doing here?"

"I called him," Lino said, not the slightest bit of remorse in his voice or face.

"You what?" He ignored me in favor of continuing to the door, determined to let Yavin come in. "Lino! You can't let him in here."

"No more secrets, Samara. I couldn't keep this from him. You're his baby sister." I stopped in the doorway between the living room and the entryway, pressing my hands to my mouth in horror.

"That wasn't your choice to make," I whispered.

He paused, turning to level me with the intensity of his stare. "Did you miss what happened last night? You're mine, and I told you when it comes to your safety, I'm in charge now. Yavin knowing the truth means he'll be on board and do what I tell him to do to protect you." Without another word for me, he turned and opened the door. Yavin immediately shoved through the gap until he stood in the entryway and stared at me with fury etched onto his face. Lino closed the door behind him quietly, giving Yavin a moment before he pushed him to interact.

"Is he dead?" Yavin asked finally. He didn't move, didn't even twitch in Lino's direction as he spoke to him. His blue-grey eyes that matched my own stared at my throat, and I instinctively reached up to shield it from the strength of that glare.

"Not yet," Lino answered quietly. "But he will be."

"Lino!" I hissed.

"Good. I want to do it," Yavin argued, turning as if he dared Lino to tell him otherwise.

"You can come, but he's mine." Yavin grunted something back, but I didn't bother to listen.

"What is my life right now?" I turned, striding into the kitchen to find Lino's stash of whiskey. The sound of their footsteps followed, and I had a moment of surprise that they'd even noticed I'd left.

"What are you doing?" Lino asked as I rummaged through the cupboards.

"I am not nearly drunk enough for this conversation," I admitted. Yavin's rough chuckle sounded behind me, as if he couldn't quite suppress it despite his shitty mood. "If you're going to discuss murder, I need to be trashed so I can pretend I was too drunk to remember what you said when the police question me."

"Samara," Yavin chuckled. Finally finding the whiskey, I tore off the cap and sucked back a swig straight from the bottle. Lino stepped up and snatched it from my hands when I went back for more, and I glared at him until Yavin stepped up and pulled me into his chest for a big brother bear hug. "Are you okay? I mean, obviously you're not but—"

"Vin, I'm fine," I groaned. "It sucked, but it's over. I just want to move on."

"Right," Yavin agreed, straightening and pulling back with his moment of sibling affection over. "Are you up to packing your things? You're going to come stay with me until this all dies down."

"Oh," I glanced at Lino, before darting my face down to the floor when he looked at me like he might lose his mind if I gave the wrong answer. "Uhh."

"She's fine with me," Lino grunted. Yavin turned to look at him in suspicion and my eyes darted between the two of them. I couldn't predict how Lino would handle the situation. Would he tell Yavin about our kiss? Would he act like it hadn't happened?

After feeling on edge about it all day long, the anxiety of him potentially telling Yavin about the kiss just felt like too much. "Yavin, I'm all settled in here. Why don't I just stay? Besides, we both know you don't want to play nursemaid and don't have a patient bone in your body. I'll demand you feed me. Lino feeds me, and I like food. No offense, but burnt toast just doesn't compare—"

"Samara, shut the fuck up," Yavin laughed, and I scrunched my nose. Lino's face was nothing but entertained and warm as he looked at me. He knew me so well, there was no doubt in my mind that he knew exactly how nervous I had to be to ramble like an idiot. "She's my sister. It's my job to take care of her, so she's coming home with me."

Lino's humor faded so quickly my breath caught, and he leveled my brother, his *other* best friend with a glare that would make most men tremble. "I promise you; she will not be walking out that door."

Yavin's head jerked back, and he stared at Lino for a moment before sighing. Given that they worked together, Yavin managed *Tease,* the Bellandi owned strip club; I knew Yavin saw Lino at his most cutthroat. Whatever he saw in Lino's face made him back down with a sigh.

"Fineee," he drew out. "But if anything happens to her on your watch, you'll have to answer to me."

I exhaled in relief, snatching the whiskey from Lino's hands.

I still needed to get drunk.

CHAPTER SIXTEEN

SAMARA

"Time to get dressed," Lino said, patting my hip to signal me to sit up. I'd been comfortable with my head resting on a pillow on his lap, and I didn't want to move.

"Why do I need to get dressed?" I'd spent a week in my pajamas or leggings and loved every minute. While I enjoyed getting all dolled up for work, that didn't carry over to other facets of my life. I was the queen of comfy. He didn't answer, instead scooting his body out from under me and bending down to pick me up and carry me to his bedroom. My apprehension rose, because unlike many it was when Lino said nothing that I really had to worry. "Lino?"

"Don't fight me on this," he said harshly. "You won't win."

"I don't understand what I'm not supposed to fight you on," I pouted. I assumed, given his brooding, that pouting was probably better than snapping. My discomfort meant those were the only two options, especially when he sat me on the bed and fumbled through my clothes in the closet. His weekly house-keeper had come, taken one look at my clothes exploding out of my suitcase, and shaken her head before tucking them all away neatly. As if they belonged there. As if I belonged there.

I didn't have much cause to go in the closet, Lino's ridiculous restriction on my walking usually meant that he grabbed my clothes and set them out in the bathroom for me. Or so I'd thought, anyway.

But the mass of white fabric he pulled out of the closet was one that I knew I had never, ever seen in my life.

It was casual and sleeveless with a plunging neckline.

Beautiful, but there was an obvious problem.

It was a wedding dress.

I swallowed loudly, looking into his stone-cold face. "What is that?" I whispered. He turned with a scoff, returning to the closet and emerging with a sundress for me to wear.

"Don't play dumb. You know exactly what this is."

"Okay," I agreed with a sigh. Apparently, we were having this conversation. "What are you doing with a wedding dress?"

"We are getting married in two hours."

I think I blinked. Several times. And then I broke off into laughter that was so strong it felt like it tore my lungs in two. I bent over, wheezing between my knees. That he had kept a straight face while he delivered that line was probably the funniest part of the joke. When I finally straightened and wiped the tears from my eyes, Lino stared at me. That breathtaking face was carved in resignation, far too serious for the joke I'd assumed it was. "What are you talking about?"

He sighed, depositing the dress on the bed next to me and kneeling on the floor. One hand went to each of my knees, pressing them apart until he could insert his body between them, and his face was nearly level with mine. "The best protection I can offer you is my name," he explained.

Understanding dawned, and I realized in that moment that while I'd thought him joking, part of me had hoped. Stupidly, I hoped it would be the declaration of love I'd always dreamed of. A misguided, but genuine, grand gesture.

In reality, it was a means to an end.

It meant nothing. Even after his kiss and words that we would explore something between us. I realized he must have known this was coming when he kissed me, and of course he had. Obviously, he would expect marriage to give him certain rights to me.

All men did.

"You're protecting me," I whispered. "By marrying me."

"Being my wife means you're completely off-limits. The man Connor owes money to can't come after you to settle the debt." His thumbs traced circles on my knees through my leggings, and I stared at him blankly.

Despite knowing that he meant well, despite him just trying to keep me safe, it felt like something broke inside me.

Reality crashed back in, filling the space where I'd let hope build temporarily. In the wake of feeling so full from the time I'd spent with Lino and all the cuddling, it seemed hollow inside me with the void that loss of hope left me with.

Empty.

"No." I pulled my legs onto the bed, crawling away to stand on the other side and go to the closet. He seemed frozen; stuck to the spot I'd left him. I hurried to shove some things back into the suitcase I'd brought with me. I knew when he kissed me that it could only end in disaster. I just hadn't expected how soon that disaster would burn everything to the ground.

"No?" he asked finally, and I looked through the closet door to see him unfurling his long, lean muscles to standing. Something in his posture gave me pause, somehow made him seem so much larger than he normally was with all his swagger.

"No," I repeated in a whisper, zipping my bag closed and going into the bedroom. I had to pass through to get to my phone downstairs so I could call Yavin to pick me up.

He sidestepped into the doorway to block me in, his dark eyes glittering dangerously.

My heart stuttered in my chest, pulsing like a warning.

Danger.

Danger.

It seemed to throb with every beat, and I backed away a step when he took one step toward me. "I do not recall asking," he said slowly.

"You don't just get to decide we're getting married! I am never getting married again," I hissed. "I've been divorced for three days!"

His gaze darkened, his lips twisting in the beginning of a snarl as savagery took over his face. "That wasn't a real marriage. No man treats his wife the way he hurt you."

My voice was barely a whisper when I risked everything to stand my ground. He'd lost his damn mind. "Neither is this."

He took another step toward me, nostrils flaring when his chest and torso pressed against mine. I dared to glare up at him when he cupped my cheek gently. It gave me a moment of comfort, a moment of reassurance that my sweet Lino was still in there. Somewhere. "You will get dressed. We will go to Matteo's where the priest is waiting for us, and when we get there you will put on the fucking dress, Samara."

"Or what?" I ground out. Something inside me needed to rebel, needed to know just how far he would take this. I didn't know if it was that part of me he'd broken by admitting our wedding would be for my safety, or it had merely stoked the flame of whatever Connor created when he betrayed me.

"You will not leave this house. You won't return to work. I will keep you locked up in a gilded cage where only I can hear you sing, Little Dove. I will not risk you, even if it means I have to make you hate me to keep you safe."

I huffed out a breath in surprise as I stared up at him in shock, my bottom lip trembling as tears burned the back of my throat. His thumb caressed my cheekbone, as if he could feel how that break inside me cracked even larger.

Like a fault line, snapping my world in two.

The two sides of the line warred within me, the one pleading me to take it for what it was. Lino would be mine, my husband.

But the other side clung to reality. That it wasn't real, and it never would be.

"Then you're no better than him!" I hissed. "Trapping me in a marriage that I don't want like this." His face contorted in pain, and I immediately regretted the words. I knew he was different to the depths of my soul, but I wouldn't let another man make me a prisoner in my own life.

His eyes darkened as he stared down at me, his jaw clenching in his anger. "I am *nothing* like him. Everything I do is to keep you safe. *Everything.* Even this."

"You wouldn't do this to me," I whispered, but the tear that wet Lino's thumb said otherwise. He would. I knew Lino meant every word he ever said to me. It turned out he'd even meant it when he said he would marry me one day, though he couldn't have known it at the time.

"When have you ever known me to say I'll do something and not follow through?" His voice turned sad, melancholy, as if he could sense just how close to the breaking point I hovered. "Let me keep you safe, *vita mia.*"

I shuddered out a breath, feeling my nostrils flare as I tried to find the words for what I needed to say. "If I do this, you'll let me leave? Go to work?"

Ever the most honest person I knew, he gave me an answer he knew I wouldn't want. "You'll have your own security, but yes. You'll be allowed to come and go as needed."

I swallowed before nodding. I knew that after what had happened to Ivory, Lino wouldn't take any chances with my safety. The wife of a Bellandi was a valuable commodity, even one who wasn't a true wife. No Bellandi would tolerate the insult that came with taking something of theirs away. "I'll never forgive you for this," I whispered. I knew the words were true. The sting of betrayal coursed through me that he would force me to do something I didn't want to do. Something I thought he would never do to me, even if it was for my own safety.

I trusted him, and he'd broken that.

"You will. It may take time, but there's no divorce for Bellandi's. We have a lifetime together." His lips touched my forehead briefly before he withdrew. He grabbed the dress off the bed, snagging one of his suits from the closet and made for the door.

"Lino!" I protested, trailing after him in a flurry of movement. "So put a guard on me. I don't have to be your wife to be protected. I'll do whatever you say to stay safe. I promise. Just please, don't make me do this," I sobbed.

He spun back to look at me, the savage look in his eyes making me flinch back a step-in self-preservation. "Get dressed," he growled, striding out the door without another word. "We're leaving in ten minutes. Ivory will help you with your makeup when we get there."

He closed the door behind him, leaving me staring at the sundress with tears on my cheeks. With a last silent sob, I went to the bathroom to blow my nose.

It would take some creative makeup for them to cover up the redness around my nose, but I knew they would do it.

If I had to get married, I wouldn't do it looking like a charity case.

Even if it was true.

∗∗∗

I got dressed, but not with the intention of going with Lino.

No matter what he threatened, I couldn't handle the thought of marrying another man who didn't love me. Of suffering through a lifetime in a marriage where I loved my husband more than he would ever love me.

I crept into the hallway as quietly as I could, making my way down the stairs to get to the living room. If I could get to my phone, I could call Yavin to come get me. He may not have been as powerful as Lino, but he would at least help me.

As soon as I made it to the bottom of the stairs, I hurried to the living room. My feet were still bare but for socks, more helpful in sneaking around the house. I let out a sigh of relief when I made it to the room undetected but whirled around in confusion when my phone wasn't sitting on the table like it should have been.

"Looking for this?" Lino asked and I whirled around to stare at him in the doorway to the hall. He'd already dressed in his suit and the dress was nowhere to be found, but my purple phone was in his hand for a moment before he tucked it into his pants pocket.

"That's the second time I've caught you with my phone," I accused. "If it wasn't password protected, I'd wonder if you'd been snooping through it."

The smirk that overtook his face lacked any of the warmth I was used to seeing on him, a sardonic look that held no amusement at my attempts to derail him from the idea of a wedding.

There wouldn't be a wedding.

"My birthday wasn't the most creative of pass codes, Little Dove." His face twitched in arrogance, and I fought back the flush of shame that heated my cheeks. "Do you know how I knew it would be yours?"

I shook my head, swallowing as he stepped toward me slowly.

"Because yours is mine." He tucked a strand of hair behind my ear, some of his tense features softening the moment he touched me. "Go get your shoes."

"No. I'm not going anywhere with you." I swatted his hand away, and the way his eyes went molten again made me swallow with anxiety. Something changed in that moment, like the flip of a switch back to the side of him that I never had to deal with. With a growl, he leaned forward and hefted me up onto his shoulder. I shrieked, punching him in his overly toned ass. "Put me down you overgrown baboon!" I screamed as he turned and strode for the front door. "Lino!"

"Quiet, Samara. It didn't have to be this way, but you're too fucking stubborn to just listen to me. So we'll do it the hard way."

"You asshole!" Cold air hit my thighs, making my skin pebble with goosebumps the moment he flung the door open and stepped outside. I jostled on his shoulder as he hurried down the stairs to where the car waited at the top of the driveway. I lifted to glance over his shoulder at where we went, finding a familiar figure jumping out of the car. He grabbed the rear door handle, and for once Lino didn't seem to protest that someone else opened a door for me. "Georgio, don't you dare!"

"Sorry, Miss Mahoney," he murmured, his face flushing in the face of my fury.

Lino tossed me off his shoulder, catching me into his arms somehow and hauling me into the car before I could even find a way to dislodge from his grip. I immediately went for the other door, tugging at it furiously when it wouldn't open. They'd enabled the damn child locks.

"Lino, so help me God, let me out of this car right now!" I demanded as he climbed in next to me, taking a seat and straightening his tie while I raged at him. "This isn't funny."

"Do I look like I'm fucking joking?" he asked, and the car jolted into motion as Georgio pulled out of the driveway. It was a short distance to Matteo's house, and wouldn't leave me with much time to convince him just how bad an idea this was. But logic had evaded me, and I felt like nothing more than a cornered animal. I flinched away when he tried to reach for me, my body coiled tight to fight him off. "Dammit, Samara! This is for your own good."

"There are better ways. This isn't right," I argued, and he reached out and wrapped his hands around me. Tugging me into his lap, he held me close while I squirmed.

"Shh. There's nothing more right than this, Little Dove," he softened, and I collapsed into him with a whimper. "It's always been you and me. It will always be you and me, Samara. You have to let me take care of you."

It felt like all the fight disappeared with those words, like they struck something inside me. It had always been the two of us, which was why it hurt so much that he would risk what we had for something so unnecessary.

His jacket was wet from my tears by the time we got to Matteo's house.

He was nice enough to pretend he didn't notice.

✳✳✳

When we finally pulled inside the front gates, Lino set me on the seat and stood from the car. I didn't flinch when he reached in to grab me. Everything in my body felt melancholic like it was totally separated from the racing thoughts in my head. Georgio followed behind us, grabbing the dress out of the passenger seat.

Don opened the front door for us, and as soon as Lino swept me inside, he set me on my feet. A glance down at my socks made me grimace. I must have looked ridiculous, stepping out of the house without shoes, but I only had a minute to feel the horror of it before Don filled my vision.

His fingers reached out, tentatively touching the light, faded bruises on my throat. The sound of footsteps coming into the foyer interrupted the moment, and he cleared his throat as his nostrils flared. He turned to stare at Ivory where she stood beside Matteo, Scar, and Enzo. "You can cover this up, yes?" he asked Ivory. She nodded, her brow furrowing as tears stung her eyes.

"Yeah Don, I can cover it up," she agreed.

"Good. My girl does not get married with any trace of that *stronzo* on her skin. Do you hear me?" he asked, and I sniffled back my tears at the rage in his voice. How pissed he had to have been to curse. Drawing me into his arms, he squeezed me so tight I thought I might stop breathing.

"I'm okay," I whispered, but he never responded. His body just shook as he ran his hands over my head.

"I hear you, sweetheart," Ivory murmured. Don pulled away, nodding to her and blinking back his own watery eyes before he turned for the kitchen. With the sudden empty space in front of me, I tried not to feel uncomfortable. I'd been in Matteo's home before, but something felt different, like there'd been a shift since the last time Ivory had invited me for lunch.

Every face was familiar—someone I knew and spent time with—but the way they looked at me had changed. Matteo's face was twisted in fury, his eyes stuck on my neck and only Ivory clearing her throat made him drop the terrifying look. Lino tugged me into his side briefly, kissing my temple as my eyes drifted down to the blanketed bundle that Matteo held in his arms.

"I'll watch over my Little Moon, while you help Samara get ready, Angel," Matteo murmured, pressing a brief kiss to his wife's lips before turning his attention back to the little bundle in his arms. She stepped forward, taking my arm and glaring at Lino briefly as if daring him to deny her right to take me away.

"You can put the dress in the first bedroom at the top of the stairs, Georgio," Ivory said, and he nodded before making his way for the stairs in haste. I had no doubt that the men couldn't wait until they could gossip like women once we were out of the way.

They were worse than most of the women I knew, honestly.

She guided me up the steps, and I resisted the urge to glance back at Lino. I wouldn't give him the satisfaction of seeing me feel so uncertain. "Just a little farther. Then you can break," she urged as she wrapped an arm around my shoulder. I nodded to her, fighting back the threat of tears.

"Angel," Matteo called and the two of us froze on the steps. I turned back to watch him raise his eyebrows at his wife, as if he could sense her sympathy for me. "She's ready in an hour, yeah?" The walls of my cage closed tighter, clutching around me with the confirmation that they all knew. They all knew I didn't want this, that I didn't want to be there.

They didn't care in the slightest.

"Yes, Teo," Ivory murmured back, and we continued on until we could hide away in the bedroom. Georgio hurried past us at the top of the stairs, and we stepped into the privacy of the bedroom a moment later. The white fabric of the dress draped over the navy blue bedding artfully, like Georgio had taken the time to arrange it just so rather than just dropping it and running like he actually had.

The door to the bathroom was propped open, and Ivory led me straight for it. "It's okay. You know Lino loves you," she reassured me, but I sniffled back the threat of tears. I couldn't cry again, couldn't actually break.

Not when I only had an hour.

"Not like this," I whimpered as she drew me in for a hug. "Congratulations," I whispered, huffing a sardonic laugh. "I couldn't see her, not with the way Matteo kept her all wrapped up, but I'm sure she's perfect."

Ivory's smooth laugh came from above my head, and it immediately brought back memories of when we'd been closer friends in high school. Of the days when she'd been infectious and happy and filled with all the joy that her relationship with Matteo had brought to my innocent friend. Since the wedding, she'd started finding her way back to that, and I couldn't have been happier for her.

"She is," she sighed, and I could feel the smile in her voice. "You could have one too, you know."

I laughed, because it was ridiculous to think of Lino and I having children. Until two days earlier, he'd never so much as kissed me. "I don't want him to resent me," I admitted. "If he marries me, what happens when he finds someone he *actually* wants to marry down the line? I'll be in the way, and it will be for the stupidest reason."

Ivory pulled back, putting her hands on my shoulders as she stared at me intently. "Trust me when I say that will never happen, okay? I get the distinct impression that Lino is a lot like his cousin, assuming you can just magically read him. It's okay that we can't, but even Matteo only told me he loved me the day before he put a ring on my finger. You just have to grab Lino and shake him and make him tell you how he feels about you."

"I don't think I want to know the answer," I admitted.

"You want him. You have always wanted him, so why have you been crying?"

Ivory turned me to the mirror as she lifted my head up and touched gentle fingers to my throat. "He threatened to lock me away. It's Lino. I just—I never thought he'd hurt me."

She sighed, dropping her fingers from my throat and shaking her head with disappointment on her face. "He shouldn't have done that. These men, they don't know how to cope with the thought that something could hurt us. That need to protect us at all costs, that's their way of saying they love us before they ever find the words." She resumed her work on my throat, working the cover up into my skin.

"That's not—"

"It's not okay. What he did to you isn't even remotely okay, and I know that right now you're wondering how you can ever get past it. But you will, and I promise you that what is waiting on the other side is going to be beautiful." With the faint bruises on my neck finally covered, she set to doing my makeup.

"And what if it's not? I'm so happy that you and Matteo got through all that, but what if that never happens for us? Where does that leave me?"

"If nothing else," she answered, and her voice was uncharacteristically soft. "You're safer *with* Lino than you are alone. Just give it a chance. You owe it to yourself to try," Ivory sighed, picking up some eyeliner. "Besides, your mother should be here soon." She winced when my eyes widened, and she drew a huge line over my eyebrow.

"What?"

"I take it he didn't tell you he invited her, then?" she asked, and her voice got a little louder with each word. Like the sadness of the moment was a thing of the past, I was going to give it a shot, and that was that.

"Uh no. Why would he invite my mother? It's cruel to—" I broke off, huffing out a breath in indignation. "Oh, that manipulative bastard!"

Ivory smiled at me. "He knows you won't make a scene in front of her."

I swallowed as she cleaned the line off my face. "Yavin?"

"Oh, fuck no," Ivory laughed. "As much as I'm sure it pains Lino to not have your brother with you, we all know just what kind of scene Yavin would make. You two will tell him later. Once it's all final."

I closed my eyes, letting her fuss over me and trying to come to terms with the obvious reality.

I was getting married.

CHAPTER SEVENTEEN

LINO

"How'd she take that?" Enzo asked the moment the girls were behind a closed door. With a sigh, I rubbed my eyes, and dropped Samara's phone onto the table in the foyer. I couldn't take any chances that she might try and call Yavin.

He couldn't know until she was legally mine, because I wouldn't let anyone stand in my way.

"About as good as expected when you have to rush into a wedding three days after your divorce for the sake of safety," I grunted. I could hear the lingering rage in my voice, the aftermath of Samara begging to not have to marry me. Her protests only threatened to wake up the worst part of me, the part of me that demanded Samara be bound to me in every way so she could never leave.

Father Alessi shook his head at me as he slipped inside the front door that Scar opened for him, signing the cross over his chest in mock indignation at the mention of Samara's divorce. Like the old bastard hadn't seen things gruesome enough to make grown men cower and not even blinked an eye.

Matteo and Enzo exchanged a glance before Enzo spoke. "So, what *exactly* did you tell her?"

"That marriage was the best way to protect her." I shrugged, looking at Father Alessi in confusion when even he winced. "What?"

"And did you perhaps mention that you've been obsessed with her since before your balls dropped?" Matteo grunted.

When I didn't answer, Enzo looked to the ceiling with a sigh. "Fucking idiots. The both of them."

"What?"

"It is a good idea to tell a woman how you feel before you marry her," Father Alessi inserted.

I scoffed. "That's unnecessary for us. Samara knows how I feel about her."

"Bro, that woman does not understand that you're even remotely interested. Let alone that this is anything other than a sacrifice on your part. Her head? She's a burden."

Matteo's eyes narrowed on Enzo. "How do you know so much about women?"

"I've got five sisters."

"Shit," I hissed, casting my eyes up to the stairs.

"Yeah, shit is right," Enzo laughed.

✳✳✳

Samara's heartbeat so hard I could feel it in her palm as I held her hands and turned her to face me. Father Alessi stood at the front of Matteo's sitting room, with us only just in front of him and our little audience on our other side. Her eyes were wide on mine when she turned, and I ignored the way Enzo and Matteo laughed silently in the corner. I ignored the way Samara's mother sniffled where she sat next to Don. I'd tried to tune out Enzo's words about Samara not knowing how I felt, tried to focus on the fact that after all those years, I would finally have what I'd always wanted.

Samara as mine.

I wouldn't lie and say that it didn't hurt to know I had to force Samara into marrying me, that it hadn't made me want to chain her to me and throw away the key. When I'd spent my life wishing this moment could ever be possible, she'd married someone else. I couldn't blame her, when I hadn't made myself an option, but I'd thought I'd been very, very clear about my intentions. Matteo and Enzo had oh-so-kindly shown me that perhaps that wasn't true. But I knew my Little Dove enough to know that even if she didn't want to think of herself as a burden to me, she was also skittish as could be.

If I pushed too hard, too fast, I'd lose her completely.

And that just wasn't an option.

The white dress hung off her light gold shoulders by the barest of straps, dripping to a slit between her breasts. The fabric was light and airy, simple, where it flowed over her hips. It was far less elaborate than I'd ever imagined I'd have when I finally had no choice but to marry someone else in a grand wedding I didn't want.

And it was all the more perfect for it, because even if it wasn't a fancy wedding, it was *ours*.

Father Alessi skipped over moments he knew wouldn't matter to us, showing just how unorthodox the priest with the mob ties was. The man had no patience for weddings, much preferring the confessions he gathered like a master of secrets. And the mob had damn good secrets.

"Lino, repeat after me," he said, giving me a brow raise that made me draw in a deep breath. He breathed out the words that would tie me to Samara, and I didn't hesitate before saying them. My eyes held hers, putting as much conviction into the words as I could and hoping that she would somehow wake up and *feel* it. Feel me.

"I, Angelino, take you Samara to be my lawfully wedded wife, to have and to hold, from this day forward. For better, for worse, for richer, for poorer, in sickness and in health, until death do us part." Her hand spasmed in mine, her eyes narrowing in on the rings that Matteo handed me. I slid the set of three bands onto her ring finger, watching her hand tremble as the oval diamond settled onto her finger, seeming massive against the delicate size of her. The two rings surrounded it with diamond studded leaves, making it look like a flower that a dove would look right at home with.

The band was gold. Her gilded cage that chained her to me for the rest of her life, setting on her finger. I knew she didn't realize the weight of the moment, the weight of what that ring would mean to her future. For Bellandi's, it was truly until death do us part.

And if she ever dared to leave me, in death or in life, I would follow her into the pits of Hell and shield her from the flames.

"Samara," Father Alessi said, and I watched as her head snapped to him. With those blue-grey eyes wide, she looked like a deer caught in the headlights. Terror flooded me, considering for the first time that she might say no.

That maybe Samara wouldn't become my wife on that day, after all.

But when Father Alessi repeated the words for Samara, she turned her gaze back to me and swallowed. Then she held her head high and repeated the words. "I, Samara, take you Angelino to be my lawfully wedded husband, to have and to hold, from this day forward, for better, for worse, for richer, for poorer, in sickness and in health, until death do us part." She hesitantly took the burnished gold wedding ring from Matteo, drawing my hand in hers and slipping it onto my ring finger.

Where I'd referred to her ring as a cage, mine felt different.

Mine felt like freedom.

Being free for the first time in forever, to openly love the woman I'd always been destined for. To have someone for myself who knew *me* down to my roots.

"You have declared your consent before the Church. May the Lord in his goodness strengthen your consent and fill you both with his blessings. What God has joined; men must not divide. Amen."

"Are you going to get to the important shit soon, Father?" Enzo teased from the back.

Father Alessi scowled at him and sighed. "I now pronounce you Mr. and Mrs. Angelino Bellandi. You may kiss your bride."

So I did, leaning forward and cupping her cheek. I pressed my lips to hers gently, sighing in relief when she lifted her face to give me better access and accepted the kiss. Accepted me. It was gentle, tentative. As the first kiss between a man and his *wife* should have been.

It was everything.

Just like her.

CHAPTER EIGHTEEN

SAMARA

I was married.

Again.

Mrs. Angelino Bellandi. The name rang in my head, a mantra repeated over and over again as I tried to remind myself that it was everything I'd ever wanted.

Signing my name on the dotted line and watching Lino return the favor with Enzo and Ivory as our witnesses, the reality of what I'd done finally sunk in. I'd married my best friend. Married the second-in-command to the mob boss who ran the city.

And what was worse, I'd married a man who didn't believe in divorce this time. It felt like signing away a piece of my soul, with the rings heavy on my finger weighing me down. If I'd thought it hard to get my divorce from Connor, looking for one from Lino would be impossible.

Standing next to Lino while everyone, save for Ivory, drank and enjoyed themselves felt surreal. Everyone treated it as if this was a genuine cause for celebration, the union of two people who had always been meant to marry each other.

No one was happier than my mother, and I didn't have it in me to break her heart.

She'd long been more of a parent to Lino than his father, offering him the affection he'd never had from his own family growing up.

I could still remember the way she used to sneak him pieces of candy when his father wasn't looking, toys that his father would have never let him have. She couldn't afford to buy them, but she did it anyway.

Because no boy should be deprived of the right to be a child, she'd say.

The dynamic should have made Lino more like a brother to me, growing up with my brother as his friend and him adored by my mother, but even their relationship hadn't been enough to curtail the attraction I felt for my poor, deprived Lino.

I treasured every display of affection he'd ever given me, because I still recalled the way he'd recoiled the first time I tried to hug him. Like it was a foreign concept.

Like he'd never just been hugged.

She came over, taking my hands in hers and grinning at me with her cheeks flushed from champagne. "I'm so happy for both of you. I never thought you would get your shit together and just *be together.* Lord knows everyone else knew you two were in love with each other from the first day you met." She pulled back, turning to Lino and pulling him into a fierce hug. "Why did you make me wait twenty years to see you marry my baby?"

He laughed against the top of her head. "I married her as soon as I could," he answered. "My father—"

"Oh, I could strangle that man. I should. It would be a gift to humanity," she hissed, backing away to cup his cheeks in her hands as she looked up at him. "You're finally officially my son now. No matter what that devil of a man tries to tell you."

Lino's face twisted with the force of her words. I knew my mother was one of the few people in his life who openly showed him how much they loved him, and I also knew that sometimes the force of that love proved too much for the man who had never known the love of a woman or girl before us.

By the time she darted away to talk to Don—who watched us from the corner with amusement—Lino just tilted my face up to his and took a kiss. He'd done it since we said, "I do." Stealing random moments of affection like he needed the touches to remember that it was real. That it wasn't a dream. That we wouldn't wake up and go back to just friends.

But I knew that wasn't the case, no matter how much I might wish it.

So I guzzled my champagne, watching Ivory laugh in the center of the room with her daughter in her arms and her husband looking over her shoulder to coo at the four-day-old baby that I wanted to hold more than anything.

But her words that I could have one stuck with me, teasing me. Luna felt like a threat, a reminder of something I would never have, but that would awaken the *want* inside me.

It was better not to want anything at all.

There was no disappointment that way.

CHAPTER NINETEEN

SAMARA

No matter what someone wanted to say about how unorthodox our relationship may have been, we were familiar with one another, probably more content in each other's presence than some newly married couples. So, we had that going for us.

We'd changed out of our fancy clothes the moment we got home, letting go of all the pretenses and going back to what we knew. There would be no romantic honeymoon for the two of us, or even a night of lovemaking.

"What are you thinking about?" Lino whispered, curled up on the couch next to me as I read on my kindle. His laptop sat on his legs where I would have loved my head to be, and he paused his typing to watch me.

"What if we fuck this up? I don't want to lose you," I whispered, voicing my fears I had for our future. Everything was uncertain, and I felt like with Lino and I's relationship shaken there was no longer a rock for me to cling to. Everything had changed, in a way I knew it would never be the same.

"You will not lose me. You're my wife."

"That doesn't mean things won't change. It doesn't mean that we won't resent each other for making this decision so suddenly. We both know I *will* resent you for the way you threatened me into it. Things are already changing," I sighed, setting my kindle on the coffee table when he moved his laptop there and shifted to lean over me.

"You'll forgive me," he repeated his words from earlier. The way he stared down at me as he lifted my chin to touch his lips to mine gently felt like he was trying to sear something into my soul. Branding me, imprinting me with something I didn't understand. "You won't have a choice. I'll spend my life wearing you down until you accept that I did what needed to be done for both of us in the long run."

"There is absolutely no benefit to you. I don't understand why you did this. What do you gain from marrying me?" I whispered. "I'm just me, Lino. Just, promise me that if you're seeing or sleeping with someone outside this marriage, we'll always be honest with each other about it? I understand this isn't a normal relationship, and we might need to adapt to suit—"

"No," Lino hissed. His lips tensed into a frown. "There is no one else for either of us. You're my *wife.* I'll not dishonor you by having affairs, and I expect the same in return."

I sighed. "I can't compete with the variety you're used to and the women who own their sexuality. I have open wounds and scars, and no one has touched me since he—" I broke off, not able to admit the truth again. It seemed that once was my threshold.

But for the first time, I knew that someone understood because he *knew.* Even without me saying the words, he knew exactly what I meant; there would never be any miscommunication on our part because of it. Being open like that left me vulnerable, bleeding out from wounds I'd wanted to call healed over the months I'd spent isolated away from men, but it also left me feeling accepted.

Understood.

"I don't need variety," Lino said softly. "I've never needed it, Little Dove."

"I don't even know if I can have sex. I haven't tried, and it might mean that you not only aren't getting variety, but you aren't getting *anything.*"

"I think you may find that you're surprised by just how patient I can be when it comes to you," he smirked at me playfully. I narrowed my eyes on him, but he ignored it in favor of going back to the work on his laptop.

Another cryptic statement that he didn't seem remotely inclined to clarify.

I nodded, moving to stand and stretch out my muscles. After having been babied unnecessarily for so long, I didn't have it in me to just sit and read, especially not when I grew more and more frustrated with Lino's evasiveness by the day. I was so tired of being sheltered and protected from whatever it was he seemed to think I couldn't handle, but there was no way to make the stubborn man tell me a thing.

I wanted to move, wanted to *do* something, but I also knew pushing Lino on that front wasn't in my best interest. Stretching seemed like a safe option. I tried not to think about the way that his eyes darted up from his computer, narrowing in on my bare midriff when I stretched up over my head.

"What are you doing?" he grunted.

I smiled at him, bending over to touch my toes. "Just stretching. My muscles feel like they've been stuck in a bed forever. Oh, wait!" I had to hope that with the way he tormented me with information, maybe, just maybe, there was another way I could return the favor.

"Samara," he warned, but his lips tipped up in amusement.

"Oh hush, Beasty. There's no reason you need to go all 'me man you woman protective on my ass.' I'm just stretching."

He chuckled, deep and throaty. "I'd like to go all caveman on your ass."

I gasped as I stood straight, staring at him open-mouthed in shock. "What has my ass ever done to you?"

"Looked too fucking good in literally *everything* you wear, to start. Do you have any idea how many times I've wanted to just slap it when you flaunt it in your tight skirts at work? Or grab a fistful in those fucking leggings?"

I smirked at him, glancing back over my shoulder to look at my legging covered ass. I nodded in agreement. "It does look good in leggings. If you keep me in bed it will get bigger, especially with the way you cook. Have you never heard of a salad?"

"I'm okay with that," he shrugged.

"What are you doing looking at my ass, anyway? Yavin will lose his shit if he finds out you've been staring at my ass."

Lino laughed. "Samara, you're my wife. I think it is safe to say your brother will lose his shit, regardless."

"Oh, my God. What are we going to tell him?" I asked, smacking my face against my hand dramatically. While not having to deal with Yavin's dramatics through the actual wedding, there would have been a positive to it.

It would be done, and I wouldn't have to worry about it.

"I'll handle it. Now, come on," he said, taking my hand. "We should cook."

"We?" I huffed a laugh. "You realize I burn water, right? You should keep me as far from the kitchen as possible."

"Oh, trust me. I learned my lesson when you tried to cook me frozen ravioli and jarred sauce and still messed that up," he teased, but he took me behind the island of the kitchen, regardless. I stood, leaning my butt against the island as he went about gathering ingredients from all corners of the kitchen. "In honor of that, I thought we would make ravioli together this time."

"I uh, okay," I swallowed. I didn't want to burn his house down. I really didn't.

It was such a lovely house.

"I got you something." His smile was infectious. "Now close your eyes." Biting my lip nervously, I did as he ordered. Something slipped over my head, settling over my tank top and leggings. Lino's strong, deft hands reached around my waist to tie it at the small of my back, and the subtle touches of his fingers against me tickled in the best of ways, dragging my body out from the pit of slumber it seemed to retreat to whenever he wasn't touching me. "Okay. Open."

There was a smile on my face, making my cheeks ache before they even opened. When they dragged open, I glanced down to my chest to see the words "I'll burn for you" stretched across my chest. I huffed a laugh, pressing my face into his chest since he seemed intent to hover too close to my body.

"It's perfect," I whispered. I'd always loved that Lino, although he was perfect, never judged me for the things I just was *not* good at. He was a literal genius, navigating the business world like he'd been born to it, and even when we were young, he'd been incredible with numbers. He could cook like a chef and loved doing it at that. He was gorgeous and worked out enough to keep his body flawless in that lean, muscled way that runners dreamed of having.

I was the opposite. I was smart, but because I'd worked to be. I didn't disappoint on *every* level, but that didn't mean that things came to me as easily as they did Lino. In my ideal world, I would have never started working in an office and pursued singing as a career. But it hadn't been meant for me, and despite my passion for it I'd found I much preferred the anonymity of open mic night instead of scheduled performances.

We both went through the process of washing our hands, Lino dragging the rings off our fingers and setting them in the bay window above the sink that looked into his backyard. It was the only hint at what the home might have been before Lino modernized it, and I loved it. On days when the dreamer in me felt stronger, I had visions of watching over our kids while they played outside, and I drank my tea.

Lino turned me to the counter, wiping it down with a clean cloth for a moment. Then he took a glass measuring cup and filled it with water, popping it in the microwave while I watched. Donning his own apron, he grabbed the flour and reached his arms around me to pour a decent-sized pile on the island counter. When the microwave went off, he grabbed the measuring cup and added two tablespoons of salt to the water, carting it over to the island and setting it near the workspace. "Can you crack eggs?" he asked with a chuckle.

"If you don't mind the shell in your ravioli, sure I can." I smiled, giggling when his face pressed into my shoulder from behind and his body shook with laughter.

"Alright. I'll do the eggs then. Make a little pool in the center of the flour."

"It gives it texture," I teased, and felt him shake his head at me. His massive fingers clasped an egg in each hand, and he tapped them against each other gently over the pile of flour. Cracking one open fully and setting the shell aside, he continued until he had four eggs in the middle.

"Add a little of the salted water. Slowly," he said. I nodded, reaching for the measuring cup and pouring a tiny stream of water into the wall with the eggs. "A little more."

His body pressed against the back of mine, taking my hands in his and setting the water to the side. It felt like he surrounded me, felt like he was *everywhere* as he guided my hands into the well and used them to mix up the eggs and water. I grimaced. I didn't think I would ever get over how gross raw food felt when you touched it.

Lino smiled into my neck, seeming to sense my displeasure. "Everything's better when it's wetter, Samara," he rasped. I snorted a laugh and felt how my laughter shook my body vibrating against his abs through his shirt and apron. "And this is about to get a lot messier." Taking my hands to the edge of the flour, he scooped some to fold it into the eggs. Flour coated our hands, sticky and messy and caked against my skin. Under any normal circumstances, I'd probably have quit. But quitting meant losing the feel of Lino pressed against me, of his breath at my ear and his hands tickling the back of mine as he guided my movements. It felt like just for a moment, we were as connected physically as we'd always felt emotionally.

I couldn't lose that. Couldn't lose the connection to my *husband* on what was technically my wedding night. I'd been honest in saying I didn't know if I could give Lino my body. I also highly suspected we wouldn't be exploring that territory just yet.

We went through the motions until the eggs disappeared and left us with flaky dough that Lino added more water too, and another egg. Kneading and pressing, every movement slid him against my back. When he pressed a light kiss to my neck just behind my ear, I thought I might melt, but he just continued kneading, as if the gentle touch hadn't turned my world upside down. But there was no doubt it had been intentional. Lino was using the contact through forming the dough to touch me, just the same as I was.

I didn't dare be the first to back down.

So I shifted my body, letting it take control in the way it had wanted since the moment Lino pressed against me. My back arched slightly as I let him guide me, the dough forming into a solid blob that he kept folding over itself and continuing on.

The groan he gave in my ear when my change in position made my ass rub against him shouldn't have felt so good. It shouldn't have vibrated through my entire body like I felt it down to my soul. But being recognized by Lino, being *seen* as something inherently female was something I'd wanted for so long, there was no stopping the visceral response I felt.

"Dough is done," he whispered finally, giving one last, lingering kiss to my cheek and backing away.

We went to wash our hands, feeling like just maybe the moment had passed. But while I washed mine, Lino leaned down and pressed a soft, lingering kiss to my lips that was one hundred times better than the kiss to my neck.

Because it lasted.

I tipped my head up farther, ignoring the way the hot water dropped from my hands as I turned my body to face him and encouraged the kiss. When his mouth opened to mine, it was all I could do not to moan as his tongue touched mine. Tentative. Like he remembered my words about not being touched since Connor, about being uncertain what I could take.

Lino wouldn't risk hurting me, wouldn't risk taking something I wasn't yet ready to give. But he could give me this, the reassurance of his kiss he was there, that he cared about me, and that we were in it together. No matter what hardships we faced along the way, or how we got things twisted up and danced around each other.

We'd never given voice to the tension between us, never acknowledged it. I didn't know why Lino refused, but it no longer mattered, apparently.

He was my husband, and I was his wife.

For better or worse.

CHAPTER TWENTY

LINO

Samara seemed almost happy to be spending time with Enzo, and that didn't sit right with me. If I hadn't trusted the man, I might have hesitated to leave. Not that I didn't trust Samara, but even I couldn't deny that our marriage hadn't been traditional. No matter how many times I might have tried to communicate my feelings for her, it always seemed like I'd be pushing too much too soon if I told her I loved her.

I couldn't afford to chase her off, and a confession of love was serious. I'd never said the words to a woman, never had the opportunity or the inclination when I'd been young enough not to fall to my father's restrictions. Young enough to think he wouldn't kill Samara if I touched her. Our friendship was offensive enough to the man, but he tolerated it so long as I didn't shame my family's name.

Because a woman with a housekeeper for a mother, a Hebrew mother at that, was just too much for him.

I would marry a good Italian woman, in his mind. It didn't matter that I never intended to marry. Matteo and I had made that promise to each other, drunk on whiskey the night before he dumped Ivory in High School. We wouldn't settle in unhappy marriages, as a fuck you to our fathers' interference when we'd been too young to fight back.

I very much looked forward to telling my father that Samara was my wife. Given Matteo's swift rise within the organization even before his father's death, which had only grown more since, my father would have no hope of telling me who I could or couldn't marry any longer. That was the point. Matteo and I had sworn that we would never be powerless, never let someone control us in any way from that day forward. We'd swept the power right out from under the old men, all so we could do as we pleased, but it had taken years.

And by the time we had enough power, Samara had married Connor. Ivory had an entire life after years without Matteo, and the stubborn man had decided his life was far too dangerous to involve her in it. So the protection continued, but at least it had been his decision that time around.

Just like I had *chosen* not to kill Connor mysteriously in his sleep and worm my way into Samara's life and bed. The thought had crossed my mind several times over the past couple years, and I now severely regretted not acting on it. Everything changed the day she told me she'd filed for divorce, and even though I gave her time to get the divorce completed, I'd started making plans and arrangements for our future. Plans that I'd thrown out the moment I learned Connor hurt her, but the end was the same.

She was mine in truth. No one could take her from me now.

"Hey, pretty lady," I said as I stepped into the kitchen. I should have been surprised to find Ivory cooking and Donatello cradling Luna, but I wasn't. From what I'd seen, I wondered if Matteo needed to worry about the older man running away with the baby he considered a granddaughter.

"Hi Lino." Ivory's face morphed into a smile. "You're still alive, I see."

I rubbed my hand over my head sheepishly. Given everything Matteo had put Ivory through in their brief, chaotic courtship, I wondered how she would react to the truth behind my marriage with Samara.

That I'd had to threaten her into it.

"Yes," I said finally. She shook her head at me, teasing but communicating just how much I should be ashamed of myself. But I wasn't. How could I be, when Samara wore my ring and bore my last name?

My wife.

It felt like I'd never get over saying it.

"Matteo's on the phone," Donatello said. "Not to be interrupted, but he shouldn't be long."

"Come help me assemble these Cubanos for lunch, and maybe I'll even let you eat one," Ivory said with a grin. I nodded, stripping off my suit jacket and rolling up my sleeves before washing my hands. As soon as I helped her pick apart the pork roast, she settled in for arranging it on the rolls. "How is she handling it?"

"Better than I expected, honestly," I sighed. "I wish I hadn't had to threaten her, but you understand why I did, right?"

Ivory paused a moment, worrying the corner of her mouth between her teeth as she thought about it. "Now? Yes. After what happened with Adrian, I completely understand going to extreme measures to keep her safe. That said, if you'd asked me before that? The answer would be a hell to the fucking no. I'm sure Samara falls in that same category. She hasn't been kidnapped or had to face the thought of abuse like that."

"He raped her, Ivory," I admitted. "That's why she finally filed for divorce." I knew it wasn't my place to tell her, but it felt like I couldn't get an accurate opinion without giving that information. "I don't want you to make a thing about it, or even let on that you know. Samara wouldn't like people knowing, but—"

"I get it," Ivory sighed, finishing with the pork and sprinkling cheese on top. "I won't say anything, but I don't think that changes much. Samara is stubborn, and I assume she didn't tell you until she had no choice?"

"You assume correctly," I grunted.

"She thinks her problems are her own. She has always thought that she should be responsible for herself and the consequences of the decisions she makes. You remember when we all went to that lake, and she climbed up on the rocks because she saw Matteo and I do it?"

"But then she got scared and didn't want to jump," I finished.

"You offered to help her down, but she wouldn't let you. Your offer to help actually *made* her jump even though she was terrified. She was that desperate to not let you help her," Ivory laughed. "I expect this is a lot like that. She'd rather flounder on her own and be afraid than reach out. In the long run, you forcing your help on her is probably a good thing because she'd never accept it any other way, but for now I think you'll have a rough road ahead of you."

I opened the jar of homemade pickles, following behind Ivory as she sprinkled the cheese. "When is anything with Samara ever easy?"

"The things worth fighting for never come easy, sweetheart," Ivory murmured. "I think you need to just be honest with her, slowly. Ease into certain aspects of the marriage and give her stubborn ass some time to acclimate. She's living with you already? So maybe start there. Get a realtor for her house and push her to sign papers to sell it. Things that make her feel like she has a say, even if she really doesn't since you're you and we both know you could sell her house out from under her if you paid the right people off."

"That makes sense," I admitted. "I'll call my realtor tomorrow morning. Get her on it, and in the meantime send some guys over to pack up the rest of her stuff."

"I know you aren't used to going without sex, but if Connor hurt her—"

"She needs time. I know. I've already waited for almost a fucking year, a little longer won't kill me." Ivory turned to stare up at me, tears pooling in her eyes.

"Almost a year?"

"Since she told me she was getting divorced. I knew that she would be mine. I wasn't about to fuck around while I waited, not when I knew our future was coming."

"Lino, I think that might be the sweetest thing I've ever heard," Matteo's gruff voice interrupted, a mocking chuckle to his lilt. But the look on his face bore nothing but open approval.

"Shoo you," Ivory laughed. "This is an important conversation. I'll send him in when we're finished."

"Fine," Matteo groaned, but he grinned as he walked past to snatch Luna out of Don's arms. "I'll spend time with the most beautiful baby in the world. She's much prettier than you anyway, Lino."

He walked down the hallway to his office, and I laughed at the way Don watched him go with his arms still out like he held the baby. He glared after Matteo, before huffing and getting back to his other duties around the house.

"If you want to know a secret, I think the best way for you to make Samara trust you sexually will be for you to put her pleasure before yours. Remind her that sex, or oral or whatever it is, *can* feel good. She's probably forgotten that after everything. If her last experience was unpleasant, it can fog everything up and make us need a reminder that sex was good before and it can be good again."

Ivory went on with more advice, giving me a treasure trove of things I would use to bring Samara around quicker.

By the time I went into Matteo's office, I felt much better about all the things with Samara.

Except for what I'd come to talk to Matteo about.

⁂

I plopped into my usual seat in Matteo's office, grinning as the man passed me his daughter. He was so hesitant to give her up, like nothing mattered more than having her in his arms as much as he could. I cooed down at the little girl, Matteo's *Little Moon*, swaying her back and forth while she stared up at me like she couldn't quite decide what to think of me.

"I know you didn't leave Samara's side to come visit Ivory and the baby, you'd have brought her along for that," Matteo grunted, sitting behind his desk and donning the persona he wore so well, that of a dictator on his throne.

"I would have," I agreed. "Has Ryker found anything?"

Matteo sighed. "You know how he is. He'll check in as soon as he has something to report, but in the meantime it's best if we don't distract him. Connor hasn't gone back to work, his cell phone was a dead end, and he hasn't gone back to his shithole apartment. Ryker tried the casinos and the illegal games, but since his well dried up with Murphy, he has no money to gamble in the first place."

I grunted, and only the precious bundle in my arms stopped me from losing my shit. Connor was far from a criminal mastermind. Some days it surprised me that the man managed to tie his shoes by himself, so how he managed to hide from Ryker of all people was beyond me. "Let's talk about Murphy then. I don't want to cause any problems for you, but if he comes after Samara, I want him to know exactly what he's risking before he does it." Matteo leaned back in his chair, thinking as he watched me. "Who's the prettiest baby ever?" I asked Luna, finally earning what seemed like a happy gurgle. I didn't speak baby, but I'd take it.

"She likes you," Matteo grunted.

"Of course, she does. I'm her fun Uncle."

Matteo huffed a laugh. "You're her cousin. Second cousin. Some shit like that."

"Shhh," I scolded. "You shouldn't swear in front of Luna." He gave me an unamused look, like the concept of not swearing in front of his daughter was ridiculous. It was. With the crimes all the men Luna would grow up around committed daily, a curse word would be the least of her problems.

"I think you should go to Murphy. Confront him, be upfront. There's no need for it to be ugly in the slightest. His issue is with Connor, not Samara. She is no longer his wife, but yours. He's a businessman, no matter how slimy he is. He'll see that going after Samara is not worth risking the wrath of the Bellandi's. The war that would ensue would cost him more than he could ever dream to weasel out of Connor or Samara if he sold her." I nodded, standing and handing Luna back to Matteo. She grabbed his finger immediately in her little fist, a daddy's girl to the core. Considering he would move the Earth itself for her, I could understand the appeal.

Even as a baby, she seemed to sense it. I wondered if she sensed the same thing in her mother. Since the sweet and innocent Ivory had killed the one and only man who dared to threaten her child.

The mama bear was strong in her.

"You're going straight there?"

"Yeah," I grunted. "Is he still holding court at that Irish pub on Clark?"

Matteo laughed, because the thought would never occur to him to hold fucking visiting hours in a restaurant. He had employees to do that for him, and Tiernan's recent attempts to take over Adrian's operation were mostly laughable. The man wasn't made to be a Boss. "He is. We'll see if he keeps up with that if he assimilates the human trafficking operation to his bookie shit. I swear he's a stain on all of us."

"Most mobsters aren't exactly known for being good people, Matteo," I laughed. "We certainly stretch the limits of the word."

He winced visibly and nodded in thought. "Do yourself a favor and make sure Samara is aware of the girls," he warned. "I never got the impression she concerned herself with the matters of our business, and I know Ivory said Samara seemed pretty in the dark when she pried the last time they had lunch. Ignorance was always bliss; I take it?"

"Yeah. The less she knew, the better. She wasn't my wife, so in the worst case she could be compelled to testify. It was just safer."

"Right, well, she's your wife now," Matteo laughed. "She'll want to know we run girls, though I would probably leave out your preference for them in the past. No woman wants to think of her husband—"

"I got it, thanks," I snarled. "I'll make sure she knows just enough that she isn't blindsided at, say the party coming up at *Indulgence*. Who knows what she could find out there, really?"

Matteo smirked, all arrogance and amusement as he stood and walked to the door. "Your first event with your wife. How adorable is that?" Matteo asked as I followed him out of the office. The sound of his ribbing continued when he found Donatello loitering in the kitchen with Ivory, but I couldn't care.

Samara would be on my arm as my wife. I never brought women as my dates to events in the past, never cared enough about any of them to make that kind of statement. But given my feelings for Samara, there was nothing but pride because the beautiful woman would be at my side.

Nothing would make me happier than knowing that men would look at her and want to be me, but none would dare to take what was mine.

I'd kill anyone who tried.

I just hoped that Samara knew that, because there was no line that I wouldn't cross when it came to her. She consumed my every thought. Drove me crazy with the fact that I had to wait, even though I understood fully.

Soon enough, we'd move past the wounds Connor had given to my woman.

And then nothing would ever come between us.

✳✳✳

I didn't waver as I strolled into Murphy's. Men like me couldn't show weakness, not even when we stormed into enemy territory. Tiernan wasn't an enemy yet, but if he won the war happening over Adrian's trafficking ring, he would be. Matteo didn't tolerate that shit in his city, and it would put them on opposite ends automatically.

Which meant making it clear to him that Samara was off limits, had a time stamp on it. He needed to understand before we came to blows, or his word would mean nothing. Even as it stood, it would probably be temporary. Nothing was safe in times of war. Even if Matteo never went after a woman for the crimes her man committed, the others didn't show the same respect.

I imagined it would make Matteo slightly more hesitant to go to war, whereas before he'd had nothing to lose, now he had a pretty wife and daughter.

But Matteo didn't lose the wars he started, and Tiernan Murphy was nothing but a shit stain compared to the men Matteo had seen dead and buried for defying his will.

"Angelino!" Tiernan said jovially, standing and smiling at me as I strolled up to the booth at the back of the pub where he conducted his business and made his deals. His copper hair almost reminded me of Samara's but had a lightness to it that hers lacked because of her Hebrew mother.

I had to wonder if her shithead father looked anything like Tiernan, given that he'd been Irish. I was grateful that he'd left, because if it hadn't been for that then Samara and her family never would have moved to Chicago, but I saw the wounds it left Samara with. Yavin said that she and her father had been practically inseparable before he left and never came home, taking the family's savings with him.

"Murphy," I greeted, standing before his table. He motioned to the chair on the other side of the table, and I slid into it and made myself comfortable.

"What brings you to my neck of the woods?"

"Connor Walsh," I said abruptly.

"Ah, he owes me a great deal of money. I know his wife is a friend of yours, which is why I thought he may be trustworthy to lend to given he had a trust fund on top of it. I've delayed hurting him out of respect, but—"

"Samara is no longer his wife, and I do not give the first shit what you do with Connor if you find him first, though I would love to participate," Murphy's brows raised, his slightly wrinkled face twisting as he worried his lip.

"I didn't realize the divorce went through. I knew Walsh fought her on it, and who can blame him, am I right? A piece like that—"

"Samara is my wife." I cut him off with a glare. "As such, I take it you understand that means she is under Bellandi protection, as she herself is a Bellandi now. If you go anywhere near her, we will consider it a declaration of war."

He held up his hands as if he was innocent, looking at his buddies who surrounded him in amusement. "I wouldn't dream of touching the wife of a Bellandi. Congratulations on your marriage then. I'll handle my problems with Walsh personally, I assure you. Now that I understand the situation clearly."

"Good," I said, sighing in relief. While I hadn't expected him to argue the point, one never knew what a power-hungry man like Murphy would do in his pursuit of more power. "How's Aoife?"

"Her father is as strict as ever. Won't let me marry her until she's 21." He rolled his eyes in reference to his future father-in-law. Aoife's father ran the Irish syndicate on the opposite side of the city, and despite Matteo having overall power in the city, he tolerated Liam O'Connell's presence out of respect for the other man. They conducted their business very similarly, transitioning to more legal pursuits slowly and only partaking in the criminal aspects when they could endeavor to ensure that innocents were not hurt unnecessarily. Aoife had no love for Murphy but had been betrothed to him at a young age as he was the son of her father's top enforcer.

She was young, raised in the life and knew her place. With no sons of his own, Liam had no choice but to pass everything down to his daughter's husband, and I often felt that his delaying on the marriage between Murphy and Aoife was because he knew he wasn't the right match for her and needed an excuse to find a way out of it.

We'd see if he found one, and what happened when he split his organization in half to benefit his daughter. I didn't think Liam realized how many of his men flocked to Murphy's way of doing things. At any rate, the Irish were none of my business.

"You are over twice her age. Perhaps he thinks she should be able to live a little before settling into the life you'll no doubt expect. Could you imagine being married at her age?"

"So long as she's virginal when we marry, it matters little to me," he shrugged, ever the misogynist. He was far from virginal, having gotten around in his forty years of life. Aoife seemed like a sweet girl, and I hoped Liam found a way out of the betrothal for her sake.

"Well, I'll let you get back to business," I said, standing when someone strolled into the pub and looked straight at Murphy.

"I appreciate you coming to clear things up, Angelino. Take care of your beautiful wife. I hope she gives you all the beautiful children men like us require." I grimaced as I smiled but nodded and turned on my heel.

Being around Tiernan Murphy always made me feel like I needed a shower. Samara's name on his lips only made me want to shower her off too, even if she hadn't been near him.

Ugh.

CHAPTER TWENTY-ONE

SAMARA

I didn't know who Lino arranged to shop for me, but I had the distinct impression that he didn't peek at the outfit they'd chosen before handing it over to me. Even before we'd delved into foreign territory, he had hated when I dressed up for work or to go out. I always thought it was because he didn't like to be reminded that I was a woman, given the platonic nature of our friendship.

I questioned that in hindsight.

But I knew he wouldn't want me to go to *Indulgence* dressed in this. It made me love the outfit even more.

Whoever she was, she'd decided to put me all in white, and I had to wonder if it was Lino's request to make me feel bridal. I hadn't had the opportunity with our wedding, despite his adorable attempt to give me a moment of it with the dress. He had no way of knowing that the big wedding Connor and I had the first time around had been at his insistence. I had zero interest in a big bridal affair.

So the thoughtful nod to our new marriage with the white, I wanted to believe it had been at Lino's insistence. So I let myself think it, even if he refused to let me out of the house once he saw me.

The strappy heels on my feet were nude, blending in with my fair skin perfectly and had just enough substance to cover the edges of the scars where they curled up from the bottoms of my feet. A double banded gold cuff on my bicep and a matching bracelet on the opposite arm were the only jewelry I wore.

No color, and it made the dark copper of my hair seem to shine brighter for it. A high-waisted, skintight white pencil skirt encased my hips and down to below my knees, and I was grateful it was an amazing quality and thick enough fabric to not be transparent as it stretched taut over my ass and thighs.

The top was strapless with a sweetheart neckline, baring a sliver of my midriff above the skirt, and an intricate balance of nude fabric and white lace that stunned.

"Samara!" Lino yelled from downstairs. "We need to talk before we go. I don't want to be late."

"Coming!" I called back, grabbing the clutch off the bed that held my phone and lipstick. With a deep sigh, I opened the door and went downstairs to greet my husband. Something about the moment, him waiting for me to get ready for his work event, felt domestic. It made the fact that we were married, regardless of the fact we hadn't consummated it, that much more real.

He stood by the island in the kitchen, sipping whiskey from a tumbler and looking delectable in his blue suit. Only a confident man could pull off a suit that was just slightly brighter than the navy I typically saw in blue suits, but Lino managed. His olive skin offset the color perfectly.

"Hi," I whispered, stepping into the kitchen. His head snapped up, drawing up my legs and to my face slowly in a slow burn that I felt spread from my toes to the top of my head.

He swallowed, tossing back the rest of his drink so quickly that I chuckled. "You can't wear that," he growled.

"Sure, I can. It's a nightclub, this is more covering than most of the dresses that will be there," I argued, planting a hand on my hip. "Besides, you bought it."

"Yes, but—"

"Angelino Bellandi," I warned him. "I can promise you I am *not* going to change. This is what I'm wearing. If you don't want to be late, then I suggest you get your balls in hand and say whatever it is you're putting off."

He snorted, but his eyes darkened as he set the tumbler down on the counter and stalked toward me. "If we don't want to be late, then I *highly* suggest you not talk about anything to do with my dick, Little Dove." I swallowed when he stopped to stand directly in front of me, his fingers touching the side of my neck and trailing down to tease the bare skin of my shoulder and over my arm.

"You're stalling," I breathed, resisting the urge to arch my neck into the touch. His hands on me, such a simple touch, shouldn't be enough to make my brain scatter. I attributed it to the fact that it had been far too long since I'd had an orgasm, even by my own hand.

It might have been time to remedy that.

"Am I?" he asked. "I don't think so. All I can think of with all this bare skin in front of me is getting my hands on you, laying you out beneath me and exploring every inch of this golden skin with my hands—" he whispered, pressing a hand to the small of my back and pulling until our bodies pressed flush together. The feel of his arousal at my belly brought a gasp from my lips, the way his breath teased my ear as he bent his neck to continue his torment. "—my tongue and my teeth," he continued. "I'd watch you writhe underneath me; make you *beg* me to give you what you need. What *only* I can give you. Don't you want that, *vita mia*?" I bit my lip, curling my hands around the back of his neck and toying with the ends of the hair at the nape of his neck.

"Such a tease," I whispered. His hand twitched against the bare skin of my back, sending a pulse of heat straight to my core. I'd never felt attraction like this. Never felt like a single touch would light me on fire. Even with the lingering traces of my anger with him for taking my choice away, for his threats to lock me up, nothing could stop the heat pooling in my core.

What would happen when he finally got me naked? When all his bare skin touched mine and he moved inside me?

I might go up in flames. I just had to hope he didn't let me burn.

His head pulled out to look down at me, and I'd never tire of the look in those eyes. The way he smoldered as he stared down at me, especially when I tugged his head down to mine and took his lips in a desperate kiss. He groaned into my mouth, devouring me, and I wanted to be consumed.

I wanted everything he offered, but fear still tickled the back of my mind. What if I'd been damaged beyond repair?

What if everything Connor said about me being a lousy lay was true, and I'd just condemned a second husband to a lifetime of bad sex?

Lino finally slid his hands down, grasping the back of my thighs and lifting until I sat on the counter in the exact same spot he'd tormented me in as we made ravioli. I willingly spread my legs, hiking the skirt up high enough to accommodate, and he slid into the space I opened. With my body flush against him, perched on the edge of the counter and trusting him, I could feel the ridge of the top of him through his slacks. Pressed up against the inside of my thigh in a torment, but I was glad because it couldn't touch *me*, not just yet.

Lino seemed to realize that I needed that boundary, and he didn't push it. Just ate at my mouth with all the ferocity he dismantled entire fortune-500 companies for takeovers. Like a conqueror staking his claim. His tongue tangled with mine and his hand mussed my hair.

But I couldn't be bothered to care. By the time he finally pulled back from my lips, his forehead pressed to mine, and he hovered there. "You have to know how much I want to take you upstairs and make love to you, Little Dove. But we have to go, and you aren't ready."

"I know," I whispered back, letting him help me slide down from the island.

"Shit, this seems like a horrible time to have this conversation now. I wish I hadn't put it off." He ran a hand through his hair as I shimmied the skirt down my hips.

"Is something wrong?"

"It's nothing that you need to be afraid of. I just, there's the side of the business that Matteo handles. But I'm not clean of it either, and I don't want anything to surprise you. This event at the club, a lot of the people who will be there are associates and allies of Matteo's. You'll be exposed to some things, and I just want you to be prepared." He took my hands in his, holding them and stroking his finger over the birthmark on my palm.

"Okay," I whispered.

"Matteo runs girls. Willing girls, but escorts. Some of them will probably work at the club tonight." My forehead wrinkled, trying to read between the lines of what he wasn't saying.

"Okay. They do the job willingly, though?"

His head jolted back, as if he couldn't believe that I even had to ask. "Of course."

"Then I don't see why I would have a problem with it honestly. You and Yavin aren't exactly pillars of the moral community. It would be hypocritical of me to judge them or you for this, but not the other things. Why? Because they have sex for money? It's their body. If they're comfortable with it, that's not my place to judge. It's frankly just none of my fucking business."

He smiled down at me, looking at me like I was some mythical unicorn. To be honest, with how catty women could be, I couldn't even be surprised. "You're incredible."

"Are you planning on sleeping with them? Is that why you thought I should know? Because we won't be faithful to this marriage?" I asked the question I didn't want the answer to. I knew what he'd said before, but after our little make-out session and I'd left him high and dry, who knew. Men were fickle, and it could have driven him over the edge.

"No. Fuck no. We are both going to be loyal to our marriage, Samara. No other women. No other men. Just you and I, but I'm not a saint. I've been with women, some I found at the club, others I found elsewhere, but—"

"But I might have run-ins with women who've had you before?" I teased, arching a brow up. "I'm not stupid and naïve. I know there were women before we became a thing, but as long as they're part of the past, that doesn't matter to me."

His lips touched mine briefly, and when he pulled away, he smiled down at me. "I don't deserve you."

"Probably not," I agreed. "I'm awesome. Now back off so I can fix my face and we can go."

He stepped back with a laugh. "Next time, I won't dread these conversations so much."

"Good. Because all I expect from you is honesty, Lino," I admitted, heading for the bathroom.

It was as simple as that.

My relationship with Lino revolved around the honesty between us, and so long as we had that, then I had faith that we could be happy together.

If only I could continue to be honest with him too.

***

Rolling up to *Indulgence* in the back of a limo was not something I'd ever experienced before. In truth, it wasn't something I ever thought I would feel. I'd started purposefully avoiding the club years prior, because while Lino never picked up a woman in front of me, it became obvious that wasn't normal. Watching him be approached time after time by woman after woman and thinking I'd never have the opportunity to stake my claim on him was something that squandered any fun I might have had on the dance floor.

I took my dance nights with friends to rival clubs, even if it meant that I felt like a traitor to Lino. It hadn't lasted long. My relationship with Connor alienated me against all those friends to where I had none. So strolling into the club with his hand on the small of my back was surreal, in a way I'd never thought to experience.

Heads turned our way as we entered, and the crush of people seeking Lino's attention started almost immediately. I had no doubt that his presence had been missed, given he'd only left on rare occasions over the weeks he'd spent taking care of me while I recovered. With my bruises faded to something I could cover up with makeup, I knew the day I returned to work approached rapidly. Even Lino couldn't justify restricting me from going back when the remaining traces of bruises were gone.

The fact that the night was a massive charity event that Matteo had asked Lino to organize to raise awareness about date rape only served to make the event more anticipated. A date rape charity event happening at a nightclub might have seemed in poor taste to some, but Lino explained that Matteo saw it as him making a statement. That shit wouldn't be tolerated at their properties, and anyone who dared would face the wrath of the Bellandi family.

"How are we doing so far?" Lino asked when Enzo met us at the foot of the stairs, walking on Lino's other side like a silent sentry as we made our way up to the VIP level.

"Great. The crooked fucks are donating even beyond the pricey admission tonight. Their statements they'll join him in the fight against date rape and sex crimes in his city. He's drawing quite the line in the sand. I just hope that we're ready to deal with the inevitable fallout," Enzo pointed out. I was inclined to agree. The thought of Lino's life in danger wasn't something I welcomed, even though I believed wholeheartedly in the cause.

I'd never been date raped or drugged, but I had listened to Ivory talking about being drugged once when she explained Matteo's connection to the charity he started. It wasn't something I would wish on anyone.

I just couldn't face the prospect of losing Lino when I only just had him as mine.

We stepped onto the VIP level, and Matteo greeted Lino with a pat on the back and a massive smile. Ivory was noticeably absent, home with newborn Luna where I was certain it would have been impossible to pry her away from even if Matteo had wanted to. There wasn't much Ivory wouldn't forgive Matteo for or tolerate in her less than ethical husband but depriving her of time with their daughter was undoubtedly one of them.

"Mrs. Bellandi," Matteo greeted, his voice too loud. Heads snapped our way, and even though the man semi-terrified me I narrowed my eyes at him in a glare. "You look lovely. Marriage to Lino suits you."

"You're a douche," I returned, making him roar with a deep laugh that echoed through the cavernous space. Even with the music pulsing on the lower level, there was no mistaking the genuine humor on his face for those who couldn't hear him.

"Always a pleasure, Samara. I hope my cousin is proving entertaining to you during your recovery," he added in a quieter voice.

Feeling thoroughly outed, I pouted at him. "He's a little tedious. Always working. If I didn't know better, I'd think his boss was a slave driver."

Lino chuckled next to me, drawing me tighter into his side and nuzzling my cheek with his nose. "Champagne?" a waitress asked as she circulated the space. Lino took two glasses and handed me one hesitantly.

"Maybe I shouldn't let you drink," he said with a smile. "You're already feeling sassy tonight. If I add alcohol, I'm a little scared what version of my Little Dove I might get." The waitress sighed at him with the way he said my nickname, and I wanted to bury my head in the sand and play ostrich.

"Are you two *trying* to embarrass me?" Matteo chuckled and then turned and stalked off to chat up some undoubtedly sketchy businessman without so much as a goodbye.

"Wouldn't dream of it," Lino laughed. "Just making it clear that you're off-limits to the men who are staring at your ass."

I giggled, turning to face him and reaching behind me to slide his hand down to the ass in question. His fingers only brushed the curve at the top, barely a touch at all, but the smile faded from his face. The hand that didn't hold my champagne rested on his chest, playing with the collar of his shirt cautiously. "Does that mean I get to mark you as off-limits too?" I teased, and he surprised me by leaning down to press a slow, sensual kiss to my lips while everyone watched.

"Consider me marked," he murmured as he pulled away. The way he looked down at me melted my heart, but it faded too quickly to be replaced by the harsher demeanor I hated to see on his face. "My father's here," he grunted, sipping his champagne like aggravation didn't pulse through his body. His free hand took mine, stroking his thumb over the birthmark. My skin tingled at the touch, the reminder of his tease before we left the house at the front of my mind, but I knew it wasn't sexual in nature. He did it to reassure himself, his comforting gesture that he'd adopted since childhood.

"Is he not supposed to be?" I asked, feigning casualness. We both knew I detested his father, and the feeling was mutual, but Lino had long ago taught me not to show my intimidation in front of the man who often commented that I needed a man to 'take me in hand.'

I wondered if he ever thought that *duty*, as he saw it, would fall to his son.

I highly doubted it.

"Angelino," his father's deep, smarmy voice said as he stepped up. "Miss Mahoney."

"Father," Lino returned. "It's Mrs. Bellandi now. I'm sure you've heard." Lino's voice was nothing but disinterested, and his father returned the bullshit show by eyeing the scantily clad women at the club as they strutted past, swaying to the music and enjoying themselves, unaware of the predator in their midst. I knew, without a doubt, that somewhere in the room, Lino's stepmother probably made her rounds. Pretending she was younger than she was, and that she wouldn't be replaced with a new model as soon as one caught her husband's fancy. Or maybe she knew it and that was why she seemed like she was on the prowl whenever I saw her.

I wouldn't put anything past the woman. She had no love for Gabriele Bellandi and the feelings were mutual. Why they'd married, I'd never know.

"I heard rumors, but I thought they were lies. Surely my oldest son wouldn't get married and not invite me?" Gabriele liked to play the role of a doting father, when it was convenient for him. I had to wonder who lingered nearby that he might want to deceive with such behavior.

"It was a last-minute decision, and since you've always been a staunch opponent of my inevitable relationship with Samara, I didn't think it prudent to invite you. The last thing I wanted on our special day was for you to cause a scene." Lino's explanation rolled off his tongue so easily, and his father turned a surprised glare to him. It wasn't often that Lino so casually opposed his father in public. I couldn't say I was present for their interactions often, so I had to wonder if it was something that had become more common in the years since my marriage to Connor—when Gabriele had declared it inappropriate for Lino to drag me along to family dinners and gatherings when I left a husband of my own at home.

Lino hadn't fought him, but I suspected it was largely because he felt it gave him a good excuse to separate me from his family. He'd known all along how much I hated those gatherings, but I'd gone to support him, anyway.

Because I knew he hated them even more than I did.

"Hm," Gabriele hummed. "Is your new wife aware that she won't be permitted to walk away from this marriage when it inevitably fails like the last? Some women just aren't suited to being wives."

I snorted on Lino's side, but held my tongue. Lino's face twisted with fury. "She's aware there is no divorce in our future. Her divorce from Connor will be irrelevant soon enough," he snarled at his father, a warning flashing in his eyes.

"And why is that?" Gabriele asked, his tone as bored as ever. He never bothered to spare me a glance, didn't consider me worth looking at. He never had, not from the days he'd called me a Jewish brat and deemed me unworthy of his pureblooded Italian son.

"Because he'll be dead," Lino stated, raising his glass of champagne to his lips and taking a sip as if he didn't vibrate with the need to strike his father.

"Well, I'll expect you both to join us for dinner on the fifteenth then?" his father asked pointedly. The one day every month where they had dinner together, where they pretended to be a family for long enough to sit down to a meal. I knew they likely saw each other during business hours, but I also knew Lino was all about the business when that happened.

"Of course," I murmured in agreement, making Lino tighten his hand at my hip. I knew what it would mean to him to have me attend those dreaded dinners with him, and that was my job as his wife. To try to make him a little more comfortable in uncomfortable situations, even if those were situations where his family scared the shit out of me.

Such was life.

"Good. I'll let you get back to business, Angelino." With another nod, the eldest Bellandi made his way for one woman dancing toward the corner of the VIP section. Smooth blond hair hung down to her waist, and she smiled openly at the older man despite the very clear age gap.

"Escort?" I asked.

Lino looked her way, considering for a moment. "Yep," he responded finally. I appreciated the honesty, that he didn't deny that he knew her by sight. To do so would have only insulted me, given that he was likely to be acquainted with the girls that Matteo ran, since it was all part of the same business.

I didn't feel a speck of jealousy.

None.

Instead of allowing it, I turned to him and nuzzled into his chest. The smell of his soap gave me the comfort I needed to brush off the stirring of unwelcome feelings. He'd been nothing but honest with me in the past, and I trusted that if he had any intention of being unfaithful, he would at least be honest with me on that front.

The women of the past didn't matter.

They didn't have him now, and they wouldn't ever if I had anything to do with it. The thought suddenly filled me with the desire to see our marriage through, like a real marriage. To have Lino as mine and not just in name.

It made me feel more determined than ever, rather than just hopeful. If nothing else, I could take the circumstances that had led me here, the lemons of a horrible marriage, and make lemonade in the form of what I'd always wanted.

"Mr. Bellandi," an older woman whispered as she approached. "Congratulations on another successful event." She reminded me very much of Lino's stepmother, with long brown hair that seemed unusual for her age. Most women in their forties started keeping it a little shorter, but she just let hers hang in a way I might have admired if her eyes didn't narrow on me briefly before dismissing me.

"Ms. Romano. Have you met my wife, Samara?" he asked, communicating that her dismissal had been preemptive. I didn't let myself think about what or who she may have seen him embracing in the past.

"I don't think I've had the pleasure," she said, holding out a hand for me to shake. I took it politely even though I wanted to ignore it, given her early dismissal. "I wasn't aware you were married, Mr. Bellandi." The way she gave me a pointed look, I knew she meant to hint at affairs, not even remotely concerned with what that knowledge being delivered in such a public setting might have done to me.

"We're newlyweds," I announced, feeling determined to take control of the conversation since she didn't seem capable of showing respect as a natural reaction to meeting someone new.

"Ah, that explains it." The smile on her face was brittle, ready to crack at any moment from how fake it was. "Where did you two meet?" she asked. "Was it here?"

"No. Lino and I have been friends since childhood," I responded. "My brother Yavin manages *Tease*."

Lino chuckled at my side, and eventually his hand found mine. "Come with me," he murmured, dragging me away from the woman I didn't want to be around, anyway. I gave her a dramatic wave, plastering a friendly smile on my face. I knew my bitterness clung to the edges, that it was clearly fake. I just didn't care. Not when she could so callously dismiss me without ever speaking to me.

I didn't understand how Lino and Matteo navigated these waters, weeding out the users and abusers. It seemed impossible, like a threat or a liar lurked on every corner. It felt like it would be impossible to trust anyone, let alone build a real, genuine family in the way they had.

"Samara, this is Emilio," Lino said, stepping up to the middle-aged man who lingered at the edges of the VIP area. "You've met before, I believe?"

"Briefly, yes. It's nice to see you again," I agreed, holding out a hand for him to shake. His brown eyes narrowed on it briefly, but he eventually reached out his own. I wasn't overly familiar with the salt and pepper haired man with the body of a linebacker even though he was old enough to be Lino's father, but I had seen him a few times in passing. Enough to know that Lino trusted him enough to let him guard his sister when her permanent security was unavailable.

"You too, Mrs. Bellandi."

"Emilio has agreed to be your full-time security," Lino said, answering the question I hadn't thought to ask even though there had to be a point to him introducing us.

He wiped his hand on his pants subtly when he drew his hand back, and I bit my lip, wiping the clammy sweat off my hand.

I felt sufficiently disgusting, but honestly. It was a nightclub, and hot as all Hell. "He'll drive you to and from work. Anytime you leave the office, you're to notify him ahead of time so that he can escort you."

I turned wide eyes up to my husband, even if I had known what was coming. "That can't be necessary."

"Those are my conditions, Little Dove. This is the only way that I can protect you and allow you the freedom to come and go as you please. I won't apologize for doing whatever it takes to keep you safe," he said, and his hand tightened around my waist.

With a sigh, I nodded. Ivory's words rang in my head, that if nothing else I was safer with Lino than alone. I had to accept that his protection came at the cost of my privacy. "Okay."

Lino let out a sigh of relief, and I felt immediate guilt that he'd anticipated me arguing the point. Deep down, I knew he honestly just wanted to protect me.

Even when he went about it in all the wrong ways.

"I'll be in touch," he said to Emilio, before he turned his attention back to me. "I want to dance with you."

Even though I wasn't much of a dancer, I let him guide me to the lower level. I knew Lino probably had business he would need to tend to, and that when the time came, I would need to navigate the waters of his club without him. Having him with me all the time—the perfect little bubble we'd existed in for half a month—couldn't last forever.

Reality hovered just on the edge of our bubble, threatening to pop it and the safe haven Lino's home had become for me. So when he tucked me into the front of his body, moving with mine to the edgy pop song I knew he probably despised, I didn't fight it.

I settled in against him, letting him guide me through the motions that didn't come naturally to me. My musical ability as a singer hadn't translated to rhythm.

"I want to sell your house," he murmured in my ear. "You don't need it now that you live with me. We can get you a good price in this market." Seduced by the movement of his body behind mine, there was no fight left in me when I murmured to him.

"Okay." It wasn't like I wanted the house where I'd been raped, anyway. It wasn't a battle worth fighting for.

Lino was.

And I intended to fight.

CHAPTER TWENTY-TWO

Lino sighed as he stood from his place in the chair at the island when the door-bell rang. He seemed determined to get some work done, avoiding me where I sat on the couch reading in favor of being in the kitchen. It was unusual for him, considering the way my stomach had started cramping up, and the separation left me feeling unusually teary. It neared the point that a jewelry commercial could set me off. I knew what loomed on the horizon, and I hated it as much as any woman. I could see him through the arched doorway, but only if I really turned my body to look at him. I did it more often than I liked to admit, enjoying the way his forehead scrunched just the slightest bit as he focused on whatever consumed his time.

I could only imagine what that was. Yavin kept me in the dark as much as Lino did, but I also wasn't totally naive or idiotic. I knew they were criminals, or at least, connected to criminals. I hoped they kept their hands clean, but the best way for me to help them through whatever they did do was to stay ignorant and give them a respite from all that. Knowing the truth, I worried I would lose that for Lino. That he would no longer see me as separate from the life that I knew often weighed on him and made those distinguished lines form at the outer corners of his eyes sooner than they probably should have.

They did nothing to detract from his breathtaking looks, and somehow in spite of them he didn't look any older than he actually was. I just knew him well enough to recognize them as they formed, because in all my life, he was easily my favorite person to look at. My favorite sight in the world, and I loved that he had become the first thing I saw in the morning and the last thing I saw at night.

"Samara baby! Where are you?" Ivory's friend Sadie shrieked, giving Lino a hasty kiss on the cheek as she hurried into the house and left him floundering at the door momentarily.

"What did I do?" he asked the ceiling, closing the front door. "Seeing as you have a guest to keep you entertained, I'll just move this to my office and give you some privacy," Lino said, turning to me. He glared at Sadie in fake annoyance, but the warmth he gave me when he strolled into the living room and kissed me briefly let me know that he was happy I had a friend to socialize with. Someone checking in on me.

"I can't believe you didn't call me! I had to hear the news from Ivory when I've been rooting for the two of you for decades, I tell you."

"It's been a crazy few days," I admitted, rubbing a hand over the back of my neck. With my hair tied up into a bun on top of my head and my glasses on my face, I felt disoriented. Sadie somehow always looked flawless, even when she showed up without makeup.

"Alright bitch you're forgiven, show me the ring!" she squealed, flopping down onto the couch next to me. She snatched the book out of my hands, sliding the bookmark off the coffee table into it in a very considerate move that kept me from clawing her face off. Then she turned my hand over, staring at the three bands on my ring finger. "Oh my God they're beautiful," she whispered.

"Aren't they? He did good."

"Well duh, only the best jeweler for the Bellandi's I tell you. How are you liking married life?"

I laughed in her face, because aside from the rare kisses and the cuddling at night, nothing had changed between Lino and me. He was everything I could ever want in a partner, but then, he always had been. "It's good. I mean, I'm sure you know that it wasn't exactly normal circumstances, but we make the best of it. Hopefully we can eventually take it to that next level, but for now it works."

"You haven't had sex?" she hissed. "I thought for sure you would have bagged and tagged that shit by now girl!"

Shaking my head with a laugh, I decided to admit the truth to Sadie. Given her occupation, there was something I'd been meaning to ask her, and I suspected that it would require honesty from me. Unfortunately. "We will. I just think I need time to get there. He's giving me that time, but I don't know how to tell him when I decide I'm ready."

"You need time to get there? Samara, you have wanted to fuck that man since you hit puberty," Sadie teased, studying my face when I didn't laugh. It wasn't like what she said was untrue in any way. I had, even if it hadn't been quite so casual as Sadie made it sound.

I'd been obsessed with him. As a teenager, every time I saw him shirtless to go for a swim in the pool it felt like my ovaries had seized and I'd had to tell them to back off. "Connor hurt me," I admitted in a rush. "I'm not over it, and I don't know if I ever will be. If it were anyone other than Lino, I don't think I'd even consider going there."

She narrowed her eyes on me, suddenly serious as she tried to read between the lines. Her nostrils flared, and her jaw tensed when she saw it. "That fucking piece of shit," she hissed. "Is he dead yet? I want to kick his corpse."

Only Sadie could make me laugh in the face of my demons, and I leaned forward until my face hit her shoulder and muffled the sound. "Not yet."

"Good. I'd really hate for him to be decomposing and shit. I do not need the nasty that is Connor on my shoes. My shoes are too fucking pretty for his innards. Even my gym shoes, and I swear sometimes those already smell like they're dead."

"Thank you," I wheezed into her shoulder, knowing she'd turned up the ridiculousness that she was for the sake of my awkwardness. It was a unique gift of Sadie's, making everyone else feel more comfortable by embarrassing herself. Or at least, the way she acted would have embarrassed a normal person.

But not Sadie.

She was a ride or die kind of woman.

She took no shit, kicked ass, and took names. And apparently didn't like to kick corpses once they started decomposing.

"Seriously though, I've been meaning to ask if you could help me. I just kind of got sidetracked with all the changes, not to mention Lino won't let me leave the house until he can arrange full-time security like a psycho." She stood, picking up my favorite violet pillow and tossing it into the air to catch it. Ever the Queen of fidgeting, I should have known she wouldn't sit on the couch with me for long.

"Yeah? How can Mama Sadie help, darling?"

"I need to know how to protect myself. I won't rely on any of the security Lino is no doubt arranging. Look at what happened to Ivory. I just, I don't ever want to be vulnerable like that again. So can you teach me to protect myself?" I asked, watching as she turned a thoughtful face my way.

"Sure," she responded, dropping to the floor and sitting with her feet pressed together in a lotus position. "I doubt Lino will object, though he might want to be the one to teach you. I have to say, it would be much more fun for him to teach you."

I had no doubt about that. None. Whatsoever. "I'm not learning to have fun. I'm learning to defend myself. I can't think when he touches me. I swear my brain turns to oatmeal in my head and there's absolutely no ability to function. I wouldn't remember a thing he tried to teach me."

"Okie dokie," she shrugged. "Your loss. If you do decide to let him spar with you at any point, can I watch? You guys have some serious unchecked chemistry, and I just broke up with Patrick. I'm having a dry spell."

"No!" Lino yelled from his office down the hall, where he'd clearly been eavesdropping like the creep he was. I knew my eyes must have darted over to the wall that separated the living room from the hallway, calculating just how hard he had to have been focusing to listen that efficiently.

"Fucking creeper!" Sadie yelled back. Never one to be daunted by the fact that she was yelling at a criminal mob guy, she grinned at me even as I had to admit that listening in was in fact creepy.

"Really? You just asked to watch Samara and I roll around on a gym mat!" he pointed out, and I hung my head as I laughed silently. "Voyeurism much?"

"Don't knock it until you try it," she teased more quietly.

What the fuck had happened to my life? Like seriously.

I just couldn't

✳✳✳

I loved Sadie.

Really, I did. Her energy was infectious, her smile made even the most callous of men melt, because she was always just so damn happy.

But during my period, she was *exhausting*. Catching the tail end of Lino's phone call and the rage in his voice hadn't helped. Connor was gone. Vanished without a trace, and in spite of how he tried to hide it, I knew it weighed on Lino every day.

By the time she left, murmuring congratulations again and giving us a warning to tell my brother as soon as possible because rumors were making their rounds, I flopped onto the couch in a puddle of nothingness.

Lino chuckled, abandoning me to my misery from the entryway. I closed my eyes, content to pretend to sleep in his absence.

I only opened my eyes when the sound of a can hitting the coaster on the coffee table snapped me out of my misery. A can of diet soda, my favorite chocolate bar, and two pain pills on a napkin sat on the table. All lined up and ready for me while Lino fetched the remote and took a seat next to me on the sofa.

I hadn't breathed a word. Hadn't mentioned my period or anything of the sort. While we'd had no conversations that dove into the intricate details of my womanhood, Lino most often gave me a refuge during that time. A place to watch a movie and curl up on the couch with my favorite treats. He'd paid far more attention than I gave him credit for, taking care of me and expecting my needs better than I could have ever hoped for in a spouse.

And he'd done all that when we were just friends.

When he settled on a lighthearted romantic comedy, my spirit soared. The ridiculous over-the-top connection was exactly what my insane brain needed. I scooped up the pills and popped both into my mouth, swallowing them with a swig of soda. "Come here," Lino murmured, patting his lap.

"Do you even know how to ask for anything?" I snapped, and I immediately winced. As true as it might have been, the appropriate time to point that out was *not* when he provided a service I desperately needed.

I couldn't even remember a time when I hadn't had Lino to baby me through my period.

He only looked at me with his brows raised. "Oh please, my darling wife. Would you bring your head over yonder so that I might ease your pains?"

I glared at him one last time before rolling my eyes. My head hit his thighs, so I stared up at him while we waited through the previews. One strong, deft hand guided my shirt up to bare my stomach, and he pressed lightly against it in an easy massage that eased some ache. One might have thought his strong, muscled thighs would be a poor pillow.

But I didn't think I ever loved a pillow so much. The movie continued, but I drifted in and out of sleep as his hands worked their magic. I couldn't have cared less that I only caught bits and pieces of the movie, that it seemed to filter in one ear and out the other. The only thing that mattered was the fact that Lino was there, his hands working at my belly to ease the pain that came every month. I didn't know a single man who cared for a woman the way he did, didn't know a single one who loved so fiercely.

As a friend, it had seemed like a horrible reality I would one day have to face. The day that he fell in love with a woman, and she wasn't me. As his wife, I hoped one day I'd be that woman. That the way he took care of me would continue into the next phase of our relationship, that everything would shift to take a new meaning as we became more intimately acquainted with one another's bodies. There was nothing I wanted more.

"Sit up and lean forward for me, Little Dove," he murmured, and the sound of his voice echoed through the fog. Like I could find him anywhere, without seeing him or feeling him.

He was just there. Always.

I did as he said, letting him pull me to sit between his legs on the couch. There was no space between us, the very back of my ass resting in his lap. His hands stroked over the skin at my nape, kneading the muscles of my neck and shoulders so intently that I moaned. "You should be careful about the sounds you make." There was humor in his voice, but there was no mistaking the way it deepened to a level that made every muscle in my core, all the muscles he'd worked to relax, tense in anticipation.

"I have my period. I think I'm safe," I teased, groaning again when his hands moved to slide up the back of my shirt and work the muscles of my shoulder blades.

"If you think there is one damn thing in this world that would stop me from getting inside you, then you're wrong. I'm dying to feel you, dying to know how wet I can make you and how much you'll squeeze my cock like a vice. The *only* thing keeping me from taking you upstairs and finding out is the fact that you just aren't ready. The only thing keeping me from you is you. You should know that I'm not afraid of a little blood," he chuckled, and I bit my lip.

"I don't want to know how familiar you are with blood," I joked, trying to lighten the conversation away from the dangerous topic of sex we might never have.

I didn't think I had too many hard no's in the bedroom, but it felt safe to say period sex was one of them.

Because yuck.

"Is that a no go for you?" he asked, and I nodded my agreement. The couple in the movie finally kissed, but for the first time it didn't feel awkward. In the past, sex scenes in movies I watched with Lino had made me want to crawl in a hole and die of humiliation. He'd always seemed just as uncomfortable with them but tolerated the romance movies for me. "We should probably have a conversation about limits."

"Limits? Are you going to need me to sign a contract too?" I whispered, wincing when he snuck a hand into my side to tickle me briefly before pulling me back and tucking me into his chest. I appreciated the move, appreciated the fact that if we were really about to have a conversation about sex, that I wouldn't have to look at his face.

"I'm not a Dom," he laughed. "But I don't want to cross any lines with you. Is there anything off limits?"

"Threesomes," I blurted. "I don't want you to let anyone else touch me or touch anyone else. I don't want to be fisted or anything too extreme—"

"I meant normal limits, Samara," he laughed. "I'm not going to just whip out some kinky shit and push it on you."

I laughed uncomfortably. "I uh, I don't think I've ever been adventurous."

"Let's start simple." He touched a finger to my lips, tapping the flesh there once to get my attention. "Can I put my cock here?" I flushed, but nodded, wondering if women ever put absolute limits on blowjobs. That finger slid down between my breasts, and I watched it glide over my shirt as my nipples pebbled in response. "Can I put it here?"

"Yes," I whispered, loving the way he groaned in my ear.

That hand slid lower, and my hips writhed on their own when he cupped me through my leggings. "Can I fuck you here?"

"Of course," I whispered with a laugh.

His other hand grabbed my ass cheek in his hand, squeezing the flesh so harshly I could feel his desperation. "What about your ass, *vita mia*? Can I fuck you there?"

I paused, biting my lip and considering. But I decided on honesty. "I've never—"

"Will you let me?" he asked, cutting off my explanation that I'd never done it.

I knew, from the way his voice morphed into a growl that he didn't want to know what I'd done or who I'd done it with. I imagined the thought felt like chewing on glass, if it was anywhere similar to how it felt for me to think of the women he'd had before me.

"Yes," I whispered. He groaned into my ear behind me, and no other questions followed. "Is that all?" I teased, wanting to push him just a little bit farther.

"Quiet Samara, or I might just forget that you aren't ready and take what's mine tonight."

Well, that escalated quickly.

With a chuckle, I reached forward to grab my candy bar. Lino stole a bite, handing it back to me while I grinned at him.

I had a feeling I would very much enjoy tormenting Lino when I *was* ready.

And I couldn't wait.

CHAPTER TWENTY-THREE

LINO

I wanted to bash my head against the wall. Why in the fuck had I asked Samara where I could fuck her? Why had I told her I couldn't wait to get inside her?

Since the day I'd had her ass on my island counter the night of the event at *Indulgence,* I'd felt incapable of functioning. I needed her with a ferocity that would have terrified her, given her history. And she had every right to be afraid of me.

I'd never hurt her like Connor had; I'd never even consider wronging her. But I wasn't a good man, and she didn't have the first concept of how deep the bad ran inside me. All the way to the core, all the way to the roots where my father and family had tarnished my soul as a child.

I'd killed my first man at six, years before Samara came into my life. She'd never known me as an innocent, only ever known the killer in me.

In the years since Matteo had taken over for his father, other people handled the dirty work. I'd already proven myself, and my expertise was far more useful in the legal businesses, but that didn't make me *clean.* It didn't erase the years I'd spent living in the trenches, fighting like every day of my life was a war zone and the only way out was to die.

Given all of that, Samara loved me. I had no doubt about that, not given the way she melted at my dirty words and my stolen kisses. Not with the way she sank into my embrace like she was always meant to be there.

But no, the real reason she should have feared me had nothing to do with the fact that I was a hardened killer under all the times she made me smile.

It was because I would never let her go.

She was mine.

And it didn't matter if there came a day when she wanted something else, when her life led her to a juncture where she wanted to leave me. I would throw away the keys to her gilded cage to keep her mine, even as I worshiped at her altar.

So when she'd suddenly taken to strutting around in shorts instead of leggings, I knew my Little Dove intentionally pushed my buttons. I knew that she had a rebellious streak just strong enough for her to want to tease and torment me, given she felt safe with the way she assumed that I thought she still had her period, but I knew the moment my woman stopped bleeding. I'd always been able to tell. I allowed it, even if my dick would probably rub raw from jerking off in the shower one too many times.

"Samara," I growled at her when she bent over in some fucking yoga pose in the living room.

"Yes, my Italian Stallion?" she hummed, the bottom of her ass peeking out at me from the fucking shorts I fully intended to rip off her one day.

"Do you want me to smack your ass?" I grunted, making her laugh out loud. The sound of it coated my heart in warmth, melting that icy interior that always seemed to thaw around her. I was convinced if it hadn't been for her, for her constant presence in my life, I'd have ended up colder than Matteo or Ryker. I'd tolerate just about anything from her, even an absurd nickname.

"Maybe," she teased with a shrug, turning her attention back to the television where she'd streamed the yoga video. The sly look on her face only drew me closer. "I like it. I think I'll call you that from now on." I stepped up behind her, sliding my hands over the bare skin at the back of her thighs and shoving the shorts up until I could see her peach of an ass.

"Do you enjoy pushing me? I think I'd prefer it when you call me *husband*." I said, bringing a hand down against her cheek that was just hard enough to turn her skin pink.

"Yes."

"It's not a nice thing to do when I can't punish you for it," I murmured, repeating the motion on the other cheek so she matched.

"You torture me all the time. Why can't I return the favor?" Her voice had gone breathy. My Little Dove liked it when I spanked her ass, and *that* was something I fully intended to remember when I could finally have her.

"I'm going to shower," I grunted, stepping back from her.

"Do you think about me? When you jerk off in there?" she asked, shocking me with her outright admission that she knew why I showered at least twice a day.

"Do you think about me when your fingers dance over that little pussy?"

"I have for years," she admitted, giving me a saucy smile.

"Same, vita mia."

***

I knew the moment Samara stepped inside the bathroom door I'd left cracked open. It was true she'd spent days tormenting me by strutting her sexy little body around the house every second of the day, and I only knew I wanted to return the favor.

Nothing seemed more appropriate than giving Samara her first glimpse of my cock.

I resisted the urge to smirk, pretending I didn't see her standing there as I leaned forward and pressed a hand against the tiled shower wall. I knew the steam in the bathroom would disguise the details, the fact that I could barely see her was enough proof of that. My eyes closed as water dripped over my face, my hand wrapping around the base of my shaft and squeezing like I imagined Samara's tight sheathe would. With my hand wet, I could always get just a little closer to imagining the real deal, to trying to imitate what the moment would feel like when I slid inside her, pushing through the inevitable resistance I would meet.

It'd been far too long for Samara, just like me. She'd be tight, and I kept my grip snug as I worked it up and down my cock in a slow rhythm meant to give her a show. To let her see and feel every detail. The feel of her eyes on me as I worked myself over was nearly too much, nearly sending me spiraling over the edge like a desperate teenager.

But knowing that Samara liked what she saw enough to stay and enjoy the show, I couldn't wait for the day when I could really study her face. Really see her reaction when I stuffed her full of every inch of me.

My pace quickened, my hand making faster work of my orgasm.

I needed her to see it, needed her to watch me come and know that it had been a product of her torment.

I also knew my Little Dove wouldn't let herself watch for much longer out of fear of getting caught.

So I pictured her laid out beneath me in bed, her legs wrapped around me tightly and clenching with every thrust—her hand tight in my hair, her whimpers sounding in my ear.

The visual was enough to send me spiraling over the edge, shooting my load all over the tile as I finished with a ragged breath.

By the time I turned to look at the door, Samara was gone.

But I intended to torment her about the fact that she'd watched.

CHAPTER TWENTY-FOUR

SAMARA

Sitting through dinner was painful.

Absolutely, miserably painful. It didn't help that Lino seemed determined to torment me, having never put on a shirt while he whipped up food for the two of us. Staring at the broad muscles of his shoulders, the way the muscles in his biceps flexed ever so slightly as he moved and shook the pans around would probably have melted me into a puddle of goo under the most normal circumstances.

But right after I'd watched him jerk off in the shower? Right after I'd seen the shadow of just how massive his package must have been for his hand to have to move quite that much.

Long, nearly violent strokes that gave the general impression I'd feel him in my throat when he finally fucked me. It made me wish we'd had the anal sex conversation *after* I'd seen that.

Because nope. Nuh-uh.

Just no.

After he'd fully tormented me, he'd sat down in the stool right next to me and tucked into his dinner. My stomach felt like it might shrivel up and die with all the need that pulsed through me, but I tried to still my body while I poked at my food.

I tried not to squirm on my stool, tried not to fidget to get even the slightest bit of friction right where I needed it so desperately.

"Is there something you need, Little Dove?" Lino asked, turning to study me intently. When my eyes met his, I knew.

Without a doubt, I knew he'd seen me. That he'd known I watched him.

My chest flushed hot, my face following as humiliation took over and my spoon clattered to the bowl, soup forgotten. "I—uh, what could I possibly need?" I decided to play innocent, hopeful that he'd let the conversation dissolve in an effort not to embarrass me further. I should have known better; Lino had always enjoyed marching me right up to the edge of my comfort zone and shoving me off it. He loved to watch my reactions, thrived on the way I struck out when I couldn't take anymore.

"Hmmm, did you enjoy watching me?" he asked, setting down his own spoon and pivoting his stool until he put his hands on my thighs and turned me to him. With our stools close enough, he shoved his knees beneath my own, using them to spread my legs. I clung to the counter with one hand and the seat of my stool with the other as the motion shifted my balance and my back hit the seat back.

"I didn't watch—"

"Don't lie to me, *vita mia*," he murmured, running the fingers of his hand over the bare skin of my thigh. The metal of his wedding ring felt cool against my fevered flesh, serving as a reminder that Lino was mine.

My husband.

Sometimes I forgot, fell back into the same thinking I'd suffered through in all the years where he'd been just a *friend*. Sometimes I got lost in the shame of being so drawn to him when we would never be.

But we were and would be.

So I raised my chin, facing him head on as I murmured, "Yes."

His eyes darkened, his fingers tightening on my thighs. He bit his lip to hide his smile, and I knew this was one of those instances where I'd surprised him. Where my reactions seemed to catch him off-guard and offered him entertainment. Even if this time that entertainment came in a far more dangerous situation.

Dangerous to my sanity.

My heart.

My very being.

But we were diving in, testing the waters of our relationship.

"Then I think," he confirmed my train of thought, those fingers gliding closer to my center and brushing the very edge of the hem of my shorts. "that perhaps you should return the favor."

I blinked up at him, feeling disoriented by the sudden shift. I'd expected him to touch me, wanted him to touch me even if I still felt uncertain about my readiness for it. "What?"

"I want to watch you touch yourself. I want to know that you're thinking of me when you make yourself come."

His free hand reached out, grasping mine in his and bringing it down between my thighs. It laid against my core, touching through the thin fabric of my shorts and adding to the warmth there. Even with as warm as I felt all over, my pussy felt like it was on fire already, just from Lino's words and the way he tormented me without *really* touching me. "I—I don't know," I stuttered, because in all honesty touching myself in front of someone wasn't an experience I'd had before.

He teased the hem of my shorts, gliding the fabric to the side so that his fingers brushed against my bare skin. I already knew I hadn't worn underwear beneath the shorts with the intent of tormenting him, so I knew how obscene I must have looked with my legs spread and pussy open to his eyes. But even with that, even though he must have known from the way he held the shorts to the side, his eyes never left mine. He never so much as glanced down while he waited for my consent. "Let me see how wet I made you, Little Dove," he whispered, leaning forward to touch his lips to mine softly for a moment. I looked down at myself, biting my lip and nodding finally. Then I slid my hand from my thigh to my center, jolting the moment my fingers touched my over-sensitized skin.

Two fingers skirted over my clit in a slow, hesitant circle. When I finally braved looking back up into Lino's face, his eyes were still on my face, still watching and waiting. "Aren't you going to watch?" I asked with more bravery than I felt in that moment, always testing and pushing back. That was the summary of our relationship, a constant push and pull of teasing, torment, affection, love, and testing boundaries.

With a groan, his eyes left mine, gliding down my body until they rested on my hand at my pussy. I knew it must have been hard to see, with his hand holding my shorts to the side and my own fingers blocking part of me from view, so I shifted my hips, tilting them up and spread my legs wider as I put more weight into the back of my stool. "Fuck," Lino groaned, emboldening me. My pace on my clit increased, my breaths coming in ragged gasps. "Not yet," he ordered. "Finger yourself."

I bit my lip but slid my hand down to slip a finger inside my entrance, my hips rolling with the need to come. "Please," I begged him, seeking the approval I didn't *need*.

But I wanted it.

Lino offered safety. A place where I could give up my control and know that I'd always be safe. He was everything I needed to feel cared for, because I knew he would always read my cues, always interpret what my body language meant before I was even conscious of what I'd done or that I had hesitations.

He was home.

"Another," he ordered gruffly. "Tell me what you're imagining."

"Your hands," I gasped. "Your fingers, stretching me. Making me feel so full."

"What else?" he rasped as I slid the second finger in, pumping them in and out of myself quickly.

"Your mouth," I whispered.

"Where is my mouth, Little Dove?" he growled. My free hand came up in answer, clutching my breast and pinching my nipple through the fabric of my shirt. He grinned, looking at me in consideration for a brief moment before he tugged my tank top down so that the mound of flesh was free to the air and pebbled from the sudden cold. His fingers touched it a moment later, making me gasp and arch my back into the touch. With a hiss, he leaned forward, and warmth enveloped my nipple as he sucked it into his mouth harshly, giving me exactly the harsh treatment that I needed.

"Lino, please," I begged again, the thought of his fingers inside me bringing me right to the edge.

"Fucking come," he ordered, and I slipped my fingers free to brush against my clit so hard I detonated in a blinding light. When I opened my eyes, it was to find Lino staring down at me, a blissful smile on his face. "Hello, beautiful," he murmured, kissing me while I chuckled. Releasing my shorts to cover me, he took my hand from between my thighs and shocked me when he sucked the two fingers, I'd had inside me into his mouth. He moaned around them, and I sighed happily. When he stretched out a hand to tuck my boob away, he leaned forward and kissed it one last time first, making me giggle and shove him away. "I need to jerk off again," he grunted, but freed my knees and turned me to my soup. He snatched the bowl, dumping the soup out in favor of grabbing hot stuff from the pot and then he kissed my cheek before darting off to go shower.

I smiled into my soup, because I'd wanted to touch him.

Wanted to feel him between my hands, but Lino seemed determined to take his time with me. To respect the boundaries that had been set long before we got together even if his natural inclination was to test them.

It only made me want to respect his good intentions, so I let him go.

I even cleaned up the dishes when I was done eating.

All domestic and shit.

***

I eyed him warily as I slid into the bathroom next to him later that night. I wasn't afraid in the slightest that he would push me sexually, not when he'd shown so much restraint when he had me half-stripped in the kitchen, but I knew he wouldn't appreciate the conversation I intended for us to have.

He snatched his toothbrush out of the holder, squeezing toothpaste onto it and shoving it in his mouth. "Lino," I sighed.

"No, Samara," he grunted, refusing to meet my eyes in the mirror.

"You're being ridiculous!" I argued. "The bruises are gone!" I lifted my head up, giving him a display as I turned my head from side to side. Nothing remained, no physical trace of Connor's abuse on my throat.

There was nothing to prevent me from returning to work, and Lino's insistence that I stay home with him for all time couldn't go on. He had a job, work to get back to, and so did I. "You're not ready," he said as he spat his toothpaste out and rinsed his mouth.

I gaped at him when he left me in the bathroom, trailing after him. He crawled into bed, snatching the television remote off the nightstand.

I did not think so.

"I'm not ready?" I hissed, snatching the remote out of his hands and tossing it into one of the armchairs at the foot of the bed. "Don't you dare put that on me. I've been ready. I've humored you. Now it is time for me to get back to my life!"

"This is your life now!" he roared, and I faltered back a step. Lino never yelled at me, never showed any inclination he was capable of it. "Do you think it is easy for me to imagine you going back to work? You'll be at risk, even with Emilio. You're my wife. You are not going to just drop back into the way things were before and pretend like nothing has changed. Everything changed the moment you married me."

My bottom lip quivered, and my nose burned with tears I wouldn't allow to come. I couldn't cry, not if he meant what it sounded like. "You promised me. You promised me if I married you that you would let me go to work and have freedom."

"I will," he sighed, scrubbing his hand over his face. "I just need more time. Another week with just the two of us before we—"

"No," I cut him off. "The bruises are gone, and I'm healed. I want to go back to work."

"Samara," he sighed.

"This is important to me. I've given you leeway in a lot of ways and forgiven things I shouldn't have. You have to give me this." He reached forward, wrapping his hands around my waist and tugging me into his lap. He shifted his body to lean further into the headboard, maneuvering me until I straddled his hips and looked down at him.

"Okay," he agreed. "Emilio will take you from here to work, and he'll stay nearby but not crowd you while you're at work. If you leave the office, you call him. I expect to hear from you throughout the day, so I know you're okay. You *will* change your name immediately."

"I think I need to go to the DMV and social security first," I told him.

"I've taken care of it. You are already legally Samara Bellandi. I'll get you your new documents from my safe before you go to work. Those are my terms. If you leave this house, you are doing it with my name and my rings on your finger, and I expect you to flaunt them proudly."

I sighed, staring down at him like he'd lost his damn mind. "You changed my name without talking to me?"

"You're my wife. There was never a chance that you wouldn't take my name, Little Dove. Do you agree to my terms or not?"

With a groan, I caved. Leaning forward to drop onto his chest, I gave again. "Yes, my Stallion." He hadn't asked anything I hadn't already known, not really. Though, the fact that his connections could get me divorced and change my name without me even knowing it happened was terrifying, it wasn't surprising.

I'd married a Bellandi, after all.

✳✳✳

Emilio had been all smiles when he picked me up from the house, an alarming contrast to his colder demeanor at the club. I shrugged it off, knowing it probably felt strange to be introduced to someone you already knew but had changed capacity in your life. I'd gone from being a friend of his boss and someone he rarely saw, to someone he would see daily and his boss' wife.

"Are you excited to go back to work, Mrs. Bellandi?" he asked from the front seat. My foot shook where I'd crossed it over my ankle, imagining the coming confrontation with Jasper. He wouldn't take the news of my marriage well, and I just couldn't wait for the day when my life returned to some semblance of normal. One where I didn't have to feel like I was just waiting for the next argument. With Jasper and Yavin still looming on the horizon, it was a miracle I didn't feel like a complete disaster.

"Yes. It will be nice to feel like I'm capable of doing something for myself again," I returned with a smile. "Lino tends to take very good care of me."

The grin he gave in return seemed overly bright. "I can imagine a man like Lino can recognize a good thing when he has it."

"That's very sweet," I murmured, and we lapsed into silence as Emilio parked the car directly in front of the building. He didn't seem concerned about the fact that he'd double parked but thrust open his driver's side door before coming around to the back to let me out.

As soon as the cold air hit my bare legs, I shuddered. There was one thing to be said about Lino's insistence that if I was going to return to work then I'd have a driver taking me to and from. It certainly prevented me from suffering in the cold of Chicago in January.

It also saved my leg muscles from the unfamiliar strain of walking in heels. It felt like it'd been so long since I'd even walked at all. As such, my calves strained against the foreign feeling of walking through the lobby with pumps on. Emilio insisted on seeing me inside, his breadth intimidating at my back as he searched the lobby for some threat. What he thought he would find in a corporate office building was a little beyond me, but I also knew that sometimes the evilest of men hid behind the most polished veneers.

Lino's father was a prime example of that. All cultured elegance that only hid the menace within until you took a close look.

"This is where you leave me," I told Emilio, turning to stop him from following me into the elevator. "Confidential appointments happen upstairs, and I can't have you compromising Lamb & Rowe's clients."

"I'm under strict orders to see you to your desk, Mrs. Bellandi," he said, staring down at me impassively. I sighed, knowing it would be far quicker to just let the man escort me upstairs. A call to Lino would delve into an argument, and the reality was I'd only *barely* gotten out of the house that morning. Despite him agreeing to it the night before, he'd seemed positively glum about the thought of me returning to work.

It was adorable, albeit frustrating as Hell.

"Fine," I sighed, dropping my head back to look at the ceiling. "What on Earth did I do to deserve this kind of crap?" I whispered.

"You married Mr. Bellandi," Emilio offered so helpfully. I leveled him with a glare.

"Do you have a wife, Emilio?" I asked him.

"No, Mrs. Bellandi. The Bellandi's are all the family I want." I pursed my lips in thought as the elevator rose to the top floor of the building.

Alrighty then.

I didn't bother to make more conversation, instead steeling myself for the inevitable confrontation that was coming with Jasper. I'd been out for weeks, and the fact that I hadn't heard from him meant that when Lino told him I wouldn't be in, *that* conversation likely hadn't gone well.

I could only imagine.

By the time the elevator doors opened, I'd straightened my spine and donned my business persona of being a shark. So I strutted my way out of the elevator and through the room to pass our little waiting room. Nothing unusual, despite my several week absence, the rings on my finger, and the suit at my back. Emilio's steps seemed unnaturally quiet compared to mine, like he always took care to be silent despite his massive size.

Inside the private space, there was a little waiting area, my work area, and then an enclosed office at the left where Jasper conducted his business. My desk sat on the opposite wall, facing his office so that I could see him through the window should he need anything, but he wasn't in there.

He stood next to my desk, looking frustrated with whoever had filled in during my absence. I didn't recognize her, and acknowledged she must have been a temp. "But I don't understand," she whispered. "I thought I was doing well."

"You're not, but that isn't why I'm saying you need to go back to the agency. You've been filling in for an employee who was out sick. You're from a temp agency, I really don't understand why you don't understand what that means," he groaned his frustration.

I cleared my throat, stepping up and taking pity on the poor girl who stared up at Jasper like stars shone out of his ass. "Sorry. I'm the employee who was sick. Thank you very much for covering for me. I'm sure Mr. Rowe truly appreciates it, but as you can see, I'm no longer sick."

"But I like it here."

"I'm sure you do," I sighed. "Pretty views, but they wouldn't have sent a newbie to come work for Mr. Rowe, so can we drop the act like you don't know how this works?" I crossed my arms over my chest, my polite smile turning condescending. I didn't want to deal with fake bullshit and drama when my life seemed to consist of nothing but real drama lately.

"Easy for you to say. I'm sure you just love it here," she snapped.

"Miss Jones, it's time to go. I'd truly like to just be done with this conversation," Jasper said coldly. "Miss Mahoney has returned from her leave—"

"Mrs. Bellandi," Emilio corrected him, and I turned wide eyes at him.

Because holy shit. Talk about letting the cat out of the bag a little early.

"Excuse me?" Jasper asked him, an uneasy chuckle coming from his throat.

"Miss Mahoney is Mrs. Bellandi now."

When I felt Jasper's eyes fall on my face, I scrunched my nose and looked at the floor like the coward I was.

I really, really was.

"Get out," Jasper hissed to the poor woman who had the brains to realize the time to gather her things had officially passed. She snatched them up, shoved them in her purse and was gone. "I'll see you in my office, *Mrs. Bellandi,*" Jasper stormed toward his office once she was gone.

"Thank you for escorting me, Emilio. But as you can see, I'm here. I think it's time you left now," I sighed, wincing.

"You'll call me when you're ready to leave or when you want to go to lunch?" he asked, and I nodded.

"Yes. I'll be staying here all day today," I explained. I wouldn't take my new freedom and throw it in Lino's face by disrespecting his desire for me to be protected. As obnoxious as it was, I also knew it was necessary given the turn my life had taken.

"I'll see you at the end of the day then, Mrs. Bellandi." Then the big man turned and strode out, the door closing sounding like it echoed through the space.

"Samara! Get your ass in here!" Jasper called, and I sighed before walking tentatively to the door. "Sit down. You have some explaining to do." I perched on the edge of the chair, worrying my hands together and contemplating what Lino may have told him. "Bellandi said you were ill. That he was taking care of you, and that I should plan on you being out for a few weeks. How does that translate to you marrying the fuck after you told me there was nothing of the sort between you two?"

"Not that I have to explain myself to you, but Connor attacked me in my home. He was after money, and apparently he owes a loan shark a very hefty sum that he can't pay," I explained, all the frustration I felt at having my decisions questioned coming out in sass. "During the attack, he strangled me. There were bruises that have only just gone away completely. Even still I have foundation on to try and cover up the last little lingering tints just to be sure. Lino married me to protect me from the consequences of Connor's debt."

"Fuck. I hope he kills him," he hissed in response. I said nothing, because I wouldn't admit that was Lino's plan from the sound of things. I trusted Jasper completely but having knowledge of a crime before it was committed would test that trust and be unfair to put him in that situation. Even if I really hoped it wouldn't come to that. I still didn't want Lino's hands stained with the taint that was Connor Walsh's death. The man wasn't worth it in the slightest. "But do you really expect me to believe that Angelino Bellandi married you solely to protect you? There would have been other ways."

"Okay, maybe not entirely for that reason," I chuckled hesitantly. "Things have certainly shifted in a way I didn't expect."

"Samara, the fact that you didn't expect it is pathetic. For someone so perceptive, I have no clue how you could think for a second that the man hasn't been in love with you for as long as I've known you. I see it every time he looks at you." For the first time, instead of pain and bitterness, those words brought me hope.

I sniffled, shoving back the sudden urge to cry. I only hoped that our relationship could be everything we always hoped it would be, tucked away in the secret alcoves of our minds.

"Now, what did I miss?"

Jasper looked like he might say something else but refrained. He took a folder from the desk, sliding it to me. "These are the numbers from the past two weeks, why don't you start by getting up to date and checking everything in your files. Check my schedule and make sure nothing is wonky. I've asked her to keep all the emails in a separate folder for you to review when you got back."

"Thank God," I sighed. I'd worried that I'd have to fix mistakes for weeks to come. At least this way I could do it relatively quickly. I stood, turning for the door.

"Samara?"

I turned back to him. "He makes you happy?" There was no annoyance or anger on his face that I'd gone against his advice and gotten involved with the man he warned me against. Nothing to indicate he was anything other than concerned for my happiness and well-being.

I nodded with a shrug. "He always has." And it was true. When I was younger, I'd been a melancholy child after my father left and we'd moved. My mother and Yavin told stories of how it was always Lino who drew me out of that mood. Even if I couldn't really remember my father anymore, I still remembered feeling cherished by him for a brief time.

"Okay then," Jasper sighed. "That's all I ever wanted for you. I just hope he realizes what a lucky bastard he is." He shifted his attention to his computer, done with the emotional conversation. Jasper Rowe didn't care for many people. He was actually anti-social and hated the way society wanted to use him to their benefit. Somehow, I'd made it onto the very short list of those who mattered to him.

"Me too," I whispered, turning to tackle the unending pile of work I knew waited for me.

CHAPTER TWENTY-FIVE

LINO

Even if it was the middle of the day, the music at Tease seemed to pulse too loud. It'd never been an issue, since I was always so used to the music here or at Indulgence, but after spending all that quiet time at home with Samara, I felt like an old man.

Yavin sitting on the other side of the desk staring at me while I went over the numbers wasn't helping the situation. I'd had to try and discreetly keep him from noticing the wedding band on my left hand, but thankfully he would never have expected me to get married.

Least of all to his little sister.

I'd tell him soon, but Samara needed to be present for it. Our marriage was *our* news to share, not mine alone, and since Yavin was important to both of us we'd do it together.

"The girls asked if you want a show," he said pointedly, glaring at me. He knew damn well that I hadn't taken any of them up in months.

Nearly a year.

I had no interest in watching them strip or the offers of more.

"I trust your judgment. You know what the clientele likes, so you can make the decisions regarding who is up to par." I shrugged him off, returning to the books in front of my face in his office. Well, Matteo's office technically, but the man never set foot inside the strip club. Even I only came rarely, so having someone we trusted running the show had proven invaluable in terms of the amount of time I saved.

It was barely lunch time, and already all I could think about was getting home to my wife. I needed to find someone to take over managing *Indulgence* on a permanent basis, because as much as I trusted Enzo, he just couldn't do it all.

I had to hope security wasn't feeling the hit while he filled in for me, but Matteo was already looking for a new manager for me to train.

"What's wrong with you? Did you turn gay all of a sudden? I haven't seen you with a woman in fuck knows how long," Yavin grunted, crossing his arms over his chest. I finished studying the books, closing it and logging off the computer.

I ignored him, continuing with what I'd come here to do. "Everything looks good here, but I'm going to see if the supplier for *Indulgence* can handle a bit more demand for liquor. We're overspending."

"Lino!" Yavin hissed, demanding my attention finally.

"What's next? We braid each other's fucking hair and talk about our feelings?" I snapped back. "I'm not interested in any of the girls."

"You haven't even looked at them, and we've hired new girls since the last time you were here. You always look over the employees to make sure we're setting the right standard. Only the best. That's what you always taught me. I could be hiring meth heads with their teeth missing for all you've cared since you walked in the front door."

I stood from behind the desk with a sigh, wincing when one of the girls in question appeared in the open doorway. Her lingerie showed everything, but regardless of the fact that she had to be one of those new girls I'd never seen before, I had zero interest in what she showed or hid.

She wasn't my wife.

"If you were hiring addicts, I'd see it in the books. People don't pay our prices for the average girls up on a pole. Now can we be done? I've got to get to the club." My apparent lack of interest in the woman in the doorway seemed to only fuel him on.

"Something's up, and I'll find out what. When I do, I'll be pissed you didn't tell me yourself."

"You need to relax, Vin." I slapped him on the shoulder as I made my way to the door. "I'll tell you what? Come over for dinner Monday and spend some time with Samara and I." Guilt flashed through me that I would be ambushing Samara with the conversation with her brother so soon, but with the risk of him poking around it seemed impossible to do anything else. Even putting it off until Monday seemed risky.

He really would be pissed if he heard it from any of the people who knew from the party at *Indulgence*.

"Fine," he sighed. "How is my sister?"

"She went back to work today. She's good, Vin. Really good. You'll see on Monday, I promise."

"And Connor?" he asked, glancing back at the girl in the doorway. She made no move to walk away or give us privacy, and I hoped to all Hell Yavin was being smart enough to keep the girls out of the business beyond what they did on stage.

"Ryker's doing his best," I reassured him, even if it grated on me. It had been over two weeks since he assaulted my woman, and there was nothing. No news, no *trace* of him whatsoever. He wasn't smart enough to pull it off on his own, and I felt a sick worry that maybe he was already dead.

And I hadn't been the one to pull the trigger.

"You better find him soon, Lino. If anything happens to her—"

"Believe me, I will do everything I can to make sure I have the opportunity to make him scream the way she probably did." With a last nod, I squeezed my way past the girl still standing in the doorway. Fishing my phone from my pocket, I texted Samara to let her know about Yavin's impromptu invite to dinner.

Already prepared for the hellcat that would unleash her fury if I told her in person when I surprised her by picking her up from work.

I wasn't afraid to admit that Samara's fury turned me on, but the last thing I wanted to do was tell Yavin I'd married his sister with a rock-hard cock.

My head dropped to my chest, annoyance leaking into my pores when the girl behind me spoke up. "Mr. Bellandi?" she asked, stepping toward me. "Your father is in one of the private rooms with a few of the other girls."

"Has he hurt them?" I asked with an eyebrow raised. I kept my attention on her face, noting the way her wide eyes made her look too young to work at *Tease*. If I hadn't had full trust in Yavin to keep to my guidelines, I might have questioned it. But while he preferred his women on the young side, he never ventured below the twenty-year-old mark.

"No, of course not," she whispered in response, but I could see the way the gears turned in her head. The way she calculated one kind of man had to question if his father would harm his employees. It was only one of those moments when I realized just how fucked up my life had been. "He's asking for you."

"And the girls are just to occupy his time?" I asked, rolling my eyes. "Lead the way."

We made our way down the hallway to the private rooms, and I hated every pulse of the music that sounded from behind the closed door at the end. I shouldn't have expected any less than for my father to demand the party room for his private show.

When I flung the door open, the pounding music and flashing lights assaulted me immediately. Three of the girls I didn't recognize surrounded the pole, winding their bodies around it and around each other in nothing but their lingerie.

With a sigh, I made my way to the control panel next to the door, stopping the deep beat immediately. All the girls froze in place, looking at me with wide eyes, but my father never turned his face away from the stage. "Get out," I ordered, and the three of them hurried for the door without a moment of hesitation. It was good to see they remembered who authorized their paychecks.

Me. Not him.

He was nothing but a retired figurehead, a man who liked to see himself as the head of a family that no longer existed. That family had died with his brother, been replaced with the family that Matteo and I built from the ground up and filled with people who were loyal to us. People who would protect each other with our lives before seeing us harmed.

Everything a family should have been.

"Do you need something?" I asked as soon as the door closed behind them. I wouldn't put it past my father to inform Yavin of my marriage if I gave any indication that Yavin didn't already know, so I made sure to school my features when he finally turned to face me. I couldn't let on that having him so close to Vin made my pulse skip with anxiety.

I owed it to Samara to give her the chance to be present when her brother found out, and I wouldn't let my father take that from her.

"Are you pleased with yourself, boy?" he asked, standing from his seat in the front. The wide chair afforded the best lap dances.

"About what exactly?" I asked, even if I knew the answer, I wouldn't give more than necessary. When it came to conversations with my father, less was more.

"Marrying that brat!" he hissed. "She has no place bearing my name. She doesn't even have the dignity to look like she could pass for Italian."

"That brat is my wife, and you will address her with respect or refrain from speaking of her at all. I would prefer the latter, since she's too good for the filth that you are." I glared at him.

"Angelino, Matteo has already sullied our blood with that woman he married. You are our only hope of bringing forward a future generation that would make your grandfather proud. It isn't too late to make the right decision. We can simply dispose of her, and you'll be free to marry someone appropriate. Elena is still willing to marry you even though you've tainted yourself with a Jew—"

His words broke off when I vaulted forward, grasping him around the throat with one hand. When he stumbled away, his back hit the edge of the stage and he hissed through his teeth in pain. I pushed further, using my grip on his throat as leverage until he bent backward and his feet slipped out from underneath him. I used my hand on his neck to pin him to the stage as I leaned down into his face. "You will not ever suggest *disposing* of my wife again. You will not suggest anything to do with her. I will not divorce her. I will not marry or impregnate another woman if she disappears, and if anything happens to her I will come for your head. Am I clear?"

He gasped; his voice lost in the pressure of my hand at his throat. "Fucking nod."

His face twisted, but he nodded his agreement regardless.

When I released him and stepped back, he collapsed to the floor in a pathetic pile. For all the times I'd suffered at his hands as a child, he'd never bothered to become anything better than a pathetic abuser who preyed on women and children.

I straightened my suit as I watched him stumble to his feet. "You would do well to remember that you have no power here. Keep our wives out of your filthy mouth, or you may quickly find you no longer have a tongue."

I ignored his sneer, turning on my heel and leaving the room. I had a wife to collect from work, and I'd be damned if the man kept me from her for any longer than he already had.

CHAPTER TWENTY-SIX

SAMARA

There was one thing to be said about going back to work.

It made me miss Lino. Which seemed ridiculous. I'd gone through most of my life without seeing him constantly. Even on the days when I did see him, his work hours often made it such that I would meet him for lunch and that would be it until the next time. Brief stolen moments in time where he liked to pretend he was normal enough to just have lunch with his friend.

Where he pretended he wouldn't be off to make money for a criminal Kingpin as soon as we finished our meal. Or where he acted like he didn't stay up most of the night in the interest of running the hottest dance club in the city.

So I felt pathetic, and sure that I'd be sitting down to a takeout dinner alone that night. Having been so desperate to get back to work, I'd given zero thought to the implications of Lino returning to work. To the fact that I'd probably almost never see him. Never see my husband. He'd crawl into bed with me long after I went to sleep, and I'd wake up and leave before he woke up. Like two ships in the night, just passing each other and never really crossing paths in any meaningful way.

But I suspected in those moments where we did manage to connect, we'd *crash* into one another with a force that took my breath away.

I was wrapping up for the day, shutting down my computer and locking up all my confidential client files for the night. I hadn't anticipated just how much the temp's unfamiliarity with the clients could impact her work, taking my knowledge of them all for granted. I'd needed to rework Jasper's calendar, taking up most of my day because she'd scheduled meetings in inappropriate timeslots.

The widow who came onto Jasper constantly couldn't have the last spot of the day, because he needed another client to get her out the door.

The doctor who often canceled when he was on call couldn't have appointments early in the day because overnight surgeries turned him into a zombie who couldn't wrap his head around the numbers Jasper threw his way.

All the little details I'd learned over my few years at Lamb & Rowe. It was no wonder she hadn't been able to do her job to Jasper's satisfaction, because she'd never stood a chance without being armed with the kind of knowledge that no temporary employee would bother to learn.

When the door to the offices opened, I sighed. "Did Lino tell you I'm incapable of finding my way to the lobby?" I asked without facing our visitor. Given the timing, I had to assume it was Emilio coming to pick me up.

"I suppose I did, yes. We both know how well I like to be told what to do, Little Dove," Lino said, making my head snap up to find him staring at me. He wore the same grey suit he'd worn when I left the house that morning, the lighter fabric working miracles against his olive skin and dark hair.

"Hi," I breathed in surprise. Biting the corner of my lip, I glanced to Jasper's occupied office before stepping around the back of my desk and snatching my purse off the top. "What are you doing here?"

"I thought I'd surprise you," he murmured, shoving his hands into his pockets —waiting for me to take the lead. Respecting my place of business and the fact that I might want to keep some distance there. It only emboldened me, so I stepped into his chest and tilted my head up to give him my lips in a casual kiss. Those strong arms of his closed around me, wrapping me up until I immediately felt like I had found my way home.

"Color me surprised," I whispered with a smile.

"I missed you," he murmured. "I'm too attached to seeing this face anytime I feel like it. I don't like it when it isn't there for me to stare at."

I giggled, pressing my face into his chest as a flush crept up my neck. "I missed you too. So fucking much."

"Bellandi," Jasper's voice snapped through the otherwise silent space, and I turned in Lino's arms to glare at my boss.

"Rowe."

"Hurt her, and I won't give a shit what your last name is. I'll bury you. You got me?" Jasper warned.

"I would never hurt her, Rowe. I'm fairly certain you know that though," Lino smirked at the other man, and I breathed a sigh of relief when Jasper shook his head and rolled his eyes.

"Thanks for coming to work today, it will set us up for Monday. Have a good weekend," Jasper said, giving me a pointed look that said, "I told you so."

I stuck my tongue out at him when he turned his back to go into his office.

And then I let Lino guide me out and take me home. I didn't bite when he talked about what we would eat for dinner, because I very much had other things in mind.

And I wanted nothing to do with food until I got them.

✱✱✱

Lino and I both headed upstairs to change, and it was customary that I would go to change in the closet while he took the bedroom. It worked for us, gave me a semblance of privacy. Even though Lino had seen my body, it seemed stupid to push those temptations when a bed was too close. I suspected that was why our only real sexual moments had happened in the kitchen. It gave me an added layer of protection, even if it was only an illusion.

Slipping my feet out of my heels, I ignored Lino asking me if I felt like ordering pizza, so he didn't have to cook. It was sweet that he wanted to go snuggle on the couch, because he'd missed me, but I focused on steadying my breaths as I turned to him. "Can you unzip me?"

He nodded wordlessly, and I turned to give him my back. He oh so carefully slid the zipper down, doing his best not to touch me. I wanted to moan my disappointment, but instead settled for a much more obvious way of getting his attention.

I slipped the cap sleeves off my shoulders, letting the black fabric slide down my body and pool at my bare feet. "Fuck, Samara. What are you doing?" I turned to face him, unbuttoning his suit jacket pointedly before I glanced up at him finally.

"I want this," I whispered. "I want to try."

"We don't have to rush, Little Dove. We have all the time in the world," he whispered, stilling my hand on his suit. I both loved and hated his patience, because while I felt like I was slowly coming apart at the seams with the need for him to take me, he was so composed.

If I couldn't feel his arousal tenting in his slacks as he hardened, I might have thought he didn't want me. But I was done assuming that, done feeling less or unattractive. Lino wanted me. Lino had touched me, and he jerked off to thoughts of me.

I wanted to find out if sex with him would make me feel as amazing as I pictured it in my mind. If he could make me come harder than I came to thoughts of him.

"Are you going to turn me down?" I asked, staring up at him from beneath my lashes and channeling all my faux bravado. "If I drop to my knees and take you down my throat, are you going to say no to me?"

"Fuck," he grunted, letting go of my hand. I continued unbuttoning the last two buttons, slipping my hands over his chest and underneath the jacket until I could shove it off his shoulders and peel it down his arms slowly. "You don't know what you're doing, *vita mia*. I don't want to scare you."

I grabbed his face in my hands, making him look at me while I whispered. "You could never scare me, not really. I might have trouble with some things, I don't know. But what I do know, is that it isn't *you* who scares me. It's not you who hurt me, who broke me. You're the one who is going to help me put the pieces back together. You're going to help fix me, Lino, but you can't do that if you don't *fucking touch me*." I pushed him, and something in his dark eyes shifted. His lips crashed against mine, all the urgency I needed to feel consuming him in that kiss. My hands went to the buttons of his shirt as he yanked at his tie, and I became painfully aware of my near nudity when his belt buckle brushed against my belly.

His tie flew across the room, his shirt landing behind him in a thump.

His belt buckle was cold in my fingers as I flicked it open, his hand replacing mine to unfasten his pants and let them fall down his thighs. He somehow even managed to look graceful when he bent and slipped off his shoes, leaving him in only his boxer briefs that clung to every corded muscle in his hips and thighs.

I wanted to run my tongue over every inch of him, explore and learn every dip and valley of his abs and the deep contours that lined up with his hip and the Adonis belt that led into his boxers like a sign that said "lick here."

I just flat out wanted him.

His mouth took mine again, his hand tangling in my hair so that he could tilt my head to the best angle and plunder me with deep strokes of his tongue that made me melt.

Made me feel loved.

I wanted it. Wanted that. So when he walked me back toward the bed, I didn't hesitate to climb up and lay out on my back for him to watch. His dark eyes narrowed, and he dragged his gaze away from my face in favor of letting it linger on the black lace bra I'd worn beneath my dress. Arching my back, I released the snap and shucked it off to throw it at him. "Are you going to stare at me all day, or are you going to come here?" I challenged him again.

He didn't need more goading. He moved, climbing into the bed slowly like a predator until he settled his weight on top of me. His bare chest touched mine, every inch of glorious skin rubbing against me as his lips found mine, and he made me feel everything.

Like I was everything to him, just like he was to me.

My world narrowed down to the feel of him on top of me, the feel of his mouth against mine. Nothing else mattered. Nothing else *existed*.

"Lino," I gasped when he pulled away, kissing his way down my neck and adding in a mix of teeth and tongue that made me writhe beneath him. "Please."

"Please what, Little Dove?"

"I want you to touch me," I whispered, and he chuckled against my skin.

"I am touching you," he argued, fingers gripping the sides of my underwear and sliding them down my hips. "I wanted to take it slow, to give you everything before I took you. But you just had to test me, hmm?" he asked, and as soon as I was underwear free, I spread my legs shamelessly.

His hands went to his boxers, shucking them down his legs and fumbling his way out of them. My eyes went to him instantly, unable to believe that somehow he looked just as big without the disguise of fog playing tricks on me. He curved up to his belly, hard and purple. Angry and swollen and desperate looking. I swallowed and bit the inside of my cheek, apprehension suddenly flooding me.

Maybe I wasn't—

Maybe I couldn't.

Shaking my head to clear it, I smiled up at Lino to try and reassure him. To try and reassure myself. He slid between my legs again, leaning over me to press a kiss to my lips. The position put him flush against my center, and the contact knocked all the breath from my lungs.

My body tensed. All arousal fled. Visions of Connor looming above me filled my head, such a vicious cycle of images that I couldn't see the end.

I wanted him off of me. I wanted it away from me. The memory of how much it had hurt, the reminder of the searing pain tearing me apart from the inside out, took over and I shoved at Lino's shoulders until he pulled away to his knees between my legs.

"Shh, Little Dove. It's okay," he soothed, but I curled my legs in on myself and hugged them to my chest. "Samara," he said more sternly. "It's me, *vita mia*. You're okay."

He didn't touch me, but I could almost feel the way his body coiled, ready to attack and wanting to do whatever he could to help, but the enemy wasn't there. There was nothing he could fight for me, no monster to slay to rescue me.

The only trace of his threat lived on in me. I tugged the sheet out from under me, pulling it to my chest to hide my body in shame. How I'd ever thought I could do this, how I'd ever thought I could push through and have something *good;* I swore I'd never know.

Good wasn't meant for girls like me.

Damaged.

Lino slid his boxer briefs up his thighs, crawling onto the bed and approaching me like I might break if he touched me. "It's okay. He won't ever hurt you again," he promised.

I huffed a humorless laugh at him, swiping tears from my cheeks angrily. "You're too smart to think that's true. He hurts me every single day. Every time he keeps me from being with you, he sinks his claws back in and—" I cut off. I didn't need to say the words for Lino to know that Connor hurt me by keeping me from Lino. His eyes were knowing as he stared at me. "I'm sorry. I thought I could—"

"Hey, don't you dare. You have nothing to be sorry for, Little Dove," he murmured, drawing my face into his chest and pressing lips to my forehead. "Talk to me. Tell me what scared you."

"I don't want to talk about this with you."

"That's a shame, because it's happening. We need to work through it together, so I can know what will trigger something for you. So what happened? You were okay; you seemed like you wanted me."

"Of course, I wanted you," I argued. "I just—" I paused. "It hurt. When he raped me. It was the worst pain I've ever known. I panicked, because the last time a man was inside me was agonizing. I don't want to live through that again, and I think—I think that's what I associate with sex now," I admitted. "Pain and violation. Humiliation."

"I would never hurt you," Lino whispered, dragging my face up to look at me.

"I know. I know that, I do. It's just there."

"Do you trust me?" he asked, taking the sheet in his hands and guiding it away. I nodded, even as my breath came in sharp pants, and I wanted to hide under the sheet again. When he pushed at my shoulders, gently guiding me onto my back again, the whimper that came from me was pathetic. Especially given that I'd admitted to trusting Lino, to knowing he wouldn't hurt me.

His lips hit the center of my cleavage, kissing and making his way down and over my stomach. When he settled between my legs, with his face hovering just above my core, I felt my eyes widen. "You don't have to do that."

"The last time a man touched you here, he took without giving. Took without your permission. He used you and didn't care that it hurt you or you didn't want it. He *hurt you.* So for now, I want to remind you that sex can feel good. That it can be amazing when it's with the right person. That it can be *everything* when it's just you and me in this bed, and to do that I'm going to put my mouth on your pretty little pussy and lick you until you scream *my name.* Until you'll never forget who is on top of you or inside of you. Until there's no one else but me, *vita mia.*" I stared down at him, watching as he held my eyes and spread my legs wider. His eyes went to my center, heating back up to molten pools of lava while he looked at me. Stroking a finger through my slit, he went slow, hesitant, *testing* to see if I'd protest the touch.

But nothing about the way he touched me was reminiscent of Connor. There was no roughness, no selfishness. Only a teasing exploration as he used his fingers to spread me open and look up into my eyes as he leaned down and ran his tongue through me. His groan vibrated in my clit, making my back arch off the bed. But I forced it flat quickly, wanting to watch him as he ate me, wanting to see that flawless face buried between my thighs.

I didn't want to miss a moment of it, but the way his tongue explored every inch of me, the way he learned which spots made me squirm, it wasn't enough. I needed more, needed something that I didn't want to admit to. Not given my history or the way I wondered if it would push me over the edge of sanity. But my hand reached down of its own accord, burying in his hair and pressing his face more firmly into me.

I just needed more, and I wanted to come. I wanted to remember what real pleasure felt like, and the sight of Lino, the knowledge that a man so powerful worshiped me with his tongue made a dark pleasure spread through me. He chuckled against me, bringing his finger up to me and sliding it inside me briefly before pulling it out and slipping his tongue down to fuck me with it.

"Oh God," I hissed, through my teeth, feeling like my eyes might roll right out of their sockets. He moaned, slipping his tongue back up to my clit and working it over gently as he thrust a finger back inside me.

Then two.

"So fucking tight, *vita mia*," he groaned, setting a furious rhythm with those fingers as he danced them against that spot inside me that made sparks fly.

"Oh fuck, please!"

"Who am I, Samara?" he asked, holding me right at the edge of an orgasm with expert skill that should have horrified me. "Who is it that's licking your pussy?"

"Lino!" I cried.

"And who the fuck am I?" he growled, a menacing warning that I felt straight down to my soul.

"My husband," I sobbed. "You're my husband, Lino."

"That's fucking right. Now, come for me, *wife*," he growled again, and it was the absolute command, the absolute *possession* in his voice that sent me spiraling over that edge finally.

My thighs tightened around his head tight enough I might have suffocated him, but he never let go. Never stopped gliding his fingers in and out of me or sucking at my clit until my limbs all collapsed back to the mattress with a thump.

When I didn't fall asleep immediately, he kissed the inside of my thigh briefly before standing from the bed. "Where are you going?" I whispered as he went for the bathroom.

He came back with a wet cloth, wiping the space between my legs clean with an intimacy I never could have expected. "I'm just going to take a shower, Little Dove," he whispered. "I'll be back before you know it."

"But what about you?"

"You just gave me the world. What more could I possibly want?" He smiled at me, stepping into the bathroom looking like he meant every word. There'd been no animosity that I hadn't returned the favor, though honestly, I would have if he'd let me recover before darting off. He'd just gotten me off again and not expected anything in return.

I didn't know what to do with that.

But I knew it got him major brownie points.

CHAPTER TWENTY-SEVEN

SAMARA

I wanted to go home from work and give Lino the orgasm he hadn't been expecting a few days before. Unfortunately, with the knowledge that Yavin would be coming over, probably within minutes of me getting home, I knew the orgasm wouldn't be happening.

I suspected I might spend the night trying to play interference with the boys, and the thought only exhausted me. After so long spent lounging around Lino's house and relaxing for the first time I could ever recall doing, the full workday and walk to the bistro where Emilio and I had lunch had worn me out. "I'm home!" I called when I opened the front door, turning to wave Emilio off. But the man stepped into the front door behind me, wanting verification that everything was fine and dandy within the house before he went on his way. Lino had stepped up security to include a guard rotation on the property, but it only consisted of one man at a time. We didn't have the interference of security within the house that served as our private sanctuary from the world, and I was grateful. I looked forward to wearing Lino's shirt to bed and coming down to eat breakfast in it the next morning, once we crossed the line into sex anyway.

I looked forward to having my ass sat on that counter and having him take me there, exactly the way he'd hinted he would do one day.

"Hey," Lino said, stepping into the entryway from the kitchen. He kissed me briefly, turning to Emilio and giving him a nod.

"See you in the morning, Mrs. Bellandi," Emilio said with a grin, stepping away and knowing he was dismissed.

"Bye!" I called, wincing from the nervous energy that made my voice shake.

"How are we doing this? We don't have a plan. We should have a plan! Why didn't we talk about what we're going to tell him?"

"Breathe," Lino chuckled. "I'll take the lead. Yavin is... he's Yavin. He's not going to take it well, but he'll get over it eventually."

I stalked past him, going for the bottle of wine resting on the counter and pouring it into a glass. "He's going to kill you." Taking swallow after swallow, I tried to down the entire glass.

"He might try," Lino admitted with a wince. "But I can't blame him. If he touched Chiara, I'd do the same." It was so rare that Lino spoke of his siblings, and with the way his father had worked to keep them alienated from one another during childhood, I couldn't blame him. Chiara spent most of her life at an all-girls boarding school, and Tomasso was the shit-head little brother who thought he was entitled to everything his father had. Gabriele had married Chiara off almost immediately after she graduated high school. It had worked out for the best, despite the arranged nature. Chiara loved her husband, from the few conversations I'd had with her at family dinners, but that had been when it was new. I hadn't been to a family dinner since I first married Connor.

The doorbell rang, signaling that the guard had given Yavin access to the property through the front gate. "Fuck," I hissed, taking another pull of wine.

"Relax, Samara. I've got it covered. What are you so worried about?"

"He's my big brother. I don't want to come between you two. I don't want to hurt him," I admitted, snuggling into his chest when he held his arms out for me.

"*Vita mia*, I hate to break it to you, but you have *always* been between Yavin and I. He just didn't want to see it." Lino's words reassured me, enabling me to let out the breath that felt trapped in my lungs. I nodded, before pulling back from his chest to put a more appropriate distance between us. No matter what news we delivered, I wouldn't throw it in Yavin's face the second he walked through the door. "You good?"

"Yeah, I'm good, my Stallion," I murmured. "I have you. How could I not be?" The smile he turned on me melted every trace of anxiety I felt until there was nothing left inside me but the love I felt for this man. "Thank you, for always being there when I need you. You make me happy in a way I never thought I'd ever feel again."

"I'm never going anywhere, Little Dove. *Never.*" His lips touched mine briefly, but with a harsh urgency that meant I could feel how much it frustrated him that he couldn't give me more. That he couldn't take the time to show me just how happy I made him. Words may not have always been our strongpoint, but we communicated with our bodies just fine. It seemed ironic, given we'd had decades to work on our verbal communication, and only weeks with our bodies speaking to one another. But I realized that our bodies had always communicated, always connected. We just didn't respond to the way they talked to one another.

To the things they said, the ways they spoke and revealed all the little secrets we kept from one another.

The knock at the door didn't make me flinch, but it did make me take a deep breath. Lino went to answer the door, leaving me standing by the counter in my work clothes. I almost wished I'd changed, but it somehow felt like the clothes put me on an equal level with the guys. Lino still wore his suit from work, and I knew Yavin would go to *Tease* after dinner, so he'd be all suited up too.

"Hey, man," Yavin's honeyed voice said through the door, and Lino stepped back with a returned greeting so that Yavin could step in.

"Baby sister," Yavin gushed. "You look so much better."

"I am. I'm all good now, I promise." I smiled at him, letting him come up and pull me into a tight hug. It took some maneuvering to hug him without letting him feel the rings on my finger. Lino had said to let him take the lead in this, and I would. Yavin would never understand coming from me, I'd never be able to make him see things from my way. For him, I'd always be that kid sister who he doted on but hated to admit was a full-grown woman who could make her own decisions.

Even if they were bad ones.

He'd hated Connor as much as Lino had, and I hadn't bothered to listen to either of them. But where my marriage with Lino was concerned, Yavin didn't have a leg to stand on. He adored Lino.

Just not with me.

"What's for dinner?" Yavin asked, turning to Lino as he released me. I held in my chuckle, because it was so predictable that the most exciting part of the evening would be Lino's cooking. Yavin was as much of a failure in the kitchen as I was, and that said something.

Lino sighed, stepping over to the island and pretending to glance in the oven window. "Lasagna. It has maybe ten minutes left." When he turned back to face my brother, his hand stretched out and tucked a loose hair behind my ear. I knew it was nothing that Yavin had never seen before, Lino had always been physically affectionate with me. Yavin had just always interpreted it as a brotherly type of affection.

But the moment Lino slid his hand around my waist and tugged me into his side, Yavin's eyes narrowed and focused in on the movement. When his eyes went back up to mine, there was nothing but suspicion and disapproval in his eyes. Whatever he found in my blank stare must have confirmed those suspicions. "No. I do not fucking think so," he hissed at me. "Go pack your shit."

"Yavin," I whispered as he stepped backward and moved to gather up whatever he could see of mine in the living room.

"She's my wife, Vin," Lino said, dropping the big ball without leading into it. I glared at him, wondering why I'd let him take the lead.

"What the fuck?" Yavin spun, his voice going hoarse with rising fury.

I held up my hand with a little smile, showing the rings I'd wanted to hide for a brief time. "We're married," I confirmed.

"You *married* my little sister? What the fuck is wrong with you? This is Samara!" Yavin's voice only rose, getting louder and louder when he leveled his attention on Lino.

"I know *exactly* who Samara is," Lino argued. "I always have, and if you'd opened your eyes, you'd know that." His hand tightened on my waist briefly before he stepped away, approaching Yavin like a cornered animal.

"How could you do this to me?" Yavin asked, turning his attention to me. "Lino? Really? The only man I really consider my friend? My brother?"

"I didn't realize that my happiness meant I was doing it to hurt you," I argued, wincing with pain. What I'd always wanted, what I'd never thought I could have, suddenly seemed so far away. And it hurt that the person standing in my way was my brother of all people. One of the few people I'd thought I could always count on to have my back. "You're asking me to put your friendship above my happiness?"

"There are millions of men in this city. You didn't have to pick him," Yavin snarled.

"Watch it," Lino argued, his face twisting in fury. "You have a problem with us? You take that up with me. The reality is that there is not a fucking person in this world who was going to keep me from making her my wife. Not you. Not my father. *No one.* You have always known that she's the most important person in my life, why did you think that was?"

Yavin winced, drawing in a deep breath. I stared at the side of Lino's face, feeling confusion seep into my bones. When we had gotten married, he'd told me it was to keep me safe, but this sounded different. This sounded like a declaration of more, of something I'd never seen coming but had been there the entire time. "If you touch her, I swear to God I'll kill you," Yavin warned.

Lino had the grace not to smirk, though I suspected if Yavin had been anyone other than my brother, his face would have twisted into cruel satisfaction. "She's my wife, Vin. She's been in my bed since I moved her in."

"Lino!" I gasped, even though I knew it was unrealistically idiotic for Yavin to think we were married and not sleeping together. He'd trapped Lino in a corner with a statement like that, because men like Lino didn't deny their intimacies with their wives. It just wasn't who they were.

They claimed. They owned. They took.

They might not go into any detail about their sex lives out of respect for the women who took their names, but that didn't mean they didn't make it clear who they took to bed each night.

"You fucking piece of shit," Yavin whispered, storming up to Lino. His fist connected with the corner of Lino's lip, and I knew both men well enough to know Lino had allowed it.

"That's the only one you get," he confirmed with his next words, but Yavin never was one to back down. To read the signals and know when to walk away from the fight that brewed.

He struck again; the second fist aimed for Lino's nose.

"Yavin!" I shrieked, sighing in relief when Lino dodged the blow.

"I mean it, Vin. I don't want to fight you. I want you to man up and think about what your sister wants. Put her first for once," Lino growled.

"She has no place with you. You do not get to drag her into your world. You want some sick fuck to take her? Like they took Ivory?" With those words, the insinuation that Lino couldn't protect me, I stepped away from the two men. I knew, from their fights when we'd been children, that getting in the way would only result in me getting hurt.

Which made them fight more, when they argued over who caused my injury.

They may have been older now but given the way the tension rose between them I had to wonder if they'd ever gotten any wiser. Lino lunged; his shoulder connected with Yavin's gut until they went sprawling to the floor with Lino on top of him. "Stop it! Both of you!"

Lino landed his first punch, connected with Yavin's cheekbone with a thump that made me wince. "Samara is my fucking wife. Nobody is going to tell me that isn't right where she was always supposed to be. Not even you." Another fist to Yavin's face.

"Lino, stop it!" I yelled, taking a step forward and hesitating. They'd both kill me if I got involved, but I couldn't just let them fight it out. Lino hauled to his feet, holding out a hand for Yavin to help him up. But my stubborn ass brother ignored it and hauled himself to his feet. I ran to Lino's side, touching a finger to the blood at the corner of his mouth and fussing over him like I always had.

Yavin stared at me like I'd grown a second head. "You go to him?" I flinched, turning my eyes to Yavin who looked like he'd have a black eye and blood trickled from his nose.

"He's my husband," I said in answer.

"So was Connor," Yavin spat. "Look where that got you."

"Get the fuck out of my house," I snarled, leaving Lino's side to shove Yavin back with two hands on his chest. "You're his best friend, and you *dare* to compare him to a man who beat me and raped me?"

Yavin blanched, and I knew in that moment Lino hadn't shared that last tidbit of my secret. "Samara—"

"What exactly does this say about you that you think your best friend is capable of doing something like that? To his *wife*, no less?" Lino stayed back, but I could feel him vibrating in fury. If he'd thought Yavin capable of hurting me, there was no way I'd be so close to him. But even with his harsh words, as horrible as they were, Lino's beast didn't see Yavin as a threat to me.

"Smalls—" Yavin wheezed, and I knew he'd reached ultimate desperation when his childhood nickname for me slipped free.

"Do not Smalls me. I have never in my life been more ashamed of you than I am in this moment. I am a grown ass woman. You do not get to piss on me and act like you own me. Lino has never touched me in a way I didn't give explicit consent to, and that is *my choice* to make. Not yours!"

"But it's Lino!" Yavin protested. "He's been my best friend since we were—"

"And who brought him home, Yavin?" I whispered. "Who introduced you to Lino? Who used to sit inside with Lino when he wasn't allowed to go play sports outside? Who kept him company when he did his hours and hours' worth of extra homework his father assigned him?" Tears stung my eyes, and I tried to choke them back, but failed when I shook my head at Yavin. "Who hugged him? Who listened to his stories about his father and kissed his boo boos when his father hit him, even if he was ten fucking years old and too old for that shit?"

Yavin took a step closer, wrapping a hand around the back of my head. "Can you give us a minute?" I asked Lino, who looked like he wanted to hesitate and looked to Yavin.

"If you try to take her from this house, I'll kill you myself," Lino warned. "She stays with me, always."

"I got it," Yavin grunted, not even bothering to look at him.

As soon as Lino had left the room, giving us the privacy I needed to openly talk to Yavin without worrying about how Lino might react, I rounded back on my idiot brother. "He was never yours, Yavin."

"I get that," he sighed, and for a moment I thought maybe that would be the end of it, that maybe he'd understand that what Lino and I had stemmed from all the moments we'd shared as children. That it had built through decades of me loving him. "But I've gone to clubs with the guy. I've seen the way women throw themselves at him, and yes, little sister, I've seen him take them home. I'm supposed to just accept that now he's fucking my sister and not be bothered by that?"

I held up a hand, closing my eyes against the torrent of images that I needed to fight off. "We weren't together, Yavin. You can't hold him accountable for something he did when he wasn't with me. He never so much as kissed me until a couple weeks ago, and I was *married* to another man. Was he supposed to become a priest?"

"It's just not the image I want to have. My best friend and my sister."

"Well for once, maybe consider the fact that this isn't about you," I hissed. "He makes me happy. He makes me feel whole again. Do you have any idea what it's like to want to be with someone for two decades and never have them? To watch them go about their life while you go about yours and be *friends* like it's enough? Because it's not, and it never would have been. I loved him enough to take him however I could have him, but I won't go back to that for you. And if you ask me to do that, I'll never forgive you."

Yavin sighed, tugging me into his chest and pressing his chin into the top of my head. "You're my baby sister. I just want what's best for you. Our life is dangerous, you have to be sure he's worth—"

"He's worth it," I returned, my voice muffled by his chest in my face.

We stood in silence for a few moments, and then he finally spoke the words I'd hoped for. "Okay."

✳✳✳

Yavin left shortly after. He didn't apologize, and neither did Lino, given that they were stupid men. "You shouldn't have fought him. He's your friend," I scolded, sitting on the bathroom counter so that I could reach the corner of Lino's mouth more efficiently. A tiny cut had formed on the very corner of his lip, and the bleeding must have stopped while I was busy telling Yavin off.

"He's my brother," Lino corrected, and I winced. The idea of him and Yavin being brothers, just made me feel more guilty about the visible rift I'd caused between them, even if I suspected it would be temporary.

"No, he isn't," I huffed a humorless laugh, even if I would have rather cried.

Lino's hands came up, trapping my face between them. "You're my wife. That means your brother is my brother." I nodded, because the reality of that felt crushing, like I could drown in the reality of what our marriage meant to my family. My mother gained her other son, my brother got the brother he always wanted.

And me?

I got everything.

I smiled up at him, dabbing at the dried blood on his lip with the washcloth one last time. "Well, if we're going to unite families with this marriage, then I think we should probably consummate it," I whispered. I felt more nervous, initiating sex the second time, because I knew to the depths of my soul that I was ready. Ready to leave the old Samara behind once and for all. Embrace the Samara who could stand up as a Bellandi with her head held high. The Samara who could be a wife to a man like Lino.

As if before, with all my bravado, I'd known I wasn't ready. Known that I needed to see Lino back down, just one more time.

Now the thought of him backing down felt agonizing, as if the thought of not having him inside me had become painful.

"Samara, there's no rush. We have all the time in the world."

"I'm ready," I whispered, holding his eyes with absolute certainty. "I'm ready to feel what it's like to have you inside me. I'm ready to take you in my mouth and to take you in my pussy," I said, fighting back the flush. It felt strange to say the words to Lino, strange to voice all the fantasies I'd let myself consider for years.

All the ways he could rock my world.

Lino groaned. "I don't think I can stop again," he admitted. "If you aren't sure—"

"I'm sure," I whispered, reaching down with my other hand to touch him through his slacks. My fingers brushed against the hard length of him, only once, before his mouth descended on mine and I tasted the coppery aftermath of his fight with Yavin. His hands went for my shirt, ripping it up and over my head. I had no choice but to reach behind me and undo my bra when his hand worked the buttons on his dress shirt and flung it to the side. Toeing off my pumps, I heard them fall to the floor with a thump. Lino's arms wrapped around me, lifting and carrying me to the bedroom, and I wound my legs around his waist tightly.

"As much as I'd love to fuck you on the counter, the first time I make love to you will be in our bed," he whispered as he dropped me onto the mattress and stripped off my pants hastily. I watched his pants follow, and he crawled up between my legs, his eyes careful on my face as he settled his weight on top of me. The moment the heat of his shaft touched me, I moaned.

No panic.

No fear.

Just us, and nothing had ever felt more right.

Reaching up a hand with a smile, I tugged his face down to mine so I could kiss him. His hips rocked against me, testing gently as he made love to my mouth in the same way I imagined he would use his cock. When I didn't protest the gentle roll of his hips, he set a smooth torturous rhythm that slid his length against me. Through me.

Building my anticipation without ever using his hand or his mouth, getting me ready for the moment when he would slide inside. He pulled his lips from mine, but kept his face close, our breaths mingling as he held my eyes. "Please," I begged, wiggling my hips slightly to torment him.

I wanted him to slip inside, wanted his control to snap, but in that moment when I felt the head of him notch against my entrance I froze. "Condom," I sighed in disappointment.

"No," he whispered. "Just us, Little Dove." I opened my mouth to protest, to ask him if that was smart. Even on birth control, there were other risks and other conversations we needed to have.

But when he pressed forward, and he finally, *finally* slid into me, my mind was gone. He groaned, tilting his head to look between our bodies, and I wished I could see. Wished I could watch him as he took me the first time, but the position made it impossible. Shoving at his chest, he went to his knees immediately and I knew I'd made him think I panicked.

His lungs heaved in relief when I smiled, looking down at where we joined to watch. His eyes slid down to the same place, and his hips rolled forward until I took a little more of him. "Okay?" he asked.

"Shut up and fuck me, Lino," I gasped, unable to believe he still had more cock to give as he stretched me open. Taking my hips in his hands, he dragged me down the bed, using my own body to get inside me.

When my ass hit his thighs, I clenched around him on a moan. "You're fucking perfect," he groaned, falling to his arms so that he held his weight just off of me. And he set a slow, torturous pace as he moved in and out of me, gliding through my wet heat and striking against the end of me until I was desperate to come.

"Harder," I begged.

"I don't want to scare you," he protested. My hips tilted up, meeting his thrust and giving him the perfect angle he'd need to take me the way I knew we both wanted.

"I'm not afraid, and you won't hurt me. It's just you and me now, Stallion," I whispered, and then immediately cried out when he tightened his fingers on my ass and *took*.

Harder, sharper drives of his cock that pounded into me with breathtaking force. He kept it slow, held my eyes the entire time, but the intensity increased until I whimpered beneath him. "Fuck, fuck, fuck," I cried out, tightening around him as I exploded into a climax.

He groaned, burying his face in my neck and filling me with heat as he came. His weight collapsed on me, and when I came down from my high, I giggled, feeling him still moving inside me in shallow thrusts like he just couldn't stop.

With my orgasm combined with his, it felt obscene.

"I'm on the pill, thanks," I said, with a laugh.

He breathed his laughter into my ear, and when he finally settled down, he looked at me thoughtfully. "That's good for now I suppose. But nothing comes between us. Not even rubber."

"You're so romantic," I cooed in a tease, screeching when he rolled me over so that I lay sprawled on top of him. With him still lodged inside me, I wondered how he still felt hard and rolled my hips to test it.

When he moaned, I decided I should get up and clean off, but his hands at my hips stopped me from separating from him, and he smirked. "Where do you think you're going?"

"To wash up?"

"Leave it. I like knowing my cum is inside you." I flushed, the filth of it seeming so wrong and sank my teeth into my bottom lip. "Besides, I'm not done with you." His hands held my ass, lifting me and setting me back down so that I rode him.

I gasped, pleasure filling me when the angle drove him right into the front wall of my pussy and stroked over that sweet spot. "Again?"

"Again," he confirmed.

CHAPTER TWENTY-EIGHT

SAMARA

I floated on cloud nine for days. The knowledge that Lino desired me constantly felt like a drug that I couldn't get enough of. Every time he turned his attention to me, every moment where his hands were on me felt precious. Like a gift I'd always wanted and never thought to receive.

So I couldn't fucking wait to get home, couldn't wait to walk through the front door and find him waiting for me. I couldn't wait for his suit to hit the floor, for the businessman to disappear and my Stallion to be left in all his glory.

Emilio walked at my side as we made our way through the front lobby, a broad smile on his face that I'd come to recognize in the past week of him driving me to and from work. He'd warmed up to me considerably once we established our roles, but I didn't miss the way he hated to be touched.

He went out of his way to avoid it, in fact.

Maybe it was just a consequence of fearing Lino might not like it, maybe he hated germs. I suspected I'd never know, because it would be too awkward to just ask. A man like him didn't seem like the type to be thrilled to admit he was afraid of germs. Weakness in his line of work wasn't something the Bellandi's would tolerate, not when his job was to protect me.

He left my side to go get the car door open, always oblivious to the glares he received as he moved for the double-parked car. He insisted Lino wouldn't tolerate having me exposed for any longer than that, and unfortunately, I knew that was likely true.

I gave a sheepish smile to a man that looked at me as I made my way through the cool air with snow falling around me. I was still steps away from where Emilio was unlocking the car and tugging at the handle when a gloved hand wrapped around my face. I instinctively made to scream, but the hand at my mouth muffled the sound.

My attacker lifted me off my feet, hauling me backward and away from the car. I was vaguely aware of the people watching in horror, of the way they stopped to stare and point and whisper. I thrust my elbow back into the ribs of the man gripping me. When his hand loosened around my mouth slightly, I bit down on it until he hissed and tugged it away. "Emilio!" I screamed finally, the sound cracking through the mostly quiet street. He still hadn't turned to look away from the car.

Why hadn't he noticed I was missing yet?

But with the sound of my scream, he seemed to snap out of his daze. His eyes darted around the crowd that had started to form, the people who never bothered to try and help me while I thrashed in my attacker's arms and he led me toward a van a few places down from the town car. When they finally landed on me, I felt a moment of panic.

The van was getting closer, too close. With the doors wide open, it wouldn't take long to toss me inside and drive off. Emilio sprinted forward, closing the distance between us. When the man tried to lift me into the back of the van, I lost sight of Emilio. Lost sight of everything but the empty cargo area. My feet caught the lip, kicking off and propelling myself back as hard as I could. It bought me enough time.

Just enough for Emilio to barrel into our sides and send us crashing to the ground. He pulled his gun from its holster, pressing it against the man's forehead until he stilled and lifted his hands. With me released, I scrambled up from the ground. "Are you alright, Mrs. Bellandi?" Emilio asked, and his voice was rough as he panted his exertion.

I knew from my experience with some of Lino's other friends that the bigger men weren't made for speed. "I'm fine," I agreed, but I crossed my arms over my chest to try and hide the trembling in my hands as I eyed the streets in hesitation.

"Call Lino," he ordered. "Now."

I closed my eyes, shuddering to think of what Lino would say.

But I called him anyway.

***

Georgio pulled the car up next to where Emilio double parked. By some miracle, Lino and Matteo had pulled strings. The entire portion of the street was closed, nobody to see the panicked look on my face. A cop sat in front of me, looking at me with sympathy as we waited for Lino.

As soon as the car came to a stop, Lino tossed his door open and vaulted out. His long legs made quick work of crossing the sidewalk and storming inside the emptied-out building that Lamb & Rowe called home.

I watched his eyes dart around the space before finally landing on me. I stood, wringing my hands in front of me as he thundered toward me. When he crashed into me, his hands wrapped me tight, one around my waist and the other around the back of my head to pull me into his torso. "Fuck," he growled.

"I'm fine," I mumbled into his shirt. "I promise. Not a mark." Matteo's Aston Martin pulled up outside, followed by the SUV I knew Scar used to drive Ivory around. "What's going on?" I asked, glancing back at Lino. "Aren't we going home?"

Lino's eyes went to where Emilio stood guard over the man who'd attacked me. He sat there silently, not speaking a word and refusing to answer any questions.

"Angel, I told you to stay in the fucking car," Matteo grunted as he and Scar traipsed after her. Those long legs of hers closed the distance between us quickly, and she tugged me into her for a hug and brushed her hands over my head. From the tears and the fear in her eyes, I knew she remembered how terrifying it had been for her when she'd been taken from her home.

"You stay in the car, Matteo Bellandi," she spat at him. He merely grinned back at his wife, and Scar stepped forward to put his hand on my shoulder.

"You okay, Mara?" he asked. I nodded back at him, staring up into his ridiculously tall face. "Good. I'm taking both of you back to the Bellandi estate. Your husbands have something they need to deal with." He glared over at where Emilio stood with the attacker.

"Lino?" I asked him, turning to look up at him, but his face was morphed into the ruthless man I knew he'd need to be to get through the night.

"Go with Scar, *vita mia*. I need to know you're safe. There's nowhere safer than Matteo's."

"But—"

"Just do this for me, Little Dove," he whispered, and I had no choice but to nod in the face of the strain in his voice. His lips touched mine, too briefly.

"Be careful," I whispered, and he nodded. As Ivory took my arm and guided me away, he and Scar exchanged a heavy look.

I didn't need to be a man to understand what it meant.

If anything happened to me, Lino would include Scar in the rampage I suspected he was about to undertake.

CHAPTER TWENTY-NINE

LINO

"Put him in the fucking trunk," I growled the moment the women were out of the building.

"Easy," Matteo tried to soothe me, but I was beyond soothing. "Ryker's still tracking Connor. We can pull him back, but—"

"No need. I've got it." His eyes widened, and he glanced down at where my hands were tightened into fists. With a nod to Georgio, the man moved to Emilio and the two of them lifted the guy off his feet to cart him outside.

"We've got it," Matteo responded, clapping a hand down on my shoulder. I knew from the fury that blazed in his piercing blue eyes that he remembered what he'd felt when Ivory was taken. Knew he remembered how much he'd struggled with the fact that he hadn't been allowed to make the fucker bleed and suffer for all eternity. He wouldn't deny me the same need for vengeance that slithered through my body like a lethal toxin that would invade every part of my life until I could release it. "No one touches our women."

"No one," I grunted, and we stormed out to the Aston side by side.

The ride to the warehouse was quick, both in distance and because of the way Matteo drove. Without Ivory in the car as precious cargo, he pushed it to the limit until we reached the worst part of town. The only people that came to this part of the city knew better than to poke their nose where it didn't belong, so when we pulled up to Georgio and Emilio hauling Samara's attacker out of the trunk, we didn't think anything of it.

Nobody would see. Nobody would care.

We were just taking out the trash, since he wouldn't leave the warehouse alive.

"In the fridge," I ordered, and the two men carted him inside. The chair in the center of the room was all prepared with ropes for us, courtesy of our meticulous torturer.

"You have me at a disadvantage," Matteo drawled as they tied him down. He went for Ryker's tools, fingering the blades affectionately. "My resident psychopath is occupied tonight, so I guess you'll have to settle for us." The man didn't respond, staring at Emilio with disdain. I went to Matteo, grabbing the sledgehammer off the floor next to the table and hefting it in my arms. As soon as Emilio and Georgio stepped back, I moved in and swung it forward with all my strength.

The crunch of his kneecap crushing beneath the force of it was satisfying in a way I'd never felt before.

I'd killed. I'd tortured. I'd done what I had to do to survive the way I was raised, but I'd never enjoyed it. But the way the man howled in pain, trying to collapse forward, *that* I enjoyed. The hammer came down on his other knee just as easily, giving me another pulse of satisfaction that both soothed me and made me feel like a monster all at once.

I used the hammer to press into his throat, tilting him back so that I could see the pain in his eyes. "You put your hands on my *wife*," I growled. "Why?"

"I didn't know who she was, I swear," he whimpered. Matteo chuckled, stripping off his suit jacket and rolling up his shirt sleeves.

"Liar," he grinned darkly, turning his attention to the man. The small knife in his hand was perfect for one thing and one thing only. As small as it was, the blade was hefty, and Ryker kept it as sharp as could be. "Should I take a finger for each lie you tell?" he asked.

The man swallowed and his eyes went to the hands tied to the arms of the chair. So easy for us to access. "Please no."

"Then why did you touch what's mine?" I asked again, pressing into his throat harder until he choked. When he didn't answer, Matteo pressed the blade to his pinky finger. Blood welled from the cut, but he didn't exert enough pressure to take it. Not yet.

"Last chance," he said with a raised brow. "We both know you aren't walking out of here alive. There's no reason it can't be a quick death if you give me what I want." When there was still no answer, I didn't need to look to see that Matteo had chopped straight through the bone. The man's resounding howl nearly covered up the sound of the bone snapping in two and it nearly covered the thud of the finger falling to the warehouse floor, but it didn't cover the wet sound his blood made as it poured out of him. "Shall we do another?" Matteo asked, and the man whimpered pathetically. "Would you like to do one, Lino?"

"Absolutely," I smiled at him.

"You're fucked in the head. What is fucking wrong with you?!" the man shouted as I took the knife from Matteo. I went to the thumb on his other hand, feeling less merciful than Matteo had evidently.

"What did you want with my wife?" I asked again, touching the blade to the thumb as he tried to bend it in—tried to protect it from me. "Even monkeys have opposable thumbs."

"Her husband paid me!" he shrieked.

"Wrong. I'm her husband," I snarled, pressing down until the bone gave way and his thumb fell to the floor. I didn't care that it bled like a motherfucker or that my suit sleeve didn't avoid the resulting mess. I'd gladly wear the blood of the men who tried to take my Little Dove away from me.

"A blond guy! He said he was her husband," he sobbed. "He paid me $1000 to bring her to the old grain mill! That's all I know. I swear."

"Get Enzo on it." I nodded to Emilio, and he darted out to make the call.

Matteo and I exchanged a look between us, and I knew he agreed with the assessment that the man didn't know anything else, but that didn't mean we could stop.

With Samara's life at risk, we had to do everything in our power to be absolutely sure.

And we did.

Hours passed before we loaded his body into the incinerator, but we did it with the assurance that Connor was a threat to Samara.

If only he'd still been at the grain mill when Enzo got there.

CHAPTER THIRTY

SAMARA

There was blood on his shirt.

So much fucking blood.

I didn't dare ask, didn't dare bring it up. His jacket was conspicuously missing and judging by the amount of red that stained his white shirt, I had to guess it was because it had been saturated completely. By the time he and Matteo pulled up to the Estate, I'd been a nervous wreck. Only Ivory and Scar's reassurance that everything would be fine had even made a dent in my growing horror with every hour that passed.

He hadn't touched me, hadn't pulled me to him like he couldn't be away from me even though I wanted to be held more than anything. Instead, we'd just gone to the car waiting in the driveway and gone home.

Like it was any other night where I'd just hung out with my friends in peace and not a night where he came home to me *covered in blood*.

He'd left me standing in the bedroom, going to shower without a word. I gave him a few minutes, staying where he'd left me and feeling stripped bare despite the clothes covering me. When I finally moved, my feet didn't carry me to the closet like I'd intended.

I went into the bathroom, dropping my clothes on the floor quickly and stepping into the massive shower behind him.

My torso pressed to his back, wrapping my hands around him to hug him tight. I tried to ignore how cold he felt, even as the water scalded us as it beat down in a steady waterfall. "Not now, Samara," he grunted.

"I need to know that you're okay," I whispered back, and he dropped his head forward. Water dripped off the side of his face, falling to the shower floor as he seemed to cave in on himself.

"I'm not. Not even remotely okay. Connor paid him to take you, and somehow we *still* don't have him."

"You'll find him," I said, leaning my face into his back. "Until then I have Emilio. Nothing will happen to me."

He spun suddenly, those brown eyes staring down at me like pools of lava. "I need you to go now, Samara. I'm too on edge tonight. I don't want to hurt you or scare you. Not after the things I did tonight. I'm too keyed up to be gentle."

"I don't want you to be gentle. This is part of you, Lino, and I want all of you," I admitted, pressing my lips to his chest softly. His chest rumbled with his growl, his hand burying in my wet hair to tug my head back so sharply. Those eyes of his burned into me, studying me for a reaction he wouldn't find. I meant it when I said that I wanted all of him to be mine, and that meant I had to be brave enough to face the side of him that intimidated me. I'd have been lying if I said that I wasn't intrigued by him.

"Last chance," he rumbled, and when I didn't protest his mouth came down on mine in a harsh claim that made me moan. His kiss was all tongue and teeth, vicious and savage as he devoured me like he could draw me into his body and make me a part of him. He spun me, pressing me against the shower wall and hiking me up to wrap my legs around his waist.

He shoved inside me without warning, and I wasn't nearly wet enough for it, but the bite of pain with the way he stretched me only added to the forbidden pleasure of it. My body clenched around him, making it impossible for him to get all the way in on the first pump, and I could feel his mounting frustration as he drew back and thrust back in. "Let me in," he groaned as he pulled his lips away from mine and bit my collarbone. I gasped, feeling myself open to him until he slid home. He didn't pause, only ground his hips into me briefly before he pulled away and pounded at me as hard as the position allowed.

With a groan of frustration, he dropped me to my feet, turned me, and bent me forward slightly until my hands touched the wall for support. He lifted my ass up until I went up on my toes, and the position immediately felt uncomfortable, off-balance. That feeling only worsened when he pounded inside, and my face smacked into the shower wall. "Lino!" I gasped, feeling him strike against the very end of me.

"You're mine," he growled.

"Yes!" I cried.

"No one will take you away from me." Another thrust, another withdrawal. "Say it, Little Dove."

"No one, my Stallion," I murmured, and his hand cracked down on my ass harshly. Instead of leaving it alone, he brought his fingers down to the place where he'd never touched me despite his promises to take me there. His fingers slid around to my pussy, soaking up the wetness from my sex and dragging it back up. "Lino, I don't think—"

"I told you to go to bed. You didn't listen, now you're going to take my cock in your ass, Little Dove."

"Lino!" I shrieked when his fingers pressed against me. His cock stilled in my pussy, stuffing me full of him but not making any move to actually fuck me. I wanted to move away, wanted to get away from the foreign, dark pleasure that tormented me, but his other arm wrapped around me to tease my clit and build up the heat that he created with his light pressure.

He waited until I writhed in his arms, and then pressed forward until his finger slid inside of me slowly, filling me with a vicious burn that made it seem like taking his dick there would be impossible. But those fingers at my clit kept working me, stroking me right up to the edge of an orgasm despite, or maybe because of, the perverse pleasure he gave me. Just when the burn dissipated, he slid another finger inside me, and it started all over again. His cock twitched inside me, as if he could feel how much my body loved the torment.

"So wet for me, Little Dove," he murmured, and his fingers drew apart inside me, stretching me open for what I knew would come next.

"Lino, please. I want to come," I begged.

"You come when you take me in your tight little ass, *vita mia*," he groaned, and his fingers pumped into me more sharply.

"Then just fucking do it already," I complained, and his dark chuckle sounded behind me as he pulled his fingers free.

"Just remember you asked for this when I split you open. Breathe," he ordered as he pressed himself against me. My flesh parted around him subtly, a slow give of tissue that made me shove a hand back at his hips to stop him. But he pressed forward, pushing through my body's resistance until he slid inside. He paused, stroking fingers at my clit until I relaxed into the discomfort and he pressed forward bit by bit. Shallow strokes that gave him just a little leeway into me with each one, I tucked my head forward and panted through it until his hips pressed against my ass and he groaned. "This ass is mine now."

"Yeah, yeah," I hissed. "Can I fucking come now, you Neanderthal?"

He laughed, and the sound was like music to my ears. Lino sounded just a little bit more human with each slide of him inside me, with each of his groans that sounded in my ear. "Yeah, *vita mia*, you can fucking come now." His fingers pressed tighter into my clit, sending me spiraling over that edge with a scream and he followed behind me with a roar.

His forehead pressed into my spine, relaxing there for the time being as the water poured down on us.

I didn't dare move for fear of awakening the beast again. With the way my body ached, I knew I wouldn't be able to take him so brutally again so soon.

But when he pulled out of me and spun me in his arms to set to cleaning me up, his eyes were warm on mine. "My stallion," I said, reaching a hand up to cup his cheek.

"My everything," he sighed back, pressing his forehead to mine and staring down at me.

My heart stuttered, remembering the words he'd spoken after Connor's assault.

His everything. My fingers traced over the tattoo on his chest, wondering, but never voicing my thoughts.

I was too flayed open, too consumed and exhausted by the day, but for the first time when he tucked me into his side when we crawled into bed, I fell asleep wondering if my years of love had really been unrequited after all.

⁕

Kicking. Clawing.

Fighting.

Arms wrapped around me. *Restraining me.*

My throat felt hoarse, my body alive and aware and pained.

Hands grabbed my wrists, gathering up my flailing limbs in a stern grip that I so desperately wanted to shake off.

"No!" I screamed. "Let go!"

"Little Dove." The soft voice permeated the fog, making me still in the arms that held me. But there was nothing but the black, no sign of my Stallion anywhere I looked. I struggled again, catching my attacker off guard. My nails raked across skin, leaving me with the too familiar feeling of blood and skin under my nails. "Samara!" Lino barked.

My eyes flew open.

Lino hovered over me, trying to restrain me as gently as possible. His eyes were wild as he inspected me. "You're okay, *vita mia*. Just a nightmare." He pulled me into his arms, against his chest, and I let him wrap me up. Let him chase away the lingering edges of the dream.

But the sight of the raised scratches at the base of his neck stared back at me.

They only bled a little, but the knowledge that I'd done that, that I'd hurt him shook me to my core. "You're okay," he repeated while I cried into his chest.

"I hurt you," I whispered, my voice catching and threatening to break.

"It's just a scratch, Little Dove. It hurt me far more to see you so scared." I let him tuck me onto my side, his arms wrapping around my middle. "I've got you. You're safe."

"I know," I murmured back. I stayed awake long after his breath evened out in sleep.

I didn't want to hurt him again.

CHAPTER THIRTY-ONE

SAMARA

The last thing I wanted to do was face Lino's father, especially not given the sex-fest that our life had become over the past few days. It felt like I could always feel the throb between my legs, the distinct soreness that told me I'd been well and thoroughly fucked. Combined with the way Lino always, always, finishes inside me that sometimes I worry about wearing dresses. After my nightmare, he seemed determined to prove to me that everything was fine—that the scratches weren't my fault. He used his body to do that, to keep me connected to him when I'd wanted to pull away physically.

"Do you want to skip it?" he asked as we sat in the car outside his father's estate.

"I think that ship sailed around the time we left the house." I laughed at him, because it seemed a little late to be asking that question. Backing out after pulling into the driveway would be viewed as nothing but a coward's move, and if there was anything his father hated, it was a coward.

And the Jews, as he'd pointed out numerous times since finding out my mother was Jewish. For a Roman Catholic who refused to even entertain the idea of his son with anyone but a good Italian girl, I knew I would have been his last choice for a wife for Lino—even if I wasn't religious myself.

I'd have been lying if I said that didn't entertain me and appeal to me on the darkest levels.

Lino chuckled in return, but the sound was uneasy. I knew these dinners were uncomfortable, even for him. As much as he loved seeing Chiara, spending time in the same room as his father and brother was far from his idea of a good

378

time. I waited in the car, letting him come around to my side and open my door for me like the gentleman he'd always been with me. Thinking of what those hands had done, hands that I hoped stayed clean from the dirtier aspects of the Bellandi business, it always struck me as odd that he could use them so gently and act so kindly. Lino had never, and probably would never, talk to me about the specifics of his family business, and honestly, I didn't want to know. Some sins were forgivable and then there were some that weren't. I just hoped his were.

When my door opened, I pivoted and twisted out of the seat. Smoothing the olive-green sweater dress down my thighs, I let Lino take my hand and guide me up to the doors to get out of the cold. Gabriele Bellandi's wife opened the door for us, smiling a thin grin. "Lino," she cooed far too familiarly. Honestly, sometimes I wondered if she hoped to upgrade to the son when Gabriele left her. Where she had once been beautiful, the stress of living a life without love could be seen on her face. It didn't make her look old, just tired. Tired and indifferent.

Unfeeling.

I pitied her some days, but most days I just wanted her to keep her hands off Lino.

It was nice that I would finally have a leg to stand on in that regard. It had never been my place to voice my opinion before, but now as his wife? Absolutely.

She took our coats, passing them off to the butler who glared at her for doing his job. "Samara, lovely to see you, my dear."

"You too, Trista," I echoed. I'd always referred to her as Mrs. Bellandi in the past, but somehow it seemed horribly awkward to call her that name when it was also my name.

Weird.

She didn't seem to notice the difference, too wrapped up in trying to get Lino's attention to pay me any mind even as she spoke. "Everyone else has already arrived. They're in the sitting room. Why don't you go on and join them? I'd just like a word with Lino."

"That's alright. I'll stay. We don't have any secrets," I returned, snuggling into his side.

Her eyes widened, narrowing in on the movement. "Samara is my wife now, Trista," he explained.

"Well," she laughed. "I had thought to warn you that your father is in a worse mood than normal, but I suspect this is probably the cause then?" Lino shrugged, as if to say that his father's mood could be attributed to anything. The sad reality was that it could, but it was unlikely anything else.

Not with the way the man hated me.

"I was under the impression your father took care of your interest in Samara many years ago," Trista said, crossing her arms over her chest. She acted like Lino owed her an explanation, but the woman had never been a mother to him. They'd married when he was already in high school, and poor Lino had been an adult when I met him because of the way his father treated him.

"He could never take away my interest. He merely made it so that it wasn't safe for her to be with me, but now I'd like to see him try and touch her. Matteo will strip him of everything and banish him from the city he loves so much. That's one thing my father never seemed to understand. Power always shifts, and he no longer controls me with empty threats," Lino said, giving my arm a tug and guiding me away to leave Trista floundering in the entryway.

"I—what was that?" I stuttered, shocked as he led me to the sitting room.

"Not here," he whispered. "I'll explain later."

"Okay," I mumbled quickly, and then we stepped into the room.

"Samara!" Chiara said instantly, jumping up to wrap me in a hug. "It's been so long!"

"Husbands," I said with a roll of my eyes. "You know how demanding they can be, I'm sure." I brushed off the absence, as if it hadn't hurt on some level to be cut out of the dinners. As much as I'd hated being near Gabriele and Tomasso, I truly had enjoyed Chiara's company.

"Ugh, say no more," she returned, casting a glance to her husband Antonio who stood behind her and leaned in to kiss my cheek. Lino shook his hand, before doing the same to his sister's cheek and giving her a brief hug.

"You look good," he said to her, touching her belly affectionately. I'd missed the baby bump there, having been so focused on the faces I hadn't seen in so long.

"Oh God! Congratulations!" I said, holding out a hand and letting it hover over her belly. I didn't want to presume to touch her without her permission, but something about the sight of her pregnant bump drew me in like it never had before. I'd never been that woman who gushed over pregnancies or babies. I'd mostly convinced myself that I didn't want children, but I also knew the reality was I hadn't wanted children with Connor.

I had a feeling Lino would be a different story when the time came. Grabbing my hands, Chiara pressed them into the little bulge and the firmness of it surprised me.

Even so small, it felt so full.

"I can't believe I missed this," I teased, rubbing a hand over it briefly before pulling back. Lino's hand came down, resting around my waist in silent support. Nobody seemed to notice the touch or the possession it communicated.

Whenever we went anywhere or saw anyone, it seemed he always needed to have his hands on me. Claiming me.

I loved it.

Loved that he cared enough to claim me. That he was proud to mark me as his.

"What's this?" Antonio asked finally, noticing the way Lino pressed into my back when it was time to move to greet Tomasso and his father. His hand reached down, taking mine in his, and eyed my rings. "I thought I'd heard you were separated."

"I was. Divorced, actually," I smiled, pausing to flounder over my words a bit.

Lino's chuckle sounded in my ear, deep and thoroughly entertained by my lack of words. "Samara and I were married a couple weeks ago."

"Holy shit," Antonio said, reaching out to clap Lino on the back. It put him tight into my space, and I felt Lino stiffen even though we both knew the movement was innocent in nature. "Congratulations are in order!"

"You—you did what?" Chiara asked, looking at Lino in shock.

"It was a small wedding," I rushed to explain. "We were actually married in Matteo's sitting room—"

"Oh, I don't care about that!" she giggled. "Weddings are such a waste. Ask me how much of mine I cared about? I'm just so happy for you! He has been wrapped around your finger for as long as I can remember! Do you remember when you were, God, must have been thirteen? I asked you what you did to get him hooked so thoroughly. You were just a wee thing."

I laughed. "I told you I had no clue what you were talking about, and I still don't. But whatever I did, I'd better hope I can keep it up."

"Will you be having kids soon? Please say yes, our kids could grow up together."

"I uh. We haven't gotten that far," I admitted, glancing back at Lino uneasily.

"Soon," Lino returned, glancing down at me with a warm look. His hand stretched around me, rubbing over my stomach in a way that felt incredibly intimate and full of promise. Everything inside me clenched, the thought of Lino's life inside me making me anxious.

Anxious to feel it.

But I knew it was too soon. We were only just figuring out how we worked together as a couple, hadn't even had our first real fight and who knew how being married would change the way we fought. Lino had been dominating as my friend. I couldn't imagine it would be any better now that I was his wife.

His family wasn't known for their leniency where women were concerned.

Tomasso finally got tired of waiting to greet us, storming over and pressing a too firm kiss to my cheek in greeting. I tried not to flinch away from the touch and the way he made me feel slimy. Despite being only seventeen, his breath smelled like a liquor cabinet. The spoiled, entitled rich boy attended the best private school in Chicago, and promptly drank away every opportunity he was given. Lino had mentioned in the past that he'd already been to rehab for a drug addiction once, and it pained me to think of how

Chiara and Lino had turned out so well in comparison, in spite of their father's interference.

There was also the questionable circumstances about Tomasso's mother's disappearance to consider. Nobody spoke of his mother, Gabriele's second wife, who disappeared shortly after she gave birth. I had to guess she'd done something unforgivable in Gabriele's eyes, and he'd gotten rid of her. Because no man in the Bellandi family ever tolerated his woman leaving him.

The only way out was through death.

So she was dead, and I'd never know what happened. I doubted even Lino knew.

"Is my new daughter-in-law planning to say hello?" Gabriele asked mockingly from his seat next to the fireplace where he held court. With a sigh, Lino took my hand and guided me to his father. I bent down, kissing him on the cheek as quickly as I could manage before standing straight. "I won't pretend to be pleased about this. Not in my own home."

"Father!" Chiara scolded, but her husband shook his head at her. Such was the legend of Gabriele's cruelty, that a husband had to worry his father-in-law would strike his pregnant daughter.

"I don't expect you to," I admitted. "That suits me just fine. You've never made any secret about your dislike for me. I don't particularly care for you either."

"Samara," Lino's voice shook with his attempt to restrain his laugh, but I ignored him in favor of holding his father's glare.

"And yet you married my eldest son. You had to know that would mean I'd be in your life. Why do such a thing if you hate me so much?" Gabriele asked, sipping at his whiskey.

"I don't recall saying I hated you. That would require me to give you more thought than you deserve," I paused, taking a deep sigh. "I'll admit, there were times I hated you. Every time I tended to Lino after you beat him. I don't think I've ever wished somebody dead, except for you."

"Perhaps you need to leash your wife, Angelino," Gabriele sneered.

Lino merely chuckled at my back. "Nah, she's much more entertaining when she runs wild. I never did care for a woman to be so beaten down she doesn't dare speak in my presence. I'm not like you," he said.

"In our lives, women are to remember their place. They do not question our decisions or the way we raise our sons. They sit at home and pop out children when we demand. Bellandi men do as they please, and you would reduce our name to a pussy-whipped weakling," Gabriele barked the words to Lino, and from the corner of my eye I saw Tomasso smirk like he knew the first thing about being a man just because he'd inherited his father's cruelty. "But you'll grow bored of her. You always did tire of your toys quickly."

Lino stepped forward, like he might intervene, but I held him back with a hand at his chest. I wouldn't, couldn't, let Gabriele see how the words affected me.

"Dinner will be ready shortly," the butler said, stepping into the room and interrupting the tension. I'd never learned his name, in all his years of working at the Bellandi household. He refused to give it. Talk about archaic and horrible. Lino sighed out his frustrations, turning his attention to me.

"Come with me before dinner," he said, taking my hand and tugging me away. "I want to show you something." I waved a brief goodbye to the others, letting him guide me into the hall and a few doors down. I knew before we got there exactly where he led me.

"It's still here," I breathed when we walked into the room. The grand piano at the back of the room never failed to take my breath away. I knew some of Lino's only memories of his mother were of her sitting at that piano, with him on the bench next to her, as she played and sang to him softly.

"Sing for me," Lino smiled, gesturing me to the piano.

Shaking my head, I backed away a step. "It's not a good time. The others—"

"It's been too long since I heard you sing, Little Dove. Please?" The pleading in his voice was enough to break me down, but my hands shook as I made my way to the bench. Flipping the keylid up over to reveal the keys, I let out a deep breath. It'd been so many years since I'd played in front of anyone, I tried to think of what song I could sing for Lino that would communicate everything I felt about myself and about him.

Eventually, I settled on a song I'd never sung for him. One that I knew would push my voice, probably too much considering how out of practice I was, but the words were about a woman overcoming and fighting for herself, and then finding healing in the arms of someone who saw the strength she held inside.

The first finger touched the keys, and then I paused. Closing my eyes, I let the feel of the keys sweep me away as I played the intro. It started slow; a soft melody that became more haunting as the song went on. When my voice joined in, it shook. The tremble almost made me fumble over the words, my fingers barely gliding over the keys the way I wanted them to.

But it solidified, my voice strengthened.

I found me. The piece of me Connor had killed every time he told me I sounded like a dying cat. Every time he told me I'd never find a career and that my friends were just afraid to hurt my feelings.

And as the song picked up the tempo, my voice grew, less hesitant and louder until I had the fleeting thought that the others would hear. I didn't care.

I hoped they heard.

By the time the last note played, a tear rolled down my cheek. Even though Lino had disguised it as a request for himself, he'd given me another piece of myself back.

"We're taking it home," Lino said, and I gave him a watery smile. When he sat next to me on the bench, I turned to straddle his lap and kissed him. I kissed him the way I'd always wanted to do all those years ago that I was never able to do. When I pulled away, the smile on his face erased anything his father had done and would say for the rest of the night.

"Okay."

CHAPTER THIRTY-TWO

SAMARA

Emilio eyed my clothes curiously a few days later. I wasn't particularly feeling up to working out with Sadie, but we'd set the date. Mondays were her only opening, because who the Hell wanted to go to the gym on a Monday? As if Mondays weren't evil enough without torture in the form of physical activity.

My hatred of working out could be seen with just a glimpse at my closet. Leggings I had in spades, but they were all cotton. Comfortable. Not the spandex from Hell that I'd had to rummage to the bottom of my drawers to find. I had precisely one sports bra, and one workout top that draped in the back to show the racerback of my bra. I'd been trapped with what I might have wanted to wear and torn the tags off when I changed into my gym clothes after work.

"Where to, Mrs. Bellandi?" he asked, opening the car door for me to slide inside.

"Fists of Fury, please."

"Sure thing," he said, but I didn't miss the way he discreetly typed a text out on his phone. Informing my husband of my itinerary, I was sure. Like Lino was unaware of the fact that I would be home later than normal. Considering that he most often stopped working before he should so he could come and have dinner with me and then settled in to work remotely, I wasn't so much of an inconsiderate asshat that I wouldn't let him know I wouldn't be home.

It still bothered me that my security felt it necessary to inform my husband of every step I took. I hoped that once everything died down with Connor, the security on me might be just a little looser. I knew it would never go away, but I could hope for less, right?

Probably not.

Even if it pissed me off to admit it.

I sighed, watching the city streets as Emilio navigated through traffic. When we finally pulled up to the gym on the other side of town, the brick exterior caught me off guard. I'd expected a monstrosity of a gym, with clean modern lines and huge windows of glass where you could see everyone's misery as they ran on the treadmill.

I'd known it was a boxing gym of course, I just didn't anticipate that it would be quite so different from a regular chain gym.

I loved it.

As soon as my door opened, I was out and striding through the front doors with Emilio rushing to keep up. The converse on my feet felt comfortable but wouldn't do for the workout I knew Sadie was about to throw my way. So I found the cubbies where people stored their belongings and swapped out my converse for a pair of violet and grey sneakers that had never seen the light of day.

I'd bought them when I intended to start going for a jog in the morning. Almost a year ago.

I hadn't gone once.

"Samara!" Sadie called, drawing my eyes over to her where she helped a man through some complicated series of punches.

I swallowed, waving back before making my way over to her. There was no question about whether or not half the guys were there to work out or check her out, considering the way they all stared as they went through the motions of jabs at their opponents or bags. "Hey, I don't mind waiting."

"Nope. You're my appointment." She grinned, tossing her dark hair behind her and gathering it up into a high ponytail that looked magazine worthy with her long, layered dark hair. Combined with the sports bra and tight, high-waisted spandex shorts, she was a poster child for a good exercise routine.

Her petite body was toned to perfection, her curves slight but seeming emphasized by the fact that she was tiny.

Below five feet tall, kind of tiny.

"Come on," she said, guiding me over to a bench where there was a case of cotton wraps. When she turned, I hung my head. I'd heard stories from Ivory about Sadie's bubble butt that brought all the boys to the gym. Seeing it for myself made me burst out laughing.

"I find it very hard to believe that your father lets you dress like that," I said, holding out a hand so that she could wrap me up in the cotton wrap.

"Psh. I'd like to see any man tell me what to do," she scoffed. "Even my daddy knows he ain't man enough for that." I roared in laughter. I'd met her father maybe twice, and he terrified me. Then again, Sadie scared the shit out of me. I had no clue who would win in a battle of wills, but it certainly sounded like it would be Sadie who came out victorious. "How goes the hunt for Connor? Ivory said something happened last week. Did they catch him?" The cotton wound around my hand quickly and efficiently.

"The guy who tried to grab me, yes. I didn't ask for details, but—"

"Yeah, he dead," Sadie huffed a laugh. "But Connor got away, I take it?"

I nodded wordlessly. "Well, that's depressing as shit. What about sex? Please tell me you've made more progress on that front," she said, switching to wrap up the other hand. I blushed, trying to avoid her gaze as it turned all-knowing. "You whore! You finally slept with Lino and you didn't call me!"

I darted my eyes around the room, wincing when I realized several of the guy watching and listening. "Sadie!" I hissed at her, burying my face in my hands.

"Oh, don't you dare," she laughed. "There ain't no shame in getting you something from a man as fine as Angelino Bellandi, especially not when he's your husband." She slid the rings off my finger, putting them up in a box on top of the shelf. My hand instantly felt naked without them, and it seemed so strange that it had only been less than three weeks since Lino first put them on. "Maybe I should—"

"Nobody touches shit here, or they know I'll rain down hell on them. They'll be safe." I nodded, letting her guide me back toward the center of the room. Emilio lurked at the edges, his eyes narrowed and oddly judgmental. "Boys!" Sadie snapped, and everyone in the gym froze. "That ring is mine. Out." I jerked my head back when the two guys sparring in one of the two rings hopped out with smiles.

"Sorry, Sandman."

"Damn right you're sorry. Get the fuck outta here," she teased, reaching out a hand to smack one on the ass as he passed. His face lit up in a smile that made her roll her eyes, and then she slid through the ropes and hopped into the center of the ring and bounced on the balls of her feet like she couldn't contain her excitement.

"I'm too pretty for you to kick my ass, right?" I teased, following much less gracefully. I nearly fell on my face when I tried to slide my last leg through the ropes.

"Aw, don't worry. Lino would kill me if I damaged that face. We aren't boxing." She said, as I tossed my own hair up. "We're just going to start really simple today. What you do to get away. That's it."

I nodded, and she closed the distance between us to step into my space. "I know you don't work out, so after this we'll set you up with a bag and work on some stamina stuff, but this is where I really need you to pay attention so I don't want you dead tired."

"I don't like the sound of me being dead tired," I admitted. "Can't we skip that part?"

"My goal is for you to get an opening and then you run like Hell. If you can't run, then this is pointless." Her hands hit her hips as she grinned at the tormented look on my face, and then she shocked me when she snapped a hand out and grabbed my wrist. "What's your instinct if Connor grabs you like this?" she asked. I was too aware of the eyes on us as she spoke to me. "Ignore them," she said. "They're nosy teenage girls!"

The sound of them going about their business reached my ears, and I breathed a sigh of relief at no longer being the center of attention. "I want to pull away."

"Wrong," she said. "He just gave you access to a very vulnerable spot on his body. Do you know what it is?" When I shook my head, she nodded down at my arm. "My wrist. Mike get your ass up here! Help me show her these moves."

She released me, and once Mike stepped into the ring, he gave me a polite smile. "Samara," he greeted. Sadie's head jerked back as she looked back and forth between us.

"You two know each other?" she asked.

I nodded, "Mike works security at this bar I go to sometimes for open mic night."

"How are you? Have you gotten that divorce yet?" he asked, crossing his arms over his chest. "I noticed you never called me."

"I—uh yeah. Lino took care of it. I'm free and clear," I answered, scrubbing a hand over the back of my neck awkwardly. As much as I hadn't wanted to admit it, the very night he'd offered to help me and told me I would take a beating before I called him, I *had* taken another beating.

And never thought to call him.

"Yeah, and then he married her ass three days later," Sadie chuckled.

"I didn't know you boxed," I said to change the conversation, glaring at Sadie.

"Mike "the Rain" Williams. He runs in the Underground Circuit," Sadie responded, and the massive man shrugged his bronzed shoulders when I gave him a questioning look. As long as I'd known him, Mike had worked at the *Bird Lounge.* There'd never been any indication of injuries when I saw him, but I suspected if he won his matches, he wouldn't need bodyguard money.

"You want me to be the attacker?" he grunted, and it became clear that he wasn't comfortable with the two sides of his life colliding. I tried to quell the curiosity about what those two sides entailed, focusing in on Sadie's response.

"Damn right," she said. "The guy she's worried about is bigger than her. I want her to see that these things work no matter size." She held out an arm, and Mike clenched his grip around her wrist. "Just watch the first time."

I nodded, and she moved so quickly there was little hope of me understanding what she'd done. Somehow, she'd twisted his arm around and gotten him down to his knees and facing away from her. When she released him, Mike stood back up. "Can you slow it down?" I asked.

Mike grabbed her wrist again, rolling his eyes at the petite woman who looked like having the ability to force a man to his knees meant nothing to her. I couldn't imagine feeling that kind of power, that kind of ability to take *my power* back in such a physical way. To never have to be afraid of Connor again.

I couldn't explain what that would mean to me.

"You're going to take your other hand and curl it over his fingers, right at the knuckles. That will give just enough hold so he can't slip away easily, okay?"

"I got it," I agreed.

"Then you swing toward the opposite side of your body. It will twist his arm around, and when that happens you grab hold of his wrist. Ready to watch?" And I did, I watched her and saw the way his arm twisted at the shoulder until he had no choice but to rotate his body and face the ground. "Once he's here, push forward. You use his arm to drive him to the ground, and he'll go to his knees. At that point, you can hold him and call for help, or you can run. It won't buy you a ton of time, but we'll get there."

"Okay." I nodded.

"She doesn't need this," Emilio interjected. "She has me to protect her."

"And Ivory had Scar," Sadie returned, shaking her head in frustration. "Shit happens, at least this way if she ever finds herself without help, she stands a chance."

I nodded, because that was all I wanted. To have a *chance* to protect myself if the worst happened, and I was on my own. "I just hope I don't freeze up in fear."

"Courage doesn't mean you aren't scared. It just means you do it anyway. Now, try on me first," Sadie said, and grabbed hold of my wrist. "Take your time, go slow. I'm not going to fight back. We'll worry about speeding it up after we've got the foundations down." So I did as she said and took my time to drive her to her knees, but I did it and didn't miss a step. "You're a natural," she reassured me even if it felt like a throwaway compliment that I hadn't earned yet. I would earn it in time. "Again," she murmured.

So I did.

Again, and again, and again.

Until it became muscle memory, and no one would ever grab my arm again without me fighting back.

CHAPTER THIRTY-THREE

LINO

Matteo and I were settled into our seats in his office by the time Don led my father inside. I knew it pained Matteo to have Gabriele in his home, in Ivory's home, after the shit he'd pulled with her in the past, but the show of power was necessary.

The reminder that Matteo occupied the Bellandi Estate, and not my father, wasn't one that would go over his head. The Estate had been the seat of our operation for generations, and it had never belonged to my father, and it never would.

"Take a seat," Matteo grunted, gesturing to the chairs in front of his desk. I relaxed, leaning against the back of the couch that I knew Ivory worked in when she could, but her workload had reduced when she hired a social media manager.

Now all she did was the cooking and photos, the parts she loved, and she let someone else handle all the obnoxious part of her business that she'd once hated.

"Lino tells me you disrespected Samara," he continued, leaning forward to tent his hands as he stared my father down. The man had never been the brightest bulb when it came to recognizing just what kind of monster Matteo hid beneath the surface, but that had changed the day Matteo shot him.

My father's face paled when confronted with what was clearly a mounting frustration for Matteo. "I've already stripped you of all your authority within the organization. I've allowed you to remain in Chicago against my better judgment. If you do not find a way to become supportive of Samara and Ivory's positions in our lives as our wives, then you will no longer be permitted to live in the city. I hear Florida is popular among aging men. Perhaps you should consider retiring there."

"Chicago is my home," Gabriele grunted, and his face twisted. "I have given my life to this city and this organization. You cannot remove me because you found a pussy you like."

Matteo sighed, standing from behind his desk and stepping around to glare at him. "I can, and I will. It is only out of respect for the men in our operation who respect you that you still breathe after you pulled a gun on my wife. If you do not plan to show them respect, then don't think of them at all. They're none of your concern. If I hear that you're badmouthing them in any way, you'll be banished from the city. If anything happens to either one of them, I'll hold you personally accountable. I suggest you keep that in mind and consider fixing your attitude. We're entering into a new generation, one that doesn't believe that blood is the ultimate bond. Our family exists because of loyalty, and you have no place in that."

"Go home," I added. "Go home and live out your years in peace in the city that you love so much. Stay out of our homes, stay away from our wives, and stay out of our business. We won't be tainted by the likes of you any longer."

My father stood from his chair, glaring over at me. The faint sign of bruises at the top of the column of his throat gave me a surge of pleasure, even if it was sick to enjoy the sight of an injury so similar to Samara's.

The man had marked me more times than I could count as a child. It seemed appropriate I finally returned the favor.

"I'll do my best to quiet my hatred for your wives and the way you've sullied the bloodline," he spat, turning on his heel and walking out the office door. Matteo sighed, leaning over the chair and squeezing the back tightly.

"He's going to be a problem."

"Yep," I agreed.

He always had.

CHAPTER THIRTY-FOUR

SAMARA

Sitting across from Linda's smiling face at the bistro made me want to sigh with contentment. "Oh honey," she whispered. "It's so good to see you smile."

"You too!" I said back, raising a brow at her. She worried about me too much, and I very much looked forward to making the point that she no longer needed to. Her eyes went to my throat, examining for any trace of the injury she'd last seen me with. "I'm good. Really," I grinned.

"Divorced?" she asked, but her eyes dropped to my rings.

"Married, but not to Connor anymore," I whispered, glancing up to thank the waitress who dropped a glass of water on the table. When he left, Linda gave me a knowing smile.

"Lino, I suspect?"

I nodded, feeling a blush rise to my cheeks. "How did you guess?"

"I was there when he came for you. I'm sure that you remember very little of it, considering the painkillers I gave you, but I remember the look on his face very vividly. He loves you. I suspect he always has," she said, sipping her white wine delicately.

"A few weeks ago, I'd have said you were crazy," I sighed, glancing out the window on my side. Emilio's reflection in the window where he sat at the bar as he watched me made me uncomfortable, but I persevered. "But now." I smiled. "Now I hope you're right."

"He hasn't told you?" she asked.

I shook my head, thinking it over. "Not in so many words, but it's all the little things, you know? He shows me how much I mean to him, and he touches me constantly like he can't get enough, and he takes care of me, and he calls me his life."

The waitress returned, giving an apologetic smile that she'd interrupted. "Are you ready to order, miss?"

"Just the salad with grilled chicken and the balsamic, please."

"Sure thing," she grinned, darting away. I turned my attention back to Linda where she smiled at me knowingly.

"Have you told him how you feel?" she asked, giving me a pointed look that told me she didn't really need to ask.

"Not yet," I admitted. "I don't want to think about what happens if I say it and he doesn't say it back. I'm happy, for the first time in a long time. I just want to hold on to that for a little while before I shake things up."

She reached across the table to take my hand in hers. "And there is nothing wrong with clinging to happiness after what you've gone through. He's your husband now. You have all the time in the world to figure it out. You should just let things move at their own pace and enjoy them for what they are instead of forcing it."

I sighed, nodding back at her and feeling like the lunch had been everything I didn't know I needed. I'd worried that seeing Linda would remind me of all the times she held ice to my bruises after Connor hit me, or the way it felt to have her fingers washing blood from my hair and pulling glass from my feet.

But instead, it felt like finally closing the book on that chapter of my life. Even with Connor still out there, he would never touch me again.

Lino would make sure of that. Connor was unfortunately Lino's problem now.

Not mine.

***

I really wanted him to get the Hell away from my desk. Under normal circumstances, I had no difficulties dismissing men who showed interest, but when it was one of Jasper's most wealthy clients who invested millions of dollars annually, I hesitated to be as outright about it as I might have been with a stranger.

I'd tried politely hinting that I needed to finish up my work for the day. I'd tried insinuating that Jasper wasn't a fan of people who used desks as furniture. I'd tried not engaging in the conversation aside from brief yes or no answers.

And yet his ass remained perched on my desk. Normally, Jasper might have waded in to rescue me by asking me to do something urgent for him that required me to go elsewhere or asking to see me in his office, but he was wrapped up in a meeting with his last client of the day, and this jerk off had been sitting on my desk since his own meeting ended nearly an hour ago.

My patience ran thin, even before he reached out a hand to touch my waist when I stood to go straighten out the waiting area. I spun, ready to tell him off myself, but Lino's deep, dangerous voice spoke too calmly before I could.

"I dare you to touch her again." There was no inflection to his voice, nothing that would have hinted at him being angry, but the way he stood inside the open door with his body too still was also nothing like a normal man.

Lino was dangerous, in a way that most men could only pretend to be. Dangerous in a way that should send most people running in the other direction when his voice went too calm and his body vibrated with the effort to keep it still.

"Relax, man. No harm done," the client said, holding up two hands as if he'd been innocent. "I've known Samara a long time. Just getting to know each other better." He obviously had no sense of self-preservation, because he touched my shoulder briefly before moving to stand from the desk.

I watched Lino's body tense, the way he prowled forward like a predator stalking an oblivious prey. The menace in every step he took was only enhanced by the way his suit clung to his body in a perfect fit, showcasing all the flawless, lean muscle of his thighs and his broad shoulders. "Do you know what happens to people who put their hands on my wife without her permission? Without *my* permission?" I went to his side, taking his hand in mine and looking to reassure him. While the touch hadn't been innocent—and would easily be described as harassment since I'd given him no indication of interest—he hadn't actually harmed me.

"Woah, man. Didn't know she was married. My bad." The client finally seemed to grasp a bit of self-preservation, but Lino was far beyond the ability to retain the beast that he'd awoken inside him. I wanted to remember that we were in my workplace, that it wasn't the time or place for Lino's display of possessiveness, but all I could focus on was how good it felt to have someone who *wanted* to claim me. Wanted to brand me with his name and tell everyone that I was his. Someone who was proud to have me as his own and would protect me, no matter what the consequences might be for either of us.

I felt lost in that feeling, lost in the need to wrap myself up in the unfamiliar sensation of being *wanted.*

Of being valued. Precious.

"If I ever see you look at her too long, let alone touch her, I'll put you in the ground myself. Do you understand me?"

"Lino!" I gasped, because even I knew that took it too far. Threatening death over a hand on the waist, that was a bit much, even for my twisted-up brain.

"You're crazy, dude," the investor laughed. "But okay, I'm not interested in another man's woman anyway. Plenty of fish in the sea." When he went to leave, Lino reached out a hand and pressed it into his chest to halt him in place. He looked down at where Lino touched him, raising a brow before hissing his own attempt to be intimidating. "Don't fucking put your hands on me."

"Like you did to my wife? Do you have any idea what kind of shit you just landed yourself in, Miller?" Lino asked, shocking me with his knowledge of the investor's name.

Keeping my distance seemed smart, so I stayed just a little behind Lino where he'd left me when he stepped into Miller's path. "How the Hell do you know my name? Your little wife been talking about me?"

"We Bellandi's tend to know everything that happens with our wives, including what clients step into this office. I can safely say that Samara has never once mentioned your name, but you did come up as a flag on the file my security guy ran for me. You've got quite a reputation for putting your hands where they aren't wanted. Several women have filed harassment suits," Lino growled. "My wife will not be one of them, because I will ruin you and then bury you if you ever touch her again. Now tell me I'm crazy again, or are you finally taking me seriously?"

"I, yeah, Mr. Bellandi. You've got it."

"Mr. Miller, is there a problem?" Jasper finally asked, stepping out the door of his office and glaring at Lino's hand on his client with a glacial look that could kill.

"No, problem, Jasper. Mr. Miller was just leaving," Lino answered for the man who scurried around Lino's outstretched hand and fled through the open door. I smiled at Jasper awkwardly, and he just rolled his eyes at me before stepping back into his office. "Let's go," Lino grunted. "Time to go home."

"Let me just shut down and make a note for the morning," I agreed, stepping around him and going to my desk. Lino paced back and forth, and I sat in my chair with an amused smirk. "You know, if I didn't know better, I'd think you were jealous," I noted, glancing up at him through my lashes. I chewed on the end of my pen, considering what I'd need to wrap up in the morning that I didn't accomplish today because of Mr. Miller's interference.

"You could at least not chew on your pen like you have an oral fixation, Samara. Fuck," he grunted in response. "I'm buying you new work clothes. Black potato sacks," he added as an afterthought. The comment made me glance down at my entirely appropriate long-sleeved black top and royal blue pencil skirt.

"I like my clothes," I argued.

"So does the entire male population that steps foot in this office," he grunted in dismay. Our conversation halted when Jasper stepped out of his office and escorted his last client to the door.

"Keep your testosterone out of my office, Bellandi. I mean it," Jasper said, pointing a finger at Lino bravely. I had to wonder if he felt like his connection to me protected him from Lino's wrath, since it would take one phone call and I knew Lino could dispose of Jasper in a heartbeat. "I told you that I couldn't have his bullshit affecting my business," he turned to me.

"I know—" I sighed, ready to apologize for the fact that Lino *had* been out of line.

Even if I liked it.

"He touched her. You're cool with that then?" Lino asked.

"Of course not, but Samara is entirely capable of handling the situation herself. She's done just fine over the last few years she's been working here." I grimaced, because *fuck* that had been the wrong thing to say.

"That happen a lot?" he asked.

"Not a lot, but I'm a young, female secretary. Men are pigs."

"Either you figure out a way to handle this, or she'll have security up here with her all day, every day, Jasper. I need to know that you have her back," Lino hissed, taking my hand and pulling me up from my chair. Shoving my purse into my hands, he guided me toward the door.

"I'll handle it," Jasper sighed, pinching his nose between his fingers. "Even if you are being ridiculous."

"I can't wait for the day that you give a shit about a woman, and I can rub it in your face," Lino said with a grin. "The day comes for all of us, and I will very much look forward to telling you that I told you so." I waved goodbye as he led me out of the office.

"Lino—" I tried hesitantly.

"Nobody puts their hands on you. Do you understand me? If someone is giving you trouble, you call me or Emilio or I swear to God Samara—"

I leaned up, pressing my lips to his to silence his tirade. "Okay," I agreed.

He eyed me suspiciously, like he couldn't quite believe it had been that simple. I didn't know why. It wasn't like I was *that* difficult. "Nobody touches me as long as the same goes for you."

"Same goes for me, Little Dove," he agreed, kissing me again, and we continued down the hall to the elevators.

There was no urgency in his step, no desperation to get home. It felt like he had no clue what was coming, what seeing him defend me had done to me. I wanted him to turn all of that frustration on me. All of that possession.

Lino had been inside me every second he could since we'd started having sex, but he was always controlled. Always worried he might hurt me with the exception of the one night in the shower.

I wanted it. I wanted it to hurt and be uncontrolled.

I wanted all of him, including the parts of him he'd shown me a glimpse of that night.

And as we walked down the hall, I decided that was the night I would get it.

***

I considered my plan all the way home. All the way through dinner.

Anxiety pulsed in my veins, even if I knew that what I was about to do had to happen. I needed to see everything that Lino was again, because if I couldn't meet the needs of that side of him, we would never be able to have a successful marriage.

There was also this dark thread within me, something I'd always known was there. The need to have a man take control, the need to not have to make decisions for once. The need to not have to fight and let someone else be in charge. I suspected it was one of the things that first attracted me to Lino, because even as a young girl I'd been intrigued by all the parts of movies that should have been horrific.

The villains who wanted the Princesses, the ones who put them in chains and gave them ultimatums that were never really choices.

Though, it was never the villains themselves who intrigued me, but the Princesses who floundered with those choices. Who fought and refused, because the villains never looked like Lino.

They never showed a gentle side, never took care of them or made promises for the future.

Even at ten, Lino had been dominant. Cool and in charge of all the other kids. They bowed down to him like he was King, and the same would be said of Matteo. But it wasn't until months after I came into his life, after he bonded with mom and Yavin, that the other side emerged. The fun-loving, carefree side of Lino was half of his personality in truth, but it wasn't the most natural version of him.

He hid that side. The villain that lurked beneath the surface, and only glances of him came out here and there. More as time went on in our marriage, like he was trying to ease me into the part of him he'd tried to hide from me for decades.

But I'd always seen it. Even when we were children, I *saw* Lino. I just let him feel like he was keeping his secrets, like he was protecting me.

And after Connor, I'd expected that dark attraction to go away. I'd felt what it was to be truly powerless. I'd felt what it was to be held down and used. How could I ever want to awaken that part of Lino that I suspected would push me right up to my boundaries and shove me over the cliff after having survived that?

But something about holding onto those desires made me feel like I had won. Like Connor hadn't broken me, hadn't changed me irrevocably after all. And giving Lino the things Connor had taken, giving him everything and knowing that no matter what I would be safe, well that felt like the ultimate way to take my body back. Because I trusted Lino more than anyone else, because I knew my body would always be safe with him.

I just had to give Lino a good shove over the edge and hope I could handle the aftermath.

So we stood in the bathroom, towel drying off after showering our day away as we usually did. There was no question that we would go to bed, that Lino would touch me the moment he could. He always did, but I'd decided that it would be on my terms. How I wanted it.

And we would decide once and for all if I could give Lino everything I knew he needed.

"You were very jealous today," I started hesitantly. For all that I knew Lino, there were some things about our relationship that just felt *new*. Even aside from the sex.

"Hmm," he hummed, but annoyance had already started creeping back into his face at the reminder.

"Does it bother you so much? To think of another man's hands on me?" I smiled at him, sitting down on the edge of the bed and leaning back. His eyes narrowed in on my breasts, my nipples pebbled in the cool air of the bedroom after the heat of our shower. "Does it torment you to think that he could have touched me here?" I asked, reaching one hand up to cup my breast. "Or here?" My hand slid down over my stomach, brushing over my belly button on it's path to get between my legs.

"Don't push me, Samara. Not tonight," he warned, those deep eyes flashing back to mine briefly.

"Maybe I want to push you," I admitted, and my hand slipped between my thighs finally. "Maybe I want you to lose control and make me feel just how frustrating it was for you to walk in and see his hand on me."

He gritted his teeth. "No. I'll hurt you."

"Good." I smiled at him. "I want it to hurt, Lino. I want to stop pretending that making love every night is enough for either of us. Our attraction to each other didn't start with stolen kisses and romance. It built in years of frustration and want. I want to feel how much you want me. I want you to just take what you want again."

"Fuck," he groaned, stalking to me. His hands took my hips, flipping me over to my stomach and tugging me to the edge of the bed so that my toes barely touched the floor. His hand gathered my wet hair up at my head, clasping it and pulling until my back arched and my breasts lifted off the bed. "Is this really what you want?" he asked, nuzzling his face into my neck.

"I want all of you, Lino. I always have. The man, the monster, and everything in between," I gasped as his fingers ran through my slick folds.

"So fucking wet," he moaned, pumping a finger in and out of me. "Do you think you deserve to come? You let him touch you. Let him put his hand on what's *mine*. I don't give a shit if it was just your waist. No man touches you but me, do you understand me?" he hissed, and I tried to nod my head. When his finger pulled free from me, I moaned at the loss.

And then his hand cracked down against my ass in a harsh slap. "Shit!" I cried out, flinching away from the pain. His hand stroked the overheated flesh, rubbing it as if he could seal in the painful heat that spread from the hand print I knew he'd left behind.

He repeated it, striking the other cheek in an even harder spank that I felt in my core. Heat bloomed in me, spreading to my already wet center as I felt like I would go mad with lust. "Do you understand me?" he asked, and even as he pulled my hair a little tighter, an edge of uncertainty crept into his voice at the end.

"I don't know," I whispered. "I don't think you've been very clear, Lino."

He stilled, going totally silent as he listened to my words and I thought for a moment I might have pressed too hard. Might have pushed too much, too fast. And then his hand came down on my ass again, and again, and again in a frenzy of movement.

I wondered if I'd be able to sit the next day, but I also didn't care. Not when his hand finally let go of my hair so he could run both hands over the skin of my ass. I collapsed face first onto the bed, loving the way he felt as he stroked the skin to a fevered pitch. "Walking into a room to find another man's hand on you, do you have the first idea what that does to me? What it reminds me of?" he growled.

"No," I gasped, thrusting back as he slid a finger inside me.

"The day you made me walk you down the aisle to marry another man, *vita mia*. The day you tormented me worse than anyone else has ever come close to doing. You have been mine since before you knew what that meant, and you made me give you away." The rough emotion that tormented his voice made me whimper, made me feel how cruel and unfair that must have been if he had truly wanted me the way I wanted him.

I'd loved Connor. Loved the promise of the life I thought he could give me, but even on my wedding day there'd been a moment when Lino first saw me in my dress that I'd wondered what it would have been like to have him waiting for me at the end of the aisle. "I'm sorry. I'm so sorry I did that to us," I admitted, moaning through the confession from the sweet torment his finger inflicted on my pussy that desperately wanted more.

"Don't be sorry, *vita mia*. You're mine now and that's all that matters. So long as you *remember* you're mine and never let another man touch you again," he warned, and I nodded, mumbling my assent that nobody would touch me.

"Nobody but you, my Stallion. Please," I begged, jutting my hips back at him. When he complied and slid his cock inside me, I moaned in relief.

"Fuck, Samara," he groaned, grasping my hips and pulling me back so that he could get deeper. "Nobody touches this. It's *mine*, and I will—" He rammed into me, hard, fast, with deep thrusts that took my breath away even as I screamed. "Never. Share. It."

"I'm so close," I moaned, wanting nothing more than the orgasm that loomed on the horizon.

So when Lino pulled out, I nearly cried in outrage. He tugged me down off the bed, shoving me to my knees in front of him. With everything we'd done, all the times he'd touched me, this was one thing he hadn't let me do yet.

I'd wondered why in those moments, wondered why he always distracted me from it.

In that moment where he shoved me to my knees, I no longer questioned it. While I would one day love having him lay out beneath me, something about being on my knees in front of him just felt right.

"Open," he ordered. Biting my lip briefly in consideration of the fact that he'd just been *inside me*, I finally opened my mouth. He thrust inside quickly, hitting the back of my throat so harshly that I gagged around him as the taste of myself exploded inside my mouth. "This mouth is mine too. The words that come out of it, the smiles, the moans, *everything* about it is mine. He does not get to look at you while you speak. He doesn't get to picture these pretty lips wrapped around him," he groaned. He paused his speech, thrusting in and out of my mouth and trying to force himself into my throat a little harder with each thrust until my eyes watered. "You wanted this? So swallow me and fucking take it, Little Dove."

Turning a watery stare up to him, I did as he told me and swallowed so that he could slide down my throat even just a little. The shallow pulses he gave me were much gentler once I gave him that, easing his way through my flesh and staring down at me. The anger in his eyes faded just enough, and he stroked a hand over my cheek adoringly. "You look so perfect with my cock in your throat, Little Dove," he whispered. "As perfect as I always knew you would be, but I'm not going to let you swallow my cum today."

He pulled free with a pop, and I licked my lips and wiggled my jaw to get some of the feeling back. Lino was just too wide to ever really be comfortable. "Are you mine?" he asked more gently.

"Always," I admitted finally, giggling when he hauled me up by my armpits and bent me over the bed again. His hand came down on my ass again at the sound of my giggle, and then he drilled inside with a hard thrust that took my feet right off the floor. "Fuck!" I shrieked, feeling that painful pinch when he hammered against the end of me without mercy. But even with that strike of pain, pleasure grew and grew to a new place I'd never experienced before. When Lino bent over my back, his chest rubbing against my spine as he fucked me into the mattress, I thought I would die of pleasure.

"That mouth is mine," he said with a hard thrust.

"Yes!" I gasped.

"This pussy is mine," he added with another.

"Yes," I repeated with a whimper.

"This ass is mine," he said, straightening off me. One hand slid underneath me, wrapping around the place where he hammered in and out of me for a few moments and just feeling the connection. His other hand wrapped around over my hip, reaching to stroke my clit in slow circles that felt agonizingly torturous in comparison to the furious way he took my pussy.

"Please, Lino," I begged.

He slid the hand that had touched himself where he slid in and out of me away, pressing a wet finger to the other part of me, and I jolted at the sensation. He made no move to force it, just applying more and more pressure slowly as he fucked me into a coma on the bed. I didn't know when, but I'd started whimpering. Three points of sensation, three points of contact, and each and every one alone was enough to drive me up the wall, but he never gave enough to make me come. "Push out, Little Dove. You can come once you take my finger in your ass again."

"Lino!" I gasped.

"Now Samara," he ordered, and the command in his voice was something I didn't seem capable of resisting when it came to Lino. That power he commanded was only stronger in bed than it was in daily life, so I pushed out.

And in his finger popped.

I stilled beneath him, my writhing suddenly stopping at the light burn that accompanied the familiar stretch.

Too full, with Lino inside of me and his finger there.

His fingers at my clit sped up as he pressed that finger forward, his hips slowing so that he could focus on all three motions.

And then I came, my scream echoing through the bedroom as I collapsed fully on the bed.

"Fuck," he grunted, pulling his hands away and gripping my hips so that he could shove himself as deep as he could go and then pull out all the way. I whimpered at the loss of him, and then he drove back inside.

He did it again and again. And I looked back to see him staring at my pussy when he pulled away. Watching me clench as if I wanted him back inside.

And I did. I *always* wanted him inside me.

When he'd finally had enough, he drove inside and fucked me with a dozen hard, brutal thrusts that had me sobbing beneath him before he exploded inside me with a groan and covered my weight with his.

I waited a few minutes for him to come down from his orgasm, and when he finally did he chuckled in my ear. The monster had left, and only Lino remained.

"You okay?" he asked.

"I'm dead," I sighed. "Just don't put fucked to death on my tombstone please." His roar of laughter after the intense sex we'd had was music to my ears.

And above all else, I had my answer.

We'd do just fine.

CHAPTER THIRTY-FIVE

Lino's father dropped by.

That never happened, in all the years I'd been hanging out with Lino on days off before he had to go to work. I couldn't say if he often stopped by on a weekday, since I tended to not be at Lino's house then, but somehow from Lino's shocked face when he opened the door to reveal his father and step-mother standing on the doorstep, I knew it was practically unheard of.

I also knew from the way his jaw clenched that whoever manned the gate that night would be in trouble. Letting his father onto the property without informing Lino was a slight to him, an insinuation that his father still had more power than Lino, but he didn't.

Not with Matteo running the shots.

To be honest, some days I was surprised that Gabriele was alive, given that he'd threatened Ivory's life. But the man felt desperate, anyone could see it glittering in his dark eyes. He'd gone from having his brother's ear and serving as his right hand, to being cast out and lingering at the fringes of the syndicate.

He wanted his power back, and his presence meant that he intended to use his son to get it.

Lino stepped back from the door, letting the couple come inside our home. His sanctuary from the things that tormented him outside the house. "Did you need something?" Lino asked through gritted teeth, closing the front door and coming to my side. I hadn't stood from my seat at the island where I'd been chatting with Lino while we ate, though I did swivel my chair to face the guests. I waited for Lino's guidance on how he wanted me to handle his father's sudden presence, because in an odd turn of events he'd come into *my* turf.

I'd always had to show respect, whether in public or in his home, because it was the expected rule for the situation. But with Gabriele coming into Lino's home—my home—it felt like there was a shift in power. I could either play the doting wife and host, or I could show Gabriele all the disrespect he'd shown me every time I was in his house.

I could make him come to me, if he wanted to bother with pleasantries.

When Lino moved to stand next to my seat, he put his hand on my shoulder. The touch was gentle, but it gave me the subtle hint that he wanted me to stay where I was. It reminded me that we'd long ago learned how to communicate without words, that as children we'd had to find ways to pass messages to each other without speaking them or writing them down.

Casual touches had become our norm, things that most people might not read into, but for us they said everything. It was no wonder they'd built into shows of affection and eventually attraction.

I crossed my legs, somehow grateful that I still wore my work clothes. The same way they served as armor at work, they felt like an armor with Gabriele. Never had he seen the Samara who lounged around with her hair in a knot on her head, glasses on her face, and in a tank top and leggings.

Never had he actually seen the real me.

The thought comforted me. That while I knew him, knew every despicable time he'd dared to lay a hand on his son, he knew absolutely nothing about me.

"Dinner the other night didn't go well. You'll have to forgive us, but the knowledge of your marriage caught us off guard. I was always under the impression that Angelino would someday settle down with an Italian woman like was expected of him," Gabriele returned, his eyes on me. There was agony in them, as if the fact that he had to speak to me as an equal was torture in and of itself. But I noticed that even as he, one might argue, apologized for his behavior, he still did it by ordering me to forgive him. Not asking, not actually apologizing. Just a demand.

"You've made that very clear," I said, intending not to give him any sort of reprieve. If he wanted me to acknowledge his pathetic attempt, he would need to try harder.

"Is there a point to this?" Lino asked, glaring at his stepmother when she moved to sit on the stool farthest from us without a word. Silent. I wasn't sure why she'd bothered to come, if she didn't intend to involve herself in the conversation. Perhaps she just wanted to see inside Lino's home, from the way her eyes glanced around and noted all the details.

Perhaps they truly had never been invited inside before.

"I wanted to offer my blessing," Gabriele said with the fake smile he gave to all the politicians who lined his pockets. To all the businessmen who paid into the Bellandi's more lucrative side businesses.

"Your blessing?" I whispered.

"You may not be Italian, but as I understand your brother has proven himself loyal to the Bellandi's and stood at Angelino's side for many years now. It's forced me to acknowledge that perhaps sometimes family doesn't necessarily mean blood. He's loyal, and I believe you will be a loyal wife to my son and do what is expected of you to bring forth the next generation." My eyes widened, his mentioning of our future children nearly making me laugh out loud. I'd never thought to see the day when Gabriele Bellandi wanted his son's blood to be tarnished by the likes of me. "Bellandi women do not work outside the home. Does that mean you've quit working?"

"No, it doesn't. Ivory works—"

He tensed his jaw at the mention of Matteo's wife. If Lino's marriage to me had been unacceptable, I couldn't imagine how it burned him that the head of the family had diluted his blood with a woman who was French and Portuguese. "Ivory is acceptable because her work occurs within the home. I understand yours does not."

"I'm not going to quit just because I got married," I protested.

"We'll consider it," Lino cut me off, making me turn a not-so-subtle glare his way. I wouldn't comment in front of his father in an attempt to create a united front, but he was couch bound if he didn't retract that statement as soon as his father left. "But I see no reason it needs to be rushed until Samara is pregnant. At any rate, when the time comes, it will be *our* decision to make. You will not have any input in it."

"I just want to be a part of your lives. Of the lives of my grandchildren—"

"If you think I would ever let you be alone with my children, you're a fucking idiot," I hissed in outrage. "Who do you think helped him every time you hit him? You never hugged your son. Never gave him any indication he was anything but a legacy and a cash cow to you. The first time I hugged him was the first time he'd been held since his mother died. You will *never* have anything to do with my kids." Lino's hand tightened on me, and he subtly shifted around to step in front of me. As if he expected his father might hurt me, and it wouldn't surprise me if he did. Gabriele's face tightened, a snarl curling his lips as he glowered at me. But when his attention shifted to Lino, something he saw there made him shift that grimace to a small smile.

"Well at least if nothing else, you'll teach my grandsons bravery and be a strong mother, since Lino clearly can't be bothered with such things. I thought I'd raised a man, not someone who hid behind his wife and let her baby him." His father turned all that ire toward him, but Lino didn't flinch. "Maybe she should be Matteo's second-in-command."

There'd been a time when his father's cruelty struck hard and deep, but it appeared that time had passed. "If you think I'm weak, you're wrong. I survived you. That took more strength than you'll ever know. Thank you for your blessing," he returned. "The door's over there."

"I truly hope Connor is found soon. It would be beneficial for us all to put this behind us," Gabriele said with a nod to me, though his face twisted like he'd swallowed glass. Nonetheless, we had his blessing. I had to hope that meant he wouldn't interfere with our marriage at the least. He turned for the door after one last lingering glare to Lino. His wife trailed after him in heels that made it difficult for her to keep up. He didn't slow, not even when he tugged the door open and stepped outside. She paused at the threshold, murmuring "good luck," before she continued on her way.

As soon as the door closed, I turned Lino to face me and buried my face in his chest. "Well that went well."

His chest shook silently, and I looked up to see him rubbing his hand over his face. "You're impossible to control, you know that?" he asked, but laughter rippled out to follow his words.

"You seem to do just fine," I murmured back, pouting when he stepped away and moved to clean up the dinner from the island counter.

"There's something on the dining room table for you. Go grab it for me, yeah?" I narrowed my eyes on him, but let my curiosity get the best of me and retreated to go see. When I made it there, all I saw was a manila envelope resting on the table. I fought back my pout. Lino didn't give me gifts often, but when he did, they were the most thoughtful gifts I ever received.

A guitar, guitar picks with doves on them, equipment I could use to record, books he thought I might like to read. While they weren't often extravagant, they showed he was thinking of me beyond the cursory gift of flowers that Connor had done when he wanted something. I strolled back to the kitchen, wanting to be with Lino when I opened the heavy packet.

"Go ahead," he chuckled, and I unwound the little string to pull out the papers inside.

The words at the top of the page shouldn't have been a surprise. "There's been an offer on my house already?" I asked. And a generous offer at that, from the numbers reflected further down the page.

"Several. This is the best one. It's a solid offer, Little Dove. We should take it."

I nodded and shrugged. "I trust your judgment. You know I hate legal shit. Do I need to sign?"

He rocked back on his heels as he looked at me, then leaned forward to grip the edge of the counter as his eyes smoldered on mine. "You aren't going to fight me? Insist that you're an independent woman and can look at your own offer?"

I chuckled. "Are we hurting for money?"

"Safe to say no." He grinned, and I knew hearing me refer to it as an us pleased him.

"Then it doesn't matter. I don't want that house; I never did. Let's sell it. Besides," I shrugged, tapping my finger on the counter. "I don't recall signing a prenup. That means what's yours is mine, and what's mine is yours."

"Should I have made you sign a prenup, Little Dove?" he whispered, stepping around the counter until he came up behind me. "Are you going to take all my money and try to run?"

"Try?" I sighed back, tipping my head to the side when his lips pressed into the flesh right below my ear.

"I will always chase you, *vita mia. Always.*"

"Hmm," I murmured in thought. "Even if I found someone else?" I knew it would be the way to push him, the way to get exactly what I was looking for in the wake of his father's interruption to our sweet evening. It seemed only natural.

He smacked the underside of my breast, making me squeal with a giggle. "I have spent a great number of years chasing men out of your life, Little Dove. Men who weren't worthy of you, boys who thought to toy with you and toss you aside. If any dared to touch you now that you're mine, I'd kill them with my bare hands." The deep growl of his voice told me he didn't find it amusing when I pushed, but I stood from the chair and pivoted to face him.

"Chasing men off?" I asked, my brow furrowing.

He nodded. "Mostly in school. Rick. David. Craig. None of them deserved you."

"Why didn't you chase off Connor?" I asked, choosing to focus on that instead of the hypocrisy that he'd been chasing off boys while he dated. As much as it pissed me off, it also felt good to know that even back then he'd wanted me, no matter what it had been that stopped him from claiming me. I hoped to understand it more someday, but today wasn't the day for that conversation. No matter how much I wanted it, the beast loomed too close to the surface for a reasonable conversation.

"By the time you met Connor, I'd decided I had to stop. That I wasn't going to interfere in your love life anymore. You have no idea how much I regret that decision, Samara. If I'd gotten rid of him like the others—"

"Don't. I don't want you to think like that. If I hadn't been with Connor, I wouldn't be who I am today. I happen to like myself for the first time in my life, I think. I'm responsible for my own choices, and I should have left him the first time he hit me. But I didn't. Or the second, or the third. I waited until it went way too far before I got out, and that's not your fault. You can't protect me from what you didn't know, my Stallion," I whispered, leaning in to touch my lips to his. "Besides, it led us here. I like where we are."

"I like where we are too," he whispered, lifting me around the waist until I perched back on the stool, and he slid between my legs. "I never want to leave where we are."

I giggled, pressing my lips to his neck as I unbuttoned his shirt. "I do have one objection."

"And what's that?"

"You have clothes on, and that's a crying shame." With a chuckle, he helped me divest him of those clothes, and just like that, I was happy with where we were.

So fucking happy

✳✳✳

Catching up on the analysis I'd missed in my absence seemed like a never-ending project. Usually, I entered values daily to keep it from getting to be too much for me to do in one sitting.

I'd never had a greater appreciation for that system but trying to get caught up meant that it felt like the rest of my job duties just fell by the wayside in the meantime. But I also knew that Jasper depended on those numbers, a quick check and balance to be sure that his people were managing funds appropriately without him having to take the time to do it himself. Being the only person he trusted with the task had always been flattering and one of the achievements in my life I felt truly proud to own.

Even if it wasn't the career path I'd ever seen for myself, I was good at it. I defied all those people who said I'd end up a cleaning lady for the rest of my life if I tried to reach too far. Like mother, like daughter, like there was something shameful about her job.

I just didn't have a domestic bone in my body. I couldn't cook, and my cleaning tended to leave a trail of dirt behind.

I couldn't handle it. It had been something Connor complained about constantly, even if we had a housekeeper. I wasn't a slob; I picked up after myself. I just didn't scrub the shower or clean the kitchen I didn't use.

Lino seemed to find it endearing, never complaining once when he had to cook every night or order in if he didn't feel like it. He'd known who I was when he married me, so committing to that woman and then complaining about those things would have been ridiculous.

Why marry someone you wanted to change?

When the door to the offices shoved open, I didn't even glance up from the files opened on my computer. "I'll be with you in just a moment," I said politely, noting down the numbers on my spreadsheet before turning my eyes up to the man who glared down at me.

I knew who he was, and I knew exactly why he could have been so angry—though how he'd found out was beyond me. "What can I do for you, Sir?" I asked, standing up from behind my desk to be level with the man. If nothing else, I hated when a man towered over me with anger in his eyes, but I swallowed down my moment of panic.

"I need to speak to Jasper Rowe, immediately," Jim Clarke hissed at me, leaning forward to grip the edge of my desk so that we were eye level. I forced a bitchy smile to my face, glancing around him to look at the closed door of Jasper's office. As if I didn't know exactly what his schedule dictated for the hour.

"I'm afraid that won't be possible. Mr. Rowe is with a client." I took my seat, picking up my highlighter and turning back to my analysis. "If you'd like to take a seat in the waiting area, he has an opening in about twenty minutes. I can see if he'd like to squeeze you in then, Mr. Clarke."

His eyes narrowed, and he studied me as if he hadn't expected me to know his name. "And how is it that a secretary knows my name?"

"I can assure you; I know every client of Lamb & Rowe. Now, the seating area is right over there"—I pointed to the four chairs at the front of the office —"If you'd like to wait. If not, I can take a message and relay it to Jasper. I'm sure he'd be happy to contact you when he has a moment."

"He will see me now!" he yelled, slamming his hands down on the edge of my desk.

"Sir, if you cannot control yourself then I'll have no choice but to call security, and if I feel threatened, I'll call *my* security as well. I can assure you; you will not find it pleasant when my husband tracks you down if I involve mine in this situation. You should take that warning very seriously, because I do not make it lightly."

He heaved a breath, standing straight even though he had no clue who my husband was. "I'll wait," he grunted, striding for the seating area.

"Wonderful." I went back to my work, ignoring the way he glowered at me as I did so.

"You seem awfully self-assured for a secretary," he commented, and I sighed before turning my attention back to him.

"I'm an Executive Assistant, not a secretary. Secretary is an outdated term that is no longer used. I could call the head of Human Resources up, if you'd like to discuss what the acceptable terms are for what Assistants do. I imagine a man like you has his own Assistant, so perhaps it would be an enlightening conversation for you," I returned with a snap that made him fight back a smile. His salt and pepper hair twinkled in the lighting when he sighed and leaned forward to drop his head into his hands.

"My wife had an affair with Mark Dobson. I want to know why Jasper doesn't keep a closer eye on his employees."

"You'll need to wait to speak with Mr. Rowe, I'm afraid. I'm not at liberty to discuss such matters with you." He fell silent, studying me intently and when Jasper escorted his client out of the office, Jasper nodded.

"Join us please," he indicated, and I sighed and pushed away from the pile of work I needed to get done.

"Right this way, Mr. Clarke," I murmured, letting him follow me into Jasper's office. As soon as we were both inside, I closed the door for privacy.

"What can I do for you, Mr. Clarke?" Jasper asked, taking his seat behind his desk. I took mine, perching on the chair that sat next to his desk and leaving Jim to claim one of the seats in front of him. My tablet in hand, I opened up my notepad and grabbed my stylus to jot down my notes quickly.

"I'd like to speak with Mark Dobson as well. I want to know why he was allowed to fuck my wife and nobody bothered to inform me!"

"Mr. Dobson is no longer an employee of Lamb & Rowe. We terminated his employment the moment Mrs. Bellandi learned of his indiscretions." I smirked at the casual way Jasper inserted my name into the conversation, a casual poke at the irate man sitting on the other side of the desk that he should remain respectful in the coming conflict.

"Mrs. Bellandi?" he asked me with an eyebrow raise.

"As in Mrs. Angelino Bellandi," I confirmed, though I hated falling back on my connection to Lino in my business hours. I also knew that anything the man did or said *would* eventually find its way back to Lino since everything did. I couldn't have him getting angry that I hadn't armed myself with the protection he gave in name or in the bodyguard who likely sat in a car waiting for my day to be finished. "I was the one who uncovered Mark Dobson's affair with your wife." The admission came too easily. "I run monthly checks on every employee's investments, to be sure that the time they log in matches the return we see. To be sure they continue to be the best of the best, you understand? Mr. Dobson logged a sudden increase in hours, but his numbers didn't change. So I checked the security footage to see what he was doing during the overtime hours."

Clarke swallowed, rolling his eyes to the ceiling. "And why wasn't I informed?"

"We aren't responsible for your wife's decisions, Mr. Clarke," Jasper said quietly. "We are responsible for the ethical practice of our employees, which is why Mark Dobson was fired immediately after we found the affair."

"You should still inform people of their wives affairs," Clarke protested.

"Unless we'd shown you photo evidence, which is not a pretty thing to see of one's spouse, we would run the risk of client's not believing us. It would turn ugly, and we hoped to keep the firm's name out of your marriage and divorce," Jasper explained leaning forward to place his elbows on the desk.

"If your wife isn't trustworthy, you should hire a private investigator. Not expect companies to do your dirty work for you," I snapped. "A company will always protect its own interest. You of all people should know that."

"Well this has been most unhelpful," Clarke sighed, standing. "I have a meeting with my divorce lawyer. I think you'll understand that I'll be transferring my accounts to another firm."

"I understand," Jasper said, not a hint of hesitation in his voice though I knew the loss of Clarke as a client would hurt. Jasper would recover, he always did, and the man was made of money in the meantime.

He hadn't gotten to the top of the Chicago's Most Eligible Bachelor list alongside Lino just by being handsome.

"Goodbye, Mr. Clarke." I nodded to him when he stepped out of the office without another glance our way. With a sigh, I jumped up from my seat and went back to my desk. I had more numbers to study than I even wanted to think about.

"You handled him well, Samara," Jasper said as I went. I smirked at him, because aside from a single moment of panic in the beginning, his anger and posturing hadn't intimidated me. I thought of how I might have reacted a few months prior and knew that healing would always be a long process.

But thanks to Lino I'd made more progress than I could have dreamed in a short time. More than I had made in months without him. The nightmares only came rarely, and I was more well-rested than I could remember being in years. Probably since the nights in school when Lino would sneak into my room and cuddle with me after his father hit him.

He was my sleep charm.

∗∗∗

Lino surprised me with a date night at *Angel's,* and I melted at the thought of really, truly having a date with my husband. While we'd gone out a few times, it had always been casual, or business related for Lino. *Angel's* felt familiar, reminding me of all our lunch dates over the years where he'd brought me to the family-owned restaurant, and I wondered how many dates had passed through the same doors on his arm.

"Mr. Bellandi," the server said immediately after we took our seats, pouring fresh water into the glasses on the table. "Could I interest you in wine this evening?" Lino went about ordering wine, knowing I didn't know the first thing about it, but knowing which ones I preferred even if I couldn't keep track.

I turned to the menu, as if I hadn't looked it over a hundred times in the past. When Lino's hand took mine and made me look over at him, I tipped my lips up at the odd look on his face. "What is it?"

"Do you have any idea how many times I took you here and wished I could just hold your hand?" He brought it to his lips, kissing the back so lightly that I giggled.

"Probably as many times as I wished you could just take me home after."

He grinned at me in response, shaking his head. "I've created a monster. How is a man supposed to keep up with you, *vita mia?*"

I snorted at him, pressing a hand to my face as I giggled. When the waiter brought our wine, we waited in silence until he'd left. "That's funny." The man was insatiable, with a stamina that still managed to shock me even though I spent many nights being woken up at random moments so he could have his way with me.

"What exactly are you insinuating, woman?" he laughed, and I rolled my eyes at him in a fight to control my giggle when the waiter returned.

"Are we ready to order?" he asked, and Lino turned to him with a broad smile that I realized he'd been using less and less in the months before my divorce. Like something had eaten away at the happy front he wore in public, and he'd gotten closer and closer to the hardened cousin who ran the show.

"I'll have the ribollita, and she'll have the beef polpette with a green salad on the side and crispy polenta," Lino ordered, and I glared at him as I shut my menu. His look dared me to say it hadn't been my order, and I couldn't help the curiosity. I didn't order the same thing frequently, so it had become a game for him to try and predict what I might order.

Somehow, he was always right.

Always.

The waiter smiled, and I knew in that moment it was someone I recognized. "You two are adorable," he murmured before he strolled off to tend to his other customers.

"Did you hear that? We're adorable." Lino teased, poking at the scowl on my face. "Was I wrong?"

"No," I grumbled.

"I don't know why you get so upset. It isn't like I've ever ordered wrong." When I stayed quiet and sipped my wine, something red and sweet that he knew I'd enjoy, he spoke again. "How was work?"

I scrunched my face up momentarily, before forcing the lie to my mouth. "It was good."

"Uh-uh, what was that face, Little Dove?"

I ran my tongue over my teeth, before diving into the most vague explanation I could find. "Do you remember a while back when I said one of the employees was sleeping with a client's wife? Well, he evidently found out today. Came to confront Jasper and the employee about it, and obviously that wasn't a fun conversation. It wasn't bad by any means, just awkward. I mean, I've seen the guy's wife with her legs spread on a desk and another man between her legs, so it was kind of hard to look at him, you know?" My words were quiet, aware of the setting of our conversation. Lino slammed his wine down to the table, the liquid splashing within the glass.

"Why was he let into the building in the first place?" Lino demanded, and I looked at him with wide eyes.

"I don't imagine Jasper wanted to tell security that a client wasn't allowed inside because an employee had fucked his wife. We were trying to keep that information quiet." I took another sip of my wine, setting it down quietly to contrast the angry way Lino had caught attention from nearby diners.

"If security isn't up to par there, you'll have to work somewhere else. I understand you want to work, and you like your job. I can find something for you that will challenge you in the same way but ensure your safety. My security at the club is top notch."

I rolled my eyes. "Right, because I totally want to watch your employees come on to you all day long, Lino. Be realistic."

"You don't have anything to worry about. I would never have an affair, Samara," Lino explained. "Besides, maybe your presence would put a stop to it more efficiently since you're so bothered by it. We could see each other throughout the day."

"I would never have an affair either, does that mean you want to watch men hit on me?" I returned, crossing my arms over my chest. Lino eyed the move, and I was struck by the familiarity of the scene. Dobson's affair had prompted Lino to try to convince me to work for him before, and it seemed it had given him another reason to push his luck.

His face turned thunderous, even as he noted the change in my posture. "You're only giving me more reason to bring you to work for me. My employees would know better than to even look at what's mine."

I smiled, leaning into the table to hold his eyes as I spoke. "Listen to me very, very carefully Angelino Bellandi. I am not leaving my job. I am not coming to work for you. I will keep working at Lamb and Rowe for as long as *I* see fit. I have conceded to you in a lot of things over the last month, but this is where I draw the line. Do not push me."

I'd expected him to argue, to make demands, but instead he nodded. "Fine, but Emilio will be guarding you more closely if I can't trust the security on the premises."

"You have got to be kidding me!" I hissed. "There are all kinds of confidentiality clauses that say he can't—"

"So Jasper will get him the paperwork to sign, but he will either be up there with you or downstairs screening all visitors going to see you or Jasper. That is the only way I'll compromise on this, Little Dove," Lino argued, leaning back in his seat as the waiter dropped our food in front of us.

"Fine. He can work with security downstairs. I'll talk to Jasper on Monday," I sighed with a roll of my eyes. The only thing that made it better was the way Lino kissed my hand one last time before tucking into his food.

I wondered if things would ever even out, if we'd ever find a pattern that worked for us where we didn't bicker with one another about my safety.

I had to hope that once Lino found Connor, things would settle down, but looking at Ivory's life I sincerely doubted it.

CHAPTER THIRTY-SIX

LINO

Walking in the front doors of Matteo's home with Samara at my side felt surreal. Of all the times I'd wished I could bring her there with her hand in mine, that I could kiss and touch her like she was mine in the same way that Ivory was Matteo's, I'd finally gotten that wish.

Our journey might have been different, it might have taken us longer to find our way to the place where we could just be together, but it was no less beautiful now that we'd made it there. If anything, I valued what we had more for the fact that I'd had to work for it, just as I had everything in my life.

People might have thought that Matteo and I had been born with a silver spoon in our mouths, and while it may have been true to some extent, we'd also had to do things that most people could never dream of to survive. We'd had to endure childhoods without love. We'd had to survive fathers who took their frustrations and disappointments out on their sons with their fists.

We'd had to bleed.

We'd had to kill.

And all of it had brought us full circle, back to the first and only women who ever made us feel anything. Samara and I hadn't had the conversation about what had kept me from claiming her all those years, but I could see from the openness in her expression that she finally started to understand that not everything was as it might have seemed. That my feelings hadn't been so straightforward, even though she hadn't been mine. It didn't change anything, couldn't erase the years of pain that came from thinking I didn't want her. Of the knowledge that I'd been with other women, and she'd been with other men when we should have been together. I knew, because there were still moments when I looked at her and saw her as she was on the day she married Connor. So serious, so serene in her gown of white that drowned her petite figure. The gown Connor's mother had convinced her was perfect for her.

And when Yavin and I walked her down the aisle, the kind of pain that had torn my chest in two was the kind that would never go away. It only got worse when Connor gave me a knowing smirk, all arrogance that Samara was officially his. Like he'd gotten one over on a Bellandi, and I hadn't made the sacrifice of giving her away to keep her safe.

Maybe one day it would all just become part of our history.

Maybe one day it wouldn't hurt so much.

Just like it no longer hurt to see my cousin nuzzle his face into his wife's neck and breathe her deep like she was the best scent in the world. I knew the feeling, wanted to spend every second of my life buried in Samara.

Luna was absent from the sitting room, but I noticed Donatello was too. It would figure that the man would manage to hog the baby when I could see her. "Samara!" Ivory hopped up from her seat, swatting Matteo's hands away when he reached for her.

Samara stepped forward to hug her, and the two of them swayed side by side as they embraced joyfully. It made me regret that I hadn't brought Samara to visit more often.

"It is much nicer to see you under these circumstances than when you're mad with anxiety. We're sisters now so you have to come and visit with me more," she whispered.

"But they're cousins," Samara returned with a half-hearted laugh, but my heart clenched at the sight of the happy tears that had started to build in her eyes. My woman didn't cry very often, didn't let emotions get the best of her when she could just shrug it off and kick ass. So the knowledge that being welcomed into my real family meant as much to her as it did to me was like a kick to the teeth.

"Please," Ivory scoffed. "They might as well be brothers, so I'm claiming sister status. There are way too many men in this fucking family. You, me, and Chiara have to stick together."

"This is getting too gushy for me." Scar stalked toward Matteo's office. Leaning in to tug Samara away from Ivory for a moment, I took her lips in a fierce kiss. Her hair felt like silk sliding through my fingers when I cradled the back of her head, feeling like I had my entire world in the palm of my hand. She giggled against my mouth, trying to tug back when she felt the appropriateness of the kiss had gone too far.

My Little Dove had never been particularly fond of public displays, often not even letting Connor kiss her at all in public. She swatted my chest playfully, narrowing her eyes. But before she could open that firecracker mouth of hers, I turned and strode down the hallway. Matteo roared out a laugh and followed behind me, leaving the women to catch up.

She still hadn't entirely forgiven me for trying to convince her to leave Jasper, but I knew it would be a slow battle I would eventually win. She was a Bellandi, and if she wanted to work that was fine, but she would eventually come to work for our family. I'd convince Matteo to hire her as a full-time lullaby singer for Luna if I had to.

The thought, the image of her singing to a baby made my heart pang in my chest.

The only thing that made me pause before I hit Matteo's office was the sound of Yavin's voice when the front door opened. It made me turn back, stalking to the sitting room where Yavin and Samara stared at one another. Crossing my arms over my chest, I watched with interest and dared Yavin to say something I didn't like. Instead, when he met my eyes, he crossed the distance between him and Samara and drew her into a hug. Whatever he said made her toss her head back with a laugh, and I relaxed, knowing I wouldn't have to beat the shit out of my friend.

But he continued on, giving me challenging smirks every time she responded to him with her own casual affection. The ridiculous display of ownership, as if a brother ever really owned his sister, made me roll my eyes and turn back down the hallway. I'd barely settled in to lean my ass against Matteo's desk when Yavin strolled in to join us, and he greeted everyone but me pointedly.

Matteo grunted. "Alright ladies, looks like we've got something to clear up."

"I don't have a problem, Matteo. I got everything I could ever want waiting for me in the other room. Yo, Yavin." I leveled him with a bright smile, daring him to start shit but he just returned my casual greeting and took his place to talk shop.

"Ryker's working on Connor still, so he'll miss out today," Scar grunted, not saying another word about the piece of shit who had hurt Samara. While there was still tension bleeding off Yavin, he turned his attitude around real quick and got down to work.

It wasn't what we'd been before I'd married his sister, but the unfortunate reality for Yavin was that if I had to choose between him and Samara, I'd choose her.

I'd always choose her.

CHAPTER THIRTY-SEVEN

SAMARA

Sadie and Duke arrived together, and I couldn't believe I hadn't expected the two of them to be there. I didn't know Duke particularly well, or at least not like I had in school, given that he'd somewhat distanced himself from Ivory during the last months where we'd grown closer, but it quickly became obvious that the love he'd had for Ivory didn't disappear. It just transferred to her daughter, in an entirely non-creepy way.

As soon as Donatello came down the stairs with the little bundle swaddled in purple, Duke had hurried over to claim his time with his "niece." Don came over to me, pressing a kiss to the top of my head in greeting before he made his way down the hall to join the men. Sadie harrumphed, moving over to the tank and grabbing Smaug. She handed me the lizard, and I giggled when he climbed onto my hand like the adventurous little thing he was.

No fear this lizard.

I wished I could be so brave one day, to just let people reach out without flinching away. But when he tilted his little head and looked up at me, my heart melted, and I stroked a finger over his head. He closed his eyes in contentment, turning in a circle on my hand before he settled down and snuggled into my hand so happily that I giggled. "Aren't you just the cutest?" I asked him.

He turned to look at Luna, sticking out his tongue for a moment that felt far too human-like.

"Yeah, he's weird," Ivory nodded. "Creepy little guy to be honest. With everything he seems to understand. But don't let him fool you, he's just as in love with Luna as the rest of us."

"Go wash your hands, and we'll wrestle her from Duke," Sadie grinned, and I jumped up to do it. I wouldn't even pretend I wasn't dying to hold that sweet little face. Somehow, in the two times I'd been in Ivory's house since Luna was born, I'd never held the baby. Between the wedding and my anxiety after the abduction attempt, I was glad I hadn't tried and tarnished my first experience with her.

When I came back, Ivory was already taking her from a pouting Duke who leveled me with a glare. "I've never held her!" I protested, holding my hands up. Laughing in response, he seemed to shake off the grumpiness and his smile became much more jovial and open. He came over, helping Ivory position my arms the proper way to hold Luna since I had no effing clue what I was doing. His hands against my bare forearms felt calloused, and I knew that he was a mixed media sculptor. Ivory had told me that the number of times he cut his hands every week was terrifying as his friend, but I hadn't expected that to translate to him having what felt like a mechanic's hands, with paint stains trapped in the cracks of his palm.

When Ivory dropped Luna into my lap, he helped me support her head with my bent arm, and her entire body from head to butt fit in the length of my forearm. Pulling back the swaddle blanket a teeny bit to get a better look at her, I watched her turn those deep baby blue eyes up to me. With the perfect little pout of a mouth, I touched a finger to her chest and wiggled it.

"Hey there, baby girl," I murmured with a smile. "You are just about the prettiest thing I think I ever saw." When I looked up to Ivory, she grinned down at me with the kind of pride that only a mother could manage.

Untucking her arm from the swaddle with a frustrated little stretch, Luna grabbed my finger tightly in her fist, holding with all her might as she just watched me. "Uh oh," Ivory whispered, a smile in her voice even before I looked at her.

But her eyes weren't on me, she watched Lino where he stood at the mouth of the hallway staring at me and Luna with a look that warmed everything inside me.

"Well, you're pregnant," Sadie said oddly.

"No, I'm not," I laughed sardonically. At least I better not have been with what I paid for birth control.

"You're about to be," Ivory roared with laughter, never taking her eyes off of Lino as he stormed toward where I sat with Luna. Duke took the hint, backing away to scoot to the other side of the couch so that Lino could sit next to me. He spread his knees and tucked me into the space between his legs, and I could feel his head on my shoulder as he stared down at the little princess. The moment felt heavy, like something had been decided right then and there without us saying a word. There was nothing I could say or do to make the moment less poignant, so I just settled against him and let it wash over me.

A strange warmth, a feeling of belonging. Nobody dared to take Luna from us until Lino declared we should get home, his voice hoarse with emotion, and I oddly wanted to cry when Ivory reclaimed Luna.

My arms suddenly felt empty. Empty in a way I'd never noticed before, as if something inside me had been woken up by holding her. Lino smiled down at me, seeming like he was somehow all-knowing about what it meant for me.

For us.

Where I was just clueless.

I didn't want to leave, wanted to stay with Luna forever, but as the others got up to leave too, I realized just how much we would be intruding on Matteo and Ivory's time with their newborn. I wouldn't have shared her at all, I suspected.

I would be selfish with my baby when the time came, and it suddenly hit me with absolute clarity that it would be a when.

No longer an if.

I'd have a baby if I had to beg.

Lino guided me to the car, and we went home together in silence. Lino seemed as wrapped up in his thoughts as I was mine, and I had to hope that it was for reasons close to mine and not the opposite.

***

We walked inside the front door, and Lino didn't waste a moment before he turned and pressed me against the back of it to plunder my mouth with his. I gasped, giving him access to anything he wanted at that moment. My heart, my soul, my body, my very *being*. Holding the baby, realizing that I wanted one of my own desperately had left me flayed wide open.

"You looked so beautiful with a baby in your arms," he murmured, leaning in to sigh into my neck. "I want a houseful of kids," he declared suddenly, and my heart stuttered in my chest.

The question erupted from my mouth before I could think better of it. "With me?"

"Of course with you, Little Dove," he laughed. "You're my wife. You'll be the mother of my children too." His look told me he thought I was ridiculous, but I still stuttered over my words. It didn't seem possible that he would want something like that with me at all.

Let alone so soon.

"Like now?"

"Very soon," he agreed on a murmur, touching his lips to mine delicately.

"How many is a houseful?" I asked, swallowing loudly. We had a huge home, surely, he couldn't mean—

"At least four, maybe six," he shrugged. "We have the room."

I gasped, shoving off the door to storm away from him and into the kitchen where I grabbed a bottle of water and took a swig. "Are you insane? Six kids?"

"Well how many do you want?" he asked, crossing his arms over his chest with an infuriating smirk on his handsome face.

"Two?" I asked.

He shook his head. "Four."

"Lino!" I laughed, giving him wide eyes. The man was infuriating, impossible. There was no way I would survive four little Lino's running around, even if my heart clenched at the thought of little boys that looked like him. They'd drive me crazy. "That's too many. I can't be a mom of four. Before today I wasn't even positive I wanted to be a mom of one."

His laughter bounced around the kitchen, and he stepped over to wrap me up in his arms. "Look at our family, Little Dove. Look at how they worship Luna. I promise you; we will not be alone. Fuck, Emilio can drive you and the kids to Matteo's house every day. We both know Ivory would love it and Don would lose his damn mind with happiness. He adores you; he loves me. He's going to worship our kids the same way he does Luna. Our babies will have my family, they'll have Yavin and your mom. They'll be *loved*, Samara. We have enough love to give."

I tucked myself against his chest, the words echoing in my head with a sudden clarity that made my heart hurt. "Okay, but on one condition."

"Anything for you, Little Dove."

"I want to adopt, at least one." He stared down at me, his body stilling and his jaw clenching. "I was lucky. I had mom after dad took off. You weren't so lucky," I stuttered. "I want to take in a little boy or a little girl who needs us. If we have all this love to give, then I want to give it to a child that's never known love."

He smiled finally, touching his forehead to mine. "Like you did with me, when you were too young to even know what you did." I sighed in relief, feeling that it wasn't anger that made his body tense. "Just when I think your heart can't get any bigger, you go and shock me."

"Is that a yes?" I whispered.

"Yeah, Little Dove. That's a yes. Anything for you," he echoed his earlier words, and I smiled up at him, feeling whole and happy.

I never wanted the feeling to end.

CHAPTER THIRTY-EIGHT

SAMARA

Jasper's behavior felt off. There was something in the way the man came in late every morning, when I knew he wasn't spending his time out clubbing. That wasn't him, and the fact that he couldn't go anywhere without cameras following him made him even more private with his life.

Women had let him down, used him for his money. The few who seemed genuinely interested in him hadn't been able to handle the stresses of his life. There was no chance he'd be out trolling for women, not given his distrust of them in general.

He reminded me of me in a lot of ways. Women only hurt you, men only hurt you. So why bother?

Looking back at the mindset now, given the happiness I'd found with Lino, I felt the need to try to convince Jasper that not all women would hurt him. That there would one day be one who would love him for him and see that he was worth all the trials and tribulations that went along with dating a man in the spotlight. But there was no point, I knew. He wouldn't hear it, not until he was ready to hear it.

And he wasn't.

I sat at my desk, staring at Jasper's door in thought and wondering how I could help someone who didn't want my help. I didn't truthfully know anyone I could set him up with. Sadie was dating someone she knew from the gym, and it made me sad to acknowledge that I had no other single friends to speak of. With Ivory and Chiara both married, that exhausted the new family I'd started forming.

When the door opened, I turned to it with a polite smile, though there was a bit of dread mixed in with it. Jasper had no standing appointments for the rest of the day, and it felt like the only ones who popped in were the ones I really didn't feel like dealing with. My eyes landed on the middle-aged woman from the club, the employee who had been catty, but surprised by Lino's marriage. With a sigh, I stood behind my desk as she approached with an overly bright smile. "Ms. Romano. Can I help you with something?"

"Samara," she said, seeming to pointedly choose to ignore my last name, like she couldn't quite stomach the thought of calling me a Bellandi. I wondered briefly if Emilio had seen her, if Lino already knew about her impromptu visit.

I couldn't imagine he would appreciate it.

She eyed me thoroughly, releasing a deep sigh. Like she was my friend. "I wondered if we might speak without Lino for a few moments. I know it's inappropriate to ambush you at work like this, but I didn't see any other way to get to you. Emilio is always with you."

I nodded, feeling like I'd swallowed glass as I gestured to the seats in the waiting area. "Why don't we take a seat?"

"Thank you." She perched on the edge of a chair, and I took the one across from her for a bit of distance. Where she looked perfect and poised, I leaned back to get comfortable, though I crossed my legs despite the relaxed position. "I just wanted to be sure you're aware of what you've married into. The Bellandi's are—"

"I know what the Bellandi's are and what they do. I believe I told you at the party that my brother is among their ranks. I've known Lino since he was just a boy. Did you know that?" I asked, tracing the birthmark in my palm with my fingers the way Lino might have in this situation. The familiar touch comforted me, gave me the feeling that he was there with me for the conversation I truly wanted no part in.

"With all respect, being the little sister of a friend of the family doesn't mean you know anything about the Bellandi's."

"You misunderstand me. Yavin didn't introduce me to Lino, it was the other way around. Lino has been my friend for longer than he's been Yavin's. I may not know every move that he makes or every decision he's ever made, but I suspect no wife does. That isn't my place in his life," I stated. "It never has been, and a ring on my finger won't change that."

"And what exactly is it that you think your place is?" she asked, a little smirk curving her lips.

"I've always been Lino's solace from that part of his life. The place he went to feel human again after something made him feel like a monster. His comfort," I answered. "The only thing that has changed is now he takes solace in me in a greater variety of ways."

"That's cute, but it won't last. He won't divorce you, obviously. You know that, but a man like Angelino doesn't stay faithful to one woman. There have been countless women who tried, and I have no doubt they were a little more creative than you in that department. He's a Bellandi, and they always wander from their wives. Lino planned to avoid that entirely, claiming he would never marry," she sighed.

"Obviously something changed," I argued.

"Yes, he needed to protect you from your first husband." She grinned at me, like she'd already won the battle I hadn't wanted to fight.

"Is there a purpose to you being here? Aside from an attempt to stir up drama. I mean, I realize that you clearly think very little of how much Lino cares for me, but regardless of what you think he isn't a man who would marry someone he doesn't want. I am important to him in ways you can't even begin to imagine." As I spoke the words, I realized how true they were. Lino had alternatives to dealing with Connor, with Yavin being part of the family I shouldn't have needed the Bellandi name to protect me. Not when Yavin could have done it nearly as effectively.

"And yet, if it hadn't been for that, who knows if he ever would have changed your relationship. I doubt it, because even he knows that he gets bored easily. If he truly found solace in you, he wouldn't have wanted to give that up for a few weeks of sex, months perhaps. Though it would be a record if it lasted that long."

My fingers dug into my palms, and I wanted nothing more than to slap her, but I refrained in the interest of keeping my face casual and bored even while I vibrated with fury. I'd spent enough time questioning our relationship; I didn't need others to do it for me, but she continued as if my opinion on the matter was entirely secondary.

"You'll serve a purpose of course. At least you'll be able to give him legitimate heirs. His father has pressured him for more years than I can count to marry for that reason. Before you know it, you'll be staying home with the children Angelino declares he wants. It will be sudden, because Lino doesn't have a patient bone in his body. You're married, so why not?" She stood, brushing her hands down her pencil skirt as she looked down at me with sympathy in her eyes.

"You're wrong," I accused, but the seed had already planted in my head. I'd hoped that Lino's sudden interest in children had come to pass for the same reason mine had, but it seemed convenient when his father and this bitch kept throwing the need for them in my face.

Men only hurt you.

Why would I have thought Lino could be any different?

"So he's told you he loves you then?" She raised an eyebrow at me sardonically, and I had to turn my head away as I considered her words. "He's very good at making you feel it without ever saying it. Any number of women will tell you that when the time comes and you declare your love for him, he'll tell you that you misunderstood his intentions. That he doesn't love you. That everything he made you feel was nothing but a twist of your imagination. He's a good time boy, Samara. I know you're already married, so the damage is done to some respect. But there's no reason you can't move forward understanding exactly what kind of marriage you'll have. It will hurt less in the end. I hope, one day, you can look back and understand I came here to save you future pain." She nodded at me, turning to stride for the door.

The sound of her heels ticking against the floor drew me from my reflection, and I stood. I plastered on my best poker face, smiling at her blandly. "Have a nice day, Ms. Romano. Thank you for coming, but I'd appreciate it if you didn't interrupt my workday again. Surely in the future you can just call Lino and tell him you'd like to do lunch. I don't imagine he'd have an issue with you telling me these things, assuming they are true."

She scowled at me before she stepped through the door, and I knew I'd been at least somewhat successful in convincing her I was unbothered. Turning back to my desk, I debated the pile of work that waited for me, but I knew I would never in a million years be able to focus with the way my heart felt like it was in my stomach.

So stupid.

He really had never told me he loved me. I'd meant it when I told Linda that it felt like he communicated it without saying it, but if other women felt that way?

Was I really any different?

He'd never actually said the words, though it felt like he had to have said them with all the declarations he'd made about our future. How it was just him and I in our marriage. But maybe it was just his attempt to control me, since Bellandi women weren't allowed affairs in spite of their husbands.

I had the horrifying thought that if all Bellandi's had affairs, what did that mean for poor Ivory? But I brushed it off in the next second. I'd seen the way that Matteo looked at her like she hung the moon and stars herself. There was no way in Hell that man was anything less than faithful to his wife. He gave her the looks and the words to back up his actions.

Unlike Lino. I got heated stares, sure. But couldn't he give those to any attractive woman? Yavin said he'd seen Lino with many women, did he make them feel the same way I felt? Had I mistaken sex for love for the second time in my life, with a second husband?

A sob stuck in my throat, but I forced it down and stepped over to Jasper's closed door. With a little push, I opened the door and peeked my head in. "I'm going to go grab a snack from downstairs. Do you want anything?"

"No, I'm good. See you soon," he said, never even looking up from his computer. Totally engrossed in whatever he worked on, but also distracted by whatever secret he kept tight to his chest. For one single moment, I decided to be pleased that he couldn't bother to pay attention to me. If he had, he'd have seen the way my soul splintered, the way the need to run pulsed through me.

Men only hurt.

I wanted to go, but with the threat of Connor looming over me, I couldn't just walk out the doors. I grabbed my phone off my desk, typing Yavin's number in and waiting for him to answer. "I need you to pick me up from work. Now," I said with a flinch. I didn't often even attempt to tell Yavin what to do, so it wasn't like me to snap at him the second he answered the phone.

"What's wrong, Smalls?" he asked, and his voice was quiet. He knew. He knew as well as anyone would know that the only person who could make me splinter like this was Lino. He'd tried to warn me, and again I hadn't listened.

"Pull up to the side door. I'll meet you there," I said, and I packed up my things and waited just a few minutes before my anxiety got the best of me.

Men only hurt.

The thought echoed in my head, feeling all the more painful because I'd thought that if nothing else, Lino would never hurt me with lies and dishonesty. He might have hurt me by not wanting me, but I couldn't exactly blame him just for not feeling the same way about me. Leading me to believe we had something more than a marriage that protected me if we didn't? That I could blame him for. Making me believe he wanted children with me and not just heirs to the Bellandi empire? That was an unforgivable sin against me.

I snagged my purse off the desk and strutted my way to the elevator, catching it on the way down. More and more people filled it as we descended during the late afternoon rush of people leaving last appointments for the day. Panic surged through me when I thought of having to sneak past Emilio, but his back was turned, and I managed to blend in with the crowd until I stepped out the side door. The need to get away from all things Lino put a tangible pressure on my chest.

Emilio never saw me standing just outside the side entrance, clinging to the building like it could save me from would-be abductors. By the time Yavin pulled up, I was a nervous mess. I had a few hours at best before they realized I was gone, and I felt horrible guilt for what it would mean for Jasper when I didn't come back.

But I already knew an hour wouldn't be enough. An hour wouldn't be enough time to process my options and try to tame my heart back into the state where it didn't care. Where it didn't want.

Where it could use Lino, just the way he used me.

"What's going on, Smalls?" Yavin whispered, reaching over to take my hand in his. I bit back a sob.

"I just need to get away for a little bit. I don't want to talk about it. I don't want to think about it. Can you just take me to *The Bird Lounge*, please? I need to listen to music."

"Yeah. Yeah, I can take you there, Samara," Yavin murmured, and he went quiet. Yavin was tumultuous and prone to fits, but he also knew when he could push the limits with me and when I was at my breaking point.

I had to hope I didn't snap this time.

CHAPTER THIRTY-NINE

LINO

The call from Emilio couldn't have come at a less convenient time. Training my new manager at Indulgence had hit critical importance. Enzo couldn't keep filling in and doing two jobs, but I also couldn't bring myself to leave Samara alone in bed at night and come to the club. It wasn't like I oversaw the nightly activities at the club anyway; I mostly worked in the office upstairs in case there was a situation that needed my attention.

Or unless something with the other side of the businesses demanded my attention. Like meetings with our gun or drug suppliers where Matteo wanted to present a united front. Those things I could and would still do, as was expected of me as one of Matteo's closest confidantes, but the mundane bullshit of running the club didn't need my attention.

My new manager was experienced and came highly recommended, it was just a new place and there were all sorts of standards involved with working for the Bellandi's. He needed to understand that when we said we'd bury him if he broke the confidentiality agreement, we meant it.

"Yeah?" I grunted as soon as the phone hit my ear.

"Mia Romano just went up to see Mrs. Bellandi about twenty minutes ago. She said you sent her, so I let her up. But now I'm thinking on it and wondering why you would send one of your father's good time girls to see your wife."

My body froze solid. The way Mia had assessed Samara at the club ran through my head, the catty way she'd tried to start shit about my marriage and fidelity. Like it was any of her business what I did with my wife or outside my marriage.

She'd been fishing for gossip, I knew. Looking for weaknesses that she could turn to my father and exploit.

I'd known better than to believe my father had truly given his blessing, but I never expected he might send a woman to do his dirty work. "Get up there now. I want to know what kind of toxic bullshit she's spinning." Samara had only just started to come around, started to believe that what we had was genuine. It had taken far too long to break down those walls she'd put up against me and all other men. I wouldn't fucking go so gently if she made me do it again.

"She just left," Emilio said. "I didn't think to stop her."

"Go to Samara then. Make sure she's okay. Call me when you have her. I want to know what that woman said to her," I snarled, turning to watch the door. I knew Mia wasn't due to work for hours yet, but it didn't stop me from wishing she was there so I could get my own answers.

"Yes, boss," Emilio grunted in my ear and the phone disconnected.

I kept it in my hand, drumming my fingers against the back of the case.

Unease slithered up my spine, the unquestionable sense that something was wrong.

But all I could do was wait.

"Is everything okay?" the new manager, Armando, asked with a glance at my phone.

"No." It was all the answer I gave, and he didn't push for me to give him more information as my head bartender ran him through the inventory while I watched, marking down the number of bottles of each kind of alcohol and matching it up with the records the bartenders kept.

I felt nauseous.

When my phone rang, I put it to my ear. "Samara?"

"She's gone, Sir. Rowe says she told him she was going to grab a snack from the third floor, but they haven't seen her." My ears rang with fury, knowing the timing was too suspect for it to be a coincidence that she wasn't where she'd said she would be. Whatever Mia had told her, it couldn't have been true, and if her lies cost me the love of my life I'd kill her myself. There was nothing I'd done to make Samara try to leave me.

Even if I had, I wouldn't let her go. I'd follow her wherever she went and bring her back to me.

But I never wanted to hurt her.

"Does Rowe have security tapes with audio up there? I want to know what the fuck she said to her." There was a moment where Emilio must have muffled the phone as he spoke to Rowe.

"No, Sir. Just video. Rowe tried calling her, but her phone is on her desk."

I nodded my head before I realized he couldn't see me. My fury spiked, even as I abandoned my manager in training and stalked for the front door. "Fuck! She left the fucking phone where I planted the tracker? I'm calling Ryker. You put in the call to Donatello. He'll mobilize people to help you search nearby. Ryker and I will take her favorite spots in the city. Access the external cameras and see if you can tell if she huffed it on foot or took a cab."

"You've got it boss."

I hung up the phone, slamming my fist into the side of the brick building as soon as I stepped out. The blood on my knuckles only made me ache for her more, for the care she would show if she knew I was injured. Samara was the only person who'd ever tended to my injuries, except for maybe my mother before I could remember.

Dialing the number, I spoke before he even greeted me. "Samara ran. I need you to find her, now," I ordered.

He grunted into the phone. "I'm on Connor's trail. You sure you want me to leave it?"

"Do you have him in your sight?" I asked.

"No. Not that close. The guy's slippery as fuck."

"Then find my wife. I'll text you a list of places she likes to go. I'll take the other half of them."

"Got it," he grunted. My fingers flew over the keyboard furiously until my driver and security stepped out of the club.

Georgio took one look at my face and retreated to get the car as I typed out the list of places Samara might go to hide. I sent the more public ones to Ryker, knowing he might scare her off if she got a good look at him. My Little Dove knew most of my family, but not Ryker, and he was one scary looking fucker.

The man scared the bravest of men, and my Little Dove was skittish even if she tried to hide it.

"Where to?" Georgio asked as he pulled up.

"Samara's old house," I hissed dialing the neighbor. When she didn't answer, I hoped to God Samara had chosen to hide out there. Somewhere relatively safe, with someone who could try and talk her down from the ledge. She'd called me without Samara's permission once, so I had to wonder why she wouldn't do it again.

All the phone calls I'd eavesdropped in on between the two women had been pleasant, with Samara doing nothing to indicate she wasn't happy with me.

When my phone rang, I answered it without glancing at the name on the screen. "Yeah?"

"Talk to me. Enzo said you just tore out of the club like a bat outta Hell." Matteo's voice held all the worry I knew I would have if he left work suddenly. There was only one thing that could make us abandon our jobs like that.

Our women.

"Samara ditched Emilio. Mia went to see her at work and then she was just gone," I answered.

"Fuck," Matteo hissed. "Don! Track Samara's phone! Now!" he yelled. In any other circumstances I'd have cursed him for making me deaf. In these, I didn't give the first fuck.

"She left the phone at her desk," I growled.

"Fuck, I told you to put one in her."

"And how did that work for you when you almost lost Ivory because of that bullshit?" I asked, and he went silent on the other side of the line. He seemed to realize that arguing with me right now would not end well for him.

"I'll get all the guys out and looking for her. We'll find her. I'll have Don check her call log." He hung up, nothing more to say about it. I tried to call Yavin, feeling so desperate to find her that I'd even tell her brother about whatever problems we had in our relationship, but his phone went straight to voicemail.

If she was okay, I'd fucking make sure she never left me again. She had to realize what this would do to me, worrying about her with Connor on the loose.

She had to be okay.

My head rested in my hands when Linda's name popped up on my phone.

I answered, hoping like Hell she had my woman in her house. "Is Samara with you?"

"No, no. Of course not. Has something happened?"

"She slipped her security," I said, but I didn't bother answering her other questions. "Call me if you hear from her." Then I hung up, because the concern in the woman's voice was real. There would be no faking that kind of worry.

"Fuck!" I roared, punching the back of the front passenger seat. I needed the pain, needed it to ground me against everything that shredded my insides.

Why the fuck couldn't she just *talk* to me?

"Where now, boss?" Georgio was brave to ask me the question.

"Sadie's gym. She probably thought Sadie would keep her safe and let her hideout until she made a plan. The crazy ass woman would too if she believed whatever bullshit Mia told her."

He hung a U-turn at the next intersection, heading straight for the gym.

I'd find her.

I had to find her.

I couldn't lose her.

Not now, not ever.

CHAPTER FORTY

SAMARA

I lost track of how long I sat in The Bird Lounge, absorbing the music and the pulse of energy it gave me before I worked up the courage to even look at my brother. The confliction on his face was obvious, the phone in his hand turned off to ignore the way people had called him repeatedly when they realized I was gone.

I wasn't ready to deal with any of them.

But I finally let him turn it back on, using it to call Jasper and listening to the sound of the ringtone while I waited. "Oh, thank fuck. Do you have Samara?" he asked, and I felt instant guilt for worrying him.

"I'm fine," I said, glancing away from the hallway to look at the stage where the singer on stage was getting ready to do his set. "I just needed some air."

"You could have at least told me what was going on, fuck Samara. Do you have any idea how worried everyone is?"

"I can imagine." I winced, but I still had no intention of calling anyone else in that moment. "I need to be away from them for a little while so I can think. Someone gave me some things to think about, so I'm taking the time to do that. You can tell them I'm okay if you want. I'm not going to tell you where I am. I might not be in tomorrow. I have to decide what the Hell I'm going to do first."

"Samar—" I hung up the phone, ignoring all the other calls, but I braved opening Yavin's text messages.

Fifteen from Lino.

Where are you?!

It isn't safe.

Please bring her back to me.

Talk to me.

Answer the fucking phone!

Bring her home.

On and on they went, over the course of the apparent four hours we'd sat in *The Bird Lounge.* My gut twisted with a mix of pain and guilt. I didn't have a home, not if what Mia had said about Lino was true. I wouldn't settle for a husband who cheated, for a man who would never love me.

I'd rather be alone.

I went back to my seat as the next singer started his set, reclaiming my lone table in the corner and getting lost in the twang of his voice while Yavin studied his phone. It was something so uncommon in Chicago, so refreshing to hear something entirely different. It sounded so sad, like it echoed the hollow feeling yawning inside my chest.

"Maybe we should call him," Yavin caved, giving me a guilty look. I hated that I'd put him in the position where he had to choose between his loyalty to me and his loyalty to Lino.

"You can text him," I agreed. "Just tell him I'm safe."

Eventually, when the singer's set finished, I stood from my table and decided to move on. Go to the bathroom and let Yavin take me to his place for the night. I stood, picking up my purse, and turning to find Lino standing in the doorway. He was drenched and rain came down in a heavy downpour through the window of the door behind him.

My eyes went to Yavin, taking in the guilty way he stared at his feet. Lino gave him a look that seemed to communicate that they'd be having words at some point, but I didn't stick around to tell Yavin how betrayed I felt. I couldn't, not with the way Lino's eyes burned into me. Not with the way the hair stood up on my arms and seemed to scream at me that I was in grave danger.

With a swallow, I turned. My feet couldn't move quickly enough, I needed to escape, needed to get away. The hall at the back had an emergency exit behind the bathrooms, and I made for it. I'd barely gotten through the door when the rain instantly pelted me and drenched my hair. My heels slipped in a puddle as I made my way down the alley, and the sound of the door blowing wide open resounded behind me with a bang.

"Samara!" he roared, and I didn't allow myself to stop. Couldn't stop.

I hadn't fortified myself, hadn't found a way to face him and see the lies in his eyes for what they were. I'd always had a blind spot where he was concerned, and I needed a plan before I dealt with him. His hand caught my arm, spinning me in place until I was pressed against his chest and all I could see was the way his lungs heaved.

With his grip still on me, he backed me up, his presence so looming and seeming so much larger than normal that I had no choice but to comply.

When my back hit the brick of the building, I gasped. His head tipped down, glaring down at me with a savage look in his eyes that made me swallow. Fear swelled.

The first time in my life I could ever remember being afraid of Lino.

Water dripped from his face, from the thick hair that was usually so flawless to splatter off my face and run inside my jacket.

It was so fucking cold.

"Lino, please," I begged. "Let me go. Just let me go."

"I will *never* let you go. Do you understand me, *vita mia?*" The whisper was anything but a sweet declaration, nothing but warning and rage in his voice. "Do you have any idea how fucking terrified I've been? Connor could have found you! He could have finished the job this time." My heart broke, the reminder that everything was fake. Everything was about my protection. Not about his feelings for me that didn't exist.

"I'm sorry I scared you. Now, as you can see, I'm fine. I was smart and I called Yavin to protect me, now *fucking let me go!*"

When his head jolted back, I realized I'd rarely, if ever, genuinely yelled at him. I'd never needed to. My tears mingled with the rain, sliding down my cheeks until it felt like my raw heart was outside my chest, on display and ready to be shredded into a million pieces. "What did she say to you?" His voice softened, some of the anger fading when he cupped my cheek.

"It doesn't matter. She didn't say anything I shouldn't have already seen. I convinced myself that you felt the same way, that this was *real*," I sobbed. "And it never was. It never will be. I appreciate that you tried to keep me safe, but I want to go to Yavin's. I think it's best I stay with him until we can get the marriage annulled. I'm sure you have the connections to—"

"Don't you fucking dare finish that sentence." He slid his body into mine, his hand reaching down to force my legs apart and make space for him between them. I glanced around the alley, grateful as all Hell that the overcast sky had gone dark.

"Stop it," I swatted at his hand when it inched my skirt up my thighs.

"You're my wife. You will always be my wife. Get that through your stubborn fucking head," he grunted, leaning down to press a kiss to my lips that I turned my head away from. "Whatever Mia told you, I can promise you it isn't true, but I can't do that unless you talk to me."

Could he see me bleeding? Could he see the way my heart bled, and my soul cracked inside my chest?

I didn't speak, couldn't voice the words when his eyes stared down at me so harshly. They softened again, and he touched his forehead to mine. "You really have no clue, do you?" he whispered, his voice suddenly filled with a pain that felt a lot like mine.

"I don't know anything, it seems," I argued defensively, trying to turn my head away from his. But his hands caught my face, framing it and holding my eyes with an intensity that scared me.

"I'm in love with you," he whispered, and I felt the sob that wracked my body at the sound of those words. Words I'd dreamed of hearing but couldn't believe. Everything was a lie. Why wouldn't this be too?

"Don't lie to me," I gasped, tugging my head back so hard that it cracked against the brick. He pressed on.

"I've been in love with you since I was a boy, Little Dove. In school, my father and uncle threatened to kill you and Ivory if we didn't stay away from you. Matteo got to have Ivory for a little while, because they never could have guessed she would come to mean so much to him. Who could have? It was high school. People don't fall in love like that when they're so young. But you?" He huffed a laugh. "My father knew what you were to me long before I did, and he was always trying to get me to push you away. When the threats against me, the beatings didn't work, he did the only thing that could keep me away from you."

"Don't," I sobbed.

"He threatened *you*. He threatened to take you from me, to kill you, to *sell* you. He threatened everything under the sun, and it got to the point that I knew he meant it. There was nothing I could do to stop him, except not be with you. I loved you too much to let him hurt you. I would have done anything to keep you safe, Samara. By the time Matteo had enough power and his father was gone, by the time I could have made you mine, you were married."

"Then why didn't you tell me how you felt when I told you about the divorce?" I whispered the words, refusing to believe the confession, the lies.

"I wanted you to be divorced before I made my move. I never planned on waiting long before we got married. Why do you think I was so fucking annoyed that you wouldn't let me hurry it along?" He chuckled, as if my inability to see how he felt was nothing but an indication of my stubbornness. As if anyone who looked could see how he felt about me. I glared at him, flinching back from his sigh. "I love you, Samara. I have always loved you. Needing to protect you only gave me an excuse to do what I already wanted."

"Lino. I can't—" I started to beg.

"Shh. I love you. I will tell you over and over again until you actually *hear* me. Until you listen." He took my hand in his, pressing it to his chest that thumped in a ferocious heartbeat that matched my own. "How can you not feel it? How can you not feel the way that we're connected, like we're two parts of the same whole?"

I clenched my eyes shut, trying to tune out the words, trying to tune out the world and just think. He took all my thoughts, turned me to mush, the second he got his hands on me. The minute he smiled.

"I love you, my wife," he repeated. "Tell me you don't love me, and I'll stop."

"Of course, I love you," I spat. "You know damn well I do!"

With a grin that broke my heart, he crashed his lips down on mine. There was no reprieve, no shoving him off.

And as soon as I felt his tongue touch my lip, I didn't even want to. I wanted to feel *something* that wasn't a lie. I shrank against him, melting into his arms despite myself. As soon as he pulled away, he hefted me into his arms. My head flew over his shoulder, facing the ground so suddenly that I screeched. "Put me down!"

"Not a fucking chance," he growled, storming down the alley and to the car that waited for him. Georgio hurried out of the driver's seat, helpfully opening the back door so that he could toss me in and climb in after me.

"Dammit, Lino. You can't just throw me in a car and take me home with you! I want to stay with Yavin." The door closed behind him with a hard thud, making me jump in my seat.

"Watch the road and call Matteo. Tell him I've got her, and he can inform everyone. Have him call Yavin and tell him I took her home."

"Yes, Sir." There was a smile in Georgio's voice as he hit buttons on the control console and spoke into the headpiece he stuck on his ear.

"Traitor!" I yelled, even if it was ridiculous. I'd always known Georgio's loyalty was to Lino, just like everyone else's, but it didn't change the fact that I liked the man. "Don't touch me!" I yelled when Lino's hands reached out to grab me. The streets of Chicago passed by in a blur as Georgio navigated through traffic like the expert he was. Lino grabbed my waist, tugging me over until I landed in his lap, and he could tug my arms behind my back and hold me like that.

"You just told me you loved me for the first time, and you thought I wouldn't shove you in the car and take you home? I won't fuck you in an alley. You deserve a castle and a knight, Samara. But you got me instead. I won't sully you more with an alley fuck where anybody could see what's mine."

I fought back the tears that burned my throat. I wouldn't give him that much of me, wouldn't cave to the lies he told, but God.

That look in his eyes as he stared up at me made my heart hurt. The thought that he could fake that— that he could look like he held the world in his hands when he looked at me, and not mean a thing.

"I love you," he murmured, and those eyes held mine, as if he could compel me to believe him.

Maybe he could, because my heart stuttered in my chest like it might try and reanimate. Come back to life. I shook my head to clear it. "Please, don't lie to me. Not about this. I can't, fuck, I can't take it. Please."

"*Vita mia*," he groaned. "You're killing me, Little Dove. Listen to me when I say I fucking love you."

Thump.

Thump.

Hope bloomed inside me when I really looked at him, really saw the way he looked at me as if he expected me to see inside him. There was no deception in his gaze, just raw, emotional love that made me want to sob in relief. "You promise?"

"I promise, Samara. I will love you until the day I die, and then I'll love you from Hell."

I swallowed, letting the confession permeate through my walls for just a moment. A tear fell, thinking that I might have wasted so much time. "You aren't going to get sick of me and go have affairs?"

"Never," he snarled. "If that's what she told you, I'll kill her myself. Nobody else, Samara. I've never felt this *right* with anyone but you."

I nodded, dropping my head to his forehead as I looked down at him. A hesitant, disbelieving smile bloomed on my face when he treated me to the full force of his grin. "You're mine, woman. All fucking mine. You know that now?"

"Yes, Lino," I murmured. "I think I get it now."

"Good," he groaned, tugging me down to him for a devouring kiss that set my blood on fire. My hips ground against him, totally lost to the sensation and not caring one bit that we had an audience. The hand that swatted at my ass said Lino wasn't quite as lost in me, that he still had some kind of common sense to stop me from grinding on his dick with Georgio in the front seat.

His hands at my waist steadied me, and I rested my head in his neck, breathing him in as if I could take him into me. As if I could take the words he'd said and somehow make myself believe they were real permanently. As if he could heal the wounds Connor had left in his wake.

By the time we pulled into the driveway, my resolve had hardened. I wasn't the pathetic woman Connor had made me. Loving Lino didn't change who I was or who I could be, because I'd *always* loved him. He was a part of me, the best part of me.

As soon as the car pulled up in front of the house, Lino had me out of the car and in his arms. His phone rang as we hurried up the front steps to the door, and he tugged it out and answered it gruffly while he unlocked the door. "Busy, Matteo. Talk to you tomorrow."

All I heard was the sound of Matteo and Ivory's laughter on the other side of the line before Lino hung up and swung the front door open. We didn't bother to head for the stairs, didn't even pretend like we would make it to the bed for what we had in mind. He peeled off his wet clothes as he walked, and I closed the door behind me. My jacket pooled on the floor when I stripped it off, stepping out of my heels simultaneously. By the time I'd made it out of the entryway, Lino stood naked and waiting for me. After I unzipped my skirt, I shoved it down my hips along with my underwear. Lino drew me into his arms to guide me where he wanted me, his hands grabbing the fabric of my shirt and pulling it apart harshly so that the sound of the fabric tearing filled the air. Only a too brief kiss landed on my lips before he spun me around and bent me over the counter. His nimble fingers divested me of my bra, and it fell down my arms until I shucked it off.

The hand that slapped against the globe of my ass shouldn't have come as a surprise, given what I'd put him through. But as the pain of Mia Romano's accusations and lies faded, I couldn't help but love Lino more for all the trouble he'd gone to. All I'd done was be out of his sight for a few hours, and he'd been mad with worry.

I tried to remember the last time someone had worried for me that way and came up empty.

There was only Lino. Always only Lino.

"You ever do that again, and I'll put a tracker in your ass," he hissed, slapping my ass again even as he reached a hand around to stroke my center. His movement was impatient, like he couldn't decide if he wanted to punish me for running or pleasure me for finally letting him in. I knew the feeling.

"You'll do no such thing!" I gasped, tossing my head back when he shoved inside me with one brutal thrust. He buried a hand in my hair, tugging me back until my hands supported me on the counter and his breath rasped against my ear.

"Ask Ivory if she would ever take hers out now, Samara. It saved her life."

"Shut up and fuck me," I grunted, wincing when the hold on my hair tightened and his hand came down on my ass again. It changed to a moan when his hips shifted to stroke over that perfect spot inside me, my orgasm building quickly under the force of his strokes and the fingers that worked my clit in a delicious roll of tight pressure.

I panted as I strove for it, and then I whimpered when he pulled out of me so suddenly that everything that had built just faded into the wind. "Lino!"

"On the counter, Little Dove," he murmured, and the harsh edges of his anger had faded to leave only the gentle man who loved me. I turned, letting him help me up so that he could slide inside me. "I need to see your eyes when you come." The height of the counter put us almost eye to eye, the tip of his nose rubbing against mine with every stroke of him inside me.

He was so hard, filling me so perfectly that it felt like there was nothing left. Like our bodies fused together and became one. He didn't kiss me except for brief touches of his lips to my lips, my face, my nose. Mostly he held my eyes and breathed the same air as me, and somehow it felt even more intimate for it. When he tugged me forward, I thought I'd fall off the counter. But he held me there, supported my weight with his body and his hands and rocked my hips to take him even deeper. "Fuck," he groaned.

"Oh God," I moaned, tossing my head back, but his hand buried in my hair, tugging my face back to his so that he could touch his forehead to mine. His eyes blazed with heat, but the undeniable presence of love in them was what sent me spiraling over the edge into my orgasm. Holding his eyes, when he roared out my name and followed me over the edge was the most intimate moment of my life.

A moment I knew I'd remember for the rest of it.

And as I caught my breath, I murmured, "I love you."

"I love you too, Little Dove," he whispered back, lifting me into his arms to carry me to bed.

I didn't remember getting there, didn't remember anything but how good Lino smelled as he carted me up the stairs.

Then I was out.

CHAPTER FORTY-ONE

SAMARA

I woke to the feeling of warmth in bed behind me. I didn't bother to open my eyes, snuggling back into Lino's broad chest and enjoying the groan he gave me in response. "Good morning, Little Dove," he murmured, his voice sleepy. I almost regretted waking him up, however unintentionally it had been. I wanted nothing more than for him to get some rest after what I'd put him through so stupidly the day before.

I couldn't imagine the kind of fear he must have felt if he really loved me, and I'd convinced myself that it was okay to believe him. That Lino wasn't some stranger who owed me nothing and wouldn't think twice about hurting me. Lino had never wanted to see me hurt, even if I'd been too emotional to see that when the blind panic had taken over and sent me running.

The walls, the self-preservation, the *fear*. I knew realistically that all of those things were a natural reaction to the kind of betrayal Connor committed against me, but I didn't want to let him ruin my life. I didn't want him to influence my decisions and keep me from what could make me happy.

Lino probably wasn't a good man. He'd likely done horrible things that I'd just turned a blind eye to and wanted to pretend didn't exist, and I was sure he had more crimes ahead of him. Especially since Connor had yet to be caught.

"Good morning," I sighed back, rolling onto my stomach so that I could look over at him. I loved the way he looked when he first woke up. Loved knowing that after so many years of him being my first good morning, I finally got to hear that sleepy voice. I finally got to see the way his hair stuck in all directions, and he looked so much younger and more carefree before the realities and pressures of his day settled over him and the businessman took over.

"Promise me you won't run again, Little Dove," he whispered, and the anguish in his voice damn near broke my heart. "My life isn't safe. You can't slip your security like that."

"I can't promise I won't test you, but I promise I won't slip security and disappear," I said in response. His hand touched my back, trailing his fingers up and down the spine at the center as he watched me. I smiled shyly. "But I won't deny that it's addictive to know you looked so hard for me. That you tried to find me, and that you were so angry with me."

"You like that I was angry with you?" His brows raised, and his fingers paused on my back.

With a swallow, I tried to explain the thoughts churning in my head. Tried to find a way to explain what it meant to me that he cared enough to do those things. "Mom always gave me freedom, you know that. Yavin is really only interested in being a brother when it suits him, and as much as I love him, he's too busy with work to ever really be there, you know?" He nodded, and a frown pursed his lips. I had to hope that eventually things between the two men in my life would settle down, and my marriage to Lino would eventually bring my brother and I closer. "He keeps me at a distance, because he can't ever tell me about his day. He thinks I'm so innocent that I've never been to a strip club, or I would be horrified by whatever he could tell me. With nothing in common, there's just not much there." I paused again, letting him consider that. I knew he and Yavin were close, but Yavin had never made as much of an effort as Lino.

Now it made sense why.

"He loves you," Lino responded.

"I know he does, and I love him. I hope now that I'm a wife of the family he feels like he can be more candid with me, but we'll see how he does with the marriage first. Anyway, Connor didn't want me to leave the house. But it wasn't because of safety, he disguised it as him wanting to be with me. But then he'd ignore me. Eventually I just stopped going out, unless I was with you. He'd guilt trip me about it when I got home, but he never showed any interest in calling me or finding out where I was. He never cared if I was safe." I cut off the ramble, because I really didn't want to go into too much detail about my marriage to Connor. No more than was necessary anyway, but some of it felt like it was important to make Lino understand what it meant to me that he looked for me. "So having you drop everything you were doing, call in a team to find me, call and text Yavin, all those things. It's endearing. It makes me feel loved. It feels good to know that someone worries about me. It makes me feel like maybe for just one second, I'm the center of your world."

"You are the center of my world, Samara. You're everything to me." I choked back tears at the declaration.

My fingers trailed over the tattoo of the eye on his chest, feeling as if I saw it for the first time. The words he'd said about it, his everything, weeks ago.

"It's me, isn't it?" I asked.

"Yes, Little Dove. It's you. Matteo and I got them together. The tattoos that reminded us of the women we thought we'd never be able to have. So that we could carry a piece of you with us always," he explained. I'd never seen Matteo's tattoo, never seen the brutal man out of his suit, so I couldn't know what tattoo he had for Ivory.

I just hoped it was as beautiful as Lino's.

"You tried to tell me how you felt, and I didn't listen," I whispered. "I'm sorry. So sorry."

"You weren't ready. That's not something you need to be sorry for, Little Dove. Our lives and our relationship haven't been easy, and they probably never will be. Not with the life I lead. I'd walk away from all of it for you if you asked me to. Now that Matteo's in charge, we could go and it would be safe."

"I would never ask you to walk away from your family. They love you, and you love them." I rolled to my side, feeling his hand settle on my hip as he smiled at me.

"I know you wouldn't, and I love you even more for it. You accept me, all of me. Just the way I am, even though you know I'm not perfect. That I'm not a good man." I wrapped my arms around his hips, snuggling into his bare chest and loving the way he smelled like him, but also like me. Like I was a part of him, right down to his scent.

"You're a good man to me. That's all that matters."

His lips touched mine, and he murmured against them with a smile. "I love you, wife."

I smiled back, jumping up from the bed and going to the closet to pull out the box I'd kept tucked behind my shoes. I had to toss the shoes out of the way to grab it, but soon had my little box of memories in hand. When I went back into the bedroom, Lino had sat up in the bed. The sheet pooled around his waist, hiding his legs while he leaned against the headboard and looked at me curiously. "I—I wanted you to have these. So that you know how I felt. You don't have to read them, but—"

"What are they?" he reached forward, tugging the small box from my hand.

"My journals. From the day we met to the day you graduated. I stopped journaling that day. I gave up on us, and I realized that I'd been chronicling our love story, or what I'd thought was our love story, to look back on one day." He took one of the purple notebooks out of the box, opening up to a random page, and I winced at the massive Mrs. Angelino Bellandi that I'd scrawled at the top of the page. It had to have been middle school for me to be that open about my feelings, that convinced that our marriage would happen. My confidence had waned as I'd gotten older and Lino dated other girls in school. I swallowed, shuffling my feet nervously as he read whatever horrifying and humiliating declarations of love were on that page specifically. When he grabbed a second and a third notebook from the box and flipped through the pages, skimming them with rapid eye movements and absorbing all my humiliating memories, I wanted to die. Wanted to crawl into a hole, but I forced myself to crawl into the bed instead.

His eyes finally turned up to meet mine, heat blazing in them briefly before he stood and strode from the room without bothering to cover up his nudity. I watched him go, staring at the box of journals and wondering if maybe I'd gone too far. If maybe they made me seem more like a creep than I'd intended given he confessed he'd had feelings for me all along. My eyes landed on the open notebook; on the sketch of our little family I'd envisioned for us. Lino and I, our four kids, and a dog.

He came back a moment later, something clutched in his hand and strode right for the bathroom. I followed with my heart in my throat, and he stood there with an arrogant, satisfied smirk on his face. Lifting the package in his hand, I felt my eyes widen on the sight of my birth control packet. "What are you doing?" I asked.

He popped a single pill out and it splashed into the toilet.

"Lino!" I protested.

"I'm done waiting," he declared, holding my eyes as he popped out a second pill. There was another splash.

"You're done waiting?" I asked.

"I have waited my entire life to have you. I'm done. Just done pretending that I'm patient. Done pretending like I can wait for you to come around to where I am in this marriage." A sequence of more splashes sounded, and I looked at the packet to find it empty. There hadn't been many pills left, admittedly, but it still seemed jarring. He'd even shoved out the placebos, as if they were an affront to him too. He tossed the empty packet into the trash and flushed the toilet before stalking toward me. I backed away until the back of my knees hit the bed and he hoisted me up and onto it. Looming over me, he grabbed my knees and spread them wide so that he could come down between them. "I'm putting a baby in your belly."

"We—I," I paused, trying to gather my thoughts as my brain raced to keep up with him. "There are things we should talk about before we take that step."

"Nope. The answers won't change anything. You want to work; we'll figure it out. You want to stay home; I'll support that choice fully. All that matters is that I love you, and we're having a baby. Did you think I'd see you hold Luna and do anything but make it so I could see you hold *our* baby like that? It drove me fucking mad to think you'd make me wait."

"And if I don't want a baby?" I whispered, but even I could feel the smile on my face. It took some of the bite out of my words undoubtedly, because Lino gave me a mischievous grin and darted his head down to lick my nipple playfully.

"I think I can convince you." Those lips wrapped around it, sucking hard enough that my back bowed.

"Okay," I gasped. "Convince me then."

His eyes danced as he released me and brought his mouth down on mine for a deep kiss.

Then he set out to convince me.

CHAPTER FORTY-TWO

Lino had convinced me. Thoroughly.

And if it were determined by the amount of sex two people could have in thirty-six hours, I'd be pregnant already.

So the phone ringing the next evening drew us out of our pleasurable little cave where we'd shut out the world. I never wanted to emerge. Never wanted to go back to work even though I knew I would need to go in the morning. Taking a day and a half off unannounced hadn't been fair to Jasper, and I was sure he would be furious with me.

Or Lino.

Or both of us.

The way that Lino's body went solid as he listened to the person on the other side of the line made me tense up, but I tried to continue with my cool down stretches after yoga. "He did what?" Lino growled, and everything in me clenched at the sound. He'd turned me into an addict, if just the sound of his savage side made me horny despite the endless supply of orgasms.

"Right. I'll be right there." He stabbed the phone with a ferocity that made me nervous. "I have to go. I don't know when I'll be home." He turned for the stairs, heading up to the bedroom, and I followed him.

"What's going on?" I asked.

"Connor went to another one of the loan sharks in the city to get more money. Enough to pay off his debt with Tiernan, but he didn't have enough property for collateral. The guy he went to has beef with the Bellandi's, so he offered up revenge on us in exchange for settling his debt." Lino swapped out his sweatpants for a fresh pair of slacks, tugging them up his legs and buttoning them at the waist quickly.

"Revenge how?" I swallowed, hating that my life and my decisions were coming down on Lino's head. I'd always known the end of my marriage would have consequences for him, I just hadn't expected to take down Matteo and Ivory with him, and I'd let myself hope that maybe, just maybe, he could protect himself against whatever damage Connor could do.

"He says he has information from the time he was married to you. Told the guy that your connection to me gave him insights that could take down the Bellandi's." The breath whooshed out of me, and I staggered to sit on the edge of the bed.

"How is that possible? I don't know anything! It's not like I could ever even tell him—"

"I believe you, Little Dove. I've always kept you in the dark. There's nothing you could have told him that's incriminating, but that doesn't mean he didn't use the connection to dig. I don't know, and I won't know until I get there." His shirt slipped on over his shoulders, and he buttoned it up hurriedly. I stood and reached out to help him, rushing through the buttons even though I needed the connection it gave me. I needed to feel like I hadn't fucked up everything.

"How do you even know about this? If the guy has beef with the Bellandi's—"

"He wants to settle our shit. He said that we could use this to settle the score between us and go about our business separately. He doesn't believe that Connor will have the information he says he has, and I sincerely doubt it. He's just exploiting the fact that everyone knows you're mine now. But he told Connor he'd think about it, we'll meet and discuss terms to get him to help us bring Connor in."

"Okay," I breathed, nodding my head and reminding myself that this was part of what I'd signed up for. I knew Lino worked late nights sometimes. I knew he had to come and go at the demands of the family often.

"I'll be back as soon as I can. Crew is on duty tonight, so he'll be available if you need anything. Don't leave the house. Order in whatever you want for dinner."

My heart ached as he slid the suit jacket up his shoulders and tugged on shoes. I wanted to hug him, wanted to thank him for the fact that even as he prepared to walk out the door and deal with a mess I'd caused, he still worried about me and my safety first.

"Don't be surprised if he checks in with you often. After the other day, I'm going to want regular updates that you're in sight."

"Lino!" I protested, wincing at the reminder. "Things are different now!"

"Don't. I know they are, but it's going to take me a while to be comfortable with it. I can't go through that fear again." He kissed me, a slow kiss that reassured me against the sting of his words. "I'll be back as soon as I can."

"I love you," I murmured as he pulled away.

"I love you too." Then he left the bedroom, making his way down the stairs. By the time I followed, I watched out the window as he climbed into the back seat of his car and Georgio waved to me through the window. As soon as the car slid out the open gate and it shut to seal me back inside the property, I plunked down onto the sofa.

I hated myself for causing problems for Lino and Matteo.

I just had to hope it would work out in the end, but it felt more like the wakeup call I'd been waiting for. The reminder that my baggage didn't only affect me.

❦

LINO DIDN'T COME HOME that night.

I waited up, couldn't seem to settle down in bed without him next to me anyway.

Curling up with a book hadn't worked. I'd been too restless to focus on the words on the screen, so it was all I could do to pick a show to stream online and binge it through the night.

I still sat there watching it when the front door opened in the early hours of the morning. When he found me sitting on the couch, he sighed, part relief and part frustration.

"You should have gone to bed," he chastised me.

"I tried, but I couldn't sleep." The admission came easy, but he made no move to close the gap between us. Anxiety rippled in my stomach, wondering if maybe I'd messed up the business enough that he would genuinely be angry with me. "What happened?"

"You don't have to worry about it," he yawned. "We've taken care of it."

"What does that mean?" I knew there was a snap to my voice. I hadn't meant to be angry, hadn't meant to give him sass, but I was so fucking tired, and I wouldn't be kept in the dark when it came to my own problems.

"They're going to let us know when he shows up," he strode for the stairs, and I followed after turning off the television.

"And what did you have to give them in exchange?"

"Samara—" he started, and I knew from the tone in his voice that he would blow me off. Tell me not to worry. Tell me it was business.

"He's my ex-husband. I'm the reason he thinks he has information at all, and I'm the only reason you're looking for him so desperately. There is zero chance that I'm going to just let you handle that! If he actually has information, what if he goes to someone else in the meantime? What if it could put you in jail? Or put Matteo in jail? That's *my fault.*"

"It's not your fault, Little Dove," he murmured, but I shook my head. Pain arched through me, and my heart twisted in my chest. The idea of leaving him, of having caused him pain or problems seemed so much harder after he'd told me he loved me. Like I'd never been meant to have it, and this was just one more thing pulling us apart. Like the universe had a sick sense of humor, because women like me didn't get to be happy. It just didn't happen for the girls from the wrong side of the tracks who had to fight their way out.

If I'd fought less, I could have ended up being one of Matteo's escorts. Maybe that was why I didn't blame them for the path they'd chosen, because I'd known it was largely luck that kept me from that fate. Luck and a brother who would have strangled me when he found out. I had no illusions that my brother wouldn't be familiar with that part of the business.

"It is, but maybe if I disappear from your life, so will Connor. There's no reason for you to concern yourself with him if I'm not here. I can just go to another city," I sighed, and my fingers toyed with the rings on my left hand. "I brought this problem into your life. It should be me who makes it go away."

"If you take off those rings, I'll have them surgically attached to your finger." I startled at the harshness in his voice. "This is my job. It is my job as your husband to protect you from all the bullshit, whether it's mine or yours. So you need to deal with that and let me fucking handle it."

He stripped off his jacket and took off his shoes. "But—"

"Samara, did I promise to love you when it was convenient? Or did I promise to love you through good and bad?" He unbuttoned his shirt, giving me a show as he threw our vows at me. I remembered them, but they were also tangled up in the web in my mind, given that I hadn't thought our marriage was real at the time. His pants followed, and he paused to study me, clearly waiting for my answer.

"Good and bad," I mumbled.

"This ain't that bad," he gave a brief chuckle. "I'm sure we'll have worse coming our way eventually. I need you to be strong, and I need you to be that rock you've always been for me. Let me come home and know that my wife has my back, that she's not going to get spooked by some drama or he said she said bullshit threat and try to leave me. Can you do that for me?"

I nodded, "I can do that." Shame filled me, I'd only promised not to leave two days before, and my instincts already had me running for the hills. "I'm sorry."

"Don't be sorry. You promised you wouldn't run, and here you are. You didn't leave even though I'm sure you wanted to. You waited for me to come home and you talked to me about the way you were feeling. That's all I can ask of you, *vita mia*." He touched his lips to my forehead, turning and striding for the bathroom. The shower came on, and I knew he wanted to clean the night off him. Crawling into bed finally, I sighed in comfort. Even the sound of the shower seemed like a relief, a reminder that he was home and we would figure it out.

When he finally crawled into bed and tugged me to rest my head on his chest, I fell asleep to the sound of his rhythmic breathing.

CHAPTER FORTY-THREE

SAMARA

I had no desire to go shopping, but having already arranged the date with Chiara, there was little choice in the matter. Lino and Emilio stood off to the side, Lino undoubtedly warning Emilio that if he lost me again, he'd strangle him judging by the fury on my husband's face. Chiara seemed blissfully ignorant to the tense conversation, waiting next to the car while they had it out. Her hand rubbed over her little belly, and I realized I couldn't wait for the day when I had a bump.

When I could openly rub my stomach, and no one would think twice or ask stupid questions. "Lino threw out my birth control," I confessed, and she turned startled eyes up to me.

She giggled furiously. "Oh God, what is it with Bellandi men?"

"At least Lino had the sense to make sure he did it in front of me. I guess at least I know what the manipulative bastard is up to unlike poor Ivory. I can't imagine what that must have felt like."

Chiara shrugged in response. "Being with men like ours, it's not a normal relationship. They can do what they want, when they want, and there's very little we can do about it. But there's something to be said for not having to stress about the kinds of decisions most married couples' debate, I think. I never have to wonder if he'll support me in a decision or if he'll resent me for it, because the asshole will let me know the minute I try to do something he doesn't like."

I laughed outright, jumping when Lino came up behind me and wrapped his arms around my waist. He watched his sister stroke her belly, and his fingers tightened on mine before they rubbed despite the impossibility of a pregnancy so soon.

"Be good," he murmured, kissing my cheek before he released me.

"I'll only spend half your money," I teased, holding up the black credit card he'd handed me that morning. "I plan on spoiling that baby. She's gotta love her Aunt Samara the mostest." His eyes warmed.

"In that case, spend it all. Just tell her it's from Uncle Lino too, yeah?" Chiara giggled, accepting the hug and kiss to the forehead that he gave her. "Samara doesn't like shopping. I expect you'll show her how it's done."

"Oh, you can count on me for that," she responded, stepping into the car as Emilio held the door open for her. I blew Lino a kiss before darting in after her, only to be thwarted when Lino's hands wrapped around my waist and hauled me back.

Screaming with laughter, I swung my hands behind me until he set me to my feet. "Where's my damn kiss?"

"Up your ass, that's where!" From the car, Chiara laughed hysterically. Emilio cleared his throat, averting his eyes as Lino grinned down at me. "Don't be such a Neanderthal."

Shaking his head briefly, he leaned down and kissed me sweetly, gently. Until his teeth bit down on my bottom lip in a nip that made me want to go back into the house with him. "Not fair," I pouted, and he patted my ass when I turned and climbed into the car. Emilio climbed into the passenger seat, letting Chiara's driver take us to the shops where I'd never bothered to attempt before. Even when Connor had insisted I dress appropriately to reflect on his family, I hadn't shopped high end. His trust fund tastes hadn't matched my bank account.

Now it seemed I didn't have anything to worry about, but I wondered if I'd ever shake the mentality that I didn't have enough money. The North Michigan shops located on Michigan Avenue on the Magnificent Mile had always seemed out of reach. Always *been* out of reach. Changing who I was and my more low-end tastes seemed absurd. Lino had fallen in love with my legging wearing ass, and he'd stay in love with me that way. I knew I'd only shop for high end clothes when I needed them for work or events with Lino, but I felt more likely to have him arrange a personal shopper.

Shopping was miserable.

I never would have guessed there might be a baby store there, but I guessed the women who shopped in those stores would or could be mothers too, even if they seemed like they belonged to another world.

"I've never seen Lino so happy," Chiara commented, and I smiled at her.

"Yeah?"

"Yeah. You've always done that for him though. I'm so glad the two of you finally pulled your heads out of your asses and got your shit together," she said, and I was shocked by how straightforward she seemed. The girl I knew before had been bookish and quiet. Totally and completely drowned and suffocated by her father's rules and stipulations for her life.

"Married life seems to be treating you well," I commented.

She giggled happily. "I got so lucky. When Gabriele arranged the marriage, I thought for sure he'd condemned me to a life with a man three times my age and cruel. The fact that I ended up with someone who grew to love me and encourage me is a miracle. Hopefully our kids won't have to go through what I did, with the arranged marriage. I can't imagine Lino or Matteo even supporting such an archaic concept when they refused to accept matches of their own."

"They seem intent on creating a new kind of family." I admired them for it, that some of their closest family weren't related by blood or marriage at all and they still had the utmost trust in each other. Much more trust than they had with their actual blood, that was for sure.

Chiara's driver pulled up in front of the building, and Emilio hopped out to take us in while he parked the car. "I'll meet you up there," he commented to Chiara, and she nodded with a smile. She trusted the man's judgment to leave her with Emilio and given that Lino had hired him to look after me I had to agree with the assessment.

Even if there was something off in the way he seemed to get lost in thought when he looked at me as he helped me out of the car.

I knew I should mention it to Lino, but it didn't feel hostile. If anything, it just seemed confused. Like he didn't quite know what to make of me.

Since I returned the sentiment, I just gave him a reassuring smile and stepped up next to Chiara to chat as we walked.

It didn't take long to recognize the store, the strollers in the window made it obvious which one would be for a baby. Looking at the little bump forming, I wondered if it wasn't too early. Seeming to sense my question, she turned to me with a sheepish grin. "I'm a little overexcited. There's nothing I've ever wanted more than to be a mother."

"It makes sense," I admitted. "Your father never would have let you be anything else, I imagine."

"There's that," she agreed, but the little smile on her face took off the sting that should have accompanied her words. "But, even still, I didn't lay in bed thinking about being a model or an astronaut. I laid there and I thought about my mother. How much I missed her, and how much I wanted to give my kids everything I'd missed out on. That was everything I wanted, and I told myself I could live with an unhappy marriage if I had that. Having a happy marriage and a baby on the way is like a dream come true." We strolled through the store, and I watched as she paused to run her hands along the wood of a white crib. The curved back hinted at a vintage design, but it was clearly new and modern in all other ways. I wanted to run my fingers along the curves with her when her eyes glazed over. "This reminds me of the crib I had. I've seen pictures."

"I think it's probably perfect then," I sighed, and she glanced down the aisle to look at the others in the line before she nodded with tears in her eyes.

"Mom had a glider. The fabric was this pale green on the seat. Do you think I'd be able to find one like it?" The gliders were much more comfortable looking and seemed more like recliners than I imagined her mother's must have been, but I swore if we couldn't find one in store, I'd find one and get my mother to help me fix it up. She deserved to have everything she dreamed of, and I wanted to help give it to her.

"I don't see one here, but we'll keep looking. I promise." It amazed me how quickly I adopted Lino's family as my own, when I'd always been content to try and keep them on the fringes of my heart. Like I'd known that I could never have them fully even though I wanted them. "Do you know what you're having?" I asked to try and alleviate the suddenly tense mood.

"A girl," she said. "The early blood test said it's a girl. I couldn't wait to find out," she laughed. I took her hand, darting to the baby clothes that hung from the displays in the center of the store. The little purple dress that had caught my attention seemed to beckon me, and I held it up for her.

"It's perfect. You should buy it; in case you have a girl." The words made my stomach clench as I looked down at the fabric, but I shook my head.

"I can't start shopping for clothes before I'm even pregnant. It's perfect for your little cupcake though." She took it, and the way her fingers clenched the fabric told me it was the first time she'd allowed herself to shop for clothes. The first time she'd let herself feel the reality of her pregnancy in such a tangible way.

"Thank you for sharing this with me." I reached out a hand, touching the little belly that seemed to beg me to touch it constantly.

"Thank you for finally letting me in." I swallowed, sucking back the tears as I realized just how many people I'd kept at arm's length. How alone I'd felt because of my own walls.

I'd never been alone.

I'd just been too blind to see it.

CHAPTER FORTY-FOUR

LINO

I hated work. I'd always loved it but knowing that Samara and my sister were out shopping on a Saturday while I got stuck working made me anxious. Enzo picked up on it. Of course, the pain in my ass.

"You're like a little slacker now," he poked me in the arm. "Always wanting to be home with the wife."

"I'm too old for this shit. I don't want to work weekends, and soon I won't have to." I shrugged, nodding my head at the manager-in-training. He came around quickly, catching on to the fact that I wanted him to take on tasks I never would have done. He needed to keep busy, and I would still keep track of most of the oversight stuff from home. I just needed someone to be in charge in the evenings.

I knew I'd still be busy, what with Matteo already eyeing a luxury apartment building that he wanted to buy. I knew nothing about being a landlord, but he relied on me to figure it out as I went. So I would.

It didn't stop me from wishing I could be home, from wishing I could convince Samara to quit her job once she was pregnant so that I could work from home and spend time with my family. My father would lose his shit if he knew I put family before the business.

It only tempted me more.

"Seriously, what has that woman done to you?" Enzo laughed, clapping me on the back. "Never seen you so distracted."

"That's because I've never had that woman waiting for me," I grinned at him, not even bothering to hide the happiness that flooded me.

His elbow in my gut made me wince, but I glanced down to the bar below.

"Look!" he hissed, his voice going low like a gossiping girl. I leaned over the rail, glancing down to see Scar taking a seat at the bar. It wasn't uncommon for him to come in for a drink during the day on his occasional day off when Ivory stayed at the Estate, but he usually came up and hung out with us while we worked.

Sitting at the bar never happened.

Sitting next to a woman never happened.

I couldn't get a good look at her, no matter how I tried, her back stayed to the VIP level. But there was no mistaking the way she radiated pure class in a pencil skirt and blouse, with raven hair that slid down to her waist. Scar bought her a drink, turning his undivided attention to the woman.

"Who do you think *that* is?" Enzo asked me.

I shrugged, even if something about her slender build seemed familiar. I couldn't place her, try as I might. Not without the face.

"Maybe she's one of the girls?" I asked. Enzo pursed his lip in thought, shaking his head after a minute.

"I'd remember that hair," he said. I didn't doubt he would, such was Enzo's memory about little details like that.

I watched for a moment, and when she finally turned her head to the side to face the bartender, I got a good look. "Fuck," I hissed. "Doesn't matter."

"Who is she?"

"No one that Scar will ever let himself touch if he finds out who she is. She's too clean for him. He'll think he doesn't deserve her." I shook my head, wishing I could get through to the stubborn man who had dedicated himself to protecting Ivory. Who'd given his life for hers without hesitation, and then somehow miraculously survived.

"I don't know man; do you see the way he's looking at her?"

"I don't blame him. She's one Hell of a woman. Only an idiot would let her walk away," I grunted, tapping the bar at the edge of the VIP area twice and heading for my office. I needed a drink if I had to watch Scar sabotage the best thing that would ever happen to him. Enzo followed, though he seemed hesitant to leave the show.

He didn't know Scar like I did, didn't know the history he had and all the ways it had left a mark on him. He'd watch all of us find our women, believing that we deserved it. In his mind, we'd given him everything. Given him a second chance at life. Pulled him off the streets and away from the mother who couldn't be bothered to care about him.

Matteo had already started trying to arrange a match for him, as his status as Ivory's bodyguard earned him a wife. But nothing would work, nothing would convince the man that he could have a woman by his side and not stain her with the things he'd done.

The things he'd survived on the streets.

Maybe the woman downstairs would be enough to pull his head out of his ass.

But more likely he'd hightail it without touching her.

Within minutes he'd come up the steps, joining Enzo and me. The look on his face confirmed everything I would ever need to know.

"Who was that?" Enzo asked, grinning at him like he'd found a juicy piece of gossip.

He sighed, looking down at the floor below and undoubtedly staring at her where even from my desk I could see she sat with her head hanging and dejected. "Someone who deserves far better than me."

Enzo's eyes glanced to me, but I shook my head.

One day, I'd force him to see that he wasn't tainted by his childhood. That he could have a life of his own and not give up his loyalty to the Bellandi's.

It was just not that day.

"Why don't you go ahead and give Ryker a call?" I asked him, putting a stop to whatever prying Enzo might have been ready to unleash on Scar. "I need an update on Connor. See what he's found." I did need the update, in all fairness. I'd intended to make the call myself, so that Ryker could hear the frustration in my voice again and know exactly what was at stake.

My sanity.

I needed him to be found. The threat he posed to Samara was just too much for me to tolerate. *Any* threat to her was too much, but the piece of shit who'd hurt her would have a special place in Hell waiting for him when I finally let him die.

Scar cleared his throat, brushing off the lingering melancholy that the woman he so clearly wanted had prompted in favor of going back into business mode for my sake. "You got it, Lino. Mia Romano just walked in. I know you were looking to have a word with her and maybe string her up in the warehouse," Scar said with an uneasy chuckle. There wasn't much that we drew the line at, but hurting women was generally one of them.

But sometimes it was unavoidable for the ones who really deserved to suffer.

Mia's crimes hadn't warranted her death, but they did warrant her getting out of my fucking club. "Send her up and then call Ryker from Enzo's office while I deal with her bullshit," I ordered, pouring myself a drink.

I didn't bother sitting, lingering at the window of my office and staring down into the club to watch as Scar approached Mia. She flinched when he barked at her and pointed up to my office, and her eyes were big when she followed his finger up. She couldn't see me, but from the look on her face I would have guessed that she knew damn well I was watching.

She heaved out a heavy breath and nodded before making her way to the staircase. I didn't move from my spot at the window as I sipped my whiskey.

The sound of her heels thumping against the floor told me the moment she stepped up to the door.

"Lino—" she sighed, anxiety in her voice.

"I think Mr. Bellandi will do just fine. Let's not pretend that we're friends." I spun to face her, setting my drink down on the corner of my desk and leveling her with a glare that I knew would make Matteo proud—all cold intensity and not a trace of any emotion. My temper normally ran hot. I usually lost myself to the fire of it and showed too much of myself, but I'd worked to school my features.

I'd learned, and I tossed all of that effort in her face.

"I just worried about her. I wanted her to understand—"

"That you think I'm the type to fuck around on my wife? Please Ms. Romano, explain to me how my sex life has ever been any of your business? Fucking my father does not make you my mother." I sneered at her, daring her to deny the accusation.

She'd long ago thought she might have a relationship with my father, that she might be wife number three. Instead, he'd married Trista and kept Mia as one of his regular side pieces. Somehow, she tolerated that place in his life, but blamed Trista for it.

I imagined she hated Samara purely on principle for being the wife that she had never had the opportunity to be.

A Bellandi wife.

"Your father broke Trista. I thought to save Samara from the same fate when you inevitably go back to the girls and the ease of your no-strings relationships. She should be prepared for what you'll do to her—"

"Don't speak like you know the first thing about me or my relationship with Samara. I wouldn't have married her if I didn't have every intention of staying loyal to her. I married her because she's the only woman I've ever loved."

Her eyes widened as I stepped around the desk to approach her. "But your father said that you only married her to protect her! He said that it wasn't a real marriage."

I smiled. The fact that she still trusted my father after all her years with him and his lies was incredible. "He played you. Used you to toy with Samara and hope that he could drive a wedge between us, but he can't. You can't. So, you've thrown yourself on the cross for nothing. Samara is still my wife. In fact, we're closer than ever thanks to you."

I leaned back on my desk, perching on the edge and crossing my arms over my chest. "I'm glad that she was strong enough to handle what I said. If what you say is true, I really hope you manage to be happy together. I'll believe it when I see it, but maybe you'll surprise me." She turned, striding for the door like the conversation was done.

Like there wouldn't be consequences for interfering in my marriage. "You won't have the opportunity to see it," I said, and her body flinched like I'd struck her. "You're fired. I highly suggest you leave Chicago before my father finds another way to use you in what's coming if he doesn't learn to shut his mouth. I want you out of my club, and if I ever see you again, I won't be so lenient. My wife does not exist to you. I do not exist to you. Understood?" I growled, and the tears in her eyes as she turned to look back at me weren't fake.

She'd invested years into the club, helping build it from the ground up.

"I understand," she mumbled, hurrying out the door and disappearing down the hall.

With a sigh, I followed. But my destination wasn't to leave.

I went for Enzo's office, and the sound of Scar's pissed off voice didn't bode well for news of Connor's whereabouts.

When we found him, I was going to cut him for every day he made me and my family hunt him down.

I just hoped he survived long enough to really, truly suffer.

CHAPTER FORTY-FIVE

SAMARA

"Hey mommy," I murmured, leaning up to kiss her cheek as she strolled into the kitchen with Lino at her back. My body winced with soreness as I stretched up onto my toes. Sadie had kicked my ass at our last session, and I would swear the muscles in my toes hurt.

I didn't even know toes had muscles before her.

"Hey, pretty girl. I'm so happy Sunday dinner is a thing again now that you two are settled. You have no idea how much I look forward to Lino's cooking during the week." She slipped onto a stool next to me, and I eyed her brightly colored skirt curiously. The tribal pattern was stunning and suited her bohemian look well.

"You're welcome anytime, Hattie," Lino murmured.

"Don't tell her that." I scowled at him. "She'll be here every night. When she tells you she loves your cooking, she really means, move me into the spare bedroom and call me mommy if it means you'll feed me."

My mother howled with laughter at my side, wrapping an arm around my shoulders and tugging me into her side dramatically.

Like it wasn't true.

"She's right," she agreed, giving Lino a beaming smile. "I best stick to once a week. I wouldn't want to intrude on the newlyweds." The buzzer sounded at the front, alerting us to the fact that our other guest had arrived at the gate. The guard was under instructions to let him through, so I knew he'd follow soon after. My stomach knotted with tension, because while the last interaction with him hadn't been hostile, it also hadn't had mom present to poke at it and Yavin and Lino still needed to have a conversation.

I hadn't been sure he'd come at all.

"That will be Yavin," Lino said, going to the door. He waited for the bell to ring at the front door.

"What's got you all twisted up?" Mom asked, and I looked at her out of the corner of my eye.

"Yavin wasn't exactly supportive of Lino and I becoming a thing."

"Oh, pish posh, I'll grab that boy around the ears and knock some sense into him. I swear, all the people in the damn world, and that boy was the only one who couldn't see you two were crazy about each other. Aside from you two, anyway." Mom's swinging arm almost caught me in the face, her enthusiasm so intense that I feared for my life. I slid off the stool, deciding it would probably be safer to put some distance between us.

If Yavin pissed her off, I'd lose my head when the arms got going.

I did not feel like being collateral damage.

When the bell rang, Lino yanked the door open. For once, I wished he would have let me answer it, but I understood his need to present himself as a barrier. As much as it infuriated me, the man needed to stake a claim, even with my brother.

I was a sister and daughter second now.

A wife first.

Soon enough, a *mother* first.

I swallowed down my apprehension, listening for Yavin to greet Lino. "Hey," he said simply.

"Hey," Lino grunted, stepping aside to let him in. Yavin went for Mom first, always respectful and pressing a kiss to her cheek before he turned his attention to me. By the time he got there, Lino had taken up residence in the kitchen, checking the dinner he'd put in the oven.

"Sis," Yavin murmured, kissing my cheek like he had Mom's. "We good?"

I rolled my eyes at the typical male show of making up without ever talking about the problem. "Sure." Even if I wanted to nag at him and rage that he'd betrayed me for calling Lino, he'd done it for the best reasons, and it had worked out just fine.

Lino loved me. I couldn't be mad about any of the circumstances that brought that knowledge to my life. I knew that a conversation still had to happen between the boys, but as far as I was concerned, I could move on if he did. "You good with them, Mom?" he asked, and I sighed before dropping into my seat.

"Don't be stupid," she spat. "Of course I'm good with them together. Only one who didn't see it coming is you." Lino snorted as he stood from checking the chicken in the oven.

"Do you need help?" I asked, looking for something to do with my hands.

"I'd like dinner to be edible, *vita mia,*" he teased. "Why don't you grab a wine?

White." I nodded moving to the wine fridge and picking the first white I saw. Lino smiled down at me as he popped the cork, and I knew he wondered if I'd ever put any thought into what wine we drank.

I wouldn't.

"If you wanted a domestic wife, you chose way wrong," I laughed, leaning up to kiss him briefly. I felt Yavin's eyes on us but chose to ignore it. I wouldn't pretend Lino wasn't my husband, wouldn't pretend we were all just friends still to make him more comfortable. I needed to settle into a normal and force him to be comfortable.

I didn't anticipate the way Lino wrapped his arms around me, staring down at me like I'd hung the moon and stars. "There was never a choice, Little Dove." The softness in his voice made me blush, knowing that he referred to the fact that we'd both known we were it for each other when we were too young to understand.

Circumstances had kept us apart.

But fuck the circumstances. We'd found our way to each other eventually.

With a blush still on my cheeks, I turned away from Lino and gathered the wine glasses from the cupboard. I poured out four glasses. When I lifted my glass to take a sip, Lino surprised me by clearing his throat. He lifted his own glass, biting his lip briefly before his eyes landed on mine and he let out a breath. "May everyone be lucky enough to hold their dreams in their arms."

I stared up at him, my throat closing with the need to cry as tears stung my eyes. Mom's sniffle beside me almost tore my attention away from Lino, but when Lino's thumb stroked away the tear that slid down my cheek, I couldn't have looked away if I'd wanted to. "You're my dream," I whispered up at him. His broad grin stole my breath, and then he sealed his lips over mine in a kiss that lingered more than Yavin would deem appropriate.

I couldn't be bothered to care. Not when I turned away to face them and saw nothing but pure joy in my mother's face as she dabbed at her nose. I took my sip of wine, resisting the urge to melt into a puddle on the floor. Yavin gave me a hesitant smile and nod, but his eyes hardened when he turned his attention to Lino.

He didn't say a word, but let Mom guide the conversation to safer topics while I set the table in the dining room.

I just had to hope that when he finally talked to Lino, that he could stop being such a brat.

For a full-grown man, he was still ridiculously talented as a brat.

CHAPTER FORTY-SIX

LINO

I waited for it all night. We all knew it was coming, and no matter how much Hattie tried to distract from it, there would never be any chance of any of us not noticing the way Yavin seemed impatient.

"Can we talk?" he finally asked after we'd brought all the dishes to the kitchen. I hated him for making Samara have to clean, because I didn't usually let her lift a finger.

"We've got it," Hattie murmured, giving me a shove to go chat with Yavin. I tried to calm down, because the man had never shown any inclination of loving a woman. He didn't understand what it was to want to give a woman an easy life.

One day he would, I hoped.

Else I'd have to kick his ass for mistreating his wife.

"Yeah," I agreed, guiding him to my office at the end of the hall. It felt like I never spent any time there now that Samara was in my life, because I preferred working in the living room where I could reach out and touch her. I turned on the light when I stepped into the room, turning to lean my ass against my desk and cross my arms over my chest while I stared at him. He ran a hand through his dark, copper-tinted hair, grimacing at me.

"Is this real for you? Or are you just playing games?" His voice was full of disbelief as if he still couldn't wrap his head around the fact that I'd married his sister. Hopefully my baby in her belly would make it feel real, real fast.

I glared at him. "When have you ever known me to play games?"

He nodded but pursed his lips in frustration. "She's been in love with you as long as I can remember," he admitted, and it surprised me that he'd noticed.

Yavin wasn't the most observant, and his mind had always been so wrapped up in trying to prove himself to Matteo and I that he neglected his family too much.

It had always been the one point of contention between us. Him wanting success more than anything, and me wishing I had his family. We'd been at odds, without ever really addressing it. "The feeling is mutual, Vin," I announced. "It always has been."

"Your father?" he asked, because where Samara *thought* she knew what kind of man Gabriele Bellandi was, Yavin actually knew. He'd seen him in action, seen him shoot a man point blank in cold blood, seen him slit a man's throat, seen him willing to gun down entire *families* if it meant he got the revenge he wanted. Matteo had put a stop to it when his father died, but the years before Matteo had been brutal.

Ugly.

War.

I hoped we never had to defend ourselves against enemies like that again, but I knew it was probably a pipe dream. The life of a Bellandi wasn't a peaceful one. "Said he'd kill her or sell her if I touched her."

"Shit," Yavin groaned, scrubbing a hand over his face. "Why didn't you ever say anything? I could have helped protect her."

"He had no reason to go near her. I didn't touch her until after I moved her in here. We both know Gabriele likes to posture, but he doesn't have any power now. Matteo stripped him of what little he had left the minute he pulled a gun on Ivory." He stepped over to my bookcase, pulling a little trinket Samara had given me off the shelf. A butterfly encased in amber, it took my breath away every time I looked at it and remembered the Christmas she'd given it to me. I didn't know what it was about it that had drawn her to it, but I knew what it meant to me.

It might not have been a dove, but it was a winged creature locked in a golden, gilded cage. It had felt like the gift was a declaration, her way of telling me it would be okay to clip her wings and make her mine.

He set it back down, glancing around the office that held pieces of Samara everywhere. "I never saw it," he admitted. "How did I not see how you felt about her?"

"You didn't want to think about it." I shrugged, because I'd always known it was true. I tried to imagine how awkward I'd feel if he'd married Chiara.

I'd probably have strangled him.

"Best friend or not, you hurt her, and I'll kick your fucking ass. I don't give a shit if you're a Bellandi. Ivory will have my back, which means Matteo will too."

"If I hurt her, I'll lay down and die," I admitted. "I'm never going to hurt her like that, Vin. I'm not perfect. We'll fight, and we'll have misunderstandings. But her heart and her body are safe with me. I think you know that."

He nodded briefly. "Good."

"There's one last thing we need to discuss before we put this shit in the past where it belongs," I said, and I shook my head in aggravation. Yavin nodded in return with a sigh. He knew damn well what was coming. "If you ever take my wife away from her security again and let hours pass before you at least tell me she's safe? We're done, Vin. You will not manage *Tease*. You will not get near Samara. I will cut you from our lives and never look back. You're my brother now, but you always have been. Do not put me in the position to be scared shit-less and wondering if she's dead in a ditch somewhere ever again."

"I got it. I knew it was wrong, she was just—" he paused. "You know how she is when she's pissed. Determined as all Hell, but she was at her breaking point. I've never seen her so close to shattering. I should have texted you and said she was safe with me but needed time. I'll do that if it happens again." Then he turned and strolled out of the room.

It wasn't a blessing.

But it wasn't a condemnation either. It would have to do for the time being.

CHAPTER FORTY-SEVEN

SAMARA

I wanted to know where we were going, wanted to understand why Lino had expected me to put on something nice but casual and dragged me out the door. The jeans clung to my legs and my hands sweated as I rubbed them over and over. He sat silent next to me, and while there was no anxiety pouring off him, I still wanted to force him to tell me what happened.

He didn't surprise me. He knew I hated surprises.

Always had and always would.

I'd been that kid who found my way into every Christmas present stash that ever existed. I'd have never slept in the days leading up to Christmas if I didn't.

Eventually when my mom realized what I did every year, she'd started letting me pick out my own damn gifts. It was easier for everyone involved.

But the last place, the absolute last place I could have ever expected to pull up was *The Bird Lounge.* My brain latched onto the fact that it was Tuesday, and open mic night had already drawn a huge crowd. "We're here to listen to music?" I asked, my voice hopeful.

Lino ignored me, stepping out of the car and going to the trunk. By the time he came to my door, he held my guitar case in his hand. "Come on, Little Dove. Come sing with me."

I took his hand, even if I wanted to run. It was time to trust him, time to let him shove me over the edge into the life that I needed to start living again.

The truth was that no matter how much I feared getting up on stage, I missed it horribly. Missed the way the crowd could get lost in the music and the way *I* got lost in it. I craved it and needed it.

I wasn't whole without it.

Stepping in through the front doors, I never could have prepared myself for the crowd that had formed. It was insane, and I'd gone to a ton of open mic nights. I'd never seen it so crowded.

Rex rushed over, taking my guitar in one hand and my hand in the other. "Thank God, I thought you weren't going to show." He tugged me up to the empty stage, sitting me down in one of the chairs that waited in the center of the stage.

"What's going on?" I asked him.

"Sugar, all these people are here to listen to you sing. They remembered you, and I have been talking about this for a week. Time's come for you to sing again and say fuck that stupid ass man who went and told you that you couldn't." Lino took a seat next to me on the stage as Rex thrust my guitar into my arms.

"I—uh, I'm sorry guys. I have no clue what's going on," I announced to a crowd that laughed in response.

"My wife had no clue we were coming tonight," Lino grinned at them. "And you'll have to forgive her. It's been a long time since she sang in public. I apologize for this, but to help her shake off the rust, I'm going to put my ass right in the front row." The crowd laughed with him as he turned and sat in the chair right in front of the stage dramatically. I laughed at the women who screamed like he was their entire world. He had that effect.

He turned to me, whispering the name of a song I'd sung for him years ago, before Connor had destroyed my confidence and made me feel like my voice wasn't worth listening to. Before I'd stopped singing altogether.

I took my pick in my hands, looking down at the purple color and the white dove that stared back at me. A piano played in the background, starting the song before I could take a moment to catch my breath.

Lino caught my eyes, nodding at me. I wanted to hate him for the way he'd ambushed me. For the fact that I hadn't had time to get my thoughts together before they'd shoved me on the stage.

I knew he'd done it intentionally so I couldn't back out.

When my cue came, I plucked the guitar strings, and started singing at the same time. My voice was too soft, too hesitant.

I knew it, the crowd knew it, but they gave me time to figure it out. It suited the song, but there was no way it would catch the attention of such a big audience.

Lino grinned at me from the front row, offering me silent support that bolstered me despite my nerves. He knew what I needed, knew that I would never come around to stepping up on the stage if left to my own devices.

So he'd gone out of his way to make the decision for me, to guide me through my nerves, and to support me through the aftermath.

Anything for you, Little Dove.

He didn't speak the words, didn't need to. It was all right there in his eyes as he stared down at me. Of all the amazing, thoughtful gifts he'd given me.

He gave me back my voice.

This was my favorite.

I found my voice, singing to him about a woman who'd been needing her man. I found my strength, and I knew that I would always need him. The crowd melted away until there was nothing but the two of us.

I sniffed back my tears when the song ended. I stood, stepping up to the mic and feeling like slow and soft just wouldn't do. I needed to sing and really take my life back.

The second song came out strong from the get-go, the guitar riffs accentuating the way I needed my voice to sound as I started the song that resonated in my soul in that moment.

A woman who survived.

A woman who fought back.

And a woman who kicked the assholes who told her no straight in the teeth.

I didn't usually sing ballads or songs that required me to belt my voice out there, because even when I'd performed regularly, I hadn't been confident enough in my voice to really project it.

But fuck that shit.

I gave it everything I had, poured my heart and soul into the words and the lyrics and the guitar.

And when the song ended, I jumped off the stage and straight into Lino's arms while the crowd cheered. I didn't care, because even though they'd been a necessary part, I hadn't sung for them.

I sang for me.

I sang for all the beaten and the bruised.

"Take me home," I whispered, and Lino nodded to Rex who gathered up my guitar and pick and handed it to me. Winding my arms around Lino's neck and my legs around his waist, I let him carry me out to the car. I didn't care what they thought as they whistled.

I had everything that mattered in my arms.

❋❋❋

Jasper forgave me for the absences the previous week, without even bothering to ask what had been so important that I had to take off unannounced.

Just more proof that there was something up with his nosey ass.

The Jasper I knew and loved would have used any excuse to poke himself into my business, and I'd given him a pretty damn good one. I tried to be patient with him, but after the way I'd taken back my confidence at *Bird Lounge*, there was no way in Hell I was letting him off the hook so easily. When we went over my notes from the previous month, he spaced out.

He was lost.

"Alright, what gives?" I asked, slamming the folder down on his desk and plopping into the seat in front of it.

"What do you mean?" he asked.

"I disappeared from work out of nowhere and nobody could find me. You yelled at me for being inconsiderate and didn't ask a single question after that. The Jasper I know would have assaulted me to get answers, for shit's sake. You aren't paying attention to work. You're distracted in a way I've never—" I cut off, thinking about how much Lino had changed after we'd gotten together.

He complained about being unable to focus, but more than that about not *wanting* to focus.

"It's nothing," he lied.

"What's her name?" I said, sliding to the edge of my chair and looking at him so intently I wanted to peer inside his soul. For once, it felt like I would be the nosy one. I freaking loved it.

"It's no one you know. Trust me."

"Hmmm," I hummed. "Okay, so give me the deal. Are you in love? Is that why you're so distracted?" He tapped his pen on the desk, trying to avoid my eyes. I waited, even though I wanted to jump down his throat.

"I don't know. I really like her, but I haven't been totally honest with her. I've kept a pretty major secret." He winced, and I tried to calm my breathing. After the gambling secret Connor had kept, secrets hit me deep. I didn't want to think of my friend and boss as capable of deceiving a woman like that.

I fiddled with my folder, straightening the pages inside it. "What kind of secret?"

"My name. She has no clue who I really am."

My jaw dropped to what felt like the floor. "Um, okay. So she doesn't know that you're richer than God and Chicago's Most Eligible Bachelor, is that what you're saying?" He stood from his seat, running his hands through his hair.

Shit, that was bad.

He'd messed up the perfect hair.

"Yeah, that. Or you know, what I look like." The admission looked painful, and I could imagine why. I'd known he felt at a loss with the dating pool, with trying to find a woman who wasn't after his money, status, or just a good lay.

But what the fuck?

"So what does she know about you? And how is that even possible?" I asked.

"Everything else! Just not my name or face. I met her on a dating app, but I uploaded some random guy's photo." Another wince.

"You have to tell her! If you don't tell her, and she somehow puts it together, she's gone, Jasper. If you want this woman permanently, then you've got to find a way to tell her and to fix it."

"I'll think of something. Maybe, or maybe I'll just continue to bury my head in the fucking sand like the coward I am," he sighed, the drama he so rarely showed evident all over his face. He sat back in the black leather chair, dropping his head into his hands. "Hit me with the numbers. I'm listening this time."

I snorted a laugh, unable to resist the urge to break into giggles. "Well, everyone's numbers are up except for one person."

"Who is it this time?"

"You, Jasper. You fucking sucked this month. Get your shit together, yeah? Whether you have to walk away or tell her just do something. You just need to decide if she's worth fighting for. I've got to tell you, if it was me? You'd have a Hell of an uphill battle to win me back after something like that."

"Ughhh," he groaned. I stood from my seat, feeling like I'd accomplished my duty of poking my nose where it didn't belong. Except in this case, it had been needed. The man was a floundering mess and needed help.

"It's cute, you know. You meeting her that way when nobody would ever expect it. It will make a good story to tell your kids one day," I said as I strolled for the door.

"Fuck, kids? Can I get through the real introduction first maybe?"

"Sure. Keep telling yourself that you're going to accept anything other than her in your life permanently. Mark my words, Jasper. You're going to marry her one day."

Leaving him gaping after me thoroughly entertained me.

By the time I hit my desk I was grinning from ear to ear as I settled back into work.

It was going to be a good day.

I just knew it.

CHAPTER FORTY-EIGHT

SAMARA

I officially loved weekends. It was rare that Lino left me to go to work, and sometimes he'd bring me along.

But not that day.

He was all mine, and I couldn't wait to just be with him for the day. "What do you want to do?" he asked. I hummed through my yoga, singing casually as I stretched up toward the ceiling in a standing side bend. Lino smiled at me, and I knew he appreciated my hums. My songs.

It came so easily since he'd taken me to the *Bird Lounge*. Like we'd finally tackled the last of my demons and moved forward into just being fucking happy and comfortable in my own skin.

"We don't have to do anything." I shrugged. "I like being with you. We could stay here, or we could go see Ivory and Luna. I never did get to see you smoosh on her the last time. Ivory says we should call you Cousin Smooshie."

He chuckled, dropping his fork to his plate and squeezing the bridge of his nose as he finished his breakfast. "Cousin Smooshie? I'd hate to know what Don and Scar are then."

"Don is Pop-Pop." I laughed, knowing it would have driven the man mad as a hatter when we'd been kids, but it seemed like he was willing to tolerate a whole new level of affection where Luna was concerned. "Scar is Captain Snuggles." I couldn't help my own roar of laughter even as I said the words. The thought of the massive man with the scar on his face and the scars in his soul as being Captain Snuggles was just too much. I didn't know him well, since he tended to be mostly a silent sentry when I spent time with Ivory and Sadie. Well, when he wasn't showing Ivory casual displays of sisterly affection that made my heart

468

ache. The bond they had was ten times what I had with Yavin, without the blood to tie them together.

If he treated his boss's wife with such heartfelt love, I could only imagine what he would give to his wife when he one day married.

"Fuck's sake," Lino grunted, standing to take care of his plate as he finished his breakfast. I ate another bite of my omelet contentedly. "You do realize we're hardened criminals, right? Not teddy bears for your entertainment."

I shrugged. "You don't seem particularly hard to me." Stepping off my mat after my last stretch, I chuckled when his groin pressed against my ass.

"Are you sure about that?" The giggle that came from my parted lips felt like pure happiness, and I never wanted the moment of bliss to end.

But the ringing of Lino's cellphone in his back pocket drew him away with a squeeze to my hips. "Yeah?" he grunted into the phone. "You're sure?" He sighed. "I'm on my way."

"It's okay," I reassured him, because he looked hesitant to leave me. I knew shit happened; work happened.

"Connor showed back up to discuss terms with the guy we made a deal with. We're going to go grab him." It didn't escape my notice that he avoided names when he talked about these people, only ever giving me vague concepts of what went on in that part of his life. My heart warmed, because I knew without a doubt that it was mostly about protecting me. The less I knew, the better.

"Okay. Just be safe. I can't lose you," I whispered, stepping up to press a kiss to his cheek.

"You'll be okay?" he asked, and the hesitance in his voice made that warm heart swell. I wanted to show him just how okay I would be, but there wasn't time.

"It's a beautiful day, so I think I'll do some more yoga outside. I'm so sore from Sadie working me over, the stretching helps. I won't leave the property, of course, but—"

"That's fine," he grunted. "Emilio is on duty. So I'll just let him know on my way out that you'll be outside so he can keep an eye out."

He turned, dashing up the stairs to get dressed. Obviously wearing a suit would be of critical importance when grabbing someone to take to an undisclosed location and kill them. I tried not to think about it.

Tried not to think about what it would be like for Lino to come home and for me to see the blood on his clothes, knowing it was my ex-husband's. Regardless of the way our marriage had ended, I'd shared my bed with him. Given him pieces of myself that I'd never shared with anyone but he and Lino.

It seemed sort of poetic in a really fucked up way that the man who killed him would be the only one who knew me better.

CHAPTER FORTY-NINE

LINO

I couldn't believe it was almost over, that Connor was almost out of our lives and his debt wouldn't threaten my woman ever again. It felt like we could finally move on with our lives, settle into a real routine.

I hopped out of the car with a smile on my face as soon as I got to the abandoned warehouse where the meet was set. Matteo and the rest of the guys came out of the woodwork, already waiting on me.

Ryker grinned, tossing me a pistol. Like I hadn't brought my own.

He didn't have much use for them, given his preference for torture and bathing in the blood of his enemies, but even he had to admit in situations like this they came in handy. He took one side, Matteo at the other, and with the rest of our guys behind us we shoved open the warehouse doors. Our contact, Gerald of all the fucking names, stood from the table and backed the fuck away as fast as could be.

"He's all yours. This means we're square, right?" The weaselly bastard asked Matteo as he made for the side door. Connor never turned to look at me, his suit clad body and blond hair setting off all the rage inside me.

"Is this some kind of fucking joke?" I asked, stepping forward to spin the bastard in his chair. Brown eyes stared up at me, full of fear and trembling. Brown eyes and about five years too young if I had to guess.

"What do you mean?" The way Gerald's brow furrowed made me hang my head in frustration.

"That isn't Connor Walsh, you fuck. Where is he?" Ryker growled at the loan shark.

I met Matteo's wide eyes when Gerald answered. "That's the man who made the deal with me. If that's not Connor Walsh, then who is he?"

"Fuck!" Ryker grunted, stepping up beside me as I went for the door.

"Samara," I said, and he nodded. There was only one reason someone would pretend to be a man I wanted dead. Fear and fury filled me in equal measure as I stormed outside.

We'd been stupid enough to fall for a fucking diversion and left my wife with only one guard to protect her.

I dug my phone out of my pocket, dialing her number to tell her to get inside.

To get to the panic room.

But it rang and rang and rang.

She was fine; she'd just left her phone in the house.

No matter how many times I told myself those same words, wincing when Ryker gunned the car and we sped off, I didn't believe them. Not for one second.

"She'll be okay," Ryker said, but even he didn't believe that. "She's tough." At least the latter was true.

But fuck. If anything happened to her, I'd burn the world to the ground.

CHAPTER FIFTY

SAMARA

The grass seemed to poke through the spandex of my workout leggings. They were the only pair I owned still, and I needed to invest in more, if I would keep up with the weekly sessions with Sadie after Lino dealt with Connor. Even though my entire body had hurt after the first couple, I found myself looking forward to the next one now. To the addictive rush of energy that followed the hard work out. I loved the way my body hardened to a more solid mass that still looked like me, and I loved the reaction of the men at the gym when I managed to do a move Sadie taught me.

Eventually, I fully expected to let her teach me to kick box. The gym was mostly filled with male boxers, but Sadie thoroughly advocated kickboxing for any of her female clients since it provided a whole-body workout. After Lino left, I'd pushed myself right out the door. I needed the distraction, needed to not think about the fact that he may endanger himself to protect me.

If he was caught because of me I'd never forgive myself.

If he was killed because of me, I'd die right along with him.

Jumping up into downward dog, I reveled in the stretch I felt through my spine, pushing it harder and harder until I felt languid. Yoga always relaxed me, and I'd enjoyed that, but it was an entirely different kind of exhilaration than it felt to workout with Sadie and enjoy the energy that came with it.

Since the entire property was fenced in, I hadn't bothered to go to the back-yard. The pool we hadn't had a chance to use took up most of it, and since it was only March it seemed unnecessary. I'd found a spot in the front where the sun hit me full force, enjoying the rare sixty-degree day for the anomaly it was. I had an unobstructed view of the gate opening, and I stood from my position to watch.

It seemed too early for Lino to return, so I had to wonder if maybe he'd sent Ivory or someone to keep me company. I smiled, thinking of how thoughtful it would be, but the smile faded from my face at the sight of the unfamiliar car. It wasn't the SUV Scar drove when he brought Ivory around, and it wasn't the town car I'd gone shopping with Chiara in.

A well-used Ford pulled through the gates, and they closed behind the car as it stopped at the top of the driveway. Apprehension slid down my spine when Emilio stepped out of the booth, he operated the gate from, crossing his arms over his chest and watching the driver's door of the Ford open up.

One suit clad leg came out slowly. Then another.

By the time Connor's blond head came out from the seat and he stood to full height, I felt like I'd swallowed my heart. My eyes went to Emilio, who had started to close the distance between us in a smooth, steady stalk. He stopped within speaking distance, but never made a move to touch me. "Gabriele sends his regards."

My heart shuddered in my chest, the feeling of betrayal making me queasy as I stared at him. Lino had trusted him to protect me. *I'd* trusted him.

Connor made his way to me, his face as thunderous as the last time I'd seen him, as fixated on me somehow being the answer to his problems. The problems he created himself, the problems that had led us down a vicious spiral in our marriage until I'd taken the brunt of his frustrations.

I turned, fleeing for the house. I had to hope that if I could just get inside, maybe Emilio didn't have a key. Even if he did, I could get to the panic room in the basement. Lino never mentioned it after the first time he'd brought me to the house, but I never forgot it was there. Never forgot how to engage the locks and shut myself away.

I'd never forget something so important.

Connor followed, sprinting after me. I cursed my shorter legs, pushing them harder when he made up distance between us too quickly. The grip of his arm on mine felt like it damn near ripped my arm out of socket, but I pushed through. "Get in the car, Mara." I kicked at his knee, swinging his arm around like Sadie had taught me and driving him to his knees.

Then I ran. I ran faster than I'd ever run in my life. My arms and legs pumped desperately. The weight that collided with my side sent me sprawling to the ground, and Emilio came down on top of me. His legs straddled my hips, his hands clasping my wrists at the side of my head to pin me. My breath came in a shuddering pant, and I tried to tune out Connor as he whimpered on the ground where I'd left him. He acted like I'd broken his arm, moaning in pain when I probably hadn't even dislocated the damn thing.

"Lino will kill you slowly, you know," I hissed, using the words as a distraction. "And Matteo will watch."

"They'll never know. You'll be long gone by the time they get back from the little stunt we arranged, and I will be conveniently unconscio—" His words faded into a shout, when I jerked my arms down to my hips and thrust my hips up in one move.

The first few times I'd done it had felt like patting my head and rubbing my tummy, but after practicing more times than I could count, it came as second nature. The force of my hips combined with the sudden loss of support at his hands threw him off balance, and he propelled forward to smack his face on the ground.

But he was still on top of me.

Still trapping me, and he'd have taken my nose with him if I hadn't turned my head at the last second. I clung to his waist, hooking the legs that I'd freed around his so that I could spin him to his back and jab my elbow into his already busted up face.

If I got away, if I *survived*, I'd kiss Sadie.

I'd owe her my life.

"Fucking bitch!" Emilio roared, grabbing my ankle as I stumbled to my feet. I went down, barely stopping my face from hitting the ground.

The shoe to my side sent such an intense pain through my torso that there was no breath.

There was nothing but agony as the second kick came, a loud crack echoing through the yard. Connor sneered down at me, grabbing me by the hair and hauling me to my feet as I wheezed and screamed in pain.

"Let go!" I grunted, stomping on his foot as I forced myself through it. I shoved my head back into his nose, wincing at the pain that exploded in my head as something wet coated my hair. For a moment, I thought it might be my blood. That somehow I'd managed to crack my head open, but when Emilio stood and wrapped his hands around my waist to lift me off my feet and haul me to the car, I got a good look at Connor's face.

His busted nose was a fountain of blood running down his face as he whimpered.

I had my answer to how I'd react if Lino came home with his blood on him.

I'd fucking celebrate.

"No!" I screamed. "*No!*" I kicked and tried to fight, but Connor finally came to his senses and grabbed my feet. With one holding my torso and one controlling my feet, there was little I could do. Nothing I could do since the position made my ribs scream, made it so I couldn't breathe past the pain. "I hope he makes you suffer," I hissed.

Connor's eyes widened before he gave me a dark, sardonic laugh. "When did you get so bloodthirsty?"

I was about to hiss an answer, ready to spit something back about the fact that I was only thirsty for *his* blood.

And Emilio's. And Gabriele's.

But there was a muffled thump and Connor crumpled to the ground. My feet went with him, and the impact jarred my body.

My torso hit the ground a few seconds later, and I wanted to cry. Wanted to scream. But there was nothing. No air in my lungs, only the pain in my ribs.

Behind me Emilio whispered a desperate, "fuck." I watched him turn to run, staring up at the sky in relief. When I finally felt like I could move, I lifted my head, finding Connor's body laid out on the ground in front of me. There was a hole in his forehead.

An entry wound.

There was another muffled thump, and the sound of Emilio shouting in pain.

The sound of men running past me caught my attention.

"Get your hands off me!" Emilio shouted.

"For once, you should hope it's me who touches you and not Lino," a man I didn't know said. His voice was rough around the edges, like he didn't speak often and had to adjust to using it.

Lino's face filled my vision, and even in my dazed reaction I think I smiled up at him.

"Thank fucking God," he hissed, tugging me into his arms. I didn't fight, didn't even react to the pain that seared my insides. All I wanted was to be in his arms.

To be safe.

"It's over, Little Dove. Connor's dead."

"Your father," I gasped.

Lino stilled, leaning against the car so that he could draw me into his lap. "What about my father?"

"Emilio said your father sent him," I whispered, finally lifting a hand to touch my ribs. Lino made no move to shift me off him, but his hand darted down to my long-sleeve shirt and lifted. I didn't bother to look, but I knew from how it hurt that there had to have been some marking. I imagined it would turn into quite a pretty boot print in time.

Lino cursed, calling, "Ryker!"

"Yeah?" That rough voice asked, and then the speaker stepped up beside us. He was shorter than Lino and Matteo, but only by a couple inches if I had to guess, and he made up for the lack of height by being ripped with muscles. His eyes were a vivid blue, striking as they narrowed on the place where my ribs hurt. His square jawline seemed savage, cut from stone, and his nose had a scar across the bridge and all those things seemed to contradict the full, almost feminine pillow lips that curled up into a sneer.

He was terrifying. but there was something soft in those intense blue eyes as he turned up to look at my face. "Get me Doc," Lino said. "And fucking find my father and you lock him in the warehouse. I want to do it; do you hear me?"

"Lino," I whimpered.

"Got it," Ryker stormed off, and his rough voice sounded as he made a call.

"I just need to do one more thing and then we can get you cleaned up before the Doc gets here," Lino murmured, shifting my weight so that he could stand with me in his arms. His hand seemed to leave a trail of red wherever it went, and he hissed.

"Not mine," I murmured, looking down at Connor's body as we passed. I wanted to kick his pretty face in, because the bullet hole wasn't enough damage for what he'd put me through.

"You did some damage, Samara," Matteo grinned at me as we passed. "Ivory and Sadie will be proud." I wanted to laugh at the ridiculousness of it but didn't dare. Not with the pain ripping me in half.

When we stepped up to where Enzo and Georgio stood over Emilio, I noted the way he held his shoulder and rocked where he sat. The glare he gave me as Lino set me to my feet in front of him made my heart clench again.

I had no idea what I'd done to make him hate me so much.

"Why?" I whispered, and my bottom lip trembled. While I hadn't had a bond with him the way that Ivory and Scar did, I would never have expected him to do something like this.

"You're a stain on the Bellandi name," he hissed through his teeth. His eyes went over my shoulder where Matteo stepped up beside me, and I winced at the vehemence in the glare he gave Emilio. "It was bad enough that one Bellandi married outside the family, but for Lino to procreate with a Jew is unthinkable. We had to get rid of you before you could get pregnant."

I'd thought it had been because Lino was of the age where men were expected to settle down, but all the inquiries and pushes about us having children, every last one had been a deception to make us want to wait. A way of fishing for information about whether it was an immediate concern. "My father encouraged this?" Lino asked, drawing the gun from inside his jacket.

Emilio sneered. "It was his idea. He found Connor long before you managed and gave him shelter in his home until we could get rid of you. He arranged the buyer, since he had the contact from his bitch of a second wife."

Lino growled, raising his arm to press the gun against Emilio's forehead. Emilio glared up at him, not bothering to beg for his life.

"I'd like to kill you slowly," he snarled, but he glanced at me. "But I think I'll save that for my father instead. You lived like a minion who didn't matter, and now you get to die like one too." There was no bang, no blast like I would have expected. Just the thump of the bullet and his eyes going lifeless as he fell to his side.

I didn't flinch. I'd never seen a man shot before, not until Connor. But anyone who could sell me to another person wasn't a man. They were rabid dogs who needed to be put down, and all I felt was pride that my husband had been the one to do it.

"Going to clean her up. Doc is on the way," Lino murmured, lifting me into his arms again.

"Good. We'll clean up out here," Matteo responded. As he said the words, a box truck pulled into the driveway. I didn't want to know or think about how many bodies they'd thrown into that box truck, so I buried my face in Lino's neck and let him take me inside.

***

The hot water felt rejuvenating. Like I'd gone into the shower one person and came out another.

"I almost lost you," Lino murmured as he towel-dried my hair.

"I thought that the loan shark was with Connor. What happened?" I asked, and Lino sighed as he tugged a shirt over my head and helped me into some sleep shorts.

"Decoy. Wasn't Connor at all, but the fucking shark was too stupid to notice the difference. We came back as soon as we realized it was a decoy, because you were the first thing I could think of that Connor would want me distracted from. I'm so sorry, Little Dove." His forehead touched mine as he lifted me and laid me out on our bed. "I fucked up."

"I'm fine," I whispered. "You came back in time, and you couldn't have known Emilio would betray you like that."

"I promised I'd protect you. I failed to do that," he grunted, and he stepped back from me. The way his shoulders slumped, I could see every bit of self-hate and blame and the way it wore on him.

"You helped me protect myself. If you hadn't encouraged me to go with Sadie —" I broke off, thinking about the reality of where I might be now if I hadn't managed to stall *just* long enough. "I don't even know how long I fought them off, but it felt like forever."

"Sadie taught you that, not me."

"And you shot them," I murmured. He'd killed two men for me, killed in cold blood and not even batted an eye. "I'm sorry that you had to do that for me."

He chuckled, stepping back into my space. "That's not a weight you need to worry about, *vita mia*. It wasn't the first time I've killed, and I'm certain it won't be the last." I stared up into those dark eyes, wondering how he could survive so much abuse as a child, survive being turned into a hardened killer, and still look down at me as if he couldn't live without me. It seemed unnatural. Like it couldn't be possible for one man to *feel* so much for me, when he should be deadened to feeling in general.

I knew he'd been well on his way as a child, but somehow, whatever this bond was between us had rescued that small piece of him. Preserved it for me. "What will you do with your father?" I asked him, staring up at him with wide eyes as the Doctor arrived.

"Don't worry about it. Trust me when I say that I won't lose any sleep over what I do to that man."

I nodded, settling in while the doctor poked and prodded at my ribs. Lino held my hand, wincing with me every time I showed any signs of pain.

He may have been brutal.

But he was *my brutal.*

And I knew in that moment that I wouldn't change him for the world.

CHAPTER FIFTY-ONE

LINO

The warehouse seemed more ominous than ever. I didn't spend a ton of time in it and had never been a critical part of the wet work. Considering that I ran the legitimate businesses, we tried to keep my hands as clean as possible. But there would always be circumstances that we couldn't control. Personal vendettas. Moments where I needed to be involved to make a show of force against the politicians and businessmen that filled my days with bullshit.

But going there knowing I'd commit patricide was a new one for me. I tried to drum up some sympathy or guilt over it, but the knowledge of what he'd done to Samara outweighed any guilt that might try to sneak in. I could tolerate a lifetime of abuse against me, but I wouldn't tolerate the fact that my wife had been hurt in his stunt.

That he'd tried to sell her.

I pulled open the door, heading for the freezer and opened that door as well. I didn't bother closing it behind me, because my father would never be so undignified to scream for help. He knew better than any just how futile it would be.

Ryker stood, leaning against the table where he kept his tools and fiddling with them like he couldn't wait to dig in. And I would let him. I wouldn't torture my father. He'd enjoy seeing me behave like a monster, even if it did mean he suffered.

Because it would mean that I was just like him in the end, that I was every-thing he'd molded me to be. I wanted him to die knowing that I was everything *she* made me. That I might kill, but I didn't enjoy it the way my father did.

"You're a stain on the Earth, and you need to be removed so our women can be safe," Ryker's voice carried all the fury he held, and I had to imagine it was largely in part due to the fact that he was so close to claiming Calla. That his self-imposed deadline would expire soon.

I might have pitied her for the shock she had coming her way, if I didn't know that Ryker would be better to her than she could ever dream.

"You don't have a woman," my father laughed, and even at his age his shirtless body was lean.

Ryker leaned in, giving my father that terrifying grin of his that showed just how closely the monster played at his surface. I honestly wasn't sure if he *had* a surface. "I'm about to."

Gabriele turned his attention to me finally. "Well?"

"What was the plan? What were you going to do with my wife?" I hissed, fury making my body lock solid. I wanted to play casual, wanted to make sure he never saw how it burned me to know that he'd so desperately tried to take away the only thing I loved.

"Walsh needed money, I needed her gone. Murphy wasn't willing to go toe to toe with Matteo over a piece of ass, so I found a private buyer in Mexico. He has a thing for redheads, and they're so rare down there." He stared at me, as if he could make me see the truth of his words. I didn't need to see them, because I could feel that they were true, and they only echoed what Emilio had told me before I shot him.

He'd intended to sell my wife to another man.

"She's worth a lot of money if you'd like to reconsider—" Ryker's fist connected with his face, so sharply that Gabriele spit out a bloody tooth.

"Did you love my mother?" I asked, and I made a good show of fidgeting with the tools on the table. Ryker's eyes lit with excitement, the messed-up dude wanting nothing more than to take out his frustrations on Gabriele. There was nothing, and I mean *nothing* the man hated more than people who preyed on women and children. I suspected it went back to his childhood, but no one would ever know.

There was probably a reason that he and Scar had an unspoken bond, that even though they didn't ever seem to speak of it, they had each other's backs.

"Of course I loved her. Why do you think I spent your entire life telling you that love weakened you?" Gabriele spat.

"And what would you have done if someone tried to sell her?" My words came out in a rough growl, because I knew what I would have done if someone tried to sell her. Even though I'd been young, I'd have tried to kill them slowly, such was the way my father had trained me from the moment I could hold a gun or a knife in my hand.

I vowed that my children would be allowed to be children, that they'd know the affection of their mother and father. Even if they would one day follow in mine and Matteo's footsteps, there was no way I could ever force that on them when the biggest concern they should have was losing a game of soccer.

"I'd have made him suffer," Gabriele snarled. I knew it was meant to push me to that edge, to the horrifying thing he'd tried to turn me into.

"Right, so you know exactly what's coming," I snarled, but I stepped back and leaned my back into the wall. As much as I wanted to torment him, I wasn't interested in becoming what he'd always wanted me to be. Someone who enjoyed torture, who thrived on it.

But he had to suffer, and I'd enjoy watching it.

I nodded to Ryker, and the man went to the door. We waited in silence, and I knew my father knew what was coming. When Ryker returned, the brand held in his hands, he strode up to Gabriele. The moment the brand touched the flesh of his chest, he gritted his teeth. His burning flesh filled the room with a putrid stink, the sound of it sizzling seemed to echo in the otherwise quiet space as Gabriele refused to scream. Once the brand pulled off his chest, the word Traitor stared back at me.

I watched, keeping my face impassive as Ryker went through tool after tool. He took everything my father had: his blood, his nails, his tongue, and eventually all his fingers. The way he worked was systematic, as if he didn't enjoy it, but I knew better. Ryker's cruel blue eyes glinted with joy every time my father grunted in pain, and when he eventually shouted when Ryker finally grabbed the fillet knife, a smile broke out on my friend's face.

"No man sells a woman, so I think it only fitting that you no longer be a man," Ryker grinned at him. I pitied him for having to look at my father after he cut his underwear away, for having to reach out with a gloved hand to hold him in the proper position while my father struggled.

The sound of his scream echoed through the room as Ryker drew the knife through his flesh. He took everything, and only when my father sobbed and slumped in the chair as his blood pooled out of him did I raise my gun and give him the mercy of death.

With that confirmed, I turned and strode out of the warehouse.

Because my wife was waiting.

✳✳✳

There was no blood on me when I came home. Nothing to show that I'd killed another man.

Three in one day wasn't a record for me, but I knew it would make Samara feel uncertain.

So I was grateful for the absence of blood. At least she wouldn't have to see the body or be reminded of what I'd done. She was flat on her back in bed, wide awake and looking up at me when I stepped in. I knew she wouldn't be able to sleep on her side, and I wondered if I should sleep in a spare room for the time being. I always pulled her into me while I slept, and I didn't want to hurt her.

"I'm going to sleep in a guest room, so I don't hurt you," I told her, feeling dejected. After nearly losing her, after nearly losing everything that mattered to me, all I wanted to do was curl up in bed with my wife and hold her. I wanted to make love to her, and from the way her eyes shone she knew as well as I did that it couldn't happen.

"I can't sleep without you," she murmured, and I tugged off my clothes against my better judgement. Her weight in the bed next to me soothed something inside me, the part of me that felt ragged and torn by the near loss of her.

She was alive.

She was with me.

That was all that mattered in the end.

"Did you—"

"Yes," I grunted in response. "I'll do anything to keep you safe. Whatever it takes. I'll kill as many men as I need to and burn the world to the ground if it means you're safe and where you belong—with me." She snuggled her face into my shoulder, and I admired the strength it must have taken, how hard it must have been, for her to fight off two fully grown men and walk away with only a broken rib.

She was so small, my tiny little spitfire of a wife.

And the men she'd fought were much bigger than her. Emilio was trained.

"I think Sadie should be the godmother," I whispered.

"Hmmm?" Her sleepy murmur made the last ragged shiver inside me melt away, and I chuckled, tucking my head down so that it touched the top of hers and her copper hair tickled my face.

"Of our first baby. Sadie should be the Godmother," I whispered.

She sniffled, and my heart broke all over again. "I think so too," she said back. It was settled, as simple as that. The woman who had taught Samara to defend herself and given her the skills she needed to survive was the only person I could even consider in light of the day we'd had. "Goodnight, my Stallion."

"Goodnight, Little Dove," I chuckled against her hair, and fell asleep with the world next to me.

EPILOGUE
SAMARA

Two months later

I walked in the front door to the scent of Lino working his magic in the kitchen. It seemed like he was always in the kitchen lately.

I wondered if it was the male version of nesting, even if he didn't know I was pregnant just yet. I wondered if he sensed the life growing inside me the way I did. Knowing how in tune with me he was, it seemed likely.

I choked down the nausea that threatened my stomach, the smell of bacon cooking turning it sour. I didn't want to let on, didn't want to give away the surprise too early. The little box in my purse made me want to thrust it at him immediately, and excitement helped chase away the nausea. I'd been lucky thus far, but I could almost feel it coming to an end. Like I'd wake up to the worst morning sickness yet in just a few days.

"How was work?" Lino asked, stepping away from the stove long enough to lean down and kiss me hello.

"It was good. Nothing unusual really." The truth was, I'd stopped loving my job. I didn't hate it, or hate the work I did, but I couldn't imagine leaving a baby behind during the day to go there.

Nothing I did felt significant. I helped rich men get richer. Helped Jasper make his clients as much money as possible.

It had never been my first choice. Or my second choice. Or even my third.

So it just seemed foolish to cling to it out of some desire for independence. Could a woman ever really be independent when she had personal security hired by her husband? When someone drove her to and from work every day? It felt like an exercise in futility, but I'd never again argue against the need for protection.

Not when I had a child to think of.

"Do you not like the job anymore?" Lino asked, eyeing me as I sat at the island.

"I do," I lied. "I like working for Jasper. It gives me more opportunity to torment him now that he's got the love bug." Lino turned, flipping the bacon and grabbed the ground beef to form patties. "Cheeseburgers again?"

He grinned at me in that mischievous way of his, and I fought the urge to sigh. The fucking man knew damn well I was pregnant. "You've been scarfing them down like a monster lately."

Sighing in frustration, I grabbed the box from my purse and set it on the counter. He grinned at me. "You can't just let it be a surprise, can you?" He washed his hands quickly, turning to the box and yanking the lid off. The stuffed horse looked tiny in his hands, but I knew it would be just the right size for our child to cuddle with. "A foal for my Stallion."

"We'll order cheeseburgers," he announced, spinning and turning off the heat on the stove.

He set the foal on the counter, and then stalked toward me. I ran for the stairs, giggling as he chased me. The happiness that exploded in my chest couldn't be stopped, couldn't be tamed.

Nothing would ever again convince me that this man didn't love me. Nothing would come between us.

Not with the way his eyes lit with joy as he followed me to the bedroom.

When I made it inside, I spun around to face him. His eyes sparkled with all the excitement I felt inside, and my face split into the widest smile I think my face had ever worn. "We're having a baby," he murmured, closing the distance between us. His hands touched my belly, sliding over the flat surface of it with awe on his face.

"We're having a baby," I confirmed.

"Ivory had the best doctor. We'll get you an appointment as soon as possible—"

"Lino, it's early. I'll call the doctor in the morning, but for now, we're fine," I reassured him with a giggle. "We'll be fine."

"I never dreamed that I could be this happy," he whispered, dropping to his knees in front of me. He lifted my shirt, pressing the side of his head to the bare skin of my belly. I ran my fingers through his hair, watching him press a kiss to the spot just above my belly button. "You're going to have the best mommy in the world," he whispered, and I resisted the urge to tell him that I doubted the baby could hear him just yet. It was too sweet to interrupt.

"I think that when life is better than you could ever dream, there's only one thing left to do."

He turned his attention back to me, standing and watching as I tugged the blouse off over my head. "And what's that, *vita mia?*"

"Make love to your wife," I whispered, sliding the zipper down on my skirt. I'd never get tired of watching his eyes heat like pools of molten lava, of knowing that I made him crave me so intensely. That he found me as addictive as I found him. Lino's shirt and sweatpants went next, his body naked thanks to his refusal to wear underwear at home recently. I loved knowing that if I tugged down his sweatpants or his shorts, he'd be naked underneath. That I could have him in my hand within seconds, and my mouth soon after.

I shucked off my bra, staring intently at the part of him I'd come to crave like a desperate addict. I couldn't go a day without him inside me, and the weeks when I'd been healing from the broken ribs proved that. I'd been like a mad woman, wanting and angry that he wouldn't give me what I needed.

Getting pregnant after that couldn't come as a surprise, not when we'd had sex constantly for days once I'd gotten the all-clear from the doctor. Lino's fingers hooked in the waistband of my underwear, guiding them down my legs slowly and teasing me as he helped me step out of them. His hand touched my jaw, cradling my face so that he could touch his lips to mine in a deep breath that felt like he inhaled me into his soul.

But it wasn't possible.

Not when I was already part of him.

Those hands came down on my hips, lifting me suddenly so that he could toss me into the middle of the bed. I shrieked when he came down on top of me, devouring me with his mouth.

My lips, my neck, my heart. He made his way to my stomach in a slow glide of lips and delicate nips with his teeth, and the way he hesitated at my stomach brought my eyes to his. He kissed the skin once, twice, three times. The joy in his eyes clouded over with worry, and I knew my stallion well enough to know that he thought of his own father. Wondered if his father had ever kissed his mother's stomach or been a good father. If he'd ever shown any promise to the child he didn't know yet. "You'll be an amazing father," I whispered, using my words and my love to chase away his doubts.

His eyes warmed, the clouds that lurked there fading away in the face of how much I loved him.

Love healed all wounds.

He lowered his mouth, and the first swipe of his tongue through me sent me soaring, sent the emotional moment to a new peak. He didn't explore, he couldn't explore something that was his, something that he knew better than I did, but he did take his time.

He worshiped every inch of me, bathing it in warmth and love until I writhed beneath him, desperate for him to send me over the edge. Burying my hand in his hair, I pressed him tighter, trying to take just a moment of control so that I could find my release. But Lino refused to allow me that control and pulled back to slap my pussy just hard enough that the skin tingled in the wake of the burn.

He grinned at me, knowing I loved it just as much as he loved doing it, and then he crawled up my body and surged inside me. He shoved my knees high, holding my legs open wide so that he could lean his weight over mine and take my mouth to silence my cry. "Fuck," he groaned, echoing the sentiment that echoed in the deepest part of me. His thrusts sent me spinning, his slow and deep rhythm as he danced his hips in and out of me a thing of absolute beauty. I tilted my head up, watching him work inside and pull back out and then turning my eyes to him.

I whimpered his name, the punishing thrusts striking the deepest part of me until I clenched around him with my orgasm, my entire body locking tight. I clutched him tight with my arms, my legs, every part of me needing him to touch mine. I needed him, wanted him.

Forever.

Once I'd come down, he flipped me over to my stomach, cocking one leg up to open me up to him and then he pounded back in. I moaned when he sealed his chest to my back, striving toward his own orgasm. Two hands clenched each side of my butt, spreading me wide so that he could get deeper. Impossibly deep. I clenched my hands into the sheets beneath me, using it to muffle my screams when he picked up the pace and lost his rhythm. Lost himself in me. "This fucking pussy," he groaned in my ear as he flooded it with heat and released me. His weight covered mine, and I couldn't resist the temptation to wiggle my hips against him.

His palm cracked down against the side of my ass.

"I love you," I giggled.

"I love you too, Little Dove. Always."

We laid like that for a few more minutes, until the sound of my stomach growling made him chuckle against me. "Guess I should feed you then."

"If I'm eating for two now, does that mean I get two cheeseburgers?" The way his body shook with his unrestrained laughter against me was my favorite feeling of all. Knowing I gave him that, just like he gave it to me.

I let myself live for that moment, for the way I knew he would make me feel for the rest of my life.

Happy. Whole.

Healed.

✳✳✳

THANK you for reading Forgivable Sins! I hope you enjoyed Lino and Samara's story. The story continues on with Grieved Loss as Ryker and Calla heal from past wounds and find solace in one another.

GRIEVED LOSS

BELLANDI CRIME SYNDICATE #3

ABOUT GRIEVED LOSS

Calla

I've never known pain like when I lost my husband, never known the fear that came with wondering how I would suddenly support my two kids. So when an anonymous benefactor stepped forward on my husband's behalf, I never questioned it.

And then Ryker comes from the shadows to show me the truth, determined to show me what his brand of love can be. He demands everything from me, my heart, my soul, my body.

And he won't stop until he's taken everything.

Ryker

For years, I watched my Sunshine from the shadows, letting her live out her simple life with the man who didn't deserve her. My loyalty to the Bellandis demanded nothing less, but when her husband is shot down in a drug deal gone bad, there's nothing that will stop me from stepping in and claiming Calla and the kids as my own.

I give her one year to grieve, to adjust to life without him. But when the year is up, rising tensions in my world threaten to steal her away from me. I won't let anything come between us.

Not even Calla herself.

Grieved Loss is a full-length standalone novel with an HEA, but the series presents a better reading experience when following the suggested reading order.

This series contains dark elements, including an over-the-top antihero who does as he pleases, and references to previous abuse in childhood. Please read at your own discretion.

SOUNDTRACK

The songs from Adelaide's playlist:
"Be Here For You" – Sam Tinnesz
"I Get Off" – Halestorm
"Goddess of the Rain" – Burn the Ballroom
"Play Dirty" – Kevin McAllister
"Grip" – Seeb, Bastille
"Chaos" – Ravenscode
"Drown" – Brian Dalton
"Devil A Pray" – Easy Mccoy
"Eye of the Storm" – Watt White
"Live in the Light" – Watt White
"Disgust Me" – New Years Day
"Nothing Is As It Seems" – Hidden Citizens
"Dance in the Rain" – Bolshiee
"Wanted" – Ben Hazelwood
"Take It All" – Pop Evil
"Animal In Me" – Solence
"Gone" – Bebe Rexha
"I Was Alive" – Dark Signal
"Underwater" – Skies Collide
"Falling Down" – Landsdowne
"Animals" – Concepts
"Better Together" – UNSECRET
"Never Have I Ever" – Danielle Bradbery

"Church" – Fall Out Boy
"The Truth" – Audiomachine
"Make Me Believe" – The Everlove
"Something to Remind You" – Staind
"Hold" – Vera Blue
"Eyes on Fire" – Blue Foundation
"Snake Charmer" – Jiovanni Daniel

PROLOGUE
RYKER

Four years ago

There was no excuse for the things I'd done. Nothing I could say to make them right. In the end, it would all be a lie anyway. I liked the feel of my knife slicing through skin and found beauty in the way blood poured onto the floor to spread like motor oil. I liked them too much to regret them, and I'd do them all over again.

To find her.

Despite all my crimes, and all my sins, I knew even then that nothing could compare to the crime of stalking Calla Latour. Following her husband came easy, even if it meant I had to work harder to stay hidden.

They frowned upon watching the police.

But stalking his innocent wife because he decided the simple life with white picket fence just wasn't enough for him? That was a crime worthy of the death sentence. It was a crime I knew I could never justify to myself.

Especially since she quickly became an addiction. I felt her burning in my veins as if I'd shot her up like a drug.

A woman like Calla was all good, all sunshine and light. I lived my life in the shadows where I belonged. But somehow it felt like my shadows changed when I first set eyes on her. Like my shadows became *her* shadows. Calla was a guiding light in my otherwise bleak existence, and I couldn't turn away.

It didn't matter that she spent most of her time in yoga pants, with her white blond hair in a ponytail, looking more and more exhausted with every hour that passed. Something about those big, dark blue eyes called to me in a way that I couldn't explain.

But I kept my distance. Because if I got too close, I would take Calla for my own. I owed everything to the Bellandi family. Her husband Chad would be useful to Matteo if he proved himself.

Very useful.

It wasn't every day that a Police Lieutenant wanted to join the Bellandi payroll, intending to make evidence disappear or stop it from being collected.

So I watched her. I made sure she wasn't meeting with anyone on her husband's behalf. Even though I knew from the first moment I followed her that the only crooked thing she had going was her smile.

She walked through the park, pushing her two-year-old son Axel in the stroller and willing him to stay asleep. She looked pained doing it, as if the toddler just never slept or gave her a moment's peace. Judging from the look on her face and the way I'd watched her snuggle with him on the couch the entire night before, I suspected it might be true. Her husband had come home after dinner, greeted her briefly, and gone up to their bed to sleep peacefully under the covers while she handled Axel.

She was too good for him. Too good for both of us.

I stayed a few paces behind her, feigning disinterest as she made her way down the path in the park near their house. The fresh air seemed to help calm Axel, as it was already their second stroll through the park for the day.

The stroller veered to the right suddenly, something shifting, so it tilted to the side. She tried to put it right, but it woke Axel anyway. Groaning, she dropped her head for a moment before she bent down to inspect the wheel. I couldn't see what happened from my spot behind them, but the way Calla buried her face in her hands and took out her phone was sign enough that something was wrong. She typed a number in, putting it to her ear as she reached down and grabbed her son from the stroller.

She bounced him rhythmically while she spoke to whoever she'd called for help—her face looking more and more harried with every second. When she finally hung up, she turned a smile to her son and shushed him before she spoke to him.

With every second she waited, her body slumped more and more. The weight of her two-year-old exhausted her, and I could practically see the way her back pained her when she tried to straighten out.

At 5'3", she was far too small to be holding Axel for lengthy periods of time like that. Yet she did it anyway, never even trying to set him down as he snuggled into her side desperately.

With a muttered, "Fuck," I knew I couldn't watch her suffer. Knew in that moment, I'd do anything to make her life just a little easier. It would end badly, there was no way approaching and talking to her would end well for me or her.

But I did it anyway.

I stepped out of the shadows of the trees, making myself visible as I walked along the path more noticeably. "Excuse me," I said, and even to me my voice sounded rough. I didn't talk much, avoided it when I could. When I was on a hunt or doing surveillance, I could go days without ever speaking a word.

I tried not to wince, tried to give her the friendliest smile I could manage. But I wasn't friendly. I didn't know how to be. I'd lost everything that made me human a long time ago.

I cleared my throat. "Do you need some help?"

She spun around, fixing that deep blue gaze on me so suddenly it was like a punch to the gut. My body stilled as my world spun, focus narrowing down on the flush that spread over her pretty cheeks and the way her pursed little mouth tipped into a blinding, ever-so-slightly crooked smile. She sucked back a sharp intake of breath that seemed to echo the raging in my blood. As if she could feel the same inexplicable urge I did, the need to claim and take and make her mine.

Those blue eyes glittered in the sunshine, my world narrowing down to the way they felt on mine. To the reminder of the kick to the teeth she'd provided from the very first moment I laid eyes on her through her living room window the day before.

"You don't mind?" she asked, but her body sagged with relief.

"Let me take a look," I agreed, going to the stroller and squatting down. Her eyes felt warm on my back, heating the chilled skin like the rays of the sun itself. I didn't imagine Calla saw many men like me in her sheltered life.

It should stay that way.

She averted her eyes as her teeth bit into her bottom lip with another flush of her cheeks. "Thank you so much for this," she sighed. "My husband is on his way, but it can be hard for him to get away from work," she explained. I resisted the urge to laugh at her attempt to let me know there was a husband in the picture. Under normal circumstances, it would have been smart. Dissuading interest early on could only benefit her, but she should have known that a man like me could take whatever he wanted. Married or not.

"It's no problem. Your boy looks like he's having a rough go of it," I grunted, finding the part where the tire had come off the rim.

"He's teething," she responded. "These teeth will be the death of me. He's usually a calm boy, but something about this time has him miserable." She wiggled her nose on his, making him squeal with laughter even as he clung to her. "Don't they, Cookie Monster?" she asked him.

I snapped the tire back onto the rim, grateful the solution came so quickly. I needed to get away from her, put distance between us before it was too late to turn back. The sound of her laughing in response to her boy's joy was something I couldn't handle. Not if I wanted to have any chance of leaving her alone.

I straightened, and the position put me closer to her than I meant to be. As my eyes slid down over her face, my gaze settled on the thumping of the pulse in her delicate neck as she stared up at me.

Axel broke my moment of fixation when he reached out his arms, straining toward me while Calla tried to contain him. "I'm so sorry," she laughed. "He isn't usually so friendly."

A boy after my own heart.

I held out my hands, lifting him under the armpits and out of Calla's arms. She looked panicked for a brief second, but then relief crossed her face as the weight left her back. I stared at the little boy in my arms, at the chocolate brown hair he'd inherited from his father, but his mother's blue eyes shone back from his face. His little hand reached up, touching the scar through my eyebrow in confusion before he laughed and punched my nose.

"Axel!" Calla scolded.

"He's alright," I said, hearing a smile in my voice for the first time in as long as I could remember.

A beautiful woman in front of me, a boy who somehow looked like me in my arms. It was everything I'd wanted once upon a time, before they took it all away.

When Axel lost interest in using me as a punching bag, Calla took him back and settled him into the seat of the stroller.

Once she'd gotten him buckled, she turned her attention back to me, smiling happily. "Thank you again. So much. Can I give you some money or—"

"You've already given me more than you know," I whispered, reaching out a hand to touch her face. "Have a good life, Tesoro." *Treasure.*

She gasped again the moment I touched her, my hand cupping her cheek as she stared up at me in confusion. I could never speak to her again, never touch her, but I'd never be able to walk away from her either.

The moment my thumb touched her high cheekbone, something in me shifted.

I was found.

CHAPTER ONE

RYKER

Two weeks later

Latour's black sedan pulled up at the back of the lot. We might have been tentatively willing to trust him in the interest of an alliance, but until the man proved himself to Matteo, he wouldn't set foot inside his home.

Or my warehouse.

When Chad got out of the car, his eyes traveled to Simon standing by the driver's side of the Lincoln as he waited for the head of the Bellandi family to emerge from the vehicle. We had designed every aspect of the meeting around the need to emphasize the power hierarchy, and the shift from what Chad felt familiar with.

The full wrath of Matteo Bellandi needed to stare Chad Latour in the face, because if he ever made the stupid mistake to cross Bellandi, it wouldn't only be the man himself who unleashed his fury on him.

I'd take away everything he should have worshiped and make him watch as I made them mine.

I watched from the sidelines, with my backup beater car behind me. I leaned my ass against it with my arms crossed over my chest, as fury filled my veins.

He was so fucking stupid. So fucking oblivious to his surroundings. How did someone survive as a cop and not realize a monster lingered just out of sight?

If Matteo hadn't needed him, I'd have slit his throat before he even saw me.

Simon opened Matteo's door finally, and the head of the Bellandi family made a grand show of unfolding his brutal body to stand next to the car. He eyed Chad's tall frame with distaste, noting the badge he wore strapped to his belt.

Our line of work made dirty cops inevitable, a necessary evil we suffered to avoid jail time. But as people who took our vows of loyalty seriously, I couldn't think of a single dirty cop who I didn't think was worse than the dirt beneath my boots. Loyalty came first. The family we chose came first. A dirty cop betrayed both.

This one was just worse than most, because he was in my way.

I watched the exchange from the shadows. Chad stretched out a hand to shake Matteo's, and my boss refused to touch him. His mouth moved, and Chad was quick to withdraw the hand.

Matteo wasn't a germaphobe. He just hated people. The cruel expression on his face never faded, never relented for even a moment to show a hint of happiness.

I'd heard stories of a time when he'd been a different man. A boy really, in love with a girl he'd never be able to keep.

I understood the feeling.

Simon nodded at me over Matteo's head, and I pushed off my car to make my way into the fray. Chad still hadn't seen me, hadn't even bothered to take his eyes off of who he saw as the threat. But while Matteo might have posed a threat, he'd never kill Chad himself.

He'd save that pleasure for me, when the time came that he stopped being useful.

I knew, because he'd told me. We were forthcoming like that.

Chad's eyes finally landed on me when my suit clad ass touched the Lincoln, and I perched on the hood. Simon glared at me as the weight of the car shifted, the tires groaning under my bulk. I ignored him, letting my fists clench around the edge of the hood.

I couldn't stand. Couldn't be too close to the fuck, because if I got any closer, I just might fuck everything up and kill him.

Owing Matteo everything meant I couldn't do that. Not yet.

Chad chuckled nervously as he turned his attention back to Matteo. "I don't think your man likes me."

I stood too much to gain from his death to entertain anything else.

"He doesn't like pigs who take their wives and sons for granted," Matteo returned. "So here is how it will go." Chad swallowed, nodding before Matteo even spoke. "You are now my bitch. If I tell you to do something, you do it. End of story. When you are not working for me, you'll be a dutiful husband to your wife. You'll treat her well, give her anything her little heart desires. But understand that my executioner will watch you and wait for you to fuck up either of these directives."

"What does my wife have to do with anything?" Chad sputtered, staring at Matteo with wide eyes and a gaping mouth.

I jumped off the Lincoln, stepping into Chad's face so he had no choice but to look at me as I spoke. "The only reason you still have a wife is because you may be useful to Matteo. Stop being useful, and you will find that you no longer have a wife and son. Because they'll be mine."

"I-what?" he asked, glancing at Matteo to see if he would agree with my demand. I knew that it wasn't normal to just claim a married woman.

I'd make her a divorcee or widow first if I could do it without hurting her.

I never wanted to hurt her.

"Just keep that in mind and know that I'll be watching everything you do. Don't fuck up, Latour," I extended a hand, patting his cheek just harshly enough that he winced. "I'll see you around."

Then I turned back for my car, listening to every word they spoke as I went. "I suggest you prove very, very useful. Persuading Ryker to wait won't be easy," Matteo said.

"I got it," Chad seethed, and I felt his eyes boring into my back as I walked. "This is fucking ridiculous. She's my goddamn wife."

"So treat her like it," Simon grunted. "Otherwise he will."

Damn fucking right I would, and I'd have the entire force of the Bellandis at my back when the time came. It was only a matter of time before Chad fucked up. They always did, and when he did, I'd be waiting.

Until then, I'd get to know my Sunshine.

CHAPTER TWO

CALLA

Three years ago

I needed to get home.

I rushed out of the corner store, waving at the man who held the door for me as I passed. My son at home alone with his father, who was also my husband, shouldn't have felt so urgent.

I wished I could enjoy my time alone, browse through the grocery store and maybe buy things that weren't on my list for once. I shouldn't have needed to get back to them and should have been able to trust my husband with our child.

Instead, my son needed me. It took fifteen minutes for Chad to get frustrated with Axel and call me. It surprised me he lasted that long with the look Axel gave me when I left.

He loved Axel, but with his work hours being so demanding, sometimes it felt like my guys didn't even know one another anymore.

In such a rush, I never noticed the figure waiting for me in the mouth of the alley that led to the parking lot at the back of the building. I never noticed the one trailing behind me either, clinging to the shadows like he lived in them.

I never did.

The moment I turned into the alley, a hand reached out from the side to grab hold of my purse and yanked it away from my body. "Hey!" I shouted, pulling back in a dramatic tug of war. Lifting the bag of groceries, I swung it for his face, the bag colliding in a resounding whack. I watched the faint hints of a face twist into a scowl as he recovered from the blow.

His fist shot through the air, aimed directly for the side of my face. I knew the moment I dropped my groceries and lifted my hand to protect myself that it would be too late. My eyes squeezed shut of their own accord, desperate to protect them in whatever way I could.

I waited for the pain to explode in my cheek, and yet the punch never came.

A grunt of pain came from in front of my clenched eyelids and made me thrust them open just in time to watch a second figure haul the thief off his feet by the throat. The savage growl my savior emitted had me stumbling back a step, staring at them in both awe and horror. Two faceless men, speaking in rough whispers that I couldn't make out. Not with the ringing of my pulse in my ears.

I ducked down, gathering up the purse I must have dropped in the altercation. I needed to be ready in case I had to make a run for it. I should already have run, but something about the sight of the unknown man gripping my attacker in such a way appealed to the darkest part of me. The same part of me that wanted justice for the attempted robbery and injury I hadn't even suffered.

Something about my savior felt familiar.

"You have a two-minute head start," he grunted, his voice deep as he lowered the other man to the pavement. When he finally released the mugger, the smaller man darted off through the alley to escape, tripping over his own feet in his urgency to get away.

I didn't want to know what happened at the end of his two minutes.

With wide eyes and shaking hands, I bent down and collected the items that had fallen free from my grocery bag.

As I shoved the last item back in, a hand stretched out from the shadows, holding the can that had rolled his way for me to take. With a nervous swallow, I stepped forward and accepted it. Our fingers brushed against each other. It was only the subtlest touch of my skin against his, but an electric current pulsed up through my arm so harshly that the can slipped through my fingers.

He moved like lightning, snatching it out of the air before it could crash to the pavement. But my eyes never left him, never left the shining blue orbs that seemed to glow even in the absence of light. The eyes of a wolf, of a predator who barely resisted the urge to devour his prey. The rest of his face remained cloaked in the shadows, a mystery despite my growing urge to see him.

Once he dropped the can in my bag for me, he retreated further into the shadows and drew the hood closer to his face. "Wait!" I called. "What's your name? I just want to thank you!"

There was no answer, though his feet paused so he could turn his head back to glance at me. He shook it side to side in a no, and I furrowed my brow with rising curiosity.

What harm could there be in a name?

"Well, my Shadow." I smiled, feeling ridiculous even as I said the words. "Thank you for saving me." He stilled for a few seconds and then nodded, turning back and continuing on his way through the alley.

I followed, determined to see where he went. There was no harm in seeing where he went, not when my car was in the same direction.

But the end of the alley was empty when I reached it. There was no trace of him, though it seemed impossible that he could have disappeared so quickly.

Just gone.

Nothing but the faint scent of metal left in his wake.

CHAPTER THREE

CALLA

One year ago

Dead.

My husband was dead.

Everybody died. Everybody left. Nothing was constant.

Why had I thought Chad would be any different?

The man across the table stared back at me, pity and sympathy shining in his eyes.

I hated it. I hated that I'd gone from having everything I could ever dream of, to being the woman people pitied.

Leaving Axel and Ines with my dad even for an afternoon felt brutal. The way they'd clung to me so desperately, afraid that I wouldn't come home. A five-year-old and one-year-old had no business knowing what that kind of pain felt like. They were too young to understand. Too young to know someone had gunned their father down in the street.

Sitting in a fancy lawyer's office where I didn't belong, waiting to receive more grievous news, it felt like the man across from me would pull the rug out from under us at any moment. It had been devastating to discover that the benefits that should have taken care of us after Chad's death would never come, that his supervisor claimed he couldn't disburse them since he didn't know *why* Chad had been in that part of town when he was meant to be on the other side of town.

It only left me with more questions.

"Mrs. Latour, your late husband arranged for a considerable trust for you and the children, should the day come when he could no longer provide for you all. Your benefactor will use it to make payments into your account monthly, and it will be enough for the three of you to live the way you've become accustomed to for at least one year."

"I-I don't understand," I mumbled, wiping my nose with the tissue in my hand. It felt like I never stopped crying, and the knowledge that Chad had gone even more out of his way to see us taken care of after his death sent me over the edge. "Where did he get that kind of money?" He'd never mentioned setting up a trust fund or anything of the sort.

"I'm not at liberty to discuss it, Mrs. Latour." The man smiled at me, his eyes kind even in the face of my confusion. "But in the meantime, I hope it helps to ease the financial burden you're confronted with after his death. You can continue to stay home with your children during this time of transition, content knowing you'll have money to pay your mortgage and put food on the table. Your benefactor is aware of all your bills and expenses, and he'll send you money accordingly."

"My benefactor. Did he know Chad?" I asked, wringing my hands together.

"Yes. He knew your late husband very well and promised he would see you and your children taken care of should something happen to him."

I nodded, but my eyes darted up into the camera at the corner of the ceiling briefly. The familiar feeling of warmth slid down my spine, the same way it had for years. I'd felt eyes on me so often it had become my new normal. At first, I'd looked over my shoulder constantly, spent nearly a year living in paranoia, but after my shadow saved me in a dark alley, I couldn't seem to muster up fear of that feeling.

A figment of my imagination looked out for me.

Even with my legging-clad ass perched on the edge of the nicest leather chair I'd ever seen and sitting in front of a stunning mahogany desk, I knew something about this situation was unusual. But the signature on the paperwork in front of me was my husband's. An exact copy of his scrawl I'd spent too much time telling him he needed to make legible.

"If he knew Chad so well, why didn't he meet with me himself? I don't understand why he wouldn't want to see me. I'd like to thank him," I said, holding my head high as I stared at the man in front of me.

He smiled, and something about him seemed so familiar. Like I'd seen him before in passing, but I couldn't place him. His brown eyes were warm on mine, his salt and pepper hair short and well-styled. He wore a fitted suit over his lean frame, the refinery of the fit and style showing just how expensive it was.

"He would like to remain anonymous for the time being, but I can promise you he only has your best interest at heart. There will come a time when it is more appropriate that the two of you meet, but for now the important thing is for you to take the time you need to heal. To grieve your loss, Mrs. Latour. I wish you the best of luck in what will undoubtedly be a hard road."

"Why isn't it appropriate that we meet now? I don't understand." My voice dropped a level, moving from the place where I'd been willing to be patient to where I wanted to demand answers as my paranoia grew.

His hands barely touched the surface of the desk as he pushed to his feet and stepped around the massive thing until I had no choice but to stand as well for fear of looking rude. "I'm not at liberty to discuss it at this time," he returned, moving toward the door of the wallpapered office.

"Should I be expecting someone to check on us? To monitor our spending?" I asked, refusing to step away from the desk. I might have stood, but I wouldn't let him dismiss me so casually after he turned my world upside down.

"We'll be in touch," he said vaguely and his hand wrapped around the doorknob.

With a sigh of frustration, I moved toward him and took his hand for a shake. "Perhaps I'll be in touch instead," I said, hinting I wouldn't just lie down and accept his non-answers. It was nice to meet you, Mr. Lombardi," I said, swallowing down the threat of tears. He'd shown me kindness when he didn't need to, understanding how uncertain I must feel in the circumstances.

"Please call me Don. The pleasure was all mine, Mrs. Latour. I hope the next time we meet is under more fortunate circumstances."

I nodded. I didn't understand what had happened to my picture-perfect life. I didn't understand why this had happened to my family.

I turned my head and looked into the camera again before I left the office, unable to stop the way my skin tingled in that too familiar way. I could practically feel the person sitting on the other side of the screen.

Watching. Waiting.

Always.

CHAPTER FOUR

CALLA

Almost one year later

I plastered a smile on my face, smiling brightly to keep the kids from noticing the horror I'd realized as soon as I opened my eyes in my eternally empty bed.

One year.

It had been one year since Chad died, since I lost my husband and my partner. Since my kids lost their father.

I went through the morning routine with a smile on my face, loving the sunshine as it streamed in through the windows of the kitchen. I scrambled eggs. I danced around in my yoga gear.

My sleepy kids groaned at my enthusiasm like they normally did. Axel held his head in his hands at the kitchen counter like he just couldn't handle the fact that morning dared to come. Even Ines dragged in the mornings, and I missed the days when I'd been able to let her sleep just a little longer before I had to carry her to the car to drop Axel off at school.

"Cheesy eggs?" Ines peeped in her tiny voice that melted my heart and the heart of anyone who heard it. A princess through and through, she already wore her rainbow unicorn dress, even if she was half asleep.

"Of course, baby," I smiled back. "Axe, can you grab me the cheese, sweetheart?"

"Okay, Mommy," he murmured, stumbling down from his seat and making for the fridge as I buttered their toast. My heart clenched. I knew the day when my boy stopped calling me mommy approached rapidly. He was already six, already such a tall boy, just like his father.

It hurt that every time I looked at the kids, I saw bits of Chad in them. Like the most bittersweet memory, like I always carried a piece of him with me. Axel had his chocolate hair and square face. Ines had his full lips and green eyes.

Even though I could pick out the traits they inherited from him, there was no doubt they were my kids. Their mannerisms, Ines's hair and Axel's eyes, they were all me. It depressed me to think that in such a brief time, it seemed like the traces of their father in their personalities had disappeared.

Chad hadn't been overly enthusiastic. He was affectionate at the start of our marriage, but that dissipated more and more with every year that passed. Even after all our years together, I couldn't pick out a single thing the kids did that reminded me of him. He was so calm and controlled, there wasn't much to mimic. That only mattered when he'd been home, which grew increasingly less and less often. The rising demands of a career that meant everything to him caused him to spend more time away from home than with his family.

My aunt had asked me once how I could miss a man who was never around when he was alive, but at least then I'd been able to convince myself I wasn't alone.

That what we did for our family, though our roles were separate, was all to work towards the same goal: a happy, safe life for our kids.

I shrugged off the melancholy thoughts and scooped eggs onto their plates, giving them each a piece of toast as I turned to wash the pan. They ate in silence as they woke up.

"Can I stay home today?" Axel asked, and the pan clanged into the sink as I dropped it. Turning back to him, I furrowed my brow in confusion.

"Are you not feeling well?"

"Mommy, I know what day it is," he said, and his little voice went so melancholy that my heart cracked in my chest.

I sighed, abandoning the pan in favor of making my way to my kids. Axel had already finished eating, because nothing could stop that boy from shoveling it into his mouth

Not even the anniversary of his father's death.

I walked around the kitchen island, needing to be within hugging distance for this conversation. "I think it's probably a good idea for you to go to school today." I knelt on the floor at his feet, taking his hands in mine and smiling through the tears burning my eyes. "You don't want to just sit at home and think about it, do you?"

"Could we go to the cemetery?" he asked, turning those deep blue eyes so like mine up to beg me.

"I tell you what," I murmured, reaching out to stroke my hand over the top of his head and brush his hair back from his face. He was due for a haircut, something I always did for him and Chad at the same time. Without Chad, it became a melancholy reminder that we both dreaded. "I have to go to the studio this morning and teach a class, but how about Ines and I pick you up after lunch? We'll go see your Dad and then get ice cream."

"Okay, mommy," he whispered, and I touched my forehead to his, sniffling back the tears one more time.

"That's my brave boy," I said, and I pulled back to stand. "Get your backpack ready for school, okay, Cookie?"

He nodded, darting into the living room to grab his stuff. I knew he needed the minute of privacy, knew that he felt like he needed to be stronger than ever without Chad. Axel became the man of the house at five, and he did the best he could to be older than he was. When I stepped around the corner of the island, Ines caught my eye. She furrowed her tiny brows in confusion and reached up a buttery hand to run her fingers through her hair. She was too young and could barely communicate with words, but she also made no secret of her not remembering her father well. There were moments when she saw Axel missing him, and I could see her trying to grasp what she didn't have.

The reality that she wouldn't be likely to have any memories of her father when she was older was something I couldn't think about without breaking down. It echoed my motherless childhood too closely.

I missed my husband. I missed having a partner. But more than anything, I missed my kids having a father.

"You almost ready, Princess?" I asked her, finishing up the pan and turning her attention back to me. Her expression smoothed out, a bright smile transforming her heart-shaped face.

"Yes, mommy," she peeped, holding up her arms in her high chair. Taking the wet washcloth, I cleaned all the evidence of her breakfast from her face and out of her hair the best I could.

"Are you ready to go see your Grandpa?" I asked as I lifted her out of the chair and carried her into the living room where Axel waited. Hanging out with my dad at his garage had quickly become my little princess's favorite pastime, and I couldn't blame her. I'd spent many years watching him restore vintage cars and handing him tools, feeling like his little helper.

The absence of my mom made it necessary.

I knew my dad probably never expected he'd have to do it all over again with his granddaughter, but I also knew he loved Ines and Axel with everything he was. He would give anything to enjoy his time with them—even be less productive at the shop.

I helped Ines into her spring jacket, zipping her up and booping her nose so she giggled and filled the silence with just a little piece of joy.

I'd take whatever I could get that day.

As soon as I bundled her up, Axel stepped forward to take her little hand in his while I grabbed her bag of toys to play with for the few hours she would spend at the shop with her Grandpa. They stood by the door and waited patiently while I grabbed my purse, and then we were out for another hectic morning of drop-offs.

Axel held his sister tight until I got the car door open and hoisted her inside. Always her protector, it overjoyed me to see just how close they'd become in the absence of Chad. I loved that he stepped up to help with Ines. I just hated that it was necessary at all.

Perhaps it was time to consider Aunt Sigrid's encouragement that the time had come to consider dating again. Even if the thought filled me with dread, didn't I owe it to my son to give him a father figure? To let him sit back and be a kid again?

I did everything I could, but for a boy who'd been raised with a hero for a father, it just wasn't enough.

I wasn't enough, and I never would be. No matter how much I wanted to be.

Once I'd gotten Ines settled into her seat, I walked around to the driver's side of the car and opened the backdoor to check that Axel fastened himself in correctly. He rolled his eyes at me. Always my independent man who knew he could do it himself. I checked every time anyway, because I would never forgive myself if I didn't and something happened. He'd understand one day.

I pressed a sloppy kiss to his cheek that made him groan. "Mommy," he protested, wiping his cheek with the sleeve of his jacket furiously. Once I climbed in the front seat and started the car, music from Ines's favorite princess movie immediately assaulted me, and Axel groaned again.

Backing out of the driveway while I changed it to the radio, Ines voiced her protest. "Princess, Mommy!"

"You know how it works, baby. You got the stereo yesterday. Today is Axel's turn." She pursed her little lips into a scowl as she glared at me, but I ignored it. I did not have time for a two-year-old tantrum today.

Nope.

I would not feed the terror that was my toddler.

Pulling up to my dad's shop a few minutes later, any threat of a meltdown disappeared the moment she saw her Grandpa strolling out the door. He tugged her door open, looking all around the interior of the car. "Where's my favorite granddaughter?" he asked. "Calla Lily, did you forget her at home?"

"Here, Grampa!" she squealed, kicking her little legs.

"Oh!" He smacked his forehead playfully. "How could I have missed the prettiest girl in the world?" His hands went to her car seat, unbuckling her and tugging him into his arms. "Have a good day at school, my Axel boy," he added, turning that warm smile to his grandson.

I'd long since been convinced that there was nothing my dad couldn't fix, so when he made Axel smile, it only confirmed my belief. The man was a miracle worker.

"I'll try, Grandpa."

"She has juice and snacks in her bag, and she brought her ponies today—" I started, wincing when he narrowed his eyes at me.

Dad shrugged me off, "Somehow, I kept you alive all your childhood. I think I've got it covered." Axel laughed in the back seat, and I twisted my face up to glare at both of them. Moms just couldn't help themselves.

"Try not to get into too much trouble today, my darling daughter." My dad's words only deepened my glare as I stuck my tongue out at him. He grabbed Ines's bag from the floor of the back seat, and then I steeled my spine as I backed out of my parking space to bring Axel to school.

I swear you get in *one* public argument with the President of the PTA, and people never let you live it down.

Psh.

Thankfully, Axel's school and the yoga studio were close to Dad's shop, so we only drove in silence for a few minutes before I parked in the studio lot and hopped out. Axel climbed out of the back, hoisting his bookbag up into place. It was too heavy for his age, but my boy wouldn't have it any other way. He let me hold his hand as we walked down the sidewalk and crossed the street. Every morning I thanked my lucky stars that I'd gotten a job at the studio right next to his school, because between dropping off Ines and then dropping off Axel, the idea of having to load myself into the car to go to some other part of town to work for a few hours exhausted me.

The wrought-iron fencing and the gate of the school came into view, and I tried not to flinch at the sight of all the moms dropping their kids off and looking immaculate in their trendy clothes.

Drop off was always painful. I was always the mom who rolled up in elastic-waist pants in a school that rolled its eyes every time I set foot inside it.

The fact was, Axel was smart. Too smart for public school, apparently.

He had a head for numbers, understanding them in a way that I had no clue where it came from. His school picked him out of the class in his first week of preschool, saying he was an exceptionally gifted boy.

He'd been reading when his classmates were learning the alphabet. He could count to one hundred when they were counting to ten. So, Chad and I had pulled the money out of nowhere, paying the tuition for the fancy private school that hosted gifted children. They strongly emphasized the importance of having a parental figure at home to encourage learning and help with the pile of home-work they sent home every night. Most days, I wondered if I should just let Axel be more of a kid, but I couldn't deny the joy he felt when he solved the latest problems they presented him with.

So I tolerated the perfect moms with the flawless blowouts and the stylish outfits and snide looks. So what if I pulled my platinum hair into a messy bun on my head? So what if my black yoga pants clung to my thighs in a way that the elite found inappropriate?

I did what I had to do to get by in the shit situation life threw at me.

"You'll pick me up early?" he asked as we stepped up to the gates, and the sadness in his voice made me glance down at him. He was normally so excited for school, darting off so quickly I sometimes had to fight to get a hug goodbye.

I sighed, nodding as I hugged him tight. "Yeah, Axe. I'll pick you up early. Just a few hours, and we'll go see your Dad. Okay?"

"Okay, Mommy."

"I love you." I didn't bother to tell him to have a good day. I wasn't that naïve.

"I love you too," he whispered, before darting inside the gates of the school. Two of his friends met up with him, flanking him in that way that only your closest friends could manage. His best friend, James, glanced back at me, giving me a wave as if to say he had it covered.

I nodded back at him, pressing a hand to my face before I stepped away and out of sight. James had been there for Axel through the funeral. He'd been there through all of it. He'd see my boy through the day.

I just had to get through mine.

Determined to do just that, I turned my back on the school and made my way back down the road to the crosswalk. On any normal day, having only ten minutes before my first class started would have stressed me out. But I couldn't wait to clear my head and lose myself in yoga. So, with that in mind, I hurried across the street—waving to the car that let me cross.

A familiar face waited for me on the other side, greeting me with a smile like every other day. "Good morning, beautiful," he murmured when my foot touched the sidewalk.

I resisted the urge to huff a laugh. "Good morning, Casey." Sometimes, I wondered if he even knew my name, or if he just ignored it. Though our inter-actions were very brief, he always inserted a compliment in his greeting.

He bit his bottom lip shyly, his fair skin looking like such a harsh contrast next to the black fabric of his suit. It didn't fit him, but there was no chance I would invite him to continue a conversation with me by making observations about his appearance. "Are you busy tonight?"

Even if I'd suspected the words might come, I hadn't ever wanted them. While Casey was an amiable man, I just wasn't interested. If I ever dated again, it would be for the sake of the kids, but even then, I wanted a man who could consume me. A man who could be consumed by me and make me feel like I was the center of his universe.

While my marriage had been content, I wished for a future one to be what you could only read about in romance books. It was a shame it didn't exist, and even if it did, it wouldn't for me. To love was to lose, and I would never put myself at risk for that again.

"I have plans with my kids," I said, not bothering to mention the rather unfortunate timing of his decision to prod into my plans and life.

"What about this weekend?" he asked, and I sighed lightly and rubbed my arms awkwardly.

His face dropped instantly, and he could read my body language well enough to know what was coming. "You should probably know I'm not interested in dating," I said, keeping my voice as soft as I could. "I have my kids, and they're all I need."

"Right," he said, rubbing his hand over the back of his head. "Of course. That makes sense." It was comical to watch how he tried to understand the rejection, but I imagined that he didn't put himself out there often. Not when it had taken him months to work up the courage to ask me.

"I'll catch you later," I said, ducking into the yoga studio to avoid the awkwardness of that conversation. I didn't get asked out often, fortunately for me. Dealing with the aftermath was shit.

Once I was inside the studio with the calming music and my mat at the front of the room, I drew in what felt like my first deep breath of the day. The scent of rose hit me, the essential oil of the night before permeating the space in a relaxing aroma.

As much as the yoga studio had started as just a job I was qualified to do, after years of staying home with the kids, I'd quickly become dependent on it. It would be a sad day when I left town and the studio behind. When I officially saved enough money despite our benefactor funds running out, we'd move somewhere smaller, somewhere new where people didn't look at us with sympathy, and memories of Chad didn't assault me every time I turned around. By the time I stripped my shoes off and dropped my purse in the back of the studio, students filled the main room and laid out their mats. I went to my own, standing and smiling at my class even though it was the last thing I felt like doing.

It felt like my theme for the day.

CHAPTER FIVE

RYKER

My knuckles dripped blood as I stepped *into* the warehouse.

That was a first.

The stupid fucker should have listened to me when I told him to stay away from my woman. Instead, he'd laid the groundwork to ask her out. The only reason he'd walked away alive was because Calla turned him down succinctly. If she hadn't, I'd be wringing blood from my clothes.

The black jeans on my legs felt too restrictive on my ass and thighs, too tight against my skin, and I knew they needed replacing. I'd gained more mass in the previous month than any other. When waiting for Calla to be mine became unbearable, I spent my days in my home gym or preparing for her insertion into my life. Toddler proofing my home proved interesting, but I wouldn't risk Ines and Axel's safety for the sake of keeping the aesthetic of my converted warehouse.

I could have worn one of my new suits, but I didn't want to waste them on wet work. They didn't belong in my filthy torture chamber and covered in the blood of my enemies.

My boots were fairly new, fortunately. My last victim had bled so much that the old ones filled with blood, and there was just no getting the metallic scent of blood out of them. When I thought of Calla or the kids stumbling on them, I physically grimaced.

I'd gone waterproof with my newest pair.

The black T-shirt clung to my chest and strained against my arms, and even I had to realize that if I wanted to have any chance of *not* terrifying the living shit out of Calla when she got a good look at me, getting bigger probably hadn't been the best way to go.

My woman was in for a shock, but she was strong. Stronger than anyone expected of her, I suspected.

Most people saw the little pescatarian, yoga instructor widow and thought life had sufficiently beaten her down. I saw how she only shone brighter for the suffering life thrust at her.

She wasn't broken. She just sacrificed every bit of herself for her kids, just the way she had even when Chad had been in the picture. But those days were done.

One more day and she would no longer be a single mother. She'd be mine. Those kids would be mine.

The way they always should have been.

"Yo, where you been?" Simon asked, grinning at me as I stepped into the freezer. Simon was classically handsome, unlike most of the rest of the Bellandis, with dark hair and eyes that attracted even the most skittish of women—lulling them into a false sense of security. Like the devil couldn't be attractive. He glanced down at the fists still clenched at my sides. "You realize you're bleeding, right?"

"Not mine," I grunted.

Simon widened his eyes on my face, staring at me like I'd lost my mind. It didn't bother me in the slightest, not with how common of an occurrence it was. "And you didn't wash your hands?"

"I'm just going to get bloody again," I told him, watching as Matteo's chest shook with a silent chuckle in the corner of the room where he lurked in the shadows. So like me in some ways, but so different in others.

Namely, he didn't have the same thirst for blood and screams that I did.

The man sitting strapped down to the wooden chair in the center of the room struggled against his binds. Matteo stepped out of the shadows as the door mostly closed behind me, leaving just a crack for some fresh air to get in. The freezer stunk like death and the floors were stained by all the blood that had spilt over the years I'd been working for the Bellandis, since Matteo's father brought me on.

Matteo hadn't technically been a grown man then, still nearly a year away from his high school graduation and entirely wrapped up in Ivory. He'd never known about the slaughter his father had allowed in exchange for my services.

"You know, there was a day when you would always beat me here," Matteo chuckled, crossing his arms over his chest and raising his brow at me.

He was right. For years, this place and the release it offered had been the only thing that kept me going.

Then, after I'd met my Sunshine, it had been the only thing to distract me from the obsession that coursed through my veins like the sweetest torment.

The moment she cast her light on the shadows I called home, the piece of me I'd thought gone forever snapped back into place.

"I think we can give him a break today," Simon laughed, stepping up to the man in the chair. He grabbed him by the hair, tugging his head back until he looked up at Simon with pleading eyes. "Don't you think so, Seamus?" he asked, and the middle-aged man nodded his head enthusiastically.

"Guess you're in luck. Tiernan's lowlife says to cut you a break. I guess it isn't every day you get ready to lock your woman and her kids in your house for the foreseeable future." Matteo smiled at me. "I do not envy you the kids. They complicate things."

I shrugged, because I didn't see it that way in the slightest. Without the kids, Calla would fight me every step of the way. She wouldn't go as quietly as Ivory had when Matteo claimed her. She'd be much more likely to claw my eyes out while I slept. With them, I had some leverage, because she would do whatever it took to keep them safe.

Even if it meant keeping them oblivious to the circumstances of their move and biting her tongue when she wanted to verbally assault me.

Underneath her peace-loving, granola crunching exterior, my Sunshine had a creative grasp on the English language.

Even if I never intended to hurt them, those kids were my leverage. It just so happened that I adored them as much as I loved their mother. I'd watched them grow, arguably a more present fixture in their lives than their biological father had been, even when he wasn't buried six feet in the ground.

They didn't know it, but I'd seen it all.

"They're mine as much as she is," I added with another shrug when Matteo looked at me expectantly. He looked thoughtful for a moment before his face broke into a dark grin that made the man in the chair tremble even more. "Is Don ready for tomorrow?" I asked, instead of letting Matteo steer the conversation further down the path of my relationship with my woman. If he hadn't had Ivory, I wouldn't have been able to tolerate his interest in her. Even with Ivory, it was difficult to resist the urge to cut him.

I didn't like people who showed an interest in Calla. I'd spent far too much time over the past year chasing off would-be suitors looking to take from her.

Nobody but me would ever touch her again, and the entire year she'd gone without sex would help make her as desperate as I felt every day when I jerked off to thoughts of her.

There was nothing I wouldn't do to claim her.

"He's ready. Not looking forward to it, but he's ready." Matteo grimaced with his words. Don had been hesitant when I first involved him in my plans, not enjoying the prospect of deceiving a grieving widow in the slightest. Personally, I thought he was more likely terrified of what would happen when Calla realized she'd been lied to and tricked into letting her stalker support her and her kids financially.

I couldn't blame him there.

"Good," I grunted. "Are we done gossiping? Can we move on to the corpse?" I asked.

Simon chuckled at me, stepping away from the chair to lean against the wall with his arms crossed over his chest. "He ain't no corpse."

"He will be soon enough," I answered, stepping over to my table of tools and picking out my favorite knife.

Matteo's levity faded to the ruthless mask he wore to rule the city, but he stayed back. Always letting me take over, because, unlike the others, I enjoyed this part.

I enjoyed every scream, and every time they begged me for mercy. Enjoyed every pulse of blood as it left their bodies.

"Where is Murphy planning to base his operation?" Matteo asked, and the silence of his answer sealed his fate.

I enjoyed every second of his torture.

CHAPTER SIX

CALLA

I carried Ines as we walked along the path in the cemetery. It had been months since we visited, months since Axel asked to talk to his Dad.

I thought about it too often, about the fact that our lives were moving on. Our time of grieving had come to an inevitable close, even though I wasn't ready. I knew I had to be. The kids deserved better than for me to cling to the memory of what we'd once had.

Of what we would never have again.

But I wanted it back. I wanted to feel what it meant to have someone sleep next to me and wake up next to me. I just couldn't ever risk losing it again.

Axel's hand was tight in mine, clutching with more strength than I'd have thought possible coming from his little hand. Even though it had been months, he remembered the walk as much as I did. There'd been weeks when we'd come every day. Weeks when we'd braved the cooling early winter air to sit on the grass for hours until our noses were red and runny.

But something about the one-year mark felt significant. Like it foretold a shift.

Like we finally had to move on fully.

The thought of leaving Chad behind made me hurt all over, and from the ashen look on Axel's face, I imagined the feeling was mutual. Ines clung to me. Even she was silent where she would have normally babbled happily. When we turned onto the grass, Axel pushed his shoulders back, releasing my hand suddenly. I tried not to wince from the loss.

He wanted to be a big boy when he talked to his father, and I had to respect that.

Even if it killed me.

Because he was my baby, and he always would be.

My heart thumped in my chest when Chad's tombstone came into view. Even though it was simple, there was no mistaking it. Not with the way the stones that surrounded it had aged. His family: his mother, his father, and his brother, had all died in a car accident before we met, leaving Chad alone. My kids were the only Latours left.

I touched the stone as we came up to it, setting Ines down. She curled her legs up underneath her, placing the flowers she'd brought on the grass gently. Axel sat in front of the stone in silence, staring at the words intently.

Father.

Husband.

Officer.

Chad's life reduced down to three words and a few scrapbooks worth of pictures.

I stood there, letting Axel have his silent conversation with his father. When he turned his blue eyes up to me finally, they seemed far too old in his little boy face. "Can I talk to him alone for a minute?" he asked.

"Sure," I said, though the request shocked me. Another moment where he wanted to show how grown-up he was, and it filled me with dread. I still remembered when he'd been a newborn who demanded to be held all the time. I still remembered when he was a teething toddler and punching handsome strangers in the park. For him, it was a lifetime ago. For me, it felt like yesterday.

I tightened my fingers around the stone, pausing. While I had every intention of giving my son the time he needed, a part of me knew I wouldn't be visiting the cemetery soon.

It was well and truly goodbye in a way that I hadn't yet let myself feel.

With a sniffle, I grabbed Ines's hand, leading her back to the path where I could keep Axel in my sight but give him the privacy he needed. I watched his lips move for a moment before I stopped watching and turned my attention down to my baby girl. "How does ice cream sound?" I asked her, tucking her platinum hair behind her ear.

"Yum!" she said with a grin.

"I think so too. I'm going to get spinach ice cream," I teased her, tapping her nose and getting a giggle.

"Eww. Cookie!"

"Spinach cookie ice cream?" I asked her with a smile.

"Nooo. Mommy silly," she laughed, hugging my leg tight.

"Okay, okay. Cookie dough it is," I murmured, bending down and tapping my cheek with my finger. "But I think you have to pay the ice cream toll first."

She smiled, pressing a sloppy kiss to my cheek.

As she went back to frolicking on the surrounding path, something drew my eyes to the familiar area in the distance, the place where my mother's grave sat. My father still visited regularly, so I knew if I wandered over I would find it maintained. Whenever we visited Chad, I couldn't bring myself to wander over.

I'd never known her, given that she'd died in childbirth, but I felt the echoes of her life through every second of mine. It was there in the way my father loved her fiercely after nearly three decades without her. It was there in the gentle smile I saw in her photos.

It was there in her absence, painted on my soul as I'd grown up without a mother to talk to me about all the things a girl needed a mother for.

Just like a boy needed a father.

"You okay?" I asked, turning to Axel when he walked up next to us. His shoulders were back, his face less pale.

Whatever he'd said to his father, he felt better for having done it.

"Yeah, Mommy. I'm good." I hugged him to my side, sniffling in his hair once before I forced it down.

"Let's go get that ice cream then," I whispered, standing up and holding out a hand for Axel to take. As my eyes settled on the area behind him, a shadow moved through the trees at the edge of the cemetery grounds. There one minute and gone the next. I smiled, thinking of the shadow who'd saved me.

Shadows couldn't exist without light.

We were slower to walk the route back to the car with Ines walking along beside us with her little legs. Where Axel was tall like his father, she'd gotten my petite build, so it felt like it took us hours to make the trip.

It didn't matter though, because with my kids on either side of me, I held my entire world in my hands.

I could survive anything if it meant giving them the best life possible.

Even being alone.

I SET my book down with a glance at the clock hanging on the wall. It was late enough that there was little to no choice. Turning the light off as I stood, I made my way to the stairs with nothing but the light from the streetlamps streaming in the windows. My fingers trailed over Chad's favored recliner as I passed, a gentle reminder that nobody had touched it in a year. Nobody dared to sit in the supple leather, although it was easily the most comfortable spot in the cozy living room. Nobody wanted to displace him from our lives.

But as I peeked inside each of the kids' bedrooms, stalling however I could, the thought sounded ridiculous even in the privacy of my mind.

Chad was dead.

He'd been dead, and nothing would ever change that. Still, I couldn't erase the memory of him falling asleep in the chair with Axel in his arms when he'd been a baby. I couldn't erase the vision of him perching on the edge every morning as he pulled on his black boots.

Nobody would ever sit in that chair again, and I couldn't live in a mausoleum. I'd have my dad help me put it on the curb over the weekend.

As I made my way into our bedroom, I stared at the massive king bed. Releasing a sigh with a sad smile, I made my way over to it. It was too big to be empty. Too big for just me.

Climbing on top of the covers on my side of the bed, I tried to will away the tension in my body. There was nothing I wanted more than to relax and just fade to sleep, but even lonely widows had needs.

Needs that went unmet with two children to think of and not wanting a relationship.

I stared at the ceiling for a moment, wishing the need away. Reading romance novels never helped my situation, but for a few moments of my day, it was nice to get lost in a world where things like true love existed.

It was nice to read about happily ever afters for couples who deserved them, for women who could let themselves be vulnerable enough to love. To read about men who would do anything for their women.

With a glance at the closed door, I let my fingers touch the tops of my thighs. They were too soft, too delicate as they slid my nightgown up to my hips. I didn't look down as I slid my hand inside my underwear, clenching my eyes tight to dispel the reality that it was my fingers that touched me. My own fingers that slid through the wetness that lingered despite my crushing loneliness. Two fingers at my clit, circling gently as my eyes clenched tighter. Shadows permeated the haze of my vision, feeling like they never left. Like my shadows were everywhere, lurking just beyond view.

My back arched as the heat of pleasure consumed me, as the building orgasm rose to my well-practiced and efficient movements.

But even with the way I knew my body so well, there was only one thing that could ever send me tumbling over the edge of oblivion. The guilt I felt with the vision never lessened, not even with all the time that had passed.

Vivid blue eyes shone through the haze of darkness inside my head, drawing a gasp from me as my back arched further and my fingers slowed to coax the last tingles of my release from my body before guilt overwhelmed me.

Vaulting myself off the bed, I made for the bathroom with guilt pulsing through my body.

It wasn't my husband's memory that got me off. Not ever.

But a shadowed stranger with blue eyes that I had no business thinking about.

The shower called to me, to the dirty feeling that crawled along my skin.

Just like always.

CHAPTER SEVEN

RYKER

I shoved open the door of the beat-up car I used whenever I needed to go beneath the radar.

My Maserati would have stuck out like a sore thumb on Calla's residential street all night. As I made my way across the road, sticking to the shadows, the hair on my head clung to my skin and tickled my neck. Still damp from my shower after I'd washed the stench of the warehouse off my skin, it was too thick to dry quickly.

I hadn't wanted to waste any more time. The only thing that had prolonged me getting to Calla's was my desire to double check that everything was ready for her and the kids' arrival the next day. I'd checked every last touch, watching Calla on the video feed on my phone.

Touching herself.

It wasn't often my Sunshine took matters into her own hands so literally, and I both cursed and thanked the panties blocking my view as she writhed on her bed. It should have been my hands sliding her nightgown up her thighs and my fingers stroking her pussy.

There should have been nothing but me dancing in her head as she came. It always made me wonder what it was she thought of, but I'd never ask.

If it wasn't me, it would mean I needed to kill someone.

The bedrooms were set, the furniture of the main space rearranged to accommodate the play area the guys would set up for the kids when I took Calla to go collect them after I explained her new reality.

Nobody saw me, despite my size, as I maneuvered through the streets like the creep I was. The house was dark, as I'd known it would be. I'd watched, waited, until the moment Calla's eyes closed, and she was lost to the land of dreams.

My Sunshine was a deep sleeper, never even sensing me when I crept into her room almost nightly.

When I made it to the front door, my key to her house was already in hand. Turning the lock, I pushed the door open and slipped inside. The motion of closing the door perfectly quietly was all too easy and familiar as I toed off my boots and clicked the lock back into place.

Navigating the stairs, I stealthily avoided the spots that squeaked, skipping the worst step altogether. I'd been doing it since the first night Calla slept alone there after Chad's death. The first night she'd finally gone back into the bedroom she'd shared with her husband when he lived.

Weeks had passed where she'd slept on the couch, as if she couldn't face the empty bed and her loneliness.

She couldn't know she wasn't alone. I was there, watching her every move. Supporting her through the transition as she came to terms with the shift in her life.

I spared a glance into each of the kids' rooms, smiling as I saw them sleeping contentedly. Even knowing what a hard day it must have been for Axel, I also knew he'd handled it well. He'd said goodbye to his father, had asked him to send someone to take care of his mother and sister.

His wish would come true the next day, though Chad probably rolled in his grave knowing that his wife was mine now.

The door to Calla's room stood wide open, the way she always left it in case either of the kids needed her in the night. It made it risky: me being in her room with her, given that Ines could easily have a nightmare and seek her mother at any moment.

It had happened twice. The first time I'd convinced the half-asleep girl she was dreaming and tucked her back into bed. The second, I hid on the floor next to Calla's bed, waiting for the two of them to resettle and fall back asleep before I snuck back out.

But nothing could keep me away.

And that night, as I sat on Calla's bed next to her and reached a hand out to hover over her sweet face pinched in frustration in her sleep, I knew it would be the last time I did this. The last time I watched her sleep and couldn't hold her. The last time I had to sneak into her bedroom.

I would never take having her in my arms for granted.

Wanting to remember the moment, I pulled my silenced phone from my pocket and took a picture of my hand against the side of her face as I tucked her hair back behind her ear. The scent of her lavender shampoo filled the air with the movement, instantly calming the raging urge to claim that roared in my veins. She tilted her head, pressing into my touch more even in her sleep like she knew it was me and emitted a happy little sigh.

The next day, Calla would be mine.

Our story would finally begin.

CHAPTER EIGHT

CALLA

The next morning felt so much lighter. Axel's mood had visibly improved the moment he finished talking to his father. By the time we made it to the ice cream parlor, he'd been smiling with Ines and doing all the goofy tricks he knew to make her squeal with laughter.

That was my boy.

I felt particularly relaxed after my yoga classes of the morning, ready to grab my baby girl from my dad and go home and bake some cookies with her to surprise Axel.

I got hung up at the studio when my Aunt Sigrid called, but I didn't mind spending extra time in the back room. It was just as relaxing as ever, with the scent of sandalwood permeating the air that day. If I hadn't wanted children with every gear in my body, I'd have wanted a home that smelled like the essential oils of the yoga studio. Something minimalist, with only the furniture necessary to live in and nothing extra. "I'm glad to hear that he could turn the day around. I worried about you three all day," she said with a somber note to her voice. She'd never been fond of Chad, always said there was just something off about him and avoided him when spending time with the kids and I, but that didn't mean that she couldn't sympathize with the loss we felt when he died.

"It was okay, in the end. It kind of felt like it was exactly what we needed. That one last day to grieve before we really start moving forward. We've just been getting by, but they deserve better," I sighed. "I just don't know how to do better for them."

"You're doing great, sweetheart. You're the best mom I know, but Axel is coming to that age where he will need a male influence in his life. Have you considered getting back out there? Dating a bit and testing the waters?" I sipped my water to stall before I swallowed and answered, even if I knew it wasn't the response she wanted.

"He has a male influence. He has Dad."

"And your father is an amazing grandfather, Calla. But the three of you need someone in that house to be there all the time. They need a father figure, and I know it hurts you to hear that. They can't have their dad, but you could meet someone amazing and give them a great step-father. You just need to open yourself up to that first."

I sighed, glancing at the door and deciding it was time to go get my girl. I was *so not* ready for this conversation, even if I had been considering the necessity of it myself. "I'm not ready to date. Maybe I'll get there eventually, but for now I just want to focus on us." I grabbed my purse off the table as I stood, cutting off her protests when I continued, "I've got to go. I'm late to pick up Ines, but I'll call you in a couple days. Okay?"

"Yeah, sweetheart," she sighed, her disappointment and pity clear in every syllable of the words. "I'll talk to you soon."

"Love you," I said as I hung up the phone and shoved the phone into my purse.

Stepping out the front door, I turned my back to the street as I dug my keys out of my purse and shoved it into the deadbolt to lock the front door. I'd only barely pulled the key free when a voice made me jump so high, I thought I might hit the overhang. "Mrs. Latour?" a male voice said, and I spun to stare up at the man I recognized all too well for only having met him once.

I'd never been able to forget the day I met Mr. Lombardi. I suspected I never would, not with the way I still felt suspicious of the situation a year later.

"Mr. Lombardi?" I asked, confusion rising as I shook off my fright.

"I apologize. I didn't mean to startle you." There was concern written on his face, much like there had been previously when we'd met in the law office and he'd given me the news of the trust.

"It's alright." I smiled at him, feeling ridiculous for the continual way I felt on edge. Like the way I felt eyes on me wherever I went couldn't possibly be anything other than Chad's work buddies monitoring the kids and I to be sure we were safe. "Can I help you with something?"

He cleared his throat, straightening his shoulders to stand taller. "Your benefactor would like to meet you, if you would please come with me."

"He—what?" I gaped in confusion.

"He feels the timing is more appropriate now that it's been a year and you are no longer in the throes of your grief." He gestured to the luxury town car parked in front of the studio.

"Now?" I asked incredulously. The audacity of the man to assume that I had nothing better to do than be summoned when it was convenient for him. I owed him an impressive deal of gratitude for the way he'd handled our expenses for the last year, but being called on made me feel like a dog that needed to be brought to heel. "I have to go get my daughter."

"Surely your father can watch her for an extra hour, Mrs. Latour." Mr. Lombardi smiled at me, raising a brow like he dared me to contradict him. I should have known that he would know where Ines went while I worked, given the fact that this mysterious benefactor paid our bills. I had a feeling he knew far more about me than I would feel comfortable with.

"I'm not comfortable riding in your car to some undisclosed location. I'm sorry if that's insulting, it's just—"

"That's alright. I would be more concerned if you got in the car. Would you like me to give you the address, and I can meet you there to make the introduction?"

I considered saying no and requesting he meet me at a location we arranged ahead of time, but the prospect of him turning away when I might finally get the answers I'd wanted for a year was an opportunity I couldn't pass up. I nodded, reassuring myself because of how accommodating he was. Serial killers didn't pay your bills for a year and then let you come with your own vehicle.

Right?

"That would be preferable, yes," I said in an attempt not to show the dark path my thoughts had taken. He slipped a card out of his pocket with a hand-written address on it and passed it to me.

"I'll see you in a little while, Mrs. Latour," he said with a slight smile before he strode for his town car. I went to the lot, dialing Dad to ask him to keep Ines for a bit longer as I went. It wasn't until I got in my car and pulled out that I realized Mr. Lombardi's town car was directly behind me and that he'd waited for me to leave.

I wasn't sure if that should feel reassuring.

But it didn't.

CHAPTER NINE

RYKER

I answered the ringing phone in my pocket. "Don?" I asked, and the man chuckled. Undoubtedly at the way my voice came out as a whisper. If he ever spoke a word of my nerves to the others, he'd doom me to a life of torment.

"I've made contact. She's driving herself as expected, but we're on our way."

"Good," I grunted before hanging up the phone and shoving it back in my pocket with a swallow.

I was going to come out of my skin.

It had been a long time since I'd felt so anxious, since I'd let someone else have enough power over me that they could riddle me with anxiety. But the knowledge that Calla was in her car, on her way to her new home, threatened to push me over the edge into a fit. They were the only people who would ever see the other side of me. The part of me I'd saved just for them.

I wanted to go to the gym on the other side of the warehouse I'd converted into a home for the four of us. Wanted to push myself until my body threatened to cave beneath the pressure.

I paced around on the rustic looking hardwood floors that I'd had refinished, my shoes tapping against the floor with every step. I hadn't wanted to wear a suit for Calla's first visit to her new home and her first impression of me in years, but we'd be picking Axel up from school shortly and that required a bit of clout. Calla's days of being the outcast in that school were done.

I'd invested enough money in the last few months that I practically owned it.

As I paced, I thought of Calla's journey to her new home. I could only imagine what would go through her mind when she traveled farther and farther outside the city limits. Would she consider turning around?

Would she register the danger she willingly drove herself into?

It wouldn't matter in the end. Calla was far too curious not to meet me now that the opportunity presented itself. She'd want to meet the man who had managed her finances so efficiently for her. She'd want to meet the man who knew her husband better than she did.

Even if she didn't know that.

So even when her instinct was to turn back, my Sunshine would keep going. I knew that, even though she would fight it, she was as drawn to me as I was to her.

Like a thread tethered us together, she felt me when I was nearby. Like my very presence was ingrained in her soul, and she couldn't seem to rid herself of me. All it took was a few minutes together four years ago, but the bond between us pulled taut, anyway.

When the sound of cars came down the dirt driveway, I chanced a glance out the smaller windows at the front of the building. Sure enough, Calla's practical sedan made its way down the road as slowly as could be. Hesitation had no doubt set in as soon as her eyes landed on the building.

From the front, it did kind of look like a convenient place to murder someone.

I supposed that's why I liked it.

It was private, with nothing nearby. The front of the house was visible from the road that nobody ever traveled down, but trees came in from the woods surrounding it to disguise most of the property. From the front, no one would ever guess just how large the building was, or that there was a beautiful yard in the back.

It hadn't always been that way, of course. What the fuck did I need a yard for?

But my boy liked sports as much as he liked numbers, and it was about time my little Princess learned to swim.

Calla's car stopped out front, but she didn't move to get out until Don parked beside her and climbed out of the car. He smiled at her broadly, trying to reassure her. She returned it with a crooked smile that showed her nerves matched my own.

Stepping away from the window, I forced myself to move into the kitchen. Then I glanced around, wondering where I should be in the house when she walked in.

Did I sit down and try to make myself not look so big?

Did I stand and just own it?

Why the fuck hadn't I given it any thought?

Shit.

I was not ready for this. But fuck it.

It was time for my Sunshine to meet me again.

CHAPTER TEN

CALLA

It was official.

I was going to die.

I'd let myself be lulled into a false sense of security, foolishly believing that Mr. Lombardi couldn't mean to hurt me, because who paid for a year of expenses just to kill someone?

Apparently, my *benefactor* did, that's who.

The drive up the dirt road hadn't boded well for me, and I should have taken the sign for what it was and turned around. Because when the building came into view, I knew I was fucked.

An old warehouse. The original function seemed indiscernible at a glance. All that remained was a generic, boxy brick structure, but even with the signs of its age, it was clearly cared for. Someone had given it a modern touch with new windows, and the shrubbery in front of the building wasn't overgrown.

A brand new and beautifully detailed massive brick fence surrounded the property, and even though the gate was thrown open when I pulled up, I wanted to crawl in a hole when I saw the guard booth tucked behind the fence, even if it was empty.

It felt like a prison, like whoever lived there put that fence to keep someone inside just as much as to keep the rest of humanity out.

What kind of monster needed to be caged inside an old warehouse? Why would Chad have been friends with someone like that?

When I finally pulled my car in front of the building, I still couldn't convince my body that it was time to get out—not when pure terror pulsed through me. The same way that my body randomly tingled with the awareness of being watched, I couldn't shake the feeling that something horrific was about to walk into my life.

Stepping foot inside that building would mean horrible things for me. And yet, I couldn't bring myself to put the car in reverse either. I couldn't walk away from whatever waited for me inside.

When Mr. Lombardi parked his car next to mine, the older man didn't hesitate to climb out of his car and make his way to me with an enormous smile. He tugged my door open, and I had the distinct impression he really was that much of a gentleman, but that the circumstances at present also just dictated he ushered me into the house.

It was disconcerting, but I somehow unbuckled my seatbelt and turned off the ignition in the car. When my legs swung out of the car, I glanced down at my yoga pant clad thighs and winced. Meeting my mysterious benefactor in workout gear had probably not been my smartest choice, but I supposed it wouldn't matter if he killed me.

And it wasn't like they'd given me much choice after picking me up from the studio and demanding I come immediately.

With a little groan of annoyance at myself, I stood from the seat and let Mr. Lombardi close the door. I took the arm he held out, letting him guide me to the front door even though I wanted to run in the other direction.

When his hand touched the door, I spun to look back at the gated driveway as the wrought iron clicked together dramatically and sealed me inside. The man at my left only patted my arm in some pathetic attempt to be reassuring, but we were so past that point it didn't matter.

"What's going on?" I asked him finally.

"I assure you, you're perfectly safe. For security reasons, it's necessary for Mr. Fiore to take certain precautions with his privacy and the safety of his home. That's all."

"Maybe I should go," I protested when he turned the knob on the door. "I can meet him in a public place. I didn't imagine this would be so private when I agreed to come here. I imagined another office, not his home." I glanced toward my car, wondering if I should just get back in and go. Something felt wrong about the entire situation, and my skin tingled as it tried to warn me of the coming danger.

"This is where he wanted the meeting to take place. He will never hurt you, please know that. I wouldn't allow myself to be involved in this if I thought otherwise," he said reassuringly. The knob turned finally, and he shoved the door in until I was peering inside.

The sight of the bright entryway and luxurious kitchen that greeted me shocked me momentarily, but it couldn't distract me from the dread I felt when I turned to face Mr. Lombardi again. "Involved in what, exactly?"

He clenched his jaw, guiding me inside the front door. It took more force than it had previously, more like my legs solidified and just couldn't be convinced to cross that final threshold.

I knew when I did, nothing would be the same ever again. I had no clue how I could know something like that, but I could feel *him* inside. Whoever he was.

Waiting.

My skin pebbled in goosebumps, the hair rising on my arms when the door closed behind me and trapped me inside the space. When the massive figure rounded the corner from behind the brick wall, the first thing I saw was the piercing blue of his eyes as he stared at me.

The same blue eyes that had haunted my dreams and consumed my pleasure for the year since Chad died.

When my eyes darted over his face to his midnight hair, there was no denying the obvious. No denying the similarity between him and the man I'd met in the park years prior, even if the one in front of me was a few years older and a few sizes broader.

I knew him.

"Hello, Tesoro."

"Mrs. Latour this is—"

"Don't call her that," the massive beast of a man growled at Mr. Lombardi.

Nerves had me biting my lip before I spoke. "But that's my name. Am I in the wrong place?" I asked, turning wide eyes back to Mr. Lombardi at my side.

"You're right where you belong." The deep voice drew my attention back to him.

"Calla," Mr. Lombardi corrected with a sheepish smile. "This is Ryker Fiore. He's been your benefactor for the last year."

"It's nice to meet you," I said, trying to smile through my discomfort.

"You can go, Don," the man named Ryker said to Mr. Lombardi.

Don nodded, touching my shoulder briefly before he turned for the door. "Wait!" I protested. "I don't think—"

"Come sit down, Sunshine. We have things to discuss."

I bristled, my annoyance allowing Don to slip out the door and close it behind him. "I do have a name, you know?" I asked him, crossing my arms over my chest.

He grinned at me, looking far too handsome although his body mass and the scars on his face made him look too menacing to ever really be beautiful.

He was dangerous, with those bright eyes that seemed too animalistic to be human, far closer to a wolf stalking prey in the night. A scar ran through his nose where it went slightly crooked like he'd broken it at some point, and a thick scar ran through his right eyebrow and left the faintest line on his cheek underneath it. He held out a hand for me, and I hesitated before I stepped forward to place mine in his.

Heat engulfed me instantly, his palm feeling like a furnace as it scalded me.

With my much smaller hand enclosed in his, he guided me down the slight step and into the living area. He towered over me as I walked beside him, and the way he clenched his teeth only exaggerated the dramatic angular lines of his square jaw.

The living room was comfortable, despite its industrial original purpose. The flat screen television was tucked under where the stairs wound against the brick wall that separated the living and kitchen spaces. A large sectional looked comfortable but stylish and modern in the space and he led me straight for it. I instantly wanted to turn and go back to the table I'd seen in the kitchen, but let him guide me to the couch, regardless.

He pressed down on my shoulder in one corner of the u-shaped sofa, letting me take my seat before he sat next to me. His knee touched mine, and the moment felt unbearably intimate.

I suspected it would have felt that way with any man, given the circumstances, but with Ryker, it just seemed more. My body came to life. It buzzed with attraction in the same way it had that day all those years ago when I hadn't been able to do anything but discourage it and feel guilty for feeling it at all. I'd been married and happily at that. Being attracted to another man wasn't something I allowed myself to feel, so I'd taken comfort in the fact that I'd never see the man again.

But I no longer had the protection of a husband to keep me from feeling something I shouldn't, and I'd walked into a situation I felt incapable of dealing with now.

Or you know, ever.

I had a feeling I'd never be ready to deal with the reality that was Ryker Fiore.

"You must have questions," he grunted finally, and I realized he still clutched my hand in his. Giving a gentle, testing tug, I pulled it back. He released it, and I used it to tuck my hair behind my ear and smile sheepishly. I felt mollified that he'd released me, that he respected my boundaries enough to let me control my body in the space he'd put me.

But when I set my hand back on my thigh, he grabbed it in his again and his hand was like a brand even through my yoga pants. I stared at the contact in confusion for a moment, before I pressed on.

I needed to get the fuck away from him, and to do that I needed to get this conversation out of the way and get the answers to the questions that had built within me for a year.

"I don't understand what's going on. You knew Chad?" I asked, and I fought the urge to flinch when his hand tightened in mine and his jaw clenched.

His blue eyes were intense on mine when he answered. "I worked with him here and there."

"You're an officer?" I asked, and his lips curved into the hint of a smile.

"Let's just say I work in criminal justice and leave it at that. Chad consulted with my boss sometimes, but I was his point of contact."

"I-okay," I whispered. "That day in the park, was it just a coincidence?"

"No, Tesoro. That was when your husband first started working with us. Sometimes my job requires me to investigate new contacts."

"You investigated me?" I said, yanking at my hand. He didn't release it, only held it securely without hurting me. "I thought you and Chad were friends. Why would you investigate his wife?"

"I never said we were friends," he growled in warning, only confirming my suspicion that the man was more animal than man. "I said I worked with him."

I turned my eyes up to his face, meeting his challenging gaze with a glare of my own. "If you weren't friends, Chad never would have trusted you to handle the money he left us. He would have left it with his partner or—"

"The money that has supported you and the kids didn't come from your husband. Don told you what he needed to in order for you to accept the money you needed." I yanked my hand from him so hard that he had no choice to release me unless he wanted to hurt me. As I stood, I took comfort that he didn't seem to want to hurt me. At least not yet.

"But his signature was on those papers," I argued, spinning back to face him once I had the luxury of distance. With his hand off of me, without his skin on mine, I could think more clearly. Somehow, the proximity to him had clouded my head and brought my body to the forefront.

"Forged." He shrugged, and I gaped at him in response. The blatant admission seemed shocking, as if there was no regret in his body that he'd deceived me for a year of my life. Given me things I hadn't asked for, and undoubtedly would expect things I didn't agree to give.

"Then I'll pay it back." As soon as I said the words, I regretted them. There was no way for me to pay back that money. Even if I gave him everything I'd saved up, it would never be enough to even cover Axel's schooling.

"I don't want your money," he said then snickered, standing from the couch to tower over me. "You needed to grieve. I gave you what you needed to do that." He stripped off his suit jacket, and my heart leapt into my throat. Tossing it over the back of the sofa, I watched as he rolled the sleeves up on his white dress shirt. His right forearm was covered in ink, an intricate tribal design that seemed to both contrast with his olive skin and somehow fade into the shadows the artist had created. Smack dab in the center of his forearm, vivid blue eyes stared back at me in the face of a lone wolf. The shadows gave the illusion of moving with his muscle as he reached for me, and I was so distracted by the art of it that I startled when his hands grasped me around the waist and he lifted me to set me back down on the couch.

"Don't touch me!" I snarled, swatting his hands away when he sat in the corner seat and leaned back.

"Then sit your pretty ass down and stay put. We both know you aren't leaving until I say you can leave."

"Excuse me?" I whispered.

He sighed. Then he dragged his hands over his face and reached over to me. Plucking me off the couch, he lifted me until my legs straddled his hips and I stared down at him. "What the fuck do you think you're doing?" I shrieked, shoving off his chest and scrambling to climb out of his lap, but those hands of his kept me rooted exactly where he wanted me. Evidently growing tired of my struggles, he stretched his hands up and caught both of mine in his and pulled them behind my back.

"Settle, Calla," he ordered. "I'm not going to hurt you."

"Then let me go!" I yelled at him, wincing when he shifted his entire body to sit straight up. The motion ground his hips between my thighs, giving me the friction I shouldn't need. Shouldn't have wanted in that moment, but there was no denying how good it felt to feel all that muscle between my legs and the way he groaned in my ear vibrated through me.

"I want you to listen to me," he said and his voice went oddly soft. I hadn't heard him speak much, but even I knew that there was something unusual about it for him. "Are you listening, Tesoro?"

"I don't have much choice, do I, asshole?" I shot back, wiggling in his lap. I stilled when I felt the bulge between my legs harden.

"That's the point, Hellcat," he laughed as I glared at him. "As we speak, my men are packing up your home." I gasped, jerking my arms against his grip, but even with only one of his hands gripping them there was zero chance of me getting free. He was relentless in the way he held me. Never hurting me, but never letting me go either. "It's already been sold to a very nice family who will appreciate it the way you used to. In a little while, we'll go get Axel from school and then pick up Ines from your father. By the time we get home, your things should be here. I've told them to prioritize unpacking the kids first. Their rooms are set up and waiting for them."

"You cannot be serious," I whispered. "I didn't sign off on selling my house. It isn't possible for it to be sold." Even as I said the words, I could already hear his response.

He'd forged Chad's signature. What was to stop him from forging mine?

"I took ownership of the house months ago, with your signature on the Deed and all the other paperwork. You'll quickly find that there is nothing that can stand in my way, Sunshine." He stared up at me, those blue eyes piercing through me as my breath disappeared from my lungs.

"Are you insane?" I whispered.

"Probably," he said with a nod. He looked as if he was thinking it over for a moment, before he shrugged his massive shoulders and continued on, "Our boy has a car and sports room that would make your father proud, and Ines's room looks like a fucking unicorn vomited in there, but I'm sure our Princess will love it."

"Our?!" I shrieked, tugging back so harshly that he readjusted his grip on my wrists.

"You're mine, Calla. That means they are too," he said simply, like it was the most obvious thing in the world.

"I am not yours," I argued. "I don't even know you."

He sighed, reaching up his free hand to cup my cheek with a warmth he didn't deserve. "This is happening, Sunshine. You can either accept that or we can do it the hard way, and we both know that the hard way won't be pleasant for the kids."

"What?" I asked.

"What do you think it will do to them to see their mother locked in this house against her will? To see you fighting me every step of the way will only traumatize them needlessly. If you fight me and I have to trap you here, what do you think that means for them? For school and seeing your father? I promise you that you will be mine, regardless."

I stumbled back when he released my wrists suddenly, falling to my back on the sofa. He moved to his knees, all languid and smooth in his movements despite the dramatic mass of his body. I had a moment to wonder what it must be like to be that large, to have to navigate the world and not fit in spaces where normal people never stopped to consider. The moment disappeared when he prowled over me, his hands resting on either side of my head and caging me in when he filled the space I'd left open after I'd fallen back. He stayed on his hands and knees, keeping a distance between our bodies even when he violated my personal space and trapped me beneath him. "I don't want to scare them," he said pointedly, his expression imploring me to see reason.

As if there was any reason to be found in the insanity he proposed.

"You're scaring *me*," I pointed out, but he didn't seem to have any qualms about that.

He looked thoughtful for a moment, before the cold blaze in his blue eyes softened again. "I don't want to scare you, Tesoro. I've told you I won't hurt you, and I mean it. But my life isn't the kind where I can just casually date you until you get used to being around me. My life is all or nothing."

"Then let me choose nothing," I hissed, pressing my hands against his chest. I both wanted and didn't want to touch him. I felt at odds with myself when presented with that striking face of his leaning closer to me as he spoke every word.

"That is *not* an option. I left you alone when you were married. Let you have your illusion of a picture-perfect life, and then I gave you time to grieve before I took what is mine. Most men in my position would not have been nearly as generous."

"Most men in your position?" I asked, and even I knew the words sounded tormented as they left my mouth. The old warehouse in the middle of nowhere, the fence, the security booth. Everything about the situation screamed that I was in over my head, that I'd walked into something I had zero chance of controlling no matter how desperately I tried to grasp the frayed edges of my life.

He let out a slow breath, seeming to debate something in his head before he dropped his forehead to rest against mine. "I'm not a good man. All you need to know for now is that there is nobody in this city who would dare to take you away from me." I stilled beneath him, staring up into his intense gaze as horror filled me. "The cost of helping you would be far too great for anyone." He vaulted up, holding out a hand to help me stand from the couch. I ignored it, standing on my own and making for the door. "Where are you going, Tesoro?" he asked with a sigh.

I didn't answer, hope surging inside me when he didn't interfere. I made it to the door, had my hand on the knob before his own came crashing down on it. I spun, glaring up at him and shoving him back.

Well, trying to shove him back, anyway. The man didn't move, just grabbed my hands in his and pinned them to his chest. Dragging me over to the kitchen table, he groaned dramatically before he picked up a piece of paper off the counter. When he handed them to me, I stared in horror at the zero where my account balance had been. There was no mistaking the glaringly obvious account number in the corner or the name of the bank where I'd stored all my savings. "What is this?"

"I've transferred your money into my account for safekeeping for the time being. When I feel it's secure, we can talk about you having access to them, but until then you should know that you have no money. No house. If you think to leave me, I'll target your dad's shop," he said, his voice cool and calculated as he delivered the crushing blow.

"Target it?" I whispered as my ears rang. This couldn't be happening, not to me. Not to us.

"Do you think his reputation would survive if he was found to be selling cars loaded with drugs? Could his good name save him from the law when they came knocking? I don't think so, not with me funding the prosecution."

"They know him. They knew Chad. They know my father would never—"

"But you're forgetting one very important detail, Sunshine. I own the police. There is nothing they can do to save your father from the frame job that they'll help me accomplish, not without going against me. Remember that detail, if you think to turn to Jason for help. I own his boss, and I'll destroy him if he tries to come between me and my woman."

The paper in my hands dropped to the table as they trembled, and I turned hate-filled wide eyes up to his. "How could you do this? I'm a person. Doesn't what I want matter to you?"

His hand lifted to cup my face, his thumb stroking over the spot on my cheekbone he'd touched all those years ago. The memory should have felt nostalgic, and it probably would have in any other circumstances. Back then, I'd thought him some kind of knight in shining armor for helping me when no one else did, for taking pity on a woman struggling with her two-year-old and alone in the park.

But in this moment it was only horrific.

"What you want means everything to me, Tesoro. One day, you'll look back and see that I've only done what I have to do so we can settle into our lives quickly and painlessly."

I huffed a breath as tears stung my eyes. He studied them, looking pained right along with me. "How is this painless?"

"I won't ever hurt you, Calla," he whispered, his voice cracking as if he was on the verge of breaking right alongside me. The hint of humanity was enough, just enough, to push me to appeal to it.

"You already are," I said on a ragged sob. "This is hurting me."

His jaw clenched, and he drew his hand away from me to step back and give me a hint of space. I looked at him hopefully, thinking for maybe just one moment that he'd listened. That he'd heard me and known I meant every word.

His hand went to his back pocket, fishing out a cell phone. He hefted it in his hand and stared at it, before his eyes came back to me. Whatever hint of kindness I'd thought I'd seen was gone, replaced by a steely determination that filled me with apprehension. "We can either go pick up the kids together, or I can have Axel pulled from school. I'll go pick him up from my man that's waiting outside, without you, and he can sit in the car wondering what the fuck is going on until you terrify him when he gets home. I don't want to go this route, Calla. The ugly way is so unnecessary and the result will be the same."

"They won't release him to you if you're not on his list of approved guardians," I returned, the wobble in my voice shocking even me. Ryker turned to the table, picking up another paper and handing it to me.

"Those are all the donations I've made to the school in the last six months. The new gymnasium they're building over the summer will be the Fiore Gymnasium. Surely you've heard of that project?" I felt my face go cold with the realization that I recognized the name from their newsletter they sent home the month before. "Make your choice."

I shook my head from side to side, refusing to believe him. Even with the striking number of zeros next to his donations, they wouldn't play games with my son's safety. I had to believe that. But when he sighed and dialed a number on his phone, his finger tapped the speakerphone so I could listen to the ring-tone. Every single one felt like a strike to my chest, making my heart skip a beat.

"Peterson School for the Gifted. Please hold," the woman's voice on the other

end of the line said. My body flinched, unable to deny that he had in fact dialed Axel's school when presented with such a blatant fact.

"No! Okay, I understand," I panicked, forcing the words out along with any of the remaining air in my lungs. "I understand," I repeated. "Please don't scare him."

Ryker pushed the end call button on the phone, tucking it back into his pocket as he took my arm in his grip. The paper with his donations on it fluttered to the floor as he guided me toward the front door.

We stepped through it, and he didn't bother locking it behind him. When I looked toward the gate, I found a man sitting in the guard booth.

Evidently Ryker only sent him away when they wanted to lure unsuspecting women inside.

Noted.

He guided me to a sleek black car that almost looked like an SUV in the driveway, opening the door and putting me inside. The interior was red and black leather and it screamed money as I settled in the seat, momentarily stunned. He took the seatbelt in his hand, reaching across my body to buckle me in like a child. As soon as the car door closed, I resisted the urge to pull it open. When he dropped into the driver's seat, it almost seemed absurd how much space he took up. It wasn't a tiny car, but it felt infinitely smaller with him inside it.

I had to wait until we were off the property, though how I would get to my kids before him when I didn't have a fucking car would take some creative maneuvering. "You can't do this. Please don't do this," I begged instead. I might not have known him, but I had little doubt that my pleas would fall on deaf ears. He didn't care what I might want or what my kids might need. Having a stranger insert himself into their lives and uproot them from their home was the absolute opposite of what they needed.

As I expected, he started up the car and the screen on the dashboard flashed with the Maserati logo. "We should get one more thing straight before we run into any problems while we're out," he announced, backing out of the front of the house and turning down the driveway. The gate opened for him before we got there, and he coasted through smoothly as he nodded at whoever the hell worked the gate.

"Is this the part where you tell me you'll kill me if I talk?" I asked tartly, crossing my arms over my chest.

He chuckled, and the humorous sound made my body vibrate with a need I didn't understand. It was rough, hoarse in a way that I suspected came from disuse. "No, Sunshine. I meant it when I said I won't hurt you. That includes murder, the last I checked."

"Funny." I gave him the finger.

"I have no such hang-ups with anyone else though, I assure you. I will not let anyone come between us. Do you understand what that means?" I shook my head, pursing my lips. It didn't sound like there could be very many interpretations of that statement, but he couldn't be that insane.

Could he?

"It means that if you go to someone for help, know that I will make them disappear. It will not be a pleasant experience for whoever helps you. So unless you want that on your conscience, I suggest you mind your tongue around other people."

I winced but nodded. "So let me get this straight. You're using my family to keep me cooperative in the privacy of your house, and you're using other people to keep me from getting help, and what? I'm supposed to like you? Is that how you see this playing out?"

He glared at me out of the side of his eye, but underneath the annoyance it felt like there was genuine amusement there. "That's about right," he said.

"Great." I grinned at him. "I'm not sure when you last dated, but in case it was the stone age maybe it's time to modernize your strategy."

"Calla," he warned with a drawl. "I swear to fuck, tame the sass unless you want me to pull over and spank your ass."

Something in my stomach clenched.

Nope. Down girl.

The psychotic man was not on the menu.

"What pray-tell are we going to tell my children then? Since they can't know you're a scary man, but apparently you won't hurt us. How do we make them understand that you didn't exist to them yesterday, but now we live with you?"

He didn't bat an eye as he shifted gears once we got off the dirt road. "You let me handle that."

"Um, no. They're my kids. If I'm supposed to do this to shelter them from the fact that you seem to think it's okay to just pluck people from their lives and make them dance for you, then I need to know what the plan is."

"You can dance for me anytime," he said instead of answering.

"Ryker!" I hissed in annoyance, but even I had to admit that in any other circumstances where he didn't make me want to stab out his eyeball, I might have been entertained by him. For a man who chuckled like he'd forgotten how to laugh, he seemed to have a smart comment for everything I said. Like he lived inside my head and could predict my words before I spoke.

And I'd officially creeped myself out.

He glanced over at me, all traces of humor gone from his eyes as they darkened. My brain shouted at me to retreat, but with him barreling down the highway there was zero chance of that. "Say it again," he ordered.

I fumbled over my thoughts, wondering what the hell had come out of my mouth to piss him off so much when he'd smiled through insults. "Ryker?" I asked finally.

He let out a deep breath, releasing some tension that had filled him so suddenly. "There was a time when I never thought I'd hear you say my name."

Half of me melted, because it was oddly sweet to see how much it affected him. But the other part screamed danger.

Because that was creepy as fuck.

"Umm. Okay. But really, what are you going to tell my kids?" I asked as the city came into view. I didn't dare glance at his speedometer to see how fast he'd driven to get there so quickly. It felt like it took me an eternity to get to his murder shack of a home, though that *might* have had something to do with the fact that I'd been scared out of my ever-loving mind.

"I'll tell Ines she has a new unicorn-vomit room and all the princess dresses she could ever want. She's two. She doesn't understand how relationships work," he answered, and I had to shrug at that one. My girl could throw a mean tantrum, but mostly she was easy to please. Throw something pink and sparkly at her and you owned her soul.

"And Axel?"

"He's a little man. I've got him covered."

"He's six," I argued.

"I've been six before. He understands men better than you think. And regardless of who his biological father was, I swear to you that boy has a lot of me in him."

"This entire thing is ridiculous. Not to mention illegal."

"Everything will be fine. You just wait and see, Sunshine," Ryker teased, setting his hand on my thigh to stroke my yoga pants affectionately. "Do you want to put your money where your mouth is?"

"Well apparently, all my money is gone, so there's that," I pointed out, making him snort a laugh.

"Okay, I didn't want your money, anyway. I think if I can convince Axel all is well, and that this is normal, I deserve a kiss."

"You sneaky fucking bastard," I growled. Glaring at him, I plucked his hand off my thigh *again* and set it back on his side of the car. "No."

"I'll get one, anyway."

I wanted to tell him he wouldn't. I should have been able to tell him he'd never get a kiss from me, but somehow, the words just didn't feel true.

I couldn't go to anyone for help. I couldn't let my kids know that the guy was crazy.

And my body seemed to think it was time to end my eighteen-month celibacy, since Chad and I hadn't had sex for nearly six months at the end of our marriage.

Ugh.

What the hell was happening?

CHAPTER ELEVEN

I was no stranger to *The Peterson School for the Gifted*. I'd hand delivered each of my more than generous monthly donations over the past few months to prepare for the coming turn of events where I had a son in the school.

I tried to picture what Principal Blanchet would say when I strolled up to pickup Axel and she realized I was connected to the woman she allowed the President of the PTA to bully. I hoped it tamed her shit down a bit, because even though she hid behind her neat and proper exterior, she acted like a bitch in heat when she saw me. Some women just thought they needed a taste of bad in their bed, but she'd never know what I felt like.

That was for sure.

What I had never done before was walk up the sidewalk to the front gate with Calla's hand held in mine. She protested, pursing her bowed lips at me and giving me a glare, but kept silent. Anyone else and I might have worried, but I knew Calla like the back of my hand. I knew all her tells, knew every step she'd take and what she would do before she tried to run.

She wouldn't get far, because I'd chase her. I would always follow her, but I'd had enough of living in the shadows of her life. It was time for me to live front and center with her, to enjoy the sun and the way she lit up the world. She just needed to accept it.

A few of the moms stopped to stare at us as we passed, and I immediately regretted not grabbing my suit jacket on the way out the door. Calla had distracted me with her pathetic half-attempt to walk out the door, like she'd genuinely thought she'd get anywhere. She would soon figure out that she wouldn't. The only reason she'd fallen back on her snarky attitude was because she knew just how helpless she was.

So she'd try to annoy me until I didn't want her anymore.

She just didn't realize that I thought her attempts to be irritating were adorable.

The closer we got to the front doors of the school, the more hesitant Calla's body language became. Every afternoon I watched her get more and more cautious when she came to Axel's school. The mornings were one thing, when she could drop him at the gate and watch him walk in, but the school refused to let a child go unless a parent or guardian physically signed them out in the office. That meant Calla had to endure the judgmental glares of other moms, because even though she had finished at the studio hours ago, she still hadn't had time to change into something these women thought appropriate.

After she finished work, she picked up Ines and ran errands, went home and cleaned, did any number of things that she would no longer have to worry about with me. She could invest time back into herself again, not because I didn't love her the way she was, but because she deserved to have a life free from stress.

She shouldn't have to run back and forth just to balance the kids and work. She had me to help with that.

"Mr. Fiore!" The Principal greeted me the very moment we walked into the front office. She stood from her seat, stepping around her desk and smiling at me with an overly enthusiastic beam that made me wince. "We weren't expecting you today."

I felt Calla's eyes on the side of my face, studying me incredulously. I bit down on the inside of my lip to hide the smile that her attention brought out. With her sweet little face pitched in a fit, she looked so much like her daughter in the beginning throes of a tantrum that I almost wanted to laugh. "I'm not here for a donation today, Miss Blanchet. We're here to add me to Axel Latour's list of approved guardians for pickup." I lifted my hand up, displaying where I held Calla's hand clutched tightly in my own.

"No, we're just here to pick him up today," Calla inserted with a white face. "You'll have to excuse him, Hulk here is a little overly enthusiastic, but I will continue to pick Axel up every day."

"Sunshine," I murmured, turning her face toward me. "I thought we talked about this."

She ignored me, pressing on with Miss Blanchet like I hadn't spoken. "Is Axel ready? I still have to pick up my daughter." The shrewd other woman narrowed her eyes on her, judgment all over her face. I'd known, from a distance, that they judged Calla for being herself and not striving harder for perfection or trying harder to find another man to marry her. But they frowned upon the fact that she had another man lined up a year after her husband's death too.

I fucking hated women like that. Who spent more time tearing each other down, no matter what the other did. Calla would be damned if she did and damned if she didn't.

I wanted to make it better, but I also knew that all the times the Principal had made it obvious she'd be available to me would not help Calla's case.

Fuck.

The Principal called Axel's class on her phone and a few minutes later Axel made his way toward us with his face pinched in concern when he saw me holding his mother's hand. Calla tightened her hand in mine, giving me a wordless plea not to scare him. Not to hurt her boy.

She'd realize soon enough that I'd die before I let anything happen to him. I might not have had someone to protect me when I was a boy, but that only gave me a stronger sense of conviction that children deserved to be protected at all costs.

Nobody would touch Axel or Ines.

Over my dead body.

Having him walk toward me for the first time, I realized just how much his face looked like mine. He had my mannerisms, my facial expressions somehow.

As if he'd seen me lurking in the shadows for the past four years and absorbed them into his own person. Like his father had never existed, and there had only ever been Calla and I.

"Hi, baby," Calla murmured, reaching her free hand out to stroke his hair back from his face. My heart melted into a giant puddle of goop. Watching the way he stared up at his mother with complete adoration, even when he was confused, I couldn't help the sense of familiarity I felt.

That was how I felt every time I looked at Calla, so I understood the look.

"Mommy?" he asked, glancing at her hand and then up to me with those dark blue eyes. He swallowed visibly, and I forced myself to clear my throat and smile at him even if I felt like I might explode with everything circling in my chest.

Being a father had been all I'd ever wanted once upon a time, and it had taken years for me to find my way back to being ready for that again. Loving people came with risks, and I knew Calla related to that better than most.

"Let's go outside, Buddy," I suggested, and Calla forced a smile down at her son as she took his hand and we went out the doors. I tried to ignore the Principal staring after us like there was an unfortunate gossip mill brewing in her head already. I'd deal with her later, because at that moment I had much more important things to do.

Like explain the new reality to my son and go get my daughter from the grandfather who would undoubtedly have some thoughts.

As soon as we were out the front gates to the school, Axel glanced over at me nervously, but we made it to the Maserati before he opened his mouth. "Who's that, Mommy?"

I bent down in front of him, dropping Calla's hand for the moment for me to focus all my attention on my boy. "My name is Ryker, and I knew your father," I said, and Axel's eyes widened for a moment before he nodded with a sniffle. I wasn't above using the things I knew Axel said, the things he wished for in his darkest moments to worm my way into their lives. "I know you wished your mom had someone who could look out for her the way she looks after you and Ines. I know it isn't exactly the same, but I will look after all of you now."

Axel looked up at me with wide eyes. "Did my Dad send you? I asked him if he could send a hero to look after my Mommy. It isn't fair that she doesn't have someone to protect her from bad guys. What if someone tries to hurt her like they did my Dad?" he asked, and I heard Calla whimper beside me. I knew it killed her to think of what would happen to the kids if something ever happened to her. That it ate her up at night to think she might be torn from their lives the same way their father had been, and still felt his absence, even if he had been a piece of shit.

"I don't know if he sent me or not, Axe," I said. "But I know that I care about your Mommy a lot, and I want to take care of her. I'll need your help though. You think we can handle her and your sister between the two of us?"

He nodded with a smile. "I'm good at taking care of Ines," he said happily. I knew at his age, I'd have been relieved to have someone looking out for me, but I also would have loved to know I still had a very important role in my family.

At least I suspected I would have, if mine hadn't been complete shit.

"Should we go pick her up? And then I have a surprise for the two of you." Axel nodded, a smile tugging at his lips before he looked to Calla.

"Can we have the surprise, Mommy?" he asked.

"Sure, Cookie Monster," she murmured back with a brief smile. Even though she tapped her foot repeatedly like she wanted to kick me in the balls, she didn't protest when I opened the back door of the Maserati and watched Axel buckle himself into his car seat before I checked to make sure everything was secure. Calla watched us like a hawk, narrowing her eyes on me when she realized I'd strapped him in properly.

I wouldn't tell her I'd practiced with a doll a few dozen times first.

I didn't need to look quite that desperate yet, though I supposed nothing was more obvious than threatening her into being with me. At any rate, Calla was vindictive enough to go spewing that fact to the guys when she met them, and they would never let me live it down.

I suddenly was very thrilled that I'd tucked the doll in Ines room like a present for my Princess.

I grabbed the door for my Sunshine, gesturing her in and buckling her up, much to Axel's entertainment as he laughed in the back seat. If I had to guess, Calla only had a few hours left in her before the claws came out and she lost her shit, so I'd have to do my best to preserve the peace just long enough that we had the kids tucked into bed first.

Calla's claws dug into my back wasn't something they needed to see.

By the time I walked around to the driver's side, I only barely caught the end of Axel's jab at his mother's sanity.

"Grandpa will like this car," he said.

"That's the hope, Little Man. That is the hope." I turned a playful grin to him before I pressed the button to start up the Maserati. The purr of the engine sounded like music to my ears and the way Axel smiled in the back seat felt like he had a lot of me and his Grandpa in him.

"Let's go get the Princess," I said, guiding the car out of the lot.

"How did you and Mommy meet?" he asked from the back seat. I took Calla's hand in mine, pulling it over to rest on my thigh and taking it with me when I needed to shift gears.

"I've known your Mommy for a long time," I admitted vaguely. "We didn't talk for a while, but I never stopped thinking about her or you and your sister."

He studied me curiously, the excitement about the surprise fading as he studied my interactions with his mother. "Then how come Mommy never talks about you?"

Calla gave me the "I told you so" look. She didn't realize just how much I knew Axel had every bit of his mother's curiosity.

"Your Mom was grieving your Dad, Axe. Sometimes women can be stubborn and not see a good thing for what it is when it looks them right in the face after something like that. She needed me to step in and push her a bit, so that's what I'm doing," I answered him with a smile. He studied me with eyes that were too wise for his age, too all-seeing to be natural. Only a boy who'd known pain and suffering could give a man like me a look like that. I would know, since I'd had the same look when I'd been even younger than him.

I navigated through the traffic, making my way to August's shop.

"Is that why she's glaring at you?" Axel asked. I gave him a grin.

"I'm stubborn? That's what you're going to call it right now?" Calla asked, and I snickered with Axel who seemed to enjoy someone other than him and his sister getting chastised for once.

"Yep," I grunted.

"My father is going to rip you to pieces," she whispered in response, and I might have been afraid for that very reason if I didn't already have my key to the castle sitting in the backseat.

When we pulled up to the front of the garage, Calla jumped out of the passenger seat as quick as she could and moved to get Axel from the back like she thought I might drive off with him. I wasn't into kidnapping kids, not unless they came along with Calla's sexy ass apparently, anyway.

I followed behind them as they hurried into the shop, and Calla kept glancing over her shoulder at me to see if I was still there. I didn't know if she expected me to wait in the car or what, but if she thought I would honestly be afraid of her father, then I needed to work on my presence a bit. I ate worse men than August Nilsson for breakfast.

"Calla Lily," her father said, stepping up and pressing a kiss to his daughter's cheek as Ines clung to her legs. "Everything alright?" he asked, eyeing me over his Calla's head.

"Yep. Everything's good," she said a little too brightly. Calla was many things, but a proficient liar wasn't one of them.

"You gonna introduce me to your friend?" he asked, and Axel threw himself into his grease covered grandfather for a hug. I could just imagine the joy that laundry proved to be for Calla.

"I'm Ryker, Sir," I said, stepping up and holding out a hand for him to shake. He eyed it warily for a moment before he finally shook it.

"Ryker says he's going to take care of Mommy!" Axel inserted in his enthusiastic voice. Calla winced visibly, and I knew she thought about how that must have made her sound. She may have stayed home with the kids when she'd married Chad, but she did it because she wanted to and because she valued her time with them more than her need to provide for herself. It hadn't been because Chad expected it, or pressured her into it, or because she wanted to live a pampered life. It was because they could afford it, and there was nothing more important to her than those kids.

Having lost her own Mom when she was born, Calla wouldn't waste a single day.

"Is that so?" August asked, crossing his arms over his chest as he raised an eyebrow at his daughter. It was the quintessential look that told her she had some explaining to do.

"It's new," I said in her defense. "I just move fast when I see something worth keeping. I'm taking a couple days off to get to know the kids. Why don't you call Calla and make plans to come to my place? Ines won't be here for a bit since Calla is taking off too, but you're always welcome with us."

I could feel Calla's glare without looking at her, but her father didn't seem to mind the way I told him our plans and ignored Calla's input. From what I knew of his relationship with Chad, it hadn't been the most open. Calla had always acted as an intermediary for their conversations, even after they'd been married for years.

That wouldn't fly with me. A grown man could have his own conversations. At least he was, if he was even remotely respectable.

Chad had been nothing but a snake in disguise.

"I'll do that," August said, and with that I turned my attention to the princess that clung to my woman's legs shyly.

"I heard you like unicorns," I said. "There's a brand new seat in my car waiting for you, and it just might have unicorns on it."

"Uni?" she asked, peeking up at me from around Calla's leg.

"Should we go see?" I asked with a smile, holding out a hand and letting her come to me. When she put her hand in mine shyly, I lifted her into my arms and plopped her onto my shoulders. She squealed with laughter, clinging to my shoulders tightly as I strode to the front of the garage and got her hooked into her car seat. I could vaguely sense Calla and her father following with Axel, but my focus was entirely on the little girl stroking the unicorn fabric happily. It was worth every penny I'd spent to have it custom made.

"Pretty uni," she said.

"Only the best for the prettiest girl in the world." She giggled when I booped her nose just like Calla did, and I turned to find Calla watching our interaction with interest. Noticing every little detail that I knew and exploited.

"Is that a Maserati Levante?" August asked, stepping forward to let his hands hover over the hood. He didn't touch her, and I knew as a car man that it was for fear of leaving greasy prints on the paint. The Maserati just wasn't the kind of car that could pull off that kind of look.

"Sure is," I said as I closed Ines's door and took Axel's hand to help him around to the other side. "When you come over, you can take it for a drive. I've got a 1970 Chevelle in my garage I'm working on fixing up. I imagine you'd enjoy getting your hands on her. She's a real beauty," I said, and he laughed at me.

"You shitting me?"

"Nope. I'm restoring the entire thing. It was in rough shape when I got my hands on it, but she's starting to shine now."

He laughed again, turning to clap a hand on Calla's shoulder so hard her body shook under the force of it. He'd always treated her like one of the boys at the shop and didn't seem to care that he stained her shirt with his greasy hands. "Well, Calla Lily," he said, the affectionate term making my heart tighten in sadness for my girl. Her mom's favorite flower had become her namesake after she died. "You're fucked. See you soon."

His laughter echoed through the garage as he abandoned his daughter to my mercy.

I grinned at her as she climbed in the passenger seat. "Why can't I drive?" she asked with her arms folded across her chest once I'd taken my spot behind the wheel.

"I'll let you drive once I'm sure you can handle a stick." Calla gasped. She would be so much fun to torment, and I'd waited long enough to do it. I smirked at her glaring face. "Don't forget, you owe me a kiss, Sunshine."

CHAPTER TWELVE

CALLA

When Ryker pulled up to the house and the gate opened, I did everything I could not to scare the kids. I didn't scream or make a fuss when it closed behind us, and I thought I deserved a damn medal for that alone.

I didn't voice my horror when he turned onto a split in the driveway that took us into the woods. Was there anything the man did that wasn't creepy as fuck?

It led us around the side of the warehouse, and when we came up to the side, the building was bigger than I'd ever expected in my first glimpse inside. And I'd thought the renovated interior had been like something out of a magazine. Pushing a button on the rearview mirror, an enormous wall of steel and glass panels slid open on a track and folded in on themselves to reveal a four-car garage that was so pristine it would make my father weep if he ever saw it.

I couldn't let him come here.

Ever.

My sensible mom-sedan looked ridiculous parked next to the Chevelle he'd mentioned, and even I felt like I might purr at the sight of it. It desperately needed a paint job, but I could see the signs of just how much work Ryker had put into restoring it already.

I wanted to hate it, but I had to admit he'd done a stunning job.

Dad made most of his money on custom builds at his shop, so I was no stranger to muscle cars and the signs of a good restoration. The fucker just had to be good at the one thing that would earn him bonus points with my Dad.

Ryker hopped out, going to the back seat and pulling Axel free before I'd even snapped myself out of my stupor. There had to be a way to get us out of

Ryker's sight, and then we could go to Jason without putting him in danger. As a Detective, he had more clout than most of the other people I might consider turning to, and the pseudo-father relationship he'd formed with the kids since Chad's death ensured he'd help us. I had no idea what Ryker was capable of, and until I did, I had to proceed with caution.

I'd never be able to live with myself if someone died because of me, but if he touched me I'd probably cut his balls off. I doubted he'd have much use for me after that. I supposed that was probably a light at the end of the tunnel.

I jumped out of the car, pulling Ines out of her seat before Ryker could get to her too. "Surprise!" she squealed, holding out her arms for the brute of a man who just swept my daughter out of my arms and carted her to the door that must have led into the main house. The door that Ryker strode through led into a hallway, and when I turned to close it behind me I watched the garage doors slide closed with mounting horror for only a moment before I turned to follow where my kids joyfully went off with a stranger.

I hadn't prepared them for strangers who clung to me, only for strangers when I wasn't around.

People like Ryker made parenting impossible. None of the rules I'd taught them seemed to apply to him, so what the hell was I supposed to tell them to make them understand that the man was dangerous, when I couldn't *actually* tell them he was dangerous?

"Do you want to see your rooms?" he asked the kids, and my eyes widened as I picked up the pace to fling myself into the door that led to the main living space. It was still as massive as it had been earlier, but the space tucked in the corner that had been empty before was filled with things from the kids' playroom at home. Ines's toy kitchen looked absurd next to the beauty of the natural stone and grey cabinets in Ryker's kitchen right next to it.

There was a little couch, an area rug, and shelves for her favorite toys. I didn't know where the couch and rug came from, because the playroom at home hadn't been that organized.

Axel's video game system was set up on the stand below the flat screen in the living room, and they had positioned a baby gate at the bottom of the stairs. Ryker opened that gate, taking the kids up. He let Axel lead the way, bringing up the rear. The wall on the side of the stairs was extreme, and I hadn't noticed earlier the way it was a recent addition. I wanted to melt that he'd thought to make his home safe for Ines, because I imagined the warehouse had been much more striking when the stairs and loft upstairs had been open the way the designer meant it to be.

I followed them up, catching the gate before it could close. The metal contraption seemed too complicated for me to figure out, so it at the very least comforted me that Ines wouldn't be at risk. There was another one at the top of the stairs, and Axel couldn't get it open. "Slide the button over and then lift and it should swing out," Ryker said, and Axe managed just fine somehow. Even though the metal of the gate seemed like a prison, apparently my six-year-old could handle it.

Watching my kids round the corner and walk around the loft was too much for me. As they walked past the office with the solid glass wall and then around the corner, I spoke. "Ryker, can we talk about this? I don't think—"

"Nope," he grunted. When he stopped at the place where the hall forked in opposite directions, I sighed.

"Mommy, do we live here now?" Axel asked, his little eyes peering up at me in confusion. Down one end of the hall toward what I assumed was the master, a mover came out of the door and gave Ryker a nod.

"Should be all set, Sir," he said as he passed us in the hall.

Ryker grinned at me before going in the opposite direction of the Master. The halls were bright, a light grey that tinted just the slightest bit blue, and with the skylights in the ceiling, natural light flooded the space and illuminated the random industrial art pieces hanging on the wall.

They were like sculptures made from wood and metal, designed to lay flat against the wall and pieced into intricate patterns. "Boss's wife's friend Duke made them," he said in explanation. He didn't seem fond of the man, but no one could deny the unique beauty of his art. "Nursery." Ryker tapped on the door on the right briefly and then turned to the one on the left. I blanched, looking down at where Axel peeked at my stomach in confusion.

Nope.

I would not relive that conversation with my son. *Ever.*

"Do you have a baby?" Axel asked, saving me from the awkwardness of not being able to ask him. What would it tell my son if I didn't even know that the man who'd moved us into his home had a baby?

Fuck sake, where had my life gone so wrong?

"Not yet," Ryker declared, shoving the door on the left open. "This is the bathroom you and Ines will share." Subway tile covered the space, making it look bright, and a blue vanity with double sinks gave it a splash of color. It was better than my master bathroom at home. "Down there are your rooms. Ines on the left, Axel on the right." Axel's curiosity outweighed his hesitation, and he fled down the hall to throw open the door.

"Mother puffin!" he yelled excitedly, and he disappeared into the room.

"I hate you," I whispered to Ryker, and Ines only giggled in response.

"Ready for your room, Princess?" Ryker asked her, tapping Ines's foot playfully.

"Uni! Uni!" she shouted, and I stepped up to peek into Axel's room with a sigh. Some boys had plastic car beds. Evidently my son had one that looked more real than any other I'd seen, built into the room and looking like a car in the shop. He had his own desk and chair, with a bookshelf, and all those things sat on a platform he had to climb three steps to get to.

He had a gentle slide that looked like a road to get down. His dressers looked like tool chests, and I just knew, I *knew* that I would never get him out of that room. Not when he could send his toy cars flying down that slide all day long.

"Mommmmyyy!" Ines shrieked, and I turned and ducked out of Axel's room to find my girl. Terror filled me, the sound of her high-pitched cry making me think the worst.

As soon as I peeked in the room, my body sagged with relief. My relief disappeared the next moment when I realized my daughter was lost to me.

She was in love.

He'd given her a fucking castle.

The prick.

Ines's bed was covered in soft pink linens, with way more pillows than any one person could need thrown on there. And it was all tucked inside a massive set of turrets like a castle. But at least they functioned as bookshelves. Some of her stuffed animals peeked over the top of the bed frame, looking oh-so-cozy as they hung out up there with plenty of personal space. To think back home, I'd had the nerve to shove them in a chest in her closet.

How dare I?

Her dolls even had a miniature princess bed and there was a massive life size unicorn standing in front of the wall opposite her bed. The one that was painted in pastel colors with a mural of a Unicorn on it.

"There's something wrong with you," I muttered to him where he stood, watching Ines dart around the room happily and hug all the toys she didn't recognize like she needed to greet them each individually.

"I am not above buying them nice things so they never want to leave," he whispered back, and his arm rounded my waist so he could pull me into his side.

I wanted to stab him. Wanted to watch him suffer for giving my kids something so perfect when they could never keep it. "It's a little over the top."

"Does it look like they're complaining?" he asked, and he guided me back to the hallway to peek into Axel's room where he was already driving his cars down the ramp. "You got homework, Buddy?" Ryker asked him, and Axel looked up at him and pursed his little face.

My boy loved homework, and I'd never seen him look even remotely disappointed that he would have to do it before. "Yeah," Axel answered.

"Ten more minutes and then we'll see if we can't get it done before dinner."

"Okay, Ryker," Axel chirped happily in response. My eyes went to his backpack that he'd tossed to the floor carelessly, and I wanted to cry. It seemed like the perfect analogy for our lives in that moment.

Discarded without thought.

"Axe, we should talk about—"

"Please don't make us go home," he whispered, and my nose burned. "It's awesome here. Ryker will protect you from the bad guys. Can we stay?"

The fact was, even if I wanted to go home, we didn't *have* a home. There was nothing waiting for us, no shelter to protect us from the storm that was Ryker as he tore our life apart. Still, I couldn't help but caution my son before he got too attached. "This isn't how these things normally go, sweetie. I just want you to be realistic. It might not work out, and I don't want you to be disappointed."

"But when we came in, Ryker said this was our home now too. Our house makes you sad. Have you seen your room? I'm sure it's amazing too!"

"I'm sure it is," I said, even if I had no intention of sleeping in it. Ines's bed looked big enough for me to curl up with her. I didn't have it in me to kill his dreams of staying in that room. Not when he so desperately wanted to stay and the house that made me sad was gone anyway.

Traces of Chad were everywhere, even a year later. It felt like walking into a tomb every time I went into our bedroom, but that didn't make it okay that Ryker would use things and toys and furniture to turn my children against me and buy their affection. That my son would so easily give in to Ryker's story about protecting us was like carburetor cleaner sprayed on an open wound, burning away at my fragile sense of self. I'd thought of myself as a somewhat successful single mother and thought I'd given my kids a sense of safety if nothing else.

Apparently, I'd been wrong.

I couldn't even begin to understand how much money he'd spent designing those rooms. We went into the hallway to give Axel a little privacy as he played, waiting for Ines to be ready to go downstairs. "If your room has a cage and chains, I swear I'll kill you," I snarled at him.

"Why would I have a cage in our bedroom?" He seemed genuinely confused that I'd suggest such a thing, and that he so clearly didn't understand the position he'd put me in was overwhelming in itself.

"Because I'm obviously a prisoner here," I spat at him. "You're even using my kids to do it."

He chuckled darkly, reaching out a hand to cup my cheek as he stared down at me and his blue eyes darkened in the absence of the kids. There was a moment where something flashed through his expression, like the hint of a dark place that threatened to pull him under, but he shook it off the next moment and his eyes blazed in desire again. "Sunshine, I don't need a cage to make you mine. I think I've proven that." He released me as suddenly as he'd touched me, stepping back and turning to go down the hall. "Come down when you're ready."

If it had been only me, that would have been never, but I knew it was only a matter of time before Ines got hungry, and a hungry terror was not something I needed to deal with.

I slumped against the wall, letting my head bang against it while I waited for the kids to emerge from their private oasis.

There was something wrong with that man.

BEDTIME WAS ALWAYS A NIGHTMARE. Axel needed a shower. Ines needed a bath. Each kid wanted their own bedtime story in their bed.

As much as I loved the quality time with them, their staggered bedtimes didn't help matters. It was late by the time the kids had eaten and settled down from the excitement of pizza for dinner that had pushed them over the edge.

We didn't eat out much, didn't do the takeout thing. So many food options were difficult for me since I didn't eat meat, so it just became easier to cook my own meals. Chad hadn't been pescatarian, but without him the kids had slowly just started eating everything I cooked since making two meals was miserable. I couldn't even remember the last time they'd had pizza, and I felt horrible for that.

With the additional full bath in the master, Axel had darted in to take his shower while I got Ines through her bath in their shared bathroom. It felt strange to see the bedtime routine cut in half, and by the time Axel came charging down the hallway in his pajamas, I was already pulling a very cranky princess from the bathtub and towel drying her hair.

"Pick out your story!" I called out to Axel.

"Okay!" he hollered back, and I resisted the urge to smile at Ines. She scowled at me when I pulled her princess nighty over her head.

"Pink!" she protested.

"I couldn't find it. You get the purple one tonight."

"Pink!" She stomped her foot.

"Uh oh! It's the bedtime dragon! Did she eat the princess again?" I teased, grabbing the comb to run through her shoulder length hair quickly.

"No dragon," she pouted.

"Then stop acting like one," I said with a smile, lifting her into my arms to go read to Axel. Normally I'd read to Ines first, but since I had every intention of curling up and hiding away in her bed, it made sense to reverse our routine.

When I walked into Axel's room, Ryker perched on the edge of the platform, reading a chapter out of the newest book Axel had brought home from the library at school. I brought Ines in, bouncing her soothingly on my lap while I waited for Ryker to finish reading. Even if I wanted to strangle him for taking story time from me. He seemed determined to insert himself into every facet of the kids' lives, like he was their father, and that just did not fly with me.

I wouldn't have been okay with a man I dated acting so high-handed with my kids, let alone a complete stranger. It was only nine o'clock at night, and I already wanted to curl up in a bed. To do that, I needed to get through the bedtime routine, but that didn't mean I wanted to lose that time with my kids.

Ryker leaned forward, kissing the top of Axel's head warmly and whispering goodnight to him.

"Goodnight, Cookie Monster. Holler if you need me," I murmured, kissing Axel's forehead and then taking Ines to her room as Ryker closed Axel's door. "I'm just going to get her settled. It could take a while."

"No worries," Ryker grinned at me, stepping into her room and pulling back the blankets of her bed. I crawled in with her, pulling the covers up over us as I picked out one of her shortest stories from her turret shelves. Ryker perched on the edge of the bed, and I tried to ignore his presence as I read my girl a story about unicorns. When I finished and closed the book, Ryker took it from my hand and replaced it on the shelf.

"I'm just going to stay with her for a bit. It's a new house and a new room," I said.

"You good, Princess?" Ryker asked, ignoring me.

"Mmm," she murmured, already half asleep. He leaned in to kiss her cheek and then grabbed me around the waist.

"Say goodnight to Ines, Sunshine," he ordered.

I kissed her but made no move to get out of the bed. Instead, I settled down deeper into the covers, tugging them up over his hands at my waist and deciding to pretend they weren't there. He flung them back easily, plucking me from the bed and tossing me over his shoulder. With me perched there and fuming silently, he reached down and fixed the blankets for Ines, tucking her in nice and tight.

"Call me if you need anything, Princess," he whispered to her.

"Night 'yker," she murmured back in that sleepy voice. He seemed satisfied with that, striding out the door, though he took the time to close it quietly.

"Do I look stupid?" he asked as he walked down the hall to the master bedroom.

"I'm guessing the answer you're looking for is a no," I said back. "If I say no, will you put me down?"

He grunted when I dug my nails into his side through his shirt. I'd initially been looking for something to pinch, but there was *nothing*.

The man didn't even seem to have skin over the solid mass of muscle. "It's time for bed," he said, and he flung open the door to the master bedroom. I'd assumed, since Axel didn't come racing out of it in terror when he took a shower, that there was nothing horrific about it. I didn't expect the lilac accents through the room, or the front, brick exterior wall to be painted white. The entire wall on the side of the house was a massive window, the view of the woods outside it reminding me just how isolated we were. When he spun to kick the door closed quietly, I got my first view of the low platform bed with sheets and a comforter that looked nearly silver in contrast to all the white and black of the room, and the pillows were my favorite lilac color too.

"I'm sorry I didn't paint it lilac. I have some limits when I sleep here too," he grunted, and he flung me off his shoulder until I thumped on the bed.

I scurried to my feet quickly, unwilling to put myself in a position where I stayed in a bed willingly. Not with the monster in the room with me, anyway.

"You should get changed for bed," Ryker growled at me.

"I'm not tired," I lied, making for the door. "Besides, I want to wait and see if the kids need me at all." He went for a panel on the wall, pressing a button and the light sound of feedback filled the room.

"Audio monitors," he grunted. "This room is soundproof, so we won't hear them without it."

"Right, well I'm still not tired," I spat, and then hesitation settled over me as I processed his words. "Why exactly does your room need soundproofing, Hulk?" I swallowed down my nerves, crossing my arms over my chest as I stared at him.

He only raised an eyebrow back at me in answer, before he pressed on like the question didn't need an answer.

It most definitely needed a damn answer.

"You were tired enough when you tried to curl up in bed with Ines." He crossed his arms over his chest, looking all too menacing as he hovered in front of the bedroom door. "Go get ready for bed, or I'll put you back in bed like that. I can't imagine those yoga pants are comfortable to sleep in, and I know you're probably dying to get out of your sports bra."

"Your understanding of female comfort is concerning," I hissed, narrowing my eyes on him. "I need to shower. I didn't get to shower after the studio today, since *someone* brought me here under the guise of a meeting and then held me hostage like a thug."

"A thug?" he asked, his scarred eyebrow raising as he studied me.

"Yes, an over-muscled thug."

"Sunshine, you have no clue who I am, but I am not a street thug."

"Of course I have no idea who you are, you just inserted yourself into my life like a crazy person. This isn't normal! What is wrong with you?"

He chuckled, hanging his head and looking at the floor before he raised it and those vibrant blue eyes met mine again. The shadows toyed with the scar that stretched over his eye with the way he angled his head, and he only looked more menacing for it. "Go shower if you're going to. Otherwise, we're going to bed."

"I don't want to sleep in the same room as you! I want to go to my home and my bed and sleep alone!" I knew my voice was bordering on hysterical, knew that the tears that burned the back of my throat wouldn't be held off forever.

I'd woken up that morning a single widow who would do anything for her kids. I didn't even know what I'd become when Ryker had suddenly appeared, but I knew that I would still do anything for my kids.

Even if it meant I had to stab Ryker in his sleep. The smile that crossed his face as he studied me didn't bode well for me.

"I'd like to see you try it, Tesoro," he murmured, stepping forward. I stood my ground, refusing to back off once we were in the privacy of his bedroom and away from my kids and the other people he could hurt.

"Try what?" I asked innocently.

"I'm trying to be patient with you, but if you try to knife me that will go out the window. Now this is the last time I'm going to tell you to go take your shower. If your sweet little ass doesn't march into the bathroom in the next thirty seconds, I'll strip you down and you can sleep naked." I didn't want to think about the fact that he knew so much about us and our lives, that he knew me well enough to know I'd considered killing him in that exact moment. His next words only confirmed just how well he knew the thoughts that circulated in my head. "You have no secrets that are safe from me."

"I'll shower in the morning," I muttered, and he groaned before stepping up and taking my hand. He guided me into the bathroom as I tried not to struggle against his grip, but it felt natural when he reached in to turn on the shower. The space was massive, with dark grey tile walls and a huge, white deep soaking tub and vanity. Modern luxury, with little industrial touches in the skylights and natural wood beams that ran along the entire ceiling of the second floor.

"You'll shower tonight. You don't like to go to bed with yoga sweat on you," he announced, and I glared back.

"I'm not taking off my clothes with you anywhere nearby, you giant meatball!" He chuckled at that, but grabbed me around the waist and pulled me into the shower spray with him. I shrieked, hot water drenching me like a drowned rat, and fled to the opposite corner of the shower.

Still chuckling, he tipped his head back and ran his fingers through his dark hair to brush the stray bits out of his face. Something about the look in his eyes and the way the water dripped off his head when he tipped his face down to look at the floor nearly broke my heart, seeing a man more broken than I'd ever thought could exist.

He ruined the sympathy that panged in my chest when he opened his mouth. "I heard cats didn't like water."

"Was that a pussy reference?" I asked with a scowl.

He roared out a laugh. For someone so intimidating, I never would have expected him to laugh as often as he did. "No, Sunshine. That was not a pussy reference," he said, and when I didn't bother to respond to that, he lifted his hands to the buttons of his shirt.

"What are you doing?" I asked with wide eyes as he undid one button at a time. The smooth expanse of his chest came into view bit by bit, filling my vision with the tantalizing lines of every muscle packed onto his body. Tugging the shirt out of his pants, he undid the last few buttons. Even as panic flooded my brain, I couldn't look away.

I didn't even know it was possible to have that many rippling abs, but it was official. There were eight of them. When he slid the shirt off his shoulders and tossed it to the corner of the massive standing shower, my eyes caught on the silver glint of barbells pierced through his nipples. The tribal wolf tattoo I'd seen on his forearm continued up and onto his chest, curving over his collarbone before stopping above his nipple. When he spun to face away from me, I got a good look at the ink on his back and the angel that seemed to nestle between his shoulder blades and extend down to his hips. It struck me as odd that a man who was a self-professed criminal would have the tattoo of an angel, but when he shoved his slacks down his legs, I didn't give the first shit.

He had a male bubble butt, but even with the boxer briefs covering it, I could see that it was just as corded with muscle as the rest of him. His thighs strained against the fabric, stretching them to the limit. "I think you need to size up, big boy," I laughed nervously. "Please keep them on."

"What's wrong, Tesoro? You don't want me to continue with the little strip tease you're enjoying so much?"

I flushed with embarrassment, but I couldn't be surprised he'd picked up on my viewing party. I hadn't been remotely subtle. "Fuck you, meatball. I'm just hoping you stay over there."

He turned around, staring at me from the other side of the shower before he closed the gap, trapping me against the wall with his hands extended so he leaned into me. He seemed so tall hovering over me, and I did everything I could to shrink into the wall.

"I'd love to fuck you, Calla," he whispered. "But I want you to be good and ready the first time I get inside you." His rough voice deepened, and I tried not to look down at the muscles of his chest in my face or the nipple piercings that I suddenly couldn't stop thinking about.

"Please tell me that's the only thing that's pierced," I blurted, my eyes widening in shock when I said the words.

He chuckled, but didn't speak. My dread mounted, because I'd seen some pretty startling pictures of dicks that were more metal than skin. "Are you asking to see my cock?"

"Nope! Definitely not. I just wanted reassurance that it wasn't some kind of monster. You know, for the rest of the female population." I flushed, and I wished I could melt into the wall. I didn't understand what it was about all the intensity the man had and why it made me act like an idiot, but there was something so unnatural about the way he fixated on me.

Like there was no one else in the world, and the only person who mattered was me. I'd never had anyone pay that close of attention to me, and it left me feeling like I was floundering and in shock, speechless where I should have just been pissed.

"It's not the only place I'm pierced," he admitted, pressing his lips to my forehead affectionately. "But I promise it isn't a monster. Not because of the piercing anyway," he said, and then he stepped back and left the shower. "I'll grab you something to wear and leave it on the counter, then I'll give you privacy to shower."

And just like that he was gone, and he left me feeling like I probably didn't want to know how his dick *was* a monster.

I needed to get the hell out of there.

❧

I'D KILL HIM.

That was certain.

I hadn't stopped to consider just what he would pick out for me to wear to bed, but I knew for a fact the lilac chemise I shrugged on hadn't been in my wardrobe.

No bra.

No underwear.

He'd be lucky if I didn't shove the nightie down his throat for him to choke on in his sleep, but as it stood it was *all* I had to wear. To get to the closet, I'd have to go through the bedroom.

My thighs were too thick for this thing and my ass jutted out obscenely. Yoga was great for toning my body, but there were just certain parts of me that got more muscular and never went away. My legs were longer than my torso called for, but I lost any length I might have gained from that because of the way the chemise stretched over my ass.

I spit out my toothpaste, rinsing my mouth and tugging my hair down from the ponytail. I had wanted nothing to do with the bed, but now I desperately wanted to use that blanket to cover up. Determined to just make a run for the closet, I took a deep breath before I flung the bathroom door open and bolted for the other door.

Ryker grimaced, vaulting up from the bed to grab me around the waist and tug me into his body. A fresh pair of boxer briefs was all he wore, leaving all that muscle pressed against most of the skin on my back that the chemise revealed where it dipped low. "Ryker!" I screamed, kicking my legs as he lifted me off the floor and turned to carry me to the bed. "No!"

"Relax, Tesoro. You're safe with me."

"Liar!" I hissed, and he dropped me onto the bed on my stomach before rolling me to my back and crawling over me. Trapped beneath him, with his thighs and his arms caging me in on both sides, I froze and panted up at him. "You can't just demand that I wear this and put me to bed. Let me change."

"No," he grunted. "It's your favorite color, and it's so perfect with your skin. You look like a fairy or something."

I glared at him, but he didn't seem affected. Instead, he just rolled me to my side and tugged me into his chest. His massive arm wrapped around me, and I considered comparing them to my thighs. I was fairly certain his arms were bigger.

One of his thighs wrapped around my legs, pinning me tightly and I tried not to think about the monster bulge against my ass or the fact that he acted like I was a fucking body pillow.

"Go to sleep, Tesoro."

"You can't just tell me to—"

"Just did," he yawned.

I pursed my lips but went silent, fully intending to wait until he fell asleep and then sneak out.

But I fell asleep far too quickly for that. His body was like a furnace against me, lulling me into a comfortable warm place where my body felt safe like the idiot it was.

CHAPTER THIRTEEN

RYKER

I never wanted to leave my bed. Calla was still snuggled against me, tucked in tight and warm against my chest and thighs, right where she was meant to be. In the night, her nightie rode up so her bare ass pressed into my groin, and I barely resisted the urge to grind my hard-on into her. Her breathing fell in the steady rhythm of sleep and the day before had been a hard one for my Sunshine. I couldn't disturb her when she rested so peacefully in my arms for the first time.

I'd watched her sleep enough times in the last year to know what it looked like, what she felt like when her brain quieted and she disappeared into the world of dreams. Dreams that didn't seem to haunt her or scare her. For my Sunshine, sleep looked like a peaceful retreat. No traces of the pissed off hellcat I'd narrowly avoided the day before.

Sweet. Pliant.

Mine.

But the sound of Axel getting up and out of bed beckoned, and the sun had long since started shining around the edges of the blackout blinds and curtains covering the window. "Calla, I have to get up," I whispered, brushing her platinum hair back from her face.

She groaned in complaint, wiggling away from me and murmuring sleepily. "Too warm," she mumbled, drawing a hoarse chuckle from my throat.

Even with my body heat still warming the bed, when I pulled away from her, she turned to follow me in her sleep, and it made it even more difficult to leave her when I glimpsed the little crooked smile on her face. Her eyes remained closed, still lost to that place where she didn't know what was going on.

But I forced myself to leave anyway, because she needed the sleep and Axel needed food.

I leaned over her, staring down at her in the same way I had for so long. The only difference was that this time I could touch her without fear. If she woke up, it wouldn't be the end of the world. I didn't have to sneak out of the house before the kids woke up or the neighbors could wonder about my car parked down the street.

Calla mumbled in her sleep again, and I smiled down at her. "Go back to sleep, Sunshine," I whispered, leaning forward to touch my lips to hers. In her sleepy state, she arched into me, taking what I gave with a brief moan. The feeling of her lips against mine was like the strongest shot to my system, and it killed me that I had to leave her. I wanted more, the first brush of my mouth on hers nothing but a tease that made me crave everything she had to give.

I'd have it all soon enough, but not right that moment. I couldn't take what I knew she would offer in her half-aware state of being. Our first time wouldn't be with her son awake and wandering the house and with her half-asleep so she could blame me when she came to her senses.

She'd be fully aware when I finally took what was mine for the first time.

I tucked her back in to fight off the chill in the room and then grabbed some sweatpants to go feed my boy.

AFTER GETTING both kids up and making them French toast for breakfast, we headed outside. The day was already warming up, and I wanted them to enjoy the beautiful weather. Having already called Axel's school and explained he wouldn't be in for the day, I didn't have it in me to wake Calla up. She was always up at the ass crack of dawn to get herself and the kids ready for their hectic mornings, and even on the weekends she had to do it to bring the kids to her dad's so she could teach morning yoga. She deserved to sleep for once.

I wouldn't want to face her wrath if I took the kids off the property without her permission. So I wrote her a note and stuck it on the nightstand, then let Axel get himself dressed. For Ines we slipped some pants on under her nighty and pulled a princess dress over her head since I wasn't comfortable getting her changed just yet. No matter how pure my intentions, when it came to the kids, I tried to remember that I was a stranger to them. I wouldn't give Calla any reason to question my behavior with them.

In time, she'd learn that I would kill anyone who even looked at a child the wrong way, but first I had to give them all the chance to get to know me.

Axel bounced happily, all his energy from the previous night bubbling up to the surface as we went through the hallway to get to the back of the house. Ines carried one of her new dolls in her hands, the one I'd practiced with in car seats, coincidentally, and I chuckled as the poor thing dragged on the floor. But she was determined to carry her, determined that it had to be *that* doll, while I carted a blanket and two more dolls in my hands.

Axel opened the door that led to the pool room, yelling in excitement. With a glass ceiling and glass paneled walls, the sun came in through the windows but let me keep the pool heated year round. And if I wanted to let in some fresh air in the summer, one of the walls opened up to accommodate that too. "This is insane!" Axel shouted.

Ines didn't look so sure, her little face pinching in distaste. I'd watched Calla attempt to get her to go into the small pool they had in the backyard last year, and even with floaties, Ines hadn't been a fan.

She'd screamed bloody murder, in fact.

I hoped the fact that she was nearly a year older would work to our advantage when she trusted me enough. "You don't come in here without your mom or me, got me?" I asked Axel in all seriousness. "Swimming is supervised. In fact, I'll make sure that door is locked."

"I get you," he said, and I realized it was the first moment he'd really heard me be anything close to serious.

Most people who knew me would have said I didn't know how to *not* be serious, that there was no humor to me or emotion aside from the glee I felt when I tormented someone who deserved it. But in reality, I'd spent most of my life grieving the things I'd never had or the things that had been taken from me.

Until Calla.

And finally, having her and the kids here with me felt like it brought me back to life. It reminded me I could laugh, and I could banter with my woman and enjoy every second.

That I could feel again.

As soon as we got to the exterior door and Axel saw the soccer net, he flung it open and ran out. "I heard you like sports." I smiled at him.

I settled Ines near the house and in the shade so that her fair skin that was so like her mother's wouldn't burn, smiling at her when her dainty hand reached up to brush against my scar in the same way her brother had all those years ago.

When I turned back to Axel, he eyed me curiously with his nose scrunched up in concentration. Like he could remember the day we'd first met, but couldn't quite grasp the faint edges of memory. I turned to grab a few soccer balls out of the bin tucked against the house. Ines sat happily with her dolls, jabbering away in her mostly pretend language without a care in the world as I tossed a ball to Axel.

"Where did you get that scar?" Axel asked as he caught it and dropped it to his feet where he slid the ball back and forth under his foot.

"Not all of us are lucky enough to have a mom who would give anything to protect us," I told him, making his lips purse into a pout. So like his mother, the curiosity would eat away at him as he tried to navigate my vague statement. But he didn't ask another question, respecting the tentative boundary I'd set.

My childhood was off limits to him. At least until he was older.

I stepped into the goal, eying him when he laughed at me. "That's not fair! You take up like the entire goal!" Glancing from side to side, I had to admit there was a decisive lack of space.

"I think we need a bigger goal," I said.

Ines giggled at the sideline as I stepped out, accepting the ball when Axel kicked it over to me. It had been a long, long time since I'd done something as simple as kick a ball back and forth.

I loved it.

And I loved the fact that it made Axel smile as he chatted and told me all about his friends at school. I already knew about them, but somehow it meant so much more to have the information come from him.

CHAPTER FOURTEEN

CALLA

Waking up happened slowly, the heat under the blankets feeling too comfortable for me to have any interest in getting out of bed. The pillow felt more comfortable than I remembered, tailor made for me in a way that seemed impossible to find.

When my eyes finally opened, I jolted up suddenly as memories of the day before crashed over me. With the chemise tangled up around my ribs, I shoved it down in a panic and looked around the room.

The empty room.

Light fought to shine in the gaps at the edges of the blinds on the massive window, and I threw the blankets off as terror filled me.

The kids.

Ryker was gone, and my kids were in the house. While I slept alone in his bed like an idiot.

Throwing open the bedroom door, I bolted for their rooms, clutching my chest when I found their beds empty.

They'd even made them up, leaving everything as pristine as when we arrived the night before. "Axel!" I yelled, turning and racing down the hallway. I rounded the corners of the loft, struggling with the gate at the top of the stairs in my hurry to get it open. I considered climbing over it, but it finally opened. I bounded down the stairs. I could see from the stairwell that the living room was empty, and the house was silent as I raced down and shoved my way through the gate at the bottom more efficiently.

"Axel!" I repeated, darting around the brick wall to glance into the kitchen and dining room. The kids' and Ryker's shoes were missing from the entryway where they'd deposited them last night when we sat down to eat pizza. "Ryker!" I screamed, turning and flying for the door that led to the garage.

My feet slapped against the tile floor, echoing along with the sound of my panicked breaths. I'd kill him. I would kill him slowly and make him suffer if he took my kids.

The garage was empty, but all three cars sat exactly where we left them. The sound of a peal of laughter came from a door further down the hall where someone left it cracked open, and I sprinted for it with my heart in my throat.

They had to be okay. I would never survive it if something happened to them.

As soon as I'd shoved the door open the rest of the way, I saw them outside the glass-enclosed pool. Ines's little blond head nearly touched the glass as she swung one of her dolls up in the air happily. Ryker picked up Axel, swinging him over his head and using all the rippling muscles in his arms to hold him there like he could fly as he ran around the yard and Axel laughed hysterically.

Fuck.

My terror fled, fury instantly filling the void it left.

Not only should my son be in school, but Ryker had scared the fucking shit out of me needlessly. I couldn't believe anyone could be so obtuse not to consider what it would do to me if I woke up to an empty house and my children gone with a self-professed criminal who made people disappear when they got in his way.

I stormed through the pool area, my feet stomping along the floor. As soon as I flung the door open, all three eyes came to me and Ines chirped happily at me. "Mommy princess," she said, pointing at me, and I realized the chemise was still the only thing I wore.

It had been the least of my concerns when I thought my children were in danger, but the way Ryker's eyes narrowed on mine as they bled to blue flames nearly made me rethink that urgency. He let Axel slide down his back until his feet touched the ground.

When my glare didn't let up, Ryker seemed to realize something was very wrong. He patted Axel on the head briefly, nodding me into the pool room with his head, and I followed. Axel eyed me like I looked as if I might explode, and the only thing that prevented it was my inability to say much in front of the kids.

What could I say that wouldn't scare them?

When Ryker pulled the door shut, he whispered with a hesitant tone. "Calla—"

"Do not ever do that to me again," I growled. "Do you have any idea what that was like? Having to wonder if you'd taken my kids? You scared the shit out of me!" My eyes burned as my throat threatened to close on itself.

"I put a note on the nightstand," he explained.

"Do you think my first inclination when I realized it was late was to look at the fucking nightstand, Ryker? All I cared about was getting to my kids and making sure you hadn't hurt them." My voice cracked, and I swallowed to clear away the emotion that clogged my throat so thoroughly.

"I would never hurt them, Tesoro," he murmured, but his voice hardened. Gradually, irritation and frustration consumed his face.

"Right. I can totally trust the man who won't let me go home," I scoffed, turning away from him and his intense stare to go to my kids. Axel had taken to drawing Ines away from the glass, entertaining her by teaching her to kick the ball into the net. Both of them pointedly ignored our argument.

I took a step toward the door, stopping with a flinch when Ryker growled behind me. His hand grabbed the back of my neck, using all the strength of his forearm to turn me back to him. I whimpered, staring up at him when my body pressed flush against his and his lips crashed down on mine.

Protesting, I shoved at his chest, but that hand stayed planted on the back of my neck and held me right where he wanted me. But he didn't push the kiss, just took a simple, chaste press of his lips on mine before he pulled away enough to stare at me while I seethed. The possessive display, and the tight hold on my neck, shouldn't have made heat pool in my center. But it did, and I hated him even more for it. "Don't you dare walk away from me, Sunshine," he whispered. "I have had far too many years of watching you walk away. That time is done. You understand me?"

I glared up at him, my breath caught in my lungs in the face of all his ferocity. "Let go of me," I said. "You'll scare the kids."

"They don't look scared to me," he chuckled, glancing over my shoulder.

With the way he controlled my neck, I could barely turn to see them for myself. I settled for glaring at him, resisting the urge to knee him in the balls. "I just want to keep them safe and happy. Can't you give me that?" I asked, glancing back for the small view I could manage.

I felt Ryker's head turn as he followed my gaze. His nostrils flared as he drew in a deep breath to steady himself. "Tell me they don't look safe or happy right now. I'll tolerate many things from you, but what I won't take is dishonesty. We will always be honest with each other, Sunshine."

I swallowed, nodding my assent. I couldn't bring myself to lie anyway, not faced with the sight of my kids playing soccer and loving every second despite the man who sought to control me.

"I will never hurt those kids. You need to understand that." I started to speak, stopping when he touched a finger to my lips. "But I'm sorry that I scared you. It wasn't my intention." The words died inside me, the look of genuine regret in his eyes taking my breath away.

"What?" I whispered, remembering how much I'd had to work to get an apology from Chad for anything, even if he had been completely in the wrong. I'd thought all men were incapable of owning their mistakes.

"I'm sorry. I won't scare you like that again. I'll wake you up and tell you next time. You just looked so peaceful, and I knew you needed the sleep."

"He should be in school," I said instead of answering the apology. I wanted to say thank you, but I couldn't quite bring myself to find the words just yet.

"Missing one day won't kill him, Sunshine. I called the school, and the Principal understood that with the move he needed a day to adjust. It's all taken care of, so you go say good morning to the kids, and I'll make you some breakfast." He leaned in, touching my lips with his once more, and I vaguely remembered him kissing me when I'd been half asleep in bed earlier. He could have easily taken advantage of me in the night.

But he hadn't, and I supposed there had to be something said for that.

I groaned inside my head. I sounded like I had Stockholm Syndrome. Grateful to my captor because he hadn't raped me yet. "I'm not hungry," I whispered when he pulled away.

He ignored me as he plowed on. "On second thought," he muttered with a glance at the clock hanging on the wall. "I'll make lunch."

"Ryker! I'm not hungry," I said.

"You need to eat. You'll need your strength," he said as he stalked off and left me floundering in the pool room. I didn't want to think about what I might need my strength for.

As I shoved open the door and gave the kids a bright smile, I tried not to think about what they'd seen and what they might think of me kissing a man who was not their father.

"Mommy, is 'yker my daddy?" Ines asked as I stepped outside. I blanched, and even Axel laughed at what must have been the horrified look on my face. I wouldn't have expected him to be so casual about the Dad word ever, let alone so soon, but Ryker had done more to show Axel he mattered than Chad had done in the last year of his life.

I rolled my eyes to the sky. Heaven help me.

RYKER WHIPPED TOGETHER A QUICK lunch of stove top macaroni and cheese. It might not have been gourmet, but it didn't come from a box and was meatless, and took more effort than Chad had ever gone to help feed the kids. I didn't like that I seemed to compare the two men so effortlessly, and that it didn't reflect positively for my husband.

Aside from the kidnapping, anyway.

After lunch, Ines quickly got cranky for her nap, so I brought her up to put her down. It only took a few minutes before she fell asleep halfway through her story, comfortably nestled into her princess castle bed like she didn't have a care in the world.

I closed the door quietly behind me, peeking into Axel's room where he'd settled in to do the reading he knew he would need to catch up on so he wouldn't be behind at school tomorrow. My responsible boy who acted far too old to be just six years old. "You good, Cookie Monster?" I asked him.

"Yeah, Mommy," he whispered, lounging in his bed and looking sleepy for a boy who hadn't napped in years. I attributed it to the excitement of the last two days, and that Ryker had been up with them and playing outside for hours before I'd woken up. I didn't remember the last time I'd slept that long or that hard. "Ryker said he was going to take a shower."

"Okay, baby," I said back, swinging his door closed in case he fell asleep. I didn't want either of them to get off-schedule, but I also didn't want Axel going back to school the next day looking like a zombie.

I debated going down the stairs. I debated grabbing both the kids and trying to get out while Ryker was distracted, but when I opened the door to the would-be nursery and snuck a peek at the front gate through the window, it was closed. A guard sat in the booth, as expected, and I sighed in frustration.

There would be no escaping so long as someone was there, at the very least, and that was assuming I could get the gate open, anyway. I drew in a ragged breath as I steadied myself. We just needed to wait for the right moment.

Instead of going downstairs, I went to the master bedroom and hoped to sneak into the closet for a sweater. I'd changed clothes when we came in for lunch right after Ines shocked me into a stupor, but the warehouse seemed to always have just the slightest chill.

"I can turn the heat on if you're cold," Ryker grunted when I tried to sneak through, scaring me so bad I jumped. A man as big as he was shouldn't have been capable of hiding, shouldn't have been so silent when he moved, but it was like he was a predator, a panther that hid in the shadows.

He stripped his T-shirt over his head when I turned to look at him, again seeming far too comfortable with his own nudity. I couldn't blame him, really. What was the point of a body like that if you didn't show it off?

"That's alright," I whispered. "I like sweaters and blankets."

"I know. There are blankets in the storage built into the couch. The cushions lift and there's a panel underneath where they tucked your throws."

I nodded, murmuring a soft "thank you."

He raised a brow at me as his hands went to his sweatpants. "Did you need something else, Sunshine?"

I shrugged, scuffing my feet nervously. I didn't know why this conversation seemed so hard to start, why it felt like it was an unreasonable request, but it wasn't. No matter what he claimed in his insanely possessive, pigheaded brain, they were *my* kids. Not his.

"I need you to make sure that what happened this morning never happens again. You can't leave with them. You can't take them places without me. If anything happened to them—"

"I already told you I was sorry for worrying you, Tesoro. I won't take them off the property without your permission, but you need to work on loosening the reins. I will be alone with them, eventually. I will drive Axe to school and bring Ines to your father if I have to work. There's no reason for you to do it all alone anymore."

"I'm not anywhere near ready for that," I protested.

"I know, but you need to work on getting there. I'll be patient for a bit, but I waited a long time to have the three of you here with me. I won't wait much longer to settle into our new routine."

He spun, heading for the bathroom like he seemed so prone to doing once he'd said his piece and knew I wouldn't like it. "Why an angel?" I asked, staring at the tattoo on his back. It suddenly seemed so important, like it held bits of the puzzle, and I needed it to figure out what drove the man who drove me up a wall.

He was insane. He was broken. He was funny. He was great with my kids.

But I had no idea who he really was, not when it came down to it. I had a feeling I only saw a carefully controlled piece of him, like the rest of the puzzle was even more horrific than what he showed me.

"You aren't the only one who has lost someone, Calla," he murmured, turning back to me briefly, and that agony filled his eyes again. So strong, so broken that I took a step toward him before I realized what I was doing.

"Who was she?" I asked, and I hated the way my heart clenched painfully. I didn't want to be jealous. Jealousy meant I cared, that somewhere underneath my hatred for the man, there was compassion.

He smiled at me sadly. "They were the only other people who ever mattered to me as much as you and those kids, which is why I never want you to worry that I would hurt them. I'd never let anything touch them."

"I'm sorry," I whispered in response, because even if I was jealous of whoever they'd been, the pain etched on his face was very real. I instantly wanted to hug him, to chase away the shadows that clung to him and bring back the man who'd tossed my son in the air and made him laugh.

I wanted to see him smile and hear that rough laugh.

And then I instantly wanted to kick myself for it.

"Me too, my Sunshine, but it also taught me to appreciate what I have now. To protect it. This house is the safest you can ever be. You'll understand everything soon enough," he murmured, stepping toward the bathroom. He paused at the last minute, turning back to gaze at me. Any hint of jealousy that I felt evaporated in response to the way he looked at me. Like he could devour me if I gave him the slightest hint of encouragement. "You should make yourself at home.

Put your things where you want them. Your moisturizer and lotion on the nightstand. I know you're all unpacked, but movers don't put things where *you* would want them. This is your home now. Get used to it."

I grimaced at his words, the harshness of them chasing away my moment of sympathy over our shared losses.

Which was the point, I suspected. Ryker, like me, hated pity and would do anything to avoid it. Even piss me off, evidently.

But something else struck me so harshly that I could practically feel the tendrils of shock creeping over my skin.

He knew what I kept on my nightstand.

CHAPTER FIFTEEN

CALLA

Spending time with Ryker and the kids, pretending everything was okay and calm, it was easy to see exactly how our lives would play out. Even in the earliest days of what he considered to be an actual relationship, he made it obvious we were his priority. He doted on me, refused to let me lift a finger, and in the absence of being busy, I grew more and more depressed with the reality of my life.

I didn't know what to do with myself, and that alone was a sad indicator of what my life had become. I didn't know how to not be busy.

After we dropped Axel at school and Ines off with my father, I glared over at Ryker. He'd told Dad that Ines would be home with us for a few days, so it seemed strange that we were back to business as usual.

Even if I couldn't go back to the studio just yet. He'd called in my absence the day before, explaining that I'd be out for the near future.

I could just imagine how my boss would rage at me for it when I went back. That she hadn't called me herself didn't bode well for me or the likelihood of my job still being there whenever I went back.

"I wasn't supposed to work today," Ryker said as he seemed to sense my glare. "Matteo knows that I'm off for now, and he wouldn't have called me in if it wasn't important."

I grunted back at him. "So why can't I go to work?" I tugged at the distressed jeans where they gaped open on my knees and clung to my skin. It seemed like it had been forever since I'd worn anything that wasn't elastic. The black T-shirt was simple, and as we drove out of the city and toward the wealthier suburbs of

Chicago, I felt underdressed. The only comfort was that Ryker wore black jeans and a black shirt with boots on his feet.

"I'll arrange your security for the next time this happens, but for today, Matteo said to just bring you to the house." He cast a glance at me from the side of his eye as he drove.

"What house?" I asked him, hating the cryptic way he seemed so desperate to avoid telling me where he was taking me. Ryker seemed comfortable in his opinions with no fear of confrontation with me, so it made the entire situation more ominous as apprehension made my palms sweat.

"Matteo's. You can meet the women. This way you're more comfortable by the time we bring the kids over," he said, turning toward a long driveway. The gate at the end was the epitome of luxury, making even Ryker's secure fortress look like child's play.

"What women?" I asked. The guard at the booth nodded to Ryker, and he returned the gesture as the gates swung open.

"The other wives, Ivory and Samara. Matteo's daughter, Luna. Ivory's friend Sadie," he explained as the gate slid closed behind us. The house in front of me was the very definition of Italian luxury, and Ryker didn't hesitate to pull the Maserati up in front. I supposed given the fact that he drove a Maserati, it shouldn't have been surprising.

I was definitely underdressed.

"Who is Matteo again?" I asked when he came to the passenger side and opened the door.

"Matteo Bellandi. My boss."

"Ryker!" I blanched. "You are not leaving me here!"

"This is the safest place you could ever be aside from with me, Sunshine. Nobody here will hurt you," he laughed.

"No one will hurt me? You're psychotic," I shot back, making him huff a soft laugh. But I didn't miss the decided shift in his personality. The dark tint to his personality seemed to grow even stronger the moment he closed the car door behind me.

I stood still, making him go through the effort of grabbing me by the elbow and leading me to the front of the house. The grey booties on my feet scuffed the ground as I tried not to move. I knew I was only prolonging the inevitable, but there was no way I could walk inside the home of Matteo fucking Bellandi.

When he'd said he was a criminal, I hadn't expected he was quite that much of a criminal that he associated with the Bellandis.

That was on another level.

"Ryker!" I whispered, protesting as he dragged me forward, but he didn't seem to care. Didn't even pause in his steps as he brought me closer and closer to what I felt certain was my doom.

I hadn't even put makeup on. Who didn't wear makeup to meet a mob boss?

Me. That's who.

He shoved the front door open and strode in like he belonged, and I resisted my urge to gasp. Fuck, he didn't even knock.

We were going to get shot.

"Calla!" a familiar voice shouted gleefully, and the sight of Samara's coppery hair came flying in through the sitting room to the entryway. She crashed into me, making Ryker grunt and step back.

"Samara?" I asked in surprise, pulling back and looking up at her the slightest bit. When my eyes went down, I realized why she seemed like she'd packed an extra punch to my ribs. "You're pregnant!" I said with a laugh. The bump on her belly was tiny, but when I touched it with delicate hands, it felt unusually firm compared to what I'd remembered. It had been years since I'd seen Samara, since I'd stopped going to yoga classes when I was pregnant with Axel, but she barely looked a day older. Her smile seemed brighter, her laughter when she squeezed my arms tight seemed more genuine.

"I am, and I heard you have two already!"

"I do," I confirmed. I nodded as a woman I didn't know stepped up. Taller and leaner, her eyes were a bright sea green as she smiled at us.

"That's Ivory," Samara introduced, and I nodded. "Matteo's wife." I blanched, darting my gaze over to Ryker where he stood like a silent sentry and watched us.

"Matteo said to tell you he'd see you at the warehouse," Ivory said to him. A huge hulk of a man stepped out of the kitchen, and Ryker moved over to touch his shoulder and whisper to him.

"Nobody likes secrets!" Samara teased, and the man who towered over even Ryker smiled at her.

"I've got her," he said to Ryker. "Sal, Dante, and Leo are on the perimeter. She's safe."

"I'm not worried about her being in danger," Ryker grunted. "I'm worried about her trying to run." When Samara and Ivory laughed, I felt like I'd entered the fucking twilight zone.

"Come on, honey. Let's get you something to drink. You look like you need wine," Ivory said, touching my arm with her hand and gesturing me into the kitchen.

"It's nine in the morning," I whispered, and she shrugged.

"So we'll do mimosas, and I'll feed you." She guided me toward the kitchen, and Ryker stepped into our path. Ivory rolled her eyes, stepping around him to leave me to his mercy.

"You don't leave Scar's sight," he announced, and I glanced over at the big guy who just grinned at me. Ryker's hand lifted to bury in my hair, tugging my head back until I met his eyes. "I mean it, Calla. Do not make me chase you," he warned.

"I'm not sure what kind of spider monkey you think I am, but I am not capable of climbing the barricades, Ryker." I rolled my eyes at him.

"I'll be back as soon as I can. Get to know Ivory and Samara. Enjoy the quiet until Sadie gets here to interrogate you."

"Fine," I sighed. I was just grateful that the legendary Matteo Bellandi wasn't there. Wives I could handle, but a mob boss I was not ready for. "We need to have a conversation when you get your meatball ass back here," I said through gritted teeth.

Scar roared out a laugh beside us, stepping into the kitchen and staring back at us. "Come on, Hellcat, you're going to do just fine here," he murmured, and Ryker glared at him over the top of my head.

"Don't push me," he grunted, and the other man just smiled in response.

"Is his ass a meatball because it's so round?!" Samara yelled from the kitchen, and I giggled when Ryker's face pinched in annoyance and he dropped his forehead on mine. It didn't stop me from seeing the way his cheeks flushed the slightest bit pink.

"Think you can maybe behave for just a few hours?"

"Probably not," I admitted with a shrug. "But you have fun doing whatever it is you do, Mr. Secret Pants. I'll just be getting all the gossip to use against you."

"Calla," he warned with a growl. When I didn't respond and didn't cower in fear dramatically, he shook his head at me and then dipped his face down and touched his lips to mine briefly before pulling away. It was an even more chaste kiss than he gave me in front of my kids, as if a public display in front of his friend was something horrific.

I imagined a man like Ryker wasn't particularly fond of showing emotion in front of others, not that there were emotions involved in what we had. Unless ownership was an emotion.

I shook my head when I realized I'd been staring after his ass when he walked away. I couldn't afford to give anyone the impression that I wanted him.

Not if I had any hope of keeping my sanity or trying to be free of the cage he'd put us in.

With a sigh, I turned and went into the kitchen, feeling like my world had been turned on its head. I hadn't expected to find Ivory putting muffins in the oven or Mr. Lombardi hovering at the edge of the room and bouncing a baby around in his arms. "Calla," he said with a smile, stepping forward. "How are you?"

"Seriously?" I asked, stepping away from him. I took a seat next to Samara at the island, watching as the woman plucked raspberries off a tray and shoved them in her mouth. "How do you think I am? You lured me into a trap!"

"Don't be mean to Don," she mumbled around the mouthful, and I had to giggle. I'd been the same way with cookies when I'd been pregnant with Axel.

She should just be grateful her craving was healthy. "He just does what Matteo and Lino ask him to."

Giving Don one last glare, I shifted my focus to Samara. As much as I wanted to poke at the man, his expression was sympathetic. "You married Lino?" I asked as the pieces finally snapped together in my head. I remembered her vaguely mentioning that she was friends with him when we'd gone to classes together, but it hadn't seemed important back then.

I could have never predicted I'd find myself in the Bellandi Estate.

"Yep," she said with a brief grin. "Ivory and I both suffered like you for a bit, but it all works out in the end."

"For what it's worth," Don interrupted, stepping to the side of the island so he could look at me. "I am very sorry for my involvement in what I'm sure feels traumatic right now."

"Don't worry about it," I mumbled. I wanted to blame him, but I couldn't when I suspected it wouldn't have made a difference if he hadn't been involved. From what I'd seen of Ryker, he would have done whatever it took to have me trapped under his thumb. Don's involvement didn't matter in the slightest, because if it hadn't been him it just would have been someone else.

The only person to blame for trapping me in a pseudo-relationship I didn't want was Ryker himself.

"Where is she?" another woman's voice asked from the entryway, and then the tiniest woman I'd ever seen stormed into the room.

"Oh, she's blond!" she yelled, stepping up and standing next to me on the stool. I knew I probably wasn't much taller than her, but her muscular and petite form looked so small from where I sat. "You're all like a complete set now! Brunette, redhead, blond." Her honey eyes were upturned almonds, and those combined with her dusky skin made her high cheekbones and strong bone structure even more prominent.

"Hush you," Samara swatted her away. "You'll scare her off."

"She's sharing a bed with Ryker. If she can survive that man, then I'm a piece of cake."

Ivory rolled her eyes as she cleaned off the counter. "That's Sadie," she said. "She's a lot. If she annoys you, just slap her."

"No, don't do that. She'll knock you on your ass and then Scar will get in trouble with Ryker," Samara laughed.

"But then we could watch them spar. That's always fun," Sadie said with a teasing grin. "I don't get to watch that nearly enough, if you know what I mean. Want to take one for the team?"

"Uh no?" I asked, and she pouted at me.

"I don't know if I like you," she whispered, but there was still a smile on her face when she took a seat. Ivory slid a mimosa in front of me, and I only stared at it for a moment before I looked back at her.

"Drink," she ordered, and I didn't need to be told twice.

I chugged it, wiping my hand across the back of my mouth when I finished. "I think she needs like six more of those," Sadie said.

"No! I can't get drunk."

Samara looked over at me with a little smirk on her face. "Oh? Would that have anything to do with the meatball ass and the fact that you want to jump on and ride him until tomorrow?"

"I changed my mind," Sadie chirped, sipping at her own mimosa delicately. "I think I do like you. I have to ask though, do your legs even wrap around him?"

I nearly spit out my first sip of my second mimosa. "I wouldn't know. I'm usually trying to get him off me. And I do not want to ride him until tomorrow!" I whispered at Samara, glancing nervously at Scar where he stood in the corner and tried not to laugh. Finally snapping my attention to Ivory, I widened my eyes at her shoulder, wondering just how much champagne she'd put in my drink. "Is that a lizard?"

"This is Smaug. He's everybody's favorite, aside from Luna over there." She gestured to the baby Don held, and he brought her over like he might drop her in my arms.

"Nope!" I squealed. "My biological clock is sensitive. I swear if I hold her, I'll be pregnant in a week and that is not happening."

Samara chuckled, but bit her tongue when I turned a glare at her. "These men don't have the best reputation for waiting long before they get us pregnant," Ivory said.

"Well, it takes two to tango, and I am not dancing."

Sadie looked over to Ivory gleefully. "I give it a week."

Ivory responded with, "two weeks."

"I give it three days," Samara said, and she shrank back from the glare I leveled her with.

"I am not having sex with Ryker," I mumbled.

"You will, and you'll love it. You'll do it constantly. Next thing you know, you'll be married, and then a month later you'll be pregnant. I swear, all they have to do is look at us and we're knocked up." Ivory's smile was warm as she dropped the lizard in my hand and went back to check the muffins. I looked down at the lizard who tilted his head and blinked at me as he settled in to sleep.

"Don't fight it," Samara whispered, suddenly seeming more serious than they'd been since I arrived. "It won't matter either way, but Ryker will take good care of you and the kids. He might not be a good man, but he'll be good to you. That's all that matters," she added.

"How can he be good to me if he doesn't give a damn about what I want?"

"So did Matteo really, and Lino," she returned. "These men aren't like normal men. The lives they live mean they take what they want. They wanted us: they took us. It really is that simple to them."

"And I'm just supposed to be okay with that?" I asked, bewildered.

"He's going to make you fall in love with him. The way that he fell for you. He won't stop until he's imprinted himself on your soul and ruined you for other men. It's much smoother when you just go with it," Ivory argued, and I glanced over at Scar where he stood for a moment. He nodded to me, as if agreeing with everything Ivory said.

I dropped my head to the table, banging it on the island while Sadie laughed.

"This isn't normal," I whispered.

"Normal is boring, baby girl. Enjoy the ride," Sadie said.

"Speaking of normal," Ivory interjected. "How's Patrick?"

Sadie's entire frame went still, and she glanced at us before shrugging and continuing on like she didn't care that a practical stranger would intrude on her private discussion. "I know he's a nice guy. I know that I should want that."

"But you don't?" I asked, sipping at my mimosa until I realized the effing thing was empty.

Again.

Shit.

She sighed dramatically, tipping her head back to stare at the ceiling. "I'm so bored. I swear all he wants to do is stay home and binge watch movies."

"What's wrong with that?" Samara asked, glaring at the smallest woman.

"Nothing, if your name is Samara," Sadie teased, dropping her head into her hands. "Women like me, I think it takes a powerful personality to handle us. Let's be honest, I'm intense on a good day. I want a man who is all about that, not one who wants me to be quiet so we can watch a movie."

"Ride or die," Samara mused thoughtfully, her face shifting into the faintest hint of a smile.

"I have to pee," I interjected suddenly, sliding off my stool. Though the motion felt graceful, eyes tracked the movement warily as Scar lunged forward and prepared to catch me.

"That wasn't so hot, huh?" I asked, getting my feet more solidly underneath me.

Ivory laughed, pressing her hand to her mouth. "Not so much, honey," she murmured.

"Fuck," I groaned as I stumbled toward the hall. It took me a moment to realize I had no clue where the Hell I was going. "I'm drunk," I announced. "Where's the bathroom in the Estate of Torment?"

Ivory reached forward, taking the mostly full mimosa she'd deposited in front of me right before my attempt to stand. She dumped it down the sink, and I watched the liquid disappear sadly. "Good call," I said as Scar caught me in his grip and guided me down the hall to the bathroom. "Why do they call you Scar?" I said, reaching up a finger to touch his face. "Ryker's the one with scars on his perfect face."

"There's more than one place to have scars, Calla Lily," Scar murmured back, and even in my drunken haze, my heart clenched at the melancholy to his words. I knew that once I wasn't drunk, his use of my father's nickname would resonate with me more.

In my drunken haze, all I felt was the fact that Ryker had bothered to talk about me with his friends. In my loopy state, it seemed sweet. "This is true," I agreed, stepping into the bathroom to do my business. It took longer than it should have, and I cursed myself for wearing jeans.

By the time I finished and Scar led me back to the kitchen, he practically had to help me back up onto the stool. His face pinched, as if it pained him to put his hands on me. "I know I'm no beauty queen, but am I that gross?" I asked, and he only chuckled at me like I was ridiculous after he got me settled.

"You're Ryker's woman. I like my hands attached to my arms, yeah?"

Samara cradled Luna in her arms next to me, and I eyed her like the temptation that she was.

No, I would not allow my biological clock to turn me into a senseless mess. Not even when drunk. When I looked up from Luna's face, Don met my eyes with a contented smile. "I never could have children of my own," he announced, and the room went still. I got the distinct impression that he'd never told the girls that, and even through the fog the moment felt important.

Like the air rippled with the significance of whatever he planned to say.

"My wife and I divorced over it, in fact. She wanted kids more than anything, and that it didn't upset me that we didn't have them became a daily fight between us." He paused, looking at me as if he expected me to understand. From the way the others looked at him, I had a feeling they were already grasping whatever I missed.

"You didn't want kids?" I picked at a raspberry before attempting to pop it into my mouth. It missed, but I pretended like nobody had seen it. Even with Sadie giggling at my side.

"They may not have come from my body, but I already had two sons. Matteo and Lino were everything I could have ever wanted. Why would it be any different for Ryker?" I stilled, the point finally settling on top of my head instead of flying right over it.

"I don't think I forgive you after all," I whispered, making his face transform with a massive smile.

"That's alright. You have an entire lifetime to do so."

Eff.

CHAPTER SIXTEEN

RYKER

I loved torturing people.

I loved the feeling of their skin splitting beneath my knife and the sounds of their screams echoing against the walls of the freezer.

But with Calla in my life, I no longer wanted to draw it out. I wanted to get the answers we needed so we could get home to the women.

I wanted Calla in my arms, and to spend every waking second striving to convince her of her new reality.

That we were inevitable, and we would be together. Hopefully, Ivory and Samara didn't do any damage to the little progress I'd made. Hopefully, they could convince her to just accept us.

To accept me.

Because I wasn't going anywhere.

I'd stalked her before she could ever be mine, and there were no limits to what I would do now that she was.

"Is Miguel planning on backing down from his war with Tiernan Murphy?" Matteo asked, and he looked bored out of his mind. He was always the best in the room at holding his mask, remaining indifferent no matter what tactics I took to get someone to talk. Simon stared at me like I'd lost my mind, and I knew I'd probably gone in a little hard.

Oops.

I supposed flaying someone alive was a tactic I usually took later in the game, rather than in the first two hours.

Matteo's eyes turned knowing as he glanced at me. "You'll have to excuse Ryker's sloppy work. He's usually an artist." He gestured down at the man's arm that had quickly turned into a piece of meat when I peeled his skin off bit by bit. "But you know how it is when you have a quality woman waiting for you."

"Please stop," Miguel's dealer begged, his eyes fixated on where his tattooed skin sat on the floor.

"Then tell me what Miguel is planning to do."

"He's leaving town! It isn't worth it for him! He has conflicts rising down in Georgia, and he can't afford the war on both fronts." I stopped carving, leaning back on my knees to look at Matteo and study his reaction to the man's confession. We could handle Tiernan Murphy, and we could probably handle Miguel Cuevas too, but Murphy would be a much easier war to win than the Cuevas cartel.

"What's so important down in Georgia that he would choose that over a trafficking ring in Chicago?" Simon asked, stepping forward to kick the fleshy part of the man's arm.

I hadn't bothered to learn his name. It wouldn't matter when he was dead, anyway.

His scream soothed a little of my wariness about being away from Calla for so long, so soon.

"A woman! It's a woman! He's fucking obsessed with the bitch, but she just won't come to heel. He doesn't need the attention she'll bring, but he can't seem to stay away from her." I stood, brushing off my pants. I felt confident that Matteo wouldn't be interested in any more garbage, because if what the guy said was true, there was nothing we could do.

As much as I might want to, we couldn't step in on behalf of a woman we'd never met.

"He's in trafficking. Why hasn't he just taken her?" Simon asked.

"She's the seventeen-year-old daughter of some Governor in his pocket. If he touches a hair on her head, he'll lose the support in Georgia. He's almost ready to take that step, but he can't do that and fight here too."

"So he's playing the doting boyfriend for her Daddy?" I asked, and fury built in my veins. I knew what Miguel Cuevas was capable of.

The poor girl would wish she was dead the moment Miguel owned her.

Matteo nodded, glancing at me like he thought I might lose my shit.

A few years ago, I might have paid her a visit and warned her. But now I had Calla and the kids to worry about, and I had to keep them safe over everything else.

Even if it broke a piece of me.

"Sandro?" Matteo called, and one of Matteo's guys stepped in the door. He was young, working his way up the ranks, but had already proven himself trustworthy. "Monitor him overnight. We'll see if he has anything else to say in the morning. Wrap up his arm so he doesn't bleed out."

"Yes, Boss," Sandro grunted, moving to grab a cloth out of the corner. It was filthy, but it didn't matter.

The guy would be dead long before infection could set in.

WHY MATTEO HAD RIDDEN with me that day, I couldn't fathom. "So?" he asked when I didn't seem ready to be chatty.

Apparently marriage had turned Matteo into the king of gossip.

"So?" I grunted back, shifting the gears in my Maserati. Simon followed with Matteo's Aston behind us, and the way he smiled behind the steering wheel made him look like a kid that had been given the keys to the kingdom.

"How is she? What you hoped?" he asked.

"Been two days," I muttered.

His grin faded. "Right." A look crossed over his face, and I knew he probably reflected on Ivory's first two days after he'd forced her to move into his home.

"She's not the moping kind. I have to worry more that she'll kill me while I sleep," I said. That brought the dark grin back to his face.

"Scar says you barely sleep, so that might prove challenging." I turned the corner to the driveway, breathing out a sigh of relief when the Estate came into view. Still standing strong, and none of the guards looked panicked like I might have expected had my woman somehow escaped.

I glanced at him out of the side of my eye, feeling my lips tip up in a smile that made him jerk his head back in shock. "I didn't say she'd be successful."

He barked a brief laugh, furrowing his brow at me as he tried to understand who I was. When the gate opened up, I drove through, and Matteo didn't stand a chance in getting out of the car before me. I threw it in park, jumping out and storming into the house.

I needed my woman. Needed to know that she hadn't left me or been hurt. I knew she couldn't logically. Nobody got in or out of Matteo's house without him knowing. But old habits were hard to break, old hurts hard to shake.

When my eyes landed on her entire body shaking as she giggled on the stool of the island, and sipped what looked to be her fourth mimosa if her swaying body was any sign, my chest sagged in relief. It fled the next moment when she pitched to the side, jarred out of her stool by Sadie's playful shove. "You're such a lightweight!" Sadie giggled, and Samara reached over to stabilize Calla but missed.

I closed the distance between us, scooping my Sunshine up before she could hit the ground. "You're drunk, Tesoro," I whispered, when she chuckled against me.

There was zero chance of me getting inside her that night. Not with the way alcohol gave her headaches if she drank and didn't go right to bed.

"You ready to go get Ines?" I asked her, and she squirmed in my arms. Like she'd be able to walk on her own. "How much did she drink?"

"Three mimosas," Ivory answered when Matteo came up behind her and tugged her into his arms for a kiss. It was the kind of kiss Calla would have thought indecent, but she'd get over that when the time came.

I'd claim her in front of anyone and everyone as soon as she was ready. Whether she liked it or not.

After he'd sufficiently kissed his wife into a stupor, he moved to Don and snatched his daughter out of his arms. "Hey, Little Moon," he whispered, and I watched Calla's eyes drift over to the interaction with longing.

She'd always wanted three kids.

She'd have them soon enough.

I carried her over to the more stable chairs in the dining area where she could still peek in on the kitchen and watch Matteo with Luna. I wasn't against encouraging that desire for another baby. Matteo grinned at me as I settled her, walking over with a calmer gait than the man usually accomplished.

Normally he didn't give a rat's ass who he terrified, but apparently he could take the time to be slightly understanding of Calla's position.

"Calla," he said in that guttural voice. Calla's head immediately lifted, and she stared at the baby in his arms with shocked eyes for a moment before her mouth dropped open.

She whispered a quiet, "Holy shit," to which Matteo only grinned in response.

"Sunshine, this is my boss Matteo," I introduced, though it seemed very obvious that the man needed no introduction. If Luna hadn't been enough of a sign of who Matteo was, then the fact that the man's face was in the news often probably was.

"Nice to meet you," she whispered, staring at the door in longing.

"Angel!" he barked suddenly, spinning to face his wife who bit her lip anxiously. "What did you tell her? She's terrified."

Ivory stifled her giggle, glancing down at Calla's pale face. "Did it occur to you, my darling husband, that perhaps you just give off that psychopath vibe?"

"She's sleeping with Ryker," Matteo returned, turning to me. His expression was pleading, and I knew he wanted me to agree with him. Undoubtedly, I was scarier at first glance.

But not by much.

I ignored him, knowing that I needed to get Calla home before she truly lost her sanity. "I just need to talk to Scar for a minute, Tesoro," I murmured, tucking her ice blond hair behind her ear when she rolled her eyes at me.

"I behaaavved," she said, and though the words were drawn out, she didn't slur. She was always so good with her words, even when she was drunk. It made sense, since she thought they were her greatest weapon.

She didn't understand that I was her greatest weapon.

With a chuckle, I turned away from the gaping women and went for where Scar just stood watching like he'd found a reality show. He followed me into the sitting room. Simon passed us as we went, and I made a mental note to hurry the conversation along. There was zero chance Simon wouldn't annoy her. "She give you any trouble?" I asked.

"None. They gossiped, told her to just let it happen, and hinted that she wants to fuck you. Then they got her drunk. Sadie said they were lowering her inhibitions so she could 'ride your meatballs until the sun came up.'"

I hung my head, sighing at the floor. Thanks to Sunshine, everyone would be talking about my meatballs.

Meatballs. A monster metal dick.

My junk was getting more and more strange by the day. If I didn't show her my cock soon, the next thing I knew, she'd claim it spit marinara.

"You going to let her ride your meatballs, Ryke?" Scar asked, trying to contain his laughter.

"Shut the fuck up," I laughed. "Thanks for keeping an eye on her."

"You know I've got your back. You deserve to be happy. She's the only person who gives you that." He shrugged, but I knew him well enough to know exactly what went through his head.

He didn't deserve the same happiness, even if our situations had been similar.

"You do too. You'll find her someday. She'll come out of nowhere and that will be that," I grunted, stepping back to the dining room to grab my woman so we could go get our kids.

Sure enough, Simon had made himself welcome in her space at the table, leaning in and whispering something to her. I fought back the rage boiling my blood. Simon was one crazy fuck, I'd give him that. But he wasn't stupid.

He'd never think to touch what was mine, and as I got closer, it became increasingly obvious. He was close, but not a single part of him touched her. She giggled at whatever shit show he told her, and then he stepped back to smile at the thunderous look on my face.

"I was just telling Calla that you like to paint in your free time," Simon said, his face contorting into a laugh. I instantly wanted to strangle him.

The only paintings I did were in blood.

"I think it's time to go get Ines, Sunshine," I murmured, closing the little distance between us and grabbing her hands. I lifted her until she stepped into my chest. I felt the room go still when I leaned over her to touch my lips to the top of her head. My heart rate and the anger that always pulsed through every muscle in my body instantly dissipated once I had my Sunshine back in my arms. She chased away the shadows.

"Why don't you two stay for dinner?" Matteo asked with a chuckle, but I leveled him with a glare. I had no intention of staying any longer, and the man knew it.

Calla tilted her head back up to look at me, her smile extra crooked with the alcohol altering her state of being.

I was ready to be back in our sanctuary.

Alone. Just the four of us.

Home.

CHAPTER SEVENTEEN

CALLA

He was a party pooper.

Practically carrying me to the car, he deposited me in the passenger seat with a disgruntled breath. I fumbled for the seat belt as my head lolled to the side, staring up at those bright blue eyes as he swatted my hand away in annoyance and took the seat belt into his own hands.

Stretching up with an arm, I touched my fingertips to his mouth.

Bubble butt. Pillow lips.

Everything about the man was a temptation. When his mouth dropped open in a moment of shock, he let go of the belt to fixate on my face as I touched him. With my finger caressing the flat tops of his bottom teeth, he nipped at it sharply until I withdrew with a pout. "You should be very careful, Tesoro. I'm not a man you should toy with."

"I don't know how to toy with a man," I admitted with a whisper. The reality of it was like a crushing weight on my chest. A more experienced woman might have known how to play with Ryker's attraction and gain freedom in that, but even in my happy haze of drunk sexual energy, I knew that wasn't me.

That wasn't us.

He'd chew me up and spit me out when he finished with me, and somehow he'd make me love every minute. Where there should have only been hate and frustration, all that remained in my buzz was the lingering effect of my attraction to a dangerous man I could never have.

Even if it seemed like I already did, we'd never stay.

Never last.

When he grabbed the seat belt and tugged it across me again, I leaned in and touched my lips to his cheek. He clenched his eyes closed like he wanted to ignore me, but he couldn't when I snatched his arm up as he pulled away. That massive hand seemed so large in mine as I entwined our fingers and guided it to the neckline of my shirt. He swallowed, and I smiled at him as I guided his fingers to slip beneath the fabric and into my bra so he cupped the top curve of my breast.

"Calla," he warned.

I pouted up at him. "Sunshine," I whispered. "I'm your Sunshine."

His eyes flared with heat at my acceptance of my nickname. "Sunshine, you'll regret this when you're sober."

"Then let's make it worth it," I whispered with a smile, guiding his hand further until the rough tips of his middle finger grazed the pucker of my nipple.

I gasped, feeling the touch buzz through my entire body like a fuse. To my horror, he pulled back with a groan and slammed the door closed before I could even react to his absence and the sudden shock of chilly air that filled the void he left. When he plopped into the seat, he swatted my hand away as I reached over to touch his denim clad thigh. "Stop that," he said. "Before I stop trying to control this situation."

"But Ryker," I complained. "Why don't you want me to touch you?"

"I want *you* to touch me. Not alcohol." I flinched back, snarling at him as I crossed my arms over my chest.

"Of course. You have morals when it's convenient for you. Taking me hostage and locking me in your home was acceptable. Putting me in a skimpy nightgown and putting your boxer covered dick-monster against my ass was peachy. But touching my freaking boob when I want it crosses a line. Got it."

He smiled at my side, reaching a hand over to rest on my jean clad thigh. I immediately cursed the thick fabric from blocking the sensation of his skin on mine. I grabbed that offending hand, guiding it to the apex of my thighs in a desperate bid for friction. "Just fuck me," I begged. The sound was needy and desperate, a combination I didn't think I'd ever been before. I had no clue what the man had done to me, but I just wanted relief.

I wanted to know why his dick was a monster.

It earned me a swift swat against my core that made me cry out in shock. "Do you have any idea how much I want to throw you in the backseat and give you more than you bargained for? Stop trying to tempt me into something we'll both regret, and be thankful that the long game is more important to me than getting inside you."

I unbuckled my seat belt, diving across the center console to put myself in his lap as he stared up at me with wide-eyed surprise. My hands went to his belt, flicking it open before he stopped me with a tight grip on my wrists and tugged my hands behind my back. "We don't have to get in the backseat," I giggled.

He shook his head, trying to ignore me as I ground my center down against him. "Calla, I swear to fuck—"

"Do it." I could almost feel myself sobering in the face of his control, but something in me wanted to test him. Wanted to push him to the limits and see just how far that control and the desire not to hurt me could be pushed. It was a dangerous game to play, but somehow seemed too important to our future.

"Take off my belt," Ryker ordered and released my hands. I went for it immediately, pulling it through the loops and not for once stopping to consider exactly why it would need to be off.

As quickly as I'd put myself in his lap, he deposited me back into my seat and buckled me in. I stared at the belt in my hands in confusion, then widened my eyes as he wrestled my wrists together and used it to secure them together. "Ryker!" I glared at him and struggled, but the belt wouldn't let loose no matter how much I pulled.

"You're adorable when you're pouting," he said, and I leveled him with my fiercest glare as I tried to shove his hand off my thigh.

"Fine then. Leave me alone. I'm too drunk for your shit."

He snorted a laugh, putting the car into gear. "Sunshine, I'll never leave you alone." Those fingers tightened on my thigh like the sweetest torment.

I'd kill him in his sleep.

That was decided.

IT DIDN'T SEEM fair that my head throbbed the next morning. It didn't seem fair that I would be punished continuously. Nothing about me and alcohol was fair.

The foggy memories of Ryker holding my hair back while I threw up made me groan, and I thanked whatever God there might have been that it was Saturday at the least. Ryker wasn't in bed, despite the early hour.

It was so early I knew even the kids wouldn't be awake. I ran down the hallway, peeking my head in their doors to make sure they were both sleeping in their beds.

When the sight of them exactly where they should be comforted me, my shoulders sagged in relief and I made my way back to the master. The pain medicine and water bottle on the nightstand beckoned me over, and I swallowed both pills with a huge gulp. I tried not to think about the fact that it was sweet or that he'd taken absurdly excellent care of me in my drunken stupor the night before.

I was fairly certain I'd tried to cuddle him like he was a teddy bear while the kids watched. I was setting an impeccable example for encouraging my kids to keep Ryker at a distance.

I didn't know where Ryker had gone, but I was in no hurry to go find him.

Especially not when my cheeks flushed in embarrassment. A glance in the mirror confirmed just how much of a hot mess I was, with my wildly tangled hair and sallow skin that made me look just as sick as I felt. With a groan, I started up the shower and went to brush the taste of my hangover out of my mouth.

I'd already been hungover by the time Ryker tucked me into bed the evening before, and it seemed like if someone could be hungover at night they should get a break from the pounding head the next morning.

But not me.

I never could handle my alcohol.

By the time I stepped into the shower, I already felt more human. Drowning myself in the scalding water helped even more, despite how much it hurt to work the conditioner into the knots of my hair.

When I finally felt like my head wouldn't explode the second I stepped out of the shower, I turned it off and went through my skin care routine. I stalled to my best ability, taking my time with tugging a comfortable dress over my head. After the jeans the day before, I was in no hurry to wear something so constricting. Even my yoga pants felt like they'd be a mistake.

I knew the moment I walked out of the master that the kids were still asleep. The sun had only just started to rise as I got dressed, and the house was mostly silent except for a subtle, rhythmic thumping from the loft space. I walked toward it, thinking I'd find Ryker downstairs, but when I peeked over the edge he was nowhere to be found.

The sound of metal clanking came through the open door to the empty office as I passed, and I stepped in to look around. Around the corner where there should have been a wall, there was nothing but a balcony overlooking wherever the sound came from.

Walking toward it, I tried to stay inconspicuous as I peered over the edge. The last thing I needed was to watch Ryker commit a crime or something and be seen doing it.

I didn't expect to see his body folded in half, hanging from a bar as he slid his knees over it and hooked them to support himself.

Once that was done, he dropped his torso down and let it dangle for a moment. Shirtless, his muscles seemed to ripple with every subtle movement he made and his grey sweatpants clung to his hips. He kept his arms in line with his torso, using nothing but those abs that flexed like they were angry to do a crunch as he hung there. When he came back down, the motion was slow, controlled. Like everything he pushed his body to do was his choice, he owned every movement he made. He wouldn't let something like gravity take away his choice on when and how he lowered. He did it again. And again. Droplets of sweat dripped down over his abs and chest, and I couldn't remember there ever being a time that I thought sweat was sexy.

Until Ryker.

I let my eyes drift away from the half-naked man who proved all too tempting with every day that passed, looking at all the other workout apparatuses in the room. It was massive, at least half the size as the garage had been. The industrial nature of the gym was more apparent than in the house, but he made it work in a way that looked like he used the bones of the warehouse to exercise.

My eyes snapped back to him when he wrapped his hands around the bar, pulling his knees free and grasping it tightly. The change in position meant I stared at his back, at the intensely masculine lines of corded muscle along his shoulders and upper back and the beautiful ink of the angel tattooed on his skin. He hung for a moment and then swung his entire body up. When the bar lifted off the posts at the side, I panicked for him. But it jumped up to the next groove and snapped into place. He continued on, one after another until he reached the top, climbing the posts with nothing but the bar in his hands on the pole and the strength in his body. Then he came back down, and when he reached the bottom post, he dropped to his feet and spun to face me, those blue eyes smoldering into mine in a way I *knew* without a doubt, that he'd known the exact moment I'd started watching him.

Fucking showoff.

It shouldn't be possible for a man to be such a beast, for muscles to tempt innocent women against their better judgment.

I would not explore the grooves of his abs with my tongue.

"Why don't you come down and join me, Tesoro?" he asked, his voice coming out with a seductive rasp and barely sounding breathless. Definitely a showoff.

"I'm not exactly dressed for death defying workout stunts today, thanks," I shot back. He grinned at me before climbing the stairs that curled around the edge of the balcony and nabbing me off the steps to haul me down into the gym. "I just showered! You're all icky," I screeched. He ignored me, carrying me over to the bar he'd been climbing like a spider monkey and wiping it down with a rag. I laughed in his face.

"You're stronger than you think," he grunted, and he touched his arms to the biceps where my sleeveless dress left them bare. "Start with the low one." Those hands of his drifted from my arms to my waist, grasping me there tightly. "I won't ever let you fall, Sunshine," he murmured. He stayed an arm's length away from me, undoubtedly giving my body the space it needed to maneuver in my misguided attempt to somehow move a fucking pole, but I reached up to grasp it regardless of how foolish it would be. He lifted me until my fingers brushed the pole, and then I wrapped my palms around it. Once I'd gripped it, he released me, stepping around to the back, and I hoped to all that was holy that my dress wasn't up around my waist.

If it was, he'd have a faceful of ass, and that was the last thing I needed.

I could feel his hands hovering just underneath me, and something in me realized that he truly meant it when he said he wouldn't let me fall. It didn't matter that his hands weren't on me, or that he didn't support me physically.

He'd catch me when I inevitably fell.

I wondered if I was losing my mind. I had to be, but I took a deep breath and swung my body in on itself in a crunch. I felt the moment the pole left the groove, felt the scrape of metal on metal and fought back the instinct to drop my grip.

There was another clash as the pole slid into the second groove, and I nearly lost my grip anyway. "I told you," Ryker's deep voice inserted behind me with a chuckle.

I laughed in response, unable to believe that I'd done something that seemed so superhuman. It didn't matter that the first and second grooves were the closest of them all, that the gaps got bigger and bigger gradually as you climbed.

It was a victory either way.

Swinging my body for the next groove, I winced when I felt the pole leave the groove too soon. I hadn't put enough effort in, hadn't gotten the momentum I needed to make the next gap. The pole clattered against the side posts, slipping from my hands as the clang vibrated through me. I screamed softly as I fell, but like he promised, Ryker snatched me out of the air.

He caught me in a single arm, cradling me so I never touched the ground as he curled his upper body over mine protectively and grabbed the pole with his other hand when it nearly hit him in the head.

I clung to his shoulder desperately until he set me to my feet.

"You're okay," he murmured, and the pole dropped to the floor with a clang. "I should go shower. I have to go out for a while again today." He made no move to pull away from me, no move to separate our faces in the slightest even though I could feel his breath on my face.

The minty freshness of it tickled my nose and something about it penetrated the haze of the day before. Something was familiar. "Thank you," I said awkwardly. "For catching me, and for taking care of me last night. I shouldn't have been drinking. It was stupid."

"I meant it when I said you were safe with me. You will always be safe with me, Sunshine. You can drink and not worry that I'll violate you. Even when you want me to," he said, and his voice tapered off into a husky chuckle. "Though maybe you should worry now that you're sober." I was fairly confident he was joking, but when one of his hands drifted down to where my dress had ridden up my thigh and he trailed his calloused hands over the sensitive skin there, I knew he wasn't joking at all. It pebbled with goosebumps in the wake of his touch, and I shivered as temptation slid through me. I'd never felt muscles like Ryker's, never touched such flawless skin. My hand slid around his collarbone, touching the space over his heart on the side of his chest free from tattoos.

There was very little hair on him, and I couldn't blame him for that decision. What was the point in such beautiful artwork inked on your skin if you couldn't see it?

"Will you take us to Matteo's again?" I asked, and the thought of my kids going to the prison of that house just felt too soon. Like they could never understand why we went places where armed guards patrolled the property. We were so far out of our comfort zone; I didn't know how to make them understand that our lives had changed irrevocably.

"No. Your security should be here soon," he told me, and that hand left my thigh. I fought the urge to put it back, to shove it up under my dress so he could touch me where I shouldn't want him, where I couldn't *crave him*. I didn't want to think of what I'd done the day before to make him think I wanted him, but the fuzzy remnants of that desire pooled in my body.

His fingers touched my chin, tilting my head to look at him as he leaned in and dragged his nose against the side of mine. "My security?" I whispered, and anger had filled my veins. More like my babysitter.

"Yes," Ryker mumbled, and any response I might have had died in my throat when his eyes blazed on mine and then darted down to glance at my lips. Leaning forward, he touched mine with his soft, full pillow lips that felt remarkably gentle against my own.

A man so hard everywhere else shouldn't have lips as plush as the ones that pressed against mine more firmly. He groaned in his chest, the sound vibrating through me so I could feel it in the depths of my soul. It felt like an imprint, like a brand rippled across my skin, tying me to him so permanently that I would never get his touch off of me.

His lips parted, his tongue teasing the seam of mine until I caved and gave him what he wanted. The moment he surged inside, the moment we crashed together, drew a whimper from me. It only seemed to spur him on, only seemed to make him go mad as he lifted me higher in his arms and brought me over to a bench where he laid me flat on my back. His mouth never left mine, never stopped devouring me as I wrapped him up in my arms and legs and distractedly noted that I could *barely* touch my toes together when they wrapped around his hips.

His hand reached up, rubbing against my nipple through the fabric of my dress and making a shock of memory spin through my mind. I'd made him touch me. His body pressed against mine, and the minute I felt the heat of his hard length touch my core, I pulled my mouth back from his.

"Stop, Ryker. We have to stop. The kids could see us," I panted, and he groaned against me, dropping his face to the crook of my neck and breathing deep.

"Fuck," he whispered. He stayed on top of me, and he looked down at me with eyes full of regret when he pulled his head back just enough to study me. I trembled. I couldn't believe I'd let him touch me, that I'd let him kiss me, like everything was fine and he hadn't ripped me out of my life. "The first time I get inside you will not be when you're drunk or on a workout bench." He seemed to scold himself more than me, and as he shoved himself up and off me, he helped to tug my dress down to cover everything that he had no business seeing. That I had no business letting him anywhere near.

I hadn't been with anyone but Chad. My husband had been the only man to ever see me naked or touch me, and now I threw myself at the first man to get anywhere near me and show me attention.

A man who had known him, but didn't seem to respect him.

"I'll meet you downstairs," Ryker said with a nod as he turned and climbed the stairs to go back to the main house. He seemed to realize that I needed a minute to wrap my head around my stupidity and desperation. I didn't under-stand what it was about Ryker that tempted me to do things I never would have even considered with anyone else. Even when Chad had been alive, I'd felt this irresistible pull to Ryker.

Like he was the one I was meant to be with, but I couldn't be.

And I wouldn't.

BY THE TIME Ryker made his way down the stairs from the bedroom, the kids were awake for the day and happily munching away at bagels. I didn't have the slightest idea where anything was in the kitchen yet, and spending my first day there without Ryker terrified me. "Good morning," Ryker grunted, seeming moodier than he normally was. I tried not to glance down at his package in his dark jeans, because honestly from what I'd felt I had no clue how he even fit that thing in there.

A moment later he snapped out of his grumpiness, grabbing a bagel off the counter and smearing cream cheese on it before he shoved a bite into his mouth. "Good morning," Axel said, and he pouted at the sight of Ryker shoving his feet into his boots. "Are you leaving?"

"Gotta take care of some business today, little man. But I'll be back as soon as I can, and my buddy Dante will come hang out with you guys while I'm gone."

"How come?" Axe asked. "Wouldn't he rather hang out with us while you're here?"

I resisted the urge to smirk, enjoying the thought of Ryker having to come up with an answer for *that*.

"Well, you know how I promised I'd protect you and your mom from bad guys?" he asked, kneeling down to be eye level with Axel. "Sometimes I have to go to work, and I can't be with you guys. I can't protect you if I'm not here, so some of my friends will keep an eye on you instead. Make sure nothing bad happens to any of you while I'm gone." I'd never been more conflicted when my son smiled happily, like the answer made perfect sense. I didn't want our security to confuse him, but I also hated that he just seemed to accept that I needed protection so readily. Protection I didn't need or want.

It felt like the sudden loss of his father had affected him more than I'd ever known, and that made me feel like a terrible mother because I hadn't seen it.

He was so like his father sometimes, so stoic and hesitant to show emotion. "Okie dokie," Axel said, shoving the last bite of bagel into his mouth and rushing off to go play video games like I'd promised he could after breakfast.

"Wash your hands!" I shouted after him, shaking my head when I heard him veer off toward the bathroom instead of the couch.

"And what about you, Princess? How did you sleep?" Ryker asked, and Ines peered up at him hesitantly.

"Bad dream," she whispered, turning to cling to me. I couldn't be surprised, with everything that had changed in the last few days I'd have been more surprised if she *didn't* have nightmares than if she did.

But Ryker winced at her confession, shaking his head with a pained smile. "Maybe tonight will be better." He patted the top of her head and then turned to look out the front door window. "Dante is here. Why don't you come meet him first, Sunshine?" he asked, and I nodded as I crossed my arms over my chest.

"Mommy will be right back, okay peanut?" I asked her, and she nodded as she went back to chewing on her bagel bite by bite.

The man stepping out of the SUV was much smaller than Ryker, not that it was a tough task. His hair had gone mostly grey, though he couldn't have been a day over forty years old. He wore a suit, and it seemed so comically overkill that I couldn't help but laugh. He'd worn a suit to come hang out with me and my two kids while he made sure I didn't run off. "Dante works for Enzo, who runs security for the Bellandis. He's the best of the best, and he'll make sure nothing happens to the three of you when I'm not around," Ryker said as I stepped outside the front door.

"Mrs. Fiore," Dante said, stepping up to hold out a hand for me to shake. "It's nice to meet you."

"Latour. My name is Calla Latour," I corrected him, and I ignored Ryker's jaw clenching with my words.

"Why don't we just go with Calla, then?" Dante asked, eyeing Ryker like he might be eaten alive. It wouldn't surprise me. He must have needed a lot of protein to maintain that body mass.

"I've got to go, but I'll be back soon. Today shouldn't take long," Ryker said, tugging me into his side and turning my face up. He kissed me before I could protest, drawing back with a grin that made me want to punch him in the throat.

"What are you doing?" I asked, deciding to be bold. It pissed me off that I would be stuck in Ryker's home when he wouldn't even be there. Disgusted me to think of myself as a prisoner, particularly when it seemed like my jailor could change with only a moment's notice. I didn't know Dante or Ryker, yet they just expected me to trust them with my kids' lives.

"Don't ask questions you know I can't answer," Ryker grunted, taking a few steps toward where the Maserati already waited for him. "As you so kindly pointed out, you aren't my wife. You can know those kinds of details once we're married." He grinned at me like he hadn't just turned my world on its head with a declaration of marriage.

He was in for a surprise, because I would never remarry.

I'd never put myself at risk for the pain that came along with losing a husband again. Not after what it had been like to bury the first.

I wouldn't do it with a second.

"Do you want me to fuck him too? Or is that only when *you're* my jailor?" I asked, intentionally being difficult. I could kill the man for putting me in this situation where I had to tolerate a stranger.

Ryker's face twisted into a scowl, and he glanced over at Dante, whose skin paled in the face of Ryker's wrath. "I like Dante. Don't make me hurt him to prove a point," Ryker growled.

"You're insane," I scoffed back at him, twisting my head away so I didn't have to look at his stupid pissed off face.

"And you're mine," he grunted, stepping back into my face to crash his lips to mine in a claiming kiss before he hurried to the car.

When the Maserati started up, he met my glare through the open window before turning and driving away. When the gate closed behind him, I turned my glare to Dante as I crossed my arms over my chest.

"I didn't choose this, you know?" I asked, and I tried not to feel any guilt when he winced visibly. I trudged on anyway. "He won't let us leave. He won't let me choose for myself, and you're okay helping him keep me locked away here?"

"I'm just doing my job, ma'am."

"Well your job sucks," I told him, turning and striding into the house. He followed only a moment later as I worked to clean Ines of the cream cheese she'd smeared all over her face. "And don't call me, ma'am," I ordered. He nodded, not looking the slightest bit bothered by my attitude problem.

It would be a long day.

CHAPTER EIGHTEEN

By the time I got to the warehouse, my skin danced with the edge of urgency I associated with being away from Calla and the kids. It was impossible to shake the feeling that someone would hurt them while I was gone or that they'd escape.

That leaving them was a mistake.

After Emilio had betrayed Lino so thoroughly, Matteo, Enzo, and I spent weeks cleaning house. Torturing our own men wasn't something we took lightly, but anyone we couldn't trust had to be tested.

We'd trusted Emilio.

He'd betrayed that trust, leaving a stain on our family and nearly costing us one of our women.

It was unforgivable.

My methods had exposed three more people who'd been complicit in the attempted sale of Samara to the cartel. To the same cartel that Miguel Cuevas ran a regional branch for.

It felt good to know that our shit was clean, that the people who remained were loyal. Even if it meant that people like Sandro looked at me like I was the devil. I supposed he wasn't fond of the fact that I haunted his nightmares, that Matteo had used me as the boogeyman to inspire honesty.

"If you betray me, I'll feed you to Ryker," had become his favorite line. I didn't mind being the threat that went bump in the night.

It was a natural evolution in my career, really.

Matteo was nowhere in sight when I stepped into the freezer and Sandro hustled out to give me privacy to work. He'd seen my blade carve through our traitors when we used them to motivate the rest of the grunts.

I went to the corner, waiting for Matteo. While I might have once waited patiently, I twirled my knife between my fingers in anxious energy. The build-up, the anticipation, should have been half the fun.

But my Sunshine had taken that from me. I couldn't even be mad about it.

It was quiet inside my head. What had once been a constant rage was gone, and I didn't feel the compulsive need to make someone bleed.

I just felt the need to fuck my woman, to remind her of exactly who she belonged to, and of what she tempted with her drunken antics. After our kiss that morning, I knew she was ready. The time had come, and I'd feel her beneath me soon enough. I just had to get home first.

And get the kids in bed.

I loved them like they were my own, but that didn't mean that it wasn't frustrating that I couldn't toss Calla over my shoulder, cart her upstairs, and fuck her until she couldn't remember her own name.

Until there was nothing left but my Sunshine and her Shadow.

Matteo and Simon finally walked in the freezer doors, and Matteo took one look at my face and laughed. "Still no, huh?" he asked.

I grunted in response, making Simon shake his head. "Bunch of crazy fucks. I swear," he muttered, moving to the other corner to watch the show. He looked like he considered leaning against the wall and then thought better of it. It was a smart choice, given that blood had a tendency to splatter. I didn't exactly spend my free time cleaning the fucking walls.

And our cleaning crew could only come *after* I'd killed the fuck in the chair.

If they came at all.

"I don't know anything else. I swear," he mumbled, his voice a rasp like he'd spent a year wandering the Sahara.

"Sandro!" Matteo yelled. "How's he supposed to talk if you don't water him?" Sandro hurried into the room with a water bottle in his hands, holding it to the man's lip so he could take greedy gulps of water.

He'd throw it up.

I'd seen enough vomit for a few days. "That's enough," I grunted, and Sandro pulled back to scurry to the very edge of the room.

"Kid's loyal," Simon chimed in. "But damn do his balls need to drop a bit. What did he think this was? Playtime with glitter and sequins?"

"He's young," Matteo returned, and there was a light bite to his words. One I recognized as a man who thought about his future sons needing to harden up for the role they'd be expected to fill.

I immediately thought of Axel, because even though he wasn't my biological child, he was mine all the same. I'd raise him in the family.

Calla wouldn't like that, but I could already see the boy was born to do it. His head for numbers meant he'd probably end up working with Lino, but he'd be in the family, regardless.

"You were fifteen when you slit a man's throat," Simon pointed out. Matteo shrugged, but we both knew that he wouldn't raise his sons the same way his father raised him. It was only Ivory who had pulled him out of the darkness he'd been destined for, and even after he'd had to walk away from her, he'd worked to guide the business to endeavors that endangered innocent people as little as possible.

He had a list of rules, of tenets that weren't to be broken.

Not if you wanted to survive in his city, anyway.

"When will Miguel leave the city?" Matteo asked.

"Within the next week," the guy admitted and his eyes went down to his arm where it remained wrapped in a towel. I stepped forward, grabbing the edge and yanking it off. It took all the dried blood, all the potential for healing, with it, and fresh blood welled to the surface immediately as he moaned in pain. "Please! I swear that's all I know."

Stalking back to my table, I picked up my filet knife from yesterday. I normally took excellent care of my tools, cleaning them after every use, so the sight of the dried blood on the blade made me pause.

Then I touched it to his cheek. "Do you think I can carve out your eyeball before you die?" I asked him, tapping the pointed tip of the blade against the spot just beneath his eye.

"He's done it before," Simon said. "Pretty sure you've taken both eyes and an arm before someone died."

"Oh, that's right," I sighed. "Guess that means you'll have plenty of time to feel pain then."

He thrashed in the chair, and I used one hand to pry his eyelid open. As the blade approached his eye, any normal man with information would have confessed. But there was nothing but silence aside from his pathetic whimpering.

"Put him down. He knows nothing else. We got what we needed anyway," Matteo sighed dramatically, and I nodded to him. My blade shifted, swiping across his throat so quickly he didn't even have time to register the change in threat. I watched the life bleed from his eyes, the same way blood poured from the straight line across his throat.

When I turned back, I tossed the knife to Sandro. "Clean that," I grunted. "And put the fucking body and the chair in the incinerator. Call the cleaners to deal with the rest of the mess," I told him.

"Yes, Ryker."

"There's a good boy," Matteo said, sarcasm in his voice as he followed me out the door. "You in a hurry?"

"Fuck you, Bellandi!" I called, climbing into the Maserati while he and Simon roared their laughter behind me.

I didn't care, because I still had to go to the store before I could go home.

THE STUFFED wolf in my hands was adorable, with vivid blue eyes that echoed the fierceness of his face.

I could only hope it would do the trick for my Princess and keep the bad dreams away. I wouldn't tolerate Ines suffering in her sleep.

With the wolf in my hands, I wasn't sure what kind of mess I'd expected to walk into when I got home, but Dante showing off pictures of his own kids and sitting at the table with a coffee in his hands wasn't it.

I'd thought my hellcat would tear him to shreds for his complicity in what she still saw as her imprisonment. Instead, she'd apparently saved all that vitriol for me, because when I stepped in the door from the garage the smile died from her face and she leveled me with a fierce glare.

Dante sensed the change in energy, wisely standing from his place at the table and moving for the front door. "Bye Dante!" Axel called, and Ines peeped up from her little corner nook where she was pretending to bake cookies.

"Bye!"

"Do you need me tomorrow?" he asked me.

"Nope," I said, taking care to control my voice. Even just the sight of my Sunshine in her floral dress was enough to make my cock go rigid in my jeans, and I still had hours to go before I could get her beneath me.

Fucking shit.

"I'll walk you out," I told Dante, retreating out the front door alongside him so we could talk in privacy. Calla's friendly nature with him rubbed me the wrong way. I couldn't help the suspicion that flooded me. "How were they?" I asked, walking him to his car in the driveway.

"Kids were great. Sweet as could be and behaved so well for their mom. Calla was prickly at first, but she seemed to mellow out as time went by and she realized I wasn't going to bite or be demanding. Honestly seems like she's starved for adult interaction. You should probably do something about that." He grinned as he got in the car. "Call me when you need me."

I stalked back into the house with a mocking set to my lips. I'd do something about it alright.

"Gonna take a shower, and then I'll come down and see what I can cook up for dinner," I told Calla when I stepped into the house. She didn't move, her glare just growing heavier and heavier on me with every moment that passed.

It was safe to say she was pissed.

I turned to Ines, leaning down and holding the wolf out to her. She looked at it for a moment, studying me in confusion. "A wolf protects his young, right?" I asked her, and I watched her eyes go over to where one of her story books about a little white wolf sat on the coffee table.

"Me?" she asked.

"Yes you, Princess. I thought he could protect you from the bad dreams." I told her, and she leapt up to wrap her arms around my neck for a hug before she snatched the wolf out of my hands.

"Ines, what do you say?" Calla asked, ever the mother.

"Thank you, 'yker!" Ines went over to show her dolls that sat on the couch her new toy, and I turned my eyes back to Calla with a smile. Hers were narrowed in on my waist, and I followed the gaze down to a red stain I hadn't noticed near the fly of my jeans.

Shit.

She swallowed visibly, licking her lips as the glare faded from her face in favor of a more nervous expression.

"Calla—" I started.

"Later," she said, nodding her head toward the kids.

I knew she was right, knew without a doubt that we could not talk about the blood on my pants in front of the kids, but I hated the look on her face. I'd need to be more careful, but I wasn't used to having to worry about someone seeing blood when I came home. The thought had never even crossed my mind.

All I'd done was slit a throat, for fuck's sake.

I went up to shower anyway, but only after I called the guard on duty to let him know to be extra alert.

I wouldn't take any chances Calla might try to take the kids and run.

I washed the filth off my skin so I could be clean enough to not to soil my family with the blood of my enemies.

CHAPTER NINETEEN

CALLA

I did not believe in violence.

I did not believe in violence.

I did not believe in violence.

Maybe if I said it enough times, I'd finally believe it.

But as I stared at the back of his giant head, all I could think was that it would make a wonderful soccer ball. We even had a net and everything.

At first, I'd thought the red stain on the fly of his jeans was lipstick. My body had filled with the fire of rage and indignation, given that he locked me away, claimed to own me, touched me, and then went out and got his rocks off with another woman when he couldn't slap his meatballs against my ass earlier that morning. Then I'd gotten even more pissed off when I realized it pissed me off, and that I was *jealous*. I shouldn't care if he got his rocks off elsewhere, since I had zero intention of riding his monster dick.

When I realized it might be blood, that pissed off had melted into full-blown fury. He'd touched my daughter. Let her hug him when he had blood on his hands.

Pants.

It didn't matter.

I didn't know if I'd rather it was blood or lipstick and that bothered me. I should have wanted it to be lipstick, because that meant he hadn't been out murdering people or doing whatever the hell it was Ryker did for the Bellandis.

He stepped outside, going to the grill where he had a piece of salmon cooking for me, kindly separated from the cheeseburgers he'd grilled for him

"

and the kids. They desperately wanted them, even though Ines had never even had a cheeseburger.

Ines pointed at the cheeseburgers on the tray when he came inside, "Meat?"

"Yeah, baby girl. Cheeseburgers are meat," Ryker answered when I stood off to the side, chopping vegetables for a salad to go with them.

"So you aren't a Pescatarian like mom then?" Axel asked, stirring macaroni with dressing.

"Hell no. Do I look like a Pescatarian? I eat meat. Next you'll tell me your Mom thinks rock music is just noise."

He faked an exaggerated, wounded expression as he held his hand to his chest and put buns on the table. I hated to admit it, but my salmon looked perfect with a teriyaki glaze that made my mouth water.

Somehow, I doubted he'd coincidentally made one of my favorites.

How the man knew so much about us was beyond me, but he knew I loved rock music judging by his arrogant smirk when he met my eyes.

I did not believe in violence.

"That's Mommy's favorite!" Axel said helpfully as he sat down at the table and grabbed a bun to squirt ketchup on.

"Well, at least she has good taste in one thing," Ryker returned, ignoring the glare I settled on him. It was like he was immune to the very glare that had often sent Chad retreating from the room.

He used the spatula to place my salmon on my plate next to his, pulling out my chair like he was a gentleman and not a brute who'd come home with a questionable red stain on his dick.

Super classy.

Blood or lipstick, there was nothing gentlemanly about that.

"Tell me if it's good, Tesoro. I've never made salmon before," he said, patting my seat for me to drop into. I did as expected, perching my ass on the very edge of the chair as I considered the conspicuous lack of knives on the table. It was like he knew his days were numbered.

"I need a knife to cut Ines cheeseburger into bites," I said through clenched teeth. He raised his eyebrows at me, handing Ines her own cheeseburger that she promptly picked up like her brother and devoured.

"You were saying?" Ryker said, making me turn back to him at the amused sound in his voice.

"Hm. I always thought meat was more satisfying when it was chopped to bits." Where I might have expected him to squirm, like most men did when faced with the even casual prospect of meatball mutilation, he just grinned at me in that dark way of his.

Like my threats were adorable.

There was something wrong with the man.

He settled in to talk to my kids about their day, talking about all the things they'd done with Dante and asking if they would like a playdate with his kids.

It was just what I needed, to meet another mob wife.

The way he stared at me told me he knew that as soon as the kids were in bed, all bets would be off. It was just a shame that his eyes seemed to light in excitement, like the coming confrontation would be entertaining.

Heaven help me.

I didn't believe in violence.

ONCE WE CLOSED the door to Axel's room behind us, Ryker gave me a manic grin and turned to stride toward the master bedroom. I had a feeling the sound-proofing there hadn't just been for sex, because he *had* to know that wasn't on the table.

Ever.

He'd be lucky if I let him keep his meatballs.

The door was open when I stalked in behind him, and he reached behind his head to tug his shirt off his shoulders and toss it to the closet. Standing in the center of the room, he crossed his arms over that chest that made my mouth water. Even as I hated that the conversation needed to happen in such close proximity to a bed, I pushed the door closed behind me as I entered. I couldn't stand the thought that when all was said and done, I'd be sleeping in the same bed as him.

Ryker did not seem the type to tolerate being kicked to the couch, and I knew he wouldn't let me sleep there either. After a year of sleeping alone, I'd never thought I might miss the ability to sleep alone. But given the filthy feeling the thought of him having touched another woman left me with, I wanted that space.

"Well, Tesoro? I'm fairly certain that you have something to say?" Ryker asked, his lips tipping up into a smirk I wanted to beat off his face.

"You came home with some other woman's lipstick all over your dick, and you touched my daughter with that all over you," I hissed through gritted teeth. I hadn't wanted to voice that, hadn't wanted to hint at it being anything other than blood. But the anger that tore through my insides felt toxic, like if I didn't shove it at him, I'd explode.

Because how fucking dare he?

I shoved him back with two hands on his chest, wincing when he didn't fucking move. It felt like shoving a building, but his hands came up to trap mine against him. He stared down at me, as if daring me to try it again, and his eyes blazed with a mixture of heat and fury. "You think I let another woman touch my cock?"

"I don't know what I think!" I snarled, jerking my arms back from him and trying to get free, but he held me steady. His grip only tightened with every second I struggled, pulling me tight until his face was directly over mine and not a spare inch remained between us. "It was blood or lipstick, and all that matters to me is that you let my daughter hug you after you were out doing fuck knows what! I can't stop you from doing anything. That's obvious. But the least you could do is shower and change before you come home instead of exposing my kids to whatever fucking diseases—"

"Enough!" he growled, and my nails dug into his chest with my answering rage. "I was not with another woman."

I swallowed, because even if I felt relief that he hadn't been out getting laid, that meant he'd made someone bleed. I pushed away, trying to put some space between us as I processed that information. Ryker had always been honest that he wasn't a good man, but somehow it felt completely different to be confronted with direct evidence of it.

My face went cold as I looked up at him, and his eyes softened momentarily, until I tried to pull away. "You hurt someone," I whispered, the sound seeming too loud in the room that had gone silent but for the quiet feedback from the audio monitor.

"No, Sunshine. I *killed* him."

CHAPTER TWENTY

CALLA

The words echoed in my head repeatedly like one of my dad's old, scratched records.

Killed.

He'd killed someone.

I staggered back a step when he released my hands, staring at him as my chest heaved. "What is wrong with you? Why?"

"Because I'm good at it. Because I enjoy it. Because sometimes the scum of the Earth need to be put down like the filthy dogs they are," he growled, prowling closer to me as I backed away.

"You killed someone," I whispered, "and you enjoyed it?"

His hand touched my cheek, his thumb dragging over the skin there like he so often did. As he stared at the contact, his face filled with awe. "He was far from the first, and he won't be the last, Sunshine. Not everything can be black and white. Sometimes, people deserve to die."

My chest rattled with a sob as his breath ruffled my hair and he pulled me against his chest and tugged me tight. "I can't do this." My voice was a broken rasp, trembling with the shivers that consumed me.

"You will. I only kill men who deserve it. Never women or children. I know that probably doesn't matter to you right now, but I promise you that once you understand, it will."

"Please, Ryker," I begged. "Just let us go. Don't make me part of this. I can't be a part of this." I shook my head, trying to push off his chest and free myself desperately from his grip.

My kids lived in the same house as a serial killer.

"You have no choice," he said, that deep voice going stern once more as his patience wore out. I had no illusions that he would tolerate my disobedience continuously. No matter his words, it was almost certain that if I became a bigger liability than I was worth, he'd get rid of me.

One of his hands lifted from my waist to cup my face, and I flinched away from him, staring at his hands in horror. His hands were covered in blood, no matter how much he scrubbed them clean.

"You are mine," he grunted, shifting my hands so that my nails released some pressure from the skin of his chest. The angry red indents drew my eyes in, and I momentarily regretted that I'd hurt him, but I found that I *liked* seeing my marks on his skin. I hated that he'd turned me into such a bloodthirsty woman that I wanted him to bleed.

But he didn't seem bothered by it either.

"I am not!" I yelled in his face.

"You are, just like I'm yours. No other woman will ever get near my cock, Sunshine. Only you."

"You think I give the first shit about other women now?! You're a murderer! The only thing I want to do with your cock is cut it off," I growled at him, and his face twisted into a triumphant smirk for a moment.

Then his lips crashed down on mine, thrusting his tongue into my mouth to cut off my protest. I hesitated only a second before I bit it sharply, and he drew back with a grin as he reached up to touch his mouth. "Do not fucking touch me," I warned him, wincing when the hand on my cheek moved to slide into my hair and grab a fistful.

Yanking my head back, he ran his teeth over the column of my throat. "I am done waiting. I'm going to take it all, Tesoro. And you're going to give it to me," he warned as he nipped at the delicate skin there. When his eyes met mine as his lips touched mine gently, they blazed like blue flames that I knew I would never escape.

He'd set me on fire and burn me alive.

I moaned when his teeth sank into my bottom lip, feeling like every nip of his teeth on me chipped away further at my defenses until he could meld his soul with mine. Like there would be no stopping him once he got what he wanted, like he really would take it all until I had nothing left. "Stop," I hissed, the sound muffled without being able to move my bottom lip with the way his teeth held it like the beast he was.

"No," he answered as he finally released my lip that felt swollen and bruised from his onslaught. "You don't want me to stop. You don't have to be ashamed of wanting me, of wanting all the things I'm going to do to you."

I moaned again when his tongue stroked inside my mouth teasingly. The moment his pillow lips sealed over mine, I was done for. My arms abandoned the flesh of his chest, reaching up to wrap around his neck as his hand slid down to my ass and he lifted me into his arms. I squeaked into his mouth, making him groan into mine. The hand in my hair abandoned it, sliding down to my thighs and jerking my dress up as he pressed me into the wall.

I didn't care about the way the bricks bit into the flesh of my back or the way my hair snagged on the ragged grooves. Not when his hand grabbed the strap of my panties and tore the fabric away from my pussy. His hand slid between my thighs, dragging a finger through my slit and sliding it inside me. At that first contact, the first touch of him against the most sensitive part of me, I didn't know if he groaned louder than I moaned, but I could hear the glide of him through me. I was too wet and shame crept in.

It disappeared when he pulled his finger free from me, and his hand went to jerking down his sweatpants. The blunt head of his cock touched me, the cool bite of metal tickled my skin as he lined himself up and slid himself against me. Through me. His mouth never left mine, kissing me mindlessly in a tangle of his tongue that I knew he would mimic with his cock if I didn't stop him.

I should have stopped him. Should have thought with my head and not the ridiculous need that he built in my center with every glide.

If I'd known how much it would hurt when he notched his head at my entrance and drove forward, I probably would have stopped him.

He split me open, taking me with hard pumps as he forced me to stretch around him. I cried into his mouth, and he pulled back to look down at me. "Too much," I whimpered, and I shoved a hand between us to touch his stomach and get him to wait.

He just needed to wait. It had been too long.

With the way our bodies pressed together and the way he used his own to support my body weight, I couldn't see him. Couldn't see the blunt instrument he tried to shove inside me. He waited just a minute before his forehead pinched and he shoved forward in a hard drive that made me see stars. "Fuck!" I screamed.

"I'm sorry," he murmured as he stilled. His hands kneaded the flesh of my ass while he waited for me to adjust. It was too full, too much. I both wanted him out and never wanted him to leave. Kissing the side of my throat, he rebuilt the heat inside of me until my hips moved against him of their own volition.

Only then did he move, drawing his hips away from me in a glide that felt like it lasted forever. When he slid back inside me, the metal of his piercing rubbed against the rear wall of my pussy and made me toss my head back on a gasp. His cock nudged the end of me, and then he withdrew again. I clung to him, wrapping my arms around his neck and holding on for my dear life. Being impaled on him felt too vulnerable, felt like I might fall to the floor and split myself in two. He seemed to sense my nervousness, so he hauled me away from the wall with a growl and made for the bed on the other side of the room. He kept me suspended in his arms, never sliding out of me as he crawled on his hands and knees to the center of the bed. As soon as he'd laid me out gently, he covered my body with his, shoved one of my knees up high and fucked me. Hard.

"Oh God," I cried, and he silenced my pleas with his mouth on mine and his teeth sinking into my bottom lip.

I stretched an arm around him, digging my nails into the globe of his ass, and tugging him tighter to me. He growled, driving deeper and harder so that every thrust shoved him to the end of me with a sharp strike of pain that somehow felt addictive.

"Fucking shit," he growled, his voice both menacing and somehow addictive. To watch him lose control, to know that I had that power over him, that was something I'd never had before.

It drove me higher and higher. Closer to the first orgasm I'd have since he trapped me in his house. Those massive hands of his tore my dress down the center, exposing my heaving breasts to his gaze. I'd never been more grateful for front clasp bras until the moment when he twisted the snap free and his finger grabbed onto my nipple. His eyes never left my face, never so much as glanced down at my breasts, as they blazed into mine.

"Tell me you're mine," he growled, and his fingertips glided down my stomach to touch my clit. His eyes followed the motion finally, abandoning my face to watch where he slid in and out of me with fierce snaps of his hips.

"Fuck you," I whispered in defiance.

"I believe we've got that covered." He shoved forward harshly, touching his finger to my clit as the head of him slammed into me. "Say it and you can come."

"Ryker!" I cried, inching away from the relentless assault of him as he pounded through my sensitive flesh. His fingers at my clit tormented me, built me higher and higher until I felt frantic with the need to come. I hated him for his control, for the calm way he worked me over until I'd have promised him my soul for an orgasm. "Please," I begged.

"Say it, Tesoro. Say the fucking words."

"I'm yours," I whimpered, and I hated myself for the weakness.

"Damn right you are, Sunshine." Those fingers circled my clit in the perfect motion, a perfect replica of what I would have done when I touched myself, and it only took two strokes before I shattered around him. My orgasm was so strong I could feel the way I pulsed around him, and he roared out my name as he flooded me with heat.

We stayed like that for a moment, catching our breaths while reality sank in and I felt my bottom lip quiver.

What the fuck had I done?

He kissed my temple, and when he pulled out of me, it seemed to take forever. The way his flesh glided against every part of me went on and on and felt too sensitive, and when he finally popped free a gush of fluid followed.

He stared down at my pussy as if fascinated as I got my first good look at where the length of him hung down his thigh, and I wanted to wince at the way it glistened.

He hadn't worn a condom.

CHAPTER TWENTY-ONE

CALLA

I blinked up at him, feeling disoriented and confused. He'd overwhelmed me, *consumed me.* There'd been nothing but him, no second thoughts about doing something I knew I'd regret.

I'd fucked a serial killer only moments after finding out he killed someone that day.

He hovered over me, crowded me even though he'd gotten what he wanted. And I'd given it up to him like an idiot.

My legs had to spread obscenely wide to accommodate his hips between them, and I suddenly wanted them closed. I wanted his eyes off me, wanted him to never see me again. He stared at me so intently it felt like he examined every piece of my flesh. So when he touched his hand to my overheated skin, rubbing his release into it with a growl, I jolted and used my legs to propel myself away from him.

I bolted from the bed, making for the bathroom where I could lock myself in until morning. I couldn't trust myself, couldn't be around him.

"Calla!" he yelled, and the thunder of his footfalls sounded behind me as he chased me. I spun, pushing the door closed, but his foot stopped it from latching and his hand curled around the edge of the door as he shoved it back open and prowled into the space. "Calla," he said calmly, and he stepped toward me slowly. There was something in his face, something so gentle it hurt as he made his way to me. The shower door rattled when my back hit it, and I stumbled forward in a moment of panic.

It brought me right into his arms, and I shoved him back. When my head twisted, I glimpsed myself in the mirror, eyes wild and panicked with the worst sex hair I'd ever seen in my life. The skin of my chest was flushed from the sex, but my face had already paled.

"Sunshine, it's okay," Ryker murmured, wrapping his arms around me. He tugged me tight to his chest, and the moment his soft cock touched me, I squeaked in the most pathetic voice I'd ever made.

"It's not okay!" I yelled as the first sob wracked my body. "What did I do? I have a husband. I can't—"

"Tesoro, he's dead." Ryker's voice stayed gentle, an agonized tremble to it as he clutched me to him against my struggles. "You're not his wife anymore."

My heart dropped into my stomach as I realized I'd always still considered myself Chad's wife. Even with him gone. "I will always be his wife," I spat, twisting my face to glare up at him when he wouldn't release me. I knew the words weren't true, but they gave me a place to hide. I couldn't remarry or date or move on with someone else I could lose. Not if I already had a husband. I needed the protection that offered me.

Ryker nodded, though his own face hardened in anger. It frustrated him that I clung to the memory of a dead man. "He never deserved you even when he was alive. I will not allow you to waste your life grieving a man who never loved you."

I blinked back tears, feeling my heart stop in my chest. "Of course he loved me. I was his wife," I whispered.

"Tesoro, he wasn't capable of love," Ryker told me, touching his thumb to my bottom lip where it quivered. "But even if he loved you, he's gone. Does he protect you? Does he provide for you? Does he feed your children and tuck them in at night? Does he bring Ines stuffed wolves and play soccer with Axel? Does he kiss you and make love to you?" he asked when I jerked my head away from his hand. "No. I do those things, Calla. He is not your husband anymore."

"Neither are you," I whispered, feeling a tear slide down my cheek. He was quick to wipe it away, to rub the salty liquid into my cheek. His hand stunk like sex, like us and I jerked my face away in disgust.

"Yet," he said, reaching in to turn on the shower. "We both know where this is going, Tesoro."

I shook my head, and he didn't press the issue further, but he didn't do what he should have done either.

He didn't free me. Didn't give me the option to make my own choice about our relationship.

I would never marry a man who killed other men. A man who could *be* killed at any moment and abandon me and the kids.

He helped me into the shower, running his soapy hands over my body quickly and then shoving one between my legs. I winced, feeling so sore and thinking he'd take more than I wanted to give, but he only cleaned me in gentle movements.

"If that happens again, wear a condom," I whispered. I wished that it wouldn't need to be said, that I'd be able to trust my self-control where he was concerned. But I'd only known the man for four days, and I'd somehow ended up climbing him like a tree. His hand stilled as he washed me for a moment, and then he shook his head behind me and resumed his gentle cleaning.

"Nothing between us," he grunted.

"It isn't fair to the kids. I'm not on birth control. There's been so much change, *too much* change, too quickly. We can't be so irresponsible to throw a baby at them right now." He was silent behind me, neither agreeing or disagreeing, so I pushed on to plead my case. "You claim you love them. Loving someone means putting their needs before your wants, Ryker. Please understand that they need time to adjust," I begged, and I felt my body relax when he touched his mouth to the top of my head and nodded.

"For now. I'll wear a condom for now," he agreed, and I sagged in relief. At least that was one concern taken care of. I mentally ran through my cycle. We should theoretically be fine, unless Ryker had super sperm that could survive for a couple of weeks.

It would be fine. I had to believe that, because I could not have a baby with a man I had every intention of leaving in the dust the first chance I got.

THE REST of the weekend passed uneventfully. Ryker seemed to realize I was too sore, too pained for him to touch me again. So he'd spent Sunday doting on the kids, giving me time to see him interact with them more.

It made me sad to realize just how much he did genuinely seem to love them. He was more engaged with them, more active in their time together than I could ever recall Chad being. He'd worked too much and been too tired when he got home to do much other than eat his dinner and fiddle on his phone.

I didn't think he'd ever changed Ines diaper. Looking back, it hadn't always been like that. He'd changed Axel, and played with him more when he'd been younger, but somewhere along the way our marriage had shifted.

He became a provider, sharing my bed but rarely touching me. He'd given me Ines only because I begged him for another baby.

It had only taken one time to get pregnant with her, and there had been a night when she was eight months old that he'd come home and made love to me. That had been the last time my husband touched me.

I felt naïve looking back, realizing I'd been so wrapped up in the kids that I never saw what was right in front of my face. Chad hadn't desired me anymore, and who could blame him? I'd gone from being a woman who cared about her appearance to one who lived in comfortable clothes and was covered in spit up.

There was unfortunately nothing sexy about motherhood or the stretch marks that marred the skin of my hips.

I snapped out of my reverie when Ines giggled happily. "Mommy dream," she said. I laughed at her, nodding my head in agreement as I booped her nose.

"I was," I whispered. "Do you want to go check on the boys?" I asked. It had taken everything in me to allow Axel and Ryker a few moments alone in the garage as they worked on the Chevelle. Given his revelation of a few days before, I'd been jumpy at even the slightest motion from him.

Ryker had taken to moving more slowly than was natural for him in his attempt to startle me less. When Axel had asked to help him with the car, I'd had no way of denying him that.

Not without admitting the truth.

Ines jumped up from our tea party in the main house, going for the door to the hall. She stopped there, letting me open it, and the sound of classic rock filtered through the open garage door. It immediately brought me back to my childhood, to my days of sitting on the garage floor in the corner and watching my Daddy chip away at car after car. My toys were always covered in grease.

When Ines ran in through the garage door, I hurried to catch up to her. Axel had his head buried in one of the toolboxes, looking confused as he stared at the treasure trove like it was candy and might jump out and bite him at the same time.

"Hey Sunshine, can you help Axel find the dial indicator?" Ryker asked. He had his head under the hood, his arms disappearing into the engine bay as he fiddled with something. I was dying to get a peek, but I crossed my arms over my chest and enjoyed the sight for a moment longer before I helped my boy.

Ryker's arms looked too good with his forearms flexed, and I had to shove down my libido that seemed to rise anytime he was anywhere near me.

I'd forgotten what sex felt like, and given the fact that I was only twenty-seven years old, that was just sad. Even if my birthday approached quickly.

With a shake of my head, I went to the toolbox, grabbing the dial indicator and handing it to Ryker. Axel smiled after me, all proud that his Mom knew her tools and car parts. His friends always thought that made me a cool mom, like I could be one of the guys.

No wonder I hadn't had sex in forever if even six-year-olds saw me as one of the guys. "Are you hungry?" I asked him as I stepped back. "Our tea party is over, and it's getting late."

Ryker nodded to me with a warm smile. "I'll be right in to get cleaned up. Axe, why don't you head upstairs and take a shower while your Mom starts dinner, yeah?" he asked.

"Okay," Axel nodded, darting out the door and into the main house.

I turned back to him, annoyance flaring at his continued insistence on acting like he was the kids' father. "Spaghetti okay? I can cook some meatballs to go with it." I tossed him a smirk.

He grimaced, glancing at Ines where her eyes darted back and forth between the two of us.

"Yeah, Sunshine. Sounds good," he lied.

When I turned and took Ines's hand as we headed for the house, I tried not to think about the fact that Ryker had known I would know what a dial indicator was.

I knew several women who had mechanic fathers. Most of them could barely change a tire.

It was just one more thing he knew that he shouldn't, one more piece of the puzzle of just how thoroughly he knew our lives. I couldn't say how much of what he'd given us was a manipulation or what was genuinely because he wanted us to be comfortable, but he'd done his research either way.

It didn't give me a happy feeling, and as I crossed the threshold to the hallway, my skin pebbled with goosebumps and a chill raked down my spine in a way that was all too familiar.

I spun, finding Ryker's gaze intense on my back.

With a swallow of nerves, I stepped into the hall and out of sight.

My hair settled immediately.

CHAPTER TWENTY-TWO

RYKER

It took everything in me not to lose my shit the moment my cell pinged with another notification. It wasn't the kind that came from my own messages, but from the app that forwarded Calla's to me.

I knew who it was. Knew he'd been texting my woman for the last hour.

Enzo looked amused at the rage on my face, like it thoroughly entertained him to see us caving to our women and the ridiculous emotions they evoked in us.

Jealousy was not my favorite look, but it seemed like it would be a permanent fixture where my Sunshine was concerned. "What did he do that you had to drag my ass out here, anyway?" I asked him, nodding to the latest fuck to land himself in my chair.

There wasn't a whole hell of a lot that a man could do to have Enzo bring him to me. The man's experience in covert operations made him one of the more straight-laced of us, but he was still crooked.

We all were.

Enzo, like most of our less enthusiastic alliances, saw the benefit to Bellandi rule in the city.

We didn't run women.

We didn't let people kill kids.

We might have been a crime syndicate, but we had standards of what was and was not acceptable. Enzo saw the value in that. He knew that if we didn't exist and maintain control of the city, someone much worse would rise up and take over.

Someone like Tiernan Murphy.

"Drugged a woman at *Indulgence*," Enzo said, crossing his arms over his chest. If that hadn't already been a big no-no for one of the Bellandi properties, it had quickly become one after Matteo learned someone drugged Ivory in a date-rape attempt during their twelve-year separation. Now the criminal kingpin hosted charity galas in his clubs to support the victims of date rape.

It might have seemed like a mind-fuck to anyone who didn't know the man, but he made it work for him. Power and money went a long way in explaining a person's eccentricities. "What's he want done? Dead? Alive?" I asked, stepping over to my tools as I examined them.

I genuinely hoped the word was dead. I was generally inclined that way, since there was one thing I didn't tolerate and that was rape.

"Warning," Enzo grinned at me, as if he could sense that I needed to kill something. Namely, one Jason Taylor. "Trouble in paradise?" he asked. I glared at him in response, because I couldn't talk about Calla in front of a guy who we'd let walk after I roughed him up. Sometimes stupid people did stupid things when they had vendettas like that, and the knowledge that I had a woman of my own wasn't something I needed to be public yet. At least not with potential enemies.

I taped up my fists, and Enzo watched with fascination. I knew the man was no stranger to it. I'd sparred with him a few times, but he disliked it. He didn't want his opponents to know what he could do before he fought them. There was logic in that, but I could always tell when he steadily approached the need for a genuine fight.

It was all in the way his eyes lit up at the sight of me taping my hands, like the violent pull we all felt toward just needing to beat something to shit suddenly became irresistible. Enzo might have been more human than me, a little less beastly when it came to the serial killer inside of him, but at the end of the day we were all just monsters who craved the beauty of blood on a canvas made out of flesh.

Enzo rolled his eyes, snatching the noise blocking earmuffs off my table and stuck them on the guy's head. I huffed a laugh at the look of panic in his eyes before Enzo wrapped a filthy rag around them. "There," he said pointedly, holding his arms out to his sides. "Light and sound deprivation. Punishment in itself. So what crawled up your ass and died?"

"Chad's partner keeps texting her to check in. Apparently, he went to the studio, and they informed him that Calla has been out for over a week. He got worried, especially when they told him her boyfriend called in for her," I grunted, landing my first strike against my victim's face. The spray of blood that came from his nose appeased me just a little, soothing the part of me that demanded blood.

Enzo howled with laughter. "Boyfriend. Fuck. The idea of your crazy ass being someone's boyfriend." He laughed again, slapping his knee with his amusement. I punched my victim in the ribs, earning a grunt and a groan of pain.

"I'm not fond of it either," I admitted with another punch. "It's temporary."

"Oh? Does that mean she's giving you all the warm fuzzy feelings already?" he asked.

"When she isn't threatening to cook my meatballs," I grunted. He looked at me like I was insane, and since we both knew I was I didn't bother to explain. After firing off a series of punches, I spoke again. "She hasn't asked him for help. She's following the plan and doing what she needs to do to protect the kids like I knew she would, but it drives me crazy. There's a man who was friends with her ex talking to her, and there's nothing I can do to stop it without telling her I've read her texts for years."

I'd hated Jason even when Chad was alive, but the way he stepped into Calla and the kids' lives after his death was like poking a bear. He'd been there for them when I couldn't be. Held them while they cried.

I'd never tolerate his presence, for that alone.

"You're all crazy with the shit you do behind their backs. My sisters would gut me if they ever found out I did something like that." He shuddered, and for once I was grateful to be an only child. Calla was mine because of my willingness to do underhanded things to *make her mine*. If I didn't stalk her, I wouldn't even know her.

And I wouldn't change having the sun in my cold, dark world for anything.

When I broke my victim's jaw, Enzo called me off, satisfied with the warning. "You can't keep bottling this shit up. You'll explode."

I hated to admit that he was right, and when my phone went off with a different tone, I grabbed it to answer.

When Matteo Bellandi called, you fucking answered.

ENZO WOULD DROP my nameless victim off at his house. He would have anyway, but my sudden call to the Bellandi estate meant that I had no choice but to haul my ass there.

I hated that it meant I had to leave Calla with Dante just a little longer, because I never wanted to be away from her, but there wasn't time to pick her up and bring her with me.

At any rate, I suspected that this meeting wouldn't be pleasant.

Pulling in to the Estate to find both Lino and Simon there, as well as the typical Don and Scar made the hackles rise on the back of my neck. We'd waited for this day, known it was coming even. But I really wished it didn't have to come when things were so precarious with Calla. The last thing I needed was a war at home while I waged a war in the streets.

I'd need a dresser in the garage for when I needed to change before I went into the house. I did enough wet work in times of peace, but in war?

I might as well bathe in blood.

Don answered the door, and there was no smile on his face. Ivory and Luna were notably absent, no doubt tucked away upstairs so they couldn't overhear something that could make Ivory nervous. I might have suspected Matteo sent them out of the house, but Scar's car confirmed they were here. Ivory went nowhere without her bodyguard, and she'd be lucky if Matteo didn't refuse to let her leave the estate altogether.

I should consider it for Calla and the kids, and if it weren't for Axel needing to go to school, I'd do it. But he'd be upset if I arranged a home tutor for him until things died down, and I couldn't explain it to him.

Not yet.

Calla would have my meatballs for that one.

We wouldn't all fit in Matteo's office, even as large as it was. Not comfortably, so they'd all set up in the sitting room at the center of the house. It seemed like I was the last to arrive, but there were no jokes about me having to escape the claws of my woman. The situation was too serious for that. Matteo didn't enter territory conflicts lightly, not when he knew that innocents would inevitably be harmed.

But the benefit outweighed the cost in some circumstances.

"Cuevas has ceded the territory to Murphy," Matteo confirmed, and it felt like the entire room sucked in a breath. It had been years since Chicago had seen a territory dispute, since Matteo took over and the other organizations thought to test him.

"Has Murphy said if he'll operate within the city?" Lino asked, always the voice of reason to Matteo's rage.

"He hasn't said anything, which I think we need to interpret as his stance. We prepare. We wait. We watch. I don't want to start a war if it isn't necessary, but if he tries to traffic people in the city—"

"We destroy him," Scar growled, looking to me and meeting my eyes. We were both more acquainted with the trafficking industry than the others; we'd seen the results of crimes like that firsthand. We'd lived that life.

We'd never let it touch our city again.

"Yes," Matteo agreed, and his eyes came to mine much like Scar's had. Matteo might not know the exact circumstances of my life before I worked for the Bellandis, but I knew he suspected.

My last name itself was hint enough to anyone who knew politicians, and since Matteo had most of them in his pocket, it was safe to say he knew politicians. He knew them better than their own wives, with all the dirt he kept on them to convince them to do his bidding.

We'd never talk about it. We didn't need to.

He knew I'd do whatever it took to make sure that Murphy never touched a woman or child in Chicago. I couldn't save the world, but I could rid it of one more piece of slime.

It wouldn't cost me any sleep at night.

CHAPTER TWENTY-THREE

RYKER

I cursed Tiernan Murphy for the fact that it was late when I got home. I hadn't been able to kiss my kids goodnight, and Dante was the only one who greeted me in the living room when I stepped inside. "Any trouble?" I asked him.

"Nope. She's sweet, now that she's stopped glaring at me like I was the devil for being complicit in this." He stood, stretching his arms above his head. "I better get home before my wife puts my balls in a vice," he said, making his way to the front door. That Dante could call my Hellcat sweet was remarkable.

"I hate to say it, but shit is about to get ugly. I'll be gone more than I planned. You good with that? Or should I find a backup?" I asked.

"Nah, that's okay. Matteo put me on your girl full-time, but if it's as bad as I think it, is you should get someone on the kids when they aren't here," Dante suggested.

"Already arranged," I said, and if he'd been most people, I would have been offended that he thought I wouldn't think of it. There was nothing that slipped my mind in terms of my family's safety.

"Call me when you need me," he said, making for his car. I watched him go, made sure that Gio closed the gate behind him and it locked safely. I wouldn't take any unnecessary risks, and I suspected that meant I would need to take more guys under my direct payroll. Being Matteo's most trusted enforcer had its perks, and the fact was, I would never lack for money.

I'd spend it all if it meant I kept my family safe.

Once I shut and locked the front door, I moved to the stairs and climbed them. I took the time to step into each of the kids' rooms, kissing their heads and silently slipping out.

By the time I made it to our room, I was exhausted and ready to drop into bed and sleep. But I wouldn't get into bed with my Sunshine without showering work off of me. Even without blood on me, it felt dirty.

It felt wrong to sully her with that part of my life. She was nestled under the covers, her head turned away from me as she slept. I sneaked into the shower.

When the scorching water poured down on me, I thought about jerking off. It had been my routine after work for years, but I couldn't bring myself to do it. Not when Calla lay in the other room, all warm and mine, just waiting for me to make love to her. I'd already decided that I would by the time I washed my hair and body, so I hurried through the motions.

Our first time shouldn't have been as rushed, as frenzied as it had been. I'd meant to take my time with her, to savor her and explore every part of her body with my own. But emotions had run high and fucking her had seemed like the best idea at the time when she stood there and challenged me so beautifully.

Stalking into the bedroom quietly, I stared at her for a moment. She'd rolled over to her back, the blanket slipping down to expose her blue nighty. She'd cocked one leg out of the blanket, looking delectable as her fair skin shone in the moonlight streaming through the window where she hadn't closed the blinds. I moved to them, shutting them as quietly as I could so I wouldn't wake her.

I wanted her sleepy and pliant. Warm and lost to the sensations I gave her.

She could regret them in the morning, and I was sure part of her would, but the more that Calla had to face this pulsing attraction between us, the sooner she could see it for what it was.

Love.

Inexplicable, illogical love.

It made no sense, defied all reason that you could fall in love with someone the first time you spoke to them, but it was there no less.

I knelt on the bed by her feet, touching my fingers to the smooth expanse of leg that beckoned to me. She jolted at my touch, like she felt that same undercurrent of electricity that I got every time I touched her. She didn't wake, proving to me she recognized my touch.

Even in her dreams, she knew who I was. Knew that I wouldn't hurt her even after I confessed to killing someone. I trailed my fingertips up her calf, watching her skin pebble in goosebumps, and when I reached her knee, I tucked a hand around the back of it and pulled it further apart from the other so I could kneel between her thighs. My hand continued a path up the top of her thigh until I reached where the nighty covered her sweet little pussy. Her hips lifted momentarily, settling back down as she whimpered in her sleep with a needy sound that made me grin. Trailing my hand over her nighty, I continued until I teased the skin of her arm in a soft caress. Up and up I went, all the way to her neck and then her bottom lip. Those pursed lips parted for me, drawing the tip of my finger in and making me groan. When I pulled my hand away, I immediately replaced it with my mouth, settling my body down to cover hers in that same moment.

My lips against hers, her shocked gasp of breath against mine felt like she breathed life into me. She invigorated me. She chased away the shadows that always controlled me.

My Sunshine.

I felt the moment she woke up, felt her confusion for only a moment before I coaxed her to open further for me. Her arms reached up, wrapping around me to touch my ribs hesitantly. But she opened, touching her tongue to my lip in encouragement. I gave her what she wanted, kissed her with everything I had.

Not with force or intensity, but by pouring all the love I felt for her into that kiss.

I pushed her to feel me, to feel my heart beating against hers as my lips drifted to touch the sensitive skin of her neck. The spot under her ear made her grind her hips against me in a desperate plea for more, and she gave a ragged gasp as her lips parted.

I kissed my way down her throat, over her collarbone and to the swell of her breasts where they heaved with her body's writhing. Her deep blue eyes stared up at me as I tugged the fabric down to bare her breasts. Her dusky nipples pebbled in the air immediately, and the sight of my olive skin against the luminescence of hers was enough to make me groan.

My Sunshine wasn't a tiny woman. She had tits and ass and a body toned from her yoga, but my hands made even her breasts look small as I cupped one in my palm. I rolled my thumb over her other nipple, drawing a whimper from her throat. "Ryker," she moaned.

Begged.

Having her beneath me, being able to touch the body I'd tormented myself by watching on my cameras for so many years, felt like a dream come true.

Finally, she was mine in truth.

I slid further down, so that my mouth leveled with her breasts and swiped my tongue across the pebbled peak as she arched her back and thrust it up into my mouth. The taste of her flooded me instantly as I wrapped my lips around it, sucking and lashing it with my tongue. When I couldn't take it anymore, I switched to the other side, giving it the same attention as I slid my hand inside her panties and stroked my fingers through her wet slit.

"Please," she whimpered when I slid a single finger inside her. She was so tight. So hot and wet and perfect for me as she clung to my finger.

Releasing her nipple with a wet pop, I turned my eyes up to hers to find her staring down at me as I slid down her body and tugged her panties off. Tossing them to the side, I laid on my stomach between her legs, settling my face so I could look at her pussy.

At my pussy.

I'd seen it from a distance when she touched herself in the privacy of her bedroom, but I'd never gotten such a thorough glimpse of all her smooth pink flesh. She squirmed underneath me, and I felt when she became uncomfortable with my attention. She didn't need to be, because there was nothing wrong with her. Not a single thing I would change.

Including the fact that she was so tiny one of my fingers could cover her pussy from clit to entrance.

I wanted to devour her, but I forced myself to touch my tongue to her clit delicately. She jerked against me like a live wire, grinding into my face with an enthusiasm that I loved. But I put my hands at her hips and held her down, forcing her to lay there and do nothing but accept my assault on her body. The taste of her, the reality that I finally had my Sunshine underneath me and her taste exploding in my mouth, was a dream come true.

She was mine, and she always would be.

I slid my finger inside her again, pumping it in and out in slow thrusts that made me nip at her clit when she tightened around me like she never wanted me to leave. When I added another finger, she whimpered, and I withdrew them both to slip my tongue inside her and fuck her with it.

I could have eaten her all night, could have lived my life with my face buried in her pussy, but with the way she whimpered I knew she needed to come.

"Ryker!" she yelped when I nipped her clit again, shoving two fingers into her and using them to stroke her g-spot while I sucked at her clit until she shattered beneath me with a scream.

As soon as she came down, I pulled my fingers free and repositioned and put my dick inside her. "Condom," she whispered. I cursed the reminder and grabbed the condoms I'd stashed in the nightstand a few days before as I pulled out. She took it from me, rolling it on as if she didn't quite trust me to do the job. I smirked when her fingers nudged my frenum piercing and her eyes went wide, but she plowed on like she hadn't touched my dick for the first time. Her hands looked so ridiculously small wrapped around me that it drove me crazy, and I shoved her to her back again.

She giggled, reaching for me as I covered her body with my weight and lined myself up to slide inside her.

Even having fucked her hard just a few days prior, she still felt tight. I doubted there would ever come a day when I didn't have to work my way inside her slowly for fear of hurting her, but she seemed to relax easier. She seemed to trust that I *would* fit inside her this time and let me make my way in with shallow thrusts until my balls rested against her ass.

I groaned, dropping my head to the crook of her neck and breathing her in. "Calla," I whispered as I moved my hips in smooth, slow glides.

I was determined to be gentle, to show her everything that our first time together should have been.

I was determined to make love to her, to make her understand just what I felt for her.

She was my love, my life, my everything.

"Ryker," she repeated in a whisper, lifting her hips to meet me thrust for thrust. I grabbed her under the ass, lifting until she tilted her hips in the perfect way for me to stroke her g-spot.

"Touch yourself, Tesoro," I whispered. "Let me see your fingers dance over that pretty little clit." She swallowed, but did as I told her. When her fingers brushed against me and where I stretched her open, she whimpered. I grabbed her hand, guiding it further so that her fingers wrapped around me as I worked myself in and out of her. "Feel how perfectly you fit me," I said, hating the fact that the condom interfered with my vision.

I wanted it to be just the two of us, with nothing in the way again. But I had to respect her reasoning.

For a time.

Once she was my wife, nothing would stop me from putting a baby in her belly.

"Oh fuck," she moaned, and her pussy tightened around me as her orgasm took her. I shoved deep, sending her back bowing into a second orgasm that drew my own from me. When my cum filled the condom, I wanted to tear a hole in it.

But I didn't for her sake. I drew her into my arms, rolling to my back so she sprawled on top of my chest. My fingers trailed up and down her spine through her nightie as sleep hovered at the edges of my vision. But I had to get rid of the condom.

When Calla let out a soft snore, I chuckled, gently rolling her to her back as I pulled out of her.

I disposed of the condom and grabbed a towel to clean her while she slept.

She wouldn't want to wake up with condom lube on her and smelling of sex.

CHAPTER TWENTY-FOUR

CALLA

I tried to fight back the panic. The thought of my father spending time with Ryker made me anxious.

I didn't know why. It wasn't like I should have cared what he thought of Ryker.

It wasn't as if I liked the ridiculous, sarcastic, arrogant Hulk of a man.

The thought I might wasn't even worth repeating. Especially not after the horrible mistake I'd made in my sleepy haze the night before. But having him touch me like that, like I was *everything,* was enough to bring me to my knees.

Even in the happiest days of our marriage, Chad had never touched me like he worshiped me. Like every inch of my skin and every freckle was precious to him and he needed to explore it.

Taking him inside me had never felt like coming home.

Not the way it did when Ryker finally took pity on me and fucked me. But it hadn't felt like he fucked me.

It felt like he made love to me and that just wasn't true. You couldn't make love to a person you didn't know. But knowing that Ryker could make me *feel* like he did, more than my husband ever had in our marriage, what did that say?

It was more evidence to Ryker's assertion that my husband didn't love me. I'd thought about it frequently since he'd said it, and every hour that passed led me closer and closer to one truth. That while I knew our marriage had been rocky at times, I'd thought we built it on a solid foundation of love that, in reality, never existed.

And that left me grieving for a man who had deceived me. Lied to me.

I just didn't know why he would do such a thing, and why I'd been so blind to it.

The knock on the front door jarred me out of my thoughts, and I jumped in place. My hip slammed into the kitchen counter, and my hand threatened to spill extra powdered sugar into the frosting I had beating in the stand mixer. "You okay, Tesoro?" Ryker asked, stepping up behind me. His arms wrapped around my waist, his lips pressing a warm kiss to the back of my neck as he leaned into me and breathed me in. I tried not to take comfort in the casual display of affection, or that Ryker seemed like he couldn't get enough of touching me.

Even when it wasn't a sexual touch, he constantly looked for ways to touch me and hold me. Like he needed the reassurance that I was with him, and he couldn't quite believe it.

"I'm fine," I said, tugging away from the comforting touch even if it threatened to break something inside me. Adding Oreo crumbles to the frosting, I tried not to be too bothered by the loss. I'd let myself be lured in with Chad's false promises and easy touches, taking them for love when they might have been nothing close to that. There was no way Ryker could love me, and I couldn't make that same mistake again.

Turning off the mixer, I took to frosting the cooled cakes while Ryker continued on like I hadn't tried to brush him off. He went for the front door, tugging it open to reveal my father standing there and looking curious.

"Oh good lord, I thought for sure I had the wrong address," he laughed, stepping inside when Ryker moved back out of the entryway. My father's eyes were wide when he looked around, taking in the absolute luxury of the converted warehouse. I didn't know why Ryker hadn't bothered to fix up the outside, though I suspected it had something to do with him liking that most people thought it was uninhabited until they came up to the gate, anyway.

But he'd spared no expense on the rest of the house.

"Grandpa!" Axel yelled, charging through the kitchen to hug my Dad's legs tight to his chest.

"Hey, Axe," my Dad said, patting his head and shoulders to return the affectionate squeeze. "Where's your sister?"

"She's playing in the living room. All wrapped up in her dollhouse," Ryker said, and he nodded his head to Axel. "Why don't you give your Grandpa a tour?"

"Really?" Axel asked, excitedly.

"Sure thing. This is your home too, little man." My father barely pressed a kiss to my cheek as Axel took his hand and dragged him into the living room. "The bathroom is down the little hall across from the front door, and you saw the kitchen and dining room," he chattered excitedly as they passed me and went for the play area and living room. Ines's new dollhouse was the latest addition Ryker had brought home with him one day, looking frilly and pink and ridiculous next to the industrial bones of the warehouse.

"Hi, Grandpa!" Ines piped up from her little corner where I hadn't been able to pull her away from the damn dollhouse for days.

"Hey, pretty girl. Axel's giving me a tour. Wanna come?" He held out a hand, and I turned my attention back to the cake as Axel led him to the stairs to show him their bedrooms, I was sure. I'd have shown them off too if I'd had something that spectacular as a kid.

When everything with Ryker inevitably crashed and burned, it would be impossible for me to give them something like that. I hated him for giving them something they'd never be able to keep.

"Do you need help with anything, Sunshine?" Ryker asked once they were out of sight. He didn't move to touch me, eyeing the way I focused on the cake and tried to get the frosting as seamless as possible on my turning table.

"Could you just check the pork? I don't want it to overcook and you know I suck at cooking meat."

"Anything for you," he murmured, touching his lips to my cheek in a kiss before he pulled the pork tenderloin from the oven to check the temperature. We stood side by side, not speaking, as seemed to be our way. I never knew what to say to him, and then I wondered why I even wanted to say anything to him at all. It seemed like an impossible task to make small talk with him. Except for the days when he had to disappear for work, we spent all our time together.

It should have felt suffocating and terrifying, but somehow it was oddly peaceful. He didn't feel the need to fill the silence with background noise, but I often wondered if he'd ever volunteer any information about himself. "Will we meet your family?" I asked him, and the pan clattered when he dropped it back into the oven.

"No," he grunted.

"Oh," I said, and annoyance colored my tone as I finished frosting and went to wash my hands.

"They're dead," he explained with a sigh, and I felt my body flinch. I'd automatically assumed that he'd intrude on our lives and insert himself without a care for what we might want, and never return the favor. Guilt flooded me for it, as he'd given us no sign that we wouldn't be the epicenter of his world.

"I'm sorry," I whispered, hanging my head over the sink with my shame. I knew what the loss of my mother had meant for my life. I couldn't fathom the loss of both my parents.

"It was years ago now," he said, stepping up behind me. The moment his powerful arms wrapped around me I felt calmed, like he soothed the part of me that had always felt a little lonely. "You're my family now." My heart stopped, the words reaching the deepest part of me that longed for that even as my breath caught in panic.

I had my father. I had my aunt. I had my kids.

I'd thought I had my husband.

But my circle was small, and I'd always been uncomfortable in sizable groups of people. I'd never made friends easily, much preferring to stay with people who I could already trust. Even before Chad's death, I'd known that loving people meant you could lose them. That it meant you could suffer the loss of that loved one. Watching my father grieve for my mother his entire life had taught me to avoid attachments, and maybe that was why I'd ended up with a man who might not have loved me.

With a man who kept his distance emotionally.

Because I'd foolishly thought it would hurt less if I lost him.

Ryker never let there be distance between us. Emotionally, he overwhelmed me and filled me with constant casual assurances that I mattered to him. Even if I didn't see how they could be legitimate. He constantly did little favors and kindnesses that made me feel cared for in a way I'd never had. Physically, he dominated me. If I didn't do what he wanted, then he manipulated my body to get what he wanted. Whether that came sexually or in terms of just picking me up and putting me where he thought I should be.

"Calla?" he whispered, and I shook my head with a slight smile.

"That's sweet," I admitted reluctantly, and I knew he could hear the disbelief in my tone. It was only a matter of time before I lost Ryker too. Before he left me, but with Ryker I would know it was because he just didn't want me. He'd gotten what he wanted, got to play house with a ready-made family for a couple weeks, and he'd realized that it wasn't for him. I didn't want to acknowledge that the thought hurt.

"I mean it, you know. The three of you are my family now. The Bellandis are my family too. You've already met them, and that's the only other family I'll ever have." The backs of his knuckles traced down my cheek lightly, and I forced myself to smile. He still had an arm wrapped around my waist, still held me tight to his chest when the kids and my Dad came thundering down the stairs. Ryker made no move to separate us, and I felt everything in me tighten in stress. Chad and I had never been fond of public displays, but even if we had been my father didn't tolerate them.

He'd always told him if he ever "caught him pawing at his daughter," he'd crush his trigger finger. He hadn't cared the least that threatening Chad had technically been threatening a police officer.

When I finally finished washing and drying my hands, I turned to face my father. Ryker moved with me, keeping himself plastered against my back like he did not understand boundaries where parents were concerned, but my father didn't look the least bit perturbed by Ryker's paw on my stomach. "Those are some bedrooms," he said with a laugh.

Ryker gave a rough chuckle in response. "I wanted them to have rooms they loved. Their own spaces in all the changes we threw at them so quickly."

"We? I don't recall having a lot to do with that," I said, lifting a disbelieving brow at him as I craned my neck to look up at him.

He chuckled, dipping his head down to touch his lips to mine briefly and a stunning smile overtook his face when he pulled back. "Okay, *I* threw at them," he admitted. I tried not to let that smile touch me, but I felt it wrap around my heart even with that effort.

I looked to my father, expecting him to admonish us for the kiss, but he didn't. He only smiled at Ryker. "You want to show me this Chevelle of yours?" he asked. Ryker separated from me just enough to grab my hand, dragging me off to guide my dad to the garage.

"I've got to keep an eye on dinner," I said with a laugh. "You guys go on ahead." The second part was much more reluctant. I didn't relish Ryker being alone with my father, and I definitely didn't want to put Ryker in a position where he had to be alone with him.

But Ryker didn't seem to mind in the slightest when he released my hand and turned to the kids. "Who's coming with us?"

"Me!" Axel shouted, but Ines shook her head and looked at me.

"You want to help me put the Oreos on the cake?" I asked her and she raced into the kitchen. I set up a chair for her to kneel on, setting the cake in front of her so she could press the Oreos onto the top. I hadn't thought to go that far with it, but I'd let my baby girl do whatever she could to help decorate if it made her happy.

The grin on her face was worth every smear of Oreo cream cheese frosting that she spread when her fingers slipped all over the place.

IT WAS safe to say my father was sufficiently enamored with Ryker. If the Maserati hadn't done it, the Chevelle would have.

If the way the kids loved him hadn't, the way Ryker spoiled them rotten with toys and rooms and the endless affection only he seemed to be able to provide them with would have.

Ines's tantrums even seemed like a thing of the past when he was around. A stern, but loving, look from Ryker was enough to dissuade my terrible two from melting down. I might have resented it, if she hadn't started respecting my warnings more too.

The full presence of two parental figures worked wonders for making sure she never wanted for attention, and the change in her behavior was obvious. It made me wonder what she would have been like with her father around, but though I hated to admit it, even I knew there wouldn't have been much difference between just me and the two of us.

By the end of our marriage, Chad had been so absent that it was almost like he wasn't there at all. To a two-year-old, I didn't imagine it felt like there was much difference between that and dead.

As horrible as that felt to think.

For Axel, there was an enormous difference. He knew what it meant when I told him his father was dead. He remembered the father who'd been present before work absorbed him.

"So, Ryker," my Dad commented as he sliced through a slice of cake slowly. "What is it you do?"

My fork clattered to my plate, and I coughed around the bite I'd been chewing and tried to clear my throat.

"You okay, Calla Lily?" Dad asked, and Ryker patted my back reassuringly. How he seemed to think anything about the moment could be comforting was beyond me. He'd confessed less than a week prior to being a murderer.

That wasn't exactly the typical dinner conversation a father wanted to have with his daughter's boyfriend slash kidnapper.

Not that he knew that, but *eff* my life.

"I work in private security. Making sure people meet the justice they deserve," Ryker answered with a smile. "I have several clients through the city, but I delegate most of my work to my employees at this point. I only consult on the particularly nasty cases."

I knew without a doubt that it was a lie, or at the very least a gross misrepresentation of what he did. If he truly believed the men he killed deserved what they got, then the justice part was true enough.

Security seemed like a stretch.

"Like a cop?" Dad asked, crossing his arms over his chest as he leaned back in his chair and studied Ryker. My dad was a shark when it came to knowing when someone lied. Being a single father to a teenage girl made that a necessary skill he honed over the years.

"The specifics are confidential, but they vary from job to job. I promise you, nothing I do will ever get me in trouble with the law." Knowing what I knew, I noticed the delicate nuances in his wording.

He didn't say it wasn't illegal, just that he wouldn't get in trouble for it.

"Calla seems to have a type then," Dad chuckled, and I huffed my own laugh and downed some more wine even if it was gross to mix it with the Oreo cake. The irony of the moment wasn't lost on me. Dad unknowingly compared my cop husband to my murderer boyfriend.

How quaint.

Ryker stroked a hand over my bare thigh under the table and took pity on my discomfort. "Are you going to let me teach you to swim soon, Princess?"

Ryker asked my girl. She shook her head viciously, picking at her food with her fingers as her appetite vanished.

I had no clue where the intense fear of the water had come from, and as grateful as I was for it some days, others I cursed it. "No," she pouted.

"I'll hold you the whole time."

"No," she repeated, smacking her hand down on the high chair tray in a rare moment of defiance against her beloved 'yker.

"We'll work on it," Ryker said with a chuckle as he turned to me. He'd wear her down, eventually. He seemed to excel at doing that.

Dad shoved his last bite of cake in his mouth, and I could already see that he was ready to go home. My old man had always been early to bed and early to rise. When he finished chewing, he studied my face intently. "You look well rested, Calla Lily," he noted. "I don't think I've seen you look so relaxed in years. Ryker must take good care of you."

"He likes to think so," I said in return, shoveling my last bite into my mouth as I stood from the table. Both men chuckled, and even Axel chimed in.

"He lets her sleep in unless he has to go to work, and she's been on vacation from the studio," Axel said.

"Sounds like he spoils her," Dad concurred, standing from the table and pressing a kiss to each of the kids' heads. "I hate to eat and run, but I need to get to bed. I promised I'd open up at six tomorrow so a friend could drop off his Cadillac." Ryker stood too, following Dad closer to the front door. He stopped next to me, wrapping an arm around my waist and tugging me into his side. "Thank you for having me over, Son," Dad said, and I swore I felt my heart pumping at my feet as my world bottomed out. He'd never, not once, even come close to calling Chad *Son*.

"Anytime, August," Ryker returned, and emotion clogged his throat. Despite my rising concern, I pressed further into his side. Given the loss of his family, I could only imagine how it felt to have someone call him Son.

"I have to say, I questioned if this was smart. It came out of nowhere," Dad said, his eyes on Ryker as he stood at the door. The kids still shoveled cake into their mouths, distracted by the sugary sweet mess of frosting.

"I'm sure it seemed that way," Ryker said evasively, but Dad's eyes came to me knowingly. He saw through some of Ryker's shit I suspected, but I also didn't think it would stop him from encouraging the relationship either. "I'm a man who sees something good and doesn't let it go. A woman like Calla has got no place living alone. It's too dangerous, and all I've ever wanted to do is keep her and the kids safe. I'm sure you've figured out that I have the resources to do that here."

Dad grinned at him. "Safe to say I figured that much, yeah. You take good care of them, I can see that, even if my Calla Lily doesn't want to admit it."

"I do my best," Ryker admitted, and I felt my throat burn with tears when something in my father's face shifted.

"All I ever wanted was a man who saw everything she was worth and wanted to protect that. Chad never appreciated her or the kids, not really. You give her that, then I'll be in your corner."

"Daddy," I whispered, feeling my heart break for him. I hadn't considered how it might hurt him to see me live out a lonely marriage, knowing his life and loneliness had influenced my relationship.

"I'll walk you out," Ryker announced, and I didn't know if I should be suspicious or just grateful for the reprieve to pull my shit together as I sniffled back my tears.

It didn't matter, because my father murmured to me softly, "See you soon, Calla Lily."

And then they both walked out the door.

CHAPTER TWENTY-FIVE

RYKER

"I could use your input on the paint job for the Chevelle. The guy I usually use had an unfortunate accident," I said, conveniently leaving out the part where he'd been using the connection to me to spy on the Bellandis for one of the rival territories outside the city.

It hadn't ended well for him. Somehow, I didn't think Calla would appreciate me telling her father the accident had involved my hatchet.

"That's too bad. I have a guy, and he'll do whatever you want, but he has an expert eye if you're willing to just let him run with it."

"If he has your trust, he has mine," I agreed, and I shuffled my feet when we stepped up to August's Mustang Cobra. The woman had me tied up in knots so hard that I couldn't even imagine how I could ask her father the question I needed.

"I'll have him call you. He'll love that car," August laughed, opening the Cobra door. He sobered. "Don't hurt her. She's been through too much, and half of it she doesn't even have the first clue that she should be upset. I don't know how he managed it, because my Calla Lily is far from stupid, but Chad twisted her up, made her think it was normal to raise their kids practically on her own. She was too young when they met, and I don't think she ever really got to experience what a healthy relationship was supposed to be before that snake dug his teeth into her."

"Calla fights for what she loves," I answered him, pushing the hair back from my face with a sigh. I needed a haircut. "She fights hard. But she never fought for him to give her more. Now, you make what you will of that, but I know what I think about it."

"You don't think she loved him?" August asked, and his eyes were intense on mine. As if he thought I might condemn his daughter for her loveless marriage.

"I think Calla believes she loved him, but actions speak louder than words. If she loved him, she'd have wanted him to be there more. She'd have pushed for him to be more active with the kids. I think Calla loved the idea of Chad, of everything he *could* give her, but she didn't want to admit she'd chosen him because she knew he never would."

August's face twisted in confusion as he studied me, and I knew he was trying to process how I knew so much about Calla so quickly. But he seemed to shrug it off when he sighed. "She's always been a loner. My girl doesn't let people in easily. I think you're good for her, so don't take this the wrong way, but you've got a hell of a road ahead of you if you think you're going to work your way under her skin." I glanced at the sky, enjoying the sight of the stars that I could never see from inside the city limits.

The light pollution of the city, the lack of true darkness and shadows, made me feel claustrophobic. It reminded me of my childhood and sleeping with the lights on so I could always see what was coming.

I found joy in the fact that I'd long since become the monster who went bump in the night.

"I know, but unlike with Chad or other people, she doesn't have much choice with me," I admitted, and I expected it might be *that* moment where I could have lost Calla's father's blessing. But just like with her, I wouldn't lie. I might omit certain truths, but there was no disguising the fact that I'd pushed my way into his daughter's life and taken her as my own. Not to some extent, anyway.

His chest heaved with a restrained chuckle as he cleared his throat. "I suppose that is a key difference, yes."

"I'm going to marry her," I admitted, pulling the ring box from my pocket where I'd kept it tucked away safely all night. "I'd like your blessing, but know that I'll marry her without it, too."

"Isn't it a little soon for marriage?" August asked, taking the box from my hand and opening it to peek inside.

"Isn't it a little soon to have her moved in with me?" I shot back, and he grinned at me as he shook his head. "I told you, I'm a man who sees something good and doesn't waste time. Calla's mine, and she's always going to be."

"You love her?" August asked.

"I would say more than you could ever understand, but I suspect that wouldn't be true." I glanced down at the wedding band he still wore even decades after Calla's mother's death.

He handed me back the ring box, running his hand over his face. "She'll kill me for it, I suspect, but if you love her like that, then you've got my blessing to marry my Calla Lily." He sat in the driver's seat, looking up at me in warning. "Just don't make me regret it."

I was smiling when he pulled the door closed and the sound of the Cobra engine engaging echoed through the space in front of the warehouse. When he drove down the driveway, the guard on duty opened it immediately.

When I finally turned back to the house, I did it feeling good about my place in Calla's life. I'd sufficiently won over nearly everyone, but her until only her aunt remained for me to contend with.

Aside from my Sunshine, I knew she'd be the hardest for me to crack.

Still, I went inside with a smile on my face, only to be hit with a fierce glare from Calla while she finished drying the pots. "What is it, Tesoro?" I asked her, stepping up to hug her. She jerked back from my touch like I'd scalded her.

"It isn't bad enough that you've taken my children from me? That you've made them love you because they know you can give them a life I have no chance of providing?"

"What are you talking about, Sunshine?" I murmured, risking it to reach out for her again. She smacked my hand away so hard that the sound echoed through the kitchen.

"You had to take my father too? Will you leave me with anything of my own when you're done with me?"

"Calla," I whispered, and I knew my voice went hoarse with the emotion that clogged my throat. She had no clue, couldn't see that I wasn't trying to take from her.

All I wanted was to give her the life I knew she dreamed of having. A husband and father to her kids who got along with her family and cared enough to facilitate that relationship. I wanted to give her everything, but as she stormed into the living room and picked Ines up off the couch to bring the kids to bed, I knew I'd pushed too hard, too fast.

Her walls were firmly in place and fighting her on it would go nowhere fast. Calla needed time to process things. Her father's heartfelt confession as he left would hit Calla right where it hurt. If there was one thing about my Sunshine I knew without a doubt, it was that her claws came out when she felt cornered.

Her walls went up because she could feel any hint of her chance at freedom disappearing with every day that passed.

I'd give her the night to lick her wounds.

After that she and I would need to have a very serious conversation about the state of our life together.

CHAPTER TWENTY-SIX

CALLA

I tried not to feel Ryker's eyes on me as I went through my yoga. If I could have done it anywhere besides the backyard, I would have. But as it stood, Axel was determined to have Ryker teach him how to throw a football properly to get that unattainable spin.

I'd tried, lord knows I'd tried over the last year. But I didn't know the first thing about football, couldn't tell you a single thing about it aside from the fact that football players wore tight pants and there was a quarterback.

Ryker knew how to throw it perfectly, just another check in the hero worship my son had going on. Even Ines enjoyed running after the ball when Ryker threw it as far as he could. The space behind the house was massive, with an enormous field cleared out where the sun shone down on it in the late afternoon.

I loved watching my baby girl giggle when Ryker picked her up and hefted her over his head like he might throw her to Axel, and I loved the broad smile that crossed my son's face every time Ryker turned his attention to him.

He needed a father.

And no matter what I might think about Ryker for me personally, I couldn't deny how incredible he was for the kids and with the kids. I'd always known being a mother meant making sacrifices, but could I sacrifice my life and my morals for them to have this with him?

For all the good he offered my children, could I condemn myself to a life of uncertainty with a man I knew was a killer in the trusted inner circle of Matteo Bellandi?

All I'd wanted for as long as I could remember was a family. A happy, whole family where the ghosts of our past didn't haunt us. As much as Dad did his best and adored me, he still mourned my mother. I'd felt that loss through my life, the lack of a mother.

I didn't want to do that to the kids, but I also wanted to have the white picket fence and an uncomplicated life. I had the distinct feeling any life I had with Ryker would never be easy.

I'd spend every day wondering if it would be the day he never came home.

I set my forearms on the mat I'd placed on the oddly flat space at the side of the field, as if Ryker had known it would be the perfect spot for me to do my yoga with just a hint of sun shining through the trees behind me. With a deep breath, I shifted my body up into a dolphin pose. When I sighed out, I kicked my legs up until the movement shifted me into an elbow stand. I held that, breathing through the feeling of Ryker's eyes on me. Eventually, I bent my knees to drop into a half scorpion, loving the way the inversion of my body made all the blood rush to my head. Normally, I hated it. I'd never been a fan of the feeling of my head drowning and losing all cognitive thought to the over-whelming pressure, but there was something so magical about the loss of thought in that moment.

Ryker's odd behavior didn't dance at the forefront of my mind. I wasn't blinded by his seemingly obsessive knowledge of us that I couldn't explain, and I didn't feel like I was losing my children to a man I didn't know.

I was just free. Free from thought and jealousy and logic.

But it eventually became too much for me, and I had no choice but to bring my legs back together into my elbow stand and drop my legs back to dolphin pose. When I stood and stretched my arms to the sky, I became acutely aware of the sweat that dripped down my spine as my head cleared and reality returned. I felt too hot in the coming moment and eventually dropped my arms to my side with a last exhale. Turning to Ryker, I found he'd stopped throwing the ball to Axel, just holding it in one of his massive palms as he stared at me. Axel stared at him, a mixture of amusement and disgust on his face, but Ines just looked confused.

"James's dad looked like that the one time he picked me up at the studio and Mommy was teaching a class," Axel inserted, and Ryker's attention finally shifted off of me to study him meaningfully.

"I'll just bet he did," Ryker grunted, finally tossing Axel the ball. "I think I'll have a word with James's father when he comes to pick you up."

Axel blushed, seeming to finally realize that Ryker might not be a fan of other men looking at me. He was too young to understand the nuances of attraction, or what it meant for Ryker to be oddly possessive of me. His father had never cared.

But I got stuck on the part about James's father picking Axel up, wracking my brain as I tried to think if I'd forgotten a birthday party. "Why is Mr. Weaver picking you up?" I asked Axel, crossing my arms over my chest. I was positive there was nothing I'd forgotten.

"James asked if I could sleepover tonight. Ryker said it was okay," Axel said, and he eyed me as he realized that might not have been a good decision, but I knew from the expression on his little face that he hadn't meant it to be hurtful. He'd asked one of the people he saw as his guardians, but it didn't change the fact that it hurt.

"I see." I nodded, turning a glare to Ryker. While my son might not have intended any harm, Ryker had to have known that it wouldn't be acceptable to me. "Axel can you take your sister inside? I'm sure you need to pack for your sleepover," I asked, and my sweet boy nodded and took his sister's hand to guide her back toward the house.

Ryker and I both watched them go, waiting until they were safely through the pool room and through the door that went to the main house. I couldn't stand the thought of them alone, when they shouldn't have had to be alone ever.

But it was unavoidable with what needed to be said.

I wouldn't make Axel feel uncomfortable, not when I genuinely couldn't blame him for being confused in our current situation. Ryker acted like he was their father, and he needed to set the expectations of what they should seek from him. Permission to go do something fell with me as his mother, and it was Ryker's fault for confusing those lines and not correcting Axel in the first place. Then he hadn't even bothered to tell me he'd given my son permission to go to a friend's house.

"Calla," he said.

"Don't," I mumbled. "You crossed a line. You should have told Axel he needed to ask me about those things. It is not your place to tell him what he can and cannot do."

"He's my son," Ryker turned to stare down at me, crossing his arms over his chest like he was the wronged party and not certifiably insane.

"You haven't even known him for two weeks!" I said sharply, stepping into his space to return his glare. "You do not get to decide like this! He is not yours, and nothing you can say or do will change the fact that he already has a father." My voice trailed off as exhaustion filled me. I was so tired from fighting him all the time, from trying to make him see my perspective and the fact that he'd ripped me from the life I'd created and just expected me to cave to his ridiculous demands. "I'm trying. God, I am fucking trying to understand what the hell is so wrong with you that you think any of this is okay." I scrubbed a hand over my face, bending down to roll up my yoga mat. "I'm trying to make it work, since you didn't give me any choice. Do you think maybe, just maybe, you could stop for once and consider what this has been like for me? I am not asking a lot by expecting you to leave the decisions regarding my children to me, and if you can't see that, then you're even more of a dick than I thought you were."

I stormed toward the house, leaving Ryker staring after me. It should have felt like a victory, like I'd successfully won a battle.

Instead, it just felt like he was preparing to win the war.

✦

I FULLY EXPECTED to have to go through the motions with Mr. Chris Weaver. Pretending that the fact that my son was going off to a sleepover wasn't an enormous deal. He'd spent the night at James's a few times, but it was the distinctly noticeable presence of Dante sitting in his car out in the driveway that made it feel very different.

Our lives were fucked.

So fucked that my son couldn't even spend the night at his friend's house without personal security staking out the property and without my six-year-old having a direct line to him through his very own cell phone. "Maybe the boys should just spend the night here," I suggested when Chris Weaver looked at me in shock as Ryker explained the security protocols.

Dante wouldn't go into their home unless there were signs of trouble, but Axel was to answer his phone calls on the hour every hour and notify him when he went to sleep. "This feels like you don't trust me to look after the boys," Chris objected, crossing his arms over his chest. He didn't say the words to Ryker, seeming to either identify me as the weak link or maybe it was because we knew each other well enough because of the kids.

He'd been there for me, helped with the kids after Chad's death and given me a shoulder to cry on after I'd tucked them into bed when it felt safe to break down. I understood why it would feel like a betrayal of trust to insinuate he couldn't keep the kids safe.

"That's not what this is," I told him with a small smile. "Ryker works in security. He's paranoid, but his job also comes along with certain dangers. He isn't trying to keep Axel safe from you, but from other parties who might seek to harm him and see an opportunity where he's unprotected. It's just a formality."

He didn't look convinced, but he sighed. I knew he adored Axel, and who could blame him? My son was impeccably well behaved for his age, too serious if anything.

"Fine," he said, touching the top of his son's head. "Maybe the next sleepover can be here. Axel has told James all about his new room."

"That would be great," I grinned.

When Chris returned the smile warmly, Ryker grunted. He touched Axel's shoulder briefly. "Why don't you show James your room now? I'd like to have that word with Mr. Weaver." Axel swallowed, but he didn't argue. I didn't blame him, because the intensity in Ryker's face was compelling, and I was very grateful for the fact that Ines was happily playing with her toys in the living room and couldn't have cared less about the conversation that happened in the kitchen.

I had a feeling it wouldn't be fun.

After Axel led James away, Ryker listened for the moment the baby gate at the top of the stairs swung closed before he spoke in a cool, quiet voice that made the hair on the back of my neck stand on its end.

"I'll lay it out for you very simply. Calla does not exist for you," he said.

"Ryker!" I whispered sharply, shoving at his shoulder. The ridiculous man just couldn't seem to help himself from behaving like an asshole.

"Excuse me?" Chris asked, furrowing his brow as he tried to make sense of Ryker's words.

"Ignore him," I hissed, glaring at Ryker out of the corner of my eye. "He hulks out randomly and has no idea when to shut his damn mouth."

Ryker didn't seem to care that I'd spoken, or hear the warning in my voice for what it was. "You make it very obvious that you want more from her. Enough that even Axel has picked up on the way you stare at her." Ryker crossed his arms over his chest. "As you can see, she is very much spoken for. Since I doubt you'll be able to let go of that attraction so easily, you deal with me from now on. You need to talk about something regarding the boys or a play date? You call me. Axel will give you my number."

"You're forbidding me from talking to your girlfriend regarding her son?" Chris asked, and from the way Ryker's face hardened I knew it had been the wrong word to use. Though what he was supposed to refer to me as, I had no clue.

Did hostage equate to girlfriend? Wife?

Who the Hell knew with his meatball ass.

"My woman," Ryker growled. "I realize for a man like you the distinction may not be significant, but know that for me it is. I won't have another man looking at my woman like she's a piece of meat."

"It's ridiculous is what it is," Chris laughed. "You don't own her. She can speak to whoever she likes."

"You have about thirty seconds to realize that you are in over your head and shut the fuck up. No, I do not own Calla, but she is mine regardless. Now tell me you understand what I'm telling you or we're going to have a far more serious problem than working out security for Axel, and you may want to think about security for yourself."

"Stop it right now. This is ridiculous," I said, giving Ryker another little shove to get him to turn his attention to me. But he held his stare with Chris, and something the other man saw in his manic blue eyes convinced him it was most definitely smart for him to agree with what Ryker said. "Chris, I'm so sorry-"

"I understand," he said finally, ignoring me entirely. He called up the stairs for James, and a moment later the boys came barreling down the stairs like only adolescent boys could do.

"Bye, Mommy!" Axel said, squeezing my legs tightly as I leaned down to kiss the top of his head.

"I'll see you tomorrow. Be a good boy."

"Bye, Ryker!" Axel said, hugging him tightly until he bounded out the door after James and his father.

"Mommy!" Ines called from the living room, finally having had enough of being ignored.

I glared at Ryker briefly, twisting my face into a glare that I felt in my soul. "I cannot believe you. You do not fucking listen to a thing I say, do you?" I asked him, leaving to go play with my daughter.

Maybe I could convince her to make voodoo dolls with me.

CHAPTER TWENTY-SEVEN

RYKER

With Ines tucked into bed and Calla having gone up to the master to take a bath with a book to read, I'd gone to the home gym to work off some energy. The thought of Calla covered in bubbles, her body slick and oiled from her bath, was enough to drive me mad.

Knowing that she hid from me because I'd sufficiently pissed her off didn't quell my need for her. I shouldn't expect anything less from her. I'd thrown her into an impossible situation without warning or regard for how she might feel about it, and I kept pushing. But it was unavoidable, given that the alternative would mean letting Calla come around to understand her place in my life slowly.

I'd rather overwhelm her and get it over with, and I'd have been lying if I said I didn't like my Hellcat when she was angry. I preferred her smiling, but there was something sexy about her when she scrunched her little face up at me in pissed off fury.

So it was only when I'd pushed myself near the point of exhaustion that I made my way up the stairs to go to the main house. I never expected to find Calla sitting in my home office, staring down at the box of cameras Enzo had dropped off at the gate earlier in the day. His guys had finally finished uninstalling all the security equipment I'd put around her house.

I'd needed them gone before the new owner finally moved in. I didn't expect her to come to the office that time of night, because my Sunshine still never sought me out. She preferred to hide in the bath or spend her time hovering over the kids rather than risk having to spend time with me.

It had never occurred to me to hide the cameras, because I'd never intended to keep my stalking a secret from Calla. But I might have held off on telling her for just a while longer.

I knew without looking what the note on the top of the box said.

I knew how incriminating it was.

"What house are these from?" Calla whispered, but from the way she refused to look at me as she clutched the tiny cameras in her hand and shuffled through the box filled with them, I knew she suspected.

"Yours," I said. I wouldn't lie to her, not ever. But the fact was that I also didn't regret what I'd done. I'd always known the day would come when I told her the truth.

I just hadn't thought it would be so soon.

I stalked toward her, fully conscious of the way sweat dripped down my chest and the fact that even in her disbelieving fury her eyes tracked the trail it left down to the waistband of my pants. Calla could never claim that the magnetic attraction between us was one-sided. I'd seen it the first time she met me, and if she hadn't been married to a man who was very useful to Matteo, I'd have made her mine.

Married or not.

But I owed Matteo everything. His father had given me my revenge, after all.

"You-you filmed us in our home?" she asked, and her voice quivered with the realization that she hadn't understood just how far my obsession went.

I nodded as I leaned over her in the chair. Her back straightened, leaning back as far as she could into the leather to avoid me as my hands grasped the arms and caged her in. "I watched you through those cameras," I confirmed. "I watched you when I snuck into your bedroom every night. I did anything I could to be with you before we were together."

Her eyes went wide only a moment before her hands went to my chest and shoved. "You're insane," she hissed.

"I'm fairly certain we've covered this, Tesoro. Who did you think it was that you felt watching you? A figment of your imagination?" I reached down to the top drawer of my desk, tugging out the massive, overflowing envelope. Opening the clasp, I let the pictures slide across the desk. Her eyes flew to them, and she reached out and grabbed one in each hand to study them.

The first photo was the one I'd taken while she slept the night before she officially became mine. The last one of her in her old home. The creeping of my ink on my wrist looked as brutal as I'd remembered next to her luminescent skin, and it felt like the perfect photo of how much she lit up my life.

The second photo was from years prior, when Chad had still been alive. Calla was still pregnant with Ines, holding her belly as she walked through the park with Axel clutching her hand. From the look of joy on her face, Ines had kicked. Calla loved being pregnant, loved feeling her children protected inside her. Like she carried the entire world within her.

I imagined it was similar to how I felt when she was in my arms.

"This was always going to end one way, Calla," I whispered, tucking her hair behind her ear as she stared at the photos in horror. She'd get over it, understand that I'd only done what was necessary to protect her from the evil in our world—the very evil her husband had dragged her into the center of when he'd gone dirty.

He'd chosen to dance with the devil and somehow thought he could do that without it putting his wife and kids in danger. His willingness to put them in danger was unforgivable, because he hadn't been capable of keeping them safe from men like me.

"I thought I was paranoid," she whispered, and my heart pounded in my chest. Even though I'd known it, the admission that she'd felt me all those years felt like the perfect affirmation of everything that pulsed between us. She'd felt me, and she'd told nobody about it.

Because she knew that I wouldn't hurt her.

On some level, she knew that the man who watched her only wanted to love her.

"Did you kill him?" she whispered, refusing to meet my eyes as she asked the question.

"No," I said firmly. "He was shot when he was going to tell one of Matteo's dealers not to be so fucking dumb and do a deal out in the open. The dealer saw his badge and panicked." I let her absorb the information of just how dirty her husband had been as a cop. She had to have processed the fact that he worked for the Bellandis, but I watched the gears turn as everything she thought she knew about her marriage vanished. "I would never have caused you pain like that. I think I've made it obvious that I wouldn't have needed to kill him to take you away if I wanted," I said, and she nodded in response. It soothed something inside me that even when she'd had her world turned on its head, she still knew that I wouldn't lie to her.

Her instincts were to trust me, even if she should have run as far as she could. I'd drag her back kicking and screaming if I had to, though. "Why? I don't understand." Her voice was so melancholy I wanted to hold her and comfort her, but I also knew she needed a sliver of space while she tried to process what she'd learned.

I gave her the only answer I could. The simple truth at its core. "You're my Sunshine," I said, perching on the edge of the desk in front of her. It made her seem even smaller somehow, like I loomed over her. I couldn't deny that something about it appealed to me. I wanted to surround her and overwhelm her until she didn't know where I ended and she began.

She knew there would be no getting away from me, not with the way the house was guarded and secured with a gate and a ten-foot fence. She stood no chance of climbing that alone, let alone with Axel and Ines in tow. But I'd *stalked* her. I'd made her question her own sanity and feel like there was something wrong with her. When all along it had just been me following her. Lurking in the shadows and watching.

Where she might have wanted to fight, she also knew there was nothing she could do to fight me.

Her life was mine now.

I saw the moment she realized all the things I knew, her favorite foods, the kids' favorite things. The fact that I knew just how to touch her to make her come apart.

Because I'd watched her do it to herself.

"I let you inside me," she whispered, her voice breaking into a quiet sob. She couldn't yell. She couldn't scream at me.

She couldn't wake Ines up.

"You did. We were always inevitable, Tesoro. I understand this must seem overwhelming to you right now, but eventually you'll understand," I said, and my voice hardened. As much as I understood it, there was a pit of anger that raged when I thought about her not wanting me. That she wasn't comforted by my presence and didn't understand that I'd done what I had to do to have her in the only capacity I could.

She didn't understand that I loved her, and I couldn't say those words. Not so soon, because it would only drive her further away.

"I will never understand this," she growled at me. "This is-this is sick, Ryker. You're sick." She tossed the photos onto the desk next to me. Standing from the chair, she made her way out of the office. When she walked out, I didn't stop her. I merely followed behind her like I had for years, lurking and studying her every move.

It wasn't until she went for the bathroom that I spoke. "Calla?" I called, and she froze mid-step with a flinch. She didn't look back at me as she hummed a response.

"Hmmm?"

"I'll break down the door. We will sleep together from now on. Understood?"

She whimpered, and her feet didn't move in either direction. Like she couldn't quite understand what she should do or where she should go.

Eventually she'd realize that the only place for her was in my arms, right where she belonged.

"Come to bed, Tesoro," I whispered, but she still didn't move.

Something in me tightened as I stripped down to my boxer briefs and stepped up behind her. The skin of her bare arms and legs felt too cold when I put one of my arms behind her knees and scooped her into my arms. She trembled against me, but ultimately let me settle her in the bed and wrap myself around her.

"You can't do this," she whispered finally, flinching when I slid my hand inside her shirt to rest against the smooth skin of her stomach. "You can't keep us here. Please, just let us go," she whimpered.

I held her tight, never letting her doubt the fact that I meant every word. "I will never let you go, Tesoro. It's time you accept that." Her body shook as she broke down into sobs, but her hands clung to my forearms where they wrapped around her torso. Clinging to me through her panic, her body gave me everything her heart wasn't ready for.

"Go to sleep, Sunshine," I murmured against her temple. One day at a time was all I could ask of her. We'd have good days and bad days as she came to terms with our relationship.

Hopefully, with everything out in the open we could move forward.

CHAPTER TWENTY-EIGHT

CALLA

I opened my eyes slowly, rolling to my side to face Ryker in the groggy, faint memory of sleep. It wasn't uncommon for me to reach out for him in the night, and I'd vaguely remember it the next morning and hate myself for it.

That I couldn't seem to resist the pull of him when my brain wasn't engaged, and that my body gravitated toward him naturally, when it should run in the other direction.

My arm smacked against the cool sheets, no sign of Ryker's overwhelming warmth. No light came in through the curtains or gave any sign that it might be morning. A glance at the alarm clock on Ryker's nightstand confirmed it was only three in the morning, and his absence suddenly felt more insidious.

Like the reason for it would slither up behind me like a venomous snake and bite me on the ass. Tugging the covers back, I crept out of bed and into the hallway. The kids slept soundly in their rooms, and the office and gym were suspiciously empty.

When I snuck a peek over the edge of the loft, the sight of Dante sitting on the couch and fiddling on his phone was all that greeted me.

It wasn't until I was halfway down the stairs that I realized I only wore my chemise, but nothing stopped me. Dante sat up straighter when he saw me come through the baby gate.

"I think you should cover up, Calla," he said instantly with a swallow, but I trudged forward and ignored the warning.

"Where's Ryker?" I asked as I wrapped my arms around my chest to fight back the cold.

Dante sighed as he stood, grabbing a blanket from under the cushions and wrapping it around my shoulders while taking great care not to touch me. "Work. Something came up, and he had to go. He didn't tell you?" he asked.

I shook my head with a sad smile. There was only one reason a man might sneak out in the middle of the night without a word.

Another woman.

I shrugged off the blanket. "He doesn't tell me much. Not really," I said, trying not to take my pain out on Dante. He really was just doing as his boss told him, and I couldn't blame him for my problems with my captor. "Goodnight, Dante."

"I'm sure it just slipped his mind, Calla. He isn't used to having to consider other people when he leaves," he said to reassure me.

"I would think leaving me sleeping alone in a bed would be a pretty obvious reminder," I whispered, making my way back up the stairs. After checking on the kids one last time to reassure myself that they were still there, I went to our bedroom and grabbed my phone off the nightstand.

I considered not calling, wondering if he'd say anything about it in the morning or just try to pretend he hadn't left me in the middle of the night. I would never sleep, never get past the anxious, uncertain frenzy of energy that whipped through me like a storm waiting to explode. With that, I dialed the number he'd programmed into my phone, realizing it was the first time I'd ever used it.

I lived with him. Shared his bed.

And I'd never spoken to him on the phone or even texted him.

He answered after a couple rings, his voice ringing in my ears. "Sunshine? What's wrong?"

"You weren't in bed," I answered with a tremble to my lips. There was a muffled grunt in the background, and Matteo's familiar voice barked out an order to be quiet. I swallowed, but the lack of sounds in the background did nothing to calm the panic in me. Were they quieting a woman? A man they intended to kill? "Where are you?"

"Working," Ryker said firmly. "You don't want the details, Tesoro."

"That's a convenient cover," I hissed.

The bastard chuckled. "While it is adorable that you're jealous, I promise you I'm working. I can make him squeal, if that would reassure you. At any rate, if I wanted to get my rocks off, I wouldn't do it with my boss."

"Don't," I snapped. "This all could have been avoided if you'd just told me you were leaving. I woke up, and you were gone. I worried."

"I didn't think you'd care, Sunshine," he murmured. The reminder of the revelation of the night before was like a shot of adrenaline to my heart.

He'd stalked me.

"I shouldn't," I whispered back. Even still that he would just slip out in the middle of the night felt wrong. It made me feel like less, nothing but a convenience. Even if that was what I was to Ryker, he took great efforts to make it so I never felt that way.

As much as I hated the stalking and the betrayal of my trust that it represented, I couldn't deny that it contributed to making me feel like I was the center of someone's universe.

I'd never understand what it must have been like to want someone so desperately that blurring the lines of right and wrong seemed acceptable.

Though, admittedly, those lines didn't seem to exist for my serial killing stalker.

"You shouldn't, but you do. More than you've even realized yet. I'll be home as soon as I can, Sunshine. Go back to sleep." Ryker hung up abruptly, not giving me a chance to respond to his last revelation.

IT HAD BEEN LONGER than I could remember since I'd been on a date.

So long it was depressing to think about, and having to put on makeup reminded me of just how long it had been since I'd bothered with anything of the sort. The champagne dress that clung to me felt like a shock, and I couldn't believe how well it fit.

I hadn't worn it since before Axel was born, but I supposed I did enough yoga to maintain the same figure. I hated the way the thin straps on my shoulders left my arms exposed. In the delicacy of the dress they seemed just a little too muscular. Too toned.

I preferred my tank tops and yoga pants where they looked right at home.

I slipped on my jacket, feeling grateful for the coverage it offered, even if I knew I wouldn't be able to have it at the restaurant.

I could hear my father and Ryker chatting downstairs, so with one last glance in the mirror I left the bedroom. As I made my way down the stairs, Ryker's eyes came to me even as he continued talking to my father quietly. There was warmth in his eyes and a mild amount of surprise lingered there. I knew he couldn't see much, that the only part of me he could see was my face and the black jacket draped over my shoulders.

When I rounded the corner at the bottom of the stairs, Ryker's eyes trailed up my bare legs where my black pumps showcased every muscle in my calves. I missed the way my body had been softer, more feminine, before I'd started teaching yoga and taken the dive into being more fit to do it for hours every day. The change felt striking, but there was no mistaking the fact that Ryker didn't mind it. He looked at me like he'd desire my body no matter how it looked, and even though I knew that had to be a fallacy, it was an appealing one.

"You look beautiful," he whispered, stepping forward to touch his lips to mine gently since my father watched on.

"Calla Lily," my father murmured as emotion made his voice crack. "You look so much like your mother." My heart stuttered in my chest, because I knew that she would have been just a year older than I was when she died.

It was a sobering thought. A woman under thirty here one moment and then gone the next. Life was too short to spend it living someone else's life.

Like I did every day I spent with Ryker.

But given everything I'd learned, the reality that he'd been stalking us for years, it made it impossible to think of finding a way out of this. How could you make someone understand his obsession wasn't healthy, and that he would be better off finding someone who he could have an actual relationship with?

"Dad," I whispered, reaching around his waist to tug him into a hug.

"You two have fun. I've got the kiddos covered. We're going to order some Chinese food and play board games until bedtime."

"Okay," I whispered, moving to each of my kids and giving them hugs and kisses goodbye.

"Princess, Mommy," Ines said with glee, running her fingers all over the satin fabric of my dress.

"You're the only Princess here, baby girl," I whispered, lingering with my lips on her head. Axel gave me a knowing look, hugging Ryker goodbye and looking positively gleeful that the man was pushing me out of my comfort zone. I didn't leave the kids for anything other than work. I never wanted to be away from them, especially not after Chad's death. So choosing to leave them voluntarily felt like a horrific step in a direction I wasn't ready for, but it wasn't like Ryker had given me much choice.

Not with his gruff command that we were going out before he told me my father was coming to babysit.

"See you in the morning, Little Man," Ryker said, stepping toward the front door and pulling it open after he squeezed Ines in for a tight hug.

I wouldn't be home to tuck my kids into bed for the first time. Even with Ryker's help, I always kissed them goodnight, and the realization made my feet stick in the kitchen. "Come on, Sunshine," Ryker said, and there was a gentle command in his voice that I couldn't argue with. I knew I'd be getting in the car even if he had to carry me there.

With a deep breath, I forced my legs to move. To carry me into the entryway so that Ryker could place his hand on the small of my back and guide me out the door. When he closed the door behind us in silence, the lock clicked closed as my father activated it behind us. It was unnecessary with all the security on the property, but I appreciated the touch.

"They'll be fine," Ryker assured me as he guided me to the car. There was patience in his steps as he went slowly for my benefit and let me take each step reluctantly.

"What if Ines needs me?" I asked him, pausing as he stopped to open the passenger door of the Maserati for me. He tucked my hair behind my ear, studying the motion intently before his bright eyes met my dark ones.

"You're her mother, Sunshine. She'll always need you, but she'll be okay with her grandpa tucking her in for one night." He kissed my forehead and gestured me into the car. With one last wistful look to the house, I nodded and climbed in. The leather immediately cushioned me, feeling somehow comforting despite the coolness of it. It was early June, and the nights still got chilly quickly. With the sun setting in the sky after a fairly overcast day, the temperature had dropped quickly.

"I hate missing bedtime," I whispered, wincing when Ryker gave me a knowing look. "If I could have had one thing with my mom, it would be for her to tuck me in at night. What if they feel like that?"

Ryker reached down to touch my cheek, brushing back the single tear that gathered. "You feel that way because you never had your mother there to tuck you in, Tesoro. Those kids know without a doubt that they'll have you back tomorrow night."

"Unless they don't," I said, turning my head back, so I severed our connection. "You never know what will happen."

Ryker closed the door, going around to his side to climb in and start up the car. I hated to admit that the sound of the Maserati engine felt like it vibrated through me, to the part of me that would always be my father's daughter who could appreciate the sound of a fantastic engine. Even if I was terrified of the driver. "You will not live your life afraid to go to dinner, Calla. I won't let you."

When Ryker turned around in the driveway, he went slow. The dirt road wouldn't be kind to the car if he went too fast, and the beauty of that car shouldn't have been wasted on a dirt road at all. It belonged in a pristine garage in the city or at the Bellandi estate.

But Ryker seemed to have a passion for an eclectic mix of old and new.

He drove through the gate, and I watched in the side mirror as the gates closed behind us. It appeased me to know that if my kids should ever be without me, they were at least as safe as possible, tucked inside the property and guarded by professionals and my father. Dante waved from outside the fence, patrolling the property as I sometimes saw the guards do.

Whoever Ryker and the Bellandi family had pissed off to warrant such security, they must have been a big fish for all the fuss.

I didn't speak to him as he drove, trying to calm my frayed nerves about being alone with him.

I was going on a date with my stalker who liked to kill people in his free time.

It sounded absurd, even in my head. I had no idea what I was to him, what the obsession meant inside that twisted head of his. For all the talking Ryker did, he said very little. From what I'd seen of him with other people, he wasn't always as talkative as he was with me and the kids, but that didn't mean that he gave me any more details about his life than he gave to absolute strangers.

It was like he was an expert at diversion, at guiding me away from topics I had a feeling he didn't want to talk about. Like his family.

"What do you need from me?" he asked as the city came into view. He drove too fast, weaving through traffic like a professional, but there was always tension in his body when he drove. Like he couldn't quite get comfortable with it, but if he had to do it, he would do it his damn way.

"Where are we going?" I asked, glancing over at him momentarily. His eyes seemed to glow in the lights shining off the dashboard, practically luminescent as he looked over at me. He held my eyes as an amused smirk crossed his face and then he turned back to the road.

"*Angel's*," he answered. My eyes widened, because I'd never been there before. Even before the kids, that had been out of Chad's price range and he'd never been one for dressing up. He'd hated the uniform he wore for work and always claimed that if he had to wear a monkey suit to work, he wouldn't wear one outside of it.

Ryker wore his suit like a second skin. Every inch of the suit was custom made to fit him, stretching over his muscles just enough to tease while still being entirely appropriate. There was no hiding that he was a beast of a man, but Ryker wasn't the type to hide who he was, anyway. He owned himself.

Dick piercing and all.

I swallowed as I glanced down at the way his pants mostly concealed what I knew was a massive cock, before darting my eyes away. I'd felt the piercing with my hand, but I still hadn't gotten a very good look at it. It seemed insane, since I'd had him inside of me.

Multiple times.

I'd felt enough to know what I was looking for when I went on google, and I had to say *that* wasn't an experience I wanted to relive. I had a feeling most cock piercings just weren't my thing.

But the frenum piercing was just right, subtle and sexy but rugged and hard.

It suited Ryker.

"That wasn't what I meant, you know?" he asked with a chuckle. I blushed, hoping he hadn't seen my wandering eyes. The amused look on his face made me think I probably hadn't been so lucky, but I pushed through it.

"What did you mean then?" I asked, staring out the window as the city streets rolled by one by one. *Angel's* loomed up ahead, looking stunning against the city backdrop. Like something out of a magazine.

"I meant to help you cope with what you learned last night," he said. The car downshifted as he moved to pull into the valet parking.

"I'm fairly certain there's nothing you can do to help with that," I huffed with a sardonic laugh. When the car came to a stop, he hopped out quickly. He ordered the boy away from my door, striding around it with confident steps to pull it open himself. Taking his hand with a deep sigh, I let him support me as I pivoted my body, and he pulled me out of the car.

"Come on, Sunshine. Let's get you inside," he whispered, rubbing his hand up and down the sleeve of my jacket as if he could warm me up through the fabric. He guided me to the front doors like that, and the valet driver pulled the Maserati away from the curb to make room for the other cars pulling up behind it.

Angel's was always busy, even on a Thursday.

Someone opened the door for us, and he guided me inside. I winced at the people waiting in the vestibule. The interior doors opened, and they allowed us inside to speak to the hostess. I noticed the interior was empty at the front aside from her and realized I was far beyond my comfort zone if people couldn't even wait inside.

"Mr. Fiore. We've been expecting you. Right this way," the hostess said with a gushing smile. Ryker nodded to her, not saying a word as he assumed his gruffer persona that I occasionally saw him use with people other than us. I had to wonder about the differences in his personality, and if it was an active decision for him to be so varied.

As we walked, I noted the restaurant was pure Italian with a classic elegance that seemed familiar even if I'd never been there. "Will this be acceptable for you, Sir?" she asked, and I wanted to laugh at the thought of calling Ryker by such a title.

Of all the men I knew, Sir suited him the least. He was a brute, a meatball, and a criminal. Not a Sir.

"This will be fine," Ryker said, moving to my chair and pulling it out for me. I looked at him in surprise, but moved to sit as he tucked it in behind me. He did it so effortlessly, so fluidly, like he'd done it hundreds of times.

I wondered if it was part of his life with the Bellandis, but got the distinct impression that he wasn't one of the refined business members of the family. Whatever Ryker did for the Bellandis, I was certain it was less cultured. That left his childhood as a possibility for being so well-practiced.

He sat down across from me, giving me a reassuring smile as the hostess excused herself and a waitress appeared to fill our water glasses. "Can I interest you in a wine list?" she asked. Ryker rattled off the name of a Pinot Grigio I'd never heard of, but I didn't care about wine enough to contradict him. Aside from at Ivory's, I hadn't had a drink since before the kids were born, always fearing that I wouldn't hear them cry if I was in the deep sleep that came with alcohol.

I'd always been a lightweight, but I hadn't been quite *that* much of a lightweight before.

When the waitress disappeared, I opened my menu and focused on it. Even if my options as a pescatarian were limited, I wouldn't waste my first time at *Angel's* on a meal I chose at the last minute. The reprieve it gave me from Ryker's intense stare was only a bonus. "Do you come here a lot?" I asked him, and I tried not to imagine all the women he'd wined and dined there.

Probably while he stalked me.

"No. I've never been here before. The Bellandis own it," he said, looking up at me from behind his menu.

"Oh, is that why she knew you by name?" I asked.

"Yes, Sunshine. She knew me by name because it is her job to know all the Bellandis on sight." I didn't bother to argue that he wasn't actually a Bellandi. I'd seen and heard enough to know that they had their own family, their own hierarchy.

They may not have been family by name, but they were a family in every way that mattered. Ryker seemed determined to apply that kind of logic to the ready-made family he'd inherited along with me.

The waitress returned with our wine, pouring it all properly in that way I never did. "Are you ready to order?" she asked.

"She'll have the pasta primavera and I'll have the ossobuco," Ryker ordered, taking the menu from my hand and handing it to the waitress along with his. I blinked at him in surprise as she walked away, unable to believe he'd been so arrogant as to order for me.

"What if I didn't want the primavera?" I asked him.

He just stared back at me with an eyebrow raised, daring me to contradict him. I wanted to, but I couldn't think of one other thing I'd seen on the menu and considered since I'd been ready to order the primavera. It didn't stop it from being so strange or prevent me from realizing that Ryker was more than comfortable displaying the intimate knowledge he had of me and my preferences.

I already knew about the stalking, so what harm was there in coming clean about it?

I sighed, shaking my head. Tears stung at the back of my throat, but I pushed them down. I couldn't show it, not in that restaurant and not in front of Ryker. Not after my breakdown the night before.

"This will break me," I whispered. "I can't handle this. How can you expect me to just be okay with this?"

"I don't want to break you, Tesoro," Ryker said, and there was an ache in his voice, as if the thought of seeing me broken would break him too. There was so much I didn't know about Ryker, so much I'd never cared to learn because I'd thought the situation with him would fizzle out and we'd be free to return to our lives in time. But something in that tone called to me, like I could feel the place of pain it stemmed from. "I just want you to bend a little for me."

"Right. Just for you," I scoffed.

"You just need to be more flexible," he said pointedly, and my cheeks flushed.

"Hilarious." I knew it was a reference to my yoga and the time he'd spent watching me. I needed the yoga to ground me, to keep me sane in a situation that was anything but. "You want me to bend about something that isn't right. How am I supposed to deal with this?" My voice dropped to a whisper before I continued. "You-you watched me. You *touched* me while I slept-"

"Hey," he said, stretching that ridiculously long arm of his across the table to grab my chin and tilt my face up to look at him. "Not like that. *Never* like that."

"And I'm just supposed to believe you?"

"I would never hurt you. You can question some things, but never question that, Sunshine." His voice hardened, like he was warning me against something that shouldn't have had to be said.

I was in some kind of twisted relationship with a man I didn't know, who had stalked me for years and wouldn't let me dump his crazy ass. My life had been so normal, and it all changed the moment Chad died.

It made me hate him just a little, that whatever business he conducted with the Bellandis had come back to bite me in the ass. Not him, but me.

I was the one paying the consequences for his decisions.

"I don't understand what this is," I said quietly. "You're taking me on a date like I matter. You claim the kids are yours now, but you aren't giving me a chance to even get to know you before you shove this down my throat. You can't expect me to just want to be with you overnight."

"Why not?" he murmured, his hand landing on my thigh from where he sat on the adjacent side of the table. "I knew I wanted you the first day I saw you." I clenched my eyes shut, hating the reminder of how insane our attraction seemed to be.

I wished I didn't feel the same, that I hadn't felt that inexplicable pull to him the first time I'd seen him in the park. I wished I hadn't been so easy to convince to spread my legs for him because I felt that same attraction he spoke of.

It made me feel weak. Like my body betrayed me and made what my brain knew was not the right decision for me.

It didn't seem to care.

Just like the way heat poured off his hand and sank into the bare skin of my thigh seemed to inch its way up to my center and stroke me as efficiently as I did when I masturbated. A hand on my thigh was all it took to make me shift in my seat.

"I need time," I whispered to him.

"I gave you a year," he said firmly.

"You gave me a year to grieve. I'm not asking to grieve Chad. I'm asking for time to adjust to whatever this is before you put these ridiculous expectations on me." The words sounded pained as I said them, and I realized the truth in them. I really wasn't asking for more time to grieve for my husband. He was gone. If nothing else, the way Ryker treated me showed me I'd put my marriage on a pedestal that it never should have been on. When Ryker was at the house, he always played with the kids or helped Axel with his homework. He would make dinner or help with the dishes, giving me soft touches here and there when I was near him like he couldn't resist the pull to touch me. There'd never been a time when Chad reacted to me that way, or had done any of the things Ryker did to help.

He'd come home, ate, and crashed on the couch with his phone in hand.

As insane and creepy as he was, Ryker treated me and my kids far better than Chad ever had.

There was something to be said for that realization and how it shook me to my core. I'd welcomed Chad into my life, dated him willingly for giving me less, and I still pushed Ryker away. His stalking and intrusive tendencies gave me a convenient excuse, but I still didn't know how long I could hold out where our relationship was concerned.

By the time our food arrived, I was an emotional mess. I did my best to hide it, but the reality of my relationship with Ryker and the fact that I felt like I might develop an attachment to him and the way he treated my kids was enough to drive me insane. It felt like he'd turned my life on its head.

He was a criminal. A murderer. A stalker.

I didn't know if I could look past that, no matter how he treated me.

"Tesoro," he whispered, dropping his fork and taking my hand in his. "One day soon, you'll have a very clear understanding of what your place in my life is. But I can see that you're shaken, and you aren't ready for me to ask you just yet. I still have one thing left I need to do before I can ask you, but I want you to think about what you need from me. What you need to know to move forward from here."

I nodded like I understood, but I didn't.

I had no clue what he could want to ask me, and I couldn't let myself think about it too hard.

At least not if I wanted to stay sane. I went back to my primavera, even if it seemed tasteless after Ryker's oddly vague statement that felt like it should have been a revelation.

But I was not going there.

Ever.

CHAPTER TWENTY-NINE

CALLA

I didn't have an enormous family. I'd never had cousins or siblings or anything beyond my one aunt. There had never been a ton of adults to play with me at family get-togethers.

Seeing my son run around on the grass of the Bellandi estate as the men chased him felt surreal. So much attention fixed on him, so much of what any onlooker who didn't know better would call love.

I knew it couldn't be. Everyone but Ryker had only met him a couple hours prior, but there was no mistaking the joy on Axel's face. There was no hiding the way he flourished under all that attention. He squealed when Enzo hauled him up into his arms and tossed him over his shoulder as he ran away from Lino where he chased them. Next to me, Samara watched and held her stomach. I remembered what it was like to be pregnant and to look forward to all those little moments.

I knew what it was like to take them for granted once they came, because the stresses of everyday life took from those precious times. It made me not see them for what they were. Watching my son laugh when Ryker stole him from Enzo was one of those moments, somehow meaningful even if I didn't understand how it could be.

Ivory turned to me, dropping Luna into my arms gently so I had no choice but to grasp her hips and tuck her into me. With her propped up on my hip, I tried not to look down at the little baby face that stared up at me, but when she grabbed a fistful of hair, there was no choice. I swallowed. I would swear I could feel my ovaries pulsing with the desire for another baby, but I was not ready to go there.

Probably not ever.

Luna gurgled at me, and I knew from conversations with Ivory that she was almost six months. "Hi," I said awkwardly.

I would not go into baby love mode.

I would not go into baby love mode.

She laughed up at me, and I felt the smile take over my face.

Shit.

"I hate you," I said, turning my attention to Ivory. She chuckled warmly, patting my arm as if she understood exactly how I felt. She couldn't possibly. Her baby was still a baby.

My first baby was *six*, and my youngest was already two. It felt like my heart tore out of my chest every day when I realized how much time had passed and that I would never get to relive those years with them. It went by too quickly.

"He's so different with you. With them," Ivory said pointedly, her eyes on the boys in the field. Even Matteo and Scar had joined in on the fun, though they'd taken to sitting at the edge and picking flowers out of the flower bed with Ines instead of running around. My daughter sitting with Matteo Bellandi and picking flowers from his immaculately groomed property was both terrifying and awe-inspiring. He'd cut the thorns off the roses before handing them to her, meticulously grooming the stems so they'd be safe for my girl to handle.

The juxtaposition between the sweetness of the action and the horrifying sight of the monstrous knife he pulled from his pocket only added to the conflict inside me.

That knife had probably cut people.

I turned my attention away from them to focus back on Ivory. "What do you mean?" I asked, bouncing Luna and making funny faces at her while she giggled in that hilarious way that only babies could ever achieve.

I dared anyone to not smile in the face of baby laughter.

It was *impossible.*

"I've known him for a while now, and he's always quiet. Reserved. He doesn't speak much, and when he does, he just says what he needs to say and that's it. Blunt. To the point," Ivory explained.

"I worried for you a little, when Lino told me that Ryker wanted to claim you. I always thought he was cold, ruthless. They all are to some extent, but not with us. I wasn't so sure that Ryker could shift to another personality. I didn't think there *was* another personality with him," Samara admitted, rubbing a hand over her belly. She finally looked at me, and there was a serene smile on her face. "But there is. He is more than I ever could have dreamed of for you."

I shrugged. "It's nice that he treats us well."

"But?" Ivory asked.

"Does it matter? With everything he's done, the stalking and the spying, and taking away my choice? I don't know if I can ever get past that." I said, and Luna seemed to realize that we weren't having as much fun as her. Her little fist came down on my chest, demanding my attention. Ryker saved her from having to continue to fight for my attention, racing over from the yard to snatch her out of my arms and put her on his shoulders. His T-shirt rode up just a little, flashing his abs to all of us as he reached up to support Luna's back before he turned.

She clung to his hair so tightly I knew it must have hurt, but giggled when he trotted through the grass to join in on Ines' flower picking. "I swear that man's muscles have muscles," Samara giggled.

I snorted a laugh, because they didn't have the first clue.

"You had sex, didn't you?" Ivory asked, and I bit my lip in humiliation. I didn't want to admit that I'd given in so easily, but it also seemed like these women were the closest thing to confidantes I would have if this would be my new life.

"We did," I admitted, and they both squealed excitedly. I shushed them furiously, wincing when Ryker's gaze came over to us knowingly. The others seemed to pick up on it too, roaring with laughter as they patted Ryker on the back like he'd won a war. "I fucking hate men," I whispered.

"We had a betting pool of how long you would hold out," Samara admitted, and I looked at her in shock. It hurt to know that they'd bet on something that shouldn't have happened. That it was just a foregone conclusion, because that was what my life had come to. "It isn't like that. Anyone can see that he adores you. When a man like Ryker turns his attention to you like that, there's not a woman whose willpower is strong enough to resist it. Honestly, I'm surprised you didn't jump him the first night."

I laughed, "I was a little busy plotting ways to stab him while he slept."

Ivory giggled at my side. "I remember those days." I ignored the fact that both of them seemed content that they totally had Stockholm Syndrome, because what could I do about it? "How was it?"

"Each time was different. The first one we were fighting, and he just shoved me up against the wall and..." I trailed off, because it felt like too much detail to say that he'd *tried* to shove his monster cock in me and had to move me to the bed before he could work his way in. "The second time I was asleep when he started touching me. It felt like he made love to me," I whispered.

"I'm sure he did," Samara said. "From what Lino said, his obsession with you has gone on for a long, long time. I don't think you would hold his interest in that way if he didn't love you, Calla."

Ryker had left Luna with her father and Scar, returning his attention to where Enzo kicked a soccer ball with Axel and laughed violently when it went soaring over his head. "Obsession isn't love."

"Normally, I'd agree with you," Ivory said. "But these men aren't normal. They love *harder* than any other men I've ever known. There's a certain obsession that goes along with that inevitably." She paused, studying me.

Samara's attention fixated on me too, and she squealed finally at whatever she saw on my face. "You *like* him!"

"Shhh!" I hissed, looking over to where Ryker studied our interaction intently, as if he could read my expressions well enough to feel the meaning of our conversation. "I don't want to," I whispered when that intense blue gaze finally left me. "I shouldn't."

"Should and shouldn't don't matter in your relationship," Ivory said. "Does he make you happy?"

"I don't know," I kicked the grass like a child as my discomfort grew. "Sometimes."

"And when he doesn't? Is it because *he* doesn't make you happy? Or because you're intentionally being difficult?" Samara said with a pointed grin. She knew me too well to believe me if I tried to argue that I wasn't difficult. "Look around you. Look at what he has to give to you and those kids. They'll never find a family who loves them more than ours and who will always be in their corner. Those men already worship them. They already see them as theirs and they protect their family above all else. He can give them a family. He can give them love. The kids see that, but he can give those things to *you* too."

I didn't have to answer, not when Ryker came flying from the field and suddenly put his shoulder in my stomach to lift me off the ground. Apparently, he'd grown tired of my conversation on the sidelines, because he turned and raced for the field where the others played. "Ryker!" I screamed, smacking his ass. I winced as pain vibrated through my palm. It was seriously not okay for one man to have an ass that hard. Enzo laughed, and I glared at him while I shook my hand out. "Asshole," I muttered to him as we passed.

His grin was full of amusement as he crossed his arms over his chest.

"Axel!" I said with a laugh when Enzo's infectious energy made me smile. "Make Ryker put me down!" With a grin, Axel bolted over to where Ryker still held me captive over his shoulder.

Ryker teased him, running in the opposite direction so fast I thought I would hurl up my lunch. How he could run like that with my entire weight settled over his shoulder, I'd never understand. The man wasn't human.

He was an animal, impossibly strong as he deftly avoided Axel's grabby hands when he finally caught up to us. I screamed when Ryker suddenly flung me forward so I slid down his torso and had to cling to his neck and wrap my legs around his waist.

"They do reach! I'll let Sadie know!" Samara yelled from the sidelines, and I flipped her off even as I howled with laughter. When Ryker finally let Axel catch us, he dropped to the ground dramatically with me underneath him, but somehow kept me from getting hurt in the impact. His weight covered mine as he shielded me from Axel, snarling at my son playfully when he tried to free me from Ryker's grasp.

I chuckled into Ryker's chest, feeling my laughter bubble at how ridiculous this must have looked. But I'd never had a moment like this, a man who would act like an idiot to entertain my children. With the sound of Ines and Luna giggling off to the side, it felt like a piece of me snapped into place.

The piece of me that knew I could have this as my life. That my kids could have this for themselves.

I wanted that. I just didn't know how to reach out, ignore how we got here, and grab it.

He tilted his head down to look at me, his eyes going to the smile on my face. His eyes lingered there until the smile drifted off my face. It felt too intense, that fixation on something as simple as a smile. His hand reached up, his thumb stroking over my bottom lip delicately. I was horribly aware of the eyes on us, of my children watching, but Ryker didn't seem to give a shit about the audience.

"Smile at me again," he whispered, and I did awkwardly behind his thumb as my cheeks turned pink from the intensity of his stare. When he pulled his thumb away, he leaned forward to touch his lips to mine. It was a gentle kiss, soft and intimate as his body relaxed into mine and his hands cupped both my cheeks. My head disappeared between them, in that way that Ryker always made me feel so small. Even smaller than I actually was. I hated that something as simple as a smile from me made him so happy and his face lit up.

How was I supposed to resist that?

"Gross!" Axel groaned, making me giggle against Ryker's lips. That giggle only seemed to spur him on, but after a brief press of his lips on mine more firmly, he drew back to stare down at me with his forehead pressed to mine. His eyes were light, as if they glowed from within, and after staring at me for a moment he jumped off me and tackled Axel to the ground as my boy screamed playfully.

He tugged Axel into his side, rubbing his fist on his head and messing up his hair. "You think it's gross that I like to kiss your Mom?" he asked him.

"Yes!" Axel laughed, shoving Ryker away.

"You better get used to it, Little Man. I'll never stop," Ryker announced, making me blush. My eyes went to Enzo, but he was busy staring at the side where Scar stared at Ryker in confusion. Something on the man's face made my heart ache, like he so desperately wanted what Ryker had.

But there was genuine fear in his eyes, as if the thought of a man like Ryker having a family was impossible to him.

A few days ago I would have agreed with him.

Now?

Now I had no clue what I thought anymore.

"Mommy! Help me!" Axel called. I lunged up from where Ryker had left me lying on the ground. When your son called you, you helped him.

So I struck Ryker in the side with all my weight, shoving him off balance as he released a deep chuckle and went tumbling to the side.

It didn't matter that it wasn't real or that I'd never have any chance of tackling the man. Not when he pretended to struggle and let Axel and I pin him to the ground. With my legs stretched over his stomach and Axel sitting on his chest in front of me, Ryker grinned up at me.

The grin only grew when Ines fell on top of the pile we formed.

I let myself feel the joy that reflected in his gaze when he wrapped his arms around all of us and pulled us tight.

Most of the time, he really did make me happy.

When I let him.

CHAPTER THIRTY

RYKER

Even in Matteo's massive sitting room, space was limited on the occasions where we all got together. There'd been just enough room for the group of us to relax on the furniture after dinner while Ines and Axel played with the toys the others had bought for them as gifts to welcome them to the family. Calla had mostly gone silent after our wrestling match, and I could practically see the way the gears turned in her head. I didn't know what Ivory and Samara had said to her, but there was a noticeable shift in the way she watched me.

There was a reason I'd decided the time had come to introduce the kids to my family, despite Calla's hesitation. I knew that the bond I shared with them was one of the best things I offered Calla. The support network we had was priceless. She'd never have to wonder what she would do if there came a day when her dad couldn't watch Ines. She'd never have to suffer through being sick and forcing a smile on her face because she had kids who needed her.

They'd need her, but they'd have other people they could spend the day with while she rested. That was if I wasn't available because of work. If I was home, she wouldn't even *need* my family, because she'd have me. But there would come a day when Luna was a little older and could play with Ines. There would come a day when Axel could watch out for his sister and his cousins like the protector I knew him to be.

Finding familial love inside the Bellandi estate had seemed like an impossibility just two years prior, but now the house burst with it. I wanted that for my woman and my kids.

I wanted them to have everything my birth family had deprived me of. A safe space to learn and grow, a place where they would know no fear.

When Yavin strolled in after dinner, the light atmosphere in the room dimmed. Yavin and Lino hadn't returned to what their relationship had been like before Samara married Lino, but they got along fine for business sake. There wasn't even any animosity between them, so much as neither was willing to be the person who stepped over the threshold to bridge that gap. I knew it drove Samara batty, especially when she rolled her eyes as Yavin walked in. He'd been invited earlier, just the same as the rest of us, but he only came when he knew we would get down to business. Like he was outside of our family, even when he had always been part of it.

I suspected it was hard for him, being the only one of us who wasn't Italian. The women weren't, but he was the only male in the inner circle who didn't have the Old World blood ties that the previous generations of Bellandis valued so highly. It didn't matter in the slightest to Matteo, who had opened the ranks of initiates looking to join people of all races and ethnicities.

He saw greater value in a man's character than his lineage, and given my history, that was something I admired.

Blood meant nothing.

Yavin glanced around the room, taking in the distinct lack of space for him to sit. I knew from the tension in his eyes it was one more nail in the coffin of his mind that he didn't belong. I scooped Calla off the seat next to me, depositing her into my lap. She squirmed for a moment, but I quickly realized it wasn't because she wanted to get off me.

She was just trying to get comfortable. I didn't imagine I made a very good cushion.

Yavin smiled at me cautiously, moving into the room and kissing Samara on the cheek. He greeted the others before he took the seat next to us. "I'm Calla," my woman said politely, stretching out a hand to greet the newcomer.

"I figured," Yavin chuckled, shaking her hand. I knew it seemed odd to him, as I couldn't remember the last time I'd shaken a woman's hand in this house. Calla hadn't quite realized that being with me meant she was family, that the Bellandis had already adopted her as one of their own.

Matteo stood suddenly, kissing Luna on her head before he dropped his Little Moon in her mother's lap and strode for the office. Yavin followed, then the others. "I gotta go talk business, Sunshine," I whispered in Calla's ear. I plopped her back onto the couch as I stood, and she pouted up at me at the disturbance.

"I was comfortable," she protested, and I grinned at her. I only had to wait a moment before she realized she'd pouted that I'd taken her off my lap, instead of the other way around. I kissed that pouty mouth firmly and then turned to stride toward Matteo's office.

We had important business to discuss, even if I hated leaving her.

But Calla was safer than she could ever be anywhere else. The security at the estate rivaled the White House, and I trusted her sanity with the women who would explain how beautiful our life together would be once she moved past the way it had started.

I only became more and more confident that we had the kind of love that Matteo had with Ivory. That Lino had with Samara. That Scar could have if he pulled his head out of his ass about a certain raven-haired woman.

Real love that lasted the test of time.

I took a seat at the edge of the room. As much as I enjoyed being in Matteo's inner circle, as much as I saw it for the honor it was, I didn't have much to contribute to the coming conversation. My expertise would come later.

When there was someone to kill or someone to find.

"Murphy hasn't reached out to give me any sign that he won't operate within Bellandi territory," Matteo said, shaking his head with a sigh. Murphy was an idiot for thinking he stood a chance of going up against Matteo and coming out alive on the other side. While his marriage to Aoife would secure his place as the heir to the Irish syndicate's resources, he had yet to marry her. Liam knew he'd made a mistake promising his only daughter to that piece of trash, and he would do everything he could to separate from him over the coming years.

He was just intelligent enough to do it without war, but he wouldn't stand by Murphy's side if he started a war with Matteo over a trafficking operation. Not when O'Connell banned the same within his own forces too.

"So what's the first step?" Yavin asked, crossing his arms over his chest and considering. He was a businessman at heart, with a head for numbers and marketing. He lacked the ruthlessness that even Lino had when pressed, because he'd never had to suffer. He hadn't had a tough childhood that made him turn his back on emotion. He was too hot headed when he needed to be cold. I had a feeling he'd learn.

None of us in this life escaped unscathed.

Not even our women.

"I need information. I won't strike first, not without confirmation that he's breaking my rules," Matteo growled and his eyes came to me. "I know the timing is shit for you. You have Calla and the kids at home. I'm not saying I need you on him 24/7, but I need you on him a couple days a week. I'll put some of my more discreet guys on him when you can't be there, but we both know you'll see things they don't."

I twisted my lips up. There'd been a day when I would have lived for this shit, but now it was just a job. "I'll start Monday. Tomorrow I need to have a conversation with my kids."

"Monday is fine," he brushed it off like I'd known he would. The information we needed would be there a day later. "Everything good?"

"Just need to talk to them before I can take things with Calla to the next level."

"Are we having another wedding here?" Lino asked with a laugh.

"Another fucking wedding," Matteo grumbled.

"That's up to her, but probably. I can't imagine she'll want another big wedding. She about died when I told her to put on a dress to go to *Angel's* the other night."

"Why didn't you ask her at *Angel's*? That's like one of the hottest proposal spots in the city," Enzo said in amusement. He raised a brow at me, and I wanted to smack the man. He knew damn well why I couldn't ask Calla to marry me in public.

"So she could throw wine in my face? No thanks," I grunted. "Can we get back to business?" I asked, giving each of them a pointed look. "You lot are worse than teenage girls. I swear. Gossiping brats."

"How did Calla like Celio and Marco?" Enzo asked.

"Oh, she loved them. She was totally thrilled about the fact that she's got more strange men watching her kids. Thanks for asking."

Matteo roared out a laugh, smacking his hand on the table, but he turned the conversation back to Murphy. Instructing Enzo through the dossier he'd gathered, on Murphy's men and who to keep an eye out for at the club, he waited until Enzo handed the packet off to Yavin.

With my part in the meeting accomplished, I sat back and enjoyed listening to the sound of the others methodically plotting a systematic dismantling of Tiernan Murphy and his buddies.

He'd disappear before he knew what hit him if Matteo had his way.

I TOOK the kids outside while Calla took a shower the next morning, antsy to have our conversation over with in case I didn't find another chance where she wasn't within hearing range. Axel looked too serious when we stepped into the field, far enough away that I knew Calla wouldn't be able to hear us even if she tried to eavesdrop. Even Ines sat quietly once I plopped them both into the center of the field and turned my back to the house.

"Let me know if your mother's coming," I told Axel. He looked over my shoulder, and then his eyes came back to me as he nodded. Those deep blue eyes were intent on mine when I pulled the ring box from the pocket of my jeans and opened it up.

"Pretty!" Ines shrieked, reaching for the ring.

I tugged it back, holding up a finger to let her down gently. "This one is for your Mommy, but if she says yes, then we'll get you one too." It just wouldn't be genuine diamonds, because as much as I wanted to spoil my Princess, that would have been overkill even for me.

"Okay," she pouted, reaching her hand down to fiddle with the grass underneath her legs.

"I'm going to ask your Mommy to marry me," I told her. She lifted her head, studying me.

"Happy after?" she asked, and I shook my head at the thought that Calla had somehow kept her so protected from all the grief of the last year that Ines still lived with her head in a fairytale. I knew she was young, but it seemed like I'd already been cynical even at two.

It was just a testament to how wonderful a mother Calla was.

"Yeah, Princess. Happily ever after. The four of us," I said, touching her head as my eyes went to Axel. "And maybe one more if I can convince your mother. Would you like that? Another sibling to help me look after?" I asked Axel.

"You want to marry Mommy?" he asked, chewing his bottom lip. I'd known it would be difficult for him to give me his permission, given the fact that he *remembered* his father. He remembered that he had a dad, and he knew that while it would never be my intent or Calla's, in some ways I would take his place. I wanted to be a better father to him than Chad had ever been, but it didn't change the fact that he'd existed. I didn't want to force that memory away from him, both for his sake and Calla's.

I knew the kids giving their permission would ease the way with Calla in terms of getting her to marry me. She'd worry about them first and foremost, and with them showing their support she'd have a lot less justification to her objections.

"Yeah, Little Man. I want to marry her," I said, keeping it simple as I let him think over what that would mean for him.

"What about my Dad?" he asked, his voice going so sad that I couldn't help but sigh.

"He's still your Dad, buddy. I know you love him. I just want to make the three of you happy and take care of you. I won't make you stop loving him or make you call me Dad. If the day comes that you want to do that, then that's great. But I can just be Ryker if you want. Even after your mom and I are married."

He nodded as he thought it over, and I watched his little brain work. "My Dad wasn't a very good father," he said, and my heart broke at what the acknowledgement seemed to take from him. "And he wasn't very good to Mommy," he whispered. He was too young to recognize that, to have to see the way his father had kept Calla at a distance. It made me wish I'd been the one to kill Chad after all.

"No. He wasn't." The words were honest, probably too blunt for how young Axel was. "But he was still your father."

"I didn't see it when he was alive, but I see the way you look at Mommy. It's different. He treated her like a problem. You treat her like she's the answer. No matter what the question is." I clapped a hand around the back of his neck, tugging him in and touching my forehead to his as rage filled me.

Rage that Chad had been so obvious in his disinterest for Calla that their insightful son had seen it at five fucking years old.

"The three of you are everything to me. I love your mommy, just like I love both of you," I said, swallowing against the emotion in my throat.

"Love you," Ines piped up, throwing her weight into my side.

Axel sniffed back his urge to cry, seeming to need to stay strong as he made a very big boy decision for his mom and their future. "You can marry her, as long as you promise that you love her."

"I promise, Little Man. There will never come a day when I don't love your mother."

"Mommy!" Ines squeaked, leaping out of my arms to race to Calla as she stepped out the door from the pool room. Axel and I stood as I discreetly tucked the ring box back in my pocket. We made our way to the girls, one grinning happily and the other narrowing her gaze on me.

I had no clue when I'd ask her or how. I'd wing it. With Calla, I never knew what each day would look like. Who knew when my Hellcat would come back out and dig her claws into my ass?

"What were you three talking about?" Calla asked, suspicion in her voice as she ran a finger through her wet hair.

"Just enjoying the sunshine," I answered before Ines could open her adorable little mouth and likely ruin the surprise. If I waited too long, I might have to do something drastic, like buy her a pony, to bribe her into secrecy.

I wasn't opposed to the idea, even if I knew nothing about horses.

How hard could it be?

CHAPTER THIRTY-ONE

CALLA

As soon as the top strap of Ines's bathing suit snapped into place, she looked up at me with terror-filled eyes. "It will be okay, Princess. Mommy and Ryker and Axel will be with you the whole time."

I watched the gears turn in her little face, wondering how she could get out of swimming since she so desperately didn't want to go in that pool. But Ryker had declared that it was time to push her to face that fear.

For once, I agreed with him. She needed to know how to swim, especially if we lived in a house with a massive pool.

"Want call 'yker, Daddy," she murmured, and I felt my face pale. It wasn't the first time she'd expressed her confusion over Ryker's place in our lives, and I couldn't blame her.

Even I felt confused.

"I don't know how to answer that, sweetheart," I whispered as I knelt in front of her. "It's complicated, but it's a big decision. I can't tell you how to feel about Ryker." I paused, watching her lips purse as she stared up at me. I knew she didn't have a clue what I was trying to tell her. How did one explain to a two-year-old that the man who acted like her father, *wasn't* her father? He hadn't been in our lives long enough to earn that title.

At least not that Ines knew about.

"Just know that it's a big step. Think hard before you say those words, okay?" I asked. When she nodded and scrunched her nose up in concentration, I stood and held out a hand. If nothing else, I hoped our little moment would distract her from her fear.

But her feet didn't budge, holding firm when I tried to guide her out of her bedroom. With a sigh and a smile, I reached down and scooped her into my arms.

She clung to me, desperately, as we made our way down the hall and stairs. Long before the pool even came into sight, she tightened her grip and held on for dear life. By the time we walked into the humid pool room, I'd already begun to second guess my decision that I needed to push her.

I never wanted my girl to be scared, and I definitely never wanted to cause it.

"Maybe this wasn't a good idea," I said, trying to ignore Ryker in favor of staring at my son. I knew without a doubt, that if I looked at Ryker with water dripping down his chest, my libido would flare to life.

I always wanted to wrap myself around the meatball like I was spaghetti.

And I'd officially traumatized myself with that thought.

"She'll be fine, Sunshine," he said, that deep voice finally drawing my eyes over to him. It made no sense. I'd seen him in less clothing than swim shorts. I'd seen him naked, for shit's sake, even if I hadn't examined his body. It wasn't like it needed a microscope to get the overall picture.

But something about him standing in the pool with the water lapping at his abs as he walked toward us made my body sing.

Why hadn't we ever gone for midnight swims?

How did one man make water droplets look lickable?

I set Ines to her feet, knowing from the previous year that if she walked in on her own it was less traumatic for everyone involved. Going down a few of the steps, I sat there and patted the space next to me for her to join me.

Sitting on the steps seemed easy enough, and it hadn't been an option in the little pool Jason had set up for me the year before.

"Come on, sweetie. Just come sit with me. That's all I want from you today," I murmured, keeping a bright smile on my face.

She shook her head at me, backing up a step as if I might reach out from the pool and drag her in.

Ryker stepped up to the edge of the pool, holding out his arms dramatically. "Come on, Princess," he said. "I won't let you fall."

She watched him, not moving for a moment before she looked at me. Her face was conflicted, as if she could feel how much it would kill me to have my daughter choose Ryker over me in that moment. Still, I smiled and nodded her on. "Go on, Ines."

Stepping forward slowly, she let Ryker gather her in his arms and step away from the edge. He held her high enough that only her feet touched the water.

Standing from the steps, I dove into the water and let the pressure drown out the threat of tears. When I surfaced, Ines had water up to her knees as Ryker led her deeper and deeper slowly.

Axel seemed to take pity on me, coming up and wrapping his arms around my stomach so he could hug me tight. "She told him she loves him," Axel whispered, and I knew without a doubt he didn't want Ryker to hear our conversation. My boy was too smart not to notice that Ryker and I never said the words to one another, especially if the kids had said them to him.

"And what about you, Cookie Monster?" I asked, booping his nose as I forced a smile to my face. "Have you told him that?"

"Not yet," Axel said in return. "Have you?"

"Have I what?" I grinned, hoping to all that was holy that he was not asking me that question.

"Told Ryker you love him. I know you do. Everyone sees it when you look at him, at least when you aren't angry," he laughed. "You never looked at Daddy like that."

I didn't ask what look he meant. I didn't think I needed to. Even I knew there was a difference between how I felt for Ryker and what I had felt for Chad.

Ryker was scary, not just because he was a serial killer and a stalker, but because of the way he turned me inside out and somehow reassembled me to feel more alive than I'd ever been before.

It seemed I wasn't the only one so deeply affected by him. Ines had been speaking little bits here and there when Chad died. "Love you," had been one of her favorite phrases.

I couldn't remember her ever saying it to Chad. Not even once.

Glancing up as Axel moved away, Ines leaned her belly over his arms and happily kicked her legs as he led her around the pool. I tried not to feel that hurt, focusing instead on the result. My daughter was in the pool, smiling and giggling without a care in the world thanks to Ryker.

As I grabbed the floaties for her arms off the ledge of the pool and stepped over with a smile to slide them onto her arms, I decided that was all that mattered.

I wouldn't change that smile for anything.

THE FEEL of weight covering me suddenly jarred me from my sleep with a shriek of terror. When my eyes opened in the unlit room, I could barely see anything. Just a shape looming above me, curling me underneath him. But I knew that body, I'd know it anywhere.

I knew the way he smelled, and I knew the way he *felt* when his skin touched mine.

"Ryker," I whispered, touching his shoulder gently. He jerked away from my touch, but never stopped cradling me underneath him. "Ryker, what's wrong?" I asked him, feeling his body jerk from side to side as if he was being struck.

But the room was silent except for his panting breaths, except for the deep shudders that shook his body as if he was being torn from the inside out.

"Ryker!" I yelled to no avail. I smacked at his shoulder gently, trying to draw his attention from whatever distressed him, but there was no response.

No sign that he was even alive, aside from his breath on my hair and the way his body moved. His hand grabbed my wrist, pinning it to the bed beside my head and holding me there. The other was pinned next, and I bucked my hips to shift his weight off of me. But he was so fucking heavy that I didn't stand a chance of moving him. Especially not if I didn't want to hurt him.

And I realized with sudden clarity that I didn't. All thoughts I'd had of stabbing him in his sleep had passed, and in reality hadn't even been real. I could never hurt the giant beast of a man who cradled me like he had to protect me from whatever haunted him. When his face shifted a little closer, I realized his eyes were closed, pinched shut as if in pain.

Asleep.

Ryker was dreaming, and the pain on his face meant it was something terrible.

"Ryker," I whispered again, a low sob sticking in my throat. I wanted to help him, wanted to pull him from whatever tormented him, but I also knew that to wake him would risk him hurting me. I knew he would never forgive himself.

"No!" he yelled suddenly, his body shifting to cover mine completely as his entire frame vibrated as if he was being struck. "You can't have her. Not her." I stilled, wondering if he dreamt about someone hurting me.

Or if there was a woman who mattered more than I did.

If I thought it sweet that he might protect me in his dreams, it tore me apart to think he might dream about protecting someone else.

His grip on my wrists tightened, near the point of bruising but never crossing over that threshold. "Not her," he murmured brokenly as his weight collapsed.

With the full force of him on top of me, I couldn't breathe. Couldn't get air into my lungs as he crushed my chest. "Ryker!" I wheezed, pinching the skin of his side so harshly that he finally woke up. He vaulted off me, falling off the foot of the bed and caught himself just before he could hit the ground.

By the time I scrambled to my feet and turned on the light, he was sitting with his head in his hands. I touched his shoulder gently, wincing when he shrugged me off and surged to his feet. His eyes searched me, and I realized quickly that he was inspecting me for injuries. Checking to see if he'd hurt me. "I'm fine," I said to reassure him. "You didn't hurt me."

His eyes landed on the reddened skin of my wrists, grabbing my hand and lifting it to look closer. "This isn't hurting you?" he asked.

"It won't even bruise, Ryker. It's nothing." I stepped into his arms, wrapping mine around his waist as best as I could as my face buried in his chest. "Talk to me."

"Talk to you about what?" he grunted, clearing his throat as he stepped out of my hold. His blue eyes were hard, cold as he looked at me.

Completely closed off. Such a contrast to the way he normally treated me, even when he wasn't speaking. It made me flinch back as a sharp pain struck my chest.

"Your nightmare. You said not her. Who—?"

"Not tonight, Calla," he growled, heading for the door to the bedroom. "Go back to sleep."

"Ryker!" I called, wincing when he stormed out and closed the bedroom door behind him. I glanced back at the bed and the mussed sheets, contemplating if I wanted to sleep alone.

He'd said we would sleep together from now on, but he'd also left me at the first hint of trouble for him. I should have known better.

And I still didn't know if there was another woman. I wanted to give him the benefit of the doubt, but I needed him to talk to me to do that.

Deciding there would be no sleep for me, I grabbed a robe and wrapped it around myself. As I passed the office, I heard Ryker working himself to death in the gym, but I ignored him in favor of going downstairs for a drink of water. When that was done, I curled up on the couch with a movie on the television.

Maybe I'd sleep.

Eventually.

CHAPTER THIRTY-TWO

It was safe to say that Calla was mad. She hadn't even woken up when I'd picked her up off the couch and brought her back to bed, irritated beyond belief with myself that I hadn't been able to just talk to her. But in the wake of my nightmare, it was all too easy to push her away.

I regretted pushing away the gentle affection she'd shown me. It had been progress; her showing that she cared about me even if she tried to fight it. I just had to hope that I hadn't done too much damage.

Having to leave to go stalk Tiernan Murphy seemed even worse than it had the day before. I should have stayed home with Calla and the kids and worked to draw her out of the funk that had taken hold. I didn't know if it was because I'd refused to talk to her, or if she genuinely felt threatened by whatever I'd done to her in my sleep, but she kept her distance to the best of her ability.

I had known something was wrong when Calla woke up before me and immediately started cooking crepes. Not that she couldn't cook, just that she hated mornings. For her to wake up and sneak out of bed before me was unheard of, and while I'd definitely appreciated the berries and cream crepes she'd made, I'd have gladly taken the smiling Calla I'd had with me over the weekend.

But like always, my past barged in and fucked everything to hell.

I kissed her tense, unwilling mouth, curling my fingers around the back of her neck to hold her still. "Try not to destroy the furniture while I'm gone, Hellcat," I murmured, a grin toying at the edges of my lips.

She didn't return it, didn't bother to call me an asshole or give me a mocking glare in response. Things were worse than I'd thought.

"I'll be back as soon as I can," I said with a sigh. I'd already said goodbye to the kids, and I hated to think of the fact that Dante would drive them to take Axel to school. While he had his own security who watched over him when he was there now, I didn't think Calla would be pleased if I suggested that she stay home while his security, Celio, took him.

She might rip off my meatballs.

"Bye," she said sternly, grabbing her purse off the hooks near the entryway. "Come on, you two!" she called. Dante strode out past me with a look full of condemnation and terror. I knew the man was not looking forward to the day he had ahead of him dealing with an angry charge.

I left the Maserati for Dante to drive, and he looked like a kid in a candy store as he hopped in the driver's seat. As much as I hated the thought of someone else driving my baby, I didn't have much choice.

I'd needed him to bring my sedan for stalking. Calla raised her brows at me when I climbed into the nondescript car, and then her face twisted with more fury. I didn't understand what was so wrong about me taking an unfamiliar car, but there was something about it that only worsened her mood.

Fucking great.

As much as I loved her, I was ready to move forward. Ready to get past the distrust and the anger. My patience was at an end, and that meant that if Calla thought I'd been pushy before, she had another thing coming.

I drove out of the gate first, pushing the sedan harder than it had been designed to go in my anger. I was also too comfortable driving my Maserati that handled the speed like a dream.

Tiernan's home was on the other side of the city, within the small territory the Irish controlled with Matteo's permission. It was only seven in the morning when I pulled up a few houses down and turned the car off. Far too early for the man who worked late into the night to be up and moving around. I didn't expect to see much for a few hours, so I settled in to look over the dossier Don had given me on Murphy.

Most of it was nothing shocking. He'd been raised in the life, his father the trusted enforcer of the head of the Irish syndicate, Liam O'Connell, until the day he died. The connection had fostered his rise to power, but what surprised me were the notes that made me believe Murphy planned to overthrow Liam. At forty-years-old, maybe he'd tired of waiting for the old man to die.

Though, if word on the street was right, he'd long since gotten tired of waiting. Certain contacts of mine suspected he'd been the one to kill Aoife's mother because she'd opposed his marriage to her daughter, but nothing had been proven. He'd hired the Russians of all people to do it and then turned on them and worked to push them out of the city. Aoife had been a child at the time, nothing more than a pawn in a political maneuver to take over after Liam died.

But the old man showed no signs of slowing down.

I snapped my attention up when Murphy's front door opened and a woman walked out. Murphy followed her, stopping to kiss her sweetly on the doorstep. I'd watched enough men over the years to know the difference between a goodbye with a one-night stand, and a goodbye with someone that mattered on some level at least. I snapped a few shots with my camera for good measure.

She giggled into his kiss, and though I couldn't hear it from my distance, I could see the way her body shook and the tip to her lips as she smiled. She pulled back just enough to talk to him, though his arms stayed wrapped around her. With him dressed in his robe, he made no move to walk her to the BMW parked in the driveway with a driver waiting for her.

I grabbed my phone, dialing Matteo quickly. "What have you got?" he answered.

"Were you aware that Murphy has a woman?" I asked, starting the car as subtly as I could as she climbed into the backseat of the BMW.

"Murphy has lots of women," Matteo laughed. "What of it?"

"This one's different." I shifted into drive. "She spent the night at his house and seems to have her own driver or security detail. I can't say which yet."

Matteo was silent on the other end. "That is interesting."

"Yeah. Get one of the others to watch Murphy for the day. He isn't going anywhere for at least thirty. I'll follow her and see what I can find." I pulled out of my parking space after giving them enough lead time to not be suspicious. Murphy was already tucked back inside his home, oblivious to the predator who could have slit his throat before he'd stepped inside if I'd wanted to act. But Matteo said we couldn't strike yet, so that was what we'd do.

"She feels that significant?"

"He could just be hiding her from O'Connell. I don't imagine Liam would take kindly to Murphy running around on his daughter even if they aren't actually together yet, but if nothing else it could be the information you need to win Liam's trust. Their operation is splintering at the seams, with the younger generation supporting Murphy and the old-timers staying behind Liam. It will explode at some point, so we might as well use it to our advantage."

Matteo sighed. "It all comes down to the women, doesn't it?" he asked.

I nodded, adding in a grunt so he could hear me when I realized he wouldn't see me. "Some men don't even protect the women they claim. Let alone the others who they don't give the first crap about."

"But we do," Matteo said, and I knew like me, he probably questioned his sanity. Our need to shelter women and children would inevitably put our own at risk. We'd lose men in the coming war, and we could only hope that we would be enough to protect the wives and kids through it.

But I'd never be able to look at myself in the mirror, let alone Calla, if I sat by and let Murphy establish his trafficking ring in our city. The thought of Calla and the kids being sold like that was enough to motivate me.

Those women and children had families who loved them too. They were just helpless to defend their loved ones.

So we did it for them. "But we do," I agreed. I hung up the phone, following the blond in the BMW to a luxury apartment building that confirmed everything I'd already suspected. The driver went upstairs with her. The personal security I'd thought him to be.

The apartment building wasn't something that an escort could afford. It wasn't something most could afford on their own.

I'd have to send one of the grunts to find out her name. I would be too memorable if anyone spotted me, and I suspected I'd be watching her regularly. With the fact that she wasn't known to O'Connell, she'd be a valuable point of contact for Murphy with his allies and men that Liam might not know about.

It was a little victory, a little sliver of information we didn't have the day before.

Hopefully, I'd have a little victory with Calla too.

CHAPTER THIRTY-THREE

CALLA

I was terrible at soccer. Absolutely and completely terrible.

With Ryker in the center of the new, larger goal he'd had delivered the day before, I wanted nothing more than to hit his striking face with the ball.

It was a shame I was horrible.

I considered asking Axel to do it for me, but I figured that might not make the best impression as a mother. Stupid responsibilities.

Ryker grinned at me as if he could sense my inner turmoil, and on the rare occasion that one of my kicks went anywhere near him, I hid behind my lack of skill.

"Oops," I shrugged when he caught the ball against his abs. He gave a light grunt that transformed into a laugh, and I glared at him. Of course, the fucking meatball couldn't even pretend to be hurt for my sake.

"Should I just lay down and you can use my head as the ball instead, Sunshine?" he chuckled, and Axel and Ines looked at me as they fought to control their giggles. Axel bent over at the waist, touching his knees as he pretended not to listen to our conversation and worked to teach Ines how to kick her smaller ball into a miniature net just for her.

"I think that might help, yes," I admitted. Ryker shook his head, tossing me the ball that I jumped away from. I'd barely settled myself down when he charged out of the net.

Those hands of his grabbed me around the waist when he collided with me, lifting me up into his arms until I had to wrap my legs around his waist as he strolled around the field. "How much longer do I have to endure before you forgive me?" he whispered, staring up at me with a bright gaze and his lips pursed into a pout that looked comical on his rugged face.

I didn't answer, trying to resist the way he looked at me. The warmth had returned to his gaze the morning before, but he acted like nothing happened.

Like he hadn't made me feel like less and kept secrets from me.

"I'm sorry I shut you out. I didn't mean to upset you. I didn't have an easy start to life and sometimes it comes up in my dreams," he said, and I felt my body soften in response to the vulnerable look in his eyes.

"You want me to believe in this relationship, or whatever you want to call it. But I have to know you to do that, and I don't. I know absolutely nothing about you aside from your criminal life. You have no family. You never talk about what you were before you joined the Bellandis. I need to know *you*, Ryker," I whispered. "Whenever I ask, you shut down. I understand not wanting to get into specifics, but I need something." My arms wrapped around the back of his neck, toying with the bottom of his hair between my fingers. "I want to know you," I admitted, even if it pained me. I knew with every layer of himself that Ryker unwrapped, I fell harder and harder.

Bit by bit. Even when I tried to ignore it and hated myself for it.

He smiled up at me, hearing the admission for what it was. A verbal acknowledgement of my growing feelings for him. "I'll tell you at some point, but for now," he reached up with a hand, supporting my weight with just the one wrapped around the back of my thigh. When he touched my cheek, I melted into that touch. "I want you to know that I give you *everything* that matters. You know me, Tesoro. My childhood contributed to the man I became, but not in a good way. The only thing that matters to you is the man I show you every day."

When he tugged my head down to his, I let him coax a kiss from me. Soft and sweet, he showed me who he was. He showed me I mattered, contrasting with the way he'd made me feel two nights prior.

"Gross! Not again!" Axel laughed. When I pulled back, Ryker turned to level Axel with a narrow-eyed stare that I had a feeling would have made most grown men cower. But my son wasn't fazed, content knowing Ryker would never hurt him.

"Are you ever going to let me kiss your mother in peace, Little Man?" he asked, setting me to my feet as my phone rang in my back pocket. He didn't let me answer, wrapping an arm around my waist and dragging me so that my feet dragged along the ground as he raced toward Axel.

"No," Axel laughed, running in the other direction when Ryker chased after him. My feet dragging undoubtedly slowed him down, but he still caught up to my boy's shorter legs quickly. Grabbing Axel around the waist, he swung him upside down as he lost his mind in a fit of giggles.

"Why am I involved in this?" I asked, laughter bubbling in my chest as Ryker moved toward Ines. She giggled, hurrying around the field as Ryker chased her.

He had to amble along like a swamp creature with both of us hindering his legs, but it only made Ines laugh harder. "Hulk! Put me down!" I laughed, wincing when he dropped me on my ass in the grass.

He'd done it delicately enough that it didn't hurt by any means, but I glared at him no less as I took my phone out of my pocket as it rang again.

When Jason's name popped up on my screen, I contemplated not answering. I didn't imagine there was a world in which Ryker would relish me talking to a man on the phone, not given all his grunty alpha bullshit with James's father.

But in the spirit of not keeping secrets when I tried to demand full truth from him, I hit the answer button. "Hey," I said.

"Calla," Jason called on the other end of the line. He sounded so uninterested, and I realized that he *always* did. I'd just never known the difference. My eyes automatically went to Ryker, watching him twirl the kids around in his arms like he was a carnival ride. "The kids sound like they're having the time of their lives," Jason laughed, undoubtedly listening to the peals of laughter.

"They're having a blast. What's up?"

"Is your Dad there? He's the only one who can make them laugh like that," Jason chuckled, thoroughly amused with his inner knowledge of our lives. I bristled, the insinuation that I couldn't make my kids laugh not lost on me. Given that he'd made similar comments in the past, I shouldn't have been surprised.

"No. I met someone and the kids adore him," I snapped, not bothering to hide the bite in my tone. "They were playing soccer, but it appears to have evolved into goofing around." I didn't know what it was, but since Ryker's insertion into my life, everything Jason texted me or said felt invasive. Perhaps it was the knowledge that he wouldn't approve of Ryker.

Or maybe it was just the fact that he expected me to be loyal to Chad until I died.

"You met someone? And you already introduced him to Chad's kids?" Jason said, his voice full of warning.

"My kids, and yup!" I popped the end of the word, feeling more and more aggravated when Ryker turned to watch me suddenly, staring at me with narrowed eyes and the humor suddenly gone from his expression.

No longer amused. The kids picked up on his disinterest immediately, the smile drifting off Axel's face.

Instantly, I grew more and more annoyed. Between Ryker's crappy jealousy and Axel's fun ending, I wanted to blame Jason for ruining what had been a pleasant moment.

One of those moments where I felt myself falling deeper and deeper in love with my stalker.

"I don't think that's smart," Jason said. "You might confuse them—"

"Not your place, Jason," I snapped, and instantly my body tightened when

Ryker's energy shifted from annoyance to pure fury. I knew he couldn't hear the other end of the conversation, but just the fact that I was on the phone with Jason seemed to be enough to bring out the beast.

He sighed on the other end, continuing on with a change of topic like he knew what was good for him. "I just wanted to wish you a happy birthday. I'm working a case and might not be able to get away tomorrow. I don't want to get too wrapped up and forget to call."

It said everything that he even could forget in the first place. We hadn't talked about it, but somehow I knew Ryker wouldn't forget my birthday.

There was no doubt he knew about it, at any rate. Not with the way he'd stalked my ass.

"Thank you," I whispered instead of responding to the feeling of despondency he left me with. As much as Jason might have aggravated me, he was the *only* connection the kids had to their father. The only other person he considered family.

"I miss you three. When can I see you?"

"I'll have to get back to you on that," I said, mumbling the words as I bit my lip. Ryker's face grew more thunderous every second I stayed on the phone, and I suddenly realized it would probably be in my best interest to end the conversation as soon as possible.

Yikes.

Spicy meatball.

"Okay, but—"

"Gotta go!" I said, pressing the end call button furiously when Ryker stormed his way to me. His eyes darkened as he stared down at me, making me swallow through my suddenly dry mouth. "Jason wants to see the kids."

"How about fuck no?" He growled, and I glanced over his shoulder. The kids watched the exchange with interest.

"Uncle Jason says hi!" I called to them, patting him on the shoulders as I put on my big girl panties and walked around his heaving torso. "You gonna Hulk out or something?"

"Calla," he warned.

"Deep breaths." I stretched up, kissing his cheek as I went to improve Axel's mood again. I practically skipped.

Given the jealousy he'd made me feel with the suspicion of him dreaming about another woman, I didn't feel even remotely guilty as I tuned him out.

An eye for an eye.

CHAPTER THIRTY-FOUR

CALLA

It was my first birthday in captivity.

I didn't expect much, didn't *want* much. Moms quickly got used to being forgotten on their days.

Who made the homemade presents with the kids for everyone else?

Moms.

Who did the shopping for other peoples' birthdays?

Moms.

It meant there was no one who put any thought into what my two-year-old could do for me. Axel was old enough to think about it now, but given that he was always with me, he was stuck too.

I never expected to wake up to a living room decorated with Calla Lilies everywhere. I wasn't prepared for the fact that Ryker had let me sleep in or that the kids were up and dressed for the day in nice clothes I'd never seen before.

There was a stack of pancakes on the table, with candles in the center and waiting for me to blow them out. My eyes watered when Ines lunged for me, wrapping her arms around my legs and shrieking. "Happy!"

My throat clogged with emotion. Chad had never once thought to do something so simple for me.

It was just another moment of realization of just how indifferent my marriage had been. I'd had my kids, and I'd thought they were all I needed.

But they weren't.

I needed more, and it was only after the realization that Ryker might love another woman that I knew I wanted it from him. Because it hurt, and it shouldn't have.

"Happy birthday, Mommy!" Axel said. He turned to Ryker excitedly. "Can she open her presents now?"

I widened my eyes at him. "Let's let your Mom wake up and eat some breakfast. Why don't we save the presents for after?" Ryker asked him, in that gentle voice that still seemed so jarring coming from the man who I never would have thought capable. When Ryker pulled out my chair, I dropped into it in a daze. "You'll have cake later, but blow out the first candles of the day, Sunshine." Looking up at him, I forced myself to blow them all out.

Aside from the day before, for three days, he'd left us during the day. Gone off to do God knows what, in a car that blended in well. Following the dream where he'd begged "not her," I'd assumed he was finally growing tired of me. That he'd been going to see the woman he actually cared about and fighting for her, despite his determination to cheer me up.

But I didn't know a single man who went to such trouble for his *girlfriend's* birthday if his heart wasn't in it. My heart pounded in my chest, and the threat of tears returned for an entirely different reason.

I couldn't deal with the uncertainty anymore. I couldn't wonder what my place was in Ryker's life.

I couldn't keep waiting for the other shoe to drop.

The kids smiled at me, chattering happily, and I forced myself to enjoy that moment with them. It was the first year Ines was old enough to understand what a birthday was. The first time she'd ever tried to say happy birthday to me, and that was a memory I would hold on to forever.

Unlike what I'd expected, I hadn't had to be the one who tried to teach her.

The pancakes were delicious, and Ryker had gone to the trouble of making a strawberry sauce for me to use instead of maple syrup. The same way I would have done for myself. I ate until I couldn't stomach anymore, pleased that it was already near lunchtime and that I wouldn't need to feed the kids another meal for a few hours.

It was close enough that this counted as lunch, especially with the way they shoved forkful after forkful into their mouths. There was no way to avoid the mess they made of themselves, and I chuckled as I stood to clean up the plates. "Sit down, Tesoro," Ryker said. "Axel and I have got it."

I gave him a wide-eyed stare as my boy gathered up his and his sister's plates and brought them into the kitchen. Axel had never washed a dish in his life, such was the frenzied life of a mom who could do it much quicker if she just did it alone.

When Axel came back with a wet towel and helped clean up his sister's hand and face, my heart melted at the gentle affection he used with Ines. "You're such a good brother," I whispered to him.

He smiled at me brightly. "I have a great mom who shows me how." I blinked back tears, moving to stand so I could go shower and get dressed. With the rest of them clothed for the day, it felt ridiculous for me to still be in my pajamas. I was also a coward and needed to flee from the emotional onslaught that threatened my sanity with Axel's words. "Where are you going?" he asked.

"To get dressed."

"Ryker says you have to wait until after presents," Axel chuckled, and the glint in his eyes was knowing.

"Uh oh," I whispered. "What is he up to now?"

"Spoiling you!" Ryker called from the kitchen, and Axel laughed. "Little Man, go grab the presents you can carry. Your mom is going to sit on the couch."

"Help!" Ines yelled, chasing after her brother as they went for the garage.

"You didn't need to go to all this trouble," I said, crossing my arms over my chest as I stepped into the kitchen. He was just finishing loading up the dishwasher, straightening to walk over to me. He wrapped his arms around me, smiling down at me like the tension between us had never happened.

I wished I could forget it the way he was, but the reality that I might have softened toward him and he'd had another woman was a threat I couldn't forget. Finally coming to terms with the fact that I'd put my marriage on a pedestal for no reason, the last thing I wanted to do was enter into another loveless marriage of convenience.

No matter how much the package might tempt me or how wonderful the man was to my kids.

"It was no trouble, Tesoro. I made you pancakes, bought some flowers, got you some gifts and the kids and I are going to make you a cake."

"Please tell me I get out of cleaning all day, because I do *not* want to clean up from that disaster," I joked. Ryker chuckled, leaning down to touch his lips to mine gently.

"You get out of cleaning all day. Happy birthday, Sunshine."

"Thank you, Ryker," I whispered up. The sound of the kids racing back into the living room from the garage made me pull away. I wanted to stay wrapped in his arms forever, but I couldn't.

Not if I wanted to maintain my sanity.

WHEN RYKER SET out to spoil a woman, he went hard.

With the kids tucked into bed, I couldn't stop staring at the trio of large canvases with our photos on them. They added life to the bedroom. With pictures someone had taken at Matteo's house less than a week prior, we looked like a real family. The kind I'd always wanted and never thought I could have. The one of Ines and I picking flowers was sweet, and the one of Ryker rubbing Axel's head and grinning at him was playful.

But it was the photo of Ryker on top of me on the ground, his eyes lit in the moment when I smiled up at him that took my breath away.

I didn't think anyone had ever looked at me the way he did in that moment, and I didn't think I'd ever looked so happy.

The other gifts downstairs were incredible. Axel had given me a yoga mat for outside so I didn't have to clean mine off before I could bring it in the house. There was a pretty dress that Ines had apparently picked out online, and although it was frilly and pink, I knew I'd wear it more than anything else in my closet. When it came to Ryker, I didn't know whether to hug him or smack him.

His actions all day, his constant attentiveness and making sure that I didn't lack for anything would have earned him a hug.

If it hadn't been for what I knew was a ridiculously expensive necklace hanging around my neck. The wire was twisted by hand, an intricate rose gold wrapping around the slice of lilac geode that hung from a rose gold chain. It was stunning.

It was completely me.

It was also way too much.

By the time Ryker stepped into the bedroom from the bathroom, I felt ready to explode. I wanted the necklace, as it was one of the most thoughtful gifts I'd ever received. I imagined it had cost more than my engagement ring from Chad, and that just made me feel like a kept woman.

I didn't like the feeling, especially not in the wake of his nightmare.

"What's wrong?" he asked, eyeing the fact that I still wore the dress Ines had given me.

Reaching up behind me, I unclasped the necklace and cradled it. "I can't accept this, Ryker. I didn't want to make it into a thing in front of the kids."

He held out his hand, letting me drop the necklace in his palm. "I thought you liked it."

"It's beautiful, but I'm not okay with the message it sends. I think it's dangerous to encourage the kids to see us like that."

His face hardened, and that steely look I was learning to fear just a little took over his eyes. "And what message is that?"

"It's not okay that they think I'm your whore! That's how the rest of the world will see this, and eventually my children will be old enough to understand what that means," I said, my frustration bleeding through every word. "I under-stand that there is probably a reason you can't be with the woman you want, but I don't appreciate being kept on the sidelines like a consolation prize. I will not live my life being second place to another woman."

"Another woman?" he growled. "That's what you think this is? Me keeping a convenient pussy on hand while I try to land the one I really want?"

"If the shoe fits, Ryker," I snapped. I went to the closet, grabbing the spare blanket off the shelf to go sleep on the couch again.

"If I wanted a convenient pussy, I wouldn't have picked you. You are far from convenient," he grunted, stepping in front of the door to block me in.

I huffed a laugh. "Oh, I'm sure. I made you work so hard for it, having sex with you less than a week after you moved me in. Totally inconvenient of me to make you wait a whole five fucking days!"

Ryker stepped forward, closing a little of the gap between us. "I love those kids. But if you were just a convenient pussy, I wouldn't have picked a woman with kids, Calla. I'd have picked a woman I could bend over my kitchen counter and fuck whenever my dick got hard."

"Do I look like her?" I whispered, and the thought was too painful. To think his seemingly endless attraction to me might be a lie he created to recreate being with someone he couldn't have *gutted* me, and that was the moment I realized just how deeply I'd fallen into his trap.

All the whispered promises and affectionate touches had reduced me to a blubbering mess who couldn't think about anything other than how good it felt to pretend I was loved.

"There is no her! Fuck, what got into your head that made you think there was?"

"Your nightmare. I told you, you said 'not her' and when I asked about it, you wouldn't talk to me. What am I supposed to think?"

He sighed, stepping over to the dresser and pulling a small box out of his sock drawer. My heart thumped in my chest when he tugged me into his chest and wrapped his palm around the front of my throat, using it to lift my head to meet his eyes. There was something terrifying about the hold, all that power wrapped around one of the most vulnerable parts of me that should have sent me scrambling away.

But no matter what, I trusted Ryker with my body. I trusted he wouldn't hurt me.

That didn't come easily, but there it was.

"There's no one else," he whispered. "The dream was about you. I just need to know you're all in before I take that leap into talking about my family and my history. Even though the nightmare was about you, the nightmares themselves come from my childhood. I can't explain one without the other. Can you understand that? I can't open up to you about that until I know you won't use it against me."

"Then where have you been the last few days? I thought you'd realized that she was the one you wanted—"

"Fuck, Sunshine. You're killing me. The timing was shit, completely, but I was working. Matteo has a job he needs me working on, that's all. I don't want anyone else." I sagged, feeling the truth in those words as they struck me. His thumb caressed my jaw before going to my lip to toy with it.

"I just, I don't understand what this is. This isn't normal. I shouldn't like you. I-I shouldn't want you."

"But you do," he whispered, hauling me up into his arms to move us to the bed. He laid out and draped me over him so that my head rested on his chest and he stared down at me.

"But I do," I admitted, and it felt like something shifted inside me. For the first time, openly acknowledging the fact that I'd somehow come to care for a man I should have hated.

There was a moment of silence as he seemed to give me time for that to sink in, and then he slid a cool metal band on my finger. I didn't dare look down at it, and there was really no need. There was only one reason for a man to ever put a ring on that finger.

"The kids—"

"Have already given me permission to marry you. As has your father," Ryker grinned at me, looking like the cat that ate the canary. I gaped up at him, floundering for a reason why this was *not* happening.

"I can't marry you."

"I don't recall asking. You said you didn't know what this was? Now you do. This is you becoming my wife. And I think if you honestly ask yourself, you know that you want that as much as I do. We'll have an amazing life together, Tesoro."

"You won't even let me go to work," I protested.

"That's not forever. Once things have settled between us, then you can go back. I didn't keep you here out of fear of you talking to the wrong person or anything like that, Sunshine. I did it so we could spend time together, and so you could be more comfortable with me quickly. I'm just eager to be happy together. That's all."

I didn't want to get married. Not to him. Not to anyone. "I don't want to be a widow ever again," I whispered.

"Sunshine, the devil himself couldn't keep me away from you if he tried," he answered, and I sucked back my argument. He wouldn't listen, that much was clear. Not unless I could really communicate it.

I had time.

I sighed, finally looking down at the ring. A massive round moonstone took center focus, with lilac geode shards on either side and a thin rose gold band that matched the necklace and fit my finger perfectly. "It's beautiful," I admitted.

"It suits you," he said.

"Of course it does, you creepy meatball. Did you go through all my jewelry that I never wear to see what I would like, if I did?" He laughed underneath me, and the sound of it seeped into me and brought a smile to my lips.

This was so messed up.

He rolled me underneath him, staring down at me with shining blue eyes that went to the smile on my face again, studying it like he had before. "It's possible," he said, and then he kissed me.

It didn't matter that I hadn't said yes, because he set to showing me exactly why he didn't need to ask.

CHAPTER THIRTY-FIVE

CALLA

He was insane. I'd said it before, and I'd say it again.

Not only had he woken up and decided it was entirely appropriate to tell the kids we were getting married, but he'd established an *insane* timeline. I'd thought we'd wait a year, let the kids adjust to living with both of us and see how the pieces fell together when I didn't want to kill him in his sleep.

Apparently that was too much to ask.

"We cannot get married next weekend," I told him, putting my hands on my hips as I stared him down. The psycho knew I was on the hunt, so after we'd tucked the kids away he'd retreated into his gym and hidden like a coward.

That's what I'd thought at least, but he just genuinely didn't seem to care that I might object to his idea of a date for our big day. Because who would mind rushing into a wedding a week after a proposal?

The fucker.

"Sure we can. Tradition seems to dictate we get married at Matteo's anyway. It's not like we need to wait for a venue." He dropped the bar onto the bench behind his head, standing and wiping the sweat from his palms. The weights on each end were frighteningly large, and I didn't even dare to see how much they weighed. The man was a beast.

"Ryker!" I shouted at him, wincing when the sound echoed in the cavernous space. "I don't even know you! You know *everything* about me, but you have never given me the chance to get to know *you.* How can I marry a man I don't know?"

"We've had this conversation. You know me, Sunshine. You know everything that matters for our marriage."

"That is not your choice to make. Literally all I know about you is that you're a criminal. Last I checked, that wasn't a check in the Pros column, you Neanderthal!"

He chuckled, stepping forward to snatch me into his arms. My hands went to his chest, feeling him slick with sweat beneath my palm. It didn't bother me, for whatever weird ass reason. Nothing about Ryker's body bothered me. "You know that I worship you," he murmured, nipping at my neck as he went to sit on the bench with me in his lap and my legs tucked around his waist. "You know that I love our kids." Another nip, and heat bloomed in me against my wishes. I shoved his face away, glaring down at him. I was determined. For once, he would not make me forget that I was angry with him and let him take me to bed. "You know that I'll do anything to keep you safe."

"You have to give me something," I begged him. He couldn't just expect me to marry a man who had an entire past—a past that caused violent nightmares—without giving me a piece of himself. "You're asking me to give you everything. All of me, without you ever giving anything in return. Please, Ryker" I whispered, and something flashed in his eyes. He groaned, dropping his head back before he stared into my eyes intently.

"I was married once before." I stilled in his lap, staring at him in horror. He'd been planning to marry me without even telling me he'd done this all before?

"What happened?" I asked instead of expressing my anger. I'd give him the chance to explain, the chance to quell my nerves. There was a pause, and I watched him debate his words before he spoke.

"She was about four months pregnant when someone ran her car off the road. She and the baby both died." The agony in his voice broke my heart, and I leaned forward to press my forehead to his.

"I'm so sorry." It didn't excuse that he hadn't planned to tell me, but I couldn't be angry in the face of his pain either. "When was this?"

"Thirteen years ago," he said, and I jerked back in shock.

"How old are you?"

He chuckled darkly, raising a brow at me. It was just another reminder I knew nothing about him. "Thirty-three."

"You were so young," I murmured, wrapping my arms around his shoulders to hold him tight.

"I was. I didn't tell you because I didn't want you to feel you had to compete with her memory. I loved Lauren, don't get me wrong, and I loved our baby. But the boy who loved her died with her. I'm not that boy anymore, and what I feel for you is different."

"I'm sure it is," I whispered, trying to quell the sadness that welled within me. It was different, because he didn't love me.

Obsession wasn't love.

He cupped my cheeks in his hands, holding me still as he looked at me. "I can already see you twisting that around," he chuckled, rubbing his thumbs over my cheeks. "I love you, Tesoro. I have loved you since the first time you smiled at me."

"Ryker—"

"Don't," he said. "I know you aren't ready to say it, but I think you need to hear it. I went to a dark place after I lost Lauren and the baby, and that's how I ended up with the Bellandis. But my life never stopped being all about the dark. Until you shone your light on my world, and I realized just how dark my shadows had become. You are the light of my life, Sunshine."

"You don't have to tell me this." Because as much as he was right, as much as I *needed* to hear it, I didn't want to.

"Sunshine and her shadow," he whispered, and it felt like the words reached straight into my chest to wrap around my heart. The familiarity of that name wasn't lost on me. "You reminded me what it could look like to just live. To love. To be free. To have Happiness."

"My shadow," I murmured, dropping my face forward to touch my forehead to his chest. "It was you. That was *years* ago."

"I've been there since the first time we met, Calla. I could never be away from you," he murmured, making my heart pang. Through my marriage, through my pregnancy with Ines, through all of it, he'd been there watching.

I shoved that down, trying not to feel the warmth that bloomed in my chest to know that while my husband might not have loved me, someone else had.

And I hadn't even known he was there.

Even in the face of that dedication, I couldn't *not* question it. "Are you sure about this? I don't think I'll survive it if another man decides he doesn't actually love me once we're married. I can't do that again, Ryker," I whispered, feeling my heart crack in my chest. I didn't want to blame Chad for the failure of my marriage, not when I was an equal part in that equation.

"You're my answer," he whispered, and there was the tiny trace of a smile on his face.

I stared at him in confusion, waiting for him to elaborate. "To what?"

"Everything," he whispered. "You're the answer to everything, Tesoro. I'll spend the rest of our lives proving it."

With a sniffle and a slight smile, I leaned in, touching my lips to his tentatively. With his hands cradling my face and his lips on mine, he overwhelmed me.

There was no part of me that felt untaken, unclaimed.

Unloved.

I'D THOUGHT Chad loved me.

I really, honestly had. To think there were relationships where people weren't too absorbed in the lives they lived separately to put the focus on one another seemed impossible.

How could you be someone's complete focus with everything else that happened in a day?

But even when he left during the day, even when we spent time apart, somehow Ryker always let me know he was thinking of me. Sweet text messages asking what the Princess and I were up to came throughout the day, and when he was home with us nothing could distract him from enjoying every second of the time we had together. It seemed like a happy little bubble that existed in the two days after his confession of love.

Like nothing could pierce the safe place we'd created within one another. I didn't want reality to intrude, because reality meant I would need to think about what our relationship meant for my life. It meant I had to consider if it could survive out in the real world.

It meant I had to wonder if it was real, and if what I had with Ryker was a lie, then I never wanted to know the truth.

So the knowledge that Ryker had arranged for us all to go to dinner with Dad and Aunt Sigrid felt like an unfortunate intrusion on my bubble. I loved her. I really did. But my aunt would tear our relationship to pieces. She'd analyze everything Ryker said and did in an attempt to rip it to shreds. She would say that he was just a rebound, that I wasn't meant to marry the first man I dated after losing Chad. A week prior, I would have agreed with her.

But Ryker made me question everything. I just had to hope he knew what he was getting into with her.

The kids bounced around in the backseat as we pulled into the parking lot of the restaurant Ryker had suggested. I knew just from looking at it that it must have been Bellandi owned. He swore it was child friendly, that Lino had encouraged Matteo to open it up to cater to the parents who wanted to go somewhere nicer but also wanted to bring their kids along.

I never would have guessed just by looking at it. I mostly assumed that if there was no animal on the sign, my kids wouldn't be welcome. Or at the very least, they wouldn't have a children's menu.

As soon as Ryker parked the car, I jumped out to get Ines out of her seat. The kids had been too antsy trying to get them dressed, and I thanked everything that was holy that Axel had seen Ryker in a suit on more than one occasion. Not that I'd put my six-year-old in a suit to go to dinner, but he *did* put on a button-up shirt with no fuss because he idolized Ryker.

And Ryker filled out a suit like no man I'd ever met.

Ines bounced up and down happily once I set her on the sidewalk and took her hand. The pretty pink and white dress Ryker surprised her with assured she would love him for the rest of the week.

The sparkly silver shoes had bought him a year.

I fought the urge to tug at my own dress, the navy fabric hanging off my shoulders felt inappropriate given I was a mom, but while it was fitted, it wasn't scandalously tight. And the length made it more appropriate as it hung down to my knees. I'd considered not wearing it, but the subtle, abstract pattern on the fabric made it too beautiful to pass up. The fact that the color was a perfect combination with my lilac geode necklace and my engagement ring was entirely coincidental, I was sure.

Ryker smiled at me, holding Axel's hand as they came around to the sidewalk. He carted Ines up into his arms, clutching her tightly as she beamed down at him with adorable baby teeth with gaps between them. They made a perfect pair, Ryker with his dark hair and olive skin and Ines all porcelain and blond.

Axel took my hand, tugging me to the door as Ryker strode toward it. For the first time, not that I'd had many opportunities, I watched women's gazes swing to him as he moved. The sight of my baby girl in his arms seemed to only amplify how handsome he was. Whereas without her, and without the warmth in his gaze as he stared down at her, he might have looked unattainable. With that steely look he so often had when he thought I wasn't watching him.

But with Ines cradled safely in his arms, women felt safer to smile at him. She became an entry point, an invitation. I knew if he even acknowledged their smiles, they'd probably approach.

It only made me chuckle, because I couldn't blame them. Every time I saw him with my kids, my ovaries burst to life as if I didn't already have my hands full as it was.

When we stepped into the restaurant, Dad and Sigrid weren't at the front. "Mr. Fiore," the host said with a smile, grabbing menus and ignoring the rest of the people waiting at the front. "Your companions are right this way." Axel looked up at me with amused eyes, nodding like the service impressed him.

Like a six-year-old knew anything about good service. I chuckled at him, mussing up his hair in a way I knew would pester him. He'd spent too long trying to get it to lay flat.

"Grandpa!" he yelled, running for where my father sat in the middle of the private room at the back. Why we needed a private room for just us was beyond me, but as the host took Ines's jacket from Ryker and hung it on a coat rack, I felt nothing but appreciation for the quiet.

"Hey, Axe," Dad stood, catching my son in a hug when he crashed into him. "Ryker, you didn't have to go to all this trouble."

"No trouble at all. I wanted to give my Sunshine a night off from cooking," Ryker smiled, stepping forward to shake Dad's hand as Sigrid came and pulled me in for a hug.

"You look beautiful, sweetie," she murmured.

"Thank you," I said, ducking my head shyly. I wasn't sure if I would ever get used to wearing dresses and makeup again after not having the time for things like that. I liked it, enjoyed feeling like I was a person again and not just a mom.

Like I could be both.

"Aunt Sigrid, this is Ryker," I said, introducing the man that I couldn't see, but I felt him when he stepped up behind me. His arm wrapped around my waist, stroking over the fabric covering my stomach as he tucked himself against my back.

"It's nice to meet you," he said, nuzzling his face against my temple until I giggled from the ticklish feeling of his scruff against me.

"You too. August hasn't been able to stop talking about you," she said, and her eyes narrowed on him.

"Could I get anyone drinks?" a waitress asked, stepping in from the door I knew must have led to the kitchens.

Ryker went about ordering a bottle of wine and water for the table, asking if anyone wanted anything else. When no one objected, "Apple juice for the kids, please," he said.

"Isn't it a little late for them to have all that sugar?" Sigrid asked as she took her seat next to my Dad. The kids each claimed a seat at one end of the table, Ines in the high chair between Sigrid and I, with Axel between his Grandpa and Ryker. Right where I knew my Little Man would want to be. The way he flourished under male attention, I knew without a doubt that he'd needed it even before his father died.

He hadn't gotten it then, but he had it now.

I couldn't be anything but grateful for that, no matter how it came to be.

"We're celebrating," Ryker said, fully humoring my aunt through her judgmental phase of the evening. She'd come out the other side and be as warm as could be, but she had to feel Ryker out as both a potential husband and a potential father for the kids. I didn't blame her for the hesitance, given that Ryker had come out of nowhere and just magically appeared in our lives.

Since she couldn't know the truth, it had to seem as simple as we'd rushed our relationship. Which we had, regardless of Ryker being a creep.

"Oh?" she asked, taking a sip of her ice water after the waitress brought it.

Ryker didn't answer until she'd retreated to the kitchen, when the kids fiddled with their children's menus. It already seemed like old news to them, regardless of the fact that Ryker had only told them a couple days before. "I've asked Calla to marry me, and she's accepted." He took my hand in his, staring down at the ring on my finger as he brushed his thumb over it and then brought my hand up to kiss the back of my knuckles.

"I didn't exactly say yes." I pointed out, but there was a light lilt to my voice. Playful, rather than admonishing.

"Is my ring on your finger?" he asked.

I rolled my eyes. "Yes."

"Then you said yes, Tesoro." He beamed down at me, releasing my hand to turn his attention to Axel as my aunt gaped at me from across the table.

"You're engaged?" she asked, shooting me a look that communicated I was insane. Her eyes were wide, with her brow raised up to her hairline as she gaped at me. "This man didn't exist a month ago."

"I know it's fast, but—"

"It's insane is what it is!" she whispered, as if the entire table couldn't hear her.

"Don't cut her off," Ryker inserted, his voice going lower as he shifted from the warm and welcoming man that could win Sigrid over to the man who would just piss her off. If she knew half of how domineering he could be, she'd *hate* him. "You give her a chance to speak for herself, and you at least listen to what she has to say before you argue with her." I'd expected Sigrid to glare at him, but a little of the anger faded from her face. "Fact is, I asked August for permission. He gave it. I asked the kids for permission. They gave it. So maybe you should take the time to get to know me and see our relationship before you condemn it as *too fast.*"

"What's the rush? If your relationship is so fabulous, take your time with it and enjoy it."

"Why waste time?" Ryker asked back. "I know I will want Calla as my wife tomorrow, and next weekend, next month, next year, fifty years from now. I will *always* want her next to me. I won't throw that time away to appease other people's opinions." Sigrid had nothing to say to that, no argument that could be made in the face of Ryker's strict condemnation of wasting time.

"We never know where life will take us," I told her. "If you'd asked me five years ago, I'd never have guessed that I'd be a widow. I regret a lot of things about my life and that marriage, but I'll never regret the marriage itself. How could I when I got Axel and Ines?" Axel looked over at me, his eyes intent on me, and he surprised me by nodding with a smile. In that moment, it felt like my son had seen what I hadn't. Like he'd seen my marriage for what it was before I was ready to. "Ryker loves the kids, and he loves me," I said, and I felt emboldened as my voice didn't waiver when I said the words. I believed them.

As insane as it was, he made me believe them every day.

"Why wouldn't I want to give that to us all?"

"They aren't talking about getting married tomorrow, Sigrid," Dad inserted, leaning back in his chair as the waitress came to take our orders. Ryker was occupied, ordering Fettuccine Alfredo for Ines and encouraging Axel to order what he wanted himself like the big boy he was.

When he finished, the waitress came to me, and I opened my mouth to place my order. "Not tomorrow. Next weekend, actually," Ryker told my father. My eyes snapped over, looking at him like he was a pushy bastard. He just didn't know how to ease someone into it, how to show any semblance of normalcy with his expectations. "You're both invited, of course," he added.

My father stared at him like he'd lost his mind for just a moment, and then he threw his head back and laughed so hard the waitress jumped at my side and her menu clattered to the floor.

"Oh, Calla Lily," he murmured when his laughter faded. I finally ordered my dinner, watching the waitress move to a shell-shocked Sigrid. "I knew he'd move fast. I didn't think he'd have you married in a month, but I knew he'd move fast. You stood zero chance against that."

"Thanks for the help, Daddy," I shot back. He laughed again, and after he ordered his food, he jumped into a conversation with Ryker about the Chevelle, of all things. Sigrid watched Ryker interact with him, and the casual way he had with the kids that spoke of just how close they'd become in their time together.

I knew what she saw.

I saw it every time I looked at them, even as it killed a part of me to admit.

A father.

CHAPTER THIRTY-SIX

RYKER

Floating on cloud nine, I went through the motions of my morning. They unfortunately did not involve the pony I'd intended to have delivered for Ines.

Apparently, ponies were brats and a ton of work.

Who knew?

It would have to wait until Ines was old enough to help, otherwise Calla might have to quickly become a cowgirl. As much as I enjoyed the thought of her in boots, I suspected she might chafe a little trying to ride a pony naked.

Boots with clothes lost some of the effect.

I'd just have to buy her the boots, anyway. I was sure we could find a use for them.

"Ryker!" Calla shrieked, following me into the bedroom where I stripped the T-shirt off my head. "We have to talk about this."

"Nothing to talk about." I told her, ignoring the way her arms flailed in frustration.

"There is a wedding dress hanging in the closet! You can't just keep steamrolling over me and getting your way. When does it stop?" she yelled, her hands landing on her hips as she glared at me. My cock hardened in my sweats, the sight of her attitude doing the same thing it always did.

It made me want to fuck her into obedience, but the kids made that difficult to do at most hours of the day. "When you're my wife," I grunted, shoving the sweats down my legs. Calla averted her gaze, her cheeks flushing like I didn't have boxer briefs on. I'd have much preferred to go without them around the house, but I didn't need to traumatize the kids with my dick swinging.

That shit was noticeable.

I made love to her most nights, but Calla was still unsure with me. Like she didn't quite know what to do, when all she had to do was be herself. Her cautious, light touches threatened to make me shoot off like a rocket. It was a crime that at her age she was still as uncertain as a virgin because of the number that shit ex had done on her.

A woman like Calla was made to take what she wanted, and I was determined that I'd teach her how to do just that.

Starting with finally getting her mouth on my cock.

"Ryker," Calla sighed, exasperation in her voice. "We are not getting married on Saturday."

"We are," I said as I walked away to grab my jeans out of the closet. I stepped into them as I made my way back into the bedroom.

"So what I want is irrelevant? Again?" There was genuine pain in her voice, like she thought I didn't care what she wanted. The truth was the opposite, I cared enough to see the difference between what she *said* she wanted and what she *actually* wanted.

I saw through her bullshit, and her strong, independent woman act. She could be all those things.

Just not when it came to me.

"You said you didn't want to be with me. I pushed you. Did it turn out so horrible?" I asked, raising an eyebrow as I stepped into her and tilted her chin up to meet my gaze. She averted her eyes, too stubborn to admit that I'd been right when I told her we would have a beautiful life together. "Did it, Sunshine?"

"No," she said grudgingly, and I could see just how much it pained her to admit that I'd been right. I knew my methods were extreme.

I just didn't care.

"This is the same situation. I'm doing what's best for us in the long-term. I know it seems fast to you, but it's not to me. I waited four years to have you."

"But I didn't," she whispered, her eyes pleading with me to understand. But I couldn't, and I wouldn't.

"I'm not saying I won't marry you. We're just getting started. I'm just asking for a little more time before we make this into something permanent."

Her eyes widened as mine narrowed on her, and I drew in a deep breath to calm myself before I said something I regretted. *That* had been the wrong thing for her to say. "This," I said, pausing for emphasis as she connected the dots, "is already permanent, Tesoro."

"I know—"

"Do you think if we're not married you have a chance of ever getting away from me?" I stepped into her, giving her no choice but to retreat until the back of her knees hit the bed. I resisted the urge to pick her up and toss her onto it, only through sheer willpower alone. I had to go to work, and the kids were downstairs with Dante. "You will never leave me. Do you understand me when I tell you that? Marriage or not, this is forever, Calla."

She swallowed. "I understand. I didn't mean," she paused, shaking her head as her face twisted. She looked dejected. "I guess it was nice to pretend that I had a choice for a little while. Thank you for reminding me what this is," she said, and the deep blue of her eyes seemed empty when she finally met my gaze again. "I wouldn't want to forget my place."

"Don't do that," I growled at her in warning. "Is it so horrible that I just want to marry you, to make you my wife?"

"It's not the fact that you want to marry me that's wrong, Ryker," she whispered, and I could hear the way tears threatened her voice, but she pushed through. "It's you not caring if it's what I want."

"Of course, I care. I *know* you want this life we can have together, Calla. You just have to pull your head out of your own ass long enough to see that the only thing holding you back is shit that doesn't matter. I took you? So fucking what? You fell in love with me anyway."

She gasped, neither confirming nor denying my words. I didn't need her to say them, because I saw it in her eyes every time she looked at me. Whether she was pissed or hurt or happy, there was no lying about the kinds of emotions that played in those deep blue pools. She fought me at every turn, *because* she loved me enough that she wanted our relationship to be everything it could. Unlike with Chad, where she'd been content to accept the status quo, because deep down she'd known that it wouldn't bring her happiness. That it couldn't.

Because he wasn't me.

She opened her mouth to speak, but I cut her off. "Don't even think about lying to me. No lies, remember?" She nodded, biting her tongue instead of spewing whatever kind of bullshit excuse she'd prepared in an attempt to deny her feelings for me. "Get over how we started, Calla. You're only hurting yourself by hanging on to hurt that you shouldn't have. If we're happy, then what difference does it make?" I asked, pressing a harsh kiss to her lips and stepping back from her. I tugged on my shirt, leaving her gaping after me as I walked out the bedroom door.

I took the time to smile and say goodbye to my kids downstairs, and then I left my Sunshine to think about what I'd said. It didn't matter what she decided, anyway. She'd be my wife come Saturday.

I just hoped she'd do it with a smile on her face.

CHAPTER THIRTY-SEVEN

CALLA

Ines pranced in front of the mirror of the guest bedroom at Matteo and Ivory's house, fluffing her lilac dress as she danced around happily. The men had taken Axel, letting him get dressed with Ryker in another room, and I wanted my girl with me while the girls went about doing my makeup.

"Where's Sadie?" Samara asked, as she finished contouring my face. When Ivory came at me with eyeliner, I shut my eyes for fear of my life.

"She already had plans with Patrick," Ivory said. "She wanted to be here so bad, but things aren't going so well—"

"It's fine." I smiled. In all honesty, I barely knew the woman. I'd only met her once, so I would have thought it more unusual if she had been there. That said, I barely knew *any* of the Bellandis. The entire situation was strange, how quickly they adopted the kids and I into their family just because Ryker said we were his.

For them, it really was that simple.

I thought about our conversation a few days prior, about how his words had struck me to the core. They were true. No matter how much I'd developed feelings for Ryker, I still couldn't seem to let go of the fact that he'd stalked me. That he'd taken away my will the day he tricked me into walking into his home, knowing he wouldn't let me leave.

He'd betrayed my trust before I'd ever known him, and no matter how he made me feel, I couldn't shake the feeling that he'd do it again. "You said that you and Matteo had a rocky start?" I asked Ivory, and she set the eyeliner down.

"It was a little different, I imagine. I already knew him. We dated in high school. He broke my heart. The usual sob story," she laughed, but there was just the hint of pain in her voice that I knew came from that place where we all clung to past hurts. No matter what made up for them after the fact.

"Don't listen to her," Samara snapped. "She's downplaying it. She knew him, and she also wanted nothing to do with him. She hated him, as I'm sure you can imagine, given what he did to her. He only made it worse once they got together, moving her in here when she didn't want to, holding her down and putting a tracker in her, and he switched out her birth control for placebos so she got pregnant."

"Oh God," I whispered, staring at Ivory. "And you forgave him?"

She shrugged, a brief smile toying at her mouth. "Something happened, and it put things into perspective for me. I love him, and I wouldn't want to die knowing that I didn't give it a shot out of fear. You only get one life, one chance, at the love these men have for their women. Don't let fear dictate that you can't have it. So he isn't normal," she shrugged again. "But he's yours."

"Don't say the love word," Samara whispered as if she wasn't standing directly behind me. "You might scare her."

"He told me he loves me already," I laughed, and Samara rolled her eyes at the mirror.

"Well, lucky you that you have a man smart enough to do that *before* the wedding. Lino didn't bother to tell me until weeks after we were already married."

Ivory giggled, shaking her head. "He thought you knew. I don't know how you didn't. Everybody knew."

"The best way to make damn sure I knew would have been to just tell me, wouldn't it?" She grimaced at the mirror, but it faded quickly when her hand came down to rest on her belly before she took out the eyeshadow.

"Could you have gotten past it without whatever put things in perspective? Could you have forgiven him?"

Ivory pulled out a lip tint, touching it to my lips lightly enough to give them some color without overwhelming my face. "I don't know," she admitted. "I hope so, because when I think about where we are now and the fact that I could have none of this? That kills me. Don't push him away, Calla. Just give him a chance to show you what things can really be like if you just stop fighting it."

"It would help if he'd stop making decisions for me," I growled, standing to peek at myself in the mirror. My dress hung in the corner, and I dreaded having to put it on, despite the fact that it was stunning. It would mean the moment of truth had come, that I'd finally have to go down the stairs and marry Ryker or make a scene that probably wouldn't end well for me.

And would scare the kids needlessly.

"Mommy pretty!" Ines said, glancing up at me from where she continued to twirl in her dress.

"He will," Samara said. "That won't ever go away completely, but it gets better. We push them, they push back harder. Once you stop pushing, things just flow."

"I hope so," I murmured, stepping into the bathroom where I put the dress on. The silk clung to my body, gliding down in a smooth line from the sweetheart neckline held up by thin straps to the floor. Only a slit in the leg went up to mid-thigh, revealing a leg and trimmed in lace.

Brushing my hands over myself, I stepped into the bedroom. "Princess!" Ines cheered, clapping her hands excitedly.

I wrung my hands as I stepped up to the mirror, looking at my reflection. I felt far more bridal in that moment than my first wedding, even though it had been in a church, and a proper wedding with a crowd of friends and family to watch.

The knock at the door jolted me out of my thoughts. "Calla?" Lino called through the door.

"Yes?" My voice shook as I answered.

"Your father is here. He'd like to see you for a minute." Lino's voice was kind through the door, and I couldn't imagine that he was the businessman who commanded the city beside his crime boss cousin. It was also hard to imagine that he'd thrown Samara over his shoulder and carted her off to Matteo's house where he manipulated her into marrying him.

"Okay. You can send him in!" I called, turning to face the door.

"No Ryker!" Samara hollered out suddenly. "She's already in her dress."

"Okay, Little Dove." Lino laughed at his wife's antics. When the door opened and my father stepped through, he stopped in his tracks and stared at me. I hadn't thought we'd have one of these moments again since it was the second wedding.

Nobody cared about the second wedding as much, right?

But the tears that formed in my Dad's eyes as he took another step forward hinted that maybe I'd been wrong in that assumption. "Calla Lily," he whispered, an ache there that brought tears to my own eyes. "You look so much like your mother."

I nodded, because I knew I'd thought the same thing when I looked in the mirror. Pictures I'd seen of my mom had shown her to be feminine and always dressed well, despite her mechanic husband.

She put in the effort every day, and maybe that was part of why Dad still missed her nearly thirty years later.

"This," he whispered, "is much better than that monstrosity of a dress you wore the first time."

I laughed as he approached and drew me into his arms for a hug. My forehead pressed against his chest, taking comfort in the familiar smell of Dad. He never could shake the smell of oil that clung to his skin.

I wouldn't have changed it for anything.

"It is so much better," I agreed, laughter making my body shake.

"The man is, too," Dad said, and I tilted my face up to look at him. Leaning down to press a kiss to my cheek, he winked at me.

"Not even a question about the fact that I'm being married at Matteo Bellandi's home? That doesn't count as a mark against Ryker?" I asked, tilting my head away as he pulled back.

"It's interesting for sure, but it doesn't matter to me. All that I care about is how much he loves you. Nothing outside of that matters to me. Love is love. I miss your mom every day. I wouldn't change anything, and not just because she gave me you. She gave me the happiest years of my life, and I love her enough that it was worth every bit of pain just to have those memories. I want that for you," he whispered, his voice hoarse with emotion as he talked about my mother.

"Is that why you gave Ryker your blessing?" I asked, fiddling with my fingers as I resisted the urge to pick the polish off in my nervousness. I would come out of my skin soon enough if I wasn't careful.

"I know this is fast for you, but I can see he loves you and the kids the same way I love you and your mother. I want that for you. I want you to have a husband who will miss you every day if something takes you away from us. I want you to have a husband worth mourning. If you don't know already that Ryker is that for you, then I'm sad for you, Calla Lily. I messed up somewhere along the line, making you so damn scared of love. Let Ryker fix that mistake for me, please," he choked out the last words.

"Daddy," I whispered as the first tear fell. He dabbed it away gently, taking care not to mess up my makeup.

"Just let him love you." He held a hand out for Ines, who raced over to put her hand in his. "Come on, pretty girl. Let's give your Mommy a minute." I read between the lines, knowing he needed to separate from me as much as he seemed to think I needed the space.

When they left the room, I realized just how deafening silence could really be.

FATHER ALESSI SPOKE, his words ringing through the yard and the small group of people who had gathered to watch us tie ourselves to one another. "Ryker, repeat after me." He went through the vows, and I had a moment where I wondered if Ryker would go through with it. If the memory of the wife he'd lost might prevent him from taking a new wife.

But the worry proved unfounded when he smiled down at me, sliding a thin rose gold band studded with diamonds onto my finger along with my engagement ring. "I, Ryker, take you Calla to be my lawfully wedded wife, to have and to hold, from this day forward. For better, for worse, for richer, for poorer, in sickness and in health, until death do us part."

My breath stalled as my heart thumped in my chest. Given that we'd both lost spouses, the until death do us part took on a new meaning that it hadn't the first time around. I knew what it was like to lose a husband.

But I knew with sudden clarity that I wouldn't *survive* losing Ryker.

I stared up at him, tears shining in my eyes. His hand reached up to stroke my cheek, as if he could see just how close I'd come to my breaking point. Closing my eyes, I leaned into his touch for just a moment before I looked to where the kids stood with my Dad and Aunt Sigrid. Even she looked pleased; even she had been won over by Ryker's gentle affection and how incredible he was with the kids.

"A once in a lifetime kind of man," she'd said as we parted ways at the restaurant a week before. "And a once in a lifetime love."

I knew she was right. I knew there would be no one who made me feel the way Ryker did. It didn't take a genius to see the way others went about their lives and how different we were.

"Calla, repeat after me," Father Alessi said with a smile. Ryker dropped his hand from my face, letting me look at the priest so I could really hear the words as he spoke them.

"I, Calla, take you Ryker, to be my lawfully wedded husband, to have and to hold, from this day forward. For better, for worse, for richer, for poorer, in sickness and in health, until death do us part." As I repeated them, it felt like a brand on my soul. Like the vows went straight to the core of me and seared themselves into me so I could never forget who I was.

Calla Fiore.

I slid the simple black band onto Ryker's finger, staring up into his face as he looked down at me with shining blue eyes. Once that was done, he ducked his head forward and stole my lips in a fierce kiss as he pulled me to him. Another brand on my soul came with it, our first kiss as husband and wife.

In the group watching, Enzo hooted. "Thatta boy!"

"I suppose saying you may now kiss your bride would be redundant," Father Alessi sighed, and I giggled in response as I tried to pull away from Ryker. Instead, his arms wrapped around my waist as he lifted my feet off the ground and spun me in a circle. "I now pronounce you Mr. and Mrs. Ryker Fiore."

When Ryker finally set me to my feet, the kids rushed into us, hugging our legs tight as we grinned down at them. It was when I looked back up at Ryker that he spoke. "Hello, wife," he whispered, and it felt like my heart stopped.

"Hello, husband," I murmured in response.

We moved away from the center of the focus of the room, Ryker glad to be out of the spotlight as much as I was. As we approached where Matteo stood with Ivory, Enzo spoke. "You know, I have yet to meet Sadie." He laughed.

Ivory eyed him curiously, and Matteo shot her a warning look with whatever he saw in his wife's sea-green eyes. "How is that even possible?" she asked instead, though the amusement never left her face.

I didn't doubt his words though, because I had a feeling anyone who met Sadie would have a very distinct impression and remember the event in significant detail. "No clue. She's just never around when I am," he shrugged. "I hear she's quite the woman."

"Don't even think about it," Matteo growled. "I will not deal with the wreckage when the two of you crash and burn."

"Relax, Teo," Enzo said mockingly. "I haven't even met the woman."

I didn't hear Matteo's response, when Ryker grabbed my hand and the kids and dragged me off into the kitchen where we could be away from the crowd. He knelt in front of the kids, the pant leg of his suit touching the floor in a way that most men might have fussed over, even though the floor was pristine. It didn't bother Ryker in the slightest. He pulled a necklace out of his pocket, a sparkly ring hanging from the chain that he clasped around Ines's neck. "I promised you there'd be one for you too, Princess." She giggled in response, grabbing the ring and pulling it away from her chest so she could look at it with a shining grin.

"Thank you!"

"And for my Little Man," Ryker said, turning his attention to Axel. "It isn't much, but you love working on the Chevelle with me so much that I thought you might like to have this." I recognized the adjustable wrench he pulled from his pocket as the one he most often used when he worked in the garage. "It was the first tool I ever bought myself after I discovered my love of cars. It only seems fitting that I pass it on to you now."

Emotion clogged my throat, the meaning behind the gift not lost on me or Axel as he held out a hand and accepted the wrench with tears in his eyes. It was the gift a father gave to his son.

"Thank you," my boy whispered, and both kids collided with Ryker's chest to hug him tight. I clenched my jaw against the threat of tears as I watched Ryker tend to my kids with such gentle affection that they'd always enjoyed.

"I'm sure your grandpa will want to see that," I said to Axel, making both kids dart into the living room to go show off their new things.

Dad's shout traveled through the doorway. "Ryker, we're gonna have some words!" he called with a laugh, kicking himself for missing the opportunity to give Axel his first tool. He might have wished he didn't miss that chance, but I wouldn't change the way it happened.

"Thank you for making them a part of today," I whispered, leaning down to touch my lips to his before he could stand. "Husband."

"Careful, wife, or we might go home early." I giggled as he stood. I couldn't wait.

WITH THE KIDS spending the night at their Grandpa's for their first ever sleep-over, the Mom in me wanted to call him and make sure everything was okay the second we got home.

I trusted my Dad with them, but Ines had never been away from me for an entire night. The way Ryker glanced at me out of the corner of his eye told me he knew just how antsy I felt as we pulled up the driveway. He smirked, and I refrained from asking.

They'd be fine, and Dad knew how to use a fucking phone if they weren't.

I took a deep breath as Ryker drove the Maserati down the side lane to park it in the garage. The rings on my finger felt heavy, as if the weight they put on my soul was tangible. I wanted to feel free, and I tried to focus on the fact that my feelings for Ryker only grew by the day. I tried not to think about that one dark cloud hanging over us in the form of his domination. I'd just give him the chance Ivory and Samara said, hoping that if I stopped pushing, so would he.

It was the only chance we had at finding our way through to the other side of our marriage.

To the beauty and the peace that I could feel hovering on the horizon. To the love that bloomed in my heart.

When we stepped out of the car, Ryker rushed around to lift me into his arms so that my legs draped over his arm and I clung to him with my arms around his chest. "It figures that the first time I have you here alone, I *want* to make love to you in our bed and not fuck you on the hood of the Chevelle."

I laughed as he stepped over the threshold, expecting him to set me to my feet once that formality was out of the way. Instead, he strode down the hall with me in his arms, showing no signs of stopping until we reached the closed door that went to the main house. There he set me down, opening the door for me and letting me walk through. "So, make love to me first, and then fuck me on the Chevelle," I teased. "If the kids are gone all night, we have some time to take advantage of." Ryker stared down at me, taking my hand in his and pulling me to the stairs so that we could race up them. With no kids to think of, we left the gates open in our haste to get to our bedroom.

"I want to fuck you in the gym and the kitchen," he whispered as we went into the bedroom finally. He closed the door behind him, and I realized how odd it seemed given that we were alone. But the thought fled from my mind the moment he turned and strode for me. He gathered the silk of the dress up in his hands, and I raised my arms to help him shimmy it off my body. His fingers traced over the curve of my bare shoulder, and I stared up at him as my hands slid the suit jacket off his broad shoulders.

"We have time," I whispered.

"We have our lives," he said back, and his stare was intense on mine. As if he could compel me to believe the words, but I wouldn't have agreed to marry him if part of me didn't think it was true already. As soon as my fingers went to the buttons on his shirt, he pushed my hands away to undo them more hastily. My hands went to his pants, unbuttoning and sliding the zipper down in my hurry to get him naked. By the time they fell to his ankles, he'd tossed his shirt to the side and moved to step out of them, kicking his shoes off. "Get on the bed, Sunshine," he whispered, but I shook my head.

"Not tonight," I said shyly, but I reached behind me and unfastened my bra. When it slid down my arms, I watched Ryker's bright eyes darken to icy pools as his gaze narrowed in on my breasts. Hooking my thumbs into the sides of my panties, I slid them down over my thighs slowly, watching his gaze lower as all that intensity shifted down my body.

"Calla, get on the bed," he repeated, his voice dropping to a growl. I shook my head again, stepping forward to hook my thumbs into the boxer briefs that covered him and slid them down until they too fell to his ankles. Then I bit my lip, glancing down at the erection that stood ready as I took his hand and guided him to the bed. I gave him a playful shove, laughing when he let himself fall to his back but tugged me down with him. Shifting his body into the center of the bed, he narrowed his eyes on me. "What are you up to, Tesoro?" he asked as I laid my body on top of him and nipped at his neck.

"I want to explore you this time," I whispered, dragging my lips down his neck in a smooth glide until they brushed over the scruff of his jaw. As soon as my lips were close enough to his, he turned his head and captured them in a fierce kiss that left my mouth feeling bruised. One hand clasped around the back of my head, he tried to contain me, tried to hold me where he wanted me. I could feel the way, with every stroke of his tongue on mine, he tried to seduce me back into the mindless puddle he usually forced me into. But I was determined to take what I wanted, to finally get my mouth on him and a much closer look at the piercing I was normally too shy to inspect.

When he finally released my mouth, I slid my body down his so that my lips touched his chest, so that my tongue dragged over his collarbone, and I felt his heart beating against my mouth. I would have sworn it beat in time with mine, that we were so connected that even our biology recognized us for what we were.

Two halves of a whole. Husband and wife.

Like the darkness in his soul called to the light in mine.

By the time my tongue danced around the bar piercing through his nipple, he jolted, grinding his hips up against mine. I repeated it on the other side quickly as his hands tightened around me, as if it took all his control not to put an end to my fun and just take what he wanted. I abandoned my play, determined to get more of it later when there was time, and he wasn't ready to fuck me yet.

I could do all I wanted to him once I'd drained him dry.

My tongue dipped into his belly button, sliding out to glide through the faint happy trail that led to his cock. I took it in hand, squeezing and pumping once as I shifted my weight down. Once I knelt between his legs, I positioned it perfectly, staring at the single barbell just below the head on the underside of his shaft.

It somehow suited him, like I couldn't imagine him without it, even though I knew there had been a day when it wasn't there. Tentatively, I leaned forward and ran my tongue over it, feeling the warm metal against me as he groaned. Glancing up to find Ryker staring down at me, I was suddenly filled with apprehension. I'd never enjoyed giving head, only done it out of obligation, and found that I wanted to make Ryker feel good. I wanted to make him as mindless as he made me.

I just didn't know how.

So, with a swallow of my nerves, I ducked my head down and wrapped my lips around the head, sucking as hard as I could. When he groaned again, I drew away in shock. Our eyes connected briefly, and when I realized it had been a groan of pleasure and not disappointment, I did it again, sliding my mouth down as far as it could go. It wasn't much, not given the length and girth that Ryker had.

I suspected it would take someone far more practiced than I to do anything impressive when it came to giving him head, but maybe I would get there one day. My hand wrapped around the base, holding him where I wanted him and working the length I couldn't reach while I glided my mouth up and down on him.

His hips shifted, his moan of "Sunshine," echoing in my ears as I strove to bring him right to the edge.

I knew I'd succeeded when he grabbed under my arms and hauled me up the bed so suddenly that I released him with a wet pop. "Hey! I wasn't done," I protested, giggling when he rolled me to my stomach and his weight came down on my back.

"You're done," he growled, bringing a hand down on my ass in a playful swat. His fingers went between my legs, finding me wet and ready. I'd never thought it could be pleasurable to give him pleasure, but when he nudged my clit, I felt like I might go off from the light touch. "So fucking wet. You like sucking my cock, Tesoro?"

"Yes," I gasped as he lifted my ass. With my legs splayed wide around his and my ass tilted up, he guided himself to my entrance and pushed inside me. The stretch to take him always bordered on painful, but once my body relaxed and accepted his intrusion there was something about it that felt complete.

Like I was right where I belonged.

"Ryke!" I cried when he finally bottomed out inside me. He leaned forward, so that the heat of his body hovered just over mine where I was plastered to the bed. His hips moved, driving his length in and out of me in slow, smooth glides that struck against the end of me with every single thrust.

"Whose pussy is this?" he asked, and I fought the urge to smile. Even with a ring on my finger, even married and with his last name, he still had the insane urge to hear me admit I was his.

I wondered if it would ever stop. If he'd ever stop being so disbelieving that this was our reality.

That I was his.

He thrust harder, making me shriek beneath him when his hand wrapped around my waist to stroke my clit. "Answer me, Calla."

"Yours. It's your pussy," I whispered, grinding myself down on him as he made love to me.

"That's right. It's mine. *You're* mine, wife," he growled, and I went careening over the edge into my orgasm with the deep sound of his words. He followed me over, and I knew from the heat that flooded me that we'd forgotten a condom again.

But I didn't have the energy to fight about it. I was just as responsible, should have realized and reminded him.

We'd worry about it another day.

As we came down from our orgasms and he pulled out of me, he seemed to realize what he'd forgotten too. He waited for my protest, waited for the verbal lashing I was sure he expected. But there was just nothing.

Nothing but us mattered in that moment.

Nothing mattered but the way he drew me into his arms and kissed me.

"You're mine too," I whispered as I rested my head on his chest. I'd need to get up and clean myself up, but I just needed a few minutes to catch my breath.

"That's right, Sunshine. Only yours."

I stretched up, running my fingers over the scar through his eyebrow and wondering what happened. I wouldn't ruin the mood or risk ending our day on a note where he shut me out, but the day would come when I needed answers.

I had a feeling the scar was part of the puzzle.

CHAPTER THIRTY-EIGHT

CALLA

I did not appreciate being woken up. Not in the slightest. I should have been sleeping until noon, not up and going to some mysterious appointment at ten in the morning.

Even the chai in my hand couldn't appease the annoyed monster that crept up my throat. Ryker was far too amused in the driver's seat, and I glared at him. "You could have left me sleeping while you did whatever this is."

"Nah, I needed my Sunshine with me today. Trust me," he chuckled. I wanted to kick him, but even if we hadn't been in the car, that would have taken effort, and I was too tired for that shit.

"Then the least you could have done was let me sleep last night."

He looked at me like I'd lost my marbles. "I didn't see you complaining when you were bent over the arm of the couch."

I flushed, but never stopped my efforts to stare him down. "I might have if I'd known you'd wake me up by nine."

"Calla," he chuckled, shaking his head. I waited for him to continue, but there was nothing else to follow. Just my name said like a benediction. We were on the outskirts of the city limits, and there wasn't much around except for a few bars and restaurants. None were overly nice, but none were sketchy either. Ryker pulled up into an empty spot, and he hopped out of the car. With it being mid-morning on a Sunday, the streets were empty as everyone either went to church or slept or just enjoyed their days at home. I wished I was one of them, snuggled up tight in bed. As much as I missed the kids, I could have easily slept until noon, eaten lunch, and then picked them up from Dad.

Such was the exhaustion after a wedding night, I supposed.

My eyes strayed to the pair of rings on my finger while I waited for Ryker to get the door for me. While he hadn't made it a rule by any means, I knew that in public places where there could be dangers associated with the Bellandis, he preferred that I wait for him to open my door. It was an easy enough concession to make, since it cost me nothing aside from a few moments of time.

When the door finally opened, Ryker stared down at me with eyes full of both excitement and dread. It did *not* give me good feelings about what we were doing, but I put my hand in his anyway. Choosing to trust that he wouldn't push too hard, that he wouldn't take advantage of me since I'd given him everything he'd asked for.

But as the car door closed behind me, he guided me to the very last building I'd expected.

The name was simple, etched on the sign up top with a tattoo gun drawing out the letters.

Ink.

"Are you getting a new tattoo?" I asked, running my thumb over the one and only tattoo I had. The arrow on my right wrist had been a spur-of-the-moment decision after Chad died, my symbol that life would propel me into something amazing, but that it'd had to pull me back first. As much as I loved having my tattoo, I couldn't help but feel a little regret over it.

Not when life had propelled me forward into a new life as a mob wife. Did that qualify as something amazing?

With the way Ryker made me feel, maybe. If I could ever really look past who he was and what he did.

"Yes," he said, and his voice went soft. "And so are you."

I laughed, thinking for sure he had to be joking, but when he guided me into the nearly empty tattoo shop, I felt panic well in my chest. Two tattoo artists stood behind the counter, smiling at us while they bent over something and conferred on it.

"Ryker," the man said, stepping around and slapping Ryker on the back of the shoulder with a familiarity that meant he knew my husband well. "Long time no see. This must be Calla."

"It's nice to meet you," I murmured, attempting to tug my hand free from Ryker's hold to shake his hand. He refused, holding me hostage. Whether it was because he didn't want me to touch the other man or because he was afraid I'd run, I didn't know. Either could be true of Ryker.

"We've got your designs ready and waiting. I have to say, Ada has outdone herself with yours. It's stunning." He complimented the woman behind me, and she shrugged her shoulders with an eye roll.

With ebony hair that fell to her butt, she stepped around the counter and took my hand. "Let's get the outline on you and see if you like it."

"I'm not getting a tattoo," I laughed. "I'm sorry to waste your time, and I'm sure Ryker will pay you for the time you spent on the design, but I didn't agree to this, and I'm not putting something permanent on my skin just because he demands it."

She chuckled, casting her eyes over to Ryker before tugging me back behind the counter, anyway. "Do you know who owns this place?" she asked.

I sighed, disbelief filling me. Of course, he would have taken me to a place where I had little to no ability to convince people I didn't want a tattoo. "Matteo Bellandi?"

"We do all the ink for everyone in the family," she said, picking up the tracing paper that was on a little platform on the counter and taking it into the back room. I sat in the chair, waiting and trying to debate what choice I had while she washed her hands and slid gloves on. I zoned out through the process, feeling her apply the stencil to the skin on the outside of my left forearm only vaguely. "Take a look," she ordered, and I stood to move to the mirror at the edge of the room.

Disbelief and fury washed over me.

"I do not fucking think so!" I yelled, and the other man who worked in the shop let out a roar of laughter from the adjacent room. It didn't matter that the tattoo was stunning, that the unalome that wound up the outer edge of my forearm and led into a lotus flower was gorgeous.

I was no expert on roman numerals, but I knew Ryker well enough to know that the roman numeral Ada had worked into the unalome was our wedding date. I stormed into the other room, staring down momentarily at the stenciled outline on his bare chest. A tribal sun, worked into the smokey haze that surrounded his existing ink there, and the same roman numeral was worked into the circle of the sun where the sun rays jutted out. It was beautiful, and it might have been sweet if he wasn't trying to force me to tattoo a wedding date on my skin.

"I am not doing this!" I growled at him, anger flooding me all over again as he stood from his chair and propelled me into the room where the woman waited to tattoo me.

"You have one for him, and now you'll have one for me," he growled right back, snatching my arm in his and pressing it to the rest where the artist needed me positioned.

"Ryker!" I shrieked.

His voice softened momentarily, but there was still a harshness in the intensity of his glare. "I need you to do this for me, Tesoro."

"I don't want to have to cover up a tattoo if we get divorced! This is ridiculous," I argued. Ada left the room, seeming to sense the danger coming before I did.

Ryker leaned forward, catching my chin in his hand and holding so firmly that I didn't dare move. "I am a Bellandi man, regardless of what my last name is.

There is no divorce in this life, Sunshine. We take the 'until death' part of our vows very seriously. So you will sit your pretty ass in that chair, Ada is going to give you the beautiful ink she designed for you, and then we will go get our children. I don't care how long it takes, because there is no other option that is acceptable to me. Understood?"

I didn't answer, clenching my jaw as I tried to jerk my head away.

"Is that understood?"

"Yes," I spat.

He released me suddenly, his eyes going more tender as he knelt in front of the chair. "Do you not like the design?"

"It's beautiful," I muttered reluctantly.

He sighed, touching my knees with his hands as Ada returned to the room. "I need you to be mine in all ways," he explained, and with the fact that the fight had disappeared from me, he seemed to decide it was safe to return to the tender man I'd convinced myself I'd married. I hated that it was partially a show, that even if that was one side of him, the man who lurked beneath the surface would always take my choice away if it suited his needs.

"I'm already your wife," I said.

"If I could tattoo my name on you, I would. Consider this a compromise." He stood, making for the door to go have his own ink done. Ada's face was solemn as she took the seat next to me, positioning my arm the way she needed it.

"I won't do this without your permission, but—"

"Just get it over with," I snapped, turning my face away so I didn't have to watch.

CHAPTER THIRTY-NINE

CALLA

I hid in the bathtub once we'd tucked the kids in, trying to wrap my head around my thoughts. I hated that Ryker had again taken my choice away from me, had violated my body in a way that I could never undo.

That I couldn't soak one of my arms only pissed me off all over again.

A tattoo should have been my choice, and if he'd needed that date on my skin, he could have at least given me the choice of where and how. But it also pissed me off that the tattoo was damn near perfect and that it combined two things I'd contemplated getting a tattoo of and put it in the one place I'd have wanted it.

So it wasn't that I didn't like the tattoo. The opposite was true, and the roman numerals in the unalome were subtle enough that most people wouldn't notice them unless they really looked. It was done tastefully, and the artwork was stunning. Ada was a very talented artist without a doubt.

It didn't stop me from feeling like every day I spent with Ryker I drowned a little more.

Like I was trying to breathe underwater, but I couldn't even bring myself to swim.

I hated that I enjoyed being with him enough to consider letting him pull me under completely, despite his flaws. He crossed the line often, but he never hurt me. He never made me feel like I was less than him, for all the ways he controlled me, more that he controlled me because I was worth *more* and it enabled him to either protect me or truly appreciate the fact that I was his.

So it was with that in mind that I went looking for him after my bath. I knew there were only two places he could be, his gym or the garage working on the

Chevelle. As I passed the gym, the distinct lack of noise coming from the door made me make my way to the garage.

The door was open to the hallway, and I stepped inside. Ryker laid under the Chevelle, only his denim-clad legs sticking out as he worked on whatever task he'd assigned himself for the day. As I stepped in, I contemplated what I wanted to say to him and how I could make him understand that I just wanted to feel like I had control in my life. Like he wouldn't just override me if I made a decision he didn't agree with.

My eyes caught on the folder resting on his tool chest, and the edge of a photo sticking out from it. Curiosity got the better of me, so after a quick glance to confirm he was still under the car, I moved toward it and flipped the folder open despite my misgivings. I half expected there to be bloody photos of a victim of the Bellandi family, but what stared back at me felt somehow infinitely worse.

A photo of a blond in profile seemed to make my heart stop in my chest. She looked so much like me, with her big blue eyes and wavy hair.

The distinction was that she was young.

Probably barely out of high school, if I had to guess, and styled perfectly with flawless makeup and clothes to accentuate the curve of her body.

I winced, scoffing in disbelief as I pushed that photo out of the way and came to another of the same woman. "What are you doing?" Ryker asked, and I jumped in place as I spun to look at him. He'd slid out from under the Chevelle, eyeing me as if I was the one in the wrong.

"You married me yesterday and forced a tattoo on me today, and you're already shopping for a younger model?" I asked, glaring at him as I snapped the folder closed. I scoffed, unable to believe how stupid I'd been. How foolish I must have been to believe that he might have cared about me.

How humiliating.

He got to his feet, approaching me, and there was a grin on his face as he put a hand on the chests on either side of me and leaned into my space. "Are you jealous, Sunshine?" he whispered, reaching up and fingering a lock of my wet hair before he flung it over my shoulder.

"You're my husband. It isn't jealousy to expect that you don't *stalk* other women, Ryker," I snarled, swatting his hand away as I continued to glare up at him.

He chuckled, stroking his thumb over my cheek. "Sheathe your claws, Hell-cat. She's a mark for work."

The breath whooshed out of me in a rush, horror filling the void as I glanced back at the folder behind me. "Are you going to—?"

"Kill her? No. I don't do women or kids. She's sleeping with a rival of Matteo's, so I'm just keeping an eye on him through her. That's all, Tesoro." The amusement never left his eyes, but he seemed genuine in his explanation.

"I don't want you stalking another woman." I winced as I spoke the words. Knowing that he'd stalked me, that his obsession with me had started in such a similar way to what he was doing with her, it felt like a betrayal of our relationship. Like it made it meaningless in the long run. Wasn't I just another mark to watch, just another woman on the other side of the camera, at one point?

It was illogical.

It was insane.

But it was true.

He shrugged, moving his greasy hands to wrap around me as he lifted me into his arms and brought me to the desk at the edge of the garage. "She hasn't given me anything useful yet. I'll put one of the other guys on her and go back to following Tiernan Murphy."

"Really?" I asked, swatting his grease covered hands away when he tried to inch the nightgown up my thighs. I'd need a shower by the time he was done with me if he kept leaving black fingerprints all over me.

"I like you jealous," he murmured, leaning down to tease my mouth with his lips. "What will you give me if I do this for you, Sunshine?"

I narrowed my eyes on him, noticing the way his eyes lit up with humor. "I suppose I can think of something," I said, feeling more playful in the face of his joy. Ryker was such a serious man, such a beast that when he turned his good humor on me in the way that he did for only the kids and I, I couldn't help but melt.

It was a real problem when I wanted to stay angry with him.

"Show me," he whispered, those stained fingers working the fabric up my leg again.

So I did.

CHAPTER FORTY

RYKER

Lino and his bodyguard, Georgio, led as we all climbed out of our cars and made our way toward the front doors of *Murphy's*. With us in suits, it must have looked like something out of a hardcore mob movie. Matteo and I went in the doors side by side after them, with Enzo and Simon taking up the rear.

As we made our way through the empty restaurant, we found Murphy already seated at his favored table in the rear. His second-in-command sat next to him, and several other allies stood behind him looking grim and terrified. They were too young, too inexperienced to present a genuine challenge to any of us. It only made sense, given that he wanted people who would be loyal to him before Liam O'Connell when it came time for him to overthrow his king. Unfortunately for Murphy, the experienced generations supported Liam whole-heartedly. He'd done well by his people, allowing them to prosper in their small territory because of his ability to form an alliance with Matteo.

Matteo and Lino each pulled out a chair on the other side of the table, taking a seat the moment Tiernan looked up from the papers in front of him. He beamed in greeting, as if he was welcoming old friends home instead of a group of rival murderers. "Gentlemen," he said, his voice too loud in the space.

"Murphy," Matteo said in greeting as Tiernan's eyes slid to the rest of us in inspection.

When they landed on me, he paused and an excited grin transformed his face. "Is this your Executioner?" Tiernan asked, leaning forward with a glint in his eye as he looked me over. "I've heard a great many tales about him."

"They're lies," I grunted, keeping my face as cold and impassive as ever as I stared back at the slime-ball who would sell my wife and children if he thought he could get away with it and make a profit off them.

"How can you be so sure? I haven't even told you what I've heard," he laughed, casting his eyes at the men who stood behind him to support their fearless imbecile of a boss.

"Because no one who has felt my knife is stupid enough to talk about it after I'm done." I spoke the truth. The men who I tortured and released were grateful that they walked away with their lives when all was said and done.

There was a tense moment of silence, and then Murphy barked a harsh laugh and jabbed a finger in my direction. "I like this guy. I don't suppose I can buy him from you?" The teasing lilt to his voice did nothing to appease the monster that rose to the surface. He struck far too close to home, too close to the truth of my life that even Matteo didn't know details of.

I was sure he'd been curious enough to dig at some point, but the specifics were limited. Even if finding my family was easy enough to do, given the prominence of the name before they died.

"Ryker is a member of my family," Matteo growled, the deep note of the threat in his menacing voice catching me by surprise. It wasn't often that he was so vehement in his defense of someone, aside from Ivory or Luna anyway, but the way that Lino's eyes glinted as he glared at Tiernan from next to me confirmed just how strongly I'd been accepted into their circle.

I'd known it, but hadn't been able to let myself feel it. Not before Calla and the kids opened me up to the kinds of things I'd never thought I could feel, the parts of me I'd thought had been killed long before.

"Loyalty." Tiernan shrugged. "We all demand it, but it is such an inconvenience when it stands in our way, is it not?" he asked. Matteo didn't answer, and I glanced to the side to meet Enzo's stare as he kept his gaze active on the rest of the room. His military training showed in every line of his body, from the way he kept his arms clasped behind his back to the way his feet remained shoulder-width apart.

If I was the brute executioner, Enzo was the shooter who would take out every enemy in the room before they could even touch their guns. Such was his reputation, and I knew from the way Murphy eyed the man warily that he'd heard it as well.

"Can we get down to business? I have places to be," Lino said, leaning forward and rapping his knuckles on the table twice.

"Yes, how is your wife? I trust she is proving to be worth the loss of your father? Such a tragedy, his untimely death," Murphy's second-in-command, Sean said from his side.

"I didn't particularly consider it a tragedy that I had to put a bullet in his brain," Lino answered casually and shrugged. "He wronged us for his own interests. We do not tolerate such betrayals." Having been the one who was there to witness Gabriele's death, I knew he didn't regret it in the slightest.

He hadn't regretted letting me torture his father before he died, either.

There was nothing a Bellandi wouldn't do for his woman and children, and Lino's father had never been a *true* Bellandi. Not with the way he beat his son and tried to get rid of Samara.

"Let's stop with the false pleasantries and dancing around our words," Matteo grunted, lifting a hand to the table to touch the surface. He immediately retracted it, rubbing his fingers together with a sneer as if he found the place distasteful or dirty.

My guess was both.

"Yes. What made you request a meeting, Matteo?" Murphy asked, daring to speak to Matteo like they were equals. They were not. Only Liam O'Connell held that honor within the Irish syndicate, and even that was only allowed because of mutual respect between the two men.

Matteo smirked, unperturbed by Tiernan's attempts to ruffle his feathers. Very little could aggravate the man who was known for ruling with a frozen fist, untouchable by even the saddest of stories. Murphy didn't have a sad story he could tell, nothing useful to implore Matteo to trust him.

He was just another asshole.

"I am aware that you have been in conflict with Cuevas for the remains of Adrian Ricci's operation. Given that he has retreated from the city, I assume it is correct that Cuevas has withdrawn himself and it is now yours?" Matteo phrased it as a question, but it was clear from the intent stare on his face that he already knew the answer. I eyed the men at Murphy's back, watching as they glanced at each other in a nervous exchange. It was laughable, really, that Murphy had selected them to be his backup for a meeting with the crime boss who controlled the city, and they couldn't refrain from shaking in their boots until after we left, even when we'd made no moves toward violence.

And we didn't intend to, not today, not in a restaurant with only the six of us present. Not on their turf.

We weren't idiots.

"That's correct." Murphy crossed his arms over his chest, leaning back in his chair. "I intend to use the earnings to purchase Aoife a lovely wedding present."

"I'm sure she'll appreciate the fact that her husband rapes and sells women for his business. What a lovely gift," I snarled. I'd never met her, had only interacted with Liam in a limited capacity occasionally, but I felt nothing but horror for the fate I knew she would face as Tiernan's wife.

He shrugged. "Men will be men."

"Sometimes men will be pigs," Simon inserted from Matteo's other side. Matteo held up a hand, silencing his bodyguard even though he looked amused at Simon's statement.

"You would let your men disrespect me in my house without reprimand?" Murphy asked him.

Matteo raised his brow, smirking cruelly. "Is it disrespect if it's true?"

I coughed to cover up the smile that came to my face, Matteo's rare moment of humor being used as a dig at the man I wanted to rip to pieces was enough to make me laugh. I held it back, but only just.

Murphy's face morphed with fury, but Matteo plowed on. "I'm sure you know I have a very strict rule of no trafficking within my city. So long as you respect the limits of my turf, we won't have a problem. But should I discover you're selling people within the area I protect, you will find you learn very quickly what the Bellandis do with pigs."

Murphy narrowed his eyes as his ruddy face reddened. "I do not take well to ultimatums."

"No ultimatum," Matteo shrugged as he stood. "These rules apply to everyone who does business in my city. One businessman to another, I merely wished to make sure you had all the information before you make a choice you will regret. A war would be costly, and it would take me away from my family more than I tolerate nowadays. Don't piss me off, Tiernan." With Matteo leading the way, we followed him toward the door.

"A man of your lineage is wasted playing dog to the Bellandis, Mr. Fiore," Murphy called as we strode for the door. "Let me know if you change your mind and would like to come join a family a little more reminiscent of home."

I didn't bother to answer as we made our way out. There was nothing else to be said. Nothing to be done, even if I wanted to break his spine for throwing out my history so casually. All we could do was wait for Murphy to break the rules.

And then we would strike.

CHAPTER FORTY-ONE

CALLA

Getting out the door that morning proved interesting, with Ryker determined to delay us until it became almost pointless for me to go to work at the studio. With him going to work too, Ines was with my Dad again, and they were both thrilled with the arrangement. It made me happy that they enjoyed being with one another, even if it was harder for me to justify working when Ryker had the means to provide for us all. Because he'd taken my options away from me for so long, I wasn't ready to willingly give up that taste of freedom. Not even when he'd dropped Ines off with Dad himself, taking a stop out of what would have been a busy morning. It seemed so simple, like trusting my husband to bring my daughter to my father's house should have been a given.

But it was the first time I trusted Ryker to take either of the kids somewhere without me, and it felt like a massive step forward in our marriage. I may not have trusted him in certain aspects, like respecting the choices I made for myself and my body, but I trusted him with those kids. There was nothing anyone could say or do that would make me question his loyalty to them and their safety.

If he loved me, the love he felt for them was like something out of this world.

By the time I'd dropped Axel off at school, ignoring the pointed glare of the Principal with a friendly wave and overly bright smile that conveyed just how little she bothered me, I was almost late for the studio. I had to run across the street to make it in time, barely stashing my things in the back before I had to go open the front door for students to trickle in. My regulars greeted me with happy smiles, congratulating me on my marriage that the other instructors must have filled them in on as a justification for my prolonged absence. I wondered if they'd known I was getting married before I did, and that made me giggle where it might have pissed me off at one point.

It seemed so absurd, it just wasn't possible not to laugh.

"Excuse me?" A woman I didn't recognize asked, stepping up beside me at the front of the room where I waited for the rest of the class to filter in before we started at eight. "Are you Calla?"

I spun to face her. She wore her sable hair in a nondescript bun, her fresh face free of makeup as if she wanted nothing more than to fade into the background. Much like me. "That's me," I said with a smile.

"I joined while you were out for your wedding," she said. "Congratulations! I just wanted to introduce myself." She turned to walk away, and I fought the urge to giggle at how nervous she must have been to walk away after an introduction she hadn't made.

"What was your name?" I asked.

She spun back, her cheeks turning pink in her embarrassment. "Oh God, I'm an idiot. I'm so sorry!" She brought a hand up to her mouth, hiding it as she giggled at herself. "I'm Ness."

"It's nice to meet you," I said in response. "I hope my class doesn't disappoint. I have to admit, I'm a little out of practice compared to how I normally am, so I hope you'll cut me a little slack."

"Of course. That's understandable. I can't imagine newlyweds have much time for yoga. Of all the more fun kinds of workouts there are to be done." She blushed again. "Oh God, that was inappropriate. I'm so sorry," she reached out, touching my arm so delicately that I couldn't help but laugh with her.

"It's fine. It's the truth," I admitted with a roll of the eyes.

"Ugh, my boyfriend too. It's the worst and the best all at the same time, I swear. Anyway, thank you for forgiving my horrible faux pas. I'll let you get to teaching the class before I make a complete fool of myself again." She shook her head, as if she couldn't quite believe how many times she'd humiliated herself in a short period of time. Something about her made me just want to reach out and hug her, to tell her it was okay to be a goofball or to say things that might make other people uncomfortable.

She reminded me of a less confident Sadie in a lot of ways, like she had no filter but couldn't quite accept that about herself. She was young, and she would get there, eventually. "It was wonderful to meet you Ness. I hope you enjoy my class." I smiled as she walked to where she'd already laid out a mat, taking a space next to a man who had to be a new student too, since I didn't recognize him. Men weren't common in my classes, so I would have remembered him if he'd been there before.

He turned to smile at me, but his eyes went to where Dante lingered in the doorway to the backroom. He'd barely spoken as he brought me to the studio, lurking behind me like the creep he was as I attempted to ignore him. As much as I liked Dante, being out and about was an entirely different experience than it was when he'd simply been spending time with us at the house.

I didn't want to make him feel weird, but I also didn't want my students to feel awkward either.

I strode over to him. "Once class starts, you can wait in the back room. I'll leave the door open so you can hear, but I don't want them to feel uncomfortable with someone watching them who isn't participating," I said, and he looked hesitant for a moment as he glanced back to the room behind him. "If you sit at that table, you should be able to monitor me without them being able to see you."

That seemed to appease him, and he nodded his assent with a smile. "Sure thing, Mrs. Fiore."

"Don't make me stab you. It tends to freak out my students." I glared as I turned and went for my mat. When I took my place at the edge, I gave myself a minute to take a deep, soothing breath before I exhaled out and smiled at the students watching me and working to center themselves despite whatever stresses worked through their brains.

It took effort. Every time. But I cleared my mind of all the noise.

And then I taught.

CHAPTER FORTY-TWO

RYKER

Following Tiernan was usually such a mindless activity that it didn't matter where my brain was. The man was so predictable it wasn't funny. Home with his side piece more often than not, though he sometimes mixed it up by bringing other women to his home a couple nights a week.

He lived the life of a man who believed variety was the spice of life.

It was his mentality, and he didn't seem to care if his woman knew it. Normally I'd have felt bad for the way he treated her, but she seemed to be aware of his promiscuous activities and infidelity, and, considering he was publicly engaged to another woman, I couldn't muster up my sympathy.

After he left home, he generally went to see Liam and Aoife a couple times a week. The rest, he went straight to *Murphy's* to conduct his loan shark business. There were no moves or even remote mentions of the trafficking operation from what I could tell, but I spent most of that day more distracted than normal.

Calla was at work. She was out of the house without me, and it had driven me mad with worry all day long. By the time I got home after picking Axel up from school, finally with permission from Calla, all I wanted to do was curl up with my family and relax. So we did just that, ordering in Chinese food and vegging out in front of the television. It wasn't something we did often, as Calla preferred to be actively involved with the kids, but from the way she rubbed at her neck and shoulders all evening, she genuinely felt sore from the way she'd suddenly thrust herself back into the physically demanding nature of her longer days. I knew she'd had two of her more advanced sessions today, on top of the long hours since she covered for the instructor who had taken over her classes in her absence to make up for her sudden time off.

When she finally finished reading Ines her story, she tucked her in even though I could see it took more energy than she had. Reaching into my Princess's bed wasn't always a simple task for me given my size, but Calla usually had no trouble. "Goodnight, Princess," I murmured, squeezing my way into the nook that her bed frame created and pressing a kiss to her forehead. "Dream of all the unicorns," I whispered, and she murmured in her half-asleep state with her arms wrapped tight around her stuffed wolf.

Calla closed the door behind us as we made our way into Axel's room. Our boy was freshly showered, waiting in bed with one of his books on his lap. Calla perched her ass on his bed next to him, snuggling in next to her son as she opened the book and started reading. Watching her read to the kids was one of my favorite moments of the day. There had been a time when I'd been forced to experience it through the window where I couldn't hear the delicate cadence of Calla's sweet, exuberant voice as she detailed the characters in the stories and tried to put on voices where appropriate. I'd never put cameras inside the kids' bedrooms for obvious reasons, so I'd never experienced *hearing* story time until the first night after I moved them in with me.

By the time Calla finished the story, Axel too was half-asleep. They were both their mother's children, sleep coming easily and quickly to them in a way I'd probably never understand. Above all else, I was happy they had that.

That their sleep was undisturbed by the horrors of the world.

"Goodnight, Axe," Calla murmured, kissing the top of his head sweetly.

"Goodnight, Little Man," I said, running a hand over his head and pushing his hair back from his face. One day soon, we'd cut it, but I had to proceed carefully and not step on his toes where his father was concerned. Axe would come to see me as his father soon enough, if he didn't already.

"Wanna be just like you when I grow up," he whispered, his eyes drifting closed as he spoke the words.

"I'm glad," I said. Warmth filled me, the confession hitting me straight in the feels as his father. Axel being like me, a man who took no shit and protected his family, would be nothing to be ashamed of. I'd teach him everything he needed to know to protect himself and the ones he loved as soon as he was old enough. I felt Calla go solid at my side, and I knew she probably had different thoughts on the subject. But discussing them in front of Axel was not an option, so she kept her mouth shut as we crept from the room.

I grinned at her, loving it when she crossed her arms over her chest and glared at me. I knew she expected me to go to our bedroom so she could reprimand me, but I wasn't having that. When she'd come into the garage a few nights before, I'd had the Chevelle jacked up, so as much as I'd wanted to *finally* fuck her on the hood, it hadn't been possible at the moment. But given the fact that I knew we had a conversation coming, I knew exactly where I wanted to be when I fucked the Hellcat right out of my Sunshine.

Near that goddamn Chevelle. That was where.

"Ryker!" she whispered, stalking after me as I turned and strode down the hallway in the opposite direction than she wanted me to go. She wouldn't risk waking up the kids, she valued their sleep even more than they did, but she stormed after me. I hurried down the steps, glancing back at her with a grin on my face that only made her scowl deepen. "Would you stop?"

I didn't, not until I made it to the garage. By the time she made it down there, she was fuming, and all I could think was that it was adding more fuel for when I fucked her. That she could work herself into a tizzy all she wanted. I hit the switch on the wall for the audio monitors to play and then turned to cross my arms over my chest with a smirk. "Did you need something, Sunshine?"

"What the fuck is wrong with you? Why would you make me chase you just to talk to you?" Her chest heaved with her frustration, and I wanted nothing more than to strip her shirt off so I could watch it happen with nothing to obstruct my view. I could picture the way her chest flushed, the way her nipples would pebble in the cool air.

"I have work to do," I shrugged, a smile teasing at my lips as she stared at me incredulously. I could see the gears turning in her pretty head, trying to figure out what kind of game I was playing with her. I didn't walk away from her. Ever. There was only one exception to that, the night she'd asked about my nightmare, and I didn't intend to repeat it. But I was already on edge after the meeting with Tiernan, and from knowing that I needed to tell Calla about the conflict so she could understand just how important it was that she and the kids stick to their personal security. I also knew that would terrify my woman, and I didn't relish the thought.

So I needed to fuck her, needed to reassure myself that she was there, and she was stronger than most gave her credit for. She'd survived her shithead husband, she would thrive with me, and nothing Tiernan Murphy could do would ever touch her.

But I also knew she wasn't *quite* at the point where I could take what I wanted just yet. "You need to set a good example for him. You're his step-father," she reminded me.

"Father," I corrected her, but she ignored it like she normally did. There would come a day when I pressed Calla to be more understanding of what I was to those kids, too. It just wasn't that day.

"The last thing he needs is to grow up looking up to you and having you teach him bad things," she pressed on.

"Name one time I haven't been a good influence on him," I said, leaning my ass against the desk as I looked at her. She blanked, her head jerking back as she tried to think of something. But I knew what she quickly realized.

While I might have been a bad influence in a lot of ways, I never exposed the kids to those things. I'd taken her. They didn't know that. They didn't know I'd given Calla no choice but to marry me, or forced her to get a tattoo for me. They didn't know about any of the qualities that would have made me a less than satisfactory role model, so while Calla might protest my parenting on principle, I was actually a pretty fucking spectacular role model, if I said so myself. I watched her flounder for a response, getting more and more frustrated when she realized there wasn't one that would prove her point.

"Listen up, Meatball," she growled. "Just because they don't know you're a poor influence doesn't make you a good one. I know, and if you ever think to expose my kids to that part of your life, I'll beat you over the head with a ball-peen hammer the next time you look in that engine bay."

Grinning at her, I couldn't help but love when she threatened me and went all violent mama bear on my meatball ass, but that she was angry that I presented myself to our kids well annoyed me. She still wanted to be the primary parent, and while I could appreciate that, it seemed ridiculous that she didn't want to share more of that burden with me. I was her husband, after all. Instead of feeding the beast that wanted to be let out of its cage, I picked up a paperweight from the desk and tossed it in the air and caught it as I shifted the conversation. "That's sweet, Hellcat. How was your day?" I asked her when she rolled her neck again.

"You already asked," she pointed out, glaring at me from a few steps away. Like the distance would protect her from me if I got grand ideas. Which I'd had long before I lured her into the garage.

"And I'm asking again. We both know you're less likely to go into details when the kids are there."

She smiled at me, rolling her eyes for a moment. "I had a couple new students sign up while I was gone, so it was nice to meet them. This one girl, she was so awkward. I felt sorry for her, because she was sweet and genuinely funny if she could just own her personality. I think it was that she was so young though. I know I was a lot less sure of who I was when I was her age. But she signed up with a friend apparently, so hopefully he can help her get more confident. He looked older," she said.

"Men do yoga?" I asked, feeling my body go solid at the declaration. I hadn't spent a ton of time watching her at the studio, since seeing her bent in all positions when I couldn't touch her had been torturous at best. I'd also never imagined there would be men in her classes. *Fuck.*

"Some do," she shrugged. "It takes all kinds, Ryker," she scolded me. "And no, as far as I know they aren't all gay, before you go there with your stereotypical macho man shit, Meatball." I smirked at her, but even her attempt at humor couldn't quell the rising beast. A man had watched my woman fold herself up like a pretzel in tight spandex clothes.

That didn't make me feel warm and fuzzy.

"Maybe you should quit," I said, and she laughed in a hysterical giggle that took my breath away. It was rare she was so open to showing how thoroughly I entertained her.

I just wished it had come when I was actually trying to be funny. Not when I was making a suggestion in all seriousness. The blank stare on my face must have alerted her to the fact that I meant business. "That's not going to happen. You only just let me go back to work."

"You stayed home when you were married to Chad. Why wouldn't you want to be a stay-at-home mom now?" I asked her, rising to stand on my feet fully. She shook her head at me, as if warning me to keep my distance, but the time rapidly approached where we were past that.

I was nearly done talking.

"Because that was my choice. In order for me to be willing to do that, let me come to that decision on my own. Don't pressure me into it, because that will only make me want to work more out of spite," she admitted.

I growled at her, closing the distance. "Do you enjoy making me crazy?" I asked, grabbing a handful of her ass in each palm as I lifted her up into my arms.

"It's very possible," she admitted. "But I would argue that you were crazy long before I knew you. You know, stalker and all."

I huffed a laugh, but I still strode to the Chevelle and set her on the hood gently. "You're the only woman I've ever stalked, Sunshine." She looked at the car beneath her ass, pursing her lips in thought for a moment before her eyes came back to me when I hooked my fingers into the waistband of her shorts and gave her a look that communicated exactly what I wanted from her.

With a huff, she lifted her ass up off the hood of the car so I could slide the shorts down her thighs. "I know you're sore already," I murmured, tossing them to the side as I spread her legs and tugged her to the very end of the hood. "But unless you give me what I want, we both know that will get worse."

She glared up at me, her mouth parting in disbelief. "Are you threatening me if I don't quit my job?" she asked.

"No, Tesoro," I growled, reaching behind her head to grab her hair in my fist and tug her head back. I slid my other hand between her thighs, slipping a finger inside her tight heat as she whimpered. "I'm telling you that if you don't quit, I'll fuck you so hard you physically *can't* go do yoga tomorrow." Thrusting my finger in and out of her at a leisurely pace, I waited for her to decide.

I knew which she'd choose, knew she would never give in to my demands through sexual blackmail.

Luckily for me, I won either way.

"You're an asshole," she hissed, and I smirked as I touched another finger to her pussy and slid it in alongside the first. She clenched down on me as she tried to fight the arousal flooding my hand, tried to deny that she craved me, craved *this*, just as much. She needed me, even if she tried to fight it and deny it.

I saw it. Just like I saw her for exactly who she was.

Mine.

"Wrong answer, Sunshine," I told her, slipping my fingers free of her so I could reach for the fly of my jeans. Once I had them undone, I tugged her down the hood of the car further and wasted no time filling the void my fingers had left. She moaned, trying to toss her head back, but I held her still with my grip on her hair, keeping her back arched as I shoved inside her. Her pussy spasmed around me, sucking me as deep as I could go.

Ever helpful once she took my cock, Calla lifted her legs high and spread them, letting me maneuver myself with more agility, but with the way frustration ate at me, I didn't want her compliant. I let go of her hair, lowering her upper body until it dropped to the hood and laid her out like a buffet, and then I tore her shirt down the center so that her tits spilled free. She gasped, staring up at me in surprise.

She even winced, no doubt from soreness, when I pressed her legs back together and put her ankles on my shoulders.

The position only made her pussy grip my cock tighter as I shoved deep, making Calla cry out beneath me as I leaned my upper body over her and bent her in half. With my hips grinding into her, I slid through every inch of her pussy in hard drives that made her gasp. I couldn't kiss her, not with the angle of my body on the hood of the car, but I stared at her as I fucked her. I willed her to feel that I wouldn't ever tolerate another man having designs on her.

That the only cock she would ever know was mine and the way I filled her so fully.

She whimpered when her orgasm neared, her fingers clenching and unclenching as she tried to find something to hold on to. My only regret was that she couldn't dig them into my ass where my jeans slid down. "Do you want to come?" I asked her, letting her thighs fall to the side so that I could stare down at where I pounded in and out of her perfect, pink little pussy. I pressed a thumb to her clit, just applying steady pressure as I took and took from her without letting her fall over that edge.

If she wanted to disobey me, then the least she could do was ask me to let her come.

She whimpered, thrusting her hips up to grind that naughty little clit on my thumb, but I chuckled and shook my head. "Please," she begged finally. "Let me come."

"If I *ever* see another man touch you, I'll kill him while you watch, Tesoro. Got it?" I asked her, and she widened her eyes at me. It wasn't often I referred to just how violent my nature could be, but I needed her to understand that there were hard limits for me. Things that would push me too far and make me expose to her just how much of a monster I was.

"Ryker!" she gasped, her lips parting as she tried to object.

"I mean it," I told her, bumping the end of her with every one of the hard drives that I made her take. Made her accept.

Just like I'd made her love me.

I was ruthless, giving her no reprieve until she gave me what I wanted. "Yes. I get it!" she cried finally, whimpering when I circled her clit in the way she needed and her back arched in her orgasm.

There were only a few more thrusts on my part before I spilled inside her with a roar. Everything went white, all of me centered on the spot where I connected with my woman. I hated immediately having to lift her off the car when I came down from my orgasm, but I couldn't let my cum leak on the paint job. Calla glared at me in an attempt to scold me as I sat her down on the desk where I'd fucked her a few days before, but I wasn't bothered by her anger. I understood it, even if I didn't agree.

Because I'd neglected a condom again.

And I couldn't lie and say it was an accident.

CHAPTER FORTY-THREE

CALLA

I smiled through my tears, staring at my son as he let me cut his hair. It wasn't like we hadn't done it since Chad died, but the previous cuts had been somber events.

This time he smiled and laughed with Ryker as I snipped away bits of his dark hair. Like he didn't have a care in the world.

It was not lost on me that Ryker gave him that. Gave *me* that.

Ines played with her stuffed wolf happily in the living room, watching her brother's hair fall to the floor in clumps as the boys talked, and I tried to soak up the happiness around me. It felt like every piece of hair that fell was the last piece of our lives floating away, leaving nothing but the new ones we could have.

That we already had, willingly or not.

When I finished with Axel's hair, my hand rubbed over his head gently as I went around to look down at him. "Go ahead and shower, my sweet boy," I whispered. He nodded, scurrying off to take a shower before bed. Ines had already fallen asleep on the couch, uninterested in the process of hair cuts. She wanted hers to grow to be longer than her waist, and she had a long way to go.

"My turn," Ryker grunted, taking the seat Axel had occupied. I smiled at him as he tugged me into his lap. Letting my feet dangle over the side as I straddled his thighs, I reached up, measuring out the length I wanted for his hair and making the first snip. "What's wrong, Sunshine?" he asked.

I sighed, continuing to cut as I tried not to make eye contact with him. I shook my head, because if Ryker had made one thing obvious in our weeks together, it was that he hated when I talked about Chad. I even understood it on some level, but I couldn't erase my worry for the kids.

"Calla," he warned.

I smiled at him. "I'm afraid you'll be angry with me. You don't like when I talk about him."

"You're sitting in my lap and thinking of another man?" he growled, making my lungs heave with a frustrated breath.

"It's not like that, I swear. I don't—" I paused, glancing into the living room to be sure Ines was still asleep. My voice dropped to a whisper when I finished the thought. "I don't miss him."

"Good," Ryker said with a smile.

"Ryker!" I slapped his chest, shaking my head at his infuriating jealousy. "He was my husband."

"And now I am, Tesoro," he said, bringing a hand up to cup my cheek as he forced me to look down at him. I abandoned my cutting, having no choice but to focus on his intent stare.

"He was their father, and now it's like he never existed. I don't want them to mourn him forever. I don't. I just—" I paused, shaking my head and trying to dislodge his focus. As always, Ryker refused, his eyes intent on my face as I tried to find the words. "I just want to do right by them, and I feel like I'm failing at that."

"Hey," Ryker whispered as his other hand caught my face and cradled it. "Don't think that."

"I would give almost anything to have had a few years to know my Mom. They had that, and I'm letting them forget him," I whispered as tears slipped down my cheeks and Ryker caught them with his thumbs.

"I'm going to be brutally honest for a second, Tesoro."

"When aren't you?" I laughed.

He chuckled, his deep voice dropping to a soft murmur as he tugged me forward and rested my forehead on his. "Chad wasn't your mother. Your mother would have loved you, and she would have treasured every moment she had with you. Your Dad wouldn't love her the way he does if that weren't true."

"Chad used all of you as a cover for who he really was. People don't suspect a cop with a wife and two kids at home to be a power-hungry sociopath. He never cared about the three of you, Sunshine, and I think you know that."

My lungs stuttered with the pain of that admission, and the fact that it wasn't entirely true. "I know he didn't love me. At least now I do, but the kids—"

"Were there to keep you happy. He didn't have to put in any effort, because you had what you wanted the most." I winced, nodding my head and sniffling back the final tears.

There was nothing else to be said with the weight of that as I went back to cutting his hair and made quick work of it. When I finished, he grabbed Ines off the couch and took her into her room and tucked her into bed.

"I'll tuck Axel in. You go shower off the itchy hair," I told him, turning to my boy's bedroom and knocking on the door. Even if he was only six, we had rules in place about privacy. The door couldn't be locked, but we still knocked before entering, in case he was changing.

So independent.

"Where's Ryker?" he asked as I settled into the bed with him.

"Showering off the itch," I said with a smile, letting him lean his head onto my shoulder as I cracked open one of his favorite books to read a chapter from. Before I started, I kissed the top of his head. "Are you happy here, Cookie Monster?"

His little head drew back as he looked at me, "Yes. Are you happy?"

I tucked his head back into my shoulder. "Yes, Cookie. I'm happy here."

And then I read my boy from a book about a wizard, feeling like my life had somehow gotten more complicated than fantasy.

NEVER HAD I ever been in love.

I loved Chad, in my way, but I was never *in* love with him, as cliché as it sounded to my head.

I'd finally fully and completely given myself to Ryker and forgiven him and convinced myself it was okay to not pick fights over stupid shit even though he pissed me off at times.

He made me laugh. He made me smile. He made me real.

And I could finally say that I was in love.

Everything I'd felt before him hadn't been real, not now that I knew the real thing. Now that I knew I would forgive him for things I had no place forgiving. He'd stalked me. He'd taken me and my kids.

But in the end, it led to being the happiest we had ever been.

I was preparing for my second class of the day and tidying up the studio room while Dante lingered in the back with the donuts we'd picked up on our way that day. Because when you were happy, sometimes you just needed a fucking chocolate donut. Or when you were sad. Or pissed.

There was never a time when a chocolate donut was inappropriate.

When my students filled in the room, I finished my tidying and went to socialize with them. Jason came in the front door, his hands tucked into his pockets and looking entirely too obvious in his white dress shirt and slacks, with his badge fastened to his belt. I stepped forward, even knowing it put me out of Dante's sight to intercept him. "Jason," I greeted with a nervous smile. "What are you doing here?"

"I won't waste time on small talk. I know you've remarried," he said, and I looked around as his voice dropped to a furious whisper. "I've arranged for Dante to be distracted in the back alley. I can help you." He took my hand, tugging me toward the front door, but I dug my feet in.

"What are you talking about? I don't need help," I told him, jerking my arm back from him and fighting to resist the urge to ask how he knew about Dante. About *anything*.

"Don't be ridiculous, Calla. Do you have any idea who that man is?" His gaze was too intent on mine, imploring me to see reason. "All you have to do is come with me and tell me what you know. I'll get you and the kids in witness protection, and we'll protect you. I promise you we will not let anything happen to you or those kids."

I didn't understand where it was coming from or how he even knew I'd gotten married. "Jason, I don't want to leave him," I told him, feeling the truth in the words. I meant it when I told myself I forgave him. That I loved him. There had been plenty of times where I might have jumped at the offer if I thought Jason could protect me, but that time had passed.

I wouldn't leave Ryker. I wouldn't break up the family I suspected would grow sooner than later, with how often Ryker conveniently forgot to wear a condom. I wouldn't take my kids from the man they were starting to see as a father.

"Calla!" he hissed, looking around the studio. "We don't have time for this. Just come with me."

"I know he may not be perfect and that he may not be who you would have chosen for me. But I love him, and I won't help you put him in prison. Now, the last I knew, you could not compel a wife to testify against her husband. You and I have nothing to talk about from here on out."

"You have to think about this," he pleaded, but my students were looking our way in curiosity and all the reassuring smiles in the world couldn't convince them there was nothing worth seeing.

"You're acting crazy. You need to leave. Please don't contact me again," I told him, and I turned my back on him and went to the rest of my class. Turning him away so harshly hurt, despite our differences. He was the last of my connection to the life I'd had with Chad, but it needed to be done. And I knew it was time to move on.

I was at the front of the room when Dante darted back into the back room, eyeing it warily as he glanced around at the students who had taken their places at their mats. "Did you see anything unusual?" he asked me.

I gave him a blank stare as I considered if I should tell him and Ryker the truth. I wanted to be honest, wanted to reassure him. But I knew Ryker well enough to know he wouldn't let it slide. He'd take away the small freedoms he'd given me if he thought someone tried to take me away from him.

I couldn't go through that again. I couldn't become a prisoner in the life I'd just started to love.

So, I shook my head, and I lied.

"Nothing unusual here. Is everything alright?" I asked. He looked mildly baffled, but went back to his seat.

It wasn't until after my class ended that I saw the text from Jason telling me to call him when I changed my mind.

Fat fucking chance of that happening.

Even if I had wanted to leave, Ryker would never let us go.

CHAPTER FORTY-FOUR

CALLA

I'd been on edge since Jason approached me, reading into every little thing Ryker did as a sign of his suspicion. I did everything I could not to act any differently than normal, going to painstaking lengths to treat him no differently than I would have before my deception. There were multiple times when I considered just coming clean, but the threat of what he might do was enough to dissuade me of it quickly.

It was inconsequential, since I'd said no. It shouldn't matter.

But I knew it did, and the guilt of my omission haunted me.

A few days later, Ryker was on the phone when I got out of the shower. My heart stuttered in my chest when he turned to look at me and his eyes were as cold as I'd ever seen. I froze, feeling like my life flashed before my eyes. I didn't think he'd hurt me, but that didn't mean I didn't fear what he *would* do if he found out I'd hidden something from him.

But I'd made my bed, and it was too late to turn back.

"Yeah, August, you know you're always welcome to come help," Ryker said into the phone, his eyes warming as his lips tipped into a smile. My breath whooshed out of me in relief, and I tugged my robe tighter around myself. "Thanks for your help," he said, stabbing the screen of his phone in frustration.

"You and my Dad talk on the phone now?" I asked, glancing at him with a little smile. He returned it, but it wasn't as warm as I'd gotten used to.

"Occasionally," he shrugged. I knew it shouldn't matter. My father was his father-in-law by all rights, but it just seemed weird that they would speak on the phone like that. Like I couldn't trust it. I narrowed my eyes on him suspiciously, wondering what he was up to. I'd been so preoccupied in my guilt, that it was entirely possible I'd missed Ryker's planning and scheming when I should have seen it right in front of my face.

If he was conspiring with my father, I'd kill them both.

"I have something to show you," Ryker grunted, tossing his cell onto the bed as he went to his nightstand. Fear pulsed again, wondering if it was the moment he confronted me about Jason. And then I wondered what I was doing in a marriage where I had to fear my husband in any way.

Who the fuck had I become that I loved him despite that fear?

When he handed me the folder of papers, I accepted it with my heart in my throat and flipped the lid. The Certificate of Adoption stared back at me, and I blinked in confusion before turning my head up to him. He'd filled everything out. Just the place for my signature remained empty.

I drew in a deep breath, trying to quell the simultaneous relief that I would not be a prisoner in my home again combined with my rage that he would be so presumptuous as to even date the fucking papers. I tossed the folder onto the bed, stepping into his space and placing my hands on his chest. "It's too soon," I said, staring up at him as I tried to make him understand. "We only just got married. They need more time to adjust before we throw this at them too."

"They're coping just fine," Ryker warned with a growl despite my attempts to keep the conversation civil.

"I don't think they're ready for this," I said, tossing a hand at the folder on the bed. "I think they need to see us together as a family more before we make this official in that way. Their father has only been gone for a year, Ryker," I murmured. "I know Axel puts on a good show, and I know he adores you, but he idolized Chad. He deserves to take the time to cope with that loss before we pressure him to move on too suddenly."

"Chad was *not* a good man to be idolized," Ryker growled, turning and leaving me in the center of the room as he went back to the nightstand.

"I didn't say that he should be, but Axel doesn't know that."

He grabbed a second folder, and he tossed it onto the bed so that photos spilled free. I opened it, dreading the contents. Nothing good ever came of the photos Ryker took.

In them, Chad stood looking stern and serious with Matteo and Simon, with Ryker, over and over again. "What is all this?" I asked.

"He made evidence disappear for Matteo. Covered up crimes and murders and pocketed money, all so he could benefit off the suffering of the people he swore to protect. I may not be a good man, but I'm loyal to the people I pledge myself to, and not just to myself."

The money Matteo passed to Chad in photo after photo couldn't be denied, but even if I didn't have the photos, I would have believed Ryker. He'd given me no reason to doubt his word, even if I couldn't trust him in other ways.

"Okay," I whispered, biting my lip as I tried to think of how to explain things to Ryker. That my ex-husband being a criminal changed nothing about the way the kids perceived him, or that they deserved time to grieve their father properly, regardless of what kind of man he was.

It wasn't for Chad. It was for the kids.

Ryker pressed on, ignorant of the fact that he wasn't making any progress in his attempt to persuade me. "At least I don't hide behind a badge and pretend to be a good man. I'm a criminal. A murderer, but I have been honest with you from day one about what I am, Calla. You made your choice."

"Did I?" I asked him. "Because I don't remember you giving me a choice."

His face hardened, and he took a step toward me. I held up a hand, for once putting my foot down. I wouldn't let him use sex to coerce me into agreeing with what he wanted. "I don't remember you telling me no when I made you mine, Sunshine."

"Sex is not consent to dating. It isn't consent to marriage, and you didn't even let me make a choice about that either. You just steamroll your way through me and what I want, and for whatever fucking reason I tolerate it," I snapped, running a hand through my wet hair as I shoved it back from my face. "I've forgiven you for everything you've done to me, but this is where I draw the line."

His chest rumbled with the threat of a growl. "He was a shitty father."

"He was," I agreed. "A shitty father and a shitty husband. But he was still their father, Ryker. You cannot change that, no matter how many papers you try to make me sign. If you want them to move forward knowing that you love them and that you are the only father they need, then you will give them time to come to that on their own terms. Not yours."

"I want all of you bound to me in every way. I won't let you cling to his memory when you're *my* wife. You sleep in my bed. You take my cock every night—"

"You just can't stop pushing, can you? I give a little and you just want to keep taking more and more!" I snapped. "When will it ever be enough?"

"When you're mine in every way."

"I'm already your wife, Ryker! For fuck's sake. This is not about me or you or even Chad. It is about you doing right by those kids. You want to be their damn father? Then act like one and put their needs first. *That* is what a real father does. Not throwing a tantrum because he can't shove adoption papers at his wife's kids to make him feel like the ready-made family he inherited is really his."

Ryker glared at me for a moment before he gathered the folders off the bed. "Fine, Calla. You want to let Axel come to me when he's ready for me to adopt him?"

I nodded, staring at him like he might snap. He was so close to the edge, balancing just before it felt like he might dive off the cliff.

He returned the nod, going for the bedroom door before he turned to stare back at me with a cruel smirk on his face. "Then I hope you're ready to deal with the alternative."

I swallowed. "What alternative?"

"You'll find out soon enough," he grunted ominously, stepping out of the bedroom and closing the door behind him. I stared at it for a moment before I crawled into bed, feeling like I'd cursed myself by admitting I loved him—even if it was only in my head.

Love gave people power over you, and the last thing Ryker Fiore needed was more control.

CHAPTER FORTY-FIVE

RYKER

I slammed the car door behind me, making my way into *Murphy's*. I knew the guys had my back, knew they'd cover my ass, but they kept their distance. Letting it look like I walked in alone.

Like I wasn't ready to throttle Antonio for being so fucking stupid that he got caught tailing Murphy's side piece.

I'd taught the goddamn idiot better than that.

The Maserati beeped behind me as the doors locked, and the front door to the pub opened when one of Murphy's men shoved it open for me. He was quick to get out of my way as I thundered through.

What the presence of Matteo and his men didn't soothe of my questionable ability to walk out, the twin guns strapped to my chest inside my shirt made up for it. I hated guns. They were the way lazy men killed, but I couldn't fight my way out of Murphy's without them if it came to that.

If Murphy hadn't requested me specifically, if he hadn't used Antonio's phone to call me directly, I might have feared for my life more. But he wanted something from me. He'd fixated on Matteo's famed Executioner at our meeting with him the week before.

He sat in the same place he always sat, staring up at me with a satisfied smirk on his face. In the corner of the room, Antonio sat in a chair with Sean's gun pressed to his head. He'd clearly been beaten and looked worse for wear, but he was a tough kid, despite being only twenty-two. He'd heal up and get back to work, I didn't doubt that.

"I am not a fan of having my woman stalked," Murphy said, pressing his hands to the table as he stood. His security looked uncomfortable with him getting closer to me as he walked around the edge of the table and stood directly in front of me. "Especially by a lackey at that. You could have at least done it personally."

I shrugged, keeping my face impassive as I stared back at him. "I was too busy keeping tabs on you to stalk your piece of ass."

Sean grunted from the corner, his face twisting in a grimace. I knew I walked the line, knew that one wrong move meant Murphy would order his men to put a bullet in my brain. But I wasn't a sheep, and I refused to act like one for anyone.

I'd learned a long time ago that the best way to survive in this world was to command respect wherever I went.

Murphy didn't glare, just stared at me in shock before his slimy face twisted into a smile and he slapped his leg as he laughed. "You've got balls. I'll give you that."

I scoffed, listening to the sound of Calla calling me Meatball on repeat in my head. Thanks to my Sunshine, I couldn't hear the word ball without thinking of her antics.

"There's no point in pretending we don't monitor our city. You live in Matteo's turf. You operate in it. That makes you his business, and he protects his interests in business," I said, staring him down. I hated having such a slime ball so close to me, knowing that he would take part in sex trafficking soon enough, if he didn't already. I'd wanted to kill him even before that, just because he coerced women into his bed through paying off their debts.

"I have to say, I expected someone a little less articulate of Matteo's famed Executioner," he commented, leaning back on the table with his arms crossed. "A mindless killer, someone who spoke with his fists rather than words." I smiled at him in response, not bothering to answer. "I didn't expect someone so intelligent."

"Making assumptions is your mistake. Preconceived notions of people only blind you to their truths."

His head jerked back as he smiled in disbelief. "A man of your talents is wasted as Bellandi's thing that goes bump in the night. He's turned you into a punchline, when you could be a man of true power, if given the proper opportunity. He's made you a dog, when you were born to be a wolf. Bellandi is too soft to do his dirty work, so he lets you do it for him."

"You're offering me a job?" I asked, and my hands twitched at my sides as Antonio's eyes met mine in shock. The kid had to know I'd never turn on Matteo, no matter what happened or what they offered me.

"I am."

"I could have been a powerful man if I'd been willing to stand on the backs of the vulnerable to do it. I was *born* to a life that makes your little operation look like child's play. What you have to offer doesn't interest me," I growled, and I watched his eyes narrow in suspicion.

"That's unfortunate," he sighed. "Take the kid, get him out of here and consider it a gesture of good will between Matteo and I. But if I catch him watching my woman again, he's a dead man. That goes for people who stalk me, too. Matteo should only assign people he views as expendable."

I glared at him as Antonio hustled from the corner and stood behind me. "If you have nothing to hide, it shouldn't matter, Murphy. But good luck. You'll have to find me before you kill me, and you didn't have the first fucking clue you were even being followed. You will never see me. They never do."

Murphy's lips twisted in a sneer, and I gave Antonio a gentle shove toward the door.

As soon as we stepped out the front door, Antonio heaved a huge breath of relief. "You're insane. You know that, right?"

I ignored him, unlocking the car and climbing into the driver's seat as he got in the passenger side.

"Just don't get blood on my wife's seat," I grunted, pulling out into traffic. The others followed, appearing from their hiding spots so we could return to the Bellandi estate to regroup.

Even with him in another vehicle, I could practically feel Matteo's fury vibrating through the air that blew in through the air conditioning in the Maserati. Antonio went silent at my side, remaining stoic despite the pain he must be in.

"Take some time off, heal up," I told him as I turned down the road that would take us to Matteo's. "When that's done, you come follow me around a bit. I'll teach you how to really blend in better so you don't get caught next time," I said. In the corner of my eye, he snapped his head to look at me sharply.

"Seriously?" he asked, his voice rising with excitement. "I thought you worked alone."

"Yeah, well, I'm getting really tired of stalking people that aren't my wife," I laughed. "I'd like someone to do it properly so I don't have to. You're as good a man as any." The harsh, impersonal words dissuaded the kid from getting too attached or thinking we had some kind of bond.

I didn't bond. I didn't do people aside from the few I considered family.

But the light in his eyes signified I had been entirely unsuccessful on that front. He didn't speak again, didn't thank me. He was too smart for that. And as soon as we pulled up to the Estate, he hurried around the back of the main house to the building where the security took their breaks. There'd be a doctor waiting for him.

Matteo's face was thunderous as he climbed out of the SUV Simon had driven him in. "When that fucker is dead, I'm going to dance on his corpse," he growled, stopping near the fountain at the front to warn me.

"That's if I leave anything to dance on." I grinned, loving the uncharacteristic fury in Matteo's body. He so often hid behind that icy exterior, sometimes it was easy to forget that it covered a well of rage just like mine.

"I can't keep this from Ivory anymore. Lino is planning on telling Samara so they know to be extra careful. Those two aren't known for keeping secrets," he warned, and I dropped my head back as frustration ate away at me.

"I have to tell Calla then. She needs to hear it from me. *Fuck,*" I groaned. Her fear for her children would mean I lost all the progress I'd worked so hard to gain.

"Good luck with that." He blew out a breath as he stepped into the house. "I do not envy you that conversation."

Neither did fucking I.

THE KIDS WERE ALREADY in bed by the time I got home, given that I'd had to talk over our options with Matteo and the others. We'd decided not to let off the pressure because, as unfortunate as it was, we couldn't be seen giving in to Murphy's demands.

We didn't back down, and we didn't take shit from a nobody who thought to climb above his place. If he'd just stayed where he belonged in his position as Liam O'Connell's second, we wouldn't have had a war on our hands.

Calla was awake, reading in bed when I strolled out of the bathroom from my shower. Even in the best scenarios, she knew not to get too close to me until after I showered when I got home. I hated tainting her with the filth of my work, so I refused to so much as hug her until I showered. Ines hugging me with blood on my clothes had been enough of a wake up call for me, even if Calla had felt the need to drive that point home. She glanced up at me nervously, smiling awkwardly before she turned her eyes back to her book.

I sighed, strolling over and taking it out of her hands to set it on her nightstand. She'd been distant since our argument over the kids' adoption papers, though we both knew it had started the day Jason snuck into the studio and spoke to her.

She still hadn't confessed, hadn't told me the truth, and her secret ate away at me every day. Even knowing that she hadn't taken him up on his offer, she still hid it from me. It made me wonder if she planned to reach out to him in the future.

I sat on the bed, and Calla straightened to lean against the headboard as she swallowed. I knew she thought this would be the night where I presented my solution to her refusal to allow me to adopt the kids. I could force it, could put the adoption through even without her signature, but it was something I wanted her to give me willingly. She needed to acknowledge that the kids were just as much mine as they were hers.

I knew she wouldn't like what I would do to buy her a little bit of time with my insane need to have all of her marked with me. I'd mostly respected her desire to wait initially, but now that we were married?

She was out of time.

"Is everything okay?" she asked.

"No, Tesoro. It isn't," I sighed. I'd never wanted to tell her about the looming war, but Matteo and I agreed that the women should all know the dangers of it. Tiernan was fond of using women against the men who loved them, so we had to take every measure possible in defense of them. "The Bellandis don't tolerate human trafficking."

"Okay," she whispered, and I knew that the information she hadn't known would come as a relief. Calla was so oblivious to that side of my life, because I'd wanted to shelter her from the horrors of it. I couldn't let anything extinguish her light. Especially not me.

"A loan shark has taken over a trafficking operation and is intending to operate within the city limits. Because Matteo doesn't allow it in his city, we're moving toward outright war between our two operations." She froze, her deep blue eyes going wide as she glanced away from me.

"Are the kids and I in danger?" she whispered, and it killed me to have to answer her honestly. To confirm the fear I saw blooming on her face. "Are *you* in danger?" Calla would always do whatever it took to protect her kids, and I could already see the gears turning. With Jason gnawing at the edges, it was beyond the least ideal time for us to be having this conversation.

But the conversation I'd had with Murphy earlier had only made one thing clear. The man fixated on me, probably saw it as a personal affront that he couldn't entice me away from Matteo. It put Calla and the kids more at the center of his focus than I wanted them to be. "You could be," I told her. "The kids have their security during the day, and you have Dante. As long as you stick with him and don't spend great amounts of time out and about, you'll be fine."

She jumped up from the bed, going to the window where she stared into the side yard. "Send us away," she said, spinning to face me. "It's the best solution. We can just leave the city for a while, and we'll come back when everything settles down."

I stood, prowling toward her as I tried to control my agitation. Everything with Calla was an excuse to flee, to shut down the connection that ran so strong between us. She was too afraid of losing me, of giving herself to me fully and then being alone again.

I understood it better than anyone. But I wouldn't tolerate it.

"I won't let anyone touch you or the kids, Sunshine," I murmured, wrapping my hand around the back of her neck as I kissed her forehead.

"And what about you? I won't stay here and watch you *die*," she argued, her voice catching as the traumatized fear she had of being alone came to the surface.

"Do you think this will be quick? A couple weeks on vacation and you come home and the war is won? Turf wars last years, they're drawn out and they are a slow process. I will not send my wife and children away for years where I cannot see them and hold them," I said, holding her tight when she tried to jerk out of my grip.

"Even if it's what's best for us?"

"Calla," I warned, fury pulsing through me at her insistence that she would be better off without me. There was no place in the world that was safer than with me. "I will *always* protect you, and there is not a single place you can go that will be safer than with me. If it comes to it, Matteo has invited all of us to stay at the Estate. But we're not at that point yet," I told her.

"It doesn't seem smart to put all of us under one roof. Wouldn't that just put a bigger target on the Estate?" she asked.

"It would," I responded. "But it would also enable us to center our defense. Nobody gets onto the Estate without Matteo's permission, Sunshine."

She quieted, and I finally let her go so she could look back out the window again. "I won't be locked in this house again, Ryker. For whatever reason. If that's how you plan to protect us, then you should just let us go. We can leave, and we'll go somewhere that no one will ever think to look."

"You're my wife," I growled. "Those vows are until death. You're naïve if you think Matteo doesn't have allies in cities all across this country, and enemies. Wherever you went, you would do it with the Bellandi name, but without Bellandi protection. They'd kill you before you even found a place to live." It hurt me to admit the truth to my Sunshine, to show her how trapped she truly was.

I didn't need a cage to trap her with me. My lifestyle did that all on its own. She nodded, turning and going back to the bed silently.

I let her curl up on her side, climbing in behind her and pressing myself against her back.

If I hadn't already wanted to slaughter Murphy slowly, the distance he put between my woman and I would have been the final straw. She made no move to sink into my touch like she normally did, too consumed by her own fear of losing someone she loved to even begin to understand her feelings for what they were.

He was a dead man, and I knew we would all fight to be the one to kill him. Hopefully, I got to play with him first. To show him exactly what it was like to be abused and maybe let someone rape him.

Tormented.

If I had my way, I'd keep him in my freezer for weeks to give him a slight taste of just what life was like for the women he sold.

And only once he truly understood would I let someone else put a bullet in his brain.

Especially when I felt the way Calla trembled with her silent tears of fear.

Death alone was too quick for him.

CHAPTER FORTY-SIX

CALLA

Being away from the kids got harder and harder with every hour that passed. After my conversation with Ryker the night before, I hated the thought of Ines being at the garage with my dad. I hated that Axel was in school.

Even knowing they had security of their own, there was nothing that would ever dissuade the worry of a mother when she felt like her babies were threatened. Nothing could quell the terror in me, but I didn't know if I had any options. Dante watched me closely. No doubt Ryker had informed him I might be a little more skittish than normal.

He must have warned him to keep a closer eye on me, because if I moved from the front of the studio where he could see me, he immediately stood and moved to the doorway with his arms crossed over his chest. Like I was stupid enough to run out of the studio and expect I'd get far. I'd considered going to the police, trusting Jason with keeping the kids and I safe, but I wasn't naïve enough to think protection came without a cost. As much as I wanted my kids to be safe from the mob war building in Chicago, the thought of losing Ryker hurt me with a depth that was physical.

I'd suffer it. For my kids. But I couldn't cross the line and see him put behind bars. I couldn't give him up and tell the police what I knew, even if it was admittedly so little it probably wouldn't amount to anything. That part of his life was so separate from the little bubble we'd created within our family, and I knew he was a different man when he stepped into that role.

I didn't want to know that man.

I just wanted my husband.

An arm came down on mine, making me gasp and jolt in place. Ness tore her hand back as I spun to look at her, jolted out of my thoughts so suddenly. "Are you alright?" she asked, and there was concern on every inch of her face. Over the past week and a half, Ness had become a friendly face at the studio. One of the students who I felt the closest connection with, though we never talked about the real specifics of our lives.

I knew she had a boyfriend and a son she didn't get to see much. It made me curious, since she never mentioned an ex or anything along those lines. It was like her son's father didn't exist, and I could relate to that.

Since I'd never once mentioned my dead first husband.

Sometimes, the past was better left in the past.

"I'm fine," I said with a fake smile. "I'm not feeling like myself today, but I promise I'm fine."

She glanced at the door to the back room where Dante watched our interaction with suspicion. Ness turned back to me, facing in a way that I knew Dante couldn't see her face or read her lips. The move was so calculated, so perceptive that it stunned me into silence. "You know, if you need help, all you need to do is ask. There's protective and then there's abuse."

I shrugged her off. "It isn't like that," I reassured her, touching her shoulder lightly. "My husband would never hurt me, and he certainly wouldn't let Dante do it either. His position is complicated, and he just wants to make sure I'm safe."

"A man can be abusive without ever laying a hand on you in anger, Calla," she said, and I looked at her with my brow furrowed for a moment. The woman who was awkward, who stumbled over her words and blushed often was gone. In her place was a woman who spoke as if she had personal experience. "I'm not saying he's abusive. I just wanted you to know that if you need help with anything, there are plenty of us who would be happy to do it. We women need to stick together, so I'm here. Even just to talk."

I nodded to her, avoiding the way Dante studied me. With a smile, I leaned in to hug her. "I appreciate that. I'll make sure to let you know if I need anything."

Seeming appeased, she stepped back and went to her yoga mat in the back of the room. Trying to make sense of when my life had gotten so complicated, I let out a deep breath as the rest of my students filtered in through the front doors. I couldn't even deny that there were definitely ways a man could abuse his wife without hurting her, and Ryker firmly crossed some of those lines.

No matter how much I reminded myself of the fact that I loved him and that he did those things to protect us, it changed nothing. He still crossed the lines, and he still had no notion of boundaries. His pressing me to let him adopt the kids proved that.

Adoption was something that should come from them. They should *want*

Ryker to adopt them, not the other way around. That he still hadn't presented his alternative to that didn't bode well for me, but I also wasn't innocent enough to think I'd dissuaded him from it fully.

Whatever alternative he finally presented, it would be nothing more than a bandage. A temporary way to fix the hole he seemed to think we could only fill when we were bound to him in every way. It drove me crazy. *He* drove me crazy.

He couldn't see that we were already his, and that we had been before there was any legal document to make it so.

I wished he could see it, and that he could stop pushing us for things we weren't ready to give. Because it meant that what we gave him wasn't enough.

That our love wasn't enough.

And that wasn't acceptable to me.

I DIDN'T KNOW what I was doing. Why I'd decided to help Ryker in the garage was beyond me. Lately it seemed like we ignored each other once the kids went to bed, his anger simmering beneath the surface and me avoiding it.

But the kids felt it. I saw the way Axel eyed us uncomfortably.

As much as I hated it, something had to be done about the path our relationship had taken. It hurt the kids to see us distant from one another, and even if I'd been willing to tolerate what the distance did to me, I couldn't handle the consequences for them. Axel looked at Ryker like he had his father, like he already had one foot out the door.

Ryker's frustration only seemed to grow with every hour that passed in silence, with me handing him tools and only asking the bare minimum of questions to fill the void. I didn't know how to close the gap between us, and I wasn't sure I wanted to.

As much as I hated it, that Ryker, who was as pushy as could be, didn't bother to fix the relationship said volumes about what he thought of the conflict. He blamed me entirely, as if our argument hadn't involved both of us. As if he hadn't crossed a line in making demands of me where my children were involved. I'd tried explaining it nicely, despite how much he aggravated me.

It hadn't mattered.

Ryker slid out from under the car, vaulting to his feet dramatically and tossing his tool onto the tool chest. Closing the distance between us, he took my hand in his and led me out of the garage. His hand was oil stained, slick as he threaded his fingers through mine and gave me no chance to protest. Keeping his steps quiet for the sleeping kids did nothing to quell the dread rising in me.

Fury rolled off of him. He was so angry with me, and I didn't want to know what was coming or how we would survive it. All I knew was I couldn't live in this uncertainty a moment longer.

Whatever came of it, we had to have the conversation we tried to avoid. He went straight for the bathroom, stripping off his clothes and getting into the shower as I washed my hands.

When he came out of the shower a few minutes later, he took my arm in his hands and studied the new tattoo he'd forced on me. He grunted, satisfied with the healing, and applied more ointment.

When he finished, I left the bathroom and went back to the bedroom to change for bed. I eyed my options in the closet, wishing I had more covering sleep options, but sleeping with Ryker in bed with me made things like sweatpants impossible. He was far too warm, like a furnace as he slept next to me.

When he came up behind me and wrapped his damp arms around my waist, I jolted in place and shrugged off his touch. The bathroom had been relatively safe, but the bedroom was the place I associated with sex. Every part of me felt too on edge to be touched, like electricity coated my skin and I'd explode at the first sign of physical pressure. We both knew that he often used sex to manipulate me. I wanted to avoid that, because I knew it accomplished nothing.

"I'm no longer allowed to touch my wife. Is that it?" he asked, and his hands gripped my arms as he spun me around to face him.

"You just startled me," I told him, giving a slight smile. It was bitter, we both knew it.

He reached out a hand, touching the corner of my mouth where I knew my smile went crooked. With a moment of silence between us, I glanced down at the fresh ink on his chest where he'd put our wedding date inside a sun. Part of me swooned over having such a physical claim over him, but the other half couldn't stop feeling anxious. The date was so recent, and it seemed like our marriage was crumbling around us. "So it has nothing to do with your visit from Jason?" he asked, and my chest heaved as my breath left me in a solid push.

"How long have you known?" I asked, staring up at him in horror. That thumb slid down over my chin, and his hand wrapped around the front of my throat as he walked me backwards.

My spine hit the wall, and I stared up at him in horror. While his hand didn't press enough to hurt, the threat felt obvious, and it made it so I couldn't turn away from the fury blazing in his bright eyes. "You thought I would put cameras in your home but not the studio? I've known since the moment he approached you."

I opened my mouth, my lip trembling as I stared up at him. "You didn't say anything," I whispered.

"Neither did you, my Sunshine. You hid it from me. He tried to take you away from me, and yet you said nothing. Why is that?" he asked, his voice quiet.

There was no mistaking the menace there, no disguising the fury that riddled his body until it was so tense he vibrated with it.

"I didn't tell him anything, and I told him I didn't want his help," I justified. I'd known that keeping the information from Ryker was a lie in its own way, but his hand on my throat while he interrogated me in anger told me I'd been right to worry what his reaction might have been.

"That's it? You told him nothing of value?" he asked, and his eyes dug into mine as if he could compel me to reconsider my words.

"Nothing that could get you in trouble," I gasped, shifting my head to ease some pressure on my throat when his hand tightened ever so slightly.

"That's not what I asked, Tesoro," he murmured, leaning down to touch his lips to my temple. He dragged them over my cheek as tears welled in my eyes. I'd felt fear before, thought I'd known what it meant to be afraid when I went to bed alone at night and worried that Chad's killer would want to finish off his family.

But it was nothing compared to the fear Ryker commanded when he turned into the man I knew he must have been underneath the facade he put on for the kids and I.

"Do you think it pleases me, knowing you told him you love me, but have never given me those words yourself?" he whispered, and my body froze.

"I didn't—" I broke off, horrified with myself when I realized that I had. I hadn't thought to ever voice those words, because to speak them gave them a new life. I didn't want to admit that I'd fallen so far that I could be in love with a man who took away my choice. At the core of our relationship, *that* was who Ryker was.

Nothing he did would ever change that, no matter how I grew to love him. So, the fact that I'd spoken the words as justification to not testify against Ryker stunned me. I'd confessed my feelings to protect him.

"You did, Sunshine. You told that *stronzo* you loved me." I swallowed, fighting back the tears that fell. The horror that Ryker knew the truth of my feelings, because I knew he wouldn't hesitate to use them against me. "If he comes near you again, I'll fucking tear him apart piece by piece," Ryker growled.

"Ryker!" I gasped, protesting when he gripped my shirt at the neck and tore it down the center.

"You are my wife. I'll not have the friend of your ex-husband interfering in our marriage and trying to take you from me. Tell me you understand me, Calla. On *this*, I will not budge. Not even for you," he ordered, and I nodded my head furiously.

"I understand," I whispered, and it seemed to calm him for a marginal second. Then he tugged me from the wall, tossing me back onto the bed as he tore the remains of my shirt from my torso and slipped off my bra with frenzied movements. "Ryker," I pleaded.

He ignored me and turned me to my stomach, grabbing my leggings and underwear at the waist and ripping them down my thighs. There was some awkwardness as he tried to pry them off my feet at that angle. His growl of frustration sounded through the room as he finally tossed the fabric to the side. There was a flash of blinding pain as his hand came down on my ass, and I shrieked, throwing an arm back to cover myself as I scrambled up to sit in the center of the bed.

"You asshole!" I screamed, kicking at the hands that reached for my ankles. He grunted, grasping one in each hand and yanking me down the bed until I laid splayed out before him. As I scrambled to sit up, his hand went back to my throat. Circling it with his palm, he used it to pin me to the mattress as I snarled up at him in fury. "You fucking hit me."

"I spanked *my* fucking ass. Have you forgotten who you belong to? You truly need a reminder so badly that you think I can't spank you when you risk *everything* we've built by keeping secrets?" I bucked my hips underneath him, trying to dislodge his grip on my neck while he settled between my thighs.

"You promised me you would never hurt me," I whispered.

"I also told you I would not tolerate dishonesty, did I not?" he asked. "I told you that you were mine, and I would kill anyone who tried to take you away from me. Yet, you thought it smart to look me in the eye for nearly two weeks and not say a word?"

I glared up at him, wanting nothing more than to smack the furious look on his face until it disappeared. With the masculine, dangerous attractiveness that Ryker wielded like a weapon, seeing him so angry only magnified that. While I hated it and hated him, my body also already betrayed me.

I wanted him, and I wanted to kill him all in the same breath.

The hand not at my throat slid through the valley between my breasts, teasing over the sensitive skin of my stomach and making me twitch with anticipation as he reached the center of me. His fingers barely teased against my flesh there, nothing but a tickle and a promise of what was to come. "I did what I thought was best for our marriage."

"Secrets will never be what is best for our marriage," he grunted, sliding a finger through my lips. The arrogant smirk that stole over his face was even more infuriating than his rage.

And it made me hate myself, because he'd barely touched me aside from manhandling me.

Yet, I was wet for him.

"Fucking soaked for me, like you always are, Sunshine," he smiled, and I jerked my hips to escape his touch.

"Like you don't keep secrets?" I accused, and his face twisted back to fury as he looked down at me.

"You will have my secrets when you can handle them, Tesoro. Not a moment before. I truly keep them to protect you, because my past is a place that no wife should ever have to know." His growl morphed into a groan as his finger dipped inside me. The towel around his waist had long since fallen to the floor when he tackled me to the bed, and his cock hung heavy between us. In that moment, no matter how much I wanted it, I saw it for the weapon it could truly be.

When he added a second finger inside me, shifting his weight down my body, I knew exactly how he intended to torment me. "Stop it," I gasped, trying to shove him off. His hand never left my throat, and I cursed just how short I was as his lips found my clit and he kissed it gently.

"I'll stop. When you beg for me to fuck you," he whispered, every syllable making his lips vibrate against me in the worst tease of my life. His fingers slid out of me before pumping back in harshly, finger fucking me harder than he ever had before. He held my eyes as he licked me from entrance to clit and then set to worshiping me in a furious energy.

He was all tongue and teeth. All anger and frustration. All ownership and possession. He brought me right up to the edge and then refused to send me spiraling over. He gave, but never enough. "Ryker!" I growled, hating his manipulations.

But I knew how the game was played, I knew he would keep going until I gave him what he wanted. Ryker was too determined to do anything less.

"Please," I begged, determined to end the suffering as quickly as possible.

I hated him, but I loved him.

I expected him to make me come. I'd given him what he wanted, but his mood was demanding as he rose from between my legs, pushed my legs wide, and shoved inside me harshly. I cried out with the intrusion, with the pain that came inevitably with taking him inside me. It had been too long since we'd had sex for his rough handling, but my body didn't care as it clutched at him and tried to take him deeper. I shoved at his chest, one thought persisting through my haze of need. "Condom," I reminded him.

"We no longer have condoms, Calla." He stressed the words with a thrust that sent him pounding through me. "I threw them out."

"What do you mean you threw them out?" I whispered, looking up at him with wide eyes. "We agreed!"

He pounded through my resistance and sensitive tissue, building my orgasm even higher despite my objection to his lack of protection. "I told you I hoped you were prepared to deal with the alternative, Sunshine. Did you think I would just accept your refusal and roll over like a puppy dog?" he asked, and his eyes went positively wolfish as he glared down at me. "You won't let me adopt *our* children officially, then we will have one of our own to bind us all together permanently."

"Stop it," I scolded him, but the words fizzled out on a moan as he worked himself in and out of me in furious strokes. He deftly avoided the spot inside me that would send me spiraling over the edge. "Children shouldn't be used like that—"

"I want us to have a child, you want a third child," he said, and I glared at him for his small reminder of just how thoroughly he'd stalked me. "I want it now," he growled, shoving deep. "And you will give me that."

His hips shifted, his body distracting me as he finally found that spot inside me and made gentle, teasing prods to it. It still wasn't enough to give me my orgasm, still made it hover just beyond my reach. "Please," I pleaded, and even I didn't know if I was begging for him to make me come or to reconsider his determination to get me pregnant.

"Tell me you love me, and I'll let you come," he grunted, slipping a teasing finger to my clit so he could torment me further.

"Fuck you," I hissed, but I moaned and writhed underneath him. Seeking just that little bit more.

"I already know it's true. You already know it's true. Just admit it, and we can move on from this madness," he said, circling that finger over me until I whimpered.

"Ryker," I whimpered, and his eyes held mine.

Watching. Waiting.

I hated him, but I loved him.

"I love you," I said with a broken sob, falling into my orgasm immediately when the words made him fill me with the heat of his own release.

He stroked inside me until I came down from it and kissed my lips gently. "I love you too, Tesoro. More than you'll ever understand." I glared up at him, feeling tears sting my eyes as he pulled out slowly. His eyes went to my core as I tried to close my legs, but he slid his hand between them as he touched his come that had slipped free. Using two fingers, he shoved it back inside me like the crazy person he was, and I laid there staring at him in horror until he turned and went to the bathroom.

The sound of water running filled the bedroom through the open door and I stared at the ceiling with blinking eyes wondering what the fuck just happened. When he came back, he cleaned me gently, while I laid there stupefied.

"Say it again," he murmured.

I waited until he laid down beside me and turned to rest my head on his chest. He didn't like that, putting a finger under my chin and tilting my face up to look him in the eye. Stretching up with one hand, I stroked the scar on his face. "I love you," I whispered. "I shouldn't, but I do."

"No more secrets, Sunshine," he whispered back to me, tugging me closer.

"Then will you tell me about this?" I asked, my thumb ran over the line.

He blew out a heavy breath but nodded. "I was just a boy. My father and brother were fond of whips. I got in the way one day, and my brother didn't pull his arm in time."

"Whips?" I whispered in shock. "Like for animals?"

"Another time, Tesoro. My life is better absorbed in small chunks. It's less traumatic for both of us that way."

I nodded, feeling heavy as Ryker's breathing evened out and he drifted off to sleep.

I dreamt of a little boy being whipped in the face.

CHAPTER FORTY-SEVEN

CALLA

I strode down the hallway of Axel's school, listening to the sound of my sneakers squeaking along the floor with the force of my steps.

Fury like I'd never known stressed each stomp, and even Dante was silent at my back.

A fight.

My harmless, smart, sweet boy punched the PTA President's son in the mouth.

The assistant nodded to me as she stood from her desk, moving to the Principal's office door. "Right this way, Mrs. Latour."

"Mrs. Fiore, and I won't even entertain the idea that you were unaware of my name change," I hissed, sidestepping her as she pulled the door open. "I filed it with the school two weeks ago."

As soon as I stepped into the office, Principal Blanchet stood from her chair and opened her mouth. "Calla, this is completely unacceptable." I held up a hand, silencing her as I moved to Axel and knelt in front of him. He let me tug the ice away from his eye, studying the swelling and purpling skin there as my rage intensified. "Mrs. Fiore!"

"You somehow failed to mention that he was injured as well," I growled as I spun on my knees and stood in front of Axel.

"I informed you he was in a fight," she said, crossing her arms over her chest.

"No," I warned. "You told me he'd struck another student on the mouth. In the future, if my son is injured in any capacity, when you call me *that* is the first thing that leaves your mouth. Is that understood?"

"He struck first. The ramifications of that didn't seem pertinent." Pearl Duncan snickered on the other side of the office where she hovered with her spawn of a son, but I ignored her in favor of making myself very clear.

"I will pull him from this school if you do not tell me I've been heard. What do you think happens to my husband's donations when Axel no longer attends the *Peterson School for the Gifted?*"

She blanched as she stared at me. "Mr. Fiore was a generous benefactor for months before he associated with you. As such, I would assume that his generosity would continue—"

"You assume wrong," I spat, turning back to Axel.

"This is all beside the point. Can we get to that little menace being punished? Look at what he did to my Oliver!" Pearl shrieked, and she clutched the strand of pearls around her neck.

"I'm talking to my son before I can even think about dealing with you," I shot over my shoulder. "What happened, Cookie Monster?" I asked Axel softly, ignoring her continued tirade behind me.

"I want him expelled!"

"Mrs. Fiore informed you she needed to discuss the situation with Axel. I suggest you quiet down and let her do that. When Mr. Fiore arrives, he won't be pleased to learn his wife and son have been disrespected," Dante warned, stepping between Pearl and I to form a physical barrier and give Axel and I a bit of privacy.

It was greatly appreciated, even if it might have seemed insignificant with Principal Blanchet's eyes on us, anyway.

"Disrespected? You dare to talk to me about disrespect when you come into my space. Do you have any idea who my husband is?" she asked, and I resisted the urge to chuckle and throw out Matteo's name.

I'd let Ryker do that when he arrived, and knowing he was already on his way gave me the courage I needed to finally stand up for myself against all the bullshit I'd endured at the hands of the bitchy, judgmental women in that school.

"Tell me what happened," I repeated, touching Axel's cheek. He turned his deep blue eyes up at me. Tears shone in them, and if I hadn't already been murderous, the sight of those alone would have made me positively stabby.

"He called you a slut," Axel whispered, and my body froze as I processed the words. "He said that you proved just how trashy you were by spreading your legs for a man like Ryker." I could see that my little boy didn't fully understand the implication or meaning of the words, but he understood enough to know it had been a terrible insult.

To both me and Ryker.

Dante's energy went haywire behind me, and I didn't dare to look at his face.

"Did he say those exact words, Cookie?" I asked Axel as calmly as I could. No matter how pissed off I was, I wouldn't do anything that gave him the impression my anger was with him.

He'd done nothing wrong, and I dared anyone to tell me that protecting his mother was wrong.

"Yes," Axel whispered. I patted his cheek gently, leaning down to kiss his forehead. Spinning around to face Pearl, I wished Dante wasn't in my way.

I wanted her to see her undoing written all over my face.

I tapped his shoulder, making my furious guard turn back to look at me. "It's alright, Dante. I'll take it from here," I said. He nodded hesitantly but stepped back to take stock behind me with Axel. My son immediately flourished under his care, letting Dante inspect the bruising in a way I couldn't.

I had a feeling he was more familiar with black eyes than I was.

I ignored Oliver's blubbering as he touched his cut lip and fixated my glare on the mother. "And I wonder where a six-year-old might have heard those words?" I asked her with pursed lips and a tilted head.

She glared back at me. "That's irrelevant."

"You're teaching your six-year-old son that a woman's value lies in who she spreads her legs for. That is hardly irrelevant, when he turns around and repeats your exact words in some pathetic, misguided attempt at bullying. You want to talk about my son being a menace? What about all the boys who have transferred schools because of Oliver's torment? He is a miserable child, just like his mother."

Axel chuckled behind me, and Dante's legs vibrated as he shook with his attempt to keep silent.

"I hardly see how I can be a miserable child. I'm a full-grown woman," Pearl scoffed with an eye roll. Always ignoring the truth of her son's bullying and always getting away with it because of how much money they donated to the school.

I suspected her biggest problem with Ryker was that his wallet was fatter than her husband's.

For people like her, it all came down to money.

"Then act like it," I spat in return.

"Are you going to expel Axel Latour or not?" she turned her attention to the Principal with a glare.

"My son will not be punished for standing up to bullies and defending his mother against the words of a catty, jealous woman who is so miserable in her own marriage that she has to condemn others for the choices they make that are *none of her fucking business.*"

"Calla, my hands are tied. I have no choice but to at least suspend Axel. He started a fight," the Principal said at my side, and my mouth pressed into a hard line at the look of glee that crossed over Pearl's face.

"You do what you have to do, but I assure you, I'll use all my resources to find a legal solution to the stain on this school." I pulled my phone out of my purse, tossing it to Axel where he sat. "Do me a favor, Cookie? Call your Aunt Samara."

"Why?" he asked, but he input my passcode and went to my contacts list, anyway.

"Because I believe Oliver's father works for Bellandi Enterprises. Let's just see what your Uncle Lino has to say—"

"That won't be necessary, Sunshine," Ryker said, stepping into the room with a smile. His eyes darkened when he glanced behind me and his gaze landed on Axel's injury. "Surely, this can be settled within this office."

"Thank you, Mr. Fiore," Principal Blanchet said with a flush to her cheeks. "The voice of reason."

"Careful, Pearl might call you a slut," I inserted with a sardonic grin. Her lips pressed into a line, but she toned down the way she practically devoured Ryker with her eyes.

For fuck's sake.

"Is that what this is about?" Ryker asked, turning his attention to Oliver. The boy cowered under Ryker's attention, even if he made no move to step toward him. "You called my wife a slut?"

"I-I—"

"Answer me honestly, boy. I don't much like liars," Ryker growled.

Oliver jumped and nodded his head. "Yes. I did."

"We have a zero-tolerance policy about violence," the Principal inserted. "I can't just let Axel off without a suspension."

"So, suspend them both," Ryker said helpfully. "I'm sure Calla would be more than willing to accept the punishment so long as it's fair. Oliver intentionally baited Axel into hitting him with an insult he knew my boy wouldn't tolerate. Unlike some, we raise our children better than that." He glared at Pearl, but didn't bother to dignify her by speaking to her directly.

Not even when she protested. Loudly. "That's preposterous! Words are not a fight."

"I agree that suspending them both is the proper course of action," Principal Blanchet agreed, taking a seat behind her desk. "One week for each of them."

"Fine," I said, nodding my head. I'd take Axel for some ice cream, and then he could spend the next week hanging out at the shop with my dad. A nice brief vacation from the hard work of school.

"You should know," Ryker said, finally looking at Pearl. She backed up a step, just like her son. "I'll be funding your opponent in the next PTA election." I resisted the urge to laugh at the horrified look on her face, and the knowledge that money bought elections, no matter the level.

As we turned to walk out of the office, there was one thought coursing through my brain. We could achieve so much when we fought other people instead of each other.

CHAPTER FORTY-EIGHT

CALLA

I fumbled through the next few days. Ryker seemed back to normal, like the fact that we'd cleared the air and accomplished something together meant all was right and well. He returned to being as warm as could be with the kids, without the dark cloud hanging over them. Like they had in the beginning of our relationship when I'd been more hesitant, they took to him like moths to the flame. I knew they needed what he gave them, but I couldn't shake the nagging feeling that something was coming for us.

That the worst wasn't over yet. I resented Ryker because he took me every night without protection. Having a baby should have been something we decided together, and taking that choice from me felt agonizing, though it wasn't like I fought too hard. I practically forgot my name once I had him inside me.

And the idea of a little boy with Ryker's eyes made me melt.

I sniffled back my tears, ignoring the way Dante watched me. He knew something was wrong, knew that the tension between Ryker and I had dissolved, but he was the one who saw me sniffle at random moments through the day. I didn't think he divulged that information to Ryker, seeming to respect that certain things I should be allowed to keep to myself. "Will it ever stop?" I asked him finally, turning to face him as I drank my chamomile tea.

"What?" he asked, standing from his seat to speak to me. My students gathered in the studio, waiting for the class to start, but as my fingers skimmed over my stomach that I knew would swell with a child soon enough, I couldn't bring myself to go out there.

I sighed, huffing a laugh. "Never mind. It doesn't matter anymore," I said, and the words were true. I knew, without a doubt, that the only way I could ever be free of Ryker was to see him in prison. And that wasn't something I could do to him. I couldn't betray him like that, not when I didn't really *want* to be free. I loved him, and I wanted to be with him.

I just wanted that to be my choice.

"Calla!" Ness called from the studio, and I stepped out. My eyes widened in shock when I took in the uniformed police filling the studio and the way my class either gaped in gossipy interest or fled the scene.

Dante was at my back a moment later, stepping in front of me as if the police might mean to harm me. "Dante Esposito, you're under arrest. Anything you say can and will be used against you in a court of law." I gaped in shock, watching as two of the officers marched up and guided Dante away from me.

"On what grounds?" he asked, shaking off their touch. He made no move to fight them, but he communicated that they had no right to touch him since he cooperated.

"Aggravated stalking of Mrs. Calla Fiore," one of them said as they neared the door.

"Wait!" I called. "He's a friend. He isn't stalking me." They glanced at one another and then continued on their way.

"You'll have to come down to the station and explain then, ma'am," he said.

"Call Ryker now!" Dante announced as he disappeared, and I glanced around nervously. If I wanted to run, I had my moment finally. My decision made, I spun, pulling out my cell phone as I made for the back room and dialed Ryker.

"The police just arrested Dante," I gasped as soon as he answered. "Should I take the car and go to the station?" It might cost me my job at the studio to leave unannounced, but I knew every second I spent unprotected was another second where I'd worry about my safety.

"No," Ryker grunted on the other end of the line. "Fuck! Do not leave the studio, Calla. I'll be there as soon as I can. I'm sending Bryan and Dario to you. They're closer and they'll get there first. You just sit tight, you got me?"

"I got you," I murmured as I hung up, staring at where the back door creaked open and contemplating calling him back immediately. When Jason stepped inside, I heaved out a breath of relief. "Was this you?" I asked, watching as he went to the door that led to the main part of the studio and tugged it closed.

"We don't have time." He said as he set two folders on the table where Dante usually sat, flipping one open. I gasped, turning my eyes away from the photos that stared up at me. I'd thought myself horrified when I found the pictures Ryker had taken of me while I slept, but nothing compared to the photos of mutilated bodies.

Nausea crept up my throat as Jason grabbed my face and forced my attention back to the photos. "What is wrong with you?" I asked Jason. Someone had carved into the face of the woman in the top left, the gashes continuing down her neck to where her throat was slit. The man next to her was beaten and bruised beyond belief, his face unrecognizable thanks to the swelling and his eyes missing from their sockets.

"*This* is who your husband is. This is what he does to people who cross the Bellandis." The photo in the bottom was of a little boy Axel's age, hand print shaped bruises curled around his throat. I touched my own, remembering the way Ryker had held me pinned to the wall as nausea filled me.

"You're wrong," I said, steeling my spine as I objected. "Ryker wouldn't. He's not capable of *that*." Even as I said the words, there was that lingering part of me that wondered. I knew he was a killer, but there was a woman.

A child.

What if I shared a bed with a man who murdered children?

Still, I closed the folder and sucked back a deep breath. The man I knew, the one who held me while I cried and laughed with my children, wasn't capable of such atrocities. "I want you to leave."

Jason sighed, closing his eyes for a moment, before he stepped forward and flipped open the top of the second folder. I didn't glance down at it, instead holding his eyes as mine flooded with tears. "Why are you doing this to me?" I repeated.

"I didn't want to show you these, but they're his *family*, Calla." Curiosity got the better of me, the family he never spoke of too enticing to resist. With a gulp, I glanced down at the photos in the second folder. These hadn't been laid out like a collage. They were just loose. The sight of the dismembered man on top was the first I saw, and I turned my face away. "This was his father." Jason reached down and snatched them up, shoving it into my face so I had no choice but to look as my body trembled with sobs. He tossed the photo to the table, showing me the second one where a woman had been strangled in the same way as the boy from the first set of pictures. "His mother," he growled as he tossed that one down. "And his older brother." I winced, the line drawn from ear to ear across the throat of a man younger than me too much to bear.

"Stop," I begged, turning away from the photos.

"You can't even look at them! Your husband killed them and you can't even look at them. They were a respectable family. His father was a senator in Maryland. He crept into their house one night and strangled his mother while she slept. She woke up before she died. She would have had to. And then once his father and brother discovered him in the house, he used the other son to control his father. He dismembered his father in front of his brother, and then Gerardo Fiore slit his own brother's throat." I froze, relief striking like a match inside me.

"My husband's name is Ryker," I told him, certain that there'd been a mixup.

Jason scoffed, shaking his head as if I were absurd. "You don't even know his real name?" he asked, and I sagged beneath the weight of that confession. "They call him Ryker because he belongs in the Rikers Island psych ward, Calla."

A buzzing rang in my ears, and that was the only defense I had for what I fixated on. "That's spelled with an I." Even to me, it seemed like such a trivial thing to fixate on.

I didn't even know his name.

"Who the fuck cares? You think those assholes are smart enough to know the difference? He slaughtered his entire family. One wife is already dead. How long until he gets rid of you?" I stared at him, I knew I did. But I didn't really see him. There was nothing but my stunned disbelief and a black fog that crept in at the edges of my vision.

I didn't know my husband at all.

"We have to get you out of here," he said, gathering up the photos and wrapping an arm around my shoulders. His dress shirt felt so warm against my chilled skin, too hot and intruding. I wanted to shrug it off, but I couldn't seem to find the will to move. "Come on, sweetheart." His voice softened as he seemed to realize that he'd broken something inside me. Something I didn't think would ever be whole again. "We have to get the kids."

"He'll never let us go," I whispered as he guided me to the back door. My legs moved as he made them, stumbling over themselves. "I can't go. It won't end well for me."

"It won't end well for you if you stay," he whispered. "Think of the kids. What do you think happens to them when Ryker gets sick of you?"

"He won't," I argued as his hand closed on the doorknob. "Ryker loves me and the kids. He won't get sick of me."

"You don't think his first wife thought the same thing?"

I didn't have to answer, because Ness flung open the door to the back room, eyeing Jason leading me to the back door. "Your new security is here. What do you want me to do?" she asked, and I knew from the judgment in her eyes she'd already decided regarding Ryker's guilt. I didn't know how she knew that my husband was a Bellandi criminal, but it explained her being so quick to offer me help.

She was insane for thinking she could help me and not get hurt, but it explained how she knew I needed that help. "I'm taking her to get the kids and go to the station. Stall them," Jason ordered as I floundered for a response.

"I'll stall them." Ness eyed his badge and then nodded, closing the door behind her as she went to the front of the studio once again. Jason's hands were tense on my shoulder as he shoved open the back door, bringing me to the unmarked car he drove that he'd tucked into the back lot. I alternated between jerking against his hold and feeling like my body was entirely disconnected from me.

"Wait," I whispered before he opened the door. "Just wait. Let me think. Jason!"

"What do you think Matteo Bellandi will do when he finds out you've been talking to the cops?" Jason asked as he put his hand on top of my shoulder and pressed me down into the seat.

"I won't testify," I whispered. It was true, even with everything I'd learned, I couldn't bring myself to help put Ryker behind bars. I didn't think I'd ever be able to look at him again, but I couldn't betray him in the way it felt like he'd betrayed me.

I didn't think there would ever be a day when I could handle his secrets.

"Let's just get the kids safe first, and then we'll figure out where to go from there," he grunted, pressing the pedal to the metal and getting us the hell out of the parking lot before anyone even saw us leave. I knew Ryker would see it all on his cameras once he realized I was gone, but I had to hope that I had the kids with me by then.

I just needed them with me so I could think straight.

I needed them safe.

CHAPTER FORTY-NINE

RYKER

The phone rang in my pocket as I strode for the car. As much as it killed me to leave Calla with men she didn't know, I'd had to wait for someone to come guard the dealer in the warehouse who was using more than he sold.

"Yeah?" I grunted into the phone as I answered. With my car door already pulled open, I sat while I waited for the person on the other end of the line to respond.

"Ryker, your wife is gone," Dario's voice said. I stilled, staring at the steering wheel in shock.

"What do you mean she's gone?" I growled, the deadly tone seeping into my voice as my body went cold.

"She isn't here. Nobody saw her leave, but we've looked everywhere."

"Look again," I said, hanging up with dread in my veins.

My fingers went through the motions, bringing up the security feed from the studio even as I couldn't think past my rage.

She'd left me.

The coincidence was too huge. She'd been alone for the first time, unguarded, and she'd made a run for it. She'd probably had a twenty-minute head start at least.

But I'd find her.

I thought the video feed would show my Sunshine sneaking out the back on her own, suspected with every bit of me that she left of her own volition. I never thought to see Jason shoving photos in her face, and while I couldn't make out what they were, the pallor of Calla's face gave me a pretty damn good idea.

Shit.

I'd explain. Whatever it was, once I found her, she'd understand.

But when he said my birth name, I watched all the life slip from my Sunshine's face as shock settled in. Of all the secrets that could bite me on the ass, *that* hadn't been the one I expected.

Calla didn't move, didn't fight or walk or anything as Jason dragged her out the back door.

Switching camera feeds came as naturally as breathing, giving me a view of the back alley where Jason's personal vehicle waited. When they got close to the car, Calla struggled finally.

She hadn't left me.

Not really, and the way Jason dared to put his hands on my woman as he shoved her into the passenger seat made my fury grow.

I called Celio and Marco to tell them to be on the alert.

No answer.

I called again.

Nothing.

Jason was a fucking dead man.

CHAPTER FIFTY

CALLA

With Axel still suspended, picking up the kids was easier than it would have been otherwise. Just one stop at Dad's shop, and I'd have them back with me and be able to think more clearly. I was early to pick them up, but my Dad never followed my work schedule enough to notice. He just knew I'd get them as soon as I was done, so when I made my way outside and buckled them into the spare car seat in the back of Jason's car, I regretted not saying goodbye to him. With everything up in the air, I didn't know how or when I'd see him again.

Ryker would know I could never stay away from my father, and he'd try to use that to contact me again. Ines was just as happy as ever, not caring that we were in an unfamiliar car or that Jason was with us. She'd never been as fond of him as Axel was, too young to see him for the connection to her father that he was.

But such was the life of a two-year-old who was as happy as my girl. Aside from her mostly random tantrums, nothing bothered her.

Axel was less unperturbed. "Where's Dante?" he asked.

"He had some stuff to take care of, so Uncle Jason offered to hang out with us for a bit. To make you and Ryker more comfortable," I said with a fake smile. The lie felt unnatural, but I didn't have a choice. Until I made up my mind, I couldn't tell him the truth.

"Okay, Mommy," he said, and despite his hesitation he didn't question me.

I didn't know how I'd gotten so lucky with such amazing kids, but as Jason drove outside of town to his house, all I could feel was immense gratitude for it.

I didn't know where we would go or what we would do. How we'd survive or if we'd find a way to be free at all.

But I knew wherever we ended up, we'd do it together.

As the shock wore off, I finally caught my breath. I could finally get enough air to just stop and think. I let out a deep breath, trying to calm the erratic beat of my heart as it warned me that something big was coming.

I couldn't do it.

I couldn't walk away from the only man I'd ever loved. There had to be an explanation.

I might not know his name, but I knew *him*.

Glancing down at the phone somehow still clutched in my hands, I discreetly called Ryker. "I made a mistake," I whispered when Jason's head snapped to me and he glared at the phone that I lifted to my ear.

"Sunshine?" Ryker said when he answered. "Where are you?" He tried to keep his voice gentle, tried not to do anything to push me over the ledge I knew he probably thought I'd walked to. But I hadn't. I never wanted to leave him.

I'd just needed space to think.

"Ryker," I whispered. "We're with Jason. He's taking us to his house—"

"Give me the fucking phone, Calla. Do not fuck this up for me," Jason warned. He reached across my body to snatch it from my hands, but I jerked away. Slapping his hand away from me, I called out to Ryker.

"Ryker, I'm sorry. I didn't—"

My voice drowned out in the next second when the entire world narrowed down to the crash of metal on metal.

To the screeching sound of a car's brakes, piercing the air.

CHAPTER FIFTY-ONE

"Calla!"

The crash that came through the phone rang through my ears as I pushed the junk car to the limit. I'd never longed for the Maserati more than I did at that moment.

Matteo and the others were behind me, catching up quickly in the vehicles that could outperform mine. I didn't even care if they passed me. I just wanted Calla and the kids to be safe.

"Calla!" I roared again as the other end of the line went silent for a moment in the aftermath of what had to be an accident. Pain thumped through my body while I waited. The thought I might lose them so soon, in an accident no less, making my body tremble with the flashbacks of all that I'd lost once before. In the same way.

She didn't speak, but I heard a door open.

And then, miraculously, I heard her voice as she spoke to the kids.

She was alive.

They were alive.

And that was all that mattered. I'd get to her soon enough, and we'd go home. I'd spank her fucking ass for letting Jason pull this shit. But they were okay.

A loud bang reverberated over the line, and then I heard her scream.

CHAPTER FIFTY-TWO

CALLA

The impact of the black SUV that came barreling through the intersection to hit the driver's side sent my head crashing into the passenger window and both the kids screamed in the back seat. I prayed that the car seats were as reliable as they seemed, and as soon as the car settled in the middle of the intersection, I unbuckled my seat belt in a daze and threw open my door. Smoke drifted up from the front tires of Jason's car, and I had Axel's door open when a bang sounded and glass shattered.

"Fuck!" Jason groaned. I snapped my head to the front, shocked to see him cradling his bleeding shoulder. "Calla, run!" he yelled, but I couldn't get Axel's seat undone. My hands shook too much in my terror, and a scream tore from my throat as arms wrapped around my waist.

"Mommy!" Axel yelled, his arms reaching for me as whoever had grabbed me dragged me away from the car while I kicked and screamed.

"Let her fucking go!" Jason yelled, and he finally shoved his door open despite the massive dent from the impact. The only thing that reassured me Ines was okay was the sound of her sharp cries through the air. It killed me I hadn't even been able to check on her before being ripped away.

When Jason moved to step toward me, I yelled at the top of my lungs. "The kids!" He hesitated in his steps, glancing back at the car in confliction. I saw the moment he realized he couldn't leave them, that he couldn't be in two places at once.

He couldn't save all three of us.

"Relax. We're under orders not to hurt you, sweet thing. Tiernan just wants to talk to your husband," the man behind me rasped in my ear. I rewarded him with a stomp of my foot on his as hard as I could. He grunted, but continued moving us backward. As we got closer and closer to a second black SUV, I glanced over his shoulder at the woman holding the door open.

Betrayal stung in a weightless feeling. A denial so instant it shocked even me. I couldn't have been so blind.

We hadn't been the best of friends, but I could never have suspected her to be capable of *this*.

"Ness?" I asked. My eyes landed on the woman standing next to her, immediately recognizing her as the woman from the photos in the garage the day after Ryker and I had been married. The blond mark he'd said he would stop stalking because it made me uncomfortable.

"Not her name," the blond sneered cruelly. Ness stayed silent, bowing her head and refusing to look me in the eye as the lackey tried to shove me into the SUV.

I caught a foot on either side of the frame and pushed back in my desperation to get away. I knew I couldn't get into that car.

I'd never come back.

We went tumbling to the ground: me landing on his chest with all my weight so that the man groaned, but another hand caught me by the hair and yanked me to my feet.

"Get in the fuckin' car," the second man rasped, dragging me over as the blond watched in fascination. I couldn't see his face, but I recognized the voice as the man who went to my yoga classes with her. Ness's eyes finally met mine, and I clawed at his hand gripping my hair, trying to get him to release me. But he held on tight, making my eyes water in pain as Ness turned away again.

"No!" I screamed.

"Shit!" the blond screamed suddenly, and she and Ness dove into the car, closing the door behind her as the driver took off.

Tires squealed.

I knew, even without looking, that Ryker had come, that the sound of doors flinging open was him coming to help.

The kids would be safe. Even if I wasn't.

Behind me there was a grunt, and the sound of a thump as something fell to the ground. With his hand still in my hair, my captor spun me to face where his comrade had climbed to his feet only a moment before.

He lay on the ground, immobile, and blood leaked from the gaping hole in his throat as if it had been torn out. Ryker stood over him, some kind of hatchet in his hand.

It dripped blood onto the pavement in a steady staccato that reverberated through the intersection. It shouldn't have been loud. Not with my captors' harsh breathing in my ear.

But I fixated on that sound until Ryker spoke. "Let. Go. Of. My. Wife," he warned, but the man holding me doubled down. He pulled a gun from his pocket and lifted it to press it to my temple. I whimpered, closing my eyes so I wouldn't have to see what came next.

So I wouldn't have to look at Ryker when I died. I wouldn't have to see the pain I knew I'd find there.

Wind grazed my cheek as something whizzed past my ear. Something wet splashed against my cheek and drew a startled gasp from my lungs. I was suddenly grateful I'd closed my eyes as the hand released my hair and the weight of the man behind me fell to the ground.

Gasping, I felt my legs collapse beneath me. I stretched up a hand to furiously scrub at what I knew had to be blood on my face. When I opened my eyes, the blank ones of the man who'd held me stared back at me, his body twisted into the position he'd fallen to. Dead. With Ryker's hatchet embedded right between his eyes.

"Can't you be normal for once?" Lino shouted, and I glanced over to the car where the kids had been. "What have you got against guns?" The car was empty, but Georgio and Matteo were in a car parked behind it, and the kids' heads bobbed in the back seat as Georgio and Matteo distracted them. I had to hope they hadn't seen anything, because it would have been traumatic enough to watch Jason be shot and me dragged off.

Watching Ryker kill the men who did it would be a whole new level.

I blinked, staring up at Ryker where he came to stand in front of me. He tore off a piece of his sleeve, using it to wipe the blood from my face. His face was gentle, though his eyes scalded me with how furious they were.

Shit.

CHAPTER FIFTY-THREE

RYKER

My wife bled from a wound on the side of her forehead. There was another man's blood splashed on her shirt that I couldn't clean as easily as I wiped it from her pale skin.

Flashbacks to the sight of Lauren crumpled and broken in the car by the time I got to her tried to draw me away from the moment. Only my pure fury could distract me from my relief that Calla stared back at me with wide eyes as I cleaned her face. When Enzo pulled up in his SUV, he jumped out and ran into the fray like only a true badass could do. With his pistol held like the military man he had once been, he heaved a sigh of relief when he saw me hunched over Calla's very alive form.

"Get the fucking cop to the warehouse," I told him, and Enzo only hesitated long enough to get Matteo's nod of approval. Cop or not, nobody fucked with our women. He'd signed his death warrant the moment he tried to take Calla away from me. That he'd almost gotten her killed in the process was just another reason for me to make him hurt before he died.

"No! Ryker, please just think about this. He's a cop," Calla whimpered, lunging to her feet in front of me. I'd known she'd fight me on it, but it didn't stop me from growing more and more furious that she would defend another man.

That she'd defend the man who tried to take her and the kids from me.

"He shoved you into a fucking car and drove off with you, Calla. I told you what I'd do if he came near you. You didn't dissuade him well enough. Now I deal with it," I growled at her, staring down at the frenzied look in her eyes. I knew Lino kept the kids occupied the best he could, but Axel made it an almost futile task by constantly trying to turn his head and see his mother.

My little man may have only been six, but I'd been much younger the first time I'd seen a dead body. He was made of more than I was, and he'd walk away knowing that I did whatever it took to protect my family.

Even if it was against Calla herself.

"He showed me your family," she whispered, and I could see the fear in her eyes. I knew part of it was because of the accident, but the knowledge of what I'd done had put distance and distrust between us I had to hope I could fix.

My eyes closed as I reached out and stroked my thumb over her cheekbone delicately, despite my anger. My poor Sunshine. A little of my rage shifted, leaving her and going to the one person I could blame for the situation.

My family had been my first kills, and the ones I enjoyed the most in all my life. I tightened my jaw, my nostrils flaring as my rage returned and I saw red. I turned my attention to where Enzo dragged Jason to his SUV. The man struggled with every bit of strength he had left, given the bullet wound in his shoulder, because he knew that he had fucked up epically.

I'd have his head.

I reached behind Calla, snatching my hatchet out of the man's face. A fresh spurt of blood made Calla gag and cover her mouth, and she turned her eyes away from the gaping gash where his nose should have been.

Turning, I strode for Jason. "Ryker!" Calla screamed, scrambling after me.

"Do not get in my way," I growled at her. She froze in place, staring at me in horror. I knew my words sounded more like a threat as my anger pulsed through me, more like I'd kill her if she got in my way than the truth. But even then, I wouldn't risk Calla getting hurt in my desire to get revenge on the man who'd taken my life, my history, and twisted it out of context to fuck with Calla's head.

To destroy my marriage and rip away everything I loved.

He tried to squirm away from Enzo when he saw me coming, his movements frantic as I approached with the hatchet in my hand. Grabbing him by the throat, I lifted him off his feet and squeezed. "Please," he begged, so desperate for the pathetic life that didn't amount to much. He had no family of his own, no one who would miss him when he was gone.

"Did you think..." I paused, tossing him until his back crashed against the back of the SUV. "That I would just let you drive off with my wife and kids?" The words came on a growl as I touched the bloodied blade of the hatchet to the side of his neck and watched him whimper.

"You don't deserve her," he spat.

"I'm very aware of that fact, but the best part about being a man like me is that I do not give the first shit if I deserve her. Because I *took* her, and I will kill every man who tries to get in my way." Calla whimpered behind me as Enzo left my side. I knew she'd disobeyed me again, could feel that she'd taken a few steps closer to me.

"No!" she yelled, and I imagined Enzo restraining her. "Stop him. I can't lose him, Enzo. Please don't let him do something that could get him arrested," she sobbed. A startled smile crossed my face with the realization that Calla wasn't concerned for Jason's life.

She was worried about losing me.

I glanced over at Matteo when the sound of sirens rang through the air, and Jason looked foolishly relieved.

The police who came wouldn't help him. I slammed the handle of the hatchet into his nose, enjoying the way it exploded in a spray of blood. "Get him the fuck out of here," I snarled, stepping away and swapping places with Enzo. The moment he released Calla, she ran forward and grabbed my shirt.

"I don't want to lose you." She gaped as she stared up at me. "Can't we just walk away from this part of your life?" I had nothing to say to that, because the reality was it was just as much a part of me as the man who loved her unconditionally.

I'd been raised in the shadows and in the shadows a part of me would always stay.

No matter how Calla tried to shine her light on me.

Enzo peeled out, getting Jason away from the scene of the crime. I led her over to where Lino waited with the kids and Calla broke free from my hold and ran for them. Axel was the first to bolt up, racing into his mother's arms as she collapsed to her knees and flung her arms around him. He cried in her embrace, burrowing into her in a way I hadn't seen him do before.

"It's okay, Cookie. Mommy's okay," she whispered with a sob.

I didn't know what had happened before we arrived or how Calla ended up fighting off her attackers, but Axel had seen bits of it. I suspected all of it. Ines quickly shoved her way in between them, crying in high-pitched sobs that made me question her ability to breathe.

By the time I found the ability to move, I dropped the hatchet on the floor of Lino's car. Then I wrapped myself around the kids' backs, closing them in tightly between us. Calla didn't protest my touching them even though we were both stained with blood. She just trembled as she clung to her children. "You were so brave," she whispered, kissing Axel's cheek.

His breath hitched in his chest, but I knew he'd be okay. I'd make sure of it, because my son would need to slowly become more and more involved in the family. Once we were at peace, I reasoned. By then he'd be old enough to understand that for every bad thing we did, there were three good ones.

I just had to make my wife see that.

"You need us?" I asked Lino.

"Nope. Matteo's got clean up covered," he answered, gesturing to where

Matteo stood shaking the Chief of Police's hand. Calla looked at him in shock, no doubt recognizing him as he nodded to her in acknowledgement. I knew the moment she realized that nobody would ever know there'd even been an accident.

"Then let's go home," I told the kids.

And so we did.

CHAPTER FIFTY-FOUR

CALLA

The reflection in the mirror didn't look like me. The massive blue eyes were too empty to be mine, too dark against the skin that was too pale—even for me. I thought back to Axel's plea as we tucked him in. It wasn't me that my son reached out to for comfort.

It was Ryker.

My husband. The murderer.

"Will the bad men who got away get caught?" Axel had asked, his face stern and solid and looking at least twice his age with the horror he'd seen that day. I'd sobbed, escaping the room so I couldn't upset him further as Ryker told him he'd make sure they could never hurt me again.

My eyes never left the bandage on the side of my head, staring at it and remembering the way it felt to have Ryker's fingers take such delicate care of me as he cleaned the wound when we got home.

Like he wasn't a killer.

I knew the moment he came up behind me in the bathroom, even without looking at him. His presence was always tangible in the air, the menace and danger and absolute power that rolled off of him was something that I'd never been able to deny. I didn't know how I'd convinced myself he wasn't all that bad. That his crimes must have been less severe. That it would somehow be okay as long as he only killed other criminals who deserved it.

Everything I'd needed to see was right in front of me, I just hadn't been able to handle the truth.

I still couldn't handle the truth. I dropped my eyes to the sink, gripping the edge of the counter as I tried to focus on my breathing. Tried to let air into my lungs that burned for it when I felt like I was dying. Like my heart was being torn from my body. Because I'd fallen in love with a monster.

"You keep a hatchet in your Maserati," I said, and the flat tone to my voice grated against me, making my head pound.

"I don't like guns," Ryker said, and there wasn't a single hint of remorse in his voice. Nothing to show that he regretted killing two men, or anything even remotely close to it. He stepped up to my side, and his hand reached out to touch the edge of the bandage. The sudden movement made me flinch back, stumbling over my own feet as I tried to put distance between us. His blue eyes darkened, his face hardening into a cruel mask. He took a step toward me, his lips parting to reveal his straight teeth as he spoke so low, so quietly I might have thought it my imagination if it hadn't been for the intensity of his gaze on mine. "You do *not ever* flinch away from me," he growled.

He closed the gap, and I held my ground. I didn't flinch the second time, but I released a slight whimper as he peeled the bandage back to expose the wound. He studied it, his fingers gently prodding the bruising around the edges as if testing the severity. I didn't know why, since he had no intention of taking me to a hospital.

I had the distinct feeling it didn't bode well for me.

"Did you really kill your family?" I whispered, and I immediately regretted the question. I couldn't handle the answer, wouldn't survive knowing—

"Yes," he said, so simply as he studied me. I couldn't breathe, couldn't think. "Shh, Tesoro," he murmured, his voice gentling with whatever he saw on my face. I still couldn't breathe, and it felt like he'd sucked all traces of life out of me with his confession. "Breathe, Sunshine," he ordered, tapping my chest as I finally heaved in a deep soul-wrecking breath.

His hand reached up, touching the pulse point on my throat and feeling it pound. Too quickly, too hard.

Too much.

Lifting me into his embrace, he brought me to the bedroom and deposited me on the bed, and the feeling of the soft sheets beneath me seemed to spur me into action. My limbs moved in a flurry of motion, struggling and shoving and kicking him off of me. "Still, Calla," he ordered. "Do not make me hold you down for this conversation." I froze immediately, hope surging with the word conversation.

I knew he'd want to punish me, as he always did, and that sex would be the answer. But there was time, time to think and find a way out of the situation. "My family," he breathed, and his eyes clenched shut. "Deserved everything they got."

I gasped when his eyes flung open, the blue of them seeming to shine even brighter than normal. "I wanted nothing to do with the family business," he scoffed. "My father and his friends had a penchant for children, and my father had the unique skill of training them to be obedient. He trained my brother and I to follow in his footsteps, and to do that he made us watch. My mother just let it happen. She didn't stop any of it." Tears flooded my eyes, but they couldn't seem to fall.

I could only imagine the horror of being raised by a man who trained children for sexual servitude. "Ryker—"

"My brother was a willing participant by the time he turned fourteen. Lost his virginity to a girl in our basement, that he and my father had painstakingly trained. I was only eight at the time. So in the face of my brother's success, as my father put it, I was the continual disappointment. Especially when I'd yet to fuck any of them by my eighteenth birthday. I didn't want to learn. I refused to train the kids they brought in. I had nightmares every night of the things they did in that basement. So, I ran. I just left. I didn't report what I'd seen, because I knew enough to know they would make me disappear before I could do something that stupid. I thought if I ran, they'd let me live my life in peace," he rasped, hanging his head in shame. "I was wrong and stupidly naïve. A year and a half later, my brother ran Lauren off the road and killed her and the baby when I refused my father's attempts to draw me back to the family business."

"I—" I didn't know what to say. What would I have done in that situation? I wanted to say that I'd have gone to the police, but having seen the power Matteo wielded over the Chief of Police, I understood with more clarity that it would have been pointless and dangerous. And the FBI offered no more help when a very powerful man, like a senator, were involved.

"After that happened, I came to the Bellandis. Matteo's father offered to help me if I agreed to work for him, so he trained me to fight. I'd already put on muscle mass since leaving home, so it was just a matter of teaching me to fight and torture and kill. I learned on the streets, and when I was ready, he gave me permission to kill them. He made it go away with the police, even if it was outside his territory. The Bellandi name reaches everywhere," Ryker explained. "So yes, Sunshine. I killed my family. I *massacred* my family, and if Franco Bellandi had allowed it, I'd have massacred all the men I knew who bought the kids my father trained."

"I'm so sorry for what you went through," I whispered, but I still couldn't move to embrace him. I felt frozen solid as I stared at him, and the horrors he must have seen at such a young age made me cry.

I wanted to comfort him, but I didn't know how to comfort something that powerful. That overwhelming.

There was nothing that could be said in the face of that kind of pain.

"You should have come to me and asked me after Jason showed you those pictures. Not let him drag you to his car and pick up the kids to leave me." The sudden shift back to anger was startling. I'd known it would come, had known that there would be hell to pay if he caught me.

"I was in shock," I whispered, and it was true. I'd never decided to leave him. I'd never made *any* decision, but I'd known I needed time to figure it out.

"You left with another man!" he yelled, and I clenched my eyes shut to avoid the intense way he glared at me. "You should have fought harder."

"It wasn't like that!" I protested. "I just needed to think, and nobody would let me think."

"You put yourself at risk. You put the kids at risk," he plowed on, as if he didn't care to hear anything I had to say. So lost in his rage, my voice went unheard.

"I was with a cop. I didn't think we would be in danger," I told him. "Who attacks a cop in the middle of the day?"

"Because you know nothing about this business," he said, reaching out a hand to stroke over my cheek. I winced, the proximity to my wound making it pulse with pain. "*That* is exactly why you stay with your fucking security and let me keep you safe. Can you take one goddamn second to think about what it was like for me to see that car, and fucking know you'd been inside it? The last accident I saw, I pulled my dead wife's body out of," he seethed.

I shuddered, an apology spilling from my lips. "I'm so sorry, Ryker."

"I don't want your fucking 'sorry,'" he growled, moving so suddenly I didn't have time to react. He shoved the dress up my thighs and tore my underwear down. "I want you to promise me you won't do that again."

I couldn't give the words he wanted, not without addressing the other secret, the other betrayal that had humiliated me and made me doubt *everything*. "I didn't even know your name," I whispered.

"The name my father gave me is not my name. I didn't hide it from you, Sunshine. I just do not think of myself as his son. Now, stop stalling and promise me," he growled as he spread my legs wider.

"Ryker," I begged, wincing when he slid his hips between my thighs and freed himself from his shorts. "I didn't know. I won't risk our safety again. I promise."

Grabbing my chin, he held my face as he stared down at me and his other hand reached down to glide himself through me. "Tell me no."

I didn't. Couldn't seem to find the words, even though there'd been no foreplay, and I knew I wasn't ready to take him. He guided himself to my entrance, shoving inside slowly. I wasn't nearly wet enough.

It burned. It hurt. It made me feel alive, made me feel something.

I whimpered, but I couldn't find the words to tell him to stop. I couldn't decide if I even wanted to, despite the pain. Part of me, deep down, knew I deserved his punishment. Knew that my lack of trust in him could have been responsible for my own death. For the kids' deaths.

"You will *never* leave me again, Tesoro. Tell me you understand," he ordered, as he finally seated himself inside me.

I shivered beneath him, feeling him press against all of me and knowing that when I told him what he wanted to know, he'd take me. He'd break me. He'd find a way to put me back together again when he was done with me, but the me that had existed that morning would be gone.

I'd be his. Even all the little pieces of my soul that I'd tried to keep for myself.

I knew, without a doubt, that it had never been meant to end any other way. Ryker didn't know how to love without *consuming*.

"I understand," I said.

He dropped his thumb to my clit, circling it as he stayed planted inside me. Building up my desire, making me wet enough that he could take me the way he wanted without doing too much damage. "I'm going to fuck you until you're pregnant," he growled, and I stared up at him with wide eyes. "I hope you weren't intending to sleep tonight, Sunshine."

I gasped when he punctuated it with a roll of his hips, testing my slickened channel. We both groaned, and he drew his hips back with a satisfied smile. Both hands went to my hips, lifting me to grind himself inside me before he drew back in a long, never ending withdrawal where I felt every inch of him. His piercing dragged through me, adding another sensation to his torment. When he shoved back inside, there was no part of me where I didn't feel him. With him kneeling between my legs, I had the perfect view of the glistening muscle, of every one of the ridges of his abs as he used them and worked them. He slid through my tender tissue, making sure I was ready one last time.

And then he fucked me, holding true to the promise in his eyes. Each thrust inside me went straight to my soul, like I could feel the very connection between us as it pulled taut. The sight of his chest starting to glisten with sweat from his exertion was a reminder of how he'd looked with blood staining the olive skin at his neck and on his hands after he saved me.

Ruthless. Savage.

Mine.

"Never again, Calla," he repeated, and as his hand reached up to touch my bottom lip. I realized he'd yet to kiss me, and the desire to feel his lips on mine was jarring. I needed it, needed to know that he still loved me despite his anger with me.

He smiled at me as his hips moved, as if he could see the desire. "What will you give me?" he asked, his cock spearing through me with every hard thrust that went straight to the end of me and drew a gasp from my lips.

I didn't know what would tumble free. Had no clue what the answer would be until the words were spoken. "A baby," I whispered. I gasped as soon as I heard the words, and his face darkened to a look of complete and utter possession.

He dropped his weight to mine, barely restraining himself from crushing me as he moved within me. I wrapped my legs around his waist, drawing him in as deep as he could go in my desperation to feel his lips on mine. "You'll already give me that, Tesoro," he whispered. "You'll sign the adoption papers too," he ordered, and I glared up at him.

I nodded my head hesitantly. "You'll ask the kids first." I still questioned if it would be the right thing to do, but in the wake of what Axel had seen, I knew it would comfort him to know that Ryker was his father legally. That he would always protect us like he had that day.

I wouldn't let my own fears get in the way of our safety and our family again.

Ryker thrust his hips inside me repeatedly, and when his lips finally touched mine, it was a mix of tongue and teeth.

Biting, licking, shredding my very soul.

I hugged him to me, needing every inch of him against me. Needing to feel him and the reminder I was alive.

That I was safe.

When he nibbled on my bottom lip, it sent me spiraling over the edge into an orgasm that stole the words from my throat and all I heard was the buzzing in my head. Ryker roared out his own climax, branding me with his heat and stroking his hands over my skin as he leaned just a little of his weight off me.

He made no motion to move, didn't seem to have any interest in separating our bodies as he rolled to his back and pulled me onto his chest without ever dislodging himself. "Mine," he murmured, and I barely heard it as I drifted off to sleep.

He woke me up an hour later.

CHAPTER FIFTY-FIVE

CALLA

Awareness came slowly, like the sun rising over the horizon. The tightness in my body, the pain in every inch of muscle seeped in through my consciousness as I tried to stretch.

"Easy," Ryker whispered. "You'll hurt for at least a few days."

I nodded my head, and even that motion felt like too much motion for my neck. Lifting my arm to touch the ridges of his abs, my arm protested the motion. My stomach muscles tightened and spasmed with the movement, but I traced his abs with a delicate finger.

Cataloguing all the little scars that littered his body. They were faint, too old to be noticeable unless I really looked for them.

But after his confession the night before, I saw them all.

I saw them for what they were. The countless abuses he'd suffered instead of hurting other children. There was no one in the world my kids would be safer with.

"He showed me pictures of other bodies too," I admitted. "Did you kill them too?"

"No," he said with a sigh.

"How can you be so sure?" I whispered back. "You know nothing about the victims. How could you possibly—"

"I know, because I don't leave bodies behind, Sunshine," he said, gently rolling me to my back so he could lean over me. He kept his weight off me, his skin barely brushing against mine as he cupped my face in his massive hands. "They couldn't have been mine."

I swallowed, picturing all the ways to dispose of a body so thoroughly. All the crime shows I'd watched, all the horrific scenarios involving acid and pigs, didn't help the vision forming in my head. "Women and kids?"

"Never, Tesoro. I have never killed a woman or a child aside from my mother."

My breath whooshed out in a rush as I contemplated my next words. I didn't know what good they would do, but it felt too significant not to mention. In my adrenaline rush and fear from the accident, I'd neglected to tell him. "Ness was there," I whispered.

"Who?" he asked.

"Remember that new student I told you about? The one who came with a man and you went into a jealous rage. That's what she told me her name was, but I don't think anything she told me was real. She was at the accident and one of the men you killed was the one who came with her. But they were with the blond from your photos," I said the words softly, guilt filling me. Maybe, if I hadn't been so jealous, the accident never would have happened. Ryker might have had eyes on her. He might have been able to expect whatever it was they were planning.

His body went still as he froze above me, staring down at me intently. "What photos?"

"The ones I saw in the garage. The woman you followed for a job for Matteo. I don't know why they were there. I didn't exactly have time to chat, but it was them."

"And you're sure? There's no doubt? This is important, Calla."

I paused, contemplating the words to make him understand. "I thought you were having an affair when I saw them. I'll never forget her face, and there was no mistaking her." Ryker kissed me gently, vaulting from the bed to stand. "Wait there's something else."

He spun, staring at me as he tugged his pants on. "What is it?" I smiled at the gruff note to his voice. The impatience as he wanted to get to work with whatever information I'd given him. If it really was that important, I imagined he needed to call Matteo.

"There was something..." I paused, biting my lip as I struggled to sit up. My body protested with every movement, and Ryker stopped to help me. I ignored the concern in his eyes to push forward. "Off with Jason. Once my shock wore off, I knew he was too impatient. It was just too sudden, too rushed. When I called you, he told me he wouldn't let me ruin it for him."

"Any idea what he meant?" he asked, his body going alert as he watched me climb from the bed. I watched the gears turn in his head, watched him try to puzzle the pieces together in a way that I was incapable of doing because I didn't have all the information.

"None, but it felt important," I told him. He leaned in, kissing me firmly before he grabbed his phone off the nightstand and turned for the door.

"Ryker," I called. "I want to know what he was up to, and why Ness played me like that. I deserve that much."

He smiled at me, a bright grin that seemed entirely disbelieving. "Why's that, Tesoro?"

My lips pressed into a thin line. The next words that left my mouth sounded so foreign, I knew that the day before had changed me. I understood the rage he felt, the pulsing need to hurt. "So that when the time comes, I'll know they deserve everything you do to them."

CHAPTER FIFTY-SIX

My waterproof boots carried me inside the warehouse, and it felt like I walked toward my destiny as the blood-stained hatchet swung at my side. We rarely went into an interrogation without all the information we could find, and what our investigator, Campbell, had dug up in Jason's finances was disturbing on so many levels.

Matteo didn't know what I knew. Not yet. He wouldn't interfere, I knew, even if the death of a cop would be inconvenient for him to cover up. Matteo pushed off the wall next to the freezer door, greeting me without the guard he never left the house without. "Simon's tying up our new friend," he explained, and I knew he didn't mean Jason.

Jason had been sitting in the warehouse since Enzo dropped him off the day before. "The driver?" I asked.

"Yes. We didn't get the women," he said with a shake of his head. "I'm sure you can imagine that Tiernan put them both under lock and key."

"I never should have stopped tailing her," I grunted, shaking my head in disgust. I'd let Calla sway me, her jealousy over me appealing to me on such a deep level that I'd not done my job properly.

"You were made," Matteo grunted. "It wouldn't have made a difference. They would have just found another way." He reached forward, touching my shoulder in a rare display of just how much he valued his family. "Calla's safe. The kids are safe. Now go in there and send Murphy a message not to fuck with our women."

I nodded, tucking my concern and regret back behind the mask of psychotic energy I wore so often. I always enjoyed torture. His eyes went over my shoulder briefly.

"You sure about this?" he asked, and I knew he was as skeptical as I'd have been if the roles were reversed.

But I'd enjoy this more than usual. I just hoped Calla could look beyond it. "Stay out of sight," I tossed over my shoulder.

We went into the freezer, one after another. Jason sat quietly, glaring at us like he might have some kind of power. I was sure he was familiar with wielding the power over others, not because he was a cop.

But because he was a dirty one.

I ignored him, stepping up to the driver where he trembled in his chair. His body was already slick with sweat, from the exertion of fighting Simon and Matteo when they snatched him out of whatever hell hole he'd desperately tried to hide in. "You are going to tell me what the fuck Tiernan wanted with my woman and my kids." I pointed the hatchet at him, watching him try to flinch back. If the chair hadn't been bolted to the floor, he might have knocked his own ass out.

Wouldn't that be anticlimactic?

"They aren't your kids!" Jason yelled from his chair, but I continued to ignore him. Matteo and Simon stayed silent in the back. Even under normal circumstances, this would have been my show. It was my wheelhouse, my warehouse, my skill set.

But given that it had been my woman in danger? It was just *mine*.

"We didn't want the kids," the driver wheezed when the blade of the hatchet touched his neck. "Just the woman."

"And why was that?" I asked, letting the blade drag across the side of his neck so that blood welled under the shallow cut.

"Murphy just wanted to talk to you," he said, glancing at Matteo in the corner. "Wanted you more agreeable to shifting your allegiance to him. He figured if he had her, then you'd consider it. She was just the leverage."

"The only thing I'd consider is how quickly I could cut him into a thousand pieces before he bled to death," I snarled, swinging my arm back as far as I could.

The guy clenched his eyes shut as he pissed himself. "Wait! He was in on it." He nodded to Jason, who shot him a horrified look. "He works for Murphy. He has for years."

"I know," I whispered with a cruel smile. I swung my hatchet through the air, colliding with the side of his neck with all the strength I had. Blood sprayed all over me, splashing onto Jason where he screamed like the girl he was. It disappointed me when the axe didn't go all the way through, so with the driver's blank eyes staring back at me, I swung again.

It was only when his head rolled to the floor that I turned my attention to

Jason. He looked at me like I was something out of his worst nightmares, and with the amount of blood I could feel on my skin, that probably wasn't far off.

"You're a fucking psychopath!" he yelled.

"Funny. Calla likes to question my sanity too," I mocked, stepping closer to him. When my blade touched his throat, I turned back to Matteo and Simon. I nodded to Matteo, and he went to the freezer door.

Calla stepped in hesitantly, her eyes instantly going to the severed head on the floor. She swallowed visibly, but made her way to me as she looked away from the head and the matching corpse.

I hadn't wanted her there, hadn't wanted her to see that part of me. But she'd already seen a glimpse the day before, and at her insistence, I couldn't say no.

Still, Matteo and Simon eyed her like she would run at any moment and they'd need to chase her down. Holding out a hand, I waited for her to put hers in it willingly and then drew her to my side. "Calla, help me," Jason rasped, pleading to my petite wife with all the emotion he could fake.

"Why?" she whispered, and the genuine pain in her voice only enraged me further. "We trusted you."

"He promised he wouldn't hurt you," Jason said. Matteo scoffed behind me, and I could practically feel him roll his eyes.

"You don't think the accident itself hurt me? You don't think watching a man drag me off was traumatic for the kids? That was Axel's greatest fear, and you helped set it up." The accusation rang through the room, her words holding strong despite the tremble to her lips. She might not have particularly liked Jason as a person, but she'd put her faith in him during a time when she needed that connection to her dead husband.

She didn't need either of them anymore.

"You deserve what's coming," she whispered, and Jason flinched like she struck him physically.

"Calla," he murmured, and for a brief moment I wondered if he actually cared about her in his own way. I quickly decided it didn't matter.

"I'll see you at home when you're done," Calla said, turning to me to kiss me briefly. "Don't take too long."

"Calla!" Jason shouted, his face twisting with outrage. "You can't just leave me here."

She turned for the freezer door, grabbing the handle and tugging it open. "Watch me," she spat as she stepped through. I had a brief glimpse of Dante waiting for her in the main part of the threshold, draping his jacket over her shoulders as she shivered. Blood and murder weren't the norm in Calla's life, and I hoped she'd never have to see something like it again.

But with war on the horizon, she needed to know exactly who I was. Exactly what I would do to protect her and the kids. With Murphy having used her to get to me once, Dante, Sadie and I would all start training her to defend herself.

She hadn't done all that poorly after the accident, but she could have done better with training.

Once the door closed completely, I waved a hand at the headless corpse and turned back to Matteo and Simon. "Do you think that was a quick death?" I asked them.

Simon looked confused, but Matteo chuckled in amusement. "It took ten seconds, so I'd say so. Yes."

"Good," I grunted, turning back to Jason. "Calla made me promise I'd make it quick when she gave me her blessing to kill you. You should be grateful she's more merciful than I am. Good thing she didn't make me promise it wouldn't be gruesome, hmm?"

"Fuck you and her mercy."

"What was he going to pay you? To betray your friend's wife and send her right into the clutches of someone who would hurt her in a heartbeat? Did you even feel a semblance of guilt? Or did you think it was okay because she wouldn't find out you'd set her up and staged the accident?"

He didn't answer me, choosing to pant his breaths like a dog in heat while he struggled against his binds. "She'll never be yours, you know? Not really," he snarled, and I knew he meant to allude to the fact that he thought Calla belonged to Chad. He might have been the first to have her, but I'd be the fucking last.

That was what mattered.

"Trust me, for that woman to walk into a blood-stained chamber with a headless corpse and kiss me? She's mine alright," I smirked, lining up my hatchet. "Any last words?"

"Murphy will gut you alive," he growled.

"I'd like to see him try," I returned, and the hatchet whizzed through the air with more force. Anger and rage for the betrayal he'd served Calla fueled my strike.

His head rolled with one.

Nothing sent a message like two heads in a box.

CHAPTER FIFTY-SEVEN

CALLA

Ines and I baked cookies so I could distract myself from the knowledge of what Ryker was doing. Of what he'd probably done before I even got home.

I had to deal with that, but I had zero clue how to go about it. The kids were happy to demand my attention, the chaos and trauma of the day before was something that would cling to all of us for a long time. I knew it without a doubt.

When the door to the garage opened, Ines hurried down off the chair where she knelt to help me form the cookies. I heard Axel drop his video game controller, and when I stepped into the living room, I found Ryker kneeling on the floor with his arms wrapped around the kids tightly. "I missed you," he rasped, and I saw the way his hands twitched on their backs as he said the words.

We weren't the only ones who had been traumatized by the day before. I went back to the kitchen, giving them the moment of privacy I suspected they needed. When Ryker finally pulled himself away, he stepped up behind me and swept the hair out of the way to kiss the top of the bandage that covered the worst of my injury. I didn't think I needed it still, but I also didn't want the kids to look at it. Hidden seemed less traumatic since the bruising around the wound itself turned a deep purple overnight. "I missed you too, Sunshine," he murmured as I leaned back into his embrace.

"And I missed you," I admitted, and the words seemed to make my body pulse with remembered pleasure of the night before. Even if my body felt like it'd been hit by a truck from the accident, and Ryker had extended that soreness to include between my legs with his rough possession all night long.

"I made it quick. For you," he whispered. I drew in a ragged breath, nodding my acknowledgement when I couldn't find the words. Ryker turned me to face him, staring down at me. "He was in on it, Calla. Don't put that shit on yourself, because he was prepared to hand you over to someone who would hurt you. A trafficker."

"I know," I murmured in response. "Did you find anything about Ness?"

He sighed. "She's apparently Tiernan's second's woman. We had no clue he even had a woman. Apparently he keeps her hidden well, because Tiernan is trying to arrange a marriage between his second and a cartel leader's sister."

I swallowed but nodded. It would explain why she didn't get to see him or her son as often as she wanted, if what she told me was true at least. I somehow doubted it. Ines crashed into our legs as Ryker reached into the bowl of cookie dough and scooped out a bite to shove into his mouth.

"Bad, 'yker!" she scolded.

Ryker laughed, mussing her blond hair as he stared down at her. "I like to live on the wild side, Princess." She darted back into the living room, so wrapped up in whatever game she played with her dolls and toy kitchen that she became immediately absorbed.

I stepped into Ryker's arms fully, wrapping my own around his waist. "I love you," I whispered, and he turned a stunning smile to me as he cupped my cheek. I knew it was the first time I said it without coercion. The first time I said it in front of the kids.

"Killer and all?" he asked.

I nodded with a chuckle. "Killer and all, my Shadow." The name echoed between us, freed from the confines of the tension that had tormented our relationship.

Sunshine and her shadow.

"What if I die?" he asked, immediately honing in on the deep wound we both knew I had to fight back every day.

"Then I'll miss you more than anything, but I'll have memories to keep me company until we're together again," I whispered, tears stinging my eyes with the thought of losing him.

"I love you too, Sunshine," he murmured, and I chuckled through my sniffles as he touched his lips to mine and Axel gagged in the next room.

"Gross!" he called, making his sister giggle.

Ryker pulled back, unfolding a stack of papers from his back pocket and stepping into the living room. I watched from the edge of the room as he knelt in front of Axel. "Is it gross if I adopt you?" he asked, and I watched Axel's eyes go to the papers in Ryker's hand. His brow furrowed, like he didn't understand.

"You want to adopt us?" he asked, and it killed me that he seemed to doubt just how amazing he was. That he doubted that anyone would be lucky to call him their son.

Ryker nodded. "Of course I want to adopt you, Little Man."

"Do I get to call you Dad?" Axel asked in a rush, and I barely restrained the sob that stuck in my throat. I'd been wrong to delay it in my fear that they weren't ready. Axel at the least was old enough to tell me what he wanted, and he'd been trying the entire time. I'd just been too focused on protecting him.

I'd underestimated just how much they loved Ryker.

"Daddy?" Ines asked, inserting herself into Ryker's arms like the demanding thing she was.

"Yeah, Princess. Daddy," Ryker whispered, leaning down to kiss the top of her head. The tears fell from my eyes when Axel's eyes came to mine and he gave me a teary smile. Axel crashed himself into Ryker's arms, hugging him tightly as he stared at me.

"Is that okay, Mommy?" my boy asked.

"If it's what you want, how could it not be?" I told him as I made my way to them. Ryker stood with both kids in his arms, heading for the couch where we snuggled up to enjoy the moment.

The cookies would wait.

CHAPTER FIFTY-EIGHT

Strolling into Matteo's office always felt ominous, like I shouldn't be there. We didn't spend enough time at the estate unless I had business, and I knew we'd need to remedy that. With everything she'd seen, Calla would need Ivory and Samara more than ever. She'd need the bond that only wives of the family could provide to one another, and the understanding that would come from the two women who had seen their fair share of blood.

Who had felt what it was to have blood splattered all over their faces.

Calla and the kids followed behind me, and I knew it had been the right choice to bring them when Ivory and Samara stepped forward and wrapped her in their embrace.

"How are you?" Ivory asked her. Tears filed Calla's eyes, but she fought them back for the kids.

"I'm okay," Calla lied. She was holding it together for the kids, but I thought for me, too. She felt like she had to be strong in the face of what happened, when really that was my job. I was there to catch her and put her back together.

She'd break down, eventually. It was unavoidable given what she'd gone through. But she'd be okay.

"The guys are in the office waiting for you," Samara said as she tended to the kids and brought them into the kitchen. The smell of Ivory's cooking came through the house, and I knew without a doubt that the three of them would be ready to explode when we went home.

Some people spoiled with love and affection.

Ivory spoiled with love and affection, food and a weird ass lizard.

I left them in the capable hands of the only women I trusted to help guide them through it, barely hearing Samara ask Calla a soft question that I felt to my bones. "Do you need to do yoga?" she asked, and it was something so jarring in its simplicity that I never could have expected Calla's voice would be teary when she answered.

"Yes," she whimpered.

Ivory distracted the kids with whatever concoction she'd cooked for them, and Samara gave my wife the only therapy she knew and welcomed. I made my way to Matteo's office, striding into all eyes turned to me.

"Calla and the kids are good?" Lino asked immediately, and I nodded in response.

"Ivory and Samara have them covered." The worst of the worst had been avoided thanks to Georgio and Lino distracting the kids. They hadn't seen much beyond the trauma of Calla being hauled away from the car after Jason was shot. It was enough, but it wasn't as bad as it could have been. I doubted Calla would have been pleased if they'd seen me split a man's face down the middle with a hatchet.

"This is why it's better to just stay single. When I think of what I'd do—" Enzo trailed off, trying to fight back that monster he kept caged inside himself. He was the only one who felt at odds with the criminal aspect of our lives, with the sheer violence, but he enjoyed it just as much as any of the rest of us.

"Your day will come," I warned him. "And then you'll understand that you will burn the world down to protect her."

Scar's eyes met mine, silently probing like he always did. Wondering how Calla and I made it work given my history. We saw ourselves as different sides of the same coin.

The boy whose family had tried to force him to rape, and the boy who had been a victim of the streets.

And all that went along with them.

"The move on Calla can be taken as nothing other than the first act of war," Matteo growled, confirming what we all knew. We'd been on the edge as it was, but a move against one of our wives was unforgivable.

"I've been calling in favors we're owed. They've all agreed to stand with us, even the ones who don't agree with our opposition to trafficking. Territory is territory, and we all know that violating it goes beyond a difference of opinions. It's an insult to the families," Don said, and I appreciated the man's proactiveness. There was *nothing* he couldn't accomplish, even in a short timeframe.

"They'll come if they're called?" Lino asked.

"Every one of them," Don agreed, his eyes moving from man to man.

We all knew the costs of war.

Death. Destruction. Loss.

"So it begins," Matteo sighed, looking ominous as he stared at each of us.

EPILOGUE
CALLA

Eight Months Later

Ines spun around in the poofiest pink dress I'd ever seen, looking like she belonged in a rose garden outside a castle.

To be fair, the Bellandi Estate wasn't exactly far off. She had a massive smile on her face as Sadie took her hand and helped her out of her shoes so they could go jump in the pink bounce house shaped like a castle that Uncle Matteo had surprised her with for her birthday. He didn't seem to care that only Axel and Ines were old enough to enjoy it alone.

Luna had squealed for joy when Aunt Sadie then snagged her from Matteo and brought her in to bounce with her lightly. I'd thought he might have a heart attack, like his precious fourteen-month-old Little Moon couldn't handle it. But he'd relented quickly when she screamed as he tried to pull her out.

It was obvious who ruled the Bellandi House, and it was no longer Matteo.

Ivory rolled her eyes, but her fingers strayed toward her stomach as she watched them interact. "How far along are you?" I asked, rubbing a hand over my own massive belly.

At eight months pregnant, it felt like I'd pop any day.

"I haven't even told Matteo yet," Ivory admitted, snapping her hand away from her belly. "It's very new."

"Obviously, if he hasn't wormed that information out of you yet," I laughed, and she turned her head to me to share in the giggle as tears filled her eyes.

"I worry with the timing," Ivory sniffled. "Everything is so uncertain right now."

"It is," I agreed, clasping her hand in mine as we stood side by side. But as I looked around the garden, filled with all our new family, I couldn't regret any of it. Dad and Don stood in the corner, drinking beer and getting trashed in a way I hadn't seen in years. Samara's mom, Hattie, lingered nearby, fretting over the two of them in that sweet, playful way only she could manage.

I hoped she'd break through, because she was the first woman I'd ever seen my father light up around. It gave me hope that maybe one day soon he wouldn't be alone, that they could find happiness in one another.

We were all proof that sometimes love came out of nowhere, that it could stomp all over us or put us back together all in one breath.

Lino strolled up to our sides, bouncing his son, Levi, on his hip as he spoke to him. Ryker and Axel came through the backyard from the gate at the side, and I heaved a breath of annoyance.

"Is that a fucking pony?" Lino roared with a laugh, and the sound of Ines screaming as she scrambled out of the bounce house and ran up to Ryker could probably be heard for miles.

"Daddy!" she screamed, and he caught her up in his arms to pick her up and swing her around. Even eight months after we'd shown the kids the adoption papers, it still made my heart melt to hear them call him Daddy. "You got me a pony!" she yelled, and even I winced from the high-pitched sound.

"I *rented* you a pony," Ryker clarified, giving Ines that stern look that dared her to pout. She refrained for him. Only for him. "Mommy would murder me if we brought it home with us."

He was absolutely right. That thing was not coming home with us. I didn't know the first thing about horses, but even I knew they were a ton of work.

The person handling the pony chuckled as Ryker set Ines in the saddle on the pony's back, and Ryker stayed right by her side as they walked around the yard. Axel approached my side, snuggling right into my arms as we watched Ryker make every one of the birthday girl dreams come true.

But then again, he did that every day.

For all of us.

"Love you, Cookie Monster," I told him, squatting down as best I could to boop his nose. He was already seven, and far too old for his age. He always had been, but after the day when he'd seen a man try to take me away, that only got worse. My little genius excelled in school at a whole new level, skipping a grade even in his school for the gifted. Ryker and I did everything we could to encourage him to just be a kid, but he seemed determined to rush through it. I knew he wanted to be a man who could protect his family, that seeing me hurt had shifted something inside him too young, too soon.

I dealt with the consequences of my choice every day.

"Love you too," he whispered, smiling up at me as Ryker and Ines finally made their way to us. Ryker's face was thunderous as Axel helped me stand back up from my squat. "You should be sitting down," he ordered, taking my arm to guide me to one of the chairs on the patio. I looked over my shoulder, rolling my eyes at Ivory who giggled and went over to help Samara carry out the cake.

"I'm pregnant, not incapable of standing," I told him, but as I lowered into the chair, I realized just how much my feet hurt.

I'd be damned if I told him that though.

It didn't matter that I didn't say the words: he saw them in the way I sighed in contentment. I glared at him, daring him to say something, but he just chuckled. Even the wildest men learned to pick their battles, and with my ass sitting in a chair, he'd won the one that mattered to him.

He was smothering me slowly, and I was terrified to see what that meant for Royce once he came.

"You know, the pony made her ridiculously happy-" he started.

"Don't you even *think* about it," I warned. "We are not getting a pony."

"You only like riding my meatballs," he teased, earning a glare as I prepared a scathing response. I couldn't voice it, couldn't warn him that his meatballs wouldn't see any action if he didn't tread carefully.

Not when Luna ran awkwardly through the yard, stopping right in front of me and reaching up to touch her hand to my belly. She'd long since been obsessed with feeling Royce kick.

So was I.

She giggled, turning those blue eyes up to me. "He's saying hi, Lunabug," I whispered.

"Hi!" she smiled, pressing her ear to my belly.

"If you listen hard enough, you'll hear him saying 'let me out! '" Ryker teased her, picking her up and hauling her up onto his shoulders.

I thought Matteo might die when Ryker put her on the pony for a ride.

I watched, grinning at Ivory as she fiddled with the impossibly beautiful cake she'd made, and feeling Royce kick my belly.

Once, my life had been black and white.

Ryker lit it up in vibrant color. And I'd never go back.

These were the moments that made a home.

THE BATH SOOTHED my aching feet. The only trouble was that I couldn't get out on my own. That and the fact that Ryker was a stickler about making sure the water wasn't too hot, so it got cold too quickly. But by the time Ryker had tucked the kids in, I was ready to come out.

He stood in the doorway, his arms crossed over his chest, and stared at me with nothing but love in his gaze. All the frustration, the anger that had once been there was gone. We had a good life with our kids, and even though life was difficult, and I knew it took its toll on his sanity, he did everything he could not to bring it home.

Even on the days when his soul looked battered, when I knew he was freshly showered and it had been a bloody day.

Stepping forward when I held out my arms, he lifted me from the tub gently and set me to my feet so he could towel me off.

I didn't remember being this horny with Axel and Ines, but that was probably in large part due to the marriage I was in. Ryker had always driven me crazy, always made me want him, but since getting pregnant it had been nonstop.

It was inconvenient, considering I'd stopped working at the studio five months ago and Ines stayed home with me during the day. Not that Ryker was around during the day anyway, and I didn't imagine he'd be easily available to stop home for a quickie while they waged war on Murphy.

When he guided me to the bedroom, he lay out on the bed like the meal he was and raised a brow at my scowl. "Oh, so you didn't want to ride me?" he chuckled. I pursed my lips, but refrained from answering as I climbed onto the bed and straddled his hips.

I both loved and hated riding him. The sight of my enormous belly hanging free and my boobs that were too fucking big made me feel insecure, but there was no mistaking that Ryker loved them. His hands ran over the tight skin of my stomach, touching where I swelled with his child. If my size was any indication, Royce would be as big as his father. But being in control meant I could find the sweet spot that seemed even more elusive and somehow even more sensitive.

I couldn't handle Ryker's mouth on my pussy, and it drove him crazy. It was too much, too intense.

Grinding my hips down on him, I let him slide against me. When I finally slid him inside me, it was to the feeling of his hands on my ass, guiding me into position as he growled beneath me. Even wet from the friction of him between my thighs, it took some time for me to work him most of the way inside before his hands shifted to my hips and he stilled me.

"Easy," he murmured, ever cautious with his pregnant wife. He wouldn't take me too hard, wouldn't give me everything out of fear of hurting the baby. I appreciated it on some levels.

But on others it made me murderous.

With every rock of my hips he prevented me from taking that last bit of him, but he gave in other ways. His eyes held mine, raging like a cold storm that communicated just how desperately he wanted me. The same way I wanted him.

So I rocked my hips over him, taking him in slow pulses I felt inside all of my body. And when I finally found my orgasm, Ryker flipped me to my back and took his with my legs spread wide and him staring down at me splayed out in front of him.

Our love was suffocating. It was too intense and too much, often, but it was also the kind of love where I could feel him wrapped around my heart, where he made me feel alive in a way I'd never had.

It was unbearable. It was perfect.

It was life in color.

I HOPE YOU LOVED RYKER & Calla's story! Please consider taking the time to drop me a review. Hearing from my readers means the world to me.

CAN'T GET ENOUGH of Ryker & Calla? Download the Exclusive Extended Epilogue and get a glimpse into their future.

>>Download the Extended Epilogue.

CONTINUE READING for a sneak peek into Shielded Wrongs, out now!

>>Get it now.

SHIELDED WRONGS SNEAK PEEK
SADIE

No air.

There was nearly no air in my lungs. No breath in my body. I flung my eyes open, fighting through the haze to see the figure looming above me.

My bedroom was dark. Not a light shining in through my curtains.

"Keep quiet, and I won't need to hurt you. We're just going for a ride." I couldn't see his face, could only barely make out the size of his body above mine and the pressure of his hands on my throat.

I could take him. I'd taken bigger men down, but there was something so distinctly different about the realness of being attacked in my bed while I slept.

The realness of thumbs crossed over the front of my throat like a vice. Of the way my lungs rattled in my chest as they fought for air.

I nodded my head, playing complacent as I considered my options. As I studied the lines of his body, the placement of his limbs and his weight.

As I took stock of every weak point I could exploit.

"Are you going to be a good girl?" he mumbled.

I nodded again, discreetly tucking my elbows into my sides. With his hips between my legs, I didn't want to contemplate the fact that he'd somehow snuck into my house and gotten on top of me while I slept.

All that mattered in that moment was breaking every bone in his body.

I hooked my right hand around his left forearm, giving him the widest eyes I could, and shuddered out a whimper. "Please," I rasped.

When a smirk dragged over his mouth, I knew that I had him right where I wanted him. Believing me weak, desperate.

"What will you give me, baby?" he asked, and I didn't stop the way my face contorted into a grimace.

I thrust my left arm up, catching him around the right side of his neck. My left foot went to his hip, using it to pivot my body in the bed beneath him until I could kick my right leg into his armpit and hold him there with a locked knee.

I twisted my left leg over his head, wrapping his shoulder up as I crossed my legs around it. With my body twisted up beneath him, I ignored his squirming attempts to push off me. I grabbed his wrist with both hands, shoving my legs down until he rolled off me to thump onto the mattress next to me.

The position meant his arm was between my legs, with me gripping it tight. I held it tight to my body as I shoved my hips up into the air, feeling nothing but glee when his elbow snapped backward and the bone broke.

"Fucking bitch!" he roared, his arm going limp in my hands as I raised my foot from the bed and smashed it down onto his nose.

"Piece of shit," I wheezed, rolling backwards and off the edge of the bed. I raced for the living room, leaving him to decide how he wanted to pick up the pieces of his pride.

I'd shatter what was left by the time I was done with him.

I scrambled for the bat tucked behind my couch, yanking it out from its hiding place. Spinning, I watched as he stumbled out of the bedroom. He grasped the doorway as he passed, leaving a red smear on the paint, and he grimaced at me with blood-stained teeth.

"You know, like you haven't pissed me off enough. Now I have to paint to cover up your nasty ass stain." I sighed.

"I'm going to bring you back to Murphy black and blue," he snarled.

I hefted my bat, holding my stance and staggering my legs for better traction. "I think it's more likely that Ryker will paint the warehouse with your blood. It's a much more welcome decor item there. You'll fit right in." I smiled, watching as he staggered forward another step.

I was too small to attack. Too small to sacrifice my balance and the strength that came from planting my weight.

He came closer.

Slowly.

Approaching a caged animal, he looked at me with rabid eyes. Men never saw that they were the animals. That they were the monsters. Women were just theirs to take and use.

Abuse.

I'd be fucking damned if I became a victim when I spent my time teaching women what to do when a man sought to hurt them.

So I waited. I itched to hit him. To make him bleed the way he would have done to me if I'd been anyone else. But he'd picked the wrong fucking woman to steal out of bed in the night.

Murphy could kiss my Filipina ass.

He raised his hand, blocking his face as he came closer.

One more step.

And I struck, swinging my bat not for his face, but for the broken elbow he kept hanging at his side like a limp dick. He roared, grabbing at it as pain exploded through his arm.

He dropped his block, and I raised a leg to my chest. Kicking down onto his kneecap, I felt it give beneath him as he collapsed to the other knee.

I swung again, catching him in the temple.

He fell to his face, staining the carpet too.

My landlord would not like me come morning.

It was a good thing he was my Dad.

I brought the bat with me as I went back to the bedroom. I didn't look at the bloodstained sheets as I snagged my phone off the nightstand.

Even in the middle of the night, she'd answer the phone. Matteo would want to kill me, but she'd answer.

"Sadie?" my best friend asked in a sleepy voice. I hated waking her up, but I had a feeling Matteo wouldn't appreciate me calling the cops for this.

"Tell Matteo one of his friends needs to be picked up," I sighed, stepping back into the living room. I watched the body on my carpet, counting every time his chest rose and fell. I wouldn't get close enough for him to catch me off guard on the chance that he only pretended to be unconscious.

Not until I got my handcuffs from the bedroom.

"I'm fine, but tell him he'll want Ryker to be ready and waiting." I added, hanging up the phone.

Backing into my bedroom, I got my handcuffs.

At least they were being used for something.

I tapped my fingers on my cheek and heaved out a sigh as I waited. Not wanting to take my eyes off the dude on my floor, I wasn't exactly sure what to do with myself.

I hated sitting still.

That was my enemy.

I stood, pacing back and forth in my living room, but keeping my distance. When the man groaned and struggled against his hands cuffed behind his back, I fought the temptation to hit him in the head again. Matteo would want him alive.

Temporarily.

His groans got louder as he came more aware with every second that passed.

I didn't have any neighbors in my apartment above the gym, thankfully. That didn't mean his voice wasn't annoying as fuck.

I went to my bedroom, grabbing a pair of Patrick's boxers off the top of the open box of stuff sitting and waiting for him to take back.

It wasn't like I could gag the dude with my own underwear.

I stepped up to his head, pinching his nose until he mouth-breathed all over me like the nasty thing he was. Shoving the boxers in, I stepped back and fought the gag that pinched my throat.

I was fairly confident the boxers were clean.

Shame.

Matteo's knock on my door was anything but subtle, and I stepped over to let in the Bellandi brigade. Ivory's body collided with mine in a rush, propelling me back into the room so quickly that I almost fell on my ass. "Woah," I laughed. "I told you, I'm fine."

"You were attacked!" she hissed, pulling back to look at me. Her brow furrowed. "Weren't you?"

"Yeah," I nodded, watching as Matteo and Ryker stepped in. The guy trailing on their heels seemed vaguely familiar from around the Bellandi Estate.

Matteo gave me a glance over, seeming to determine I was safe enough. "What's that in his mouth?" he asked, bending down to inspect the dude with the twitchy eyeballs. He'd wake up soon enough.

"Patrick's boxers," I said, and Ryker huffed out a laugh.

"You good, Short Stuff?" he asked, blue eyes studying my face.

"I'm good, Meatball. Assuming you guys are going to clean up the blood. It just does not go with my color palette."

Ryker laughed. "Yeah, she's good." Stepping over to the body, he hauled him up into his arms. Seemed the stalker was in a hurry to get back to the Warehouse.

"This is Bryan. He's going to keep an eye on you from now on until things settle down," Matteo said, coming over to wrap Ivory in his arms.

"On that note, I'm out!" Ryker called as he stepped into the hallway. The man had a brain.

If only Matteo had been that smart.

"Um, fuck no?" I asked, glancing at Ivory. Had she lost her ever-loving mind that she thought I'd be okay with a babysitter?

"Ivory wants you to come stay with us. I do not think that would be wise, seeing how I'd probably feed you to Ryker by the end of the week," Matteo admitted. "You would still need security while you were out of the house at any rate."

"Please, Sadie. Do this for me," Ivory begged. "This will get ugly. You need to protection if they're going to come after all of us."

"Did you miss the part where I defended myself just fine? Not sure if you noticed, but he is concussed because I bashed his head in with a bat, he has a broken arm and probably leg too. I'm just fine on my own," I told her, waving my hands in the air as I spoke. She eyed them and backed off, seeing the writing on the wall.

"She's pissed," Ivory said to Matteo.

"Thank you, Angel. I deducted as much on my own," he whispered to her, affection and amusement in his voice.

"Miss Hicks, I can sleep on the couch. I'll try to be as unobtrusive as I can," Bryan said.

"Look, Bry. There is no way that anybody is sleeping on my couch. I live alone for good reason. I will walk from my bathroom to my bedroom, buck ass naked. I am not Chef Ivory over here, and I am not going to feed you. You are not staying here."

"Unfortunately for Bryan, he takes orders from me," Matteo inserted.

"Right, so I hope you know that I will sneak out every chance I get. I will draw dicks on his face while he sleeps, and I'll steal his clothes while he's in the shower for good measure. Are you sure he's up to the task? He seems a little green to me. I promise you I will attempt to torment him every second of the day if you leave him here," I said.

Matteo glared at me. "Bryan, go home," he said finally, tugging his phone from the pocket of the jeans he'd slipped on before coming here. The other man looked grateful before he slipped out the door.

"What? You promised me you'd protect her!" Ivory whispered, looking at him like he'd lost his mind.

"Oh, she'll be protected all right. I just know I'm going to regret this. Fucking woman will be the death of me," he muttered as he stepped out the front door of the apartment.

"Love you too!" I called as the door closed behind him. "Who's he calling?" I asked, watching as Ivory bounced on her heels. "Do you have to pee?"

"No, I do not have to pee. Stop acting like I'm pregnant. I'm not," she said.

I raised my brow at her. "Yet."

"Hush," she scolded. She slid over to the door, pressing her ear to it as she tried to listen to her husband on the phone. Her full lips twisted into a pout when she couldn't hear Matteo's side of the conversation, glaring at me.

"Well?"

"Nothing. I can't hear a damn thing. I don't understand why he's keeping secrets like this. I want to know who's coming!" she said.

She jumped back when Matteo opened the door carefully. He knew Ivory well enough to know she'd be trying to eavesdrop. She wasn't exactly good at it. "Who did you call?" she asked.

He leveled her with a look that said she needed to learn some patience. The oaf of a man preaching patience was ridiculous, given the way he'd taken Ivory without care for giving her the time she needed to adjust to being with him. "You should pack a bag, Sadie. Staying here is a security threat. I can't see your new babysitter letting that fly."

"I'm not going anywhere," I argued, crossing my arms over my chest and staring him down.

"Suit yourself. I'm not the one who will have to deal with the consequences of not doing what you're told. I suggest you at least put some more clothes on. I don't imagine you'll want him to throw you on the back of his bike in shorts."

"I have time." I shrugged. Nobody, even in the middle of the night, could get through Chicago traffic so quickly.

"You have less than five minutes. He was close, and traffic isn't an issue for him," Matteo flopped down onto my couch, making himself comfortable as he waited out whatever fucking friend he was so confident I wouldn't torment.

"I'll just make him miserable too, you know? It doesn't matter who you assign to me. I will make it my mission to drive them crazy," I said.

He smirked, glancing up at me with vivid blue eyes. "I'd like to see you try to get away with that shit with him."

"Go put on a bra at least," Ivory said. "Trust me when I say you'll want the girls up where they belong-"

"Don't even start," Matteo warned. "He is here to protect her, not be her plaything."

"After all I did for you." I gasped in mock indignation, pressing a hand to my chest. That he could think so little of me.

Like I cared.

I went to put on a bra anyway, because after Ivory drew attention to it, I felt weird being in a room with Matteo without one. I grimaced at her as I stepped back into the living room.

Bras were the devil.

The knock on the door sent Ivory springing to her feet as she raced for it. Peeking through the hole in the door, she grinned as she spun back to look at me.

It really said something about our lives that she could smile so happily while blood stained my carpet next to my feet.

She tugged the door open, stepping aside for the powerhouse of a man to step over the threshold. He emerged from the shadows of the hallway, stepping into the well-lit room and towering over me as he approached. It took a big man to stand in the same room as Matteo Bellandi and not seem small.

He managed.

Motorcycle boots covered his feet, and jeans hugged his legs in that oh-so-sexy but not quite tight way. The black t-shirt that clung to his broad shoulders couldn't quite contain the beast of a man.

"Sadie, this is Lorenzo Vescovi," Ivory gushed, knowing that the sound of the name would turn me into a puddle.

"Enzo," I whispered, staring up at the hazel eyes that stared down at me as he stepped closer.

"Hello, *Carina*," he said in a deep rumble of a voice.

Fuck.

ALSO BY ADELAIDE FORREST

Bellandi Crime Syndicate

Bloodied Hands

Forgivable Sins

Grieved Loss

Shielded Wrongs

Insta-Love Novellas

The Men of Mount Awe

Deliver Me from Evil

Kings of Conquest - Cowritten with Lyric Cox

Claiming His Princess

Stealing His Princess - Coming Soon

9 780578 305806